The Wheel of Time®

By Robert Jordan

New Spring: The Novel
The Eye of the World
The Great Hunt
The Dragon Reborn
The Shadow Rising
The Fires of Heaven
Lord of Chaos
A Crown of Swords
The Path of Daggers
Winter's Heart
Crossroads of Twilight
Knife of Dreams

By Robert Jordan and Brandon Sanderson

The Gathering Storm
Towers of Midnight
A Memory of Light

By Robert Jordan and Teresa Patterson

The World of Robert Jordan's The Wheel of Time

By Robert Jordan, Harriet McDougal, Alan Romanczuk, and Maria Simons

The Wheel of Time Companion

Praise for
Robert Jordan and
The Wheel of Time®

"His huge, ambitious Wheel of Time series helped redefine the genre." —George R. R. Martin, internationally bestselling author of *A Game of Thrones*

"Anyone who's writing epic secondary world fantasy knows Robert Jordan isn't just a part of the landscape, he's a monolith within the landscape." —Patrick Rothfuss, internationally bestselling author of The Kingkiller Chronicle

"*The Eye of the World* was a turning point in my life. I read, I enjoyed. (Then continued on to write my larger fantasy novels.)" —Robin Hobb, *New York Times* bestselling author of The Farseer Trilogy

"Robert Jordan's work has been a formative influence and an inspiration for a generation of fantasy writers." —Brent Weeks, *New York Times* bestselling author of *The Way of Shadows*

"Jordan has come to dominate the world Tolkien began to reveal." —*The New York Times*

"One of fantasy's most acclaimed series." —*USA Today*

"Robert Jordan was a giant of fiction whose words helped a whole generation of fantasy writers, including myself, find our true voices. I thanked him then, but I didn't thank him enough." —Peter V. Brett, internationally bestselling author of The Demon Cycle

"[Robert Jordan's] impact on the place of fantasy in the culture is colossal. . . . He brought innumerable readers to fantasy. He became the *New York Times* Best Seller List's face of fantasy." —Guy Gavriel Kay, internationally bestselling author of *Tigana*

"Jordan's writing is so amazing! The characterization, the attention to detail!" —Clint McElroy, cocreator of the #1 podcast *The Adventure Zone*

"The Wheel of Time [is] rapidly becoming the definitive American fantasy saga. It is a fantasy tale seldom equaled and still less often surpassed in English."
—*Chicago Sun-Times*

"Hard to put down for even a moment. A fittingly epic conclusion to a fantasy series that many consider one of the best of all time." —*San Francisco Book Review* on *A Memory of Light*

THE GATHERING STORM

ROBERT JORDAN

AND

BRANDON SANDERSON

A TOM DOHERTY ASSOCIATES BOOK
NEW YORK

THE GATHERING STORM

Copyright © 2009 by Bandersnatch Group, Inc.

Excerpt from *Towers of Midnight* copyright © 2010 by Bandersnatch Group, Inc.

The phrase "The Wheel of Time" and the snake-wheel symbol are trademarks of Bandersnatch Group, Inc.

Maps by Ellisa Mitchell
Interior illustrations by Matthew C. Nielsen and Ellisa Mitchell

A Tor Book
Published by Tom Doherty Associates
120 Broadway
New York, NY 10271

www.tor-forge.com

Tor® is a registered trademark of Macmillan Publishing Group, LLC.

ISBN 978-1-250-25260-9

Our books may be purchased in bulk for promotional, educational, or business use. Please contact your local bookseller or the Macmillan Corporate and Premium Sales Department at 1-800-221-7945, extension 5442, or by email at MacmillanSpecialMarkets@macmillan.com.

First Edition: November 2009
First Premium Mass Market Edition: May 2020

Printed in the United States of America

0 9 8 7 6 5 4

FOREWORD

In November 2007, I received a phone call that would change my life forever. Harriet McDougal, wife and editor of the late Robert Jordan, called to ask me if I would complete the last book of The Wheel of Time.

For those who did not know Mr. Jordan had passed away, it pains me to be the one to break the news. I remember how I felt when—while idly browsing the Internet on September 16, 2007—I discovered that he had died. I was shocked, stunned, and disheartened. This wonderful man, a hero to me in my writing career, was gone. The world suddenly became a different place.

I first picked up *The Eye of the World* in 1990, when I was a teenage fantasy addict visiting my corner bookstore. I became a fan instantly and eagerly awaited *The Great Hunt*. Over the years, I've read the books numerous times, often re-reading the entire series when a new book was released. Time passed, and I decided I wanted to become a fantasy author—influenced, in large part, by how much I loved The Wheel of Time. And yet, never did I think that I would one day get that phone call from Harriet. It came to me as a complete surprise. I had not asked, applied, or dared wish for this opportunity—though when the request was made, my answer was immediate. I love this series as I have loved none other, and the characters feel like old, dear friends from my childhood.

I cannot replace Robert Jordan. Nobody could write this book as well as he could have. That is a simple fact. Fortunately, he left many notes, outlines, completed scenes, and dictated explanations with his wife and assistants. Before his passing, he asked Harriet to find someone to complete the series for his fans. He loved you all very much and spent the very last weeks of his life dictating events for the final volume. It was to be called *A Memory of Light*.

Eighteen months later, we are here. Mr. Jordan promised that the final book would be big. But the manuscript soon grew prohibitively huge; it would be three times the size of a regular Wheel of Time book, and the decision was made by Harriet and Tor to split *A Memory of Light* into thirds. There were several excellent breaking points that would give a full and complete story in each third. You may think of *The Gathering Storm* and its two followers as the three volumes of *A Memory of Light* or as the final three books of The Wheel of Time. Both are correct.

As of this writing, I am halfway done with the second third. We are working as quickly as is reasonable, and we don't want you to have to wait too long to get the ending we were all promised nearly twenty years ago. (Mr. Jordan did write this ending himself before he passed away, and I have read it. And it is fantastic.) I have not tried to imitate Mr. Jordan's style. Instead, I've adapted my style to be appropriate to The Wheel of Time. My main goal was to stay true to the souls of the characters. The plot is, in large part, Robert Jordan's, though many of the words are mine. Imagine this book as the product of a new director working on some of the scenes of a movie while retaining the same actors and script.

But this is a big project, and it will take time to complete. I beg your patience as we spend these next few years perfecting this story. We hold in our hands the ending of the greatest fantasy epic of our time, and I intend to see it done *right*. I intend to remain true to Mr. Jordan's wishes and notes. My artistic integrity, and love for the books, will not let me do anything less. In the end, I let the words herein stand as the best argument for what we are doing.

This is not my book. It is Robert Jordan's book, and to a lesser extent, it is your book.

Thank you for reading.

BRANDON SANDERSON
June 2009

For Maria Simons and Alan Romanczuk,
without whom this book wouldn't have been possible

Contents

Ravens and crows. Rats. Mists and clouds. Insects and corruption. Strange events and odd occurrences. The ordinary twisted and strange. Wonders!

The dead are beginning to walk, and some see them. Others do not, but more and more, we all fear the night.

These have been our days. They rain upon us beneath a dead sky, crushing us with their fury, until as one we beg: "Let it begin!"

—Journal of the Unknown Scholar,
entry for The Feast of Freia, 1000 NE

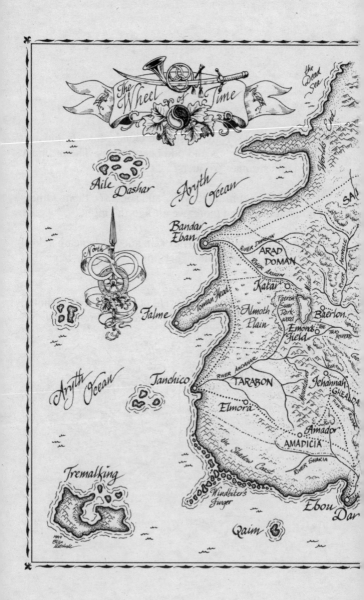

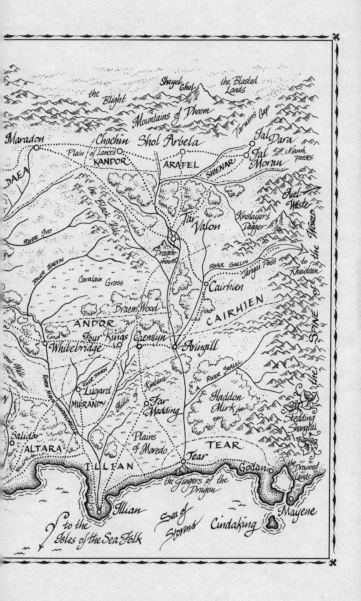

PROLOGUE

What the Storm Means

Renald Fanwar sat on his porch, warming the sturdy blackoak chair crafted for him by his grandson two years before. He stared northward.

At the black and silver clouds.

He'd never seen their like before. They blanketed the entire horizon to the north, high in the sky. They weren't gray. They were *black* and *silver*. Dark, rumbling thunderheads, as dark as a root cellar at midnight. With striking silver light breaking between them, flashes of lightning that gave off no sound.

The air was *thick*. Thick with the scents of dust and dirt. Of dried leaves and rain that refused to fall. Spring had come. And yet his crops didn't grow. Not a sprout had dared poke through the earth.

He rose slowly from his chair, wood creaking, chair rocking softly behind him, and walked up to the edge of the porch. He chewed on his pipe, though its fire had gone out. He couldn't be bothered to relight it. Those clouds transfixed him. They were so black. Like the smoke of a brushfire, only no brushfire smoke ever rose that high up in the air. And what to make of *silver* clouds? Bulging between the black ones, like places where polished steel shone through metal crusted with soot.

He rubbed his chin, glancing down at his yard. A small, whitewashed fence contained a patch of grass and shrubs. The shrubs were dead now, every one of them. Hadn't lasted through that winter. He'd need to pull them out soon. And the grass . . . well, the grass was still just winter thatch. Not even any weeds sprouted.

A clap of thunder shook him. Pure, sharp, like an enormous crash of metal against metal. It rattled the windows of the house, shook the porch boards, seemed to vibrate his very bones.

He jumped back. That strike had been close—perhaps on his property. He itched to go inspect the damage. Lightning fire could destroy a man, burn him out of his land. Up here in the Borderlands, so many things were unintentional tinder—dry grass, dry shingles, dry seed.

But the clouds were still distant. That strike *couldn't* have been on his property. The silver and black thunderheads rolled and boiled, feeding and consuming themselves.

He closed his eyes, calming himself, taking a deep breath. Had he imagined the thunder? Was he going off the side, as Gaffin always joked? He opened his eyes.

And the clouds were right there, directly above his house.

It was as if they had suddenly rolled forward, intending to strike while his gaze was averted. They dominated the sky now, sweeping distantly in either direction, massive and overwhelming. He could almost feel their weight pressing the air down around him. He drew in a breath that was heavy with sudden humidity, and his brow prickled with sweat.

Those clouds churned, dark black and silver thunderheads shaking with white blasts. They suddenly boiled downward, like the funnel cloud of a twister, coming for him. He cried out, raising a hand, as a man might before a powerfully bright light. That blackness. That endless, suffocating *blackness*. It would take him. He knew.

And then the clouds were gone.

His pipe hit the porch's floorboards, clicking softly, tossing burned tabac out in a spray across the steps. He hadn't realized he'd let it slip free. Renald hesitated, looking up at empty blue sky, realizing that he was cringing at nothing.

The clouds were off on the horizon again, some forty leagues distant. They thundered softly.

He picked up his pipe with a shaking hand, spotted from age, tanned from years spent in the sun. *Just a trick of your mind, Renald,* he told himself. *You're going off the side, sure as eggs is eggs.*

He was on edge because of the crops. That had him on edge. Though he spoke optimistic words for the lads, it just wasn't natural. Something should have sprouted by now.

He'd farmed that land for forty years! Barley didn't take this long to sprout. Burn him, but it didn't. What was going on in the world these days? Plants couldn't be depended on to sprout, and clouds didn't stay where they should.

He forced himself to sit back down in his chair, legs shaking. *Getting old, I am. . . .* he thought.

He'd worked a farm all of his life. Farmsteading in the Borderlands was not easy, but if you worked hard, you could grow a successful life while you grew strong crops. "A man has as much luck as he has seeds in the field," his father had always said.

Well, Renald was one of the most successful farmers in the area. He'd done well enough to buy out the two farms beside his, and he could run thirty wagons to market each fall. He now had six good men working for him, plowing the fields, riding the fences. Not that he didn't have to climb down in the muck every day and show them what good farming was all about. You couldn't let a little success ruin you.

Yes, he'd worked the land, lived the land, as his father always used to say. He understood the weather as well as a man could. Those clouds weren't natural. They rumbled softly, like an animal growling on a dark night. Waiting. Lurking in the nearby woods.

He jumped at another crash of thunder that seemed too close. Were those clouds forty leagues away? Is that what he'd thought? Looked more like ten leagues away, now that he studied them.

"Don't get like that," he grumbled at himself. His own voice sounded good to him. Real. It was nice to hear something other than that rumbling and the occasional creak of shutters in the wind. Shouldn't he be able to hear Auaine inside, getting supper ready?

"You're tired. That's it. Tired." He fished in his vest pocket and pulled out his tabac pouch.

A faint rumbling came from the right. At first, he assumed it was the thunder. However, this rumbling was too grating, too regular. That wasn't thunder. It was wheels turning.

Sure enough, a large, oxen-drawn wagon crested Mallard's Hill, just to the east. Renald had named that hill himself. Every good hill needed a name. The road was Mallard's Road. So why not name the hill that too?

He leaned forward in his chair, pointedly ignoring those

clouds as he squinted toward the wagon, trying to make out
the driver's face. Thulin? The smith? What was he doing,
driving a wagon laden halfway to the heavens? He was supposed to be working on Renald's new plow!

Lean for one of his trade, Thulin was still twice as muscled as most farmhands. He had the dark hair and tan skin
of a Shienaran, and kept his face shaved after their fashion,
but he did not wear the topknot. Thulin's family might trace
its roots back to Borderland warriors, but he himself was
just a simple country man like the rest of them. He ran the
smithy over in Oak Water, five miles to the east. Renald had
enjoyed many a game of stones with the smith during winter
evenings.

Thulin was getting on—he hadn't seen as many years as
Renald, but the last few winters had prompted Thulin to
start speaking of retirement. Smithing wasn't an old man's
trade. Of course, neither was farming. *Were* there really any
old man's trades?

Thulin's wagon approached along the packed earthen
road, approaching Renald's white-fenced yard. *Now, that's
odd,* Renald thought. Behind the wagon trailed a neat string
of animals: five goats and two milkcows. Crates of black-
feathered chickens were tied on the outside of the wagon,
and the bed of the wagon itself was piled full of furniture,
sacks and barrels. Thulin's youthful daughter, Mirala, sat
on the seat with him, next to his wife, a golden-haired
woman from the south. Twenty-five years Thulin's wife, but
Renald still thought of Gallanha as "that southern girl."

The whole family was in the wagon, leading their best
livestock. Obviously on the move. But where? Off to visit
relatives, perhaps? He and Thulin hadn't played a round of
stones in . . . oh, three weeks now. Not much time for visiting, what with the coming of spring and the hurried planting. Someone would need to mend the plows and sharpen
the scythes. Who would do it if Thulin's smithy went cold?

Renald tucked a pinch of tabac into his pipe as Thulin
pulled the wagon up beside Renald's yard. The lean, gray-
haired smith handed the reins to his daughter, then climbed
down from the wagon, feet throwing puffs of dust into the air
when he hit the ground. Behind him the distant storm still
brewed.

Thulin pushed open the fence gate, then strode up to the

porch. He looked distracted. Renald opened his mouth to give greeting, but Thulin spoke first.

"I buried my best anvil in Gallanha's old strawberry patch, Renald," the big smith said. "You remember where that is, don't you? I packed my best set of tools there as well. They're well greased and inside my best chest, lined to keep it dry. That should keep the rust off of them. For a time at least."

Renald closed his mouth, holding his pipe half-full. If Thulin was burying his anvil . . . well, it meant he wasn't planning to come back for a while. "Thulin, what—"

"If I don't return," Thulin said, glancing northward, "would you dig my things out and see that they're cared for? Sell them to someone who cares, Renald. I wouldn't have just anyone beating that anvil. Took me twenty years to gather those tools, you know."

"But Thulin!" Renald sputtered. "Where are you going?"

Thulin turned back to him, leaning one arm on the porch railing, those brown eyes of his solemn. "There's a storm coming," he said. "And so I figure I've got to head on to the north."

"Storm?" Renald asked. "That one on the horizon, you mean? Thulin, it looks bad—burn my bones, but it does—but there's no use running from it. We've had bad storms before."

"Not like this, old friend," Thulin said. "This ain't the sort of storm you ignore."

"Thulin?" Renald asked. "What are you talking about?"

Before he could answer, Gallanha called from the wagon box. "Did you tell him about the pots?"

"Ah," Thulin said. "Gallanha polished up that set of copper-bottom pots that your wife always liked. They're sitting on the kitchen table, waiting for Auaine, if she wants to go claim them." With that, Thulin nodded to Renald and began to walk back toward the wagon.

Renald sat, stupefied. Thulin always *had* been a blunt one; he favored saying his mind, then moving on. That was part of what Renald liked about him. But the smith could also pass through a conversation like a boulder rolling through a flock of sheep, leaving everyone dazed.

Renald scrambled up, leaving his pipe on the chair and following Thulin down into the yard and to the wagon. *Burn it,* Renald thought, glancing to the sides, noticing the brown grass and dead shrubs again. He'd worked hard on that yard.

The smith was checking on the chicken crates tied to the sides of his vehicle. Renald caught up to him, reaching out a hand, but Gallanha distracted him.

"Here, Renald," she said from the wagon box. "Take these." She held out a basket of eggs, one lock of golden hair straying from her bun. Renald reached over to take the basket. "Give these to Auaine. I know you're short on chickens on account of those foxes last fall."

Renald took the basket of eggs. Some were white, some were brown. "Yes, but where are you *going*, Gallanha?"

"North, my friend," Thulin said. He walked past, laying a hand on Renald's shoulder. "There will be an army gathering, I figure. They'll need smiths."

"Please," Renald said, gesturing with the basket of eggs. "At least take a few minutes. Auaine just put some bread in, one of those thick honey loaves that you like. We can discuss this over a game of stones."

Thulin hesitated.

"We'd better be on the move," Gallanha said softly. "That storm is coming."

Thulin nodded, then climbed up into the wagon. "You might want to come north too, Renald. If you do, bring everything you can." He paused. "You're good enough with the tools you have here to do some small metalwork, so take your best scythes and turn them into polearms. Your two best scythes; now don't go skimping around with anything that's a second best or a third best. Get your best, because it's the weapon you're going to use."

Renald frowned. "How do you know that there will be an army? Thulin, burn me, I'm no soldier!"

Thulin continued as if he hadn't heard the comments. "With a polearm you can pull somebody off of a horse and stab them. And, as I think about it, maybe you can take the third best and make yourself a couple of swords."

"What do I know about making a sword? Or about using a sword, for that matter?"

"You can learn," Thulin said, turning north. "Everyone will be needed, Renald. Everyone. They're coming for us." He glanced back at Renald. "A sword really isn't all that tough to make. You take a scythe blade and straighten it out, then you find yourself a piece of wood to act as a guard, to keep the enemy's blade from sliding down and cutting your hand. Mostly you'll just be using things that you've already got."

Renald blinked. He stopped asking questions, but he couldn't stop thinking them. They bunched up inside his brain like cattle all trying to force their way through a single gate.

"Bring all your stock, Renald," Thulin said. "You'll eat them—or your men will eat them—and you'll want the milk. And if you don't, then there'll be men you can trade with for beef or mutton. Food will be scarce, what with everything spoiling so much and the winter stores having run low. Bring everything you've got. Dried beans, dried fruit, everything."

Renald leaned back against the gate to his yard. He felt weak and limp. Finally, he forced out just one question. "Why?"

Thulin hesitated, then stepped away from the wagon, laying a hand on Renald's shoulder again. "I'm sorry to be so abrupt. I . . . well, you know how I am with words, Renald. I don't know what that storm is. But I know what it means. I've never held a sword, but my father fought in the Aiel War. I'm a Borderlander. And that storm means the end is coming, Renald. We need to be there when it arrives." He stopped, then turned and looked to the north, watching those building clouds as a farmhand might watch a poisonous snake he found in the middle of the field. "Light preserve us, my friend. We need to be there."

And with that, he removed his hand and climbed back into the wagon. Renald watched them ease off, nudging the oxen into motion, heading north. Renald watched for a long time, feeling numb.

The distant thunder cracked, like the sound of a whip, smacking against the hills.

The door to the farmhouse opened and shut. Auaine came out to him, gray hair in a bun. It had been that color for years now; she'd grayed early, and Renald had always been fond of the color. Silver, more than gray. Like the clouds.

"Was that Thulin?" Auaine asked, watching the distant wagon throw up dust. A single black chicken feather blew across the roadway.

"Yes."

"And he didn't stay, even to chat?"

Renald shook his head.

"Oh, but Gallanha sent eggs!" She took the basket and began to transfer the eggs into her apron to carry them inside. "She's such a dear. Leave the basket there on the ground; I'm sure she'll send someone for it."

Renald just stared northward.

"Renald?" Auaine asked. "What's gotten into you, you old stump?"

"She polished up her pots for you," he said. "The ones with the copper bottoms. They're sitting on her kitchen table. They're yours if you want them."

Auaine fell silent. Then he heard a sharp sound of cracking, and he looked over his shoulder. She had let her apron grow slack, and the eggs were slipping free, plopping to the ground and cracking.

In a very calm voice, Auaine asked, "Did she say anything else?"

He scratched his head, which hadn't much hair left to speak of. "She said the storm was coming and they had to head north. Thulin said we should go too."

They stood for another moment. Auaine pulled up the edge of her apron, preserving the majority of the eggs. She didn't spare a glance for those that had fallen. She was just staring northward.

Renald turned. The storm had jumped forward again. And it seemed to have grown *darker* somehow.

"I think we ought to listen to them, Renald," Auaine said. "I'll . . . I'll go fix up what we'll need to bring with us from the house. You can go around back and gather the men. Did they say how long we'll be gone?"

"No," he said. "They didn't even really say why. Just that we need to go north for the storm. And . . . that this is the end."

Auaine inhaled sharply. "Well, you just get the men ready. I'll take care of the house."

She bustled inside, and Renald forced himself to turn away from the storm. He rounded the house and entered the barnyard, calling the farmhands together. They were a stout lot, good men, all of them. His own sons had sought their fortunes elsewhere, but his six workers were nearly as close to him as sons. Merk, Favidan, Rinnin, Veshir and Adamad gathered round. Still feeling dazed, Renald sent two to gather up the animals, two more to pack what grain and provisions they had left from the winter and the final man off to fetch Geleni, who had gone into the village for some new seed, just in case the planting had gone bad on account of their stores.

The five men scattered. Renald stood in the farmyard for a moment, then went into the barn to fetch his lightweight forge and pull it out into the sunlight. It wasn't just an anvil, but a full, compact forge, made for moving. He had it on rollers; you couldn't work a forge in a barn. All that dust could take fire. He heaved the handles, wheeling it out to the alcove set off to the side of the yard, built from good bricks, where he could do minor repairs when he needed to.

An hour later, he had the fire stoked. He wasn't as skilled as Thulin, but he'd learned from his father that being able to handle a little of your own forgework made a big difference. Sometimes, you couldn't squander the hours it would take to go to town and back just to fix a broken hinge.

The clouds were still there. He tried not to look at them as he left the forge and headed into the barn. Those clouds were like eyes, peeping over his shoulder.

Inside the barn, light sprinkled down through cracks in the wall, falling on dust and hay. He'd built the structure himself some twenty-five years back. He kept planning to replace some of those warped roofing planks, but now there wouldn't be time.

At the tool wall, he reached for his third-best scythe, but stopped. Taking a deep breath, he took the best scythe off the wall instead. He walked back out to the forge and knocked the haft off the scythe.

As he tossed the wood aside, Veshir—eldest of his farmhands—approached, pulling a pair of goats. When Veshir saw the scythe blade on the forge, his expression grew dark. He tied the goats to a post, then trotted over to Renald, but said nothing.

How to make a polearm? Thulin had said they were good for yanking a man off his horse. Well, he would have to replace the snath with a longer straight shaft of ashwood. The flanged end of the shaft would extend beyond the heel of the blade, shaped into a crude spearpoint and clad with a

piece of tin for strength. And then he would have to heat the
blade and bang off the toe about halfway, making a hook
that could tug a man off his horse and maybe cut him at the
same time. He slid the blade into the burning coals to heat
it, then began to tie on his apron.

Veshir stood there for a minute or so, watching. Finally,
he stepped up, taking Renald by the arm. "Renald, what are
we doing?"

Renald shook his arm free. "We're going north. The storm
is coming and we're going north."

"We're going north for just a storm? It's insanity!"

It was nearly the same thing Renald had said to Thulin.
Distant thunder sounded.

Thulin was right. The crops . . . the skies . . . the food going bad without warning. Even before he'd spoken to Thulin,
Renald had known. Deep within, he'd known. This storm
would not pass overhead then vanish. It had to be confronted.

"Veshir," Renald said, turning back to his work, "you've
been a hand on this farm for . . . what, fifteen years now?
You're the first man I hired. How well have I treated you
and yours?"

"You've done me well," Veshir said. "But burn me, Renald, you've never decided to *leave* the farm before! These
crops, they'll wither to dust if we leave them. This ain't no
southerner wetfarm. How can we just go off?"

"Because," Renald said, "if we don't leave, then it won't
matter if we planted or not."

Veshir frowned.

"Son," Renald said, "you'll do as I say, and that's all we'll
have of it. Go finish gathering the stock."

Veshir stalked away, but he did as he was told. He was a
good man, if hotheaded.

Renald pulled the blade out of the heat, the metal glowing white. He laid it against the small anvil and began to
beat on the knobby section where heel met beard, flattening
it. The sound of his hammer on the metal seemed louder
than it should have been. It rang like the pealing thunder,
and the sounds blended. As if each beat of his hammer was
itself a piece of the storm.

As he worked, the peals seemed to form words. Like
somebody muttering in the back of his head. The same
phrase over and over.

The storm is coming. The storm is coming. . . .

He kept on pounding, keeping the edge on the scythe, but straightening the blade and making a hook at the end. He still didn't know why. But it didn't matter.

The storm was coming and he had to be ready.

Watching the bowlegged soldiers tie Tanera's blanket-wrapped body across a saddle, Falendre fought the desire to begin weeping again, the desire to vomit. She was senior, and had to maintain some composure if she expected the four other surviving *sul'dam* to do so. She tried to tell herself she had seen worse, battles where more than a single *sul'dam* had died, more than one *damane*. That brought her too near thinking of exactly how Tanera and her Miri met their deaths, though, and her mind shied from it.

Huddling by her side, Nenci whimpered as Falendre stroked the *damane*'s head and tried to send soothing feelings through the *a'dam*. That often seemed to work, but not so well today. Her own emotions were too roiled. If only she could forget that the *damane* was shielded, and by whom. By what. Nenci whimpered again.

"You will deliver the message as I directed you?" a man said behind her.

No, not just any man. The sound of his voice stirred the pool of acid in her belly. She made herself turn to face him, made herself meet those cold, hard eyes. They changed with the angle of his head, now blue, now gray, but always like polished gemstones. She had known many hard men, but had she ever known one hard enough to lose a hand and moments later take it as if he had lost a glove? She bowed formally, twitching the *a'dam* so that Nenci did the same. So far they had been treated well for prisoners under the circumstances, even to being given washwater, and supposedly they would not remain prisoners much longer. Yet with this man, who could say what might make that change? The promise of freedom might be part of some scheme.

"I will deliver your message with the care it requires," she began, then stumbled over her tongue. What honorific did she use for him? "My Lord Dragon," she finished hurriedly. The words dried her tongue, but he nodded, so it must have sufficed.

One of the *marath'damane* appeared through that impossible hole in the air, a young woman with her hair in a long braid. She wore enough jewelry for one of the Blood, and of all things, a red dot in the middle of her forehead. "How long do you mean to stay here, Rand?" she demanded as if the hard-eyed young man were a servant rather than who he was. "How close to Ebou Dar are we here? The place is full of Seanchan, you know, and they probably fly *raken* all around it."

"Did Cadsuane send you to ask that?" he said, and her cheeks colored faintly. "Not much longer, Nynaeve. A few minutes."

The young woman shifted her gaze to the other *sul'dam* and *damane*, all taking their lead from Falendre, pretending there were no *marath'damane* watching them, and especially no men in black coats. The others had straightened themselves as best they could. Surya had washed the blood from her face, and from her Tabi's face, and Malian had tied large compresses on them that made them appear to be wearing odd hats. Ciar had managed to clean off most of the vomit she had spilled down the front of her dress.

"I still think I should Heal them," Nynaeve said abruptly. "Hits to the head can cause odd things that don't come on right away."

Surya, her face hardening, moved Tabi behind her as if to protect the *damane*. As if she could. Tabi's pale eyes had widened in horror.

Falendre raised a pleading hand toward the tall young man. Toward the Dragon Reborn, it seemed. "Please. They will receive medical aid as soon as we reach Ebou Dar."

"Give over, Nynaeve," the young man said. "If they don't want Healing, they don't want it." The *marath'damane* scowled at him, gripping her braid so hard that her knuckles turned white. He turned his own attention back to Falendre. "The road to Ebou Dar lies about an hour east of here. You can reach the city by nightfall if you press. The shields on the *damane* will evaporate in about half an hour. Is that right for the *saidar*-woven shields, Nynaeve?" The woman scowled at him in silence. "Is that right, Nynaeve?"

"Half an hour," she replied finally. "But none of this is right, Rand al'Thor. Sending those *damane* back. It isn't right, and you know it."

For a moment, his eyes were even colder. Not harder. That would have been impossible. But for that long moment, they seemed to hold caverns of ice. "Right was easy to find when all I had to care for was a few sheep," he said quietly. "Nowadays, sometimes it's harder to come by." Turning away, he raised his voice. "Logain, get everyone back through the gateway. Yes, yes, Merise. I'm not trying to command you. If you'll deign to join us, though? It will be closing soon."

Marath'damane, the ones who called themselves Aes Sedai, began filing through that mad opening in the air, as did the black-coated men, the Asha'man, all mingling with the hook-nosed soldiers. Several of those finished tying Tanera to the saddle of the horse. The beasts had been provided by the Dragon Reborn. How odd, that he should give them gifts after what had happened.

The hard-eyed young man turned back to her. "Repeat your instructions."

"I am to return to Ebou Dar with a message for our leaders there."

"The Daughter of the Nine Moons," the Dragon Reborn said sternly. "You will deliver my message to her."

Falendre stumbled. She was not in any way worthy to speak to one of the Blood, let alone the High Lady, daughter of the Empress, might she live forever! But this man's expression allowed no argument. Falendre would find a way. "I will deliver your message to her," Falendre continued. "I will tell her that . . . that you bear her no malice for this attack, and that you desire a meeting."

"I *still* desire one," the Dragon Reborn said.

As far as Falendre knew, the Daughter of the Nine Moons had never known about the original meeting. It had been arranged in secret by Anath. And that was why Falendre *knew* for certain that this man must be the Dragon Reborn. For only the Dragon Reborn himself could face one of the Forsaken and not only survive, but come out the victor.

Was that really what she had been? One of the Forsaken? Falendre's mind reeled at the concept. Impossible. And yet, here was the Dragon Reborn. If he lived, if he walked the land, then the Forsaken would, too. She was muddled, her thoughts going in circles, she knew. She bottled up her terror—she would deal with that later. She needed to be in control.

She forced herself to meet those frozen gemstones this man had for eyes. She had to preserve some dignity if only to reassure the four other surviving *sul'dam*. And the *damane*, of course. If the *sul'dam* lost composure again, there would be no hope for the *damane*.

"I will tell her," Falendre said, managing to keep her voice even, "that you *still* desire a meeting with her. That you believe there must be peace between our peoples. And I am to tell her that Lady Anath was . . . was one of the Forsaken."

To the side, she saw some of the *marath'damane* push Anath through the hole in the air, maintaining a stately bearing despite her captivity. She always *had* tried to dominate above her station. Could she really be what this man said she was?

How was Falendre to face the *der'sul'dam* and explain this tragedy, this terrible mess? She itched to be away from it, to find someplace to hide.

"We *must* have peace," the Dragon Reborn said. "I will see it happen. Tell your mistress that she can find me in Arad Doman; I will quell the battle against your forces there. Let her know that I give this as a sign of good faith, just as I release you out of good faith. It is no shame to be manipulated by one of the Forsaken, particularly not . . . that creature. In a way, I rest more easily, now. I worried that one of them would have infiltrated the Seanchan nobility. I should have guessed that it would be Semirhage. She always preferred a challenge."

He spoke of the Forsaken with an incredible sense of familiarity, and it gave Falendre chills.

He glanced at her. "You may go," he said, then walked over and passed through the rip in the air. What she would give to have that traveling trick for Nenci. The last of the *marath'damane* passed through the hole, and it closed, leaving Falendre and the others alone. They were a sorry group. Talha was still crying, and Malian looked ready to sick up. Several of the others had had bloodied faces before they washed, and faint red smears and flakes of crusted blood still marred their skin. Falendre was glad she had been able to avoid accepting Healing for them. She had seen one of those *men* Healing members of the Dragon's party. Who knew what taint it would leave on a person to be beneath those corrupt hands?

"Be strong," she commanded the others, feeling far more uncertain than she sounded. He had actually let her free! She'd barely dared hope for that. Best to be away soon. Very soon. She chivvied the others onto the horses he had given, and within minutes they were riding south, toward Ebou Dar, each *sul'dam* riding with her companion *damane* at her side.

The events of this day could mean having her *damane* stripped from her, being forbidden to hold the *a'dam* ever again. With Anath gone, punishment would be demanded of someone. What would High Lady Suroth say? *Damane* dead, the Dragon Reborn insulted.

Surely losing access to the *a'dam* was the worst that could happen to her. They wouldn't make one such as Falendre *da'covale*, would they? The thought made the bile twist inside of her again.

She would have to explain the events of this day very carefully. There *had* to be a way she could present these matters in a way that would save her life.

She had given her word to the Dragon to speak directly to the Daughter of the Nine Moons. And she would. But she might not do so immediately. Careful consideration would have to be given. Very careful consideration.

She leaned in close to her horse's neck, nudging her mount forward, ahead of the others. That way, they wouldn't see the tears of frustration, pain and terror in her eyes.

Tylee Khirgan, Lieutenant-General of the Ever Victorious Army, sat her horse atop a forested hilltop, looking north-ward. Such a different place this land was. Her homeland, Maram Kashor, was a dry island on the very southeastern tip of Seanchan. The lumma trees there were straight, tow-ering monsters, with fronds sprouting from the top like the hair crest of a member of the High Blood.

The things that passed for trees in this land were gnarled, twisting, branching shrubs by comparison. Their limbs were like the fingers of old soldiers, gone arthritic from years holding the sword. What had the locals called these plants? Brushwood trees? So odd. To think that some of her ances-tors might have come from this place, traveling with Luthair Paendrag to Seanchan.

Her army marched down the road below, throwing dust

into the air. Thousands upon thousands of men. Fewer than she'd had before, but not by many. It had been two weeks since her fight with the Aiel, where Perrin Aybara's plan had worked impressively. Fighting alongside a man like him was always a bittersweet experience. Sweet for the sheer genius of it. Bitter for the worry that one day, they would face each other on the battlefield. Tylee was not one who enjoyed a challenge in a fight. She'd always preferred to win straight out.

Some generals said that never struggling meant never being forced to improve. Tylee figured that she and her men would do *their* improving on the practice field, and leave the struggling to her enemies.

She would not like to face Perrin. No, she would not. And not just because she was fond of him.

Slow hoofbeats sounded on the earth. She glanced to the side as Mishima rode his horse, a pale gelding, up next to hers. He had his helm tied to his saddle, and his scarred face was thoughtful. They were a pair, the two of them. Tylee's own face bore its share of old scars.

Mishima saluted her, more respectful now that Tylee had been raised to the Blood. That particular message, delivered by *raken,* had been an unexpected one. It was an honor, and one she still wasn't accustomed to.

"Still mulling over the battle?" Mishima asked.

"I am," Tylee said. Two weeks, and still it dominated her mind. "What do you think?"

"Of Aybara, you mean?" Mishima asked. He still spoke to her like a friend, even if he kept himself from meeting her eyes. "He is a good soldier. Perhaps too focused, too driven. But solid."

"Yes," Tylee said, then shook her head. "The world is changing, Mishima. In ways we cannot anticipate. First Aybara, and then the oddities."

Mishima nodded thoughtfully. "The men don't want to speak of them."

"The events have happened too often to be the work of delusion," Tylee said. "The scouts are seeing *something.*"

"Men don't just vanish," Mishima said. "You think it's the One Power?"

"I do not know what it is," she said. She glanced over the trees around her. Some trees she'd passed earlier had begun to send out spring growth, but not a one of these had done so. They looked skeletal, though the air was warm enough for it to be planting season already. "Do they have trees like this in Halamak?"

"Not exactly like them," Mishima said. "But I've seen their like before."

"Should they have budded by now?"

He shrugged. "I'm a soldier, General Tylee."

"I hadn't noticed," she said dryly.

He grunted. "I mean that I don't pay attention to trees. Trees don't bleed. Perhaps they should have budded, but perhaps not. Few things make sense on this side of the ocean. Trees that don't bud in spring, that's just another oddity. Better that than more *marath'damane* acting like they were of the Blood, everyone bowing and scraping to them." He shuddered visibly.

Tylee nodded, but she didn't share his revulsion. Not completely. She wasn't certain what to think of Perrin Aybara and his Aes Sedai, let alone his Asha'man. And she didn't know much more about trees than Mishima. But it felt to her that they should have started to bud. And those men the scouts kept seeing in the fields, how could they vanish so quickly, even with the One Power?

The quartermaster had opened up one of their packs of travel rations today and found only dust. Tylee would have started a search for a thief or a prankster if the quartermaster hadn't insisted that he'd checked that pack just moments before. Karm was a solid man; he'd been her quartermaster for years. He did not make mistakes.

Rotting food was so common here. Karm blamed the heat of this strange land. But travel rations couldn't rot or spoil, at least not this unpredictably. The omens were all bad, these days. Earlier today, she'd seen two dead rats lying on their backs, one with a tail in the mouth of the other. It was the worst omen she'd ever seen in her life, and it still chilled her to think of it.

Something was happening. Perrin hadn't been willing to speak of it much, but she saw a weight upon him. He knew much more than he had spoken.

We can't afford to be fighting these people, she thought. It was a rebellious thought, one she wouldn't speak to Mishima. She didn't dare ponder it. The Empress, might

she live forever, had ordered that this land be reclaimed.
Suroth and Galgan were the Empire's chosen leaders in the
venture, until the Daughter of the Nine Moons revealed
herself. While Tylee couldn't know the High Lady Tuon's
thoughts, Suroth and Galgan were united in their desire to
see this land subdued. It was practically the only thing they
did agree upon.

None of them would listen to suggestions that they should
be looking for allies among the people of this land, rather
than enemies. Thinking about it was close to treason. Insubordination, at least. She sighed and turned to Mishima,
prepared to give the order to begin scouting for a place to
camp for the night.

She froze. Mishima had an arrow through his neck, a
wicked, barbed thing. She hadn't heard it strike. He met her
eyes, stunned, trying to speak and only letting out blood.
He slid from the saddle and collapsed in a heap as something enormous charged through the underbrush beside
Tylee, cracking gnarled branches, throwing itself at her.
She barely had time to pull free her sword and shout before
Duster—a good, solid warhorse that had never failed her in
battle—reared in panic, tossing her to the ground.

That probably saved her life, as her attacker swung a
thick-bladed sword, cutting into the saddle where Tylee
had been. She scrambled to her feet, armor clanking, and
screamed the alert. "To arms! Attack!"

Her voice joined hundreds who made the same call at
virtually the same time. Men screamed. Horses whinnied.

An ambush, she thought, raising her blade. *And we
walked right into it! Where are the scouts? What happened?* She launched herself at the man who had tried to
kill her. He spun, snorting.

And for the first time, she saw just what he was. Not quite
a man—instead, some creature with twisted features, the
head covered in coarse brown hair, the too-wide forehead
wrinkled with thick skin. Those eyes were disturbingly
human-like, but the nose below was flattened like that of
a boar and the mouth jutted with two prominent tusks. The
creature roared at her, spittle spraying from its nearly human lips.

Blood of my Fathers Forgotten, she thought. *What have
we stumbled into?* The monster was a nightmare, given a

body and let loose to kill. It was a thing she had always
dismissed as superstition.

She charged the creature, knocking aside its thick sword
as it tried to attack. She spun, falling into Beat the Brushes,
and separated the beast's arm from its shoulder. She struck
again, and its head followed the arm to the ground, cut free.
It stumbled, somehow still walking three steps, before collapsing.

The trees rustled, more branches snapping. Just down
from her hillside, Tylee saw that hundreds of the creatures
had broken out of the underbrush, attacking the line of her
men near the middle, causing chaos. More and more of the
monsters poured between the trees.

How had this happened? How had these things gotten so
close to Ebou Dar! They were well inside the Seanchan defensive perimeter, only a day's march from the capital.

Tylee charged down the hillside, bellowing for her honor
guard as more of the beasts roared out of the trees behind her.

Graendal lounged in a stonework room lined with adoring
men and women, each one a perfect specimen, each one
wearing little more than a robe of diaphanous white cloth.
A warm fire played in the hearth, illuminating a fine rug
of blood red. That rug was woven in the design of young
women and men entangled in ways that would have made
even an experienced courtesan blush. The open windows let
in afternoon light, the lofty position of her palace giving a
view of pines and a shimmering lake below.

She sipped sweetbristle juice, wearing a pale blue dress
after the Domani cut—she was growing fond of their fashions, though her dress was far more filmy than the ones
they wore. These Domani were too fond of whispering
when Graendal preferred a nice sharp scream. She took another sip of juice. What an interestingly sour flavor it had. It
was exotic during this Age, since the trees now grew only
on distant islands.

Without warning, a gateway spun open in the center of
the room. She cursed under her breath as one of her finest
prizes—a succulent young woman named Thurasa, a member of the Domani merchant council—nearly lost an arm to
the thing. The gateway let in a sweltering heat that marred the

perfect mix of chill mountain air and fireplace warmth she
had cultivated.

Graendal kept her composure, forcing herself to lounge
back in her overstuffed velvet chair. A messenger in black
strode through the portal, and she knew what he wanted
before he spoke. Only Moridin knew where to find her, now
that Sammael was dead.

"My Lady, your presence is required by—"

"Yes, yes," she said. "Stand straight and let me see you."

The youth stood still, just two steps into the room. And
my, he was attractive! Pale golden hair as was so rare in
many parts of the world, green eyes that shimmered like
moss-grown pools, a lithe figure taut with just enough
muscle. Graendal clicked her tongue. Was Moridin trying
to tempt her by sending his very most pretty, or was the
choice coincidental?

No. Among the Chosen, there were no coincidences.
Graendal nearly reached out with a weave of Compulsion
to seize the boy for herself. However, she restrained herself. Once a man had known that level of Compulsion, there
was no way to recover him, and Moridin might be angered.
She did need to worry about his whims. The man never had
been stable, even during the early years. If she intended to
see herself as Nae'blis someday, it was important not to rile
him until it was time to strike.

She turned her attention away from the messenger—if
she couldn't have him, then she wasn't interested in him—
and looked through the open gateway. She hated being
forced to meet with one of the other Chosen on their terms.
She hated leaving her stronghold and her pets. Most of all,
she hated being forced to grovel before one who should
have been her subordinate.

There was nothing to be done about it. Moridin was
Nae'blis. For now. And that meant, hate it or not, Graendal
had no choice but to answer his summons. So she set aside
her drink, then stood and walked through the gateway, her
diaphanous pale blue gown shimmering with golden embroidery.

It was distractingly hot on the other side of the gateway. She immediately wove Air and Water, cooling the air
around her. She was in a black stone building, with ruddy
light coming in the windows. They had no glass in them.

That reddish tint implied a sunset, but it was barely mid-afternoon back in Arad Doman. Surely she hadn't traveled *that* far, had she?

The room was furnished only with hard chairs of the deepest black wood. Moridin certainly was lacking in imagination lately. Everything of black and red, and all focused on killing those fool boys from the village of Rand al'Thor. Was she the only one who saw that al'Thor himself was the real threat? Why not just kill him and be done with it?

The most obvious answer to that question—that none of them so far had proven strong enough to defeat him—was one she did not enjoy contemplating.

She walked to the window and found the reason for the rust-colored light. Outside, the claylike ground was stained red from the iron in the soil. She was on the second level of a deep black tower, the stones drawing in the burning heat of the sky. Very little vegetation sprouted outside, and that which did was spotted with black. So, it was the deep northeastern Blight. It had been some time since she'd been here. Moridin seemed to have located a fortress, of all things.

A collection of shoddy huts stood in the shadow of the fortress, and a few patches of blightstrain crops marked fields in the distance. They were probably trying a new strain, coaxing it to grow in the area. Perhaps several different crops; that would explain the patches. Guards prowled the area, wearing black uniforms despite the heat. Soldiers were necessary to fight off attacks from the various Shadowspawn that inhabited the lands this deep within the Blight. Those creatures obeyed no master save for the Great Lord himself. What was Moridin doing all the way out here?

Her speculation was cut short as footsteps announced other arrivals. Demandred entered through the doorway to the south, and he was accompanied by Mesaana. Had they arrived together, then? They assumed that Graendal did not know of their little alliance, a pact that included Semirhage. But honestly, if they wanted to keep that a secret, couldn't they see that they shouldn't answer a summons together?

Graendal hid a smile as she nodded to the two of them, then selected the largest and most comfortable-looking of the room's chairs to sit in. She ran a finger along the smooth, dark wood, feeling the grain beneath the lacquer. Demandred and Mesaana regarded her coldly, and she knew them

well enough to pick out hints of their surprise at seeing her.
So. They had anticipated this meeting, had they? But not
Graendal's presence at it? Best to pretend that she herself
was not confused. She smiled knowingly at the two of them
and caught a flash of anger in Demandred's eyes.

That man frustrated her, though she would never admit it
out loud. Mesaana was in the White Tower, pretending to be
one of what passed for an Aes Sedai in this Age. She was obvious and easy to read; Graendal's agents in the White Tower
kept her well apprised of Mesaana's activities. And, of course,
Graendal's own newly minted association with Aran'gar was
helpful as well. Aran'gar was playing with the rebel Aes Sedai,
the ones who were besieging the White Tower.

Yes, Mesaana did not confuse her, and the others were
equally easy to track. Moridin was gathering the Great
Lord's forces for the Last Battle, and his war preparations left
him very little time for the south—though his two minions,
Cyndane and Moghedien, occasionally showed their faces
there. They spent their time rallying the Darkfriends and
occasionally trying to follow Moridin's orders that the two
ta'veren—Perrin Aybara and Matrim Cauthon—be killed.

She was certain Sammael had fallen to Rand al'Thor
during the struggle for Illian. In fact—now that Graendal
had a clue that Semirhage had been pulling strings with the
Seanchan—she was confident she knew the plans of every
one of the other seven remaining Chosen.

Except Demandred.

What was that blasted man up to? She'd have traded all of
her knowledge of Mesaana's and Aran'gar's doings for even
a hint of Demandred's plans. He stood there, handsome and
hawk-nosed, his lips drawn in perpetual anger. Demandred
never smiled, never seemed to enjoy anything. Though he
was one of the foremost generals among the Chosen, warfare had never seemed to bring him joy. Once she had heard
him say that he would laugh the day he could snap the neck
of Lews Therin. And only then.

He was a fool to bear that grudge. To think he might have
been on the other side—might have become the Dragon
himself, had things turned out differently. Still, fool or not,
he was extremely dangerous, and Graendal did *not* like
being ignorant of his plans. Where had he set up? Deman-

dred liked having armies to command, but there were none left moving in the world.

Save perhaps for those Borderlanders. Could he have managed to infiltrate *them*? That certainly would have been a coup. But surely she'd have heard something; she had spies in that camp.

She shook her head, wishing for a drink to wet her lips. This northern air was too dry; she much preferred the Domani humidity. Demandred folded his arms, remaining standing as Mesaana seated herself. She had chin-length dark hair and watery blue eyes. Her floor-length white dress bore no embroidery, and she wore no jewelry. A scholar to the core. Sometimes Graendal thought Mesaana had gone over to the Shadow because it offered a more interesting opportunity for research.

Mesaana was fully dedicated to the Great Lord now, just like the rest of them, but she seemed a second-rate member of the Chosen. Making boasts she couldn't fulfill, allying herself to stronger parties but lacking the skill to manipulate them. She'd done evil works in the Great Lord's name, but had never managed the grand achievements of Chosen like Semirhage and Demandred. Let alone Moridin.

And, as Graendal began to think on Moridin, the man entered. Now, *there* was a handsome creature. Demandred looked like a knob-faced peasant compared with him. Yes, this body was *much* better than his previous one. He was almost pretty enough to be one of her pets, though that chin spoiled the face. Too prominent, too strong. Still, that stark black hair atop a tall, broad-shouldered body. . . . She smiled, thinking of him kneeling in a filmy outfit of white, looking at her adoringly, his mind wrapped in Compulsion to the point that he saw nobody—nothing—other than Graendal.

Mesaana rose as soon as Moridin entered, and Graendal reluctantly did likewise. He wasn't her pet, not yet. He was Nae'blis, and he had begun to demand more and more shows of obedience from them in recent days. The Great Lord gave him the authority. All three of the other Chosen reluctantly bowed their heads to him; only to him among all men would they show deference. He noted their obedience with stern eyes as he stalked to the front of the room, where the wall of charcoal black stones was set with a mantel. What had possessed someone to build a fortress out of *black* rock in the Blight's heat?

Graendal sat back down. Were the other Chosen coming? If not, what did it mean?

Mesaana spoke before Moridin could say anything. "Moridin," she said, stepping forward, "we need to rescue her."

"You will speak when I give you leave, Mesaana," he replied coldly. "You are not yet forgiven."

She cringed, then obviously grew angry at herself for it. Moridin ignored her, glancing over at Graendal, eyes narrow. What was that look for?

"You may continue," he finally said to Mesaana, "but remember your place."

Mesaana's lips formed a line, but she did not argue. "Moridin," she said, tone less demanding. "You saw the wisdom in agreeing to meet with us. Surely that was because you are as shocked as we are. We do not have the resources to help her ourselves; she is bound to be well guarded by Aes Sedai and those Asha'man. You need to help us free her."

"Semirhage deserves her imprisonment," Moridin said, resting his arm on the mantel, still turned away from Mesaana.

Semirhage, captured? Graendal had just barely learned that the woman was impersonating an important Seanchan! What had she done to get herself captured? If there were Asha'man, then it seemed she'd managed to be taken by al'Thor himself!

Despite her startlement, Graendal maintained her knowing smile. Demandred glanced at her. If he and Mesaana had asked for this meeting, then why had Moridin sent for Graendal?

"But think of what Semirhage might reveal!" Mesaana said, ignoring Graendal. "Beyond that, she is one of the Chosen. It is our duty to aid her."

And beyond that, Graendal thought, *she is a member of the little alliance you two made. Perhaps the strongest member. Losing her will be a blow to your bid for control of the Chosen.*

"She disobeyed," Moridin said. "She was not to try to kill al'Thor."

"She didn't intend to," Mesaana said hastily. "Our woman there thinks that the bolt of Fire was a reaction of surprise, not an intention to kill."

"And what say you of this, Demandred?" Moridin said, glancing at the shorter man.

"I want Lews Therin," Demandred said, his voice deep, his expression dark, as always. "Semirhage knows that. She also knows that if she'd killed him, I would have found her and claimed her life in retribution. Nobody kills al'Thor. Nobody but me."

"You or the Great Lord, Demandred," Moridin said, voice dangerous. "His will dominates us all."

"Yes, yes, of course it does," Mesaana cut in, stepping forward, plain dress brushing the mirror-bright black marble floor. "Moridin, the fact remains that she didn't intend to kill him, just to capture him. I—"

"Of course she intended to capture him!" Moridin roared, causing Mesaana to flinch. "That was what she was *ordered* to do. And she failed at it, Mesaana. Failed spectacularly, leaving him wounded despite my express command that he wasn't to be harmed! And for that incompetence, she will suffer. I will give you no aid in rescuing her. In fact, I *forbid* you to send her aid. Do you understand?"

Mesaana flinched again. Demandred did not; he met Moridin's eyes, then nodded. Yes, he was a cold one. Perhaps Graendal underestimated him. He very well might be the most powerful of the three, more dangerous than Semirhage. She was emotionless and controlled, true, but sometimes emotion was appropriate. It could drive a man like Demandred to actions that a more coolheaded person couldn't even contemplate.

Moridin looked down, flexing his left hand, as if it were stiff. Graendal caught a hint of pain in his expression.

"Let Semirhage rot," Moridin growled. "Let her see what it is to be the one questioned. Perhaps the Great Lord will find some use for her in the coming weeks, but that is *his* to determine. Now. Tell me of your preparations."

Mesaana paled just slightly, glancing at Graendal. Demandred's face grew red, as if he was incredulous that they would be interrogated in front of another Chosen. Graendal smiled at them.

"I am perfectly poised," Mesaana said, turning back to Moridin with a sweep of her head. "The White Tower and those fools who rule it will shortly be mine. I will deliver not just a broken White Tower to our Great Lord, but an entire brood of channelers who—one way or another—will serve our cause in the Last Battle. This time, the Aes Sedai will fight for us!"

"A bold claim," Moridin said.

"I will make it happen," Mesaana said evenly. "My followers infest the Tower like an unseen plague, festering inside of a healthy-looking man at market. More and more join our cause. Some intentionally, others unwittingly. It is the same either way."

Graendal listened thoughtfully. Aran'gar claimed that the rebel Aes Sedai would eventually secure the Tower, though Graendal herself wasn't certain. Who would be victorious, the child or the fool? Did it matter?

"And you?" Moridin asked Demandred.

"My rule is secure," Demandred said simply. "I gather for war. We will be ready."

Graendal itched for him to say more than that, but Moridin did not push. Still, it was much more than she'd been able to glean on her own. Demandred apparently held a throne and had armies. Which were gathered. The Borderlanders marching through the east seemed more and more likely.

"You two may withdraw," Moridin said.

Mesaana sputtered at the dismissal, but Demandred simply turned and stalked away. Graendal nodded to herself; she'd have to watch him. The Great Lord favored action, and often those who could bring armies to his name were best rewarded. Demandred could very well be her most important rival—following Moridin himself, of course.

He had not dismissed her, and so she remained seated as the other two withdrew. Moridin stayed where he was, one arm leaning against the mantel. There was silence in the too-black room for a time, and then a servant in a crisp red uniform entered, bearing two cups. He was an ugly thing, with a flat face and bushy eyebrows, worth no more than a passing glance.

She took a sip of her drink and tasted new wine, just slightly tart, but quite good. It was growing hard to find good wine; the Great Lord's touch on the world tainted everything, spoiling food, ruining even that which never should have been able to spoil.

Moridin waved the servant away, not taking his own cup. Graendal feared poison, of course. She always did when drinking from another's cup. However, there would be no reason for Moridin to poison her; he was Nae'blis. While most of them resisted showing subservience to him, more and more he was exerting his will on them, pushing them into positions as his lessers. She suspected that, if he wished, he could have her executed in any manner of ways and the Great Lord would grant it to him. So she drank and waited.

"Did you glean much from what you heard, Graendal?" Moridin asked.

"As much as could be gleaned," she answered carefully.

"I know how you crave information. Moghedien has always been known as the spider, pulling strings from afar, but you are in many ways better at it than she. She winds so many webs that she gets caught in them. You are more careful. You strike only when wise, but are not afraid of conflict. The Great Lord approves of your initiative."

"My dear Moridin," she said, smiling to herself, "you flatter me."

"Do not toy with me, Graendal," he said, voice hard. "Take your compliments and be silent."

She recoiled as if slapped, but said no more.

"I gave you leave to listen to the other two as a reward," Moridin said. "Nae'blis has been chosen, but there will be other positions of high glory in the Great Lord's reign. Some much higher than others. Today was a taste of the privileges you might enjoy."

"I live only to serve the Great Lord."

"Then serve him in this," Moridin said, looking directly at her. "Al'Thor moves for Arad Doman. He is to live unharmed until he can face me at that last day. But he *must not* be allowed to make peace in your lands. He will attempt to restore order. You must find ways to prevent that from happening."

"It will be done."

"Go, then," Moridin said, waving a hand sharply.

She rose, thoughtful, and started toward the door.

"And Graendal," he said.

She hesitated, glancing at him. He stood against the mantel, back mostly to her. He seemed to be staring at nothing, just looking at the black stones of the far wall. Strangely, he looked a great deal like al'Thor—of whom she had numerous sketches via her spies—when he stood like that.

"The end is near," Moridin said. "The Wheel has groaned its final rotation, the clock has lost its spring, the serpent heaves its final gasps. He must know pain of heart. He must know frustration, and he must know anguish. Bring these to him. And you will be rewarded."

She nodded, then made her way through the provided gateway, back to her stronghold in the hills of Arad Doman.

To plot.

Rodel Ituralde's mother, now thirty years buried in the clay hills of his Domani homeland, had been fond of a particular saying: "Things always have to get worse before they can get better." She'd said it when she'd yanked free his festering tooth as a boy, an ailment he'd earned while playing at swords with the village boys. She'd said it when he'd lost his first love to a lordling who wore a hat with feathers and whose soft hands and jeweled sword had proven he'd never known a real battle. And she'd say it now, if she were with him on the ridge, watching the Seanchan march upon the city nestled in the shallow valley below.

He studied the city, Darluna, through his looking glass, shading the end with his left hand, his gelding quiet beneath him in the evening light. He and several of his Domani kept to this small stand of trees; it would take the Dark One's own luck for the Seanchan to spot him, even with looking glasses of their own.

Things always had to get worse before they could get better. He'd lit a fire under the Seanchan by destroying their supply depots all across Almoth Plain and into Tarabon. He shouldn't be surprised, then, to see a grand army like this one—a hundred and fifty thousand strong at least—come to quench that fire. It showed a measure of respect. They did not underestimate him, these Seanchan invaders. He wished that they did.

Ituralde moved his looking glass, studying a group of riders among the Seanchan force. They rode in pairs, one woman of each pair wearing gray, the other red and blue. They were far too distant, even with the glass, for him to make out the embroidered lightning bolts on the dresses of those in red and blue, nor could he see the chains that linked each pair together. *Damane* and *sul'dam*.

This army had at least a hundred pairs, probably more. If that weren't enough, he could see one of the flying beasts above, drawing close for its rider to drop a message to the general. With those creatures to carry their scouts, the Seanchan army had an unprecedented edge. Ituralde would have traded ten thousand soldiers for one of those flying beasts. Other commanders might have wanted the *damane*, with their ability to throw lightnings and cause the earth to heave, but battles—like wars—were won by information as often as they were by weapons.

Of course, the Seanchan had superior weapons as well as superior scouts. They also had superior troops. Though Ituralde was proud of his Domani, many of his men were ill trained or too old for fighting. He almost lumped himself in that latter group, as the years were beginning to pile on him like bricks on a pallet. But he gave no thought to retiring. When he'd been a boy, he'd often felt a sense of urgency—a worry that by the time he came of age, the great battles would all be done, all the glory won.

Sometimes, he envied boys their foolishness.

"They march hard, Rodel," Lidrin said. He was a youth with a scar across the left side of his face, and he wore a fashionable thin black mustache. "They badly want to capture that city." Lidrin had been untested as an officer before this campaign began. He was a veteran now. Although Ituralde and his forces had won nearly every engagement they'd had with the Seanchan, Lidrin had seen three of his companion officers fall, poor Jaalam Nishur among them. From their deaths, Lidrin had learned one of the bitter lessons of warfare: winning didn't necessarily mean living. And following orders often didn't mean either winning or living.

Lidrin didn't wear his customary uniform. Neither did Ituralde or any of the men with him. Their uniforms had been needed elsewhere, and that left them with simple worn coats and brown trousers, many borrowed or bought from locals.

Ituralde raised his looking glass again, thinking on Lidrin's comment. The Seanchan did indeed march with speed; they were planning to take Darluna quickly. They saw the advantage it would offer, for they were a clever foe, and they had returned to Ituralde an excitement he had assumed that he'd left behind years ago.

"Yes, they push hard," he said. "But what would you

do, Lidrin? An enemy force of two hundred thousand behind you, another of a hundred and fifty thousand ahead of you. With enemies on all sides, would you march your men maybe just a little too hard if you knew that you'd find refuge at the end?"

Lidrin did not respond. Ituralde turned his looking glass, examining spring fields clustered with workers going about their planting. Darluna was a large city for these parts. Nothing here in the west could match the grand cities of the east and south, of course, regardless of what people from Tanchico or Falme would like to claim. Still, Darluna had a sturdy granite wall a good twenty feet tall. There was no beauty to the fortification, but the wall was solid, and it wrapped a city big enough to make any country boy gawk. In his youth, Ituralde would have called it grand. That was before he'd gone to fight the Aiel at Tar Valon.

Either way, it was the best fortification to be found in the area, and the Seanchan commanders no doubt knew it. They could have chosen to hunker down on a hilltop; fighting surrounded would make full use of those *damane*. However, that would not only leave no retreat, but would leave them minimal opportunities for supply. A city would have wells and perhaps leftover winter stores inside the wall. And Darluna, which had had its garrisons pressed into service elsewhere, was far too small to offer serious resistance. . . .

Ituralde lowered his looking glass. He didn't need it to know what was happening as the Seanchan scouts reached the city, demanding that the gates be opened to the invading force. He closed his eyes, waiting.

Lidrin exhaled softly beside him. "They didn't notice," he whispered. "They're moving the bulk of their forces up to the walls, waiting to be let in!"

"Give the order," Ituralde said, opening his eyes. There was one problem with superior scouts like the *raken*. When you had access to a tool so useful, you tended to rely upon it. And reliance like that could be exploited.

In the distance, the "farmers" on the fields tossed aside their tools and pulled bows from hidden clefts in the ground. The gates to the city opened, revealing the soldiers hiding inside—soldiers that the Seanchan *raken* scouts had claimed were a four-day ride away.

Ituralde raised his looking glass. The battle began.

The Prophet's fingers bit dirt, tearing trenches in the soil as he scrambled up to the top of the forested hillside. His followers straggled behind. So few. So few! But he would rebuild. The glory of the Dragon Reborn followed him, and no matter where he went, he found willing souls. Those with hearts that were pure, those who had hands that burned to destroy the Shadow.

Yes! Think not of the past, think of the future, when the Lord Dragon would rule all of the land! When men would be subject only to him, and to his Prophet beneath him. Those days would be glorious indeed, days when none would dare scorn the Prophet or deny his will. Days when the Prophet wouldn't have to suffer the indignity of living near the very camp—the *very* one—as Shadowspawn like that creature Aybara. Glorious days. Glorious days were coming.

It was difficult to keep his thoughts on those future glories. The world around him was filthy. Men denied the Dragon and sought the Shadow. Even his own followers. Yes! That must have been why they had fallen. That must have been why so many died when assaulting the city of Malden and its Darkfriend Aiel.

The Prophet had been so certain. He had assumed that the Dragon would protect his people, lead them to a powerful victory. Then the Prophet would finally have gotten his wish. He could have killed Perrin Aybara with his own hands! Twist that too-thick bull's neck in his fingers, twist it around, squeezing, feeling the bones crack, the flesh wring, the breath stop.

The Prophet reached the top of the ridge and brushed the dirt from his fingers. He breathed in and out, scanning around him, underbrush rustling as his few remaining followers climbed up toward him. The canopy was dense overhead, and very little sunlight peeked through. Light. Radiant light.

The Dragon had appeared to him the night before the attack. Appeared in glory! A figure of light, glowing in the air in shimmering robes. Kill Perrin Aybara! the Dragon had commanded. Kill him! And so the Prophet had sent his very best tool, Aybara's own dear friend.

That boy, that tool, had failed. Aram was dead. The Prophet's men had confirmed it. Tragedy! Was that why they had not prospered? Was that why, out of his thousands of followers, he now only had a bare handful? No. No! They must have turned against him, secretly worshipping the Shadow. Aram! Darkfriend! That was why he had failed.

The first of his followers—battered, dirtied, bloodied, exhausted—reached the top of the ridge. They wore threadbare clothing. Clothing that did not set them above others. The clothing of simplicity and goodness.

The Prophet counted them off. Fewer than a hundred. So few. This cursed forest was so dark, despite the daylight. Thick trunks stood shoulder-to-shoulder, and the sky overhead had grown dim with cloud cover. The underbrush of thin-branched boneweed shrubs matted together, forming an almost unnatural barrier, and those shrubs scratched like claws on his skin.

With that underbrush and the sharp earthen bank, the army could not follow this way. Though the Prophet had escaped from Aybara's camp barely an hour before, he already felt safe. They would go north, where Aybara and his Darkfriends would not find them. There, the Prophet could rebuild. He had stayed with Aybara only because his followers had been strong enough to keep Aybara's Darkfriends away.

His dear followers. Brave men, and true, every one. Killed by Darkfriends. He mourned them, bowing his head and muttering a prayer. His followers joined him. They were weary, but the light of zeal shone in their eyes. Any who were weak, or who lacked dedication, had fled or been killed long ago. These were the best, the mightiest, the most faithful. Each one had killed many Darkfriends in the name of the Dragon Reborn.

With them, he could rebuild. But first he had to escape Aybara. The Prophet was too weak, now, to face him. But later he would kill him. Yes . . . Fingers on that neck . . . Yes . . .

The Prophet could remember a time when he'd been called something else. Masema. Those days were growing very blurry to him, like memories from a former life. Indeed, just as all men were reborn into the Pattern, so had Masema been reborn—he had cast off his old, profane life and had become the Prophet.

The last of his followers joined him atop the cliff face. He spat at their feet. They had failed him. Cowards. They should have fought better! He should have been able to win that city.

He turned north and pushed his way forward. This landscape was growing familiar to him, though they had nothing like it up in the Borderlands. They would climb to the highlands, then cross over and enter Almoth Plain. There were Dragonsworn there, followers of the Prophet, even if many didn't know of him. There he could rebuild quickly.

He pushed through a patch of the dark brush and entered a small clearing. His men followed quickly. They would need food, soon, and he would have to send them hunting. No fires. They couldn't afford to alert—

"Hello, Masema," a quiet voice said.

He hissed, spinning, his followers bunching around him and pulling out weapons. Swords for some, knives, quarterstaffs, and the occasional polearm. The Prophet scanned the dim afternoon clearing, searching for the one who had spoken. He found her standing on a little outcrop of rock a short distance away, a woman with a prominent Saldaean nose, slightly tilted eyes, and shoulder-length black hair. She wore green, with skirts divided for riding, her arms folded in front of her.

Faile Aybara, wife of the Shadowspawn, Perrin Aybara. "Take her!" the Prophet screamed, pointing. Several of his followers scrambled forward, but most hesitated. They had seen what he had not. Shadows in the forest behind Aybara's wife, a half-circle of them. They were the shapes of men, with bows pointed into the clearing.

Faile waved with a sharp motion, and the arrows flew. Those of his followers who had run at his bidding fell first, crying out in the silent forest before falling to the loamy earth. The Prophet bellowed, each arrow seeming to pierce his own heart. His beloved followers! His friends! His dear brothers!

An arrow slammed into him, throwing him backward to the ground. Around him, men died, just as they had earlier. Why, why hadn't the Dragon protected them? Why? Suddenly, the horror of it all returned to him, the sinking terror of watching his men fall in waves, at watching them die at the hands of those Darkfriend Aiel.

It was Perrin Aybara's fault. If only the Prophet had seen earlier, back in the early days, before he'd even recognized the Lord Dragon for who he was!

"It's my fault," the Prophet whispered as the last of his followers died. It had taken several arrows to stop some of them. That made him proud.

Slowly, he forced himself back to his feet, hand to his shoulder, where the shaft sprouted. He'd lost too much blood. Dizzy, he fell to his knees.

Faile stepped down off her stone and entered the clearing. Two women wearing trousers followed. They looked concerned, but Faile ignored their protests that she stay back. She walked right up to the Prophet, then slid her knife from her belt. It was a fine blade, with a cast hilt that showed a wolf's head. That was well. Looking at it, the Prophet remembered the day when he'd earned his own blade. The day his father had given it to him.

"Thank you for helping to assault Malden, Masema," Faile said, stopping right in front of him. Then she reached up and rammed that knife into his heart. He fell backward, his own blood hot on his chest.

"Sometimes, a wife must do what her husband cannot," he heard Faile tell her women as his eyes fluttered, trying to close. "It is a dark thing we did this day, but necessary. Let no one speak of it to my husband. He must never know."

Her voice grew distant. The Prophet fell.

Masema. That had been his name. He'd earned his sword on his fifteenth birthday. His father had been so proud.

It's over, then, he thought, unable to keep his eyes open. He closed them, falling as if through an endless void. *Did I do well, Father, or did I fail?*

There was no answer. And he joined with the void, tumbling into an endless sea of blackness.

CHAPTER
I

Tears from Steel

The Wheel of Time turns, and Ages come and pass, leaving memories that become legend. Legend fades to myth, and even myth is long forgotten when the Age that gave it birth comes again. In one Age, called the Third Age by some, an Age yet to come, an Age long past, a wind rose around the alabaster spire known as the White Tower. The wind was not the beginning. There are neither beginnings nor endings to the turning of the Wheel of Time. But it was *a* beginning.

The wind twisted around the magnificent Tower, brushing perfectly fitted stones and flapping majestic banners. The structure was somehow both graceful and powerful at the same time; a metaphor, perhaps, for those who had inhabited it for over three thousand years. Few looking upon the Tower would guess that at its heart, it had been both broken and corrupted. Separately.

The wind blew, passing through a city that seemed more a work of art than a workaday capital. Each building was a marvel; even the simple granite shopfronts had been crafted by meticulous Ogier hands to evoke wonder and beauty. Here a dome hinted at the form of a rising sun. There a fountain sprang from the top of a building itself, cresting what appeared to be two waves crashing together. On one cobbled street, a pair of steep three-story buildings stood opposite one another, each crafted into the form of a maiden. The marble creations—half-statue, half-dwelling—reached with stone hands toward one another as if in greeting, hair billowing behind, immobile, yet carved with such delicacy that every strand seemed to undulate in the wind's passing.

The streets themselves were far less grand. Oh, they had been laid out with care, radiating from the White Tower like streaks of sunlight. Yet that sunlight was dimmed by refuse and clutter, hints at the crowding the siege had caused. And perhaps the crowding wasn't the only reason for the disrepair. The storefront signs and awnings hadn't seen wash or polish in far too long. Rotting garbage piled where it had been dumped in alleys, drawing flies and rats but driving away all others. Dangerous toughs lounged on the street corners. Once, they'd never have dared do that, and certainly not with such arrogance.

Where was the White Tower, the law? Young fools laughed, saying that the city's troubles were the fault of the siege, and that things would settle down once the rebels were quelled. Older men shook their gray-streaked heads and muttered that things had never been this bad, even when the savage Aiel had besieged Tar Valon some twenty years previously.

Merchants ignored both young and old. They had their own problems, mainly on Southharbor, where trade into the city by way of the river had nearly come to a halt. Thick-chested workers toiled beneath the eyes of an Aes Sedai wearing a red-fringed shawl; she used the One Power to remove wards and weaken the stone, while the workmen broke the rock apart and hauled it away.

The workmen had sleeves rolled up, exposing curls of dark hair along burly arms, as they swung pick or hammer, pounding at the ancient stones. They dripped sweat onto rock or into the water below as they dug at the roots of the chain that blocked passage into the city by river. Half of that chain was now indestructible *cuendillar*, called heartstone by some. The effort to tear it free and allow passage into the city was an exhausting one; the harbor stoneworks— magnificent and strong, shaped by the Power itself—were only one of the more visible casualties of the silent war between the rebel Aes Sedai and those who held the Tower.

The wind blew through the harbor, where idling porters stood watching the workers chip the stones away, one by one, sending flakes of gray-white dust to float on the water. Those with too much sense—or perhaps too little—whispered that such portents could mean only one thing. Tarmon Gai'don, the Last Battle, must quickly be approaching.

The wind danced away from the docks, passing over the tall white bulwarks known as the Shining Walls. Here, at least, one could find cleanliness and attention in the Tower Guard who stood watch, holding bows. Clean-shaven, wearing white tabards free from stain or wear, the archers watched over their barricades with the dangerous readiness of snakes prepared to strike. These soldiers had no intention of letting Tar Valon fall while they were on duty. Tar Valon had repelled every enemy. Trollocs had breached the walls, but been defeated in the city. Artur Hawkwing had failed to take Tar Valon. Even the black-veiled Aiel, who had ravaged the land during the Aiel War, had never taken the city. Many claimed this as a great victory. Others wondered what would have happened if the Aiel had actually *wanted* to cross into the city.

The wind passed over the western fork of the River Erinin, leaving the island of Tar Valon behind, passing the Alindaer Bridge soaring high to the right, as if taunting enemies to cross it and die. Past the bridge, the wind swept into Alindaer, one of the many villages near Tar Valon. It was a village mostly depopulated, as families had fled across the bridge for refuge in the city. The enemy army had appeared suddenly, without warning, as if brought by a blizzard. Few wondered at it. This rebel army was headed by Aes Sedai, and those who lived in the White Tower's shadow rarely gambled on just what Aes Sedai could and couldn't do.

The rebel army was poised, but uncertain. Over fifty thousand strong, it camped in a massive ring of tents around the smaller camp of Aes Sedai. There was a tight perimeter between the inner camp and the outer one, a perimeter that had most recently been intended to exclude men, particularly those who could wield *saidin*.

Almost, one could think that this camp of rebels intended to set up permanently. It had an air of common daily life about its workings. Figures in white bustled about, some wearing formal novice dresses, many others clothed in near approximations. Looking closely, one could see that many of these were far from young. Some had already reached their graying. But they were referred to as "children," and obedient they were as they washed clothing, beat rugs, and scrubbed tents beneath the eyes of serene-faced Aes Sedai. And if those Aes Sedai glanced with uncommon frequency at the nail-like profile of the White Tower, one would be mistaken in assuming them uncomfortable or nervous. Aes Sedai were in control. Always. Even now, when they had suffered an indelible defeat: Egwene al'Vere, the rebel Amyrlin Seat, had been captured and imprisoned within the Tower.

The wind flicked a few dresses, knocked some laundry from its hangings, then continued westward in a rush. Westward, past towering Dragonmount, with its shattered and smoking apex. Over the Black Hills and across the sweeping Caralain Grass. Here, pockets of sheltered snow clung to shadows beneath craggy overhangs or beside the occasional stands of mountain blackwood. It was time for spring to arrive, time for new shoots to peek through the winter's thatch and for buds to sprout on the thin-branched willows. Few of either had actually come. The land was still dormant, as if waiting, holding its breath. The unnatural heat of the previous autumn had stretched well into winter, pressing upon the land a drought that had baked the life from all but the most vigorous plants. When winter had finally arrived, it had come in a tempest of ice and snow, a lingering, killing frost. Now that the cold had finally retreated, the scattered farmers looked in vain for hope.

The wind swept across brown winter grass, shaking the trees' still-barren branches. To the west, as it approached the land known as Arad Doman—cresting hills and short peaks—something suddenly slammed against it. Something unseen, something spawned by the distant darkness to the north. Something that flowed against the natural tide and currents of the air. The wind was consumed by it, blown southward in a gust, across low peaks and brown foothills to a log manor house, isolated, set upon the pine-forested hills in eastern Arad Doman. The wind blew across the manor house and the tents set up in the wide, open field before it, rattling pine needles and shaking tents.

Rand al'Thor, the Dragon Reborn, stood, hands behind his back as he looked out the open manor window. He still thought of them that way, his "hands," though he now had only one. His left arm ended in a stump. He could feel the smooth, *saidar*-healed skin with the fingers of his good hand. Yet he *felt* as if his other hand should be there to touch.

Steel, he thought. *I am steel. This cannot be fixed, and so I move on.*

The building—a thick-logged structure of pine and cedar after a design favored by the Domani wealthy—groaned and settled in the wind. Something on that wind smelled of rotten meat. Not an uncommon scent, these days. Meat spoiled without warning, sometimes only a few minutes after butchering. Drying it or salting it didn't help. It was the Dark One's touch, and it grew with each passing day. How long until it was as overwhelming, as oily and nauseating, as the taint that had once coated *saidin,* the male half of the One Power?

The room he stood in was wide and long, thick logs making up the outer wall. Planks of pine—still smelling faintly of sap and stain—made up the other walls. The room was furnished sparsely: fur rug on the floor, a pair of aged crossed swords above the hearth, furniture of wood with the bark left on in patches. The entire place had been decorated in a way to say that this was an idyllic home in the woods, away from the bustle of larger cities. Not a cabin, of course—it was far too large and lavish for that. A retreat.

"Rand?" a soft voice asked. He didn't turn, but felt Min's fingers touch his arm. A moment later, her hands moved to his waist and he felt her head rest upon his arm. He could feel her concern for him through the bond they shared.

Steel, he thought.

"I know you don't like—" Min began.

"The boughs," he said, nodding out the window. "You see those pines, just to the side of Bashere's camp?"

"Yes, Rand. But—"

"They blow the wrong direction," Rand said.

Min hesitated, and though she gave no physical reaction, the bond brought him her spike of alarm. Their window was on the upper floor of the manor, and outside of it, banners set above the camp flapped against themselves: the Banner of Light and the Dragon Banner for Rand, a much smaller blue flag bearing the three red kingspenny blossoms to mark the presence of House Bashere. All three flew proud . . . yet just to the side of them, the needles on the pines blew in the *opposite* direction.

"The Dark One stirs, Min," Rand said. He could almost think these winds a result of his own *ta'veren* nature, but

the events he caused were always possible. The wind blowing in two directions at once . . . well, he could feel the
wrongness in the way those pines moved, even if he did
have trouble distinguishing the individual needles. His eyesight hadn't been the same since the attack on that day he'd
lost his hand. It was as if . . . as if he looked through water
at something distorted. It was getting better, slowly.

This building was one in a long line of manors, estates
and other remote hiding places Rand had used during
the last few weeks. He'd wanted to keep moving, jumping from location to location, following the failed meeting
with Semirhage. He'd wanted time to think, to consider,
and hopefully time to confuse the enemies that might be
searching for him. Lord Algarin's manor in Tear had been
compromised; a pity. That had been a good place to stay.
But Rand had to keep moving.

Below, Bashere's Saldaeans had set up a camp on the
manor's green—the open patch of grass out front, bounded
by rows of fir and pine trees. Calling it the "green" seemed
an irony, these days. Even before the army's arrival, it hadn't
been green—it had been a patchy brown, winter thatch broken only occasionally by hesitant new shoots. Those had
been sickly and yellow, and they had now been trampled by
hooves or booted feet.

Tents covered the green. From Rand's vantage on the
second floor, the neat lines of small, peaked tents reminded
him of squares on a stones board. The soldiers had noticed
the wind. Some pointed, others kept their heads down, pol-
ishing armor, carrying buckets of water to the horselines,
sharpening swords or lance points. At least it was not the
dead walking again. The most firm-hearted of men could
lose their will when spirits rose from their graves, and Rand
needed his army to be strong.

Need. No longer was it about what Rand wanted or what
he wished. Everything he did focused only on need, and
what he needed most was the lives of those who followed
him. Soldiers to fight, and to die, to prepare the world for
the Last Battle. Tarmon Gai'don was coming. What he
needed was for them all to be strong enough to win.

To the far left of the green, running below the modest hill
where the manor rested, a twisting stream cut the ground,
sprouting with yellow stickfinger reeds and scrub oak that

had yet to send out spring buds. A small waterway, to be certain, but a fine source of fresh water for the army.

Just outside the window, the winds suddenly righted themselves, and the flags whipped around, blowing in the other direction. So it hadn't been the needles after all, but the banners that had been in the wrong. Min let out a soft sigh, and he could feel her relief, though she still worried about him. That emotion was perpetual, lately. He felt it from all of them, each of the four bundles of emotions tucked away in the back of his mind. Three for the women he had allowed to place themselves there, one for the woman who had forced her way in against his will. One of them was drawing closer. Aviendha, coming with Rhuarc to meet with Rand at the manor house.

Each of the four women would regret their decision to bond him. He wished he could regret his decision to let them—or, at least, his decision to allow the three he loved. But the truth was that he needed Min, needed her strength and her love. He would use her as he used so many others. No, there was no place in him for regret. He just wished he could banish guilt as easily.

Ilyena! a voice said distantly in Rand's head. *My love.* . . . Lews Therin Telamon, Kinslayer, was relatively quiet this day. Rand tried not to think too hard about the things Semirhage had said on the day when Rand had lost his hand. She was one of the Forsaken; she would say anything if she thought it would bring her target pain.

She tortured an entire city to prove herself, Lews Therin whispered. *She has killed a thousand men a thousand different ways to see how their screams would differ from one another. But she rarely lies. Rarely.*

Rand pushed the voice away.

"Rand," Min said, softer than before.

He turned to look at her. She was lithe and slight of build, and he often felt that he towered over her. She kept her hair in short ringlets, the color dark—but not as dark as her deep, worried eyes. As always, she had chosen to wear a coat and trousers. Today, they were of a deep green, much like the needles on the pines outside. Yet, as if to contradict her tailored choice, she had had the outfit made to accentuate her figure. Silver embroidery in the shape of bonabell flowers ran around the cuffs, and lace peeked out from the sleeves beneath. She smelled faintly of lavender, perhaps from the soap she'd taken to most recently.

Why wear trousers only to trim herself up with lace? Rand had long abandoned trying to understand women. Understanding them would not help him reach Shayol Ghul. Besides, he didn't need to understand women in order to use them. Particularly if they had information he needed.

He gritted his teeth. *No,* he thought. *No, there are lines I will not cross. There are things even I will not do.*

"You're thinking about her again," Min said, almost accusatory.

He often wondered if there was such a thing as a bond that worked only one way. He would have given much for one of those.

"Rand, she's one of the Forsaken," Min continued. "She would have killed all of us without a second thought."

"She wasn't intending to kill me," Rand said softly, turning away from Min and looking out the window again. "Me she would have held."

Min cringed. Pain, worry. She was thinking of the twisted male *a'dam* that Semirhage had brought, hidden, when she'd come impersonating the Daughter of the Nine Moons. The Forsaken's disguise had been disrupted by Cadsuane's *ter'angreal,* allowing Rand to recognize Semirhage. Or, at least, allowing Lews Therin to recognize her.

The exchange had ended with Rand losing a hand but gaining one of the Forsaken as his prisoner. The last time he'd been in a similar situation, it hadn't ended well. He still didn't know where Asmodean had gone or why the weasel of a man had fled in the first place, but Rand did suspect that he had betrayed much about Rand's plans and activities.

Should have killed him. Should have killed them all.

Rand nodded, then froze. Had that been Lews Therin's thought or his own? *Lews Therin,* Rand thought. *Are you there?*

He thought he heard laughter. Or perhaps it was sobbing.

Burn you! Rand thought. *Talk to me! The time is coming. I need to know what you know! How did you seal the Dark One's prison? What went wrong, and why did it leave the prison flawed? Speak to me!*

Yes, that was definitely sobbing, not laughter. Sometimes it was hard to tell with Lews Therin. Rand continued to think of the dead man as a separate individual from himself, regardless of what Semirhage had said. He had cleansed *saidin*! The taint was gone and it could touch his mind no longer. He was *not* going to go insane.

The descent into terminal madness can be . . . abrupt. He heard her words again, spoken for the others to hear. His secret was finally out. But Min had seen a viewing of Rand and another man melded together. Didn't that mean that he and Lews Therin were two separate people, two individuals forced into one body?

It makes no difference that his voice is real, Semirhage had said. *In fact, it makes his situation worse. . . .*

Rand watched a particular group of six soldiers inspect the horselines that ran along the right side of the green, between the last line of tents and the line of trees. They checked the hooves one at a time.

Rand couldn't think about his madness. He also couldn't think about what Cadsuane was doing with Semirhage. That left only his plans. *The north and the east must be as one. The west and the south must be as one. The two must be as one.* That was the answer he'd received from the strange creatures beyond the red stone doorway. It was all he had to go on.

North and east. He had to force the lands into peace, whether they wanted it or not. He had a tenuous balance in the east, with Illian, Mayene, Cairhien and Tear all under his control in one way or another. The Seanchan ruled in the south, with Altara, Amadicia and Tarabon under their control. Murandy might soon be theirs, if they were pressing in that direction. That left Andor and Elayne.

Elayne. She was distant, far to the east, but he could still feel her bundle of emotions in his head. At such a distance, it was difficult to tell much, but he thought she was . . . relieved. Did that mean that her struggle for power in Andor was going well? What of the armies that had besieged her? And what *were* those Borderlanders up to? They had left their posts, joining together and marching south to find Rand, but giving no explanation of what they wanted of him. They were some of the best soldiers west of the Spine of the World. Their help would be invaluable at the Last Battle. But they had left the northlands. Why?

He was loath to confront them, however, for fear it could mean yet another fight. One he couldn't afford at the moment. Light! He would have thought that, of all people, he could have depended on the Borderlanders to support him against the Shadow.

No matter, not for the moment. He had peace, or something close to it, in most of the land. He tried not to think about the recently placated rebellion against him in Tear or the volatility of the borders with Seanchan lands, or the plottings of the nobility in Cairhien. Every time he thought he had a nation secure, it seemed a dozen others fell apart. How could he bring peace to a people who refused to accept it?

Min's fingers tightened on his arm, and he took a deep breath. He did what he could, and for now, he had two goals. Peace in Arad Doman and a truce with the Seanchan. The words he'd received beyond the doorway were now clear: He could not fight both the Seanchan and the Dark One. He had to keep the Seanchan from advancing until the Last Battle was over. After that, the Light could burn them all.

Why had the Seanchan ignored his requests for a meeting? Were they angered that he had captured Semirhage? He had let the *sul'dam* go free. Did that not speak of his good faith? Arad Doman would prove his intentions. If he could end the fight in Almoth Plain, he could show the Seanchan that he was serious in his suits for peace. He would *make* them see!

Rand took a deep breath, studying out the window. Bashere's eight thousand soldiers were erecting peaked tents and digging an earthen moat and wall around the green. The growing bulwark of deep brown contrasted with the white tents. Rand had ordered the Asha'man to help with the digging, and though he doubted they enjoyed the humble work, it did speed the process greatly. Besides, Rand suspected that they—like he himself—secretly savored any excuse to hold *saidin*. He could see a small group of them in their stiff black coats, weaves spinning around them as they dug up another patch of ground. There were ten of them in the camp, though only Flinn, Naeff and Narishma were full Asha'man.

The Saldaeans worked quickly, wearing their short coats as they cared for their mounts and set pickets. Others took shovelfuls of dirt from the Asha'man mound and used it to pack into the bulwark. Rand could see there was that displeasure on the faces of many of the hawk-nosed Saldaeans. They didn't like making camp in a wooded area, even one as sparsely flecked with pine as this hillside. Trees made cavalry charges difficult and could hide enemies as they approached.

Davram Bashere himself rode slowly through the camp, barking orders through that thick mustache of his. Beside him walked Lord Tellaen, a portly man in a long coat and wearing a thin Domani mustache. He was an acquaintance of Bashere's.

Lord Tellaen put himself at risk by housing Rand; sheltering the troops of the Dragon Reborn could be seen as treason. But who was there to punish him? Arad Doman was in chaos, the throne under threat from several rebel factions. And then there was the great Domani general Rodel Ituralde and his surprisingly effective war against the Seanchan to the south.

Like his men, Bashere went about unarmored in a short blue coat. He also wore a pair of the baggy trousers that he favored, the bottoms tucked into his knee-high boots. What did Bashere think of being caught in Rand's *ta'veren* web? In being, if not in direct opposition to the will of his queen, at least uncomfortably to the side of it? How long had it been since he had reported to his rightful ruler? Hadn't he promised Rand that his queen's support would be speedy in coming? How many months ago had that been?

I am the Dragon Reborn, Rand thought. *I break all covenants and vows. Old allegiances are unimportant. Only Tarmon Gai'don matters.* Tarmon Gai'don, and the servants of the Shadow.

"I wonder if we'll find Graendal here," Rand said thoughtfully.

"Graendal?" Min asked. "What makes you think she might be?"

Rand shook his head. Asmodean had said Graendal was in Arad Doman, though that had been months ago. Was she still here? It seemed plausible; it was one of the few major nations where she could be. Graendal liked to have a hidden base of power far from where the other Forsaken lurked; she wouldn't have set up in Andor, Tear or Illian. Nor would she have been caught in the lands to the southwest, not with the Seanchan invasion.

She would have a hidden retreat somewhere. That was how she operated. Probably in the mountains, secluded, somewhere here in the north. He couldn't be sure she was in Arad Doman, though it felt *right* to him, from what he knew of her. From what Lews Therin knew of her.

But it was only a possibility. He would be careful, watching for her. Each of the Forsaken that he removed would make the Last Battle that much easier to fight. It would—

Soft footsteps approached his closed door.

Rand released Min and they both spun, Rand reaching for his sword—a useless gesture, now. The loss of his hand, though it wasn't his primary sword hand, would leave him vulnerable if he were to face a skilled opponent. Even with *saidin* to provide a far more potent weapon, his first instinct was for the sword. He'd have to change that. It might get him killed someday.

The door opened and Cadsuane strode in, as confident as any queen at court. She was a handsome woman, with dark eyes and an angular face. Her dark gray hair was up in a bun, a dozen tiny golden ornaments—each one a *ter'angreal* or *angreal*—hanging in their places atop it. Her dress was of a simple, thick wool, tied at the waist with a yellow belt, with more yellow embroidery across the collar. The dress itself was green, which was not uncommon, as that was her Ajah. Rand sometimes felt that her stern face—ageless, like that of any Aes Sedai who had worked long enough with the Power—would have fit better in the Red Ajah.

He relaxed his hand on his sword, though he did not release it. He fingered the cloth-tied hilt. The weapon was long, slightly curved, and the lacquered scabbard was painted with a long, sinuous dragon of red and gold. It looked as if it had been designed specifically for Rand— and yet it was centuries old, unearthed only recently. *How odd, that they should find this now,* he thought, *and make a gift of it to me, completely unaware of what they were holding. . . .*

He had taken to wearing the sword immediately. It felt *right* beneath his fingers. He had told no one, not even Min, that he had recognized the weapon. And not, oddly, from Lews Therin's memories—but Rand's own.

Cadsuane was accompanied by several others. Nynaeve was expected; she often followed Cadsuane these days, like a rival cat she found encroaching on her territory. She did it for him, likely. The dark-haired Aes Sedai had never quite given up being Wisdom of Emond's Field, no matter what she said, and she gave no quarter to anyone she thought was abusing one under her protection. Unless, of course, Nynaeve herself was the one doing the abusing.

Today, she wore a dress of gray with a yellow sash at the waist over her belt—a new Domani fashion, he had heard—and had the customary red dot on her forehead. She wore a long gold necklace and slim gold belt, with matching bracelets and finger rings, both studded with large red, green and blue gems. The jewelry was a *ter'angreal*—or, rather, several of them and an *angreal* too—comparable to what Cadsuane wore. Rand had occasionally heard Nynaeve muttering that *her ter'angreal*, with the gaudy gems, were impossible to match to her clothing.

Where Nynaeve wasn't a surprise, Alivia was. Rand hadn't been aware that the former *damane* had been involved in the . . . information gathering. Still, she was supposed to be even stronger than Nynaeve in the One Power, so perhaps she had been brought for support. One could never be too careful where the Forsaken were concerned.

There were streaks of white in Alivia's hair, and she was just a bit taller than Nynaeve. That white in her hair was telling—any white or gray on a woman who wielded the One Power meant age. A great deal of it. Alivia claimed to be four centuries old. Today, the former *damane* wore a strikingly red dress, as if in an attempt to be confrontational. Most *damane*, once unleashed, remained timid. Not so with Alivia—there was an intensity to her that almost suggested a Whitecloak.

He felt Min stiffen, and he felt her displeasure. Alivia would help Rand die, eventually. That had been one of Min's viewings—and Min's viewings were never wrong. Except that she'd said she'd been wrong about Moiraine. Perhaps that meant that he wouldn't have to . . .

No. Anything that made him think of living through the Last Battle, anything that made him hope, was dangerous. He had to be hard enough to accept what was coming to him. Hard enough to die when the time came.

You said we could die, Lews Therin said in the back of his mind. *You promised!*

Cadsuane said nothing as she walked across the room, helping herself to a cup of the spiced wine that sat on a small serving table beside the bed. Then she sat down in one of the red cedar chairs. At least she hadn't demanded that he pour the wine for her. That sort of thing wasn't beyond her.

"Well, what did you learn?" he asked, walking from the window and pouring himself a cup of wine as well. Min walked to the bed—with its frame of cedar logs and a skip-peeled headboard stained deeply reddish brown—and sat down, hands in her lap. She watched Alivia carefully.

Cadsuane raised an eyebrow at the sharpness in Rand's voice. He sighed, forcing down his annoyance. He had asked her to be his counselor, and he had agreed to her stipulations. Min said there was something important he would need to learn from Cadsuane—that was another viewing—and in truth, he had found her advice useful on more than one occasion. She was worth her constant demands for decorum.

"How did the questioning go, Cadsuane Sedai?" he asked in a more moderate tone.

She smiled to herself. "Well enough."

"Well enough?" Nynaeve snapped. *She* had made no promises to Cadsuane about civility. "That woman is infuriating!"

Cadsuane sipped her wine. "I wonder what else one could expect from one of the Forsaken, child. She has had a great deal of time to practice being . . . infuriating."

"Rand, that . . . creature is a *stone*," Nynaeve said, turning to him. "She's yielded barely a single useful sentence despite days of questioning! All she does is explain how inferior and backward we are, with the occasional aside that she's eventually going to kill us all." Nynaeve reached up to her long, single braid—but stopped herself short of tugging on it. She was getting better about that. Rand wondered why she bothered, considering how obvious her temper was.

"For all the girl's dramatic talk," Cadsuane said, nodding to Nynaeve, "she has a reasonable grasp on the situation. Phaw! When I said 'well enough' you were to interpret it as 'as well as you might expect, given our unfortunate constraints.' One cannot blindfold an artist, then be surprised when he has nothing to paint."

"This isn't art, Cadsuane," Rand said dryly. "It's torture." Min shared a glance with him, and he felt her concern. Concern for him? He wasn't the one being tortured.

The box, Lews Therin whispered. *We should have died in the box. Then . . . then it would be over.*

Cadsuane sipped her wine. Rand hadn't tasted his—he already knew that the spices were so strong as to render the drink unpalatable. Better that than the alternative.

"You press us for results, boy," Cadsuane said. "And yet you deny us the tools we need to get them. Whether you name it torture, questioning, or *baking*, I call it foolishness. Now, if we were allowed to—"

"No!" Rand growled, waving a hand . . . a stump . . . at her. "You will *not* threaten or hurt her."

Time spent in a dark box, being pulled forth and being beaten repeatedly. He would *not* have a woman in his power treated the same way. Not even one of the Forsaken. "You may question her, but some things I will not allow."

Nynaeve sniffed. "Rand, she's one of the *Forsaken*, dangerous beyond reason!"

"I am aware of the threat," Rand said flatly, holding up the stump where his left hand had been. The metallic gold and red tattoo of a dragon's body sparkled in the lamplight. Its head had been consumed in the Fire that had nearly killed him.

Nynaeve took a deep breath. "Yes, well, then you *must* see that normal rules shouldn't apply to her!"

"I said no!" Rand said. "You will question her, but you will not hurt her!" *Not a woman. I will keep to this one shred of light inside me. I've caused the deaths and sorrows of too many women already.*

"If that is what you demand, boy," Cadsuane said tersely, "then that is what shall be done. Just don't whine when we are unable to drag out of her what she had for breakfast yesterday, let alone the locations of the other Forsaken. One begins to wonder why you insist we continue this farce at all. Perhaps we should simply turn her over to the White Tower and be done with it."

Rand turned away. Outside, the soldiers had finished with the horselines. They looked good. Even and straight, the animals given just the right amount of slack.

Turn her over to the White Tower? That would never happen. Cadsuane wouldn't let Semirhage out of her grip until she got the answers she wanted. The wind still blew outside, his own banners flapping before his eyes.

"Turn her over to the White Tower, you say?" he said, glancing back into the room. "Which White Tower? Would you entrust her to Elaida? Or did you mean the others? I doubt that Egwene would be pleased if I dropped one of the Forsaken in her lap. Egwene might just let Semirhage go and take *me* captive instead. Force me to kneel before the White Tower's justice and gentle me just to give her another notch in her belt."

Nynaeve frowned. "Rand! Egwene would never—"

"She's Amyrlin," he said, downing his cup of wine in one gulp. It was as putrid as he recalled. "Aes Sedai to the core. I'm just another pawn to her."

Yes, Lews Therin said. *We need to stay away from all of them. They refused to help us, you know. Refused! Said my plan was too reckless. That left me with only the Hundred Companions, no women to form a circle. Traitors! This is their fault. But . . . but I'm the one who killed Ilyena. Why?*

Nynaeve said something, but Rand ignored her. *Lews Therin?* he said to the voice. *What was it you did? The women wouldn't help? Why?*

But Lews Therin had begun sobbing again, and his voice grew distant.

"Tell me!" Rand yelled, throwing his cup down. "Burn you, Kinslayer! Speak to me!"

The room fell silent.

Rand blinked. He'd never . . . never tried speaking to Lews Therin out loud where others could hear. And they knew. Semirhage had spoken of the voice that he heard, dismissing Rand as if he were a common madman.

Rand reached up, running a hand through his hair. Or he tried to . . . but he used the arm that was only a stump, and it accomplished nothing.

Light! he thought. *I'm losing control. Half the time, I don't know which voice is mine and which is his. This was supposed to get better when I cleansed* saidin! *I was supposed to be safe. . . .*

Not safe, Lews Therin muttered. *We were already mad. Can't turn back from that now.* He began to cackle, but the laughter turned to sobs.

Rand looked around the room. Min's dark eyes were so worried he had to turn away. Alivia—who had watched the exchange about Semirhage with those penetrating eyes of hers—seemed too knowing. Nynaeve finally gave in and tugged on her braid. For once, Cadsuane didn't chastise him for his outburst. Instead she just sipped her wine. How could she stand the stuff?

The thought was trivial. Ridiculous. He wanted to laugh. Only, the sound wouldn't come out. He couldn't summon even a wry humor, not anymore. *Light! I can't keep this up. My eyes see as if in a fog, my hand is burned away, and the old wounds in my side rip open if I do anything more strenuous than breathe. I'm dry, like an overused well. I need to finish my work here and get to Shayol Ghul.*

Otherwise, there won't be anything left of me for the Dark One to kill.

That wasn't a thought to cause laughter; it was one to cause despair. But Rand did not weep, for tears could not come from steel.

For the moment, Lews Therin's cries seemed enough for both of them.

CHAPTER
2

The Nature of Pain

E gwene stood up straight, backside aflame with the
now-familiar agony of a solid beating beneath the
hands of the Mistress of Novices. She felt like a rug
that had just been pounded free of its dust. Despite that,
she calmly straightened her white skirts, then turned to the
room's mirror and calmly dabbed the tears from the corners of her eyes. Only one tear in each eye this time. She
smiled to her reflection, and her twin selves nodded to one
another in satisfaction.

A small, dark-paneled room reflected behind her on the
mirror's silvery surface. Such a stern place it was, a sturdy
stool in the corner, the top darkened and smoothed from
years and years of use. A blockish desk, set with the Mistress of Novices' thick tome. The narrow table directly
behind Egwene had some carvings, but its leather pad-
ding was far more distinctive. Many a novice—and not a
few Accepted—had bent down across that table, bearing
the punishment for disobedience. Egwene could almost
imagine that the table's dark color had come from repeated
tearstains. Many of her own had been shed there.

But none today. Only two tears, and neither had fallen
from her cheeks. Not that she didn't hurt; her entire body
seemed to burn from the pain. Indeed, the severity of those
beatings had increased the longer she continued to defy the
powers in the White Tower. But as the beatings had grown
more frequent and more painful, Egwene's resolve to endure had grown as well. She hadn't yet managed to embrace
and accept the pain as the Aiel did, but she felt that she

was close. The Aiel could laugh during the most cruel of tortures. Well, she could smile the moment she stood up.

Each lash she endured, each pain she suffered, was a victory. And victory was always a reason for happiness, no matter how one's pride or one's skin burned.

Standing beside the table behind Egwene, reflected in the mirror, was the Mistress of Novices herself. Silviana looked down at the leather strap in her hands, frowning. Her ageless square face seemed just faintly confused; she regarded the strap as one might a knife that refused to cut or a lamp that refused to light.

The woman was of the Red Ajah, a fact reflected in the trim on the hem of her simple gray dress and the fringed shawl on her shoulders. She was tall and stocky and she had her black hair back in a bun. In most ways Egwene considered her a superior Mistress of Novices. Even if she *had* administered a ridiculous number of punishments to Egwene. Perhaps because of that. Silviana did her duty. Light knew there were few enough in the Tower lately of whom that could be said!

Silviana looked up and met Egwene's eyes in the mirror. She quickly put down the strap and washed all emotion from her face. Egwene turned around calmly.

Uncharacteristically, Silviana sighed. "When will you give this up, child?" she asked. "You've proven your point quite admirably, I must say, but you must know that I will continue to punish you until you submit. Proper order must be maintained."

Egwene held in her shock. The Mistress of Novices rarely addressed Egwene except to offer instruction or reprobation. Still, there had been cracks before. . . .

"Proper order, Silviana?" Egwene asked. "As it has been maintained elsewhere in the Tower?"

Silviana's lips drew back in a line. She turned and made a notation in her book. "I will see you in the morning. Off to dinner with you."

The morning punishment would be because Egwene had called the Mistress of Novices by her name without adding the honorific "Sedai" to the end. And likely because both knew that Egwene would not curtsy before she left.

"I will return in the morning," Egwene said, "but dinner

must wait. I have been ordered to attend Elaida this evening as she eats." This session with Silviana had gone long—Egwene had brought quite a list of infractions with her—and now she wouldn't have time to eat. Her stomach complained at the prospect.

Silviana showed just a brief moment of emotion. Was it surprise? "And you said nothing of this earlier?"

"Would it have changed anything if I had?"

Silviana did not respond to the question. "You will eat after attending the Amyrlin, then. I shall leave instructions for the Mistress of the Kitchens to hold you some food. Considering how often you are being given Healing these days, child, you will need to take your meals. I won't have you collapsing from lack of nourishment."

Stern, yet fair. A pity this one had found her way to the Red. "Very well," Egwene said.

"And after eating," Silviana said, raising a finger, "you shall return to me for showing disrespect to the Amyrlin Seat. She is never to be known as simply 'Elaida' to you, child." She turned down to her ledger, adding, "Besides, Light only knows what kind of trouble you'll be in by this evening."

As Egwene left the small chamber behind—entering a wide, gray-stoned hallway with floor tiles of green and red—she considered that last comment. Perhaps it *hadn't* been surprise that Silviana had shown upon hearing of Egwene's visit to Elaida. Perhaps it had been sympathy. Elaida would not react well when Egwene stood up to her the way she had to all others in the Tower.

Was that why Silviana had decided to bring Egwene back for a final strapping after eating? With the orders Silviana had given, Egwene would be *required* to take food before returning for her punishment, even if Elaida heaped the strappings upon her.

It was a small kindness, but Egwene was grateful for it. Enduring the daily punishments was difficult enough without skipping meals.

As she pondered, two Red sisters—Katerine and Barasine—approached her. Katerine held a brass cup. Another dose of forkroot. Elaida wanted to make certain that Egwene couldn't channel a trickle during the meal, it seemed. Egwene took the cup without protesting and downed it in a single gulp, tasting the faint, yet characteristic, hint of mint. She handed the cup back to Katerine with an offhanded gesture, and the woman had no choice but to accept it. Almost as if she were a royal cupbearer.

Egwene didn't head for Elaida's quarters immediately. The overly long punishment's intrusion into the dinner hour ironically left her with a few spare moments—and she didn't want to arrive early, for that would show Elaida deference. So instead she lingered outside the door of the Mistress of Novices with Katerine and Barasine. Would a certain figure come to visit the study?

In the distance, small clusters of sisters walked the hallway's tiles of green and red. There was a furtive cast to their eyes, like hares venturing into a clearing to nibble at leaves, yet fearing the predator who hid in the shadows. Sisters in the Tower these days always wore their shawls, and they never went about alone. Some even held the Power, as if afraid of being jumped by footpads here in the White Tower itself.

"Are you pleased with this?" Egwene found herself asking. She glanced at Katerine and Barasine; both were, coincidentally, also part of the group that had first captured Egwene.

"What was that, child?" Katerine asked coolly. "Speaking to a sister without being asked a question first? Are you so eager for more punishment?" She wore a conspicuous amount of red, her dress a bright crimson slashed with black. Her dark hair curled slightly in its cascade down her back.

Egwene ignored the threat. What more could they do to her? "Set aside the bickering for a moment, Katerine," Egwene said, watching a group of Yellows pass, their step quickening as they saw the two Reds. "Set aside the posturing for authority and the threats. Put these things away and *look*. Are you proud of this? The Tower spent centuries without an Amyrlin being raised from the Red. Now, when you finally have a chance, your chosen leader has done *this* to the Tower. Women who won't meet the eyes of those they do not know familiarly, sisters who travel in clusters. The Ajahs behave as if they are at war with one another!"

Katerine sniffed at the comment, though the lanky Barasine hesitated, glancing over her shoulder at the group of

Yellows hurrying down the corridor, several of them firing glances back at the two Reds.

"This was not caused by the Amyrlin," Katerine said. "It was created by your foolish rebels and their betrayal!"

My rebels? Egwene thought with an inward smile. *So you now see them as "mine," rather than regarding me as just a poor Accepted who was duped? That's progress.*

"Were we the ones who pulled down a sitting Amyrlin?" Egwene asked. "Were we the ones who turned Warder against Warder, or the ones who failed to contain the Dragon Reborn? Have we chosen an Amyrlin who is so power-hungry, she's ordered the construction of her own *palace*? A woman who has every sister wondering if she'll be the next to be stripped of the shawl?"

Katerine didn't respond, as though realizing that she shouldn't be drawn into an argument with a mere novice. Barasine still watched the distant Yellows, her eyes wide. Worried.

"I should think," Egwene said, "that the Red should not be the ones sheltering Elaida, but should instead provide her fiercest critics. For Elaida's legacy will be your own. Remember that."

Katerine glanced at her, eyes flaring, and Egwene suppressed a cringe. Perhaps that last had been too straightforward.

"You will report to the Mistress of Novices tonight, *child*," Katerine informed her. "And explain how you showed disrespect to sisters and to the Amyrlin herself."

Egwene held her tongue. Why was she wasting her time trying to convince Reds?

The aged wooden door behind her snapped shut, making Egwene jump and glance over her shoulder. The tapestries to either side stirred slightly, then went still. Egwene hadn't realized that she'd left the door open just a crack as she'd left. Had Silviana listened to the conversation?

There was no more time to dawdle. It appeared that Al-viarin wasn't going to come this evening. Where was she? She always arrived for punishment right around the time that Egwene finished. Egwene shook her head, then strode away down the hallway. The two Reds followed—they stayed with her increasingly now, following her, watching her, at all times except when Egwene visited the quarters of other Ajahs for training. She tried to act as if those two sisters were an honorary retinue, rather than her jailers. She also tried to ignore the pain of her backside.

All signs indicated that Egwene was winning her war against Elaida. Earlier, at lunch, Egwene had heard the novices gossiping about the dramatic failure Elaida had suffered in failing to keep Rand captured. The event was several months past, now, and was supposed to have been secret. And then there was the rumor of Asha'man bonding sisters who had been sent to destroy them. Another mission of Elaida's that wasn't supposed to be known. Egwene had taken steps to keep these failures strong in the minds of the Tower's occupants, much as she had with Elaida's irregular treatment of Shemerin.

Whatever the novices were gossiping about, the Aes Sedai were hearing. Yes, Egwene was winning. But she was beginning to lose the satisfaction she'd once felt at that victory. Who could take joy in seeing the Aes Sedai unraveling like aged canvas? Who could feel glad that Tar Valon, the grandest of all great cities, was piled with refuse? As much as Egwene might despise Elaida, she could not exult at seeing an Amyrlin Seat lead with such incompetence.

And now, tonight, she would face Elaida in person. Egwene walked slowly through the hallways, pacing herself so as to not arrive early. How should she proceed at the dinner? During her nine days back in the Tower, Egwene had not so much as glimpsed Elaida. Attending the woman would be dangerous. If she offended Elaida just a hair too much, she could find herself being sent for execution. And yet, she could not simper and pander. She would *not* bow before the woman, not if it cost her life.

Egwene turned a corner, then pulled up short, nearly stumbling. The hallway ended abruptly in a stonework wall set with a bright tile mural. The image was that of an ancient Amyrlin, sitting on an ornate golden seat, holding forth her hand in warning to the kings and queens of the land. The plaque at the bottom declared it to be a depiction of Caraighan Maconar, ending the rebellion in Mosadorin. Egwene vaguely recognized the mural; the last she'd seen it, it had been on the wall of the Tower library. But when she'd seen it there, the Amyrlin's face hadn't been a mask of blood. The dead bodies depicted hanging from the eaves hadn't been there either.

Katerine stepped up beside Egwene, face paling. Nobody liked to speak of the unnatural way rooms and corridors changed places in the Tower. The transformations made for a solemn reminder that squabbles over authority were secondary to larger, horrible troubles in the world. This was the first time Egwene had seen not only a corridor moved, but a depiction altered as well. The Dark One stirred, and the very Pattern itself was shaking.

Egwene turned and stalked away from the misplaced mural. She couldn't focus on those problems right now. You scrubbed a floor clean by first picking a single spot and getting to work. She'd picked her spot. The White Tower *had* to be made whole.

Unfortunately, this detour was going to take more time. Egwene reluctantly hastened her pace; it wouldn't do to be early, but she'd prefer not to be late either. Her two watchers hurried as well, skirts swishing as they backtracked through several corridors. As they did, Egwene caught sight of Alviarin hurrying around a corner, head down, walking toward the study of the Mistress of Novices. So she was going to her punishment after all. What had caused her to delay?

Two more turns and one flight of cold stone steps later, Egwene found herself cutting through the Red Ajah section of the Tower, as that now provided the quickest route up to the Amyrlin's quarters. Red tapestries hung on the walls, accented by crimson tiles on the floor. The women walking the corridors wore expressions of a near uniform austerity, their shawls draped carefully over their shoulders and arms. Here, in their own Ajah's quarters where they should be confident, they seemed insecure and suspicious, even of those servants who bustled about, bearing the Flame of Tar Valon on their chests. Egwene passed through the hallways, wishing she didn't have to hurry so, as it made her look cowed. There was nothing to be done about it. At the center of the Tower, she climbed several flights of stairs, eventually reaching the hallway that led to the Amyrlin's quarters.

Her busyness with novice chores and lessons had left her with little time to consider her confrontation with the false Amyrlin. This was the woman who had pulled down Siuan, the woman who had beaten Rand, and the woman who had

pushed the Aes Sedai themselves to the very brink of collapse. Elaida needed to know Egwene's anger, she needed
to be humiliated and made ashamed! She. . . .

Egwene stopped in front of Elaida's gilded door. *No.*

She could imagine the scene easily. Elaida enraged,
Egwene banished to the dark cells beneath the Tower. What
good would that do? She could *not* confront the woman, not
yet. That would only lead to momentary satisfaction followed by a debilitating failure.

But light, she couldn't bow to Elaida either! The Amyrlin
did no such thing!

Or . . . no. The Amyrlin did what was required of her.
Which was more important? The White Tower, or Egwene's
pride? The only way to win this battle was to let Elaida
think that *she* was winning. No . . . No, the only way to win
was to let Elaida think there *was no battle*.

Could Egwene keep a civil tongue long enough to survive this night? She wasn't certain. However, she *needed* to
leave this dinner with Elaida feeling that she was in control,
that Egwene was properly cowed. The best way to achieve
that while maintaining some measure of pride would be to
say nothing at all.

Silence. That would be her weapon this evening. Steeling
herself, Egwene knocked.

Her first surprise came when an Aes Sedai opened the
door. Didn't Elaida have servants to perform that function?
Egwene didn't recognize the sister, but the ageless face
was obvious. The woman was of the Gray, as indicated by
her shawl, and she was slender with a full bust. Her golden
brown hair fell to the middle of her back, and she had a
haunted cast to her eyes, as if she'd been under great strain
recently.

Elaida sat inside. Egwene hesitated in the doorway, looking in at her rival for the first time since departing from the
White Tower with Nynaeve and Elayne to hunt the Black
Ajah, a turning point that seemed an eternity ago. Handsome and statuesque, Elaida seemed to have lost a small
measure of her sternness. She sat, secure and smiling
faintly, as if thinking on some joke that only she understood. Her chair was almost a throne, carved, gilded and
painted with red and white. There was a second place set at
the table, presumably for the nameless Gray sister.

Egwene had never visited an Amyrlin's own quarters before, but she could imagine what Siuan's might have looked like. Simple, yet not stark. Just enough ornamentation to indicate that this was the room of someone important, but not enough to become a distraction. Under Siuan, everything would have served a function—perhaps several functions at once. Tables with hidden compartments. Wall hangings that doubled as maps. Crossed swords over the hearth that were oiled, should the Warders need them.

Or perhaps that was just fancy. Regardless, not only had Elaida taken different rooms for her quarters; her decorations were notably rich. The entire suite hadn't been decorated yet—there was talk that she was adding to her rooms day by day—but what was there was very lavish. New silk brocades, all of red, hung from the walls and ceilings. The Tairen rug underfoot depicted birds aflight, and was so finely woven that it could almost be mistaken for a painting. Scattered through the room were pieces of furniture of a dozen different styles and makes, each one lavishly carved and inlaid with ivory. Here a series of vines, there a knobby ridged design, there crisscrossing serpents.

More infuriating than the extravagance was the stole across Elaida's shoulders. It was striped with six colors. Not seven, but six! Though Egwene had not chosen an Ajah herself, she would have taken the Green. But that didn't stop her from feeling a surge of anger at seeing that shawl with blue removed. One did not simply *disband* one of the Ajahs, even if one were the Amyrlin Seat!

But Egwene held her tongue. This meeting was about survival. Egwene could bear straps of pain for the good of the Tower. Could she bear Elaida's arrogance as well?

"No curtsy?" Elaida asked as Egwene entered the room. "They *said* that you were stubborn. Well, then, you shall visit the Mistress of Novices when this supper is through and inform her of the lapse. What do you say to that?"

That you are a plague upon this structure as vile and destructive as any disease that has struck city and people in all years past. That you—

Egwene broke her gaze away from Elaida's. And—feeling the shame of it vibrate through her very bones—she bowed her head.

Elaida laughed, obviously taking the gesture the right

way. "Honestly, I expected you to be more trouble. It appears that Silviana *does* know her duty. That is well; I had worried that she, like far too many in the Tower lately, had been shirking. Well, be busy with you. I won't wait all night to dine."

Egwene clenched her fists, but said nothing. The back wall was set with a long serving table bearing several silver platters, their polished domed lids dripping with condensation from the heated contents. There was also a silver soup tureen. To the side, the Gray sister hovered near the door. Light! The woman was terrified. Egwene had rarely seen such an expression on a sister. What was causing it?

"Come, Meidani," Elaida said to the Gray. "Are you going to hover all night? Sit down!"

Egwene covered a moment of shock. Meidani? She was one of those sent by Sheriam and the others to spy on the White Tower! As Egwene checked the contents of each platter, she shot a glance over her shoulder. Meidani had found her way to the small, less ornate seat at Elaida's side. Did the Gray always wear such finery to supper? Her neck sparkled with emeralds and her muted green dress was of the most expensive silk, accentuating a bosom that might have been average on another woman, but that seemed ample on Meidani's slender body.

Beonin said she'd warned the Gray sisters that Elaida knew they were spies. So why hadn't Meidani fled the Tower? What was holding her here?

Well, at least now the woman's expression of terror made sense. "Meidani," Elaida said, sipping from a goblet of wine, "you are rather wan this day. Have you been getting enough sun?"

"I have been spending a great deal of time with historical records, Elaida," Meidani said, voice uneven. "Have you forgotten?"

"Ah, that is right," Elaida said musingly. "It will be good to know how traitors have been treated in the past. Beheading seems too easy and simple a punishment to me. Those who split our Tower, those who flaunt their defection, a very *special* reward will be needed for them. Well, continue your search then."

Meidani sat down, hands in lap. Anyone other than an Aes Sedai would have had to mop her brow free of sweat.

Egwene stirred the silver tureen, hand clutching the ladle with a white-knuckled grip. Elaida *knew*. She knew that Meidani was a spy, and yet she still invited the woman to dinner. To play with her.

"Hurry up, girl," Elaida snapped at Egwene.

Egwene plucked up the tureen, the handles warm beneath her fingers, and walked over to the small table. She filled the bowls with a brownish broth bobbing with Queen's Crown mushrooms. It smelled so heavily peppered that any other flavor would be indistinguishable. So much food had gone bad that without spice, the soup would be inedible.

Egwene worked mechanically, like a wagon wheel rolling behind the oxen. She didn't have to make choices; she didn't have to respond. She just worked. She filled the soup bowls precisely, then fetched the bread basket and placed one piece—not too crusty—on each small porcelain bread saucer. She returned with a circular dab of butter for each, cut quickly but precisely from the larger brick with a couple of flicks of the knife. One did not spend long as an innkeeper's daughter without learning to serve a proper meal.

Even as she worked, she stewed. Each step was agony, and not because of her still-burning backside. That physical pain, oddly, seemed insignificant now. It was secondary to the pain of remaining silent, the pain of not allowing herself to confront this awful woman, so regal, so arrogant.

As the two women began their soup—pointedly ignoring the weevils in their bread—Egwene retreated to the side of the room and stood, hands clasped before her, posture stiff. Elaida glanced at her, then smiled, apparently seeing another sign of subservience. In reality, Egwene didn't trust herself to move, for she feared that any activity would end with her slapping Elaida across the face. Light, but this was hard!

"What talk is there in the Tower, Meidani?" Elaida asked, dipping her bread in the soup.

"I . . . don't have much time to listen. . . ."

Elaida leaned forward. "Oh, surely you know something. You have ears, and even Grays must gossip. What are they saying about those rebels?"

Meidani paled further. "I . . . I . . ."

"Hmm," Elaida said. "When we were novices, I don't remember you being so slow of wit, Meidani. You haven't impressed me these last few weeks; I begin to wonder why you were ever given the shawl. Perhaps it never belonged on your shoulders in the first place."

Meidani's eyes opened wide.

Elaida smiled at her. "Oh, I'm only teasing you, child. Back to your meal."

She joked! Joked about how she had stolen the shawl from a woman, humiliating her to such an extent that she fled the Tower. Light! What had happened to Elaida? Egwene had met this woman before, and Elaida had struck her as stern, but not tyrannical. Power changed people. It appeared that in Elaida's case, holding the Amyrlin Seat had taken her sternness and solemnity and replaced them with a heady sense of entitlement and cruelty.

Meidani looked up. "I . . . I have heard sisters express worry about the Seanchan."

Elaida waved an indifferent hand, sipping her soup. "Bah. They are too distant to be of danger to us. I wonder if they're secretly working for the Dragon Reborn. Either way, I suspect that the rumors about them are largely exaggerated." Elaida glanced at Egwene. "It's a source of constant amusement to me that *some* will believe anything that they hear."

Egwene couldn't speak. She could barely have sputtered. How would Elaida feel about these "exaggerated" rumors if the Seanchan slapped a cold *a'dam* around her idiot neck? Egwene could sometimes feel that band on her own skin, itching, impossible to move. Sometimes, it still made her faintly sick to move around freely, as if she felt that she should be locked away, chained to the post on the wall by a simple loop of metal.

She *knew* what she had dreamed, and knew those dreams to be prophetic. The Seanchan would strike at the White Tower itself. Elaida, obviously, discounted her warnings.

"No," Elaida said, waving for Egwene to bring another ladle of soup. "These Seanchan are not the problem. The *real* danger is the complete lack of obedience shown by the Aes Sedai. What will I have to do to end those foolish talks at the bridges? How many sisters will have to do penance before they acknowledge my authority?" She sat, tapping her spoon against her soup cup. Egwene, at the serving table, picked up the tureen, retrieving the ladle from its silver holder.

"Yes," Elaida mused, "if the sisters had been *obedient*, then the Tower wouldn't be divided. Those rebels would have obeyed rather than running off like a silly flock of startled birds. If the sisters were *obedient*, we would have the Dragon Reborn in our hands, and those horrid men training in their 'Black Tower' would have been dealt with long ago. What do you think, Meidani?"

"I . . . obedience is certainly important, Elaida."

Elaida shook her head as Egwene ladled soup into her bowl. "Anyone would admit *that*, Meidani. I asked what should be done. Fortunately, I have an idea myself. Doesn't it strike you as strange that the Three Oaths contain no mention of obedience to the White Tower? Sisters cannot lie, cannot make a weapon for men to kill other men, and cannot use the Power as a weapon against others except in defense. Those oaths have always seemed too lax to me. Why no oath to obey the Amyrlin? If that simple promise were part of all of us, how much pain and difficulty could we have avoided? Perhaps some revision is in order."

Egwene stood still. Once, she herself hadn't understood the importance of the oaths. She suspected that many a novice and Accepted had questioned their usefulness. But she had learned, as every Aes Sedai must, their importance. The Three Oaths were what *made* the Aes Sedai. They were what kept the Aes Sedai doing what was best for the world, but more than that, they were a shelter from accusations.

Changing them . . . well, it would be an unprecedented disaster. Elaida should *know* that. The false Amyrlin just turned back to her soup, smiling to herself, no doubt contemplating a fourth oath to demand obedience. Couldn't she see how that would undermine the Tower itself? It would transform the Amyrlin from a leader to a despot!

Egwene's rage boiled within her, steaming like the soup in her hands. This woman, this . . . creature! *She* was the cause of the problems in the White Tower, *she* was the one who caused division between rebels and loyalists. *She* had taken Rand captive and beaten him. She was a disaster!

Egwene felt herself shaking. In another moment, she'd burst and let Elaida hear truth. It was boiling free from her, and she could barely contain it.

No! she thought. *If I do that, my battle ends. I lose my war.*

So Egwene did the only thing she could think of to stop herself. She dumped the soup on the floor.

Brownish liquid sprayed across the delicate rug of red, yellow and green birds aflight. Elaida cursed, jumping up from her seat and backing away from the spill. None of the liquid had gotten on her dress, which was a shame. Egwene calmly snatched a serving towel off of the table and began to mop up the spill.

"You clumsy idiot!" Elaida snapped.

"I'm sorry," Egwene said, "I wish that hadn't happened." And she did. She wished none of this evening had occurred. She wished Elaida weren't in control; she wished the Tower had never been broken. She wished she hadn't been forced to spill the soup on the floor. But she had. And so she dealt with it, kneeling and scrubbing.

Elaida sputtered, pointing. "That rug is worth more than your entire village, wilder! Meidani, help her!"

The Gray didn't offer a single objection. She scurried over and grabbed a bucket of chilled water, which had been cooling some wine, and hurried back to help Egwene. Elaida moved over to a door on the far side of the room to call for servants.

"Send for me," Egwene whispered as Meidani knelt down to help clean.

"What?"

"Send for me to give me instruction," Egwene said quietly, glancing at Elaida, whose back was turned. "We need to speak."

Egwene had originally intended to avoid the Salidar spies, letting Beonin act as her messenger. But she had too many questions. Why hadn't Meidani fled the Tower? What were the spies planning? Had any of the others been adopted by Elaida and beaten down as soundly as Meidani?

Meidani glanced at Elaida, then back at Egwene. "I may not seem it sometimes, but I'm still Aes Sedai, *girl*. You cannot order me."

"I am your Amyrlin, Meidani," Egwene said calmly, wringing a towelful of soup into a pitcher. "And you would do best to remember it. Unless you want the Three Oaths replaced with vows to serve Elaida for eternity."

Meidani glanced at her, then cringed at Elaida's shrill

calls for servants. The poor woman had obviously seen a hard time lately.

Egwene laid a hand on her shoulder. "Elaida *can* be unseated, Meidani. The Tower *will* be reunited. I will see it happen, but we must keep courage. Send for me."

Meidani looked up, studying Egwene. "How . . . how do you do it? They say you are punished three and four times a day, that you need Healing between so that they can beat you further. How can you take it?"

"I take it because I must," Egwene said, lowering her hand. "Just as we all do what we must. Your service here watching Elaida is difficult, I can see, but know that your work is noticed and appreciated."

Egwene didn't know if Meidani really had been sent to spy on Elaida, but it was always better for a woman to think that her suffering was for a good purpose. It seemed to have been the right thing to say, for Meidani straightened, taking heart and nodding. "Thank you."

Elaida was returning, behind her three servants.

"Send for me," Egwene ordered Meidani again, voice a whisper. "I am one of the few in this Tower who has a good excuse to move between the various Ajah quarters. I can help heal what has been broken, but I will need your help."

Meidani hesitated, then nodded. "Very well."

"You!" Elaida snapped, stepping up to Egwene. "Out! I want you to tell Silviana to strap you as she's never strapped a woman before! I want her to punish you, then Heal you on the spot, then beat you again! Go!"

Egwene stood, handing her towel to one of the servants. Then she walked to the exit.

"And don't think that your clumsiness has allowed you to escape your duties," Elaida continued from behind. "You will return and serve me again on another date. And if you so much as spill another *drop*, I will have you locked away in a cell with no windows or lights for a week. Do you understand?"

Egwene left the room. Had this woman ever been a true Aes Sedai, in control of her emotions?

Yet Egwene herself had lost control of her emotions. She should never have let herself get to a point where she'd been forced to drop the soup. She had underestimated how infuriating Elaida could be, but that would not happen again.

She calmed herself as she walked, breathing in and out. Rage did her no good. You didn't get mad at the weasel who was sneaking into your yard and eating your hens. You simply laid a trap and disposed of the animal. Anger was pointless.

Hands still smelling faintly of pepper and spices, she made her way down to the lowest level of the Tower, to the novices' dining hall beside the main kitchens. Egwene had worked in those kitchens herself frequently during the last nine days; every novice was required to work chores. The smells of the place—charcoal and smoke, simmering soups and sharp, unscented soaps—were very familiar to her. The smells weren't that different, actually, from the kitchen of her father's inn back in the Two Rivers.

The white-walled room was empty, the tables sitting unattended, though there was a small tray on one of them, covered with a pot lid to keep it warm. Her cushion was there as well, left by the novices to soften the hard bench. Egwene approached, but ignored the cushion as she always did, though she was grateful for the gesture. She sat and removed the lid from the meal. Unfortunately, all she found was a bowl of the same brownish soup. There was no hint of the roast, gravy or long, thin buttered beans that had made up the rest of Elaida's meal.

Still, it was food, and Egwene's stomach was grateful for it. Elaida hadn't ordered that she *immediately* go for punishment, and so Silviana's order that she eat first took precedence. Or, at least, there was enough of an argument there to protect her.

She ate quietly, alone. The soup was indeed spicy, and it tasted as much of pepper as it had smelled, but she didn't mind. Other than that, it was actually quite good. She'd also been left a few slices of bread, though she'd gotten the ends of the loaf. All in all, not a bad meal for someone who had thought she might get nothing.

Egwene ate contemplatively, listening to Laras and the scullions bang pots at washing up in the other room, surprised at how calm she felt. She had changed; something was different about her. Watching Elaida, finally confronting the woman who had been her rival all of these months, forced her to look at what she was doing in a new light.

She had imagined herself undermining Elaida and seizing

control of the White Tower from within. Now she realized that she didn't need to undermine Elaida. The woman was fully capable of doing that herself. Why, Egwene could picture the reaction of the Sitters and Ajah heads when Elaida announced her intention to change the Three Oaths!

Elaida would topple eventually, with or without Egwene's help. Egwene's duty, as Amyrlin, wasn't to speed that fall—but to do whatever she could to hold the Tower and its occupants together. They couldn't afford to fracture further. Her duty was to hold back the chaos and destruction that threatened them all, to reforge the Tower. As she finished off her soup, using the last piece of bread to wipe the remnants from the bowl, she realized she had to do *whatever* she could to be a strength to the sisters in the Tower. Time was growing very short. What was Rand doing to the world without guidance? When would the Seanchan attack to the north? They'd have to cut through Andor to get to Tar Valon, and what destruction would that cause? Surely she had some time to reforge the Tower before the attack came, but no moments to waste.

Egwene took her dish into the kitchen proper and washed it herself, earning a nod of approval from the hefty Mistress of the Kitchens. After that, Egwene made her way up to Silviana's study. She needed to get her punishment done quickly; she still intended to visit Leane tonight, as was her custom. Egwene knocked, then entered, finding Silviana at her desk, leafing through a thick tome by the light of two silver lamps. When Egwene entered, Silviana marked the page with a small length of red cloth, then shut it. The worn cover read *Meditations on the Kindling Flame,* a history of the rise of various Amyrlins. Curious.

Egwene sat down on a stool before the desk—not flinching at the immediate sharp pain of her backside—and spoke calmly about the evening, omitting the fact that she'd dropped the bowl of soup on purpose. She did, however, say that she'd dropped it after Elaida had talked of revoking and changing the Three Oaths.

Silviana looked very thoughtful at that.

"Well," the woman said, standing up and fetching her lash, "the Amyrlin has spoken."

"Yes, I have," Egwene said, standing up and positioning herself on the table, skirts and shift up for the beating.

Silviana hesitated, and then the strapping began. Oddly, Egwene felt no desire to cry out. It hurt, of course, but she just couldn't scream. How ridiculous the punishment was!

She remembered her pain at seeing the sisters pass in the hallways, regarding one another with fear, suspicion and distrust. She remembered the agony of serving Elaida while holding her tongue. And she remembered the sheer horror at the idea of everyone in the Tower being bound by oath to obey such a tyrant.

Egwene remembered her pity for poor Meidani. No sister should be treated in such a way. Imprisonment was one thing. But beating a woman down, toying with her, hinting at the torture to come? It was insufferable.

Each of these things was a pain inside of Egwene, a knife to the chest, piercing the heart. As the beating continued, she realized that nothing they could do to her body would *ever* compare to the pain of soul she felt at seeing the White Tower suffer beneath Elaida's hand. Compared with those internal agonies, the beating was ridiculous.

And so she began to laugh.

It wasn't a forced laugh. It wasn't a defiant laugh. It was the laughter of disbelief. Of incredulity. How could they think that beating her would solve anything? It was ludicrous!

The lashing stopped. Egwene turned. Surely that wasn't all of it!

Silviana was regarding her with a concerned expression. "Child?" she asked. "Are you all right?"

"I am quite well."

"You . . . are certain? How are your thoughts?"

She thinks I've broken under the strain, Egwene realized. *She beats me and I laugh from it.*

"My thoughts are well," Egwene said. "I don't laugh because I've been broken, Silviana. I laugh because it is absurd to beat me."

The woman's expression darkened.

"Can't you see it?" Egwene asked. "Don't you feel the pain? The agony of watching the Tower crumble around you? Could any beating compare to that?"

Silviana did not respond.

I understand, Egwene thought. *I didn't realize what the Aiel did. I assumed that I just had to be harder, and that was what would teach me to laugh at pain. But it's not hardness at all. It's not strength that makes me laugh. It's understanding.*

To let the Tower fall, to let the Aes Sedai fail—the pain of that would destroy her. She had to stop it, for she was the Amyrlin Seat.

"I cannot refuse to punish you," Silviana said. "You realize that."

"Of course," Egwene said. "But please remind me of something. What was it you said about Shemerin? Why was it Elaida got away with taking the shawl from her?"

"It was because Shemerin accepted it," Silviana replied. "She treated herself as if she really *had* lost the shawl. She didn't fight back."

"I will not make the same mistake, Silviana. Elaida can *say* whatever she wants. But that doesn't change who I am, or who any of us are. Even if she tries to change the Three Oaths, there will be those who resist, who hold to what is correct. And so, when you beat me, you beat the Amyrlin Seat. And that should be amusing enough to make us both laugh."

The punishment continued, and Egwene embraced the pain, took it into herself, and judged it insignificant, impatient for the punishment to cease.

She had a lot of work to do.

CHAPTER
3

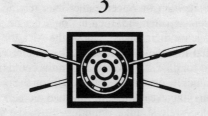

The Ways of Honor

Aviendha crouched with her spear-sisters and some True Blood scouts atop the low, grassy hill, looking down at the refugees. They were a sorry lot, these Domani wetlanders, with dirtied faces that had not seen a sweat tent in months, their emaciated children too hungry to cry. One sad mule pulled a single cart among the hundred struggling people; what they hadn't piled in the vehicle they carried. There wasn't much of either. They plodded northeast along a pathway that couldn't quite be called a road. Perhaps there was a village in that direction. Perhaps they were just fleeing the uncertainty of the coastal lands.

The hilly landscape was open save for the occasional stand of trees. The refugees hadn't seen Aviendha and her companions, despite the fact that they were less than a hundred paces away. She'd never understood how wetlanders could be so blind. Didn't they watch, noting any oddities on the horizon? Couldn't they see that traveling so near to a hilltop practically invited scouts to spy on them? They should have secured the hill with their own scouts before coming anywhere near.

Didn't they care? Aviendha shivered. How could you *not* care about eyes watching you, eyes that might belong to a man or Maiden holding a spear? Were they so eager to wake from the dream? Aviendha did not fear death, but there was a very big difference between embracing death and wishing for it.

Cities, she thought, *they're the problem.* Cities were stinking, festering places, like sores that never healed. Some were better than others—Elayne did an admirable job with

Caemlyn—but the best of them gathered too many people and taught them to grow comfortable staying in one place. If those refugees had been accustomed to travel and had learned to use their own feet, rather than relying on horses as wetlanders so often did, then it would not be so difficult for them to leave their towns. Among the Aiel, the craftsmen were trained to defend themselves, the children could live off the land for days, and even blacksmiths could travel great distances quickly. An entire sept could be on the move within an hour, carrying everything they needed on their backs.

Wetlanders were strange, doubtless. Still, she felt pity for the refugees. The emotion surprised her. While she was not heartless, her duty lay elsewhere, with Rand al'Thor. She had no reason to feel heartsore for a group of wetlanders she'd never met. But time spent with her first-sister, Elayne Trakand, had taught her that not all wetlanders were soft and weak. Just most of them. There was *ji* in caring for those who could not care for themselves.

Watching these refugees, Aviendha tried to see them as Elayne would, but she still struggled to understand Elayne's form of leadership. It was not the simple leadership of a group of Maidens on a raid—that was both instinctive and efficient. Elayne would not watch these refugees for signs of danger or hidden soldiers. Elayne would feel a responsibility to them, even if they were not of her own people. She would find a way to send food, perhaps use her troops to secure a safe area for them to homestead—and in doing so, acquire a piece of this country for herself.

Once, Aviendha would have left these thoughts to clan chiefs and roofmistresses. But she wasn't a Maiden any longer, and she had accepted that. She now lived under a different roof. She was ashamed that she had resisted the change for so long.

But that left her with a problem. What honor was there for her now? No longer a Maiden, not quite a Wise One. Her entire identity had been wrapped up in those spears, her *self* forged into their steel as surely as the carbon that strengthened them. She had grown from childhood certain that she would be *Far Dareis Mai*. Indeed, she had joined the Maidens as soon as possible. She had been proud of her life and of her spear-sisters. She would have served her clan and sept until the day when she finally fell to the spear, bleeding her last water onto the parched earth of the Three-fold Land.

This was not the Three-fold Land, and she had heard some *algai'd'siswai* wonder if the Aiel would ever return there. Their lives had changed. She didn't trust change. It couldn't be spotted or stabbed; it was more silent than any scout, more deadly than any assassin. No, she'd never trust it, but she would accept it. She would learn Elayne's ways and how to think like a chief.

She *would* find honor in her new life. Somehow.

"They are no threat," whispered Heirn, crouching with the True Bloods on the other side of the Maidens.

Rhuarc watched the refugees, alert. "The dead walk," the Taardad clan chief said, "and men fall at random to Sightblinder's evil, their blood corrupted like the water of a bad well. Those might be poor folk fleeing the ravages of war. Or they might be something else. We keep our distance."

Aviendha glanced at the increasingly distant line of refugees. She did not think Rhuarc was right; these were not ghosts or monsters. There was always something . . . wrong about those. They left her with an itch, as if she were about to be attacked.

Still, Rhuarc was wise. One learned to be careful in the Three-fold Land, where a tiny twig could kill. The group of Aiel slipped off the hilltop and down onto the brown-grassed plain beyond. Even after months spent in the wetlands, Aviendha found the landscape strange. Trees here were tall and long-limbed, with too many buds. When the Aiel crossed patches of yellow spring grass among the fallen winter leaves, they all seemed so full of water that she half-expected the blades and leaves to burst beneath her feet. She knew the wetlanders said that this spring was unnaturally slow starting, but already it was more fertile than her homeland.

In the Three-fold Land, this meadow—with the hills to provide watchpoints and shelter—would have immediately been seized by a sept and used for farming. Here, it was just one of a thousand different untouched patches of land. The fault lay again in those cities. The nearest ones were too distant from this location to make it a good spot for a wetlander farmstead.

The eight Aiel quickly crossed the grasses, weaving between hillsides, moving with speed and stealth. Horses

could not match a man's feet, what with their thunderous
galloping. Terrible beasts—why did the wetlanders insist
on riding them? Baffling. Aviendha could begin to understand how a chief or queen must think, but she knew that
she'd never completely understand wetlanders. They were
just too strange. Even Rand al'Thor.

Especially Rand al'Thor. She smiled, thinking of his
earnest eyes. She remembered the scent of him—wetlander
soaps, which smelled of oil, mixed with that particular earthy
musk that was all his own. She *would* marry him. She was
as determined as Elayne in that regard; now that they were
first-sisters, they could marry him together as was proper.
Only, how could Aviendha marry anyone, now? Her honor
had been in her spears, but Rand al'Thor now wore those at
his waist, beaten and forged into a belt buckle, given to him
by her own hand.

He had offered her marriage once. A man! Offering marriage! Another of those strange wetlander customs. Even disregarding the strangeness of it—disregarding the insult his
proposal had shown Elayne—Aviendha could never have accepted Rand al'Thor as her husband. Couldn't he understand
that a woman must bring honor to a marriage? What could a
mere apprentice offer? Would he have her come to him as an
inferior? It would shame her completely to do that!

He must not have understood. She did not think him cruel,
only dense. She would come to him when *she* was ready,
then lay the bridal wreath at his feet. And she couldn't do that
until she knew who she was.

The ways of *ji'e'toh* were complex. Aviendha knew how
to measure honor as a Maiden, but Wise Ones were different
creatures entirely. She had thought she was gaining some
small amount of honor in their eyes. They had allowed her,
for instance, to spend a great deal of time with her first-sister
in Caemlyn. But then, suddenly, Dorindha and Nadere had
arrived and informed Aviendha that she had been ignoring
her training. They had seized her like a child caught listening furtively outside the sweat tent, towing her away to join
the rest of her clan as they left for Arad Doman.

And now . . . and now the Wise Ones treated her with
less respect than they had before! They offered her no
teaching. Somehow, she had misstepped in their eyes. That
made her stomach twist. To shame herself before the other

Wise Ones was almost as bad as showing fear before one as brave as Elayne!

So far, the Wise Ones had allowed Aviendha some honor by letting her serve punishments, but she didn't know *how* she had shamed herself in the first place. Asking would—of course—only bring more shame. Until she unwove the problem, she could not meet her *toh*. Worse, there was a real danger of her making the mistake again. Until she sorted out this problem, she would remain an apprentice, and she would *never* be able to bring an honorable bridal wreath to Rand al'Thor.

Aviendha gritted her teeth. Another woman might have wept, but what good would that have done? Whatever her mistake, she had brought it upon herself, and it was her duty to right it. She *would* find honor again and she *would* marry Rand al'Thor before he died at the Last Battle.

That meant that whatever it was she had to learn, she needed to do so quickly. Very quickly.

They met up with another group of Aiel waiting in a small clearing amid a stand of pine trees. The ground was thick with discarded brown needles, the sky broken by the towering trunks. The group was small by the standards of clans and septs, barely two hundred people. In the middle of the clearing stood four Wise Ones, each wearing the characteristic brown woolen skirt and white blouse. Aviendha wore similar attire, which now felt as natural to her as the *cadin'sor* once had. The scouting party split up, men and Maidens moving to join members of their clans or societies. Rhuarc joined the Wise Ones, and Aviendha followed him.

Each of the Wise Ones—Amys, Bair, Melaine, and Nadere—gave her a glance. Bair, the only Aiel with the group who wasn't Taardad or Goshien, had arrived only recently, perhaps to coordinate with the others. Whatever the reason, none of them seemed pleased. Aviendha hesitated. If she left now, would it seem as if she were trying to avoid their attention? Did she instead dare stay, and risk incurring their further displeasure?

"Well?" Amys said to Rhuarc. Though Amys had white hair, she looked quite young. In her case, this wasn't due to working the Power—her hair had started turning silver when she'd been a child.

"It was as the scouts described, shade of my heart,"

Rhuarc said. "Another pitiful band of wetlander refugees. I saw no hidden danger in them."

The Wise Ones nodded, as if this was what they had expected. "That is the tenth band of refugees in less than a week," said aged Bair, her watery blue eyes thoughtful.

Rhuarc nodded. "There are rumors of Seanchan attacks on harbors to the west. Perhaps the people move inland to avoid the raids." He glanced at Amys. "This country boils like water spilled on a hearthstone. The clans are uncertain what Rand al'Thor wishes of them."

"He was very clear," Bair noted. "He will be pleased that you and Dobraine Taborwin secured Bandar Eban, as he asked."

Rhuarc nodded. "But still, his intentions are not clear. He asked for us to restore order. Are we then to be like wetlander city guardsmen? That is no place for the Aiel. We are not to conquer, so we do not get the fifth. And yet it feels very much like conquest, what we do. The *Car'a'carn*'s orders can be clear yet confusing at the same time. He has a gift in that area, I think."

Bair smiled, nodding. "Perhaps he intends for us to do something with these refugees."

"And what would we do?" Amys asked, shaking her head. "Are we Shaido, expected to make *gai'shain* from wetlanders?" Her tone left little doubt as to what she thought of both Shaido *and* the idea of making wetlanders *gai'shain*.

Aviendha nodded in agreement. As Rhuarc said, the *Car'a'carn* had sent them to Arad Doman to "restore order." But that was a wetlander concept; Aiel brought their own order with them. There was chaos to war and battle, true, but each and every Aiel understood his place, and would act within that place. The little children understood honor and *toh*, and a hold would continue to function after all of the leaders and Wise Ones were killed.

It was not so with wetlanders. They ran about like a basket of wild lizards suddenly dropped onto hot stones, taking no care for provisions when they fled. As soon as their leaders were occupied or distracted, banditry and chaos ruled. The strong took from the weak, and even blacksmiths were not safe.

What could Rand al'Thor expect the Aiel to do about it? They could not teach *ji'e'toh* to an entire nation. Rand al'Thor had told them to *avoid* killing Domani troops. But those troops—often corrupt and turned to banditry themselves—were part of the problem.

"Perhaps he will explain more when we arrive at this manor house of his," said Melaine, shaking her head, red-gold hair catching the light. Her pregnancy was just beginning to show beneath her Wise One blouse. "And if he does not, then surely it is better for us to be here in Arad Doman than to spend yet more time lounging back in the land of the treekillers."

"As you say," Rhuarc agreed. "Let us move on, then. There is still a distance to run." He moved off to speak with Bael. Aviendha took a step away, but a harsh glance from Amys made her freeze.

"Aviendha," said the hard, white-haired woman. "How many Wise Ones went with Rhuarc to scout this refugee train?"

"None but me," Aviendha admitted.

"Oh, and are you a Wise One now?" Bair asked.

"No," Aviendha said, quickly, then shamed herself further by blushing. "I spoke poorly."

"Then you shall be punished," Bair said. "You are no longer a Maiden, Aviendha. It is not your place to scout; that is a task for others."

"Yes, Wise One," Aviendha said, looking down. She had not thought that going with Rhuarc would bring her shame—she had seen other Wise Ones do similar tasks.

But I am not a Wise One, she reminded herself. *I am an apprentice only.* Bair had not said that a Wise One could not scout; only that it had not been Aviendha's place to go. It was about Aviendha herself. And about whatever it was she had done—or perhaps continued to do—to provoke the Wise Ones.

Did they think she had grown soft by spending time with Elayne? Aviendha herself worried that that was true. During her days in Caemlyn, she had begun to find herself enjoying the silks and baths. By the end, she had objected only feebly when Elayne had come up with an excuse to dress her in some impractical and frivolous garment with embroidery and lace. It was well that the others had come for her.

The others just stood there, looking at her expectantly, faces like red desert stones, impassive and stern. Aviendha gritted her teeth again. She would complete her apprenticeship and find honor. She *would*.

The call came to begin moving, and *cadin'sor*-clad men and women did so, running together in small groups. The Wise Ones moved as easily as the soldiers, despite their bulky skirts. Amys touched Aviendha's arm. "You will run with me so that we can discuss your punishment."

Aviendha fell into pace beside the Wise One at a brisk jog. It was a speed any Aiel could maintain almost indefinitely. Her group, from Caemlyn, had met up with Rhuarc as he was traveling from Bandar Eban to meet with Rand al'Thor in the eastern part of the country. Dobraine Taborwin, a Cairhienin, was still maintaining order in the capital city, where he'd reportedly located a member of the Domani ruling body.

Perhaps the group of Aiel could have Traveled through a gateway the rest of the distance. But it was not far—only a few days by foot—and they had left early enough to arrive at the appointed time without using the One Power. Rhuarc wanted to scout for himself some of the landscape near the manor house Rand al'Thor was using as a base. Other bodies of Goshien or Taardad Aiel would join them at the base, using gateways, if needed.

"What do you think of the *Car'a'carn*'s demands of us here in Arad Doman, Aviendha?" Amys asked as they ran.

Aviendha stifled a frown. What of her punishment? "It is an irregular request," she said, "but Rand al'Thor has many strange ideas, even for a wetlander. This will not be the most unusual duty he has set for us."

"And the fact that Rhuarc finds the duty discomforting?"

"I doubt that the clan chief is uncomfortable," Aviendha said. "I suspect that Rhuarc speaks what he has heard others say, passing the information to the Wise Ones. He does not wish to shame others by revealing who has spoken of their fears."

Amys nodded. What was the purpose of the questions? Surely the woman had guessed the same thing. She would not come to Aviendha for counsel.

They ran in silence for a time, with no mention of punishments. Had the Wise Ones forgiven her unknown slight? Surely they wouldn't dishonor her in that way. Aviendha had to be given time to think out what she had done, otherwise her shame would be unbearable. She might err again, this time worse.

Amys gave no clue as to her thoughts. The Wise One had been a Maiden once, like Aviendha. She was hard, even for an Aiel. "And al'Thor himself?" Amys asked. "What do you think of him?"

"I love him," Aviendha said.

"I did not ask Aviendha the silly girl," Amys said curtly. "I asked Aviendha the Wise One."

"He is a man of many burdens," Aviendha said more carefully. "I fear that he makes many of those burdens heavier than they need be. I once thought that there was only one way to be strong, but I have learned from my first-sister that I was wrong. Rand al'Thor . . . I do not think he has learned this yet. I worry that he mistakes hardness for strength."

Amys nodded again, as if in approval. Were these questions a test of some sort?

"You would marry him?" Amys asked.

I thought we weren't talking about Aviendha the "silly girl," Aviendha thought, but of course didn't say it. One did not say such things to Amys.

"I *will* marry him," she said instead. "It is not a possibility, but a certainty." The tone earned her a glance from Amys, but Aviendha held her ground. Any Wise One who misspoke deserved to be corrected.

"And the wetlander Min Farshaw?" Amys asked. "She obviously loves him. What will you do about her?"

"She is my concern," Aviendha said. "We will reach an accommodation. I have spoken with Min Farshaw, and I believe she will be easy to work with."

"You would become first-sisters with her as well?" Amys asked, sounding just faintly amused.

"We will reach an accommodation, Wise One."

"And if you cannot?"

"We will," Aviendha said firmly.

"And how can you be so certain?"

Aviendha hesitated. Part of her wished to return only silence to that question, passing the leafless brush thickets and giving Amys no answer. But she was just an apprentice, and while she could not be forced to speak, she knew that Amys would keep pushing until the answer came out. Aviendha hoped she would not incur too much *toh* by her response.

"You know of the woman Min's viewings?" Aviendha said. Amys nodded.

"One of those viewings relates to Rand al'Thor and the three women he will love. Another relates to my children by the *Car'a'carn*."

She said no more, and Amys pressed no more. It was enough. Both knew that one would sooner find a Stone Dog who would retreat than find a viewing of Min's that went wrong.

On one hand, it was good to know that Rand al'Thor would be hers, although she would have to share him. She did not begrudge Elayne, of course, but Min . . . well, Aviendha did not really know her. Regardless, the viewing was a comfort. But it was also bothersome. Aviendha loved Rand al'Thor because *she* chose to, not because she was destined to. Of course, Min's viewing didn't guarantee that Aviendha would actually be able to marry Rand, so perhaps she had misspoken to Amys. Yes, he would love three women and three women would love him, but would Aviendha find a way to marry him?

No, the future was not certain, and for some reason that brought her comfort. Perhaps she should have worried, but she did not. She would get her honor back, and then she would marry Rand al'Thor. Perhaps he would die soon after, but perhaps an ambush would come and she would fall to an arrow this day. Worrying solved nothing.

Toh, however, was another matter.

"I misspoke, Wise One," Aviendha said. "I implied that the viewing said I would marry Rand al'Thor. That is not true. All three of us will love him, and while that implies marriage, I do not know for certain."

Amys nodded. There was no *toh*; Aviendha had corrected herself quickly enough. That was well. She would not add more shame on top of what she had already earned.

"Very well, then," Amys said, watching the path ahead of her. "Let us discuss today's punishment."

Aviendha relaxed slightly. So she still had time to discover what she had done wrong. Wetlanders often seemed confused by Aiel ways with punishment, but wetlanders had little understanding of honor. Honor didn't come from *being* punished, but *accepting* a punishment and bearing it restored honor. That was the soul of *toh*—the willing lowering of oneself in order to recover that which had been lost. It was strange to her that wetlanders couldn't see this; indeed, it was strange that they didn't follow *ji'e'toh* instinctively. What was life without honor?

Amys, rightly, wouldn't tell Aviendha what she had done wrong. However, she was having no success thinking through the answer on her own, and it would cause less shame if she discovered the answer through conversation. "Yes," Aviendha said carefully. "I should be punished. My time in Caemlyn threatened to make me weak."

Amys sniffed. "You are no more weak than you were when you carried the spears, girl. A fair bit stronger, I should think. Your time with your first-sister was important for you."

So that wasn't it. When Dorindha and Nadere had come for her, they had said she needed to continue her training as an apprentice. Yet in the time since the Aiel had departed for Arad Doman, Aviendha had been given no lessons. She had been assigned to carry water, to mend shawls, and to serve tea. She had been given all manner of punishments with little explanation of what she had done wrong. And when she did something obvious—like going scouting when she shouldn't have—the severity of her punishment was always greater than the infraction should have merited.

It was almost as if the punishment *was* the thing the Wise Ones wanted her to learn, but that could not be. She was not some wetlander who needed to be taught the ways of honor. What good would constant and unexplained punishment do, other than to warn of some grave mistake she had made?

Amys reached to her side, untying something hanging at her waist. The woolen bag she held up was about the size of a fist. "We have decided," she said, "that we have been too lax in our instruction. Time is precious and we have no room left for delicacy."

Aviendha covered her surprise. Their previous punishments were *delicate*?

"Therefore," Amys said, handing over the small sack, "you will take this. Inside are seeds. Some are black, others are brown, others are white. This evening, before we sleep, you will separate the colors, then count how many there are of each one. If you are wrong, we will mix them together and you will start again."

Aviendha found herself gaping, and she nearly stumbled to a stop. Hauling water was necessary work. Mending clothing was necessary work. Cooking meals was important work, particularly when no *gai'shain* had been brought with the small advance group.

But this . . . this was *useless* work! It was not only unimportant, it was frivolous. It was the kind of punishment reserved for only the most stubborn, or most shameful, of people. It almost . . . almost felt as though the Wise Ones were calling her *da'tsang*!

"By Sightblinder's eyes," she whispered as she forced herself to keep running. "What did I *do*?"

Amys glanced at her, and Aviendha looked away. Both knew that she didn't want an answer to that question. She took the bag silently. It was the most humiliating punishment she had ever been given.

Amys moved off to run with the other Wise Ones. Aviendha shook off her stupor, her determination returning. Her mistake must have been more profound than she had thought. Amys' punishment was an indication of that, a hint.

She opened the bag and glanced inside. There were three little empty *algode* bags inside to help with the separation, and thousands of tiny seeds nearly engulfed them. This punishment was *meant* to be seen, meant to bring her shame. Whatever she'd done, it was offensive not just to the Wise Ones, but to all around her, even if they—like Aviendha herself—were ignorant of it.

That only meant she had to be more determined.

CHAPTER
4

Nightfall

Gawyn watched the sun burn the clouds to death in the west, the final light fading. That haze of perpetual gloom kept the sun itself shrouded. Just as it hid the stars from his sight at night. Today the clouds were unnaturally high in the air. Often, Dragonmount's tip would be hidden on cloudy days, but this thick, gray haze hovered high enough that most of the time, it barely brushed the mountain's jagged, broken tip.

"Let's engage them," Jisao whispered from where he crouched beside Gawyn on the hilltop.

Gawyn glanced away from the sunset, back toward the small village below. It should have been still, save perhaps for a goodman checking on his livestock one last time before turning in. It should have been dim, unlit save for a few tallow candles burning in windows as people finished evening meals.

But it was not dim. It was not quiet. The village was alight with angry torches carried by a dozen sturdy figures. By that torchlight and the light of the dying sun, Gawyn could make out that each was wearing a nondescript uniform of brown and black. Gawyn couldn't see the three-starred insignia on their uniforms, but he knew it was there.

From his distant vantage, Gawyn watched a few latecomers stumble from their homes, looking frightened and worried as they gathered with the others in the crowded square. These villagers welcomed the armed force with reluctance. Women clutched children, men were careful to keep their eyes downcast. "We don't want trouble," the postures said. They'd undoubtedly heard from other villages that these invaders were orderly. The soldiers paid for goods they took, and no young men were pressed into service—though they weren't turned away either. A very odd invading army indeed. However, Gawyn knew what the people would think. This army was led by Aes Sedai, and who could say what was odd or normal when Aes Sedai were involved?

There were no sisters with this particular patrol, thank the Light. The soldiers, polite but stern, lined up the villagers and looked them over. Then a pair of soldiers entered each house and barn, inspecting it. Nothing was taken and nothing was broken. All very neat and cordial. Gawyn could almost hear the officer offering apologies to the village mayor.

"Gawyn?" Jisao asked. "I count barely a dozen of them. If we send Rodic's squad to come in from the north, we'll cut off both sides and smash them between us. It's getting dark enough that they won't see us coming. We could take them without so much as running up a lather."

"And the villagers?" Gawyn asked. "There are children down there."

"That hasn't stopped us other times."

"Those times were different," Gawyn said, shaking his head. "The last three villages they've searched point a direct line toward Dorlan. If this group vanishes, the next one will wonder what it was they nearly uncovered. We'd draw the entire army's eye in this direction."

"But—"

"No," Gawyn said softly. "We have to know when to fall back, Jisao."

"So we came all this way for nothing."

"We came all this way for an opportunity," Gawyn said, backing away from the hilltop, making certain he didn't show a profile on the horizon. "And now that I've inspected that opportunity, we're not going to take it. Only a fool looses his arrow just because he's got a bird in front of him."

"Why wouldn't you loose it if it's right there in front of you?" Jisao asked as he joined Gawyn.

"Because sometimes the prize isn't worth the arrow," Gawyn said. "Come on."

Below, waiting in the dark with lanterns hooded, were

some of the very men the soldiers in the village were searching for. Gareth Bryne must have been very displeased to learn there was a harrying force hiding somewhere nearby. He'd been diligent in trying to flush it out, but the countryside near Tar Valon was liberally sprinkled with villages, forests and secluded valleys that could hide a small, mobile strike force. So far, Gawyn had managed to keep his Younglings out of sight while pulling off the occasional raid or ambush on Bryne's forces. There was only so much you could do with three hundred men, however. Particularly when you faced one of the five Great Captains.

Am I destined to end up fighting against each and every man who has been a mentor to me? Gawyn took the reins of his horse and gave a silent order to withdraw by raising his right hand, then gestured sharply away from the village. The men moved without comment, dismounting and leading their mounts for both stealth and safety.

Gawyn had thought he was over Hammar and Coulin's deaths; Bryne himself had taught Gawyn that the battlefield sometimes made allies into sudden foes. Gawyn had fought his former teachers, and Gawyn had won. That was the end of it.

Recently, however, his mind seemed determined to dredge up those corpses and carry them about. Why now, after so long?

He suspected his sense of guilt had to do with facing Bryne, his first and most influential instructor in the arts of war. Gawyn shook his head as he guided Challenge across the darkening landscape; he kept his men away from the road in case Bryne's scouts had placed watchers. The fifty men around Gawyn walked as quietly as possible, the horses' hoofbeats deadened by the springy earth.

If Bryne had been shocked to discover a harrying force striking at his outriders, then Gawyn had been equally shocked to discover those three stars on the uniforms of the men he slew. How had the White Tower's enemies recruited the greatest military mind in all of Andor? And what was the Captain-General of the Queen's Guard doing fighting with a group of Aes Sedai rebels in the first place? He should have been in Caemlyn protecting Elayne.

Light send that Elayne *had* arrived in Andor. She couldn't still be with the rebels. Not with her homeland lacking a queen. Her duty to Andor outweighed her duty to the White Tower.

And what of your duty, Gawyn Trakand? he thought to himself.

He wasn't certain he had duty, or honor, left to him. Perhaps his guilt about Hammar, his nightmares of war and death at Dumai's Wells, were due to the slow realization that he might have given his allegiance to the wrong side. His loyalty belonged to Elayne and Egwene. What, then, was he still doing fighting a battle he didn't care about, helping a side that—by all accounts—was *opposed* to the one Elayne and Egwene had chosen?

They're just Accepted, he told himself. *Elayne and Egwene didn't choose this side—they are just doing what they've been ordered to do!* But the things that Egwene had said to him all those months ago, back in Cairhien, suggested that she had made her decision willingly.

She had chosen a side. Hammar had chosen a side. Gareth Bryne had, apparently, chosen a side. But Gawyn continued to want to be on *both* sides. The division was ripping him apart.

An hour out of the village, Gawyn gave the order to mount and take to the road. Hopefully, Bryne's scouts wouldn't think to search the land outside the village. If they did, the tracks of fifty horsemen would be hard to miss. There was no avoiding that. The best thing now was to reach firm ground, where the signs of their passing would be hidden by a thousand years of footfalls and traffic. Two pairs of soldiers rode off in front and two pairs hung back to watch. The rest maintained their silence, though their horses now pounded a thunderous gallop. None asked why they were withdrawing, but Gawyn knew that they were wondering, just as Jisao had.

They were good men. Perhaps too good. As they rode, Rajar pulled his mount up beside Gawyn's. Just a few months ago, Rajar had been a youth. But now Gawyn couldn't think of him as anything other than a soldier. A veteran. Some men gained experience through years spent living. Other men gained experience through months spent watching their friends die.

Glancing upward, Gawyn missed the stars. They hid their faces from him behind those clouds. Like Aiel behind black veils. "Where did we go wrong, Rajar?" Gawyn asked as they rode.

"Wrong, Lord Gawyn?" Rajar asked. "I don't know that we did anything wrong. We couldn't have known which villages that patrol would choose to inspect, or that they wouldn't turn along the old Wagonright Road, as you had hoped. Some of the men may be confused, but it was right to withdraw."

"I wasn't talking about the raid," Gawyn said, shaking his head. "I'm talking about this whole bloody situation. You shouldn't have to go on supply raids or spend your time killing scouts; you should have become a Warder to some freshly minted Aes Sedai by now." *And I should be back in Caemlyn, with Elayne.*

"The Wheel weaves as the Wheel wills," the shorter man said.

"Well, it wove us into a hole," Gawyn muttered, glancing at the overcast sky once again. "And Elaida doesn't seem too eager to pull us out of it."

Rajar looked at Gawyn reproachfully. "The White Tower's methods are its own, Lord Gawyn, and so are its motives. It isn't for us to question. What good is a Warder who questions the orders of his Aes Sedai? A good way to get both of you killed, that is."

You're not a Warder, Rajar. That's the problem! Gawyn said nothing. None of the other Younglings seemed to be plagued with these questions. To them, the world was much simpler. One did as the White Tower, and the Amyrlin Seat, commanded. Never mind if those commands seemed designed to get you killed.

Three hundred youths against a force of over fifty thousand hardened soldiers, commanded by Gareth Bryne himself? Will of the Amyrlin or not, that was a deathtrap. The only reason the Younglings had survived as long as they had was because of Gawyn's familiarity with his teacher's ways. He knew where Bryne would send patrols and outriding scouts, and knew how to evade his search patterns.

It was still a futile effort. Gawyn didn't have nearly the troops needed for a true harrying force, particularly with Bryne entrenched in his siege. Beyond that, there was the remarkable matter of the army's complete lack of a supply line. How were they getting food? They purchased supplies from the surrounding villages, but not nearly enough to feed themselves. How could they possibly have carried all they needed while still moving quickly enough to appear, without warning, in the middle of winter?

Gawyn's attacks were next to meaningless. It was enough to make a man think that the Amyrlin just wanted him, and the other Younglings, out of the way. Before Dumai's Wells, Gawyn had suspected that was the case. Now he was growing certain. *And yet you continue to follow her orders,* he thought to himself.

He shook his head. Bryne's scouts were getting dangerously close to his base of operations, and Gawyn couldn't risk killing any more of them without giving himself away. It was time to head back to Dorlan. Perhaps the Aes Sedai there would have a suggestion on how to proceed.

He hunkered down on his horse and continued riding into the night. *Light, I wish I could see the stars,* he thought.

CHAPTER
5

A Tale of Blood

Rand crossed the trampled manor green, banners flapping before him, tents surrounding him, horses whinnying in their pickets on the far west side. In the air hung the scents of an efficient war camp: smoke and savor from the stewpots were much stronger than the occasional whiff of horse dung or an unwashed body.

Bashere's men maintained a tidy camp, busying themselves with the hundreds of little tasks that allowed the army to function: sharpening swords, oiling leathers, mending saddles, fetching water from the stream. Some practiced charges to the left, on the far side of the green, in the space between tent lines and the scraggly trees growing alongside the stream. The men held gleaming lances at the level as their horses trampled the muddy ground in a long swath. The maneuvers not only kept their skills sharp, but exercised the horses as well.

As always, Rand was trailed by a flock of attendants. Maidens were his guards, and the Aiel watched the Saldaean soldiers with wariness. Beside him were several Aes Sedai. They were always about him, now. The Pattern had no place for his onetime insistence that all Aes Sedai be kept at arm's length. It wove as it willed, and experience had shown that Rand needed these Aes Sedai. What he wanted no longer mattered. He understood that now.

It was little comfort that many of these Aes Sedai in his camp had sworn allegiance to him. Everyone knew that Aes Sedai followed their oaths in their own ways, and they would decide what their "fealty" to him would require.

Elza Penfell—who accompanied him this day—was one

of those who had sworn to him. Of the Green Ajah, she had a face that might be considered pretty, if one didn't recognize the ageless quality that marked her as Aes Sedai. She was pleasant, for an Aes Sedai, despite the fact that she had helped kidnap Rand and lock him in a box for days, to be pulled out only for the occasional beating.

In the back of his mind, Lews Therin growled.

That was past. Elza had sworn. That was enough to allow Rand to use her. The other woman attending him today was less predictable; she was a member of Cadsuane's retinue. Corele Hovian—a slim Yellow with blue eyes, wild dark hair, and a perpetual smile—had sworn no oaths to do as he said. Despite that, he felt a temptation to trust her, since she had once tried to save his life. It was only because of her, Samitsu and Damer Flinn that Rand had survived. One of two wounds in Rand's side that would not heal—a gift from Padan Fain's cursed dagger—still lingered as a reminder of that day. The constant pain of that festering evil overlaid the equal pain of an older wound beneath, the one Rand had taken while fighting Ishamael so long ago.

Soon, one of those wounds—or perhaps both—would spill Rand's blood onto the rocks of Shayol Ghul. He wasn't certain if they would be what killed him or not; with the number and variety of the different factors competing to take Rand's life, even Mat wouldn't have known which one was the best bet.

As soon as Rand thought of Mat, the colors swirled in his vision, forming into the image of a wiry, brown-eyed man wearing a wide-brimmed hat and tossing dice before a small crowd of watching soldiers. Mat wore a grin and seemed to be showing off, which was not unusual, though there didn't seem to be any coin changing hands for his throws.

The visions came whenever he thought of Mat or Perrin, and Rand had stopped dismissing them. He did not know what caused the images to appear; probably his ta'veren nature interacting with the other two ta'veren from his home village. Whatever it was, he used it. Just another tool. It appeared that Mat was still with the Band, but was no longer camped in a forested land. It was hard to tell from the angle, but he looked to be outside a city somewhere. At least, that was a large road in the near distance. Rand had not seen the small, dark-skinned woman with Mat for some time. Who was she? Where had she gone?

The vision faded. Hopefully, Mat would return to him soon. He would need Mat and his tactical skills at Shayol Ghul.

One of Bashere's quartermasters—a thick-mustached man with bowlegs and a squat body—saw Rand and approached with a quick step. Rand waved the Saldaean back; he had no mind for supply reports at the moment. The quartermaster saluted immediately and retreated. Once, Rand might have been surprised at how quickly he was obeyed, but no longer. It was right for the soldiers to obey. Rand was a king, though he didn't wear the Crown of Swords at the moment.

Rand passed through the green, filled with tents and horse pickets now. He left the camp, passing the unfinished earthen bulwark. Here, pine trees continued down the sides of the gentle slope. Tucked into a stand of trees just to the right was the Traveling ground, a square section of ground roped off to provide a safe location for gateways.

One hung in the air at that moment, an opening to another place. A small group of people was making their way through, walking out onto the pinecone-strewn ground. Rand could see the weaves that made up the gateway; this one had been crafted with *saidin*.

Most of the people in the group wore the colorful clothing of Sea Folk—the men bare-chested, even in the chill spring air, the women in loose bright blouses. All wore loose trousers, and all had piercings in their ears or noses, the complexity of the adornments an indication of each person's relative status.

As he waited for the Sea Folk, one of the soldiers who guarded the Traveling ground approached Rand with a sealed letter. The letter would be one sent via Asha'man from one of Rand's interests in the east. Indeed, as he opened it, he found it was from Darlin, the Tairen king. Rand had left him with orders to gather an army and prepare it for marching into Arad Doman. That gathering had been completed for some time now, and Darlin wondered— yet again—about his orders. Could no one simply do as they were told?

"Send a messenger," Rand said to the soldier, impatiently

tucking the letter away. "Tell Darlin to continue recruiting. I want him to draft every Tairen who can hold a sword and either train him for combat or set him to work in the forges. The Last Battle is close. Very close."

"Yes, my Lord Dragon," the soldier said, saluting.

"Tell him that I will send an Asha'man when I want him to move," Rand said. "I still intend to use him in Arad Doman, but I need to see what the Aiel have discovered first."

The soldier bowed and retreated. Rand turned back to the Sea Folk. One of them approached him.

"Coramoor," she said, nodding. Harine was a handsome woman in her middle years, with white streaking her hair. Her Atha'an Miere blouse was of a bright blue, colorful enough to impress a Tinker, and she had an impressive five gold rings in each ear as well as a nose chain strung with gold medallions.

"I did not expect you to come and meet us personally," Harine continued.

"I have questions for you that could not wait."

Harine looked taken aback. She was the Sea Folk ambassador to the Coramoor, which was their name for Rand. They were angry with Rand for the weeks he had spent without a Sea Folk minder—he had promised to keep one with him at all times—yet Logain had mentioned their hesitation to send Harine back. Why was that? Had she achieved greater rank, making her too important to attend him? *Could* one be too important to attend the Coramoor? Much about the Sea Folk made little sense to him.

"I will answer if I can," Harine said guardedly. Behind her, porters moved the rest of her belongings through the gateway. Flinn stood on the other side, holding the portal open.

"Good," Rand said, pacing back and forth before her as he spoke. At times, he felt so tired—so weary to his bones—that he knew he had to keep moving. Never stopping. If he did, his enemies would find him. Either that, or his own exhaustion, both mental and physical, would drag him down.

"Tell me this," he demanded as he paced. "Where are the ships which have been promised? The Domani people starve while grain rots in the east. Logain said you had agreed to my demands, but I have seen nothing of your ships. It has been weeks!"

"Our ships are swift," Harine said testily, "but there is a great distance to travel—and we must go *through* seas controlled by the Seanchan. The invaders have been extremely diligent with their patrols, and our ships have had to turn back and flee on several occasions. Did you expect that we would be able bring your food in an instant? Perhaps the convenience of these gateways has made you impatient, Coramoor. We must deal with the realities of shipping and war even if you do not."

Her tone implied that he *would* have to deal with those realities in this case. "I expect results," Rand said, shaking his head. "I expect no delays. I know you do not like being forced to keep your agreement, but I will suffer no lagging to prove a point. People die because of your slowness."

Harine looked as if she'd been slapped. "Surely," she said, "the Coramoor does not imply that we would not keep to our Bargain."

The Sea Folk were stubborn and prideful, Wavemistresses more than most. They were like an entire race of Aes Sedai. He hesitated. *I should not insult her so, not because I am frustrated about other things.* "No," he finally said. "No, I do not imply that. Tell me, Harine, were you punished much for your part in our agreement?"

"I was hung up by my ankles naked and strapped until I could scream no more." As soon as the words left her mouth, her eyes opened in shock. Often, when influenced by Rand's *ta'veren* nature, people said things they did not intend to admit.

"So harsh?" Rand said, genuinely surprised.

"It was not so bad as it could have been. I retain my position as Wavemistress for my clan."

But it was obvious she had lost a great deal of face, or incurred great *toh*, or whatever the blasted Sea Folk called honor. Even when he wasn't present, he caused pain and suffering!

"I am glad you have returned," he forced himself to say. No smile, but a softer tone. That was the best he could do. "You have impressed me, Harine, with your levelheadedness."

She nodded in thanks to him. "We will keep our Bargain, Coramoor. You needn't fear."

Something else struck him, one of the original questions he'd come to ask her. "Harine. I would ask you a somewhat delicate question about your people."

"You may ask," she said carefully.

"How do the Sea Folk treat men who can channel?"

She hesitated. "That is not a matter for the shorebound to know."

Rand met her eyes. "If you agree to answer, then I will answer a question for you in return." The best way to deal with the Atha'an Miere was not to push or bully, but to offer trade.

She paused. "If you give me two questions," she said, "I will answer."

"I will give you one question, Harine," he said, raising a finger. "But I promise to answer you as truthfully as I can. It is a fair bargain, and you know it. I have little patience right now."

Harine touched her fingers to her lips. "It is agreed, then, under the Light."

"It is agreed," Rand said. "Under the Light. My question?"

"Men who can channel are given a choice," Harine said. "They can either step from the bow of their ship holding a stone which is also tied to their legs, or they can be dropped off on a barren isle with no food or water. The second is considered the more shameful option, but some few do take it, to live for a brief time longer."

Not much different from what his own people did in gentling men, truth be told. "*Saidin* is cleansed now," he said to her. "This practice must stop."

She pursed her lips, regarding him. "Your . . . man spoke of this, Coramoor. Some find it difficult to accept."

"It is true," he said firmly.

"I do not doubt that you believe it to be so."

Rand gritted his teeth, forcing down another burst of anger, his hand forming a fist. He had *cleansed* the taint! He, Rand al'Thor, had performed a deed the likes of which had not been seen since the Age of Legends. And how was it treated? With suspicion and doubt. Most assumed that he was going mad, and therefore seeing a "cleansing" that had not really happened.

Men who could channel were always distrusted. Yet they
were the only ones who could confirm what Rand said! He'd
imagined joy and wonder at the victory, but he should have
known better. Though male Aes Sedai had once been as
respected as their female counterparts, that had been long
ago. The days of Jorlen Corbesan had been lost in time.
All people could remember now was the Breaking and the
Madness.

They hated male channelers. Yet, in following Rand,
they served one. Did they not see the contradiction? How
could he convince them that there was no longer reason to
murder men who could touch the One Power? He *needed*
them! Why, there might be another Jorlen Corbesan among
the very men the Sea Folk tossed into the ocean!

He froze. Jorlen Corbesan had been one of the most talented Aes Sedai before the Breaking, a man who had crafted
some of the most amazing *ter'angreal* Rand had ever seen.
Except Rand had *not* seen them. Those were Lews Therin's
memories, not his. Jorlen's research facility of Sharom had
been destroyed—the man himself killed—by the backlash
of Power from the Bore.

Oh, Light, Rand thought with despair. *I'm losing myself.
Losing myself in him.*

The most terrifying part was that Rand could no longer
make himself wish to banish Lews Therin. Lews Therin
had known a way to seal the Bore, if imperfectly, but Rand
had no idea how to approach the task. The safety of the
world might depend on the memories of a dead madman.

Many of the people around Rand appeared shocked, and
Harine's eyes were both uncomfortable and a little frightened. Rand had been muttering to himself again, he realized, and he cut off abruptly.

"I accept your answer," he said stiffly. "What is your
question of me?"

"I will ask it later," she said. "Once I have had a chance
to consider."

"As you wish." He turned away, his retinue of Aes Sedai,
Maidens and attendants following. "The Traveling ground
guards will see you to your room and carry your luggage."
There was a veritable mountain of *that.* "Flinn, to me!"

The elderly Asha'man jumped through the gateway, motioning for the last of the porters to trot back to the docks

on the other side. He let the portal twist back into a slash of light and vanish, then hurried after Rand. He spared a glance and a smile for Corele, who had bonded him as her Warder.

"I apologize for taking so long to return, Lord Dragon." Flinn had a leathery face and only a few wisps of hair on his head. He looked a lot like some of the farmers Rand had known back in Emond's Field, though he had been a soldier for most of his life. Flinn had come to Rand because he wanted to learn Healing. Rand had turned him into a weapon instead.

"You did as ordered," Rand said, walking back toward the green. He wanted to blame Harine for the prejudices of an entire world, but that was not fair. He needed a better way, a way to *make* everyone see.

"I've never been exceptional at making gateways," Flinn continued. "Not like Androl. I needed to—"

"Flinn," Rand said, cutting in. "Enough."

The Asha'man blushed. "I apologize, my Lord Dragon."

To the side, Corele laughed softly, patting Flinn on the shoulder. "Don't mind him, Damer," she said in a lilting Murandian accent. "He's been as surly as a winter thunderhead all morning."

Rand glared at her, but she just smiled good-naturedly. Regardless of what the Aes Sedai thought of men who could channel in general, the ones who had taken Asha'man as Warders seemed as protective of them as mothers of their children. She had bonded one of his men, but that did not change the fact that Flinn *was* one of his men. An Asha'man first and foremost, a Warder second.

"What do you think, Elza?" Rand said, turning from Corele to the other Aes Sedai. "About the taint and what Harine said?"

The round-faced woman hesitated. She walked with hands behind her back, dark green dress marked only by subtle embroideries. Utilitarian, for an Aes Sedai. "If my Lord Dragon says that the taint has been cleansed," the woman said carefully, "then it is certainly improper to express doubt of him where others can hear."

Rand grimaced. An Aes Sedai answer for certain. Oath or no oath, Elza did as she wished.

"Oh, we were both there at Shadar Logoth," Corele said, rolling her eyes. "We saw what you did, Rand. Besides, I can feel male power through dear Damer here when we link. It *has* changed. The taint is gone. Right as sunlight, it is, though channeling the male half still feels like wrestling with a summer whirlwind."

"Yes," Elza said, "but be that as it is, you must realize how difficult it will be for others to believe this, Lord Dragon. During the Time of Madness, it took decades for some people to accept that the male Aes Sedai were doomed to go insane. It will likely take longer for them to overcome their distrust, now that it has been ingrained for so long."

Rand gritted his teeth. He had reached a small hill at the side of the camp, just beside the bulwark. He continued up to the top, Aes Sedai following. Here, a short wooden platform had been erected—a fire tower for launching arrows over the bulwark.

Rand stopped at the top of the hill, Maidens surrounding him. He barely noticed the soldiers who saluted him as he looked over the Saldaean camp with its neat tent lines.

Was this all he would leave to the world? A taint cleansed, yet men still killed or exiled for something they could not help? He had bound most nations to him. Yet he knew well that the tighter one tied a bale, the sharper the snap of the cords when they were cut. What would happen when he died? Wars and devastation to match the Breaking? He hadn't been able to help that last time, for his madness and grief at Ilyena's death had consumed him. Could he prevent something similar this time? Did he have a choice?

He was *ta'veren*. The Pattern bent and shaped around him. And yet, he had quickly learned one thing from being a king: the more authority you gained, the less control you had over your life. Duty was truly heavier than a mountain; it forced his hand as often as the prophecies did. Or were they both one and the same? Duty and prophecy? His nature as a *ta'veren* and his place in history? *Could* he change his life? Could he leave the world better for his passing, rather than leaving the nations scarred, torn and bleeding?

He watched the camp, men moving about their tasks, horses nosing at the ground, searching for patches of winter grass that had not already been chewed to their roots.

Though Rand had ordered this army to travel light, there were still camp followers. Women to help with meals and laundry, blacksmiths and farriers to tend horses and equipment, young boys to run messages and to train on the weapons. Saldaea was a Borderland, and battle was a way of life for its people.

"I envy them, sometimes," Rand whispered.

"My Lord?" Flinn asked, stepping up to him.

"The people of the camp," Rand said. "They do as they are told, working each day under orders. Strict orders, at times. But orders or not, those people are more free than I."

"You, Lord?" Flinn said, rubbing his leathery face with an aged finger. "You are the most powerful man alive! You're *ta'veren*. Even the Pattern obeys your will, I should think!"

Rand shook his head. "It doesn't work that way, Flinn. Those people out there, any one of them could just ride away. Escape, if they felt like it. Leave the battle to others."

"I've known a few Saldaeans in my day, my Lord," Flinn said. "Forgive me, but I have doubts that any one of them would do that."

"But they *could*," Rand said. "It's possible. For all their laws and oaths, they are free. Me, I *seem* as if I can do as I wish, but I am tied so tightly the bonds cut my flesh. My power and influence are meaningless against fate. My freedom is all just an illusion, Flinn. And so I envy them. Sometimes."

Flinn folded his hands behind his back, obviously uncertain how to respond.

We all do as we must, Moiraine's voice from the past returned to his memory. *As the Pattern decrees. For some there is less freedom than for others. It does not matter whether we choose or are chosen. What must be, must be.*

She had understood. *I'm trying, Moiraine,* he thought. *I will do what must be done.*

"My Lord Dragon!" a voice called. Rand turned toward the sound and saw one of Bashere's scouts running up the hill. The Maidens cautiously allowed the youthful, dark-haired man to approach.

"My Lord," the scout said, saluting. "There are Aiel on the outskirts of the camp. We saw two of them prowling through the trees about half a mile down the slope."

The Maidens immediately began to move their hands, speaking in their clandestine handtalk.

"Did any of those Aiel wave at you, soldier?" Rand asked dryly.

"My Lord?" the man asked. "Why would they do that?"

"They're Aiel. If you saw them, that means they wanted you to—and that means they're allies, not foes. Inform Bashere that we'll be meeting with Rhuarc and Bael shortly. It is time to secure Arad Doman."

Or maybe it was time to destroy it. Sometimes, it was difficult to tell the difference.

Merise spoke. "Graendal's plans. Tell me again what you know of them." The tall Aes Sedai—of the Green Ajah, like Cadsuane herself—maintained a stern expression, arms folded beneath her breasts, a silver comb slid into the side of her black hair.

The Taraboner woman was a good choice to lead the interrogation. Or, at least, she was the best choice Cadsuane had. Merise didn't show a bit of discomfort at being so near to one of the most feared beings in all of creation, and she was relentless in her questioning. She did try a little too hard to prove how stern she was. The way she kept her hair pulled back into its bun with such force, for instance, or the way she flaunted her Asha'man Warder.

The room was on the second floor of Rand al'Thor's Domani mansion, the outer wall made of thick round pine logs, the inner walls of wood planks, all stained a matching dark color. This chamber, which had once been a bedroom, had been emptied of nearly all furniture; there was not even a rug on the sanded wood floor. In fact, the only furniture in it now was the stout chair Cadsuane sat in.

Cadsuane sipped her tea, intentionally projecting an air of composure. That was important, especially if one wasn't anything *near* composed on the inside. At the moment, for instance, Cadsuane wanted to crush the teacup between her hands, then perhaps spend an hour or so stamping on the shards.

She took another sip.

The source of her frustration—and the object of Merise's questioning—hung in the air, held upside down by

weaves of Air with her arms tied behind her back. The captive had short wavy hair and dark skin. Her face matched
Cadsuane's own for composed serenity, despite her circumstances. Wearing a simple brown dress—the hem held up
around her legs by a weave of Air to keep it from obscuring
her face—held bound and shielded, the prisoner somehow
seemed the one in control.

Merise stood in front of the prisoner. Narishma leaned
against the wall, the only other one in the room.

Cadsuane did not control the questioning herself, not yet.
Letting another lead the interrogation worked to her advantage; it let her think and plan. Outside the room, Erian,
Sarene, and Nesune held the prisoner's shield, two more
than were normally considered necessary.

One did not take chances with the Forsaken.

Their prisoner was Semirhage. A monster who many
thought was simply a legend. Cadsuane did not know how
many of the stories about the woman were true. She did
know that Semirhage was not easily intimidated, unsettled
or manipulated. And that was a problem.

"Well?" Merise demanded. "My question: you have an
answer?"

Semirhage regarded Merise, icy contempt in her voice as
she spoke. "Do you know what happens to a man when his
blood is replaced with something else?"

"I did not—"

"He dies, of course," Semirhage said, cutting Merise off
with words like knives. "The death often happens instantly,
and quick deaths are of little interest. With experiment, I
discovered that some solutions can replace blood more effectively, allowing the subject to live for a short time after
the transfusion."

She fell silent.

"Answer the question," Merise said, "or out the window
you will hang again and—"

"The transfusion itself requires use of the Power, of
course," Semirhage interrupted again. "Other methods are
not quick enough. I invented the weave myself. It can suddenly and instantly pull the blood from a body and deposit
it in a bin, while at the same time taking a solution and
pressing it into the veins."

Merise gritted her teeth, glancing at Narishma. The Asha'man wore a coat and trousers of black, as usual, his long dark hair in braids woven with bells on the ends. He lounged against the log wall. He had a boyish face, but displayed a growing edge of danger. Perhaps that came from training with Merise's other Warders. Perhaps it came from associating with people who would put one of the Forsaken to the question.

"My warning—" Merise began again.

"I had one subject survive an entire hour after the transfusion," Semirhage said in a calm, conversational tone. "I count it as one of my greatest victories. He was in pain the entire time, of course. True pain, agony that he could feel in every *vein* of his body, right down to the near-invisible ones in his fingers. I know of no other way to bring such suffering to every part of the body at once."

She met Merise's eyes. "I will show you the weave someday."

Merise paled just slightly.

With a whip of her hand, Cadsuane wove a shield of Air around Semirhage's head to block her from hearing, then wove Fire and Air into two small balls of light, which she placed directly in front of the Forsaken's eyes. The lights weren't bright enough to blind or damage her eyes, but they would keep her from seeing. That was a particular trick of Cadsuane's; too many sisters would think to deafen a captive, yet leave them capable of watching. One never knew who had learned to read lips, and Cadsuane had little inclination to underestimate her current captive.

Merise glanced at Cadsuane, a flash of annoyance in her eyes.

"You were losing control of her," Cadsuane said firmly, setting her tea on the floor beside her chair.

Merise hesitated, then nodded, looking truly angry. Likely at herself. "This woman, nothing works on her," she said. "She never changes the tone of her voice, no matter what we do to her. Every punishment I can think of only creates more threats. Each one more gruesome than the last! Light!" She gritted her teeth again, refolding her arms and breathing deeply through her nose. Narishma straightened as if to walk over to her, but she waved him back. Merise was appropriately firm with her Warders, though she did snap at anyone else who tried to keep them in their places.

"We *can* break her," Cadsuane said.

"Can we, Cadsuane?"

"Phaw! Of course we can. She is human, just like anyone else."

"True," Merise said. "Though she's lived for three thousand years. Three *thousand*, Cadsuane."

"She spent the bulk of that time imprisoned," Cadsuane said with a dismissive sniff. "Centuries locked up in the Dark One's prison, likely in a trance or hibernation. Subtract those years, and she's no older than any of us. A fair sight younger than some, I would imagine."

It was a subtle reminder of her own age, something rarely discussed among Aes Sedai. The entire conversation about age was, in fact, a sign of how uncomfortable the Forsaken made Merise. Aes Sedai were practiced at appearing calm, but there was a reason that Cadsuane had kept those holding the shield outside the room. They gave away too much. Even the normally unflappable Merise lost control far too often during these interrogations.

Of course, Merise and the others—like all the women in the Tower these days—still fell short of what an Aes Sedai should be. These younger Aes Sedai had been allowed to grow soft and weak, prone to bickering. Some had allowed themselves to be bullied into swearing fealty to Rand al'Thor. Sometimes, Cadsuane wished she could simply send them all to penance for a few decades.

Or maybe that was just Cadsuane's age speaking. She was old, and that was making her increasingly intolerant of foolishness. Over two centuries ago, she'd sworn to herself that she'd live to attend the Last Battle, no matter how long that took. Using the One Power lengthened one's years, and she'd found that determination and grit could stretch those years even further. She was one of the oldest people alive.

Unfortunately, her years had taught her that no measure of planning or determination could make life turn out as you wanted. That didn't stop her from being annoyed when it didn't. One might have thought that the years would also have taught her patience, but it had done the opposite. The older she grew, the less inclined she was to wait, for she knew she didn't have many years left.

Anyone who claimed that old age had brought them patience was either lying or senile.

"She *can* and *will* be broken," Cadsuane repeated, "I am
not going to allow a person who knows weaves from the
Age of Legends to simply dance herself to execution. We
are going to pull every scrap of knowledge from that woman's brain, if we have to turn a few of her own 'creative'
weaves on her."

"The *a'dam*. If only the Lord Dragon would let us use it
on her . . ." Merise said, glancing at Semirhage.

If ever Cadsuane had been tempted to break her word, it
was regarding that. Slip an *a'dam* on the woman . . . but no,
in order to force someone to talk with an *a'dam*, you had to
give them pain. It was the same as torture, and al'Thor had
forbidden it.

Semirhage had closed her eyes against Cadsuane's lights,
but she was still composed, controlled. What was going on
in that woman's mind? Did she wait for rescue? Did she
think to force them to execute her so that she could avoid
true torture? Did she really assume that she'd be able to
escape, then wreak vengeance on the Aes Sedai who had
questioned her?

Likely the last—and it was hard not to feel at least a hint
of apprehension. The woman knew things about the One
Power that hadn't survived even in legends. Three thousand years was a long, long time. Could Semirhage break
through a shield in a way that was unknown? If she could,
why hadn't she already? Cadsuane wouldn't be entirely
comfortable until she was able to get her hands on some of
that forkroot tea.

"Your weaves, you can release them, Cadsuane," Merise
said, standing. "I have composed myself. I fear we will have
to hang her out the window for a time, as I said. Perhaps
we can threaten her with pain. She can't know of al'Thor's
foolish requirements."

Cadsuane leaned forward, releasing the weaves that hung
the lights before the Forsaken's eyes, but not removing the
shield of Air that kept her from hearing. Semirhage's eyes
snapped open, then quickly found Cadsuane. Yes, she knew
who was in charge. The two locked eyes.

Merise continued to question, asking about Graendal.
Al'Thor thought the other Forsaken might be somewhere

in Arad Doman. Cadsuane was far more interested in other questions, but Graendal made an acceptable starting point.

Semirhage responded to Merise's questions with silence this time, and Cadsuane found herself thinking about al'Thor. The boy had resisted her teaching as stubbornly as Semirhage resisted questioning. Oh, true, he had learned some minor things—how to treat her with a measure of respect, how to at least feign civility. But nothing more.

Cadsuane hated admitting failure. And this was *not* a failure, not yet, but she was close. That boy was destined to destroy the world. And maybe save it, too. The first was inevitable; the second conditional. She could wish the two were reversed, but wishes were about as useful as coins carved from wood. You could paint them however you wanted, but they remained wood.

She gritted her teeth, putting the boy out of her mind. She needed to watch Semirhage. Each time the woman spoke, it could be a clue. Semirhage returned her stare, ignoring Merise.

How did you break one of the most powerful women who had ever lived? A woman who had perpetrated countless atrocities during the days of wonder before, even, the Dark One's release? Meeting those black, onyx eyes, Cadsuane realized something. Al'Thor's prohibition on hurting Semirhage was meaningless. They could not break this woman with pain. Semirhage was the great torturer of the Forsaken, a woman intrigued by death and agony.

No, she would not break that way, even if the means had been allowed them. With a chill, looking into those eyes, Cadsuane thought she saw something of herself in the creature. Age, craftiness and unwillingness to budge.

That, then, left a question for her. If given the task, how would Cadsuane go about breaking herself?

The concept was so disturbing that she was relieved when Corele interrupted the interrogation a few moments later. The slender, cheerful Murandian was loyal to Cadsuane and had been on duty watching over al'Thor this afternoon. Corele's word that al'Thor would be meeting soon with his Aiel chiefs brought an end to the interrogation, and the three sisters maintaining the shield entered and towed

Semirhage off to the room where they would set her bound and gagged with flows of Air.

Cadsuane watched the Forsaken go, carried on weaves of Air, then shook her head. Semirhage had been only the day's opening scene. It was time to deal with the boy.

CHAPTER
6

When Iron Melts

R odel Ituralde had seen a lot of battlefields. Some
things were always the same. Dead men like piles of
rags, lying in heaps. Ravens eager to dine. Groans,
cries, whimpers and mumbles from those unlucky enough
to need a long time to die.

Each battlefield also had its own individual print. You
could read a battle like the trail of passing game. Corpses
lying in rows that were disturbingly straight indicated a
charge of footmen who had been pressed against volleys
of arrows. Scattered and trampled bodies were the result
of infantry breaking before heavy cavalry. This battle had
seen large numbers of Seanchan crushed up against the
walls of Darluna, where they had fought with desperation.
Hammered against the stone. One section of wall was completely torn away where some *damane* had tried to escape
into the city. Fighting in streets and among homes would
have favored the Seanchan. They hadn't made it in time.

Ituralde rode his roan gelding through the mess. Battle
was always a mess. The only neat battles were the ones
in stories or history books. Those had been cleansed and
scoured by the abrasive hands of scholars looking for con-
ciseness. "Aggressor won, fifty-three thousand killed" or
"Defender stood, twenty thousand fallen."

What would be written of this battle? It would depend
on who was writing. They would neglect to include the
blood, pounded into the earth to make mud. The bodies,
broken, pierced and mangled. The ground torn in swaths
by enraged *damane*. Perhaps they would remember the
numbers; those often seemed important to scribes. Half of

Ituralde's hundred thousand, dead. On any other battlefield, fifty thousand casualties would have shamed and angered him. But he'd faced down a force three times his size, and one with *damane* at that.

He followed the young messenger who had fetched him, a boy of perhaps twelve, wearing a Seanchan uniform of red and green. They passed a fallen standard, hanging from a broken pole with the tip driven into mud. It bore the sign of a sun being crossed by six gulls. Ituralde hated not knowing the houses and names of the men he was fighting, but there was no way to tell with the foreign Seanchan.

The shadows cast by a dying evening sun striped the field. Soon a blanket of darkness would cradle the bodies, and the survivors could pretend for a time that the grassland was a grave for their friends. And for the people their friends had killed. He rounded a small hillock, coming to a scattered pattern of fallen Seanchan elite. Most of these dead wore those insectlike helms. Bent, cracked, or dented. Dead eyes stared blankly from openings behind twisted mandibles.

The Seanchan general was alive, if just barely. His helmet was off, and there was blood on his lips. He leaned against a large, moss-covered boulder, back supported by a bundled cloak, as if he were waiting for a meal to be delivered. Of course, that image was marred by his twisted leg and the broken haft of a spear punching through the front of his stomach.

Ituralde dismounted. Like most of his men, Ituralde wore worker's clothing—simple brown trousers and coat, borrowed off of the man who had taken Ituralde's uniform as part of the trap.

It felt odd to be out of uniform. A man like this General Turan did not deserve a soldier in drab. Ituralde waved the messenger boy to stand back, out of earshot, then approached the Seanchan alone.

"You're him, then," Turan said, looking up at Ituralde, speaking with that slow Seanchan drawl. He was a stout man, far from tall, with a peaked nose. His close-cropped black hair was shaved two finger widths up each side of his head, and his helm lay beside him on the ground, bearing three white plumes. He reached up with an unsteady black-gloved hand and wiped the blood from the corner of his mouth.

"I am," Ituralde said.

"They call you a 'Great Captain' in Tarabon."

"They do."

"It's deserved," Turan said, coughing. "How did you do it? Our scouts. . . ." His cough consumed him.

"*Raken*," Ituralde said once the cough subsided. He squatted down beside his foe. The sun was still a sliver in the west, lighting the battlefield with a glimmer of golden red light. "Your scouts see from the air, and truth is easy to hide from a distance."

"The army behind us?"

"Women and youths, mostly," Ituralde said. "A fair number of farmers as well. Wearing uniforms taken from my troops here."

"And if we'd turned and attacked?"

"You wouldn't have. Your *raken* told you that you were outnumbered. Better to chase after the smaller force ahead of you. Better than that to head for the city your scouts say is barely defended, even if it means marching your men near to exhaustion."

Turan coughed again, nodding. "Yes. Yes, but the city was empty. How did you get troops into it?"

"Scouts in the air," Ituralde said, "can't see inside buildings."

"You ordered your troops to hide inside for that long?"

"Yes," Ituralde said. "With a rotation allowing a small number out each day to work the fields."

Turan shook his head in disbelief. "You realize what you have done," he said. There was no threat in his voice. In fact, there was a fair amount of admiration. "High Lady Suroth will never accept this failure. She will *have* to break you now, if only to save face."

"I know," Ituralde said, standing. "But I can't drive you back by attacking you in your fortresses. I need you to come to me."

"You don't understand the numbers we have . . ." Turan said. "What you destroyed today is but a breeze compared to the storm you've raised. Enough of my people escaped today to tell of your tricks. They will not work again."

He was right. The Seanchan learned quickly. Ituralde had been forced to cut short his raids in Tarabon because of the swift Seanchan reaction.

"You know you can't beat us," Turan said softly. "I see it in your eyes, Great Captain."

Ituralde nodded.

"Why, then?" Turan asked.

"Why does a crow fly?" Ituralde asked.

Turan coughed weakly.

Ituralde did know that he could not win his war against the Seanchan. Oddly, each of his victories made him more certain of his eventual failure. The Seanchan were smart, well equipped and well disciplined. More than that, they were persistent.

Turan himself must have known from the moment those gates opened that he was doomed. But he had not surrendered; he had fought until his army broke, scattering in too many directions for Ituralde's exhausted troops to catch. Turan understood. Sometimes, surrender wasn't worth the cost. No man welcomed death, but there were far worse ends for a soldier. Abandoning one's homeland to invaders . . . well, Ituralde couldn't do that. Not even if the fight was impossible to win.

He did what needed to be done, when it needed to be done. And right now, Arad Doman needed to fight. They would lose, but their children would always know that their fathers *had* resisted. That resistance would be important in a hundred years, when a rebellion came. If one came.

Ituralde stood up, intending to return to his waiting soldiers.

Turan struggled, reaching for his sword. Ituralde hesitated, turning back.

"Will you do it?" Turan asked.

Ituralde nodded, unsheathing his own sword.

"It has been an honor," Turan said, then closed his eyes. Ituralde's sword—heron-marked—took the man's head a moment later. Turan's own blade bore a heron, barely visible on the gleaming length of blade the Seanchan had managed to pull. It was a pity that the two of them hadn't been able to cross swords—though, in a way, these past few weeks had been just that, on a different scale.

Ituralde cleaned his sword, then slid it back into its sheath. In a final gesture, he slid Turan's sword out and rammed it into the ground beside the fallen general. Ituralde then remounted and, nodding farewell to the messenger, made his way back across the shadowed field of corpses.

The ravens had begun.

"I've tried encouraging several of the serving men and Tower Guards," Leane said softly, sitting beside the bars of her cell. "But it's hard." She smiled, glancing at Egwene, who sat on a stool outside the cell. "I don't exactly feel alluring these days."

Egwene's responding smile was wry, and she seemed to understand. Leane wore the same dress that she'd been captured in, and it had not yet been laundered. Every third morning, she removed it and used the morning's bucket of water—after washing herself clean with a damp rag—to clean the dress in her basin. But there was only so much one could do without soap. She'd braided her hair to give it a semblance of neatness, but could do nothing about her ragged nails.

Leane sighed, thinking of those mornings spent standing in the corner of her cell, hidden from sight, wearing nothing while she waited for the dress and shift to dry. Just because she was Domani didn't mean she liked parading about without a scrap on. Proper seduction required skill and subtlety; nudity used neither.

Her cell wasn't bad as cells went—she had a small bed, meals, plenty of water, a chamber pot that was changed daily. But she was never allowed out, and was always guarded by two sisters who kept her shielded. The only one who visited her—save for those trying to pry information from her regarding Traveling—was Egwene.

The Amyrlin sat on her stool, expression thoughtful. And she *was* Amyrlin. It was impossible to think of her any other way. How could a child so young have learned so quickly? That straight back, that poised expression. Being in control wasn't so much about the power you had, but the power you implied that you had. It was much like dealing with men, actually.

"Have you . . . heard anything?" Leane asked. "About what they plan to do with me?"

Egwene shook her head. Two Yellow sisters sat chatting nearby on the bench, lit by a lamp on the table beside them. Leane hadn't answered any of the questions her captors put to her, and Tower law was very strict about the questioning of fellow sisters. They couldn't harm her, particularly not with the Power. But they *could* just leave her alone, to rot.

"Thank you for coming to see me these evenings," Leane said, reaching through the lattice of bars to take Egwene's hand. "I believe I owe my sanity to you."

"It is my pleasure," Egwene said, though her eyes showed a hint of the exhaustion she undoubtedly felt. Some of the sisters who visited Leane mentioned the beatings Egwene was suffering as "penances" for her insubordination. Odd, how a novice to be instructed could be beaten but a prisoner to be interrogated could not. And despite the pain, Egwene came to visit Leane in the cell virtually every night.

"I *will* see you free, Leane," Egwene promised, still holding her hand. "Elaida's tyranny cannot last. I'm confident it won't be long now."

Leane nodded, letting go and standing up. Egwene took hold of the bars and pulled herself to her feet, cringing ever so slightly at the motion. She nodded farewell to Leane, then hesitated, frowning.

"What is it?" Leane asked.

Egwene took her hands off of the bars and looked at her palms. They seemed to be coated with a reflective, waxy substance. Frowning, Leane looked at the bars, and was shocked to see Egwene's handprints on the iron.

"What in the Light—" Leane said, poking at one of the bars. It bent beneath her finger like warm wax on the lip of a candle's bowl.

Suddenly, the stones beneath Leane's feet shifted, and she felt herself sinking. She cried out. Globs of melted wax starting to rain down from the ceiling, splattering across her face. They weren't warm, but they were somehow liquid. They had the color of stone!

She gasped, panicked, stumbling and sliding as her feet sank deeper in the too-slick floor. A hand caught hers; she looked up to where Egwene had grabbed her. The bars melted out of the way as Leane watched, the iron drooping to the sides, then liquefying.

"Help!" Egwene screamed at the Yellows outside. "Burn you! Stop staring!"

Leane scrambled for purchase, terrified, trying to pull herself along the bars toward Egwene. She grasped only wax. A lump of bar came loose in her hand, squishing between her fingers, and the floor warped around her, sucking her down.

And then threads of Air seized her, yanking her free. The room lurched as she was tossed forward into Egwene, knocking the younger woman backward. The two Yellows—white-haired Musarin and short Gelarna—had jumped to their feet, and the glow of *saidar* surrounded them. Musarin called for help, watching the melting cell with wide eyes.

Leane righted herself, scrambling off of Egwene, her dress and legs coated with the strange wax, and stumbled back away from the cell. The floor here in the hallway felt stable. Light, how she wished she could embrace the source herself! But she was too full of forkroot, not to mention the shield.

Egwene climbed to her feet with a hand from Leane. The room fell still, lamp flickering, all of them staring at the cell. The melting had stopped, the bars split, the top halves frozen with drips of steel on their tips, the lower halves bent inward. Many had been flattened to the stones by Leane's escape. The floor inside the room had bowed inward, like a funnel, the rocks stretching. Those stones bore gashes where Leane's scrambling had scored them.

Leane stood, her heart beating, realizing that only seconds had passed. What should they do? Scuttle away in fear? Was the rest of the hallway going to melt, too?

Egwene stepped forward, tapping her toe against one of the bars. It resisted. Leane took a step forward, and her dress *crunched*, bits of stone—like mortar—falling free. She reached down and brushed at her skirt, and felt rough rock coating it instead of wax.

"These sorts of events are more frequent," Egwene said calmly, glancing at the two Yellows. "The Dark One is getting stronger. The Last Battle approaches. What is your Amyrlin doing about it?"

Musarin glanced at her; the tall, aging Aes Sedai looked deeply disturbed. Leane took Egwene's lead, forcing herself to be calm as she stepped up beside the Amyrlin, chips of stone falling from her dress.

"Yes, well," Musarin said. "You shall return to your rooms, novice. And you . . ." She glanced at Leane, then at the remains of the cell. "We will . . . have to relocate you."

"And get me a new dress as well, I assume," Leane said, folding her arms.

Musarin's eyes flickered at Egwene. "Go. This is no longer your business, child. We will care for the prisoner."

Egwene gritted her teeth, but then she turned to Leane. "Stay strong," she said, and hurried away, heading down the hallway.

Exhausted, disturbed by the stone-warping bubble of evil, Egwene walked with swishing skirts toward the Tower wing that contained the novices' quarters. What would it take to convince the foolish women that there wasn't time to spare for squabbling!

The hour was late, and few women walked the corridors, none of them novices. Egwene passed several servants bustling at late-night duties, their slippered feet falling softly on the floor tiles. These sectors of the Tower were populated enough that lamps burned on the walls, trimmed low, giving an orange light. A hundred different polished tiles reflected the flickering flames, looking like eyes that watched Egwene as she walked.

It was hard to comprehend that this quiet evening had turned into a trap that nearly killed Leane. If even the ground itself could not be trusted, then what could? Egwene shook her head, too tired, too sore, to think of solutions at the moment. She barely noticed when the floor tiles turned from gray to a deep brown. She just continued on, into the Tower wing, counting the doors she passed. Hers was the seventh . . .

She froze, frowning at a pair of Brown sisters: Maenadrin—a Saldaean—and Negaine. The two had been speaking in hushed whispers, and they frowned at Egwene as she passed them. Why would they be in the novices' quarters?

But wait. The novices' quarters didn't have brown floor tiles. This section should have had nondescript gray tiles. And the doors in the hallway were spaced far too widely. This didn't look at all like the novices' quarters! Had she been so tired that she'd walked in completely the wrong direction?

She retraced her steps, passing the two Brown sisters again. She found a window and looked out. The rectangular white expanse of the Tower wing extended around her, just as it should. She wasn't lost.

Perplexed, she looked back down the hallway. Maenadrin had folded her arms, regarding Egwene with a set of dark eyes. Negaine, tall and spindly, stalked up to Egwene. "What business have you here this time of night, child?" she demanded. "Did a sister send for you? You should be back in your room for sleep."

Wordlessly, Egwene pointed out the window. Negaine glanced out, frowning. She froze, gasping softly. She looked back in at the hallway, then back out, as if unable to believe where she was.

In minutes, the entire Tower was in a frenzy. Egwene, forgotten, stood at the side of a hallway with a cluster of bleary-eyed novices as sisters argued with one another in tense voices, trying to determine what to do. It appeared that two sections of the Tower had been swapped, and the slumbering Brown sisters had been moved from their sections on the upper levels down into the wing. The novices' rooms—intact—had been placed where the section of Brown sisters had been. Nobody remembered any motion or vibration when the swap happened, and the transfer appeared seamless. A line of floor tiles had been split right down the middle, then melded with tiles from the section that had shifted.

It's getting worse and worse, Egwene thought as the Brown sisters decided—for now—that they would have to accept the switch. They couldn't very well move sisters into rooms the size that novices used.

That would leave the Browns divided, half in the wing, half in their old location—with a clump of novices in the middle of them. A division aptly representative of the less-visible divisions the Ajahs were suffering.

Eventually, exhausted, Egwene and the others were sent off to sleep—though now she had to trudge up many flights of stairs before reaching her bed.

CHAPTER
7

The Plan for Arad Doman

A storm is coming," Nynaeve said, looking out the window of the manor.

"Yes," replied Daigian from her chair by the hearth without bothering to glance at the window. "I think you might be right, dear. I swear, it seems as if it has been overcast for weeks!"

"It has been a single week," Nynaeve said, holding her long, dark braid in one hand. She glanced at the other woman. "I haven't seen a patch of clear sky in over ten days."

Daigian frowned. Of the White Ajah, she was plump and curvaceous. She wore a small stone on her forehead as Moiraine had so long ago, though Daigian's was an appropriately white moonstone. The tradition apparently had something to do with being a Cairhienin noblewoman, as did the four colored slashes the woman wore on her dress.

"Ten days, you say?" Daigian said. "Are you certain?"

Nynaeve was. She paid attention to the weather; that was one of the duties of a village Wisdom. She was Aes Sedai now, but that didn't mean she stopped being who she was. The weather was always there, in the back of her mind. She could sense the rain, sun, or snow in the wind's whispers.

Lately, however, the sensations hadn't been like whispers at all. More like distant shouts, growing louder. Or like waves crashing against one another, still far to the north, yet harder and harder to ignore.

"Well," Daigian said, "I'm certain this isn't the only time in history that it has been cloudy for ten days!"

Nynaeve shook her head, tugging on her braid. "It's not normal," she said. "And those overcast skies aren't the storm I'm talking about. It's still distant, but it's coming. And it is going to be terrible. Worse than any I've ever seen. Far worse."

"Well, then," Daigian said, sounding slightly uncomfortable, "we will deal with it when it arrives. Are you going to sit down so that we can continue?"

Nynaeve glanced at the plump Aes Sedai. Daigian was extremely weak in the Power. The White might just be the weakest Aes Sedai that Nynaeve had ever met. By traditional—yet unspoken—rules, that meant that Nynaeve should be allowed to take the lead.

Unfortunately, Nynaeve's position was still questionable. Egwene had raised her to the shawl by decree, just as she'd raised Elayne: there had been no testing, nor had Nynaeve sworn on the Oath Rod. To most—even those who accepted Egwene's place as the true Amyrlin—those omissions made Nynaeve something less than Aes Sedai. Not an Accepted, but hardly equal to a sister.

The sisters with Cadsuane were particularly bad, as they hadn't declared for either the White Tower or the rebels. And the sisters sworn to Rand were worse; most were still loyal to the White Tower, not seeing a problem with supporting both Elaida and Rand. Nynaeve still wondered what Rand had been thinking, allowing sisters to swear fealty to him. She'd explained his mistake to him on several occasions—quite rationally—but talking to Rand these days was like talking to a stone. Only less effective and infinitely more infuriating.

Daigian was still waiting for her to sit. Rather than provoke a contest of wills, Nynaeve did so. Daigian was still suffering from having lost her Warder—Eben, an Asha'man—during the fight with the Forsaken. Nynaeve had spent that fight completely absorbed by providing Rand with immense amounts of *saidar* to weave.

Nynaeve could still remember the sheer joy—the awesome euphoria, strength, and sheer feel of *life*—that had come from drawing that much power. It frightened her. She was glad the *ter'angreal* she'd used to touch that power had been destroyed.

But the male *ter'angreal* was still intact: an access key to a powerful *sa'angreal*. As far as Nynaeve knew, Rand had not been able to persuade Cadsuane to return it to him. As well she shouldn't. No human being, not even the Dragon Reborn, should channel that much of the One Power. The things one could be tempted to do. . . .

She'd *told* Rand that he needed to forget about the access key. Like talking to a stone. A big, red-haired, iron-faced idiot of a stone. Nynaeve harrumphed to herself. That caused Daigian to raise an eyebrow. The woman was quite good at controlling her grief, though Nynaeve—whose room in the Domani mansion was beside Daigian's—heard the woman crying to herself at night. It was not easy to lose one's Warder.

Lan. . . .

No, best not to think of *him* at the moment. Lan would be fine. Only at the end of his journey of thousands of miles would he be in danger. It was there he intended to throw himself at the Shadow like a lone arrow loosed at a brick wall . . .

No! she thought to herself. *He will not be alone. I saw to that.*

"Very well," Nynaeve said, forcing herself to focus, "let us continue." She showed no deference to Daigian. She was doing this woman a favor, distracting her from her grief. That was how Corele had explained it, anyway. It wasn't, certainly, for *Nynaeve*'s benefit that they met. She had nothing to prove. She *was* Aes Sedai, no matter what the others thought or implied.

This was all just a ruse to help Daigian. That was it. Nothing else.

"Here is the eighty-first weave," the White said. The glow of *saidar* sprang up around her, and she channeled, crafting a very complex weave of Fire, Air and Spirit. Complex, but useless. The weave created three burning rings of fire in the air which glowed with unusual light, but what was the point of that? Nynaeve already knew how to make fireballs and balls of light; why waste time learning weaves that repeated what she already knew, only in a far more complicated way? And why did each ring have to be a slightly different color?

Nynaeve waved an indifferent hand, repeating the weave exactly. "Honestly," she said, "that one seems the most useless of the bunch! What is the point of all of these?"

Daigian pursed her lips. She said nothing, but Nynaeve knew that Daigian thought that this all should be far more difficult for Nynaeve than it was. Eventually, the woman spoke. "You cannot be told much about the testing. The only thing I can say is that you will need to repeat these weaves exactly, and do so while undergoing extreme distraction. When the time comes, you will understand."

"I doubt it," Nynaeve said flatly, copying the weave three times over while she spoke. "Because—as I *believe* I've told you a dozen times already—I'm not going to be taking the test. I'm already Aes Sedai."

"Of course you are, dear."

Nynaeve ground her teeth. This had been a bad idea. When she'd approached Corele—supposedly a member of Nynaeve's own Ajah—the woman had refused to acknowledge her as an equal. She'd been pleasant about it, as Corele often was, but the implication had been clear. She'd even seemed sympathetic. Sympathetic! As if Nynaeve needed her pity. She had suggested that if Nynaeve knew the hundred weaves each Accepted learned for the test to become Aes Sedai, it might help with her credibility.

The problem was, this placed Nynaeve in a situation where she was all but treated as a student again. She *did* see the use in knowing the hundred weaves—she'd spent far too short a time studying them, and virtually every sister knew it. However, by accepting the lessons, she hadn't meant to imply that she *saw* herself as a student!

She reached for her braid, but stopped herself. Her visible expressions of emotion were another factor in how she was treated by the other Aes Sedai. If only she had that ageless face! Bah!

Daigian's next weave made a popping sound in the air, and once again the weave itself was needlessly complex. Nynaeve copied it with barely a thought, committing it to memory at the same time.

Daigian stared at the weave for a moment, a distant look on her face.

"What?" Nynaeve asked testily.

"Hmm? Oh, nothing. I just . . . the last time I made that weave, I used it to startle . . . I . . . never mind."

Eben. Her Warder had been young, maybe fifteen or sixteen, and she had been very fond of him. Eben and Daigian had played games together like a boy and an elder sister rather than Aes Sedai and Warder.

A youth of only sixteen, Nynaeve thought, *dead. Did Rand have to recruit them so young?*

Daigian's face grew stiff, controlling her emotions far better than Nynaeve would have been able to.

Light send that I'm never in the same situation, she thought. *At least not for many, many years.* Lan wasn't her Warder yet, but she meant to have him as soon as possible. He was already her husband, after all. It still angered her that Myrelle had the bond.

"I might be able to help, Daigian," Nynaeve said, leaning forward, laying her hand on the other woman's knee. "If I were to attempt a Healing, perhaps. . . ."

"No," the woman said curtly.

"But—"

"I doubt you could help."

"Anything can be Healed," Nynaeve said stubbornly, "even if we don't know how yet. Anything save death."

"And what would you do, dear?" Daigian asked. Nynaeve wondered if she refused to call her by name on purpose, or if it was an unconscious effect of their relationship. She couldn't use "child," as she would with an actual Accepted, but to call her "Nynaeve" might imply equality.

"I could do something," Nynaeve said. "This pain you feel, it *has* to be an effect of the bond, and therefore something to do with the One Power. If the Power causes your pain, then the Power can take that pain away."

"And why would I want that?" Daigian asked, in control once again.

"Well . . . well, because it's pain. It hurts."

"It should," Daigian said. "Eben is dead. Would *you* want to forget your pain if you lost that hulking giant of yours? Have your feelings for him cut away like some spoiled chunk of flesh in an otherwise good roast?"

Nynaeve opened her mouth, but stopped. Would she? It wasn't that simple—her feelings for Lan were genuine, and not due to a bond. He was her husband, and she loved him. Daigian had been possessive of her Warder, but it had been the affection of an aunt for her favored nephew. It wasn't the same.

But *would* Nynaeve want that pain taken away? She closed her mouth, suddenly realizing the honor in Daigian's words. "I see. I'm sorry."

"It is nothing, dear," Daigian continued. "The logic of it seems simple to me at times, but I fear that others do not accept it. Indeed, some might argue that the logic of the issue depends on the moment and the individual. Shall I show you the next weave?"

"Yes, please," Nynaeve said, frowning. She herself was so strong in the Power—one of the strongest alive—that she often took little thought for her ability. It was much as a very tall man rarely paid attention to other people's heights; everyone else was shorter than he, and so their different heights didn't matter much.

What was it like to be this woman, who had spent longer as an Accepted than anyone else in memory? A woman who had barely attained the shawl, doing so—many said—by an eyelash and a whisper? Daigian had to show deference to all other Aes Sedai. If two sisters met, Daigian was always the lesser. If more than two sisters met, Daigian served them tea. Before the more powerful sisters, she was expected to scrape and grovel. Well, not that, she *was* Aes Sedai, but still. . . .

"There is something wrong with this system, Daigian," Nynaeve said absently.

"With the testing? It seems appropriate that there should be *some* kind of test to determine worthiness, and the performing of difficult weaves under stress strikes me as fulfilling that need."

"I didn't mean that," Nynaeve said, "I mean the system that determines how we are treated. By each other."

Daigian flushed. It was inappropriate to refer to another's power, in any way. But, well, Nynaeve had never been very good at conforming to other people's expectations. Particularly when they expected foolishness. "There you sit," she said, "knowing as much as any other Aes Sedai—knowing *more* than many, I'd wager—and the moment any Accepted just off apron strings gains the shawl, you have to do what she says."

Daigian's blush deepened. "We should move on."

It just wasn't right. Nynaeve let the matter drop, however. She'd stepped in this particular pit once before in teaching the Kinswomen to stand up for themselves in front of Aes Sedai. Before long, they'd been standing up to Nynaeve too, which had *not* been her intention. She wasn't certain she wanted to attempt a similar revolution among the Aes Sedai themselves.

She tried to turn back to the tutoring, but that sense of an impending storm kept drawing her eyes to the window. The room was on the second floor and had a good view of the camp outside. It was by pure happenstance that Nynaeve caught a glimpse of Cadsuane; that gray bun set with innocent-looking *ter'angreal* was obvious even from a distance. The woman was crossing the courtyard, Corele at her side, walking at a fair clip.

What is she doing? Nynaeve wondered. Cadsuane's pace made her suspicious. What had happened? Something to do with Rand? If that man had gotten himself hurt again . . .

"Excuse me, Daigian," Nynaeve said, standing. "I just remembered something that I must see to."

The other woman started. "Oh. Well, all right then, Nynaeve. We can continue another time, I suppose."

It wasn't until Nynaeve had hurried out the door and down the stairs that she realized Daigian had actually used her name. She smiled as she walked out onto the green.

There were Aiel in the camp. That itself wasn't uncommon; Rand often had a complement of Maidens to act as guards. But these Aiel were men, wearing the dusty brown *cadin'sor* and carrying spears at their sides. A fair number of them wore the headbands bearing Rand's symbol on them.

That was why Cadsuane had been in such a hurry; if the Aiel clan chiefs had arrived, then Rand would be wanting to meet with them. Nynaeve strode across the green—which wasn't very green at all—in a huff. Rand hadn't sent for her. Probably not because he didn't want to include her, but because he was just too wool-headed to think of it. Dragon Reborn or not, the man rarely thought to share his plans with others. She would have thought that after all this time, he would have realized the importance of getting advice from someone a little more experienced than he. How many times now had he gotten himself kidnapped, wounded or imprisoned because of his rashness?

All these others in camp might bow and scrape and dote on him, but Nynaeve knew that he was really just a sheepherder from Emond's Field. He still got into trouble the same way he had when he and Matrim had pulled pranks as boys. Only now instead of flustering the village girls he could throw entire nations into chaos.

On the far northern side of the green—directly opposite the manor house, close to the front of the bulwark—the Aiel newcomers were setting up their camp, complete with tan tents. They arranged them differently than the Saldaeans; instead of straight rows, the Aiel preferred small groups, organized by society. Some of Bashere's men called greetings to passing Aiel, but none moved to help. Aiel could be a prickly bunch, and while Nynaeve found the Saldaeans to be far less irrational than most, they *were* Borderlanders. Skirmishes with Aiel had been a way of life for them in earlier years, and the Aiel War itself was not so distant. For now, they all fought on the same side, but that didn't keep the Saldaeans from stepping a little more carefully now that the Aiel had arrived in force.

Nynaeve scanned for signs of Rand or any Aiel she knew. She doubted that Aviendha would be with the group; she would be back in Caemlyn with Elayne, helping secure the throne of Andor. Nynaeve still felt guilty for leaving them, but *somebody* had needed to help Rand cleanse *saidin*. That wasn't the sort of thing you left him to do alone. Now, where *was* he?

Nynaeve stopped at the boundary between the Saldaeans and the new Aiel camp. Soldiers carrying lances nodded to her in respect. Aiel in brown and green glided across the grass, their motions smooth as water. Women in blues and greens carried wash from the stream beside the manor house. Broad-needled pines shivered in the wind. The camp bustled like the village green at Bel Tine. Which way had Cadsuane gone?

She sensed channeling in the northeast. Nynaeve smiled, setting off with a determined step, yellow skirt swishing. The channeling would either be an Aes Sedai or a Wise One. Sure enough, she soon saw a larger Aiel tent erected at the corner of the green. She strode straight for it, her stares—or perhaps her reputation—encouraging Saldaean soldiers to get out of her way. The Maidens guarding the entrance did not try to stop her.

Rand stood inside, wearing black and red, leafing through maps on a sturdy wooden table, his left arm held behind his back. Bashere stood at his side, nodding to himself and studying a small map he held before him.

Rand looked up as Nynaeve entered. When had he started looking so much like a Warder, with that instant glance of assessment? Those eyes which picked out every threat, body tense as if expecting an attack at any time? *I should never have let that woman take him from the Two Rivers,* she thought. *Look what it's done to him.*

She immediately frowned at her own foolishness. If Rand had stayed in the Two Rivers, he would have gone mad and perhaps destroyed them all—assuming, of course, the Trollocs, the Fades or the Forsaken themselves hadn't accomplished the task first. If Moiraine hadn't come for Rand, he'd now be dead. With him would have gone the light and hope of the world. It was just hard to abandon her old prejudices.

"Ah, Nynaeve," Rand said, relaxing and turning back to his maps. He motioned for Bashere to inspect one of them, then turned back to her. "I was about to send for you. Rhuarc and Bael are here."

Nynaeve raised an eyebrow, folding her arms. "Oh?" she asked flatly. "And here I'd assumed that all the Aiel in the camp meant we had been attacked by Shaido."

His face hardened at her tone, and those eyes of his grew . . . dangerous. But then he lightened, shaking his head, almost as if to clear it. Some of the old Rand—the Rand who had been an innocent sheepherder—seemed to return. "Yes, of course you would have noticed," he said. "I'm glad you are here. We will begin as soon as the clan chiefs return. I insisted they see their people settled before we began."

He waved for her to sit; there were cushions on the floor, but no chairs. Aiel spurned those, and Rand would want them to be comfortable. Nynaeve eyed him, surprised at how tight her own nerves had become. He was just a wool-headed villager, no matter how much influence he'd found. He *was.*

But she could not shake away that look in his eyes, that flash of anger. Holding a crown was said to change many men for the worse. She intended to see that didn't happen to Rand al'Thor, but what recourse would she have if he suddenly decided to have her imprisoned? He wouldn't do that, would he? Not Rand.

Semirhage said he was mad, Nynaeve thought. *Said that . . . he heard voices from his past life. Is that what is happening when he cocks his head, as if listening to things that nobody else can hear?*

She shivered. Min was there in the tent, of course, sitting and reading a book in the corner: *The Wake of the Breaking.* Min looked too intently at the pages; she'd listened to the exchange between Rand and Nynaeve. What did she think of the changes in him? She was closer to him than anyone—close enough that, if they'd all been back in Emond's Field, Nynaeve would have given the two of them a tongue-lashing strong enough to make their heads spin. Even though they *weren't* in Emond's Field and she was no longer Wisdom, she'd made certain that Rand knew of her displeasure. His response had been simple: "If I marry her, my death will bring her even more pain."

More idiocy, of course. If you were planning to go into danger, then it was all the *more* reason to get married. Obviously. Nynaeve seated herself on the floor, arranging her skirts, and pointedly did *not* think of Lan. He had such a long distance to cover, and. . . .

And she had to make *sure* that she was given his bond before he reached the Blight. Just in case.

Suddenly, she sat upright. Cadsuane. The woman wasn't there; besides guards, the tent contained only Rand, Nynaeve, Min and Bashere. Was she off planning something that Nynaeve—

Cadsuane entered. The gray-haired Aes Sedai wore a simple tan dress. She relied on presence, not clothing, to draw attention, and of course her hair sparkled with its golden ornaments. Corele followed her in.

Cadsuane wove a ward against eavesdropping, and Rand did not object. He should stick up for himself more—that woman practically had him tamed, and it was unsettling how much he let her get away with. Like questioning Semirhage. The Forsaken were far too powerful and dangerous to treat lightly. Semirhage should have been stilled the moment they captured her . . . though Nynaeve's opinion in that regard was directly related to her own experience in keeping Moghedien captive.

Corele gave Nynaeve a smile; she tended to have one of

those for everyone. Cadsuane, as usual, ignored Nynaeve. That was fine. Nynaeve had no need for her approval. Cadsuane thought she could order everyone around just because she'd outlived every other Aes Sedai. Well, Nynaeve knew for a fact that age had little to do with wisdom. Cenn Buie had been as old as rain, but had about as much sense as a pile of rocks.

Many of the camp's other Aes Sedai and camp leaders trickled into the tent over the next few minutes; perhaps Rand really *had* sent messengers, and would have called for Nynaeve. The newcomers included Merise and her Warders, one of whom was the Asha'man Jahar Narishma, bells tinkling on the ends of his braids. Damer Flinn, Elza Penfell, a few of Bashere's officers also arrived. Rand glanced up when each one entered, alert and wary, but he quickly turned back to his maps. Was he growing paranoid? Some madmen grew suspicious of everyone.

Eventually, Rhuarc and Bael made their appearance, along with several other Aiel. They stalked through the tent's large entrance like cats on the prowl. In an odd turn, a batch of Wise Ones—whom Nynaeve had been able to sense when they got close—were among the group. Often, with Aiel, an event was either considered clan chief business or Wise One business—much as things happened back in the Two Rivers with the Village Council and the Women's Circle. Had Rand asked for them all to attend, or had they decided to come together for reasons of their own?

Nynaeve had been wrong about Aviendha's location; she was shocked to see the tall, red-haired woman hovering at the back of the group of Wise Ones. When had she left Caemlyn? And why was she carrying that worn cloth with a frayed edge?

Nynaeve didn't get a chance to ask Aviendha any questions, as Rand nodded to Rhuarc and the others, motioning for them to sit, which they did. Rand himself remained standing beside his map table. He placed his arms behind his back, hand clasping stump, a thoughtful look on his face. He offered no preamble. "Tell me of your work in Arad Doman," he said to Rhuarc. "My scouts inform me that this land is hardly at peace."

Rhuarc accepted a cup of tea from Aviendha—so she

was still considered an apprentice—and turned to Rand.
The clan chief did not drink. "We have had very little time,
Rand al'Thor."

"I don't look for excuses, Rhuarc," Rand said. "Only results."

This brought flashes of anger to the faces of several of
the other Aiel, and the Maidens at the doorway exchanged a
furious burst of hand signals.

Rhuarc himself displayed no anger, though Nynaeve did
think his hand tightened on his cup. "I have shared water
with you, Rand al'Thor," he said. "I would not think that
you would bring me here to offer insults."

"No insults, Rhuarc," Rand said. "Just truths. We don't
have time to waste."

"No time, Rand al'Thor?" Bael said. The clan chief of the
Goshien Aiel was a very tall man, and he seemed to tower,
even when sitting down. "You left many of us in Andor for
months with nothing to do but polish spears and scare wetlanders! Now you send us to this land with impossible orders, then follow a few weeks later and demand results?"

"You were in Andor to help Elayne," Rand said.

"She did not want or need help," Bael said with a snort.
"And she was right to refuse aid. I'd rather run across the
entire Waste with a single skin of water than have leadership of my clan handed to me by another."

Rand's expression grew dark again, his eyes stormy, and
Nynaeve was again reminded of the tempest brewing to the
north.

"This land is broken, Rand al'Thor," Rhuarc said, his
voice calmer than Bael's. "It is not making excuses to explain that fact, and it is not cowardice to be cautious about
a difficult task."

"We *must* have peace here," Rand growled. "If you can't
manage—"

"Boy," Cadsuane said, "perhaps you want to stop and
think. How often have you known the Aiel to fail you? How
often have you failed, hurt, or offended them?"

Rand snapped his mouth closed, and Nynaeve gritted her
teeth at not having spoken up herself. She glanced at Cadsuane, who had been given a chair to sit upon—Nynaeve
couldn't recall ever seeing her sit on the floor. The chair had
obviously been taken from the manor; it was constructed

from pale elgilrim horns—which stretched out like open palms—and had a red cushion. Aviendha handed Cadsuane a cup of tea, which she sipped carefully.

With obvious effort, Rand pulled his temper back under control. "I apologize, Rhuarc, Bael. It has been a . . . wearing few months."

"You have no *toh*," Rhuarc said. "But please, sit. Let us share shade and speak with civility."

Rand sighed audibly, then nodded, seating himself before the other two. The several Wise Ones in attendance—Amys, Melaine, Bair—didn't seem inclined to participate in the discussion. They were observers, much—Nynaeve realized—as she herself was.

"We *must* have peace in Arad Doman, my friends," Rand said, unrolling a map between them on the tent rug.

Bael shook his head. "Dobraine Taborwin has done well with Bandar Eban," he said, "but Rhuarc spoke rightly when he called this land broken. It is like a piece of Sea Folk porcelain dropped from the tip of a high mountain. You told us to discover who was in charge and see if we could restore order. Well, as far as we can tell, *no one* is in charge. Each city has been left to fend for itself."

"What of the Council of Merchants?" Bashere said, sitting down with them, knuckling his mustache as he studied the map. "My scouts say that they still hold some measure of power."

"In the cities where they rule, this is true," Rhuarc said. "But their influence is weak. There is only one member still in the capital, and she has little control there. We have stopped the fighting in the streets, but only with great effort." He shook his head. "This is what comes from trying to control more lands than holds and clan. Without their king, these Domani do not know who is in charge."

"Where is he?" Rand asked.

"Nobody knows, Rand al'Thor. He vanished. Some say months ago, others say it has been years."

"Graendal might have him," Rand whispered, studying the map intently. "If she's here. Yes, I think she probably is. But where? She won't be in the king's palace, that's not her way. She will have some place that is *hers*, a place where she can display her trophies. A location that would make a trophy itself, but not a place that one would think of immediately. Yes, I know. You're right. That's how she did it before. . . ."

Such familiarity! Nynaeve shivered. Aviendha knelt beside her, holding out a cup of tea. Nynaeve took it, meeting the woman's eyes, then began to whisper a question. Aviendha shook her head curtly. Later, her expression seemed to imply. Aviendha rose and retreated to the back of the room and then, grimacing, took out her frayed cloth and began pulling the threads out one at a time. What was the point of that?

"Cadsuane," Rand said, stopping his whispering, speaking up. "What do you know of the Council of Merchants?"

"They are mostly women," Cadsuane said, "and women of great cunning at that. However, they are also a selfish lot. It is their duty to choose the king, and with Alsalam's disappearance, they should have found a replacement. Too many of them see this as an opportunity, and that keeps them from reaching an agreement. I can assume that they've separated in face of this chaos to secure power in their home cities, fighting for position and alliances as they each offer their own choice of king for the others to consider."

"And this Domani army fighting the Seanchan?" Rand asked. "Is that their doing?"

"I know nothing of that."

"You speak of the man Rodel Ituralde," Rhuarc said.

"Yes."

"He fought well twenty years ago," Rhuarc said, rubbing his square chin. "He is of the ones you call a Great Captain. I should like to dance the spears with him."

"You will not," Rand said sharply. "Not while I live, at least. We will secure this land."

"And you expect us to do this without fighting?" Bael asked. "This Rodel Ituralde reportedly fights like a sandstorm against the Seanchan, drawing their ire better— even—than you yourself, Rand al'Thor. He will not sleep while you conquer his homeland."

"Once again," Rand said, "we are *not* here to conquer."

Rhuarc sighed. "Then why send us, Rand al'Thor? Why not use your Aes Sedai? They understand wetlanders. This country is like an entire *kingdom* of children, and we are too few adults to bring them to obedience. Particularly if you forbid us to spank them."

"You can fight," Rand said, "but only when you need to. Rhuarc, this has gone beyond the ability of Aes Sedai to fix. You *can* do this. People are intimidated by the Aiel; they will do as you say. If we can stop the Domani war with the Seanchan, perhaps this Daughter of the Nine Moons will see that I am serious in my desire for peace. Then maybe she'll agree to meet with me."

"Why not do as you've done before?" Bael asked. "Seize the land for your own?"

Bashere nodded, glancing at Rand.

"It won't work, not this time," Rand said. "A war here would take too many resources. You spoke of this Ituralde— he's holding off the Seanchan with virtually no supplies and few men. Would you have us engage a man that re- sourceful?"

How thoughtful Bashere seemed, as if he were indeed considering engaging this Ituralde. Men! They were all the same. Offer them a challenge, and they'd be curious, no matter that the challenge would likely end with them spitted on a lance.

"There are few men alive like Rodel Ituralde," Bashere said. "He would be a great help to our cause, for certain. I've always wondered if I could beat him."

"No," Rand said again, looking over the map. From what Nynaeve could see, it showed troop concentrations, marked with annotations. The Aiel were an organized mess of char- coal marks across the top of Arad Doman; Ituralde's forces were deep into Almoth Plain, fighting Seanchan. The mid- dle of Arad Doman was a sea of chaotic black annotations, likely the personal forces of various nobles.

"Rhuarc, Bael," Rand said. "I want you to seize the mem- bers of the Council of Merchants."

The tent was silent.

"Are you certain that is wise, boy?" Cadsuane finally asked.

"They're in danger from the Forsaken," Rand said, idly tapping the map with his fingers. "If Graendal really has taken Alsalam, then getting him back will do us no good. He'll be so far beneath her Compulsion that he'll barely have the mind of a child. She's not subtle; she never has been. We need the Council of Merchants to choose a new king. That's the only way to bring this kingdom peace and order."

Bashere nodded. "It's bold."

"We are not kidnappers," Bael said, frowning.

"You are what I say you are, Bael," Rand said quietly.

"We are still free people, Rand al'Thor," Rhuarc said.

"I will change the Aiel with my passing," Rand said with a shake of his head. "I don't know what you'll be once this is all through, but you cannot remain what you were. I will have you take up this task. Of all those who follow me, I trust you the most. If we're going to take the members of the Council without throwing this land further into war, I will need your cunning and stealth. You can prowl into their palaces and manors as you infiltrated the Stone of Tear."

Rhuarc and Bael regarded one another, sharing a frown.

"Once you take the Council of Merchants," Rand continued, apparently unconcerned about their worries, "move the Aiel into the cities where those merchants ruled. Make sure those cities don't degenerate. Restore order as you did in Bandar Eban. From there, begin hunting bandits and enforcing the law. Supplies will soon arrive from the Sea Folk. Take cities on the coast first, then move inland. Within a month's time, the Domani should be flowing *toward* you, rather than running away from you. Offer them safety and food, and order will take care of itself."

A surprisingly rational plan. Rand really did have a clever mind, for a man. There was a lot of good in him, perhaps the very soul of a leader, if he could keep his temper in check.

Rhuarc continued to rub his chin. "It would help if we had some of your Saldaeans, Davram Bashere. Wetlanders do not like following Aiel. If they can pretend that wetlanders are in charge, then they will be more likely to come to us."

Bashere laughed. "We'll also make nice targets. As soon as we seize a few members of the merchant council, the rest will send assassins after us for certain!"

Rhuarc laughed as if he thought that a grand joke. The Aiel sense of humor was its own sort of oddity. "We will keep you alive, Davram Bashere. If we do not, we will stuff you and set you on that horse of yours, and you will make a grand quiver for their arrows!"

Bael laughed loudly at this, and the Maidens by the doors began another round of handtalk.

Bashere chuckled, though he didn't seem to understand

the humor either. "You sure this is what you want to do?" he asked Rand.

Rand nodded. "Divide some of your forces, send them with Aiel groups as Rhuarc decides."

"And what of Ituralde?" Bashere asked, looking back at the map. "There won't be peace for long once he realizes we've invaded his homeland."

Rand tapped the map softly for a moment. "I will deal with him personally," he finally said.

CHAPTER
8

Clean Shirts

A dockmaster's sky, it was called. Those gray clouds, blotting out the sun, temperamental and sullen. Perhaps the others—here in the camp just outside of Tar Valon—hadn't noticed the persistent clouds, but Siuan had. No sailor would miss them. Not dark enough to promise a storm, not light enough to imply smooth waters either.

A sky like that was ambiguous. You could set out and never see a drop of rain or a hint of stormwinds. Or, with barely a moment's notice, you could find yourself in the middle of a squall. It was deceitful, that blanket of clouds.

Most ports charged a daily fee to each vessel moored in their harbors, but on days of storm—when no fisher could make a catch—the fee would be halved, or spared entirely. On a day like this, however, when there were gloomy clouds but no proof of storms, the dockmasters would charge a full day's rent. And so the fisher had to make a choice. Stay in the harbor and wait, or go fishing to recoup the dock fees. Most days like this didn't turn stormy. Most days like this were safe.

But if a storm did come on a day like this, it tended to be very bad. Many of the most terrible tempests in history had sprung from a dockmaster's sky. That's why some fishers had another name for clouds like those. They called them a lionfish's veil. And it had been days since the sky had offered anything different. Siuan shivered, pulling her shawl close. It was a bad sign.

She doubted many fishers had chosen to go out this day.

"Siuan?" Lelaine asked, voice tinged with annoyance. "Do hurry up. And I don't want to hear any more superstitious nonsense about the sky. Honestly." The tall Aes Sedai turned away and continued along the walk.

Superstitious? Siuan thought indignantly. *A thousand generations of wisdom isn't superstition. It's good sense!* But she said nothing, and hurried after Lelaine. Around her, the camp of Aes Sedai loyal to Egwene continued its daily activities, as steady as a clock's gears. If there was one thing Aes Sedai were good at, it was creating order. Tents were arranged in clusters, by Ajah, as if to imitate the White Tower's layout. There were few men, and most of those who passed—soldiers on errands from Gareth Bryne's armies, grooms caring for horses—were quick to be about their duties. They were far outnumbered by worker women, many of whom had gone so far as to embroider the pattern of the Flame of Tar Valon on their skirts or bodices.

One of the only oddities about the village—if one ignored the fact that there were tents instead of rooms and wooden walkways instead of tiled hallways—was the number of novices. There were hundreds and hundreds. In fact, the number had to be over a thousand now, many more than the Tower had held in recent memory. Once the Aes Sedai were reunited, novices' quarters that hadn't been used in decades would have to be reopened. They might even need the second kitchen.

These novices bustled around in families, and most of the Aes Sedai tried to ignore them. Some did this out of habit; who paid attention to novices? But others did so out of displeasure. By their estimation, women aged enough to be mothers and grandmothers—indeed, many who *were* mothers and grandmothers—shouldn't have been entered into the novice book. But what could be done? Egwene al'Vere, the Amyrlin Seat, had declared that it should happen.

Siuan could still sense shock in some of the Aes Sedai she passed. Egwene was to have been carefully controlled. What had gone wrong? When had the Amyrlin gotten away from them? Siuan would have taken more smug delight from those looks if she hadn't herself worried about Egwene's continued captivity in the White Tower. That was a lionfish's veil indeed. Potential for great success, but also for great disaster. She hurried after Lelaine.

"What is the status of the negotiations?" Lelaine asked, not bothering to look at Siuan.

You could go to one of the sessions yourself and find out, Siuan thought. But Lelaine wanted to be seen supervising, not taking an active hand. And asking Siuan, in the open, was also a calculated move. Siuan was known as one of Egwene's confidants and still carried some measure of notoriety for having been Amyrlin herself. The things Siuan said to Lelaine weren't important; being seen saying them, however, increased the woman's influence in camp.

"They don't go well, Lelaine," Siuan said. "Elaida's emissaries never promise anything, and seem indignant any time we raise important topics, like reinstating the Blue Ajah. I doubt they have any real authority from Elaida to make binding agreements."

"Hmm," Lelaine said thoughtfully, nodding to a group of novices. They bobbed into curtsies. In a shrewd decision, Lelaine had begun talking very acceptingly of the new novices.

Romanda's dislike of them was well known; now that Egwene was gone, Romanda had begun to imply that once reconciliation was achieved, this "foolishness" with the aged novices would have to be dealt with swiftly. However, more and more of the other sisters were seeing Egwene's wisdom. There was great strength among the new novices, and not a few would be raised to Accepted the moment the White Tower was achieved. Recently—by offering tacit acceptance of these women—Lelaine had given herself yet another tie to Egwene.

Siuan eyed the retreating family of novices. They had curtsied to Lelaine almost as quickly and as deferentially as they would have to the Amyrlin. It was becoming clear that, after months at a stalemate, Lelaine was winning the battle against Romanda for superiority.

And that was a very large problem.

Siuan didn't dislike Lelaine. She was capable, strong-willed and decisive. They had been friends once, though their relationship had changed drastically with Siuan's changed position.

Yes, she might say she liked Lelaine. But she *didn't* trust the woman, and she particularly didn't want to see her as Amyrlin. In another era, Lelaine would have done well in the position. But this world *needed* Egwene, and—friendship or not—Siuan couldn't afford to let this woman displace the rightful Amyrlin. And she had to make certain Lelaine wasn't taking action to prevent Egwene's return.

"Well," Lelaine said, "we shall have to discuss the negotiations in the Hall. The Amyrlin wants them to continue, so we certainly can't let them stop. Yet there must be a way to make them effective. The Amyrlin's desires must be seen to, wouldn't you say?"

"Undoubtedly," Siuan replied flatly.

Lelaine eyed her, and Siuan cursed herself for letting her emotions show. Lelaine needed to believe that Siuan was on her side. "I'm sorry, Lelaine. That woman has me in a fury. Why does Elaida hold talks if she won't concede a single point?"

Lelaine nodded. "Yes. But who can say why Elaida does what she does? The Amyrlin's reports indicate that Elaida's leadership of the Tower has been . . . erratic at best."

Siuan simply nodded. Fortunately, Lelaine didn't seem to suspect Siuan's disloyalty. Or she didn't care about it. It was remarkable how innocuous the women thought Siuan was, now that her power had been so greatly reduced.

Being weak was a new experience. From her very early days in the White Tower, sisters had noted her strength and her sharpness of mind. Whispers of her becoming Amyrlin had begun almost immediately—at times, it seemed that the Pattern itself had pushed Siuan directly into the Seat. Though her hasty ascent to Amyrlin while so young had come as a surprise to many, she herself had not been shocked. When you fished with squid as bait, you shouldn't be surprised to catch fangfish. If you wanted to catch eels, you used something else entirely.

When she'd first been Healed, her reduced power had been a disappointment. But that was changing. Yes, it was infuriating to be beneath so many, to lack respect from those around her. However, because she was weaker in power, many seemed to assume she was weaker in political skill as well! Could people really forget so quickly? She was finding her new status among the Aes Sedai to be liberating.

"Yes," Lelaine said as she nodded to another group of novices, "I believe that it is time to send envoys to the kingdoms that al'Thor hasn't conquered. We may not hold the White Tower itself, but that is no reason to abandon our political stewardship of the world."

"Yes, Lelaine," Siuan said. "But are you certain that Romanda won't argue against that?"

"Why would she?" Lelaine said dismissively. "It wouldn't make sense."

"Little Romanda does makes sense," Siuan said. "I think she disagrees just to spite you. But I *did* see her chatting with Maralenda earlier in the week."

Lelaine frowned. Maralenda was a distant cousin to the Trakand line.

Siuan covered a smile. It was amazing how much you could accomplish when people dismissed you. How many women had *she* dismissed because they lacked visible power? How often had *she* been manipulated much as she now manipulated Lelaine?

"I shall look into it," Lelaine said. It didn't matter what she discovered; as long as she was kept busy worrying about Romanda, she wouldn't be able to spend as much time stealing power from Egwene.

Egwene. The Amyrlin needed to hurry up and finish with her plotting in the White Tower. What good would it do to undermine Elaida if the Aes Sedai outside crumbled while Egwene wasn't watching? Siuan could only keep Romanda and Lelaine distracted for so long, particularly now that Lelaine held such a distinct advantage. Light! Some days, she felt that she was trying to juggle buttered live silverpike.

Siuan checked the position of the sun behind that dock-master's sky. It was late afternoon. "Fish guts," she muttered. "I'll need to be going, Lelaine."

Lelaine glanced at her. "You have washing, I presume? For that ruffian of a general of yours?"

"He's *not* a ruffian," Siuan snapped, then cursed herself. She'd lose much of her advantage if she kept snapping at those who thought themselves her betters.

Lelaine smiled, eyes twinkling as if she knew something special. Insufferable woman. Friend or not, Siuan had half a mind to wipe . . .

No. "I apologize, Lelaine," Siuan forced out. "I get on edge, thinking of what that man demands of me."

"Yes," Lelaine said, downturning her lips. "I've considered on this, Siuan. The Amyrlin may have suffered Bryne's bullying of a sister, but I won't stand for it. You're one of my attendants now."

One of your attendants? Siuan thought. *I thought that I was just supposed to support you until Egwene returned.*

"Yes," Lelaine mused, "I should think it's time to put an end to your servitude to Bryne. I shall pay off your debt, Siuan."

"Pay off my debt?" Siuan said, feeling a moment of panic. "Is that wise? Not that I wouldn't mind being free of that man, of course, but my position offers me quite useful opportunities for listening in on his plans."

"Plans?" Lelaine asked, frowning.

Siuan cringed inwardly. The last thing she wanted was to imply wrongdoing on Bryne's part. Light, the man was strict enough to make *Warders* look sloppy in keeping their oaths.

She should just let Lelaine end this foolish servitude, but the thought made her stomach churn. Bryne was already disappointed that she'd broken her oath to him months before. Well, she *hadn't* broken that oath—she'd just postponed her period of service. But try convincing the stubborn fool of that fact!

If she took the easy way out now, what would he think of her? He'd think that he'd won, that she'd proven herself unable to keep her word. There was no way she'd let that happen.

Besides, she wasn't about to let Lelaine be the one who freed her. That would just move her debt from Bryne to Lelaine. The Aes Sedai would collect it in far more subtle ways, but each coin would end up being paid one way or another, if only through demands of loyalty.

"Lelaine," Siuan said softly, "I don't suspect the good general of anything. However, he controls our armies. Can he really be trusted to do as required without any supervision?"

Lelaine sniffed. "I'm not certain *any* man can be trusted without direction."

"I hate doing his laundry," Siuan said. Well, she did. Even if she wouldn't be stopped from doing it for all of the gold in Tar Valon. "But if the duty keeps me close, with a listening ear. . . ."

"Yes," Lelaine said, nodding slowly. "Yes, I see that you are right. I will not forget your sacrifice, Siuan. Very well, you are dismissed."

Lelaine turned, glancing down at her hand, as if longing for something. Probably wishing for the day when—as
Amyrlin—she could offer her Great Serpent ring for a
kiss when she parted ways with another sister. Light, but
Egwene needed to return soon. Buttered silverpike! Buttered, flaming silverpike!

Siuan made her way toward the edge of the Aes Sedai
camp. Bryne's army surrounded the Aes Sedai camp in
a large ring, but she was on the far side of the ring from
Bryne. It would take a good half-hour to walk to his command post. Fortunately, she found a wagon driver who was
taking a load of supplies, brought through a gateway, to the
army. The short, grizzled man immediately agreed to let
her ride with the turnips, though he did seem puzzled why
she didn't go get a horse, as befitted an Aes Sedai's station.
Well, it wasn't *that* far, and riding with vegetables was a
fate *far* less undignified than being forced to jounce around
on the back of a horse. If Gareth Bryne wanted to complain
about her tardiness, then he'd get an earful, he would!

She settled back against a lumpy sack of turnips, brown-
skirted legs hanging over the back of the wagon. As the
cart rolled up a slight incline, she could see over the Aes
Sedai camp—with its white tents and citylike organization.
Ringed around it was the army, with smaller tents in neat
straight lines, and ringed around *them* was a growing ring
of camp followers.

Beyond it all, the landscape was brown, the winter snows
melted, but spring sprouts scarce. The countryside was
pocketed with thickets of scrub oak; shadows in valleys and
twisting lines of chimney smoke pointed to distant villages.
It was surprising how familiar, how welcome, these grasslands felt. When she had first come to the White Tower,
she'd been sure she'd never come to love this landlocked
countryside.

Now she had lived much more of her life in Tar Valon
than she had in Tear. It was difficult at times to recall that
girl who had sewn nets and gone on early-morning trawl-
ing trips with her father. She'd become something else, a
woman who traded in secrets rather than fish.

Secrets, those powerful, dominating secrets. They had
become her life. No love save for youthful dalliances. No
time for entanglements, or much room for friendships.

She'd focused on only one thing: finding the Dragon Reborn. Helping him, guiding him, hopefully controlling him.

Moiraine had died following that same quest, but at least she had been able to go out and see the world. Siuan had grown old—in spirit, if not in body—cooped up in the Tower, pulling her strings and nudging the world. She'd done some good. Time would tell if those efforts had been enough.

She didn't regret her life. Yet, at this moment, passing army tents—holes and broken ruts in the path shaking the cart, making it rattle like dried fishbones in a kettle—she envied Moiraine. How often had Siuan bothered to look out of her window toward the beautiful green landscape, before it all had started going sickly? She and Moiraine had fought so hard to save this world, but they had left themselves without anything to enjoy in it.

Perhaps Siuan had made a mistake in staying with the Blue, unlike Leane, who had taken the opportunity in their stilling and Healing to change to the Green Ajah. *No,* Siuan thought, wagon rattling, smelling of bitter turnips. *No, I'm still focused on saving this blasted world.* There would be no switching to the Green for her. Though, thinking of Bryne, she did wish that the Blue were a little more like the Green in certain ways.

Siuan the Amyrlin hadn't had any time for entanglements, but what of Siuan the attendant? Guiding people with quiet manipulations required a lot more skill than bullying them with the power of the Amyrlin Seat, and it was proving more fulfilling. But it also left her without the crushing weight of responsibility she'd felt during her years leading the White Tower. Was there, perhaps, room in her life for a few more changes?

The wagon reached the far side of the army camp, and she shook her head at her own foolishness as she hopped down, then nodded her thanks to the wagon driver. Was she a girl, barely old enough for her first full-day blackfish trawl? There was no use in thinking of Bryne that way. At least not right now. There was too much to do.

She walked along the perimeter of the camp, army tents to her left. It was growing dark, and lanterns burning precious oil illuminated disorganized shanties and tents to her right. Ahead of her, a small circular palisade rose on the army side. It didn't enclose the entire army—in fact, it was only big enough for several dozen officer tents and some larger command tents. It was to act as a fortification in an emergency, but always as a center of operations—Bryne felt it good to have a physical barrier separating the larger camp from the place where he held conference with his officers. With the confusion of the civilian camp, and with such a long border to patrol, it would be too easy for spies to approach his tents otherwise.

The palisade was only about three-quarters done, but work was progressing quickly. Perhaps he would choose to surround the entire army, eventually, if the siege continued long enough. For now, Bryne felt that the small, fortified command post would not only suggest security to the soldiers, but also lend them a sense of authority.

The eight-foot wooden stakes rose from the ground ahead, a line of sentinels standing side by side, points raised to the sky. While holding a siege one generally had a lot of manpower for work like this. The guards at the palisade gate knew to let her pass, and she quickly made her way to Bryne's tent. She *did* have washing to do, but most of it would probably have to wait until the morning. She was supposed to meet Egwene in *Tel'aran'rhiod* as soon as it grew dark, and the glow of the sunset was already beginning to fade.

Bryne's tent, as usual, shone with only a very faint light. While people outside squandered their oil, he scrimped. Most of his men lived better than he did. Fool man. Siuan pushed her way into the tent without calling. If he was foolish enough to change without going behind the screen, then he was foolish enough to be seen doing it.

He was seated at his desk working by the light of a solitary candle. He appeared to be reading scout reports.

Siuan sniffed, letting the tent flaps droop closed behind her. Not a single lamp! That man! "You will ruin your eyes reading by such poor light, Gareth Bryne."

"I have read by the light of a single candle for most of my life, Siuan," he said, turning over a page and not looking up. "And I'll have you know that my eyesight is the same as it was when I was a boy."

"Oh?" Siuan said. "So you're saying that your eyesight was poor to begin with?"

Bryne grinned, but continued his reading. Siuan sniffed again, loudly, to make sure he heard. Then she wove a globe of light and sent it hovering over beside his desk. Fool man. She wouldn't have him going so blind he fell in battle to an attack he didn't see. After setting the light beside his head—perhaps too close for him to be comfortable with it without scooting over—she walked over to pluck clothing off the drying line she'd strung across the center of the tent. He'd voiced no complaint about her using the *inside* of his tent for drying laundry, and hadn't taken it down. That was a disappointment. She'd been anticipating chastising him for that.

"A woman from the camp outside approached me today," Bryne said, shifting his chair to the side, then picking up another stack of pages. "She offered me laundry service. She's organizing a group of washwomen in the camp, and she claimed that she could do my wash more quickly and effectively than a single distracted maidservant could."

Siuan froze, sparing a glance at Bryne, who was looking through his papers. His strong jaw was lit on the left by the even white light of her globe and on the right by the flickering orange candlelight. Some men were made weak by age, others were made to look tired or slovenly. Bryne had simply become distinguished, like a pillar, crafted by a master stonemason, then left to the elements. Age hadn't reduced Bryne's effectiveness or his strength. It had simply given him character, dusting his temples with silver, creasing his firm face with lines of wisdom.

"And what did you tell this woman?" she asked.

Bryne turned a page over. "I told her that I was satisfied with my laundry." He looked up at her. "I have to say, Siuan, that I'm surprised. I had assumed that an Aes Sedai would know little of work such as this, but rarely have my uniforms known such a perfect combination of stiffness and comfort. You are to be commended."

Siuan turned away from him, hiding her blush. Fool man! She had caused kings to kneel before her! She manipulated the Aes Sedai and planned for the deliverance of mankind itself! And he complimented her on her *laundering* skills?

The thing was, from Bryne, that was an honest and meaningful compliment. He didn't look down on washwomen, or on runner boys. He treated all with equity. A person didn't gain stature in Gareth Bryne's eyes by being a king or queen; one gained stature by keeping to one's oaths and doing one's duty. To him, a compliment on laundry well done was as meaningful as a medal awarded to a soldier who had stood his ground before the enemy.

She glanced back at him. He was still watching her. Fool man! She hurriedly took down another of his shirts and began folding it.

"You never did explain to my satisfaction why you broke your oath," he said.

Siuan froze, looking at the back wall of the tent, splayed with shadows of the still-hanging laundry. "I thought that you understood," she said, continuing to fold. "I had important information for the Aes Sedai in Salidar. Besides, I couldn't very well let Logain run about free, now could I? I had to find him and get him to Salidar."

"Those are excuses," Bryne said. "Oh, I know that they're true. But you're Aes Sedai. You can cite four facts and use them to hide the real truth as effectively as another might use lies."

"So you claim I'm a liar?" she demanded.

"No," he said. "Just an oathbreaker."

She glanced at him, eyes widening. Why, she'd let him hear the rough side of. . . .

She hesitated. He was watching her, bathed in the glow of the two lights, eyes thoughtful. Reserved, but not accusatory. "That question drove me here, you know," he said. "It's why I hunted you all that way. It's why I finally swore to these rebel Aes Sedai, though I had little wish to be pulled into yet another war at Tar Valon. I did it all because I needed to understand. I had to know. Why? Why did the woman with those eyes—those passionate, haunting eyes—break her oath?"

"I told you I was going to return to you and fulfill that oath," Siuan said, turning away from him and snapping a shirt in front of her to unwrinkle it.

"Another excuse," he said softly. "Another answer from an Aes Sedai. Will I ever have the full truth from you, Siuan Sanche? Has anyone ever had it?" He sighed, and she heard papers rustle, the candle's light flickering in the faint stir of his movements as he turned back to his reports.

"When I was still an Accepted in the White Tower,"

Siuan said softly, "I was one of four people present when a Foretelling announced the imminent birth of the Dragon Reborn on the slopes of Dragonmount."

His rustling froze.

"One of the three others present," Siuan continued, "died on the spot. Another died soon after. I'm confident that she—the Amyrlin Seat herself—was murdered by the Black Ajah. Yes, it exists. If you tell anyone that I admitted that fact, I'll have your tongue.

"Anyway, before she died, the Amyrlin sent Aes Sedai out hunting the Dragon. One by one, those women vanished. The Blacks must have tortured their names out of Tamra before killing her. She would not have given up those names easily. I still shiver, sometimes, thinking about what she must have gone through.

"Soon, there were just the two of us left who knew. Moiraine and me. We weren't supposed to hear the Foretelling. We were just Accepted, in the room by happenstance. I believe that Tamra was somehow able to withhold our names from the Blacks, for if she hadn't, we'd have undoubtedly been murdered like the others.

"That left two of us. The only two in all of the world who knew what was coming. At least, the only two who served the Light. And so I did what I had to, Gareth Bryne. I dedicated my life to preparing for the Dragon's coming. I swore to see us through the Last Battle. To do whatever was necessary—*whatever* was necessary—to bear the burden I had been given. There was only one other person I knew I could trust, and she is now dead."

Siuan turned, meeting his eyes across the tent. A breeze rippled the walls and fluttered the candle, but Bryne sat still, watching her.

"So you see, Gareth Bryne," she said. "I *had* to delay fulfilling my oath to you because of other oaths. I swore to see this through to the end, and the Dragon has not yet met his destiny at Shayol Ghul. A person's oaths must follow their order of importance. When I swore to you, I did *not* promise to serve you immediately. I was intentionally careful on that point. You will call it an Aes Sedai wordplay. I would call it something else."

"Which is?" he asked.

"Doing what was necessary to protect you, your lands

and your people, Gareth Bryne. You blame me for the loss of a barn and some cows. Well, then I suggest that you consider the cost to your people should the Dragon Reborn fail. Sometimes, prices must be paid so that a more important duty can be served. I would expect a soldier to understand that."

"You should have told me," he said, still meeting her eyes. "You should have explained who you were."

"What?" Siuan asked. "Would you have believed me?"

He hesitated.

"Besides," she said frankly, "I didn't trust you. Our previous meeting had not been particularly . . . amicable, as I recall. Could I have taken that risk, Gareth Bryne, on a man I did not know? Could I have given him control over the secrets I alone know, secrets that needed to be passed on to the new Amyrlin Seat? Should I have spared even a moment when the entire world was wearing the hangman's noose?"

She held those eyes, demanding an answer.

"No," he finally admitted. "Burn me, Siuan, but no. You shouldn't have waited. You shouldn't have made that oath in the first place!"

"*You* should have been more careful to listen," she said, finally breaking his gaze with a sniff. "I suggest that if you swear someone into service in the future, you be careful to stipulate a time frame for that service."

Bryne grunted and Siuan whipped the final shirt off of the drying line, causing it to shake, making a blurry shadow on the back wall of the tent.

"Well," Bryne said, "I told myself I'd only hold you to work as long as it took me to get that answer. Now I know. I would say that—"

"Stop!" Siuan snapped, spinning on him and pointing.

"But—"

"Don't say it," she threatened. "I'll gag you and leave you hanging in the air until sundown tomorrow. Don't think that I won't."

Bryne sat, silent.

"I'm not finished with you yet, Gareth Bryne." She whipped the shirt in her hands, then folded it. "I shall tell you when I am."

"Light, woman," he muttered, almost under his breath. "If I'd known you were Aes Sedai before chasing you to Salidar . . . if I'd known what I was doing. . . ."

"What?" she demanded. "You wouldn't have hunted me down?"

"Of course I would have," he said indignantly. "I'd have just been more careful, and perhaps come better prepared. I went off hunting boars with a rabbit knife instead of a spear!"

Siuan set the folded shirt on top of the others, then picked up the stack. She gave him a suffering look. "I will do my best to pretend that you *didn't* just compare me to a boar, Bryne. Kindly be a little more cautious with your tongue. Otherwise, you'll find yourself without a maidservant, and you'll *have* to let those ladies in the camp take up your laundry."

He gave her a bemused look. Then he just laughed. She failed at keeping her own grin to herself. Well, after that exchange, he would know who was in control of this association.

But . . . Light! Why had she told him about the Foretelling? She'd rarely told anyone about that! As she packed the shirts in his trunk, she glanced at Bryne, who was still shaking his head and chuckling.

When other oaths no longer have a hold on me, she thought. *When I'm certain the Dragon Reborn is doing what he is supposed to, perhaps there will be time. For once, I'm actually starting to look forward to being done with this quest.* How remarkable.

"You should be bedding down, Siuan," Bryne said.

"It's early yet," she said.

"Yes, but it's sunset. Every third day you bed down uncharacteristically early, wearing that odd ring you have hidden between the cushions of your pallet." He turned over a paper on his desk. "Please give my kind regards to the Amyrlin."

She turned toward him, slack-jawed. He *couldn't* know about *Tel'aran'rhiod*, could he? She caught him smiling in satisfaction. Well, perhaps he didn't know about *Tel'aran'rhiod*, but he'd obviously guessed that the ring and her schedule had something to do with communicating with Egwene. Sly. He glanced over the top of his papers at her as she passed, and his eyes had a twinkle to them.

"Insufferable man," she muttered, sitting down on her pallet and dismissing her globe of light. Then she sheepishly fished out the ring *ter'angreal* and put it around her neck, turned her back on him and lay down, trying to will herself to sleep. She made certain to rise early every third day so that she'd be tired at night. She wished she could put herself to sleep as easily as Egwene did.

Insufferable . . . *insufferable* man! She'd have to do something to get back at him. Mice in the bedsheets. That would be a good payback.

She lay for too long a time, but eventually coaxed herself to sleep, smiling faintly to herself at the prospect of an apt revenge. She awoke in *Tel'aran'rhiod* wearing nothing but a scandalous, barely covering shift. She yelped, immediately replacing that—through concentration—with a green dress. Green? Why green? She made it blue. Light! How was it that Egwene was always so good at controlling things in *Tel'aran'rhiod* while Siuan could barely keep her clothing from switching at every idle thought? It must have something to do with the fact that Siuan had to wear this inferior *ter'angreal* copy, which didn't work as well as the original. It made her look insubstantial to others who saw her.

She was standing in the middle of the Aes Sedai camp, surrounded by tents. The flaps of any given structure would be open one moment, then closed the next. The sky was troubled by a violent, yet strangely silent, storm. Curious, but things were often strange in *Tel'aran'rhiod*. She closed her eyes, willing herself to appear in the study of the Mistress of Novices in the White Tower. When she opened her eyes, she was there. A small, wood-paneled room with a stout desk and a table for strappings.

She would have liked to have the original ring, but Elayne had taken that one with her. She should be thankful for even a small catch, as her father had been fond of saying. She *could* have been left without any of the rings. The Sitters thought this one had been with Leane when she'd been captured.

Was Leane all right? At any moment, the false Amyrlin could opt for execution. Siuan knew all too well how spiteful Elaida could be; she still felt a stab of sorrow when she thought of poor Alric. Had Elaida felt a single moment of guilt over murdering a Warder in cold blood, before the woman she was tearing down had been properly deposed?

"A sword, Siuan?" Egwene's voice suddenly asked. "That's novel."

Siuan looked down, shocked to find herself holding a bloody sword, likely intended for Elaida's heart. She made it vanish, then regarded Egwene. The girl looked the part of the Amyrlin, wearing that magnificent golden gown, her brown hair in an intricate arrangement set with pearls. Her face wasn't ageless yet, but Egwene was getting *very* good at the calm serenity of an Aes Sedai. In fact, she seemed to have grown measurably better at that since her capture.

"You look well, Mother," Siuan said.

"Thank you," Egwene said, with a faint smile. She showed more of herself around Siuan than she did the others. They both knew how heavily Egwene had relied on Siuan's teaching to get where she was.

Though she'd probably have made it there anyway, Siuan admitted. *Just not quite as quickly.*

Egwene glanced at the room around them, then grimaced faintly. "I realize I suggested this location last time, but I have seen enough of this room lately. I will meet you in the novices' dining hall." She vanished.

An odd choice, but very unlikely to conceal unwanted ears. Siuan and Egwene weren't the only ones who used *Tel'aran'rhiod* for clandestine meetings. Siuan closed her eyes—she didn't need to, but it seemed to help her—and imagined the novices' dining hall, with its rows of benches and its bare walls. When she opened her eyes, she was there, as was Egwene. The Amyrlin settled back and a majestic stuffed chair appeared behind her, catching her gracefully as she sat. Siuan didn't trust herself to do anything so complicated; she simply sat down on one of the benches.

"I think we may want to start meeting more frequently, Mother," Siuan said, tapping the table as she ordered her thoughts.

"Oh?" Egwene asked, sitting up straighter. "Has something happened?"

"Several somethings," Siuan said, "and I'm afraid a few of them smell as ripe as last week's catch."

"Tell me."

"One of the Forsaken was in our camp," Siuan said. She hadn't wanted to think about *that* too frequently. The knowledge made her skin crawl.

"Is anyone dead?" Egwene asked, voice calm though her eyes looked to be steel.

"No, bless the Light," Siuan said. "Other than those you already know about. Romanda made the connection. Egwene, the creature had been with us for some time, in hiding."

"Who?"

"Delana Mosalaine," Siuan said. "Or her serving woman, Halima. Most likely Halima, as I've known Delana for a great long time." Egwene's eyes widened just faintly. Halima had waited on Egwene. Egwene had been touched and served by one of the Forsaken. She took the news well. Like an Amyrlin.

"But Anaiya was killed by a man," Egwene said. "Were those murders different?"

"No. Anaiya wasn't murdered by a man, but by a woman wielding *saidin*. It must have been—it's the only thing that makes sense."

Egwene nodded slowly. Anything was possible where the Dark One was concerned. Siuan smiled in satisfaction and pride. This girl was learning to be Amyrlin. Light, she *was* Amyrlin!

"There's more?" Egwene asked.

"Not much more on this topic," Siuan said. "They got away from us, unfortunately. Disappeared the very day we discovered them."

"What warned them, I wonder."

"Well, that involves one of the other things I need to tell you." Siuan took a deep breath. The worst of it was out, but this next part wouldn't be much easier to stomach. "There was a meeting of the Hall that day, attended by Delana. In that meeting, an Asha'man announced that he could sense a man channeling in the camp. We think that is what informed her. It wasn't until after Delana fled that we made the connection. It was that same Asha'man who told us that his fellow had encountered a woman who could channel *saidin*."

"And why was an Asha'man in the camp?" Egwene asked coolly.

"He'd been sent as an envoy," Siuan explained. "From the Dragon Reborn. Mother, it appears some of the men who follow al'Thor have bonded Aes Sedai."

Egwene blinked a single time. "Yes. I had heard rumors

of this. I had hoped that they were exaggerated. Did this Asha'man say who gave Rand permission to commit such an atrocity?"

"He's the Dragon Reborn," Siuan said, grimacing. "I don't think he feels he *needs* permission. But, in his defense, it appears he didn't know it was happening. The women his men bonded were sent by Elaida to destroy the Black Tower."

"Yes." Egwene finally showed a sliver of emotion. "So the rumors are accurate. All too accurate." Her beautiful dress retained its shape, but bled to a deep brown in color, like Aiel clothing. Egwene didn't seem to notice the change. "Will Elaida's reign of disasters never cease?"

Siuan just shook her head. "We've been offered forty-seven Asha'man to bond as restitution, of sorts, for the women al'Thor's men bonded. Hardly a fair trade, but the Hall decided to accept the offer nonetheless."

"As well they should have," Egwene said. "We shall have to deal with the Dragon's foolishness at a later date. Perhaps his men acted without his direct orders, but Rand must take responsibility. Men. Bonding women!"

"They claim *saidin* is cleansed," Siuan said.

Egwene raised an eyebrow, but did not object. "Yes," she said, "I suppose that might be a reasonable possibility. We will need further confirmation, of course. But the taint arrived when all seemed won; why should it not leave when all seems to be approaching pure madness?"

"I hadn't considered it that way," Siuan said. "Well, what should we do, Mother?"

"Let the Hall deal with it," Egwene said. "It seems they have matters in hand."

"They'd be better at *keeping* them in hand if you'd return, Mother."

"Eventually," Egwene said. She sat back and laced her fingers in her lap, somehow looking far older than her face would suggest. "My work is here, for now. You'll have to see that the Hall does as it should. I have great faith in you."

"And it's appreciated, Mother," Siuan said, keeping her frustration inside. "But I'm losing control of them. Lelaine has begun to set herself up as a second Amyrlin—and is doing it by pretending to support you. She's seen that appearing to act in your name serves herself."

Egwene pursed her lips. "I would have thought Romanda would take the advantage, considering that she discovered the Forsaken."

"I think she assumed she'd hold the advantage," Siuan said, "but she spent too long basking in her victory. Lelaine has, with no small effort, become the most devoted servant of the Amyrlin who has ever lived. You would think that you and she were the closest of confidants, to hear her speak! She's appropriated me as her attendant, and each time the Hall meets it's 'Egwene wanted this' and 'Remember what Egwene said when we did that.'"

"Clever," Egwene said.

"Brilliant," Siuan said, sighing. "But we knew one of them was eventually going to claw her way ahead of the other. I keep diverting her toward Romanda, but I don't know how long I can keep her distracted."

"Do your best," Egwene said. "But don't worry if Lelaine refuses to be diverted."

Siuan frowned. "But she's usurping your place!"

"By building upon it," Egwene said, smiling. She finally noticed that her dress had changed to brown, for she switched it back in a heartbeat, not breaking the conversation. "Lelaine's gambit will only succeed if I fail to return. She is using *me* as a source of authority. When I return, she'll have no choice but to accept my leadership. She'll have spent all of her effort building me up."

"And if you don't return, Mother?" Siuan asked softly.

"Then it will be better for the Aes Sedai to have a strong leader," Egwene said. "If Lelaine has been the one to secure that strength, then so be it."

"She has good reason to make *certain* you don't return, you know," Siuan said. "At the very least, she's betting against you."

"Well, she can't very well be blamed for that." Egwene let down her guard enough to show a grimace. "I'd be tempted to bet against myself, if I were on the outside. You'll simply have to deal with her, Siuan. I can't let myself be distracted. Not when I see so much potential for success here, and not when there is an even greater price for failure."

Siuan knew that stubborn set to Egwene's jaw. There would be no persuading her tonight. Siuan would simply have to try again during their next meeting.

All of it—the cleansing, the Asha'man, the crumbling of the Tower—made her shiver uncomfortably. Though she'd been preparing for these days for most of her life, it was still unsettling to have them finally arrive. "The Last Battle really is coming," Siuan said, mostly to herself.

"It is," Egwene said, voice solemn.

"And I'm going to face it with barely a lick of my former power," Siuan said, grimacing.

"Well, perhaps we can get you an *angreal* once the Tower is whole again," Egwene said. "We'll be using everything we have when we ride against the Shadow."

Siuan smiled. "That would be nice, but not necessary. I'm just grumbling out of habit, I suppose. I'm actually learning to deal with my . . . new situation. It's not so difficult to stomach, now that I see that it has some advantages."

Egwene frowned, as if trying to figure out what advantages there could be in lessened power. Finally, she shook her head. "Elayne once mentioned a room to me in the Tower, filled with objects of power. I assume it really exists?"

"Of course," Siuan said. "The basement storeroom. It's in the second level of the basement, on the northeast side. Little room with a plain wooden door, but you can't miss it. It's the only one in the hallway that is locked."

Egwene nodded to herself. "Well, I can't defeat Elaida through brute force. Still, it is nice to know of that. Is there anything else remarkable to report?"

"Not at the moment, Mother," Siuan said.

"Then return and get some sleep." Egwene hesitated. "And next time, we'll meet in two days. Here in the novices' dining hall, though we may want to begin meeting out in the city. I don't trust this place. If there was a Forsaken in our camp, I'd bet half my father's inn that there's one spying on the White Tower too."

Siuan nodded. "Very well." She closed her eyes, and soon found herself blinking awake back in Bryne's tent. The candle was out, and she could hear Bryne breathing quietly from his pallet on the other side of the tent. She sat up and looked across at him, though it was too dark to see anything more than shadows. Strangely, after talking about Forsaken and Asha'man, the sturdy general's presence comforted her.

Is there anything else remarkable to report, Egwene? Siuan thought idly, rising to change out of her dress behind the screen and put on her sleeping gown. *I think I might be in love. Is that remarkable enough?* To her, it seemed stranger than the taint being cleansed or a woman channeling *saidin.*

Shaking her head, she tucked the dream *ter'angreal* back in its hiding place, then snuggled down beneath her blankets.

She'd forgo the mice, just this once.

CHAPTER
9

Leaving Malden

A cool spring breeze tickled Perrin's face. Such a breeze should have carried with it the scents of pollen and crisp morning dew, of dirt overturned by sprouts pushing into the light, of new life and an earth reborn.

This breeze carried with it only the scents of blood and death.

Perrin turned his back to the breeze, knelt down and inspected the wagon's wheels. The vehicle was a sturdy construction of hickory, wood darkened with age. It appeared to be in good repair, but Perrin had learned to be careful when dealing with equipment from Malden. The Shaido didn't scorn wagons and oxen as they did horses, but they—like all Aiel—believed in traveling light. They hadn't maintained the wagons or carts, and Perrin had found more than one hidden flaw during his inspection.

"Next!" he bellowed as he checked the first wheel's hub. The comment was directed at the crowd of people waiting to speak with him.

"My Lord," a voice said. It was deep and rough, like wood scraping against wood. Gerard Arganda, First Captain of Ghealdan. His scent was of well-oiled armor. "I must press the issue of our departure. Allow me to ride ahead with Her Majesty."

The "Her Majesty" he referred to was Alliandre, Queen of Ghealdan. Perrin continued working with the wheel; he wasn't as familiar with carpentry as he was with smithing, but his father had taught each of his sons to recognize signs

of trouble in a wagon. Better to fix the problem before leaving than to be stranded halfway to the destination. Perrin
ran his fingers across the smooth, brown hickory. The grain
was clearly visible, and he tested for cracks with questing fingers, searching each point of stress. All four wheels
looked good.

"My Lord?" Arganda asked.

"We all march together," Perrin said. "That's my order,
Arganda. I won't have the refugees thinking that we're
abandoning them."

Refugees. There were over a hundred thousand of those
to care for. A hundred thousand! Light, that was far more
than lived in the entire Two Rivers. And Perrin was in
charge of feeding every one of them. Wagons. Many men
didn't understand the importance of a good wagon. He lay
down on his back, preparing to inspect the axles, and that
gave him a view of the overcast sky, partially blocked by
Malden's nearby city wall.

The city was large for one this far north in Altara. It was
almost more of a fortress than a city, with daunting walls
and towers. Until the day before, the land around this city
had been home to the Shaido Aiel, but they were gone now,
many killed, others fled, their captives freed by an alliance
between Perrin's forces and the Seanchan.

The Shaido had left him two things: a scent of blood on
the air and a hundred thousand refugees to care for. Though
he was happy to give them their freedom, his goal in liberating Malden had been far different: the rescue of Faile.

Another Aiel group had been advancing on his position,
but they'd slowed, then camped, and were no longer rushing toward Malden. Perhaps they'd been warned by Shaido
fleeing the battle that they had a large army before them,
one that had defeated the Shaido despite their channelers. It
seemed this new group behind Perrin had as little desire to
engage him as he had to engage them.

That gave him time. A little bit, at least.

Arganda was still watching. The captain wore his polished breastplate and had his slotted helmet under his arm.
The squat man wasn't a puffed-up fluff of an officer, but a
common man who had risen through the ranks. He fought
well and did as instructed. Usually.

"I'm not going to bend on this, Arganda," Perrin said, pulling himself along the damp ground beneath the wagon.

"Could we at least use gateways instead?" Arganda asked, kneeling down, graying hair—shorn short—nearly brushing the ground as he peeked under the wagon.

"The Asha'man are near dead from fatigue," Perrin snapped. "You know that."

"They're too tired for a large gateway," Arganda said, "but maybe they could send a small group. My lady is exhausted from her captivity! Surely you don't mean for her to march!"

"The refugees are tired too," Perrin said. "Alliandre can have a horse to ride, but she's leaving when the rest of us do. Light send that's soon."

Arganda sighed, but nodded. He stood up as Perrin ran fingers along the axle. He could tell stress in wood with a glance, but he preferred touch. Touch was more reliable. There was always a crack or a splintering where wood weakened, and you could feel it near to breaking. Wood was reliable like that.

Unlike men. Unlike himself.

He gritted his teeth. He didn't want to think about that. He had to keep working, had to keep doing *something* to distract himself. He liked to work. He'd been given far too few opportunities for it lately. "Next!" he said, voice echoing against the bottom of the wagon.

"My Lord, we should attack!" a boisterous voice declared from beside the vehicle.

Perrin thumped his head back against the well-trampled grass, closing his eyes. Bertain Gallenne, Lord Captain of the Winged Guards, was to Mayene what Arganda was to Ghealdan. Aside from that single similarity, the two captains were about as different as men could be. Perrin could see Bertain's large, beautifully worked boots, with clasps shaped like hawks, from beneath the wagon.

"My Lord," Bertain continued. "A fine charge from the Winged Guard would scatter that Aiel rabble, of this I'm certain. Why, we easily dealt with the Aiel here in the city!"

"We had the Seanchan, then," Perrin said, finishing with the rear axle and wriggling his way to the front to check the other one. He wore his old, stained coat. Faile would chastise him for that. He was supposed to present himself as a lord. But would she really expect him to wear a fine coat if he was going to spend an hour lying in the muddy grass, looking at the bottoms of wagons?

Faile wouldn't want him to be in the muddy grass in the first place. Perrin hesitated, hand on the front axle, thinking of her raven hair and distinctive Saldaean nose. She held the sum total of his love. She was everything to him.

He had succeeded—he'd saved her. So why did he feel as if things were nearly as bad as they had been? He should rejoice, he should be ecstatic, should be relieved. He'd worried so much about her during her captivity. And yet now, with her safety secure, everything still felt wrong. Somehow. In ways he couldn't explain.

Light! Would *nothing* just work as it was supposed to? He reached down for his pocket, wanting to finger the knotted cord he'd once carried there. But he'd thrown that away. *Stop it!* he thought. *She's back. We can go back to the way it was before. Can't we?*

"Yes, well," Bertain continued, "I suppose the departure of the Seanchan could be a problem in an assault. But that Aiel group camped out there is smaller than what we already defeated. And if you are worried, you could send word to that Seanchan general and bring her back. Surely she would wish to fight alongside us again!"

Perrin forced himself back to the moment. His own foolish problems were irrelevant; right now, he needed to get these wagons moving. The front axle was good. He turned and pushed himself out from underneath the wagon.

Bertain was of medium height, though the three plumes rising from his helmet made him look taller. He had on his red eye patch—Perrin didn't know where he'd lost the eye—and his armor gleamed. He seemed excited, as if he thought Perrin's silence meant they would attack.

Perrin stood, dusting off his plain brown trousers. "We're leaving," he said, then held up a hand to forbid further argument. "We defeated the septs here, but we had them dosed with forkroot and there were *damane* on our side. We're tired, wounded, and we have Faile back. There's no further reason to fight. We run."

Bertain didn't look satisfied, but he nodded and turned away, stomping across the muddy ground toward where his men sat their mounts. Perrin looked at the small group of people who waited in a cluster around the wagon to speak with him. Once, this kind of business had frustrated Perrin. It seemed like pointless work, as many of the supplicants already knew what his answer would be.

But they needed to hear those answers from him, and Perrin had come to understand the importance of that. Besides, their questions helped distract him from the strange tension he felt at having rescued Faile.

He walked toward the next wagon in line, his small entourage following him. There were a good fifty of the wagons set in a long caravan train. The first ones were loaded with salvage from Malden; the middle ones were in the process of being treated likewise, and he had only two left to inspect. He had wanted to be well out of Malden before sunset. That would probably carry him far enough away to be safe.

Unless these new Shaido decided to give chase in revenge. With the number of people Perrin had to move, a blind man would be able to track them.

The sun drooped toward the horizon, a shining spot behind the cloud cover. Light, but this was a mess, with the chaos of organizing refugees and separate army camps. Getting away was supposed to be the easy part!

The Shaido camp was a disaster. His people had scavenged and packed many of the abandoned tents. Now cleared, the ground around the city was trampled weeds and mud, littered with refuse. The Shaido, being Aiel, had preferred to camp *outside* the city walls, rather than within them. They were a strange people, no denying that. Who would spurn a nice bed, not to mention a better military position, to stay outside in tents?

Aiel despised cities, though. Most of the buildings had either been burned during the initial Shaido assault or looted for riches. Doors beaten down, windows shattered, possessions abandoned on the streets and trampled by *gai'shain* running back and forth to fetch water.

People still scurried about like insects, moving through the city gates and around the former Shaido camp, grabbing what they could to stow it for transport. They'd have to leave the wagons behind once they decided to Travel— Grady couldn't make a gateway big enough to pass a wagon through—but for now, the vehicles would be a big help. There were also a good number of oxen; someone else was inspecting those, making certain they were fit to pull the wagons. The Shaido had let many of the city's horses run off. A shame, that. But you made use of what you had.

Perrin reached the next wagon, beginning his inspection with the vehicle's long tongue, to which oxen would be harnessed. "Next!"

"My Lord," said a scratchy voice, "I believe that I am next."

Perrin glanced over at the speaker: Sebban Balwer, his secretary. The man had a dry, pinched face and a perpetual stoop that made him look almost like a roosting vulture. Though his coat and breeches were clean, it seemed to Perrin that they should shed puffs of dust each time Balwer stepped. He smelled musty, like an old book.

"Balwer," Perrin said, running his fingers over the tongue, then checking the harness straps, "I thought you were speaking with the captives."

"I have, indeed, been busy with my work there," Balwer said. "However, I grew curious. Did you have to let the Seanchan take *all* of the captive Shaido channelers with them?"

Perrin glanced at the musty secretary. The Wise Ones who could channel had been knocked unconscious by forkroot; they'd been given over to the Seanchan while still unconscious, to do with as they pleased. The decision had not made Perrin popular with the Aiel among his allies, but he would *not* have those channelers running about to take revenge on him.

"I don't see why I would want them," he said to Balwer.

"Well, my Lord, there is much of great interest to learn. For instance, it appears that many of the Shaido are ashamed of their clan's behavior. The Wise Ones themselves were at odds. Also, they have had dealings with some very curious individuals who offered them objects of power from the Age of Legends. Whoever they were, they could make gateways."

"Forsaken," Perrin said with a shrug, stooping down on one knee to check the right front wheel. "I doubt we'll figure out which ones. Probably had a disguise on."

From the corner of his eyes, he saw Balwer purse his lips at that comment.

"You disagree?" Perrin asked.

"No, my Lord," he said. "The 'objects' the Shaido were given are very suspect, by my estimation. The Aiel were duped, though for what reason, I cannot yet fathom. However, if we had more time to search the city. . . ."

Light! Was *every* person in the camp going to ask him for something they knew they couldn't have? He got down on the ground to check the back of the wheel hub. Something about it bothered him. "We already know that the Forsaken oppose us, Balwer. They won't rightly welcome Rand in with open arms to seal them away again, or whatever it is he's going to do."

Blasted colors, showing Rand in his mind's eye! He pushed those away again. They appeared whenever he thought of Rand or Mat, bringing visions of them.

"Anyway," Perrin continued, "I don't see what you need me to do. We'll take the Shaido *gai'shain* with us. The Maidens captured their fair share. You can interrogate them. But we're leaving this place."

"Yes, my Lord," Balwer said. "It's just a shame we lost those Wise Ones. My experience has been that they are those among the Aiel with the most . . . understanding."

"The Seanchan wanted them," Perrin said. "So they got them. I wouldn't let Edarra bully me on the point, and what is done is done. What do you expect of me, Balwer?"

"Perhaps a message could be sent," Balwer said, "to ask some questions of the Wise Ones when they awake. I. . . ." He stopped, then stooped down to glance at Perrin. "My Lord, this is rather distracting. Couldn't we find someone else to inspect the wagons?"

"Everyone else is either too tired or too busy," Perrin said. "I want most of the refugees waiting in the camps to move when we give the marching order. And most of our soldiers are scavenging the city for supplies—each handful of grain they find will be needed. Half the stuff's spoiled anyway. I can't help with that work, since I need to be where people can find me." He'd accepted that, cross though it made him.

"Yes, my Lord," Balwer said. "But surely you can be somewhere accessible *without* crawling under wagons."

"It's work I can do while people talk to me," Perrin said. "You don't need my hands, just my tongue. And that tongue is telling you to forget the Aiel."

"But—"

"There is nothing more I can do, Balwer," Perrin said firmly, glancing up at him through the spokes of the wheel. "We're heading north. I'm done with the Shaido; they can burn for all I care."

Balwer pursed his thin lips again, and he smelled just slightly of annoyance. "Of course, my Lord," he said, giving a quick bow. Then he withdrew.

Perrin squirmed out and stood up, nodding to a young woman who stood in a dirty dress and worn shoes at the side of the line of wagons. "Go fetch Lyncon," he said. "Tell him to have a look at this wheel hub. I think the bearing's been stripped, and the blasted thing looks ready to roll right off."

The young woman nodded, running away. Lyncon was a master carpenter who had been unfortunate enough to be visiting relatives in Cairhien when the Shaido attacked. He'd had the will beaten nearly out of him. Perhaps he should have been the one to inspect the wagons, but with that haunted look in his eyes, Perrin wasn't sure how far he trusted the man to do a proper inspection. He seemed good enough at fixing problems when they were pointed out to him, though.

And the truth was, as long as Perrin kept moving, he felt he was doing something, making progress. Not thinking about other issues. Wagons were easy to fix. They weren't like people, not at all.

Perrin turned, glancing across the empty camp, pocked with firepits and discarded rags. Faile was walking back toward the city; she'd been organizing some of her followers to scout the area. She was striking. Beautiful. That beauty wasn't just in her face or her lean figure, it was in how easily she commanded people, how quickly she always knew what to do. She was clever in a way Perrin never had been.

He wasn't stupid; he just liked to think about things. But he'd never been good with people, not like Mat or Rand. Faile had shown him that he didn't need to be good with people, or even with women, as long as he could make *one* person understand him. He didn't have to be good at talking to anyone else as long as he could talk to her.

But now he couldn't find the words to say. He worried about what had happened to her during her captivity, but the possibilities didn't bother him. They made him angry, but none of what had happened was her fault. You did what you had to to survive. He respected her for her strength.

Light! he thought. *I'm thinking again! Need to keep working.* "Next!" he bellowed, stooping down to continue his inspection of the wagon.

"If I'd seen your face and nothing else, lad," a hearty voice said, "I'd assume that we'd lost this battle."

Perrin turned with surprise. He hadn't realized that Tam al'Thor was one of those waiting to speak with him. That crowd had thinned, but there were still some messengers and attendants. At the back, the blocky, solid sheepherder leaned on his quarterstaff as he waited. His hair had all gone to silver. Perrin could remember a time when it had been a deep black. Back when Perrin had just been a boy, before he'd known a hammer or a forge.

Perrin's fingers reached down, touching the hammer at his waist. He'd chosen it over the axe. It had been the right decision, but he'd still lost control of himself in the battle for Malden. Was that what bothered him?

Or was it how much he'd enjoyed the killing?

"What do you need, Tam?" he asked.

"I'm only bringing a report, my Lord," Tam said. "The Two Rivers men are organized for the march, each man with two tents on his back, just in case. We couldn't use water from the city, on account of the forkroot, so I sent some lads to the aqueduct to fill some barrels there. We could use a wagon to bring them back."

"Done," Perrin said, smiling. Finally, someone who did things that were needed without having to ask first! "Tell the Two Rivers men that I intend to have them back home as soon as possible. The moment Grady and Neald are strong enough to make a gateway. That could be a while, though."

"That's appreciated, my Lord," Tam said. It felt so strange for him to use a title. "Can I speak to you alone for a moment, though?"

Perrin nodded, noticing that Lyncon was coming—his limp was distinctive—to look at the wagon. Perrin moved with Tam away from the group of attendants and guards, walking into the shadow of Malden's wall. Moss grew green against the base of the massive blocks making up the fortification; it was strange that the moss was far brighter than the trampled, muddied weeds under their feet. Nothing but moss seemed green this spring.

"What is it, Tam?" Perrin asked as soon as they were far enough away.

Tam rubbed his face; there was gray stubble coming in. Perrin had pushed his men hard these last few days, and there hadn't been time for shaving. Tam wore a simple blue wool coat, and the thick cloth was probably a welcome shield against the mountain breeze.

"The lads are wondering, Perrin," Tam said, a little less formal now that they were alone. "Did you mean what you said about giving up on Manetheren?"

"Aye," Perrin said. "That banner has been nothing but trouble since it first came out. The Seanchan, and everyone else, might as well know. I'm no king."

"You have a queen who's sworn you as her liege."

He considered Tam's words, working out the best response. Once that kind of behavior had made people think he was slow of thought. Now people assumed his thoughtfulness meant that Perrin was crafty and keen minded. What a difference a few fancy words in front of your name made!

"I think you're right, in what you did," Tam said, surprisingly. "Calling the Two Rivers Manetheren would not only have antagonized the Seanchan, but the Queen of Andor herself. It would imply that you meant to hold more than just the Two Rivers, that perhaps you wanted to conquer all that Manetheren once held."

Perrin shook his head. "I don't mean to conquer anything, Tam. Light! I don't mean to hold what people say I've got. The sooner that Elayne takes her throne and sends a proper lord out to the Two Rivers, the better. We can be done with all of this Lord Perrin business and things can go back to normal."

"And Queen Alliandre?" Tam asked.

"She can swear to Elayne instead," Perrin said stubbornly. "Or maybe directly to Rand. He seems to like scooping up kingdoms. Like a child playing a game of wobbles."

Tam smelled concerned. Troubled. Perrin looked away. Things should be simpler. They *should* be. "What?"

"I just thought you were over this," Tam said.

"Nothing has changed from the days before Faile was

taken," Perrin said. "I still don't like that wolf head banner either. I think maybe it's time to take that one down too."

"The men believe in that banner, Perrin, lad," Tam said quietly. He had a soft way about him, but that made you listen when he spoke. Of course, he also usually spoke sense. "I pulled you aside because I wanted to warn you. If you provide a chance for the lads to return to the Two Rivers, some will go. But not many. I've heard most swear that they'll follow you to Shayol Ghul. They know the Last Battle is coming—who couldn't know that, with all of the signs lately? They don't intend to be left behind." He hesitated. "And neither do I, I reckon." He smelled of determination.

"We'll see," Perrin said, frowning. "We'll see."

He sent Tam off with orders to requisition a wagon and take it for those water barrels. The soldiers would listen; Tam was Perrin's First Captain, though that seemed backward to Perrin. He didn't know much of the man's past, but Tam had fought in the Aiel War, long ago; he'd held a sword before Perrin had been born. And now he followed Perrin's orders.

They all did. And they wanted to keep doing so! Hadn't they learned? He rested back against the wall, not walking back to his attendants, standing in the shadow.

Now that he seized upon it, he realized that was a part of what was bothering him. Not the whole of it, but some, tied in with what was troubling him. Even now that Faile had returned.

He hadn't been a good leader lately. He'd never been a model one, of course, not even when Faile had been there to guide him. But during her absence, he'd been worse. Far worse. He'd ignored his orders from Rand, ignored everything, all to get her back.

But what else was a man supposed to do? His wife had been kidnapped!

He'd saved her. But in doing so, he'd abandoned everyone else. And because of him, men were dead. Good men. Men who had trusted in him.

Standing in that shadow, he remembered a moment— only a day past—when an ally had fallen to Aiel arrows, his heart poisoned by Masema. Aram had been a friend, one that Perrin had discarded in his quest to save Faile. Aram had deserved better.

I should never have let that Tinker pick up a sword, he thought, but he didn't want to deal with this problem right now. He *couldn't.* There was too much to do. He moved away from the wall, planning to inspect the last wagon in line.

"Next!" he barked as he began again.

Aravine Carnel stepped forward. The Amadician woman no longer wore her *gai'shain* robes; instead she had on a simple light green dress, not clean, that had been pulled out of the salvage. She was plump but her face still bore a haggard cast from her days as a captive. There was a determination about her. She was surprisingly good at organization, and Perrin suspected she was of noble heritage. She had the scent of it about her: self-confidence, an ease giving commands. It was a wonder those things had survived her captivity.

As he knelt down to look at the first wheel, he figured it was odd that Faile had chosen Aravine to supervise the refugees. Why not one of the youths from *Cha Faile*? Those dandies could be annoying, but they'd shown a surprising measure of competence.

"My Lord," Aravine said, her practiced curtsy another indication of her background. "I have finished organizing the people for departure."

"So soon?" Perrin asked, looking up from the wheel.

"It was not so difficult as we expected, my Lord. I commanded them to gather by nationality, then by town of birth. Not surprisingly, the Cairhienin form the largest bulk of them, followed by Altarans, then Amadicians, with some smattering of others. A few Domani, some Taraboners, the occasional Borderlander or Tairen."

"How many can stand a day or two of marching without a ride in the wagons?"

"Most of them, my Lord," she said. "The sick and elderly were expelled from the city when the Shaido took it. The people here are accustomed to being worked hard. They're exhausted, Lord, but none too eager to be waiting here with those other Shaido camped not half a day's march away."

"All right," Perrin said. "Start them marching immediately."

"Immediately?" Aravine asked with surprise.

He nodded. "I want them on that road, marching northward, as soon as you can get them going. I'll send Alliandre and her guard to lead the way." That ought to keep

Arganda from complaining, and it would get the refugees out of the way. The Maidens would be far better, and far more efficient, at gathering supplies alone. The scavenging was nearly finished anyway. His people would have to survive on the road for only a few weeks. After that, they could jump via gateway to someplace more secure. Andor, perhaps, or Cairhien.

Those Shaido behind had him anxious. They could decide to attack at any time. Better to get away and remove the temptation.

Aravine curtsied and hurried away to make preparations, and Perrin thanked the Light for someone else who didn't see a need to question or second-guess him. He sent a boy to inform Arganda of the impending march, then finished his inspection of the wagon. After that, he stood up, wiping his hands on his trousers. "Next!" he said.

Nobody stepped forward. The only people remaining around him were guards, messenger boys and a few wagoneers waiting to hitch up their oxen and move the wagons off for loading. The Maidens had made a large pile of foodstuffs and supplies in the middle of the former camp, and Perrin could make out Faile there working to organize it.

Perrin sent the ring of attendants with him over to help her, then found himself alone. With nothing to do.

Just what he'd wanted to avoid.

The wind blew past again, carrying that awful stench of death. It also carried memories. The fury of the battle, the passion and thrill of each swing. Aiel were excellent warriors—the best the land knew. Each exchange had been close, and Perrin had earned his share of cuts and bruises, though those had since been Healed.

Fighting the Aiel had made him feel alive. Each one he'd slain had been an expert with the spears; each one could have killed him. But he'd won. During those moments of fighting, he'd felt a driving passion. The passion of finally *doing* something. After two months of waiting, each blow had meant a step closer to finding Faile.

No more talking. No more planning. He'd found purpose. And now it was gone.

He felt hollow. It was like . . . like the time when his father had promised him something special as a gift for Winternight. Perrin had waited months, eager, doing his chores to earn the unknown gift. When he'd finally received the small wooden horse, he'd been excited for a moment. But the next day, he'd been shockingly melancholy. Not because of the gift, but because there had no longer been anything to strive for. The excitement was gone, and only then had he realized how much more precious he'd found that anticipation than the gift itself.

Soon after that he'd begun visiting Master Luhhan's forge, eventually becoming his apprentice.

He was glad to have Faile back. He rejoiced. And yet, now what was there for him? These blasted men saw him as their leader. Some even thought of him as their king! He'd never asked for that. He'd had them put away the banners every time they put them out, up until Faile had persuaded him that using them would be an advantage. He still didn't believe that the wolfhead banner belonged there, flapping insolently above his camp.

But could he take it down? The men *did* look to it. He could smell pride on them every time they passed it. He couldn't turn them away. Rand would need their aid—he'd need everyone's aid—at the Last Battle.

The Last Battle. Could a man like him, a man who didn't want to be in charge, lead these forces to the most important moment in their lives?

The colors swirled, showing him Rand, sitting in what appeared to be a stone Tairen home. Perrin's old friend had a dark cast to his expression, like a man troubled by weighty thoughts. Even sitting like that, Rand looked regal. *He* was what a king was supposed to be, with that rich red coat, that noble bearing. Perrin was just a blacksmith.

He sighed, shaking his head and dispelling the image. He needed to seek out Rand. He could feel something tugging at him, *pulling* him.

Rand needed him. That had to be his focus now.

CHAPTER
10

The Last of the Tabac

Rodel Ituralde puffed quietly on his pipe, smoke curling from it like the sinuous coils of a snake. The smoke tendrils wrapped around themselves, pooling at the ceiling above him, then leaking out through cracks in the roof of the ramshackle shed. The boards in the walls were warped from age, opening slits to the outside, and the gray wood was cracked and splintering. A brazier burned in the corner and winds whistled through the cracks in the walls. Ituralde faintly worried those winds would blow over the entire building.

He sat on a stool, several maps on the table before him. At the corner of the table, his tabac pouch weighed down a wrinkled piece of paper. The small square was weathered and folded from being carried in his inside coat pocket.

"Well?" Rajabi asked. Thick of neck and determined of attitude, he was brown-eyed, with a wide nose and a bulbous chin. He was completely bald now, and faintly resembled a large boulder. He tended to act like a boulder, too. It could take a lot of work to get him rolling, but once you did, he was bloody hard to stop. He had been one of the first to join Ituralde's cause, for all the fact that he had been poised to rebel against the king just a short time before.

It had been nearly two weeks since Ituralde's victory at Darluna. He'd extended himself far for that victory. Perhaps too far. *Ah, Alsalam,* he thought. *I hope this was all worth it, old friend. I hope you haven't just gone mad. Rajabi might be a boulder, but the Seanchan are an avalanche, and we've brought them thundering down upon us.*

"What now?" Rajabi prodded.

"We wait," Ituralde said. Light, but he hated waiting. "Then we fight. Or maybe we run again. I haven't made up my mind yet."

"The Taraboners—"

"Won't come," Ituralde said.

"They promised!"

"They did." Ituralde had gone to them himself, had roused them, had asked them to fight the Seanchan just one more time. They'd yelled and cheered, but had not followed with any haste. They would drag their feet. He'd gotten them to fight "one last time" on half a dozen different occasions now. They could see where this war was going, and he could no longer depend on them. If he'd ever been able to in the first place.

"Bloody cowards," Rajabi muttered. "Light burn them, then! We'll do it alone. We have before."

Ituralde took a long, contemplative puff on his pipe. He'd chosen to finally use the Two Rivers tabac. This pipeful was the last in his store; he'd been saving it for months, now. Good flavor. Best there was.

He studied his maps again, holding a smaller one up before him. He could use better maps, that was certain. "This new Seanchan general," Ituralde said, "is marshaling over three hundred thousand men, with a good two hundred *damane*."

"We've beat large forces before. Look what we did at Darluna! You crushed them, Rodel!"

And doing so had required every bit of craftiness, skill and luck Ituralde could muster. Even then, he'd lost well over half his men. Now he ran, limping, before this second, larger force of Seanchan.

This time, they weren't making any mistakes. The Seanchan didn't rely solely on their *raken*. His men had intercepted several foot scouts, and that meant dozens *hadn't* been caught. This time, the Seanchan knew Ituralde's true numbers and his true location.

His enemies were done being herded and goaded; instead they hunted him, relentlessly, avoiding his traps. Ituralde had planned to retreat deeper and deeper into Arad Doman; that would favor his forces and stretch the Seanchan supply lines. He'd figured he could keep it up for another four or five months. But those plans were useless now; they'd been made before Ituralde had discovered there was an entire bloody army of Aiel running about Arad Doman. If the reports were to be believed—and reports about Aiel were often exaggerations, so he wasn't sure how much *to* believe—there were upwards of a hundred thousand of them holding large sections of the north, Bandar Eban included.

A hundred thousand Aiel. That was as good as two hundred thousand Domani troops. Perhaps more. Ituralde well remembered the Blood Snow twenty years ago, when it had seemed he'd lost ten men for each Aiel who fell.

He was trapped, a walnut crushed between two stones. The best he'd been able to do was retreat here, to this abandoned *stedding*. That would give him an edge against the Seanchan. But only a small one. The Seanchan had a force six times the size of his own, and the greenest of commanders knew that fighting those odds was suicide.

"Have you ever seen a master juggler, Rajabi?" Ituralde asked, studying the map.

From the corner of his eye, Ituralde saw the bull-like man frown in confusion. "I've seen gleemen who—"

"No, not a gleeman. A master."

Rajabi shook his head.

Ituralde puffed in thought before speaking. "I did, once. He was the court bard of Caemlyn. Spry fellow, with a wit that might better have belonged in a common room, for all the way he was decorated. Bards don't often juggle; but this fellow didn't mind the request. He liked juggling to please the young Daughter-Heir, so I understand."

He removed the pipe from his mouth, tapping down the tabac.

"Rodel," Rajabi said. "The Seanchan. . . ."

Rodel held up a finger, situating his pipe before continuing. "The bard started by juggling three balls. Then he asked us if we thought he could do another. We cheered him on. He went to four, then five, then six. With each ball he added, our applause grew greater, and he always asked if we thought he could do another. Of course we said yes.

"Seven, eight, nine. Soon he had ten balls going in the air, flying in a pattern so complex that I couldn't track them. He had to strain to keep them going; he kept having to reach down and grab balls that he nearly missed. He was too lost in concentration to ask us if he should add another, but the crowd called for it. Eleven! Go for eleven! And so, his assistant tossed another ball into the mess."

Ituralde puffed.

"He dropped them?" Rajabi asked.

Rodel shook his head. "That last 'ball' wasn't actually a ball at all. It was some kind of Illuminator's trick; once it got halfway to the bard, it flashed and gave off a sudden burst of light and smoke. By the time our vision cleared, the bard was gone, and ten balls were lined up on the floor. When I looked around, I found him sitting at one of the tables with the rest of the diners, drinking a cup of, wine and flirting with Lord Finndal's wife."

Poor Rajabi looked completely dumbfounded. He liked his answers neat and straightforward. Ituralde usually felt the same way, but these days—with their unnaturally overcast skies and sense of perpetual gloom—made him philosophic.

He reached out and took the worn, folded sheet of paper off the table from beneath his tabac pouch. He handed it to Rajabi.

"'Strike hard against the Seanchan,'" Rajabi read. "'Push them away, force them into their boats and back across their bloody ocean. I'm counting on you, old friend. King Alsalam.'" Rajabi lowered the letter. "I know of his orders, Rodel. I didn't come into this because of him. I came because of you."

"Yes, but *I* fight because of him," Ituralde said. He was a king's man; he always would be. He stood up, tapping out his tabac and grinding the embers beneath the heel of his boot. He set the pipe aside and took the letter from Rajabi, then walked to the door.

He needed to make a decision. Stay and fight, or flee for a worse location, but gain a little more time?

The shack groaned and wind shook the trees as Ituralde stepped outside into the overcast morning. The shed wasn't Ogier-built, of course. It was too flimsy for that. This *stedding* had been abandoned for a long time. His men camped amid the trees. Hardly the best location for a war camp, but one made soup with the spices on hand; the *stedding* was far too useful to pass up. Another man might have fled to a city and hidden behind its walls, but here in these trees, the One Power was useless. Negating the Seanchan *damane* was better than walls, no matter how high.

We have to stay, Ituralde thought, watching his men work, digging in, erecting a palisade. He hated the thought of cutting down trees in a *stedding*. He'd known a few Ogier in his time, and respected them. These massive oaks probably held some lingering strength from the days when the Ogier had lived here. Cutting them down was a crime. But you did what you had to. Running might gain him more time, but it might just as easily *lose* him time. He had a few days here before the Seanchan hit him. If he could dig in well, he might force them into a siege. The *stedding* would make them hesitant, and the forests would work to the advantage of Ituralde's smaller force.

He hated letting himself get pinned in. That was probably why he'd considered for so long, even though, deep down, he'd already known that it was time to stop running. The Seanchan had finally caught him.

He continued along the ranks, nodding to working men, letting himself be seen. He had forty thousand troops left, which was a marvel, considering the odds they had faced. These men should have deserted. But they'd seen him win impossible battle after impossible battle, tossing ball after ball into the air to greater and greater applause. They thought he was unstoppable. They didn't understand that when one tossed more balls into the air, it wasn't just the *show* that became more spectacular.

The fall at the end grew more spectacular as well.

He kept his dark thoughts to himself as he and Rajabi continued through the forested camp, inspecting the palisade. It was progressing nicely, the men setting thick tree trunks into freshly dug troughs. After his inspection, Ituralde nodded to himself. "We stay, Rajabi. Pass the word."

"Some of the others say that staying here means dying for sure," Rajabi responded.

"They're wrong," Ituralde said.

"But—"

"Nothing is sure, Rajabi," Ituralde said. "Fill these trees inside the palisade with archers; they'll be almost as effective as towers. We'll need to set up a killing field outside. Cut down as many trees around the palisade here as possible, then set the logs inside as barriers, a second line of retreat. We'll hold strong. Perhaps I'm wrong about those Taraboners, and they'll ride to aid us. Or maybe the king has a hidden army stashed away to defend us. Blood and ashes, maybe we'll fight them off here on our own. We'll see how much they like fighting without their *damane*. We'll survive."

Rajabi straightened visibly, growing confident. That was the kind of talk Ituralde knew he expected. Like the others, Rajabi trusted the Little Wolf. They didn't believe he *could* fail.

Ituralde knew better. But if you were going to die, you did it with dignity. The young Ituralde had often dreamed of wars, of the glory of battle. The old Ituralde knew there was no such thing as glory to be had in battle. But there *was* honor.

"My Lord Ituralde!" a runner called, trotting along the inside of the unfinished palisade wall. He was a boy, young enough that the Seanchan would probably let him live. Otherwise Ituralde would have sent the lad, and those like him, away.

"Yes?" Ituralde asked, turning. Rajabi stood like a small mountain at his side.

"A man," the boy said, puffing. "The scouts caught him walking into the *stedding*."

"Come to fight for us?" Ituralde said. It was not uncommon for an army to draw recruits. There were always those tempted by the lure of glory, or at least by the lure of steady meals.

"No, my Lord," the boy said, puffing. "He says he's come to see you."

"Seanchan?" Rajabi barked.

The boy shook his head. "No. But he's got nice clothes."

Some lord's messenger, then. Domani, or perhaps a Taraboner renegade. Whoever he was, he could hardly make their situation worse. "And he came alone?"

"Yes, sir."

Brave man. "Bring him, then," Ituralde said.

"Where will you receive him, my Lord?"

"What?" Ituralde snapped. "You think I'm some fancy merchant with a palace? The field here will do. Go get him, but take your time getting back. And make sure he's properly guarded."

The boy nodded and ran off. Ituralde waved over some soldiers and sent them running for Wakeda and the other officers. Shimron was dead, burned to char by a *damane*'s fireball. Too bad, that. Ituralde would rather have kept him than many of the others.

Most of the officers arrived before the stranger. Lanky Ankaer. One-eyed Wakeda, who might otherwise have been a handsome man. Squat Melarned. Youthful Lidrin, who continued to follow Ituralde after his father's death.

"What is this I hear?" Wakeda asked, folding his arms as he strode up. "We're staying in this death trap? Rodel, we don't have the troops to resist. If they come, we'll be trapped here."

"You're right," Ituralde said simply.

Wakeda turned to the others, then back to Ituralde, a little of his irritation deflated in the face of Ituralde's frank answer. "Well . . . why don't we run, then?" He blustered a lot less now than he had just months ago, when Ituralde had first begun this campaign.

"I won't give you sugar and lies," Ituralde said, looking at them each in turn. "We're in a bad shape. But we'll be in a *worse* shape if we run. We've got no more holes to hide in. These trees will work to our advantage, and we can fortify. The *stedding* will negate the *damane*, and that alone is worth the price of staying. We fight here."

Ankaer nodded, seeming to understand the gravity of the situation. "We have to trust him, Wakeda. He's led us right so far."

Wakeda nodded. "I suppose."

Bloody fools. Four months ago, half of them would have killed him on sight for staying loyal to the king. Now they thought he could do the impossible. It was a pity; he was beginning to think he could have brought them back to Al-salam as loyalists. "All right," he said, pointing at various spots along their fortification. "Here's what we're going to do to shore up the weak points. I want . . ."

He trailed off as he saw a group approaching through the clearing. The messenger boy, accompanied by a squad of soldiers, escorting a man in red and gold.

Something about the newcomer drew Ituralde's eyes. Perhaps it was the height; the young man was as tall as an Aiel, and fair of hair like them as well. But no Aiel dressed

in a fine red coat with sharp golden embroidery. There was
a sword at his side, and the way the newcomer walked made
Ituralde think he knew how to use it. He strode with firm,
determined steps, as if he thought the soldiers around him
an honor guard. A lord, then, and one accustomed to command. Why had he come in person, rather than sending a
messenger?

The young lord stopped a short length in front of Ituralde
and his generals, looking at each of them in turn, then focused on Ituralde. "Rodel Ituralde?" he asked. What accent
was that? Andoran?

"Yes," Ituralde said cautiously.

The young man nodded. "Bashere's description was accurate. You appear to be boxing yourself in, here. Do you
honestly expect to hold against the Seanchan army? They
are many times your size, and your Tarabon allies do not
appear . . . eager to join you in your defense."

He had good intelligence, whoever he was. "I am not in
the habit of discussing my defenses with strangers." Ituralde
studied the young lord. He was fit—lean and hard, though
it was difficult to tell with the coat on. He favored his right
hand, and on closer inspection, Ituralde noticed that the left
hand was missing. Both of his forearms had some kind of
strange red and gold tattoo on them.

Those eyes. Those were eyes which had seen death a
number of times. Not just a young *lord*. A young *general*.
Ituralde narrowed his eyes. "Who are you?"

The stranger met his eyes. "I am Rand al'Thor, the
Dragon Reborn. And I need you. You and your army."

Several of those with Ituralde cursed, and Ituralde
glanced at them. Wakeda was incredulous, Rajabi surprised, young Lidrin openly dismissive.

Ituralde looked back at the newcomer. The Dragon Reborn? This youth? He supposed it could be possible. Most
rumors agreed that the Dragon Reborn was a young man
with red hair. But, then, rumors also claimed he was ten
feet tall, and still others said his eyes glowed in dim light.
And then there were the stories of him appearing in the
sky at Falme. Blood and ashes, Ituralde didn't know if he
believed that the Dragon *had* been reborn in the first place!

"I haven't time to argue," the stranger said, face impassive. He seemed . . . older than he looked. He didn't appear

to care that he was surrounded by armed soldiers. In fact, his coming alone . . . it should have seemed like such a foolish act. Instead it made Ituralde thoughtful. Only one such as the Dragon Reborn himself could stride into a war camp like this, completely alone, and *expect* to be obeyed.

Burn him, if that fact by itself didn't make Ituralde want to believe him. Either this man was who he claimed to be or he was an utter lunatic.

"If we go outside the *stedding*, I will prove I can channel," the stranger said. "That should count for something. Give me leave, and I'll have ten thousand Aiel here and several Aes Sedai, all of whom will swear to you that I am who I say."

The rumors also said Aiel followed the Dragon Reborn. The men around Ituralde coughed and glanced about uncomfortably. Many had been Dragonsworn before coming to Ituralde. With the right words, this Rand al'Thor—or whoever he was—might be able turn Ituralde's camp against itself.

"Even if we assume that I believe you," Ituralde said carefully, "I don't see that it matters. I have a war to fight. You have other business to concern you, I assume."

"*You* are my concern," al'Thor said, eyes so hard that they seemed ready to burrow into Ituralde's skull and search about inside for anything of use. "You must make peace with the Seanchan. This war gains us nothing. I want you up on the Borderlands; I can't spare men to guard the Blight, and the Borderlanders themselves have abandoned their duties."

"I have orders," Ituralde said, shaking his head. Wait. He wouldn't do as this youth asked if he *didn't* have orders. Except . . . those eyes. Alsalam had had eyes like that, when they were both younger. Eyes that demanded obedience.

"Your orders," al'Thor said. "They are from the king? That is why you throw yourselves against the Seanchan as you do?"

Ituralde nodded.

"I've heard of you, Rodel Ituralde," al'Thor said. "Men I trust, men I respect, trust and respect *you*. Rather than fleeing and hiding, you hunker down here to fight a battle you know will kill you. All because of your loyalty to your king. I commend that. But it is time to turn away and fight a battle that means something. One that means *everything*. Come with me, and I'll give you the throne of Arad Doman."

Ituralde stood up sharply, alert. "After commending my loyalty, you expect me to unseat my own king!"

"Your king is *dead*," al'Thor said. "Either that, or his mind has been melted like wax. More and more, I think Graendal has him. I see her touch on the chaos in this land. Whatever orders you have likely came from her. Why she wants you fighting the Seanchan, I haven't yet been able to determine."

Ituralde snorted. "You speak of one of the Forsaken as if you've had her as a dinner guest."

Al'Thor met his eyes again. "I remember each of them— their faces, their mannerisms, the way they speak and act—as if I've known them for a thousand years. I remember them better than I remember my own childhood, sometimes. I am the Dragon Reborn."

Ituralde blinked. *Burn me,* he thought. *I believe him. Bloody ashes!* "Let's . . . let's see this proof of yours."

There were objections, of course, mostly from Lidrin, who thought it too dangerous. The others were shaken. Here was the man they'd sworn themselves to without ever meeting him. There seemed to be a . . . a *force* about al'Thor, drawing Ituralde in, demanding that he do as asked. Well, he'd see the proof, first.

They sent runners for horses to ride out of the *stedding*, but al'Thor spoke as if Ituralde was his man already. "Perhaps Alsalam lives," al'Thor said as they waited. "If so, I can see that you would not want his throne. Would you like Amadicia? I will need someone to rule there and keep an eye on the Seanchan. The Whitecloaks fight there now; I'm not sure if I'll be able to stop that conflict before the Last Battle."

The Last Battle. Light! "I won't take it if you kill the king there," Ituralde said. "If the Whitecloaks have already killed him, or if the Seanchan have, then perhaps."

King! What was he saying? *Burn you!* he thought to himself. *At least wait until the proof is given before agreeing to accept thrones!* There was a way about this man, the way he discussed events like the Last Battle—events that mankind had been fearing for thousands of years—as if they were items on the daily camp report.

Soldiers arrived with their horses, and Ituralde mounted, as did al'Thor, Wakeda, Rajabi, Ankaer, Melarned, Lidrin and a half-dozen lesser officers.

"I've brought a large number of Aiel into your lands," Rand al'Thor said as they began to ride. "I had hoped to use them to restore order, but they are taking longer than I'd wished. I'm planning to secure the members of the merchant council; perhaps once I have them in hand, I'll be able to improve the stability of the area. What do you think?"

Ituralde didn't know what to think. Securing the merchant council? That sounded like kidnapping them. What had Ituralde gotten himself into? "It could work," he found himself saying. "Light, it's probably the best plan, all things considered."

Al'Thor nodded, looking forward as they passed out of the palisade and moved out along a trail toward the edge of the *stedding*. "I'll have to secure the Borderlands, anyway. I will care for your homeland. Burn those Borderlanders! What are they up to? No. No, not yet. They can wait. No, he'll do. He can hold it. I'll send him with Asha'man." Suddenly, al'Thor turned to Ituralde. "What could you do if I gave you a hundred men who could channel?"

"Madmen?"

"No, most of them are stable," al'Thor said, taking no apparent offense. "Whatever madness they incurred before I cleansed the taint is still there—removing the taint didn't heal them—but few of them were far gone. And they won't get worse, now that *saidin* is clean."

Saidin? Clean? If Ituralde had his own men who could channel. . . . His own *damane*, in a way. Ituralde scratched his chin. It was coming at him quickly—but, then, a general had to be able to react quickly. "I could use them well," he said. "Very well."

"Good," al'Thor said. They had left the *stedding*; the air felt different. "You've got a lot of land to watch, but many of the channelers I'll give you can spin gateways."

"Gateways?" Ituralde asked.

Al'Thor glanced at him, then seemed to grit his teeth, closing his eyes, shaking as if nauseated. Ituralde sat upright, suddenly alert, hand on his sword. Poison? Was the man wounded?

But no, al'Thor opened his eyes, and there seemed to be a look of ecstasy in those depths. He turned, waving his hand, and a line of light split the air in front of him. Men around Ituralde cursed, backing up. It was one thing for a man to claim he could channel; it was another to see him do so in front of you!

"That's a gateway," al'Thor said as the line of light turned around, opening a large black hole in the air. "Depending on the Asha'man's strength, a gateway can be made wide enough to drive wagons through. You can travel nearly anywhere with speed, sometimes instantly, depending on circumstances. With a few trained Asha'man, your army could dine in Caemlyn in the morning, then have lunch in Tanchico a few hours later."

Ituralde rubbed his chin. "Well now, *that*'s a thing to see. A thing to see indeed." If this man spoke truthfully, and these gateways really *did* work. . . . "With *this* I could clear the Seanchan out of Tarabon, and maybe off the land entirely!"

"No," al'Thor snapped. "We make peace with them. From what my scouts say, it's going to be hard enough to bring them to agreement without promising them your head. I won't rile them further. There is no *time* for squabbling. We have more important matters to be about."

"Nothing is more important than my homeland," Ituralde said. "Even if those orders are forged, I know Alsalam. He would agree with me. We won't stand for foreign troops on the soil of Arad Doman."

"A promise, then," al'Thor said. "I will see the Seanchan out of Arad Doman. I promise you this. But we don't fight them away any further than that. In exchange, you go to the Borderlands and protect against an invasion there. Hold back the Trollocs if they come, and lend me some of your officers to help secure Arad Doman. It will be easier to restore order if the people see that their own lords are working with me."

Ituralde considered, though he knew already what his answer would be. That gateway could spirit his men away from this death trap. With Aiel on his side—with the Dragon Reborn as an ally—he really *did* have a chance of keeping Arad Doman secure. An honorable death was a good thing.

But the ability to keep on fighting with honor . . . that was a prize far more precious.

"Agreed," Ituralde said, holding out a hand.

Al'Thor took it. "Go break camp. You're to be in Saldaea by nightfall."

CHAPTER
II

The Death of Adrin

I think he should be beaten again, said Lerian, moving
her fingers in the complex motions of Maiden handtalk.
*He is like a child, and when a child touches something
dangerous, the child is beaten. If a child hurts himself because he was not taught properly to stay away from knives,
then the shame is upon his parents.*

The previous beating did not seem to do any good, Surial
replied. *He accepted it like a man, not a child, but did not
change his actions.*

Then we must try again, Lerian replied.

Aviendha dropped her rock into the pile by the watch-
post, then turned around. She did not acknowledge the
Maidens who watched the way into the camp, and they did
not acknowledge her. Speaking to her while she was being
punished would only heighten her shame, and her spear-
sisters would not do that.

She also didn't indicate that she understood their conversation. While nobody expected a former Maiden to forget
handtalk, it was best to be unobtrusive. The handtalk belonged to the Maidens.

Aviendha selected a large stone from a second pile,
then began to walk back into camp. If the Maidens continued their conversation, she could not tell, as she could
no longer see their hands. But their discussion lingered
with her. They were angered that Rand al'Thor had gone
to meet with the general Rodel Ituralde without guards. It
was not the first time he had acted so foolishly, and yet he
seemed unwilling—or unable—to learn the proper way.
Each time he put himself in danger without protection, he

insulted the Maidens as surely as if he had slapped each
one in the face.

Aviendha probably had some small *toh* toward her spear-
sisters. Teaching Rand al'Thor of Aiel ways had been her
task, and she had quite obviously failed. Unfortunately, she
had a much greater *toh* toward the Wise Ones, even if she
still didn't know the reason. Her lesser duty to her spear-
sisters would have to wait for an appropriate time.

Her arms ached from carrying rocks. They were smooth
and heavy; she had been required to dig them out of the
river beside the manor house. Only her time spent with
Elayne—when she had been forced to bathe in water—had
given her the strength to walk into that river. In that, she
had not shamed herself. And at least this river was a small
one—wetlanders might inaccurately call it a stream. A
stream was a tiny mountain runoff in which you could dip
your hands or fill a waterskin. Anything too large to step
across was definitely a river.

The day was overcast, as usual, and the camp was subdued. Men who had bustled just days before—when the Aiel
had arrived—were more lethargic now. The camp wasn't
by any means unkempt; Davram Bashere was too careful a commander to allow that, wetlander though he was.
However, the men *did* move more slowly. She had heard
some of them complain that the dark sky was dampening
their moods. How strange wetlanders were! What did the
weather have to do with one's mood? She could understand
being displeased that no raids were approaching, or that a
hunt had gone poorly. But because there were clouds in the
sky? Was shade so poorly appreciated here?

She shook her head, continuing on her way. She had chosen stones which would strain her muscles. To do otherwise
would have been to make light of her punishment, and she
wouldn't do that—although each step pained her honor. She
had to cross through the entire camp, in full sight, doing
work that was useless! She would rather have been naked
before them all outside of the sweat tent. She would rather
have run a thousand laps, or been beaten so hard that she
couldn't walk.

She reached the side of the manor house and deposited
her stone with a hidden sigh of relief. Two wetlander soldiers from Bashere's army stood guarding the door into the

manor, a counterpart to the two Maidens at the other end of Aviendha's trek. As she stooped and picked up a large stone from a second pile by the wall, she overheard them speaking.

"Burn me, but it's hot," one of the men complained.

"Hot?" the other replied, glancing at the overcast sky. "You're jesting."

The first guard waved his hand at himself, puffing out and sweating. "How can you not feel that?"

"You must have a fever or something."

The first guard shook his head. "I just don't like the heat, that's all."

Aviendha picked up her rock and began to walk back across the green. After some contemplation, she had determined that being a wetlander required one common attribute: a fondness for complaining. During her first months in the wetlands, she had considered this shameful. Did that guard not care that he was losing face in front of his fellow by exposing his weakness?

They were all like that, even Elayne. If you listened to her talk about the aches, sicknesses and frustrations of her pregnancy, you would almost think she was approaching death! However, if complaining was something that Elayne did, then Aviendha refused to accept it as a sign of weakness. Her first-sister would not act in such a shameful way.

Therefore, there had to be some hidden honor in it. Perhaps the wetlanders exposed their weaknesses to their companions as a means of offering friendship and trust. If your friends knew of your weaknesses, it would give them an advantage should you dance the spears with them. Or, perhaps, the complaining was a wetlander way of showing humility, much as the *gai'shain* showed honor by being subservient.

She had asked Elayne about her theories and had received only a fond laugh in return. Was it some aspect of wetlander society that she was forbidden to discuss with outsiders, then? Had Elayne laughed because Aviendha had figured out something she was not meant to?

Either way, it was certainly a way to show honor, and that satisfied Aviendha. If only her own problems with the Wise Ones were as simple! It was expected that the wetlanders would act in erratic, unnatural ways. But what was she to do when Wise Ones behaved so strangely?

She was growing frustrated—not with the Wise Ones, but with herself. She was strong and brave. Not as brave as some others, of course; she could only wish to be as bold as Elayne. Still, Aviendha could think of only a few problems which she hadn't been able to solve with the application of spears, the One Power or her wits. Yet she had failed utterly at deciphering her current predicament.

She reached the other side of the camp and deposited her stone, then brushed off her hands. The Maidens stood motionless and contemplative. Aviendha moved to the other pile and picked up an oblong rock with a jagged edge. It was three handspans wide, and the smooth surface threatened to slip in her fingers. She had to shift it several times before getting a good purchase. She headed back across the trampled winter thatch, past Saldaean tents, toward the manor house.

Elayne would say that Aviendha hadn't thought the problem through. Elayne was calm and thoughtful when other people were tense. Aviendha sometimes grew frustrated with how much her first-sister liked to talk before committing to action. *I need to be more like her. I need to remember that I'm not a Maiden of the Spear any longer. I can't charge in with weapon held high.*

She needed to approach problems as Elayne did. That was the only way she was going to get her honor back, and only then could she claim Rand al'Thor and make him hers as much as he was Elayne's or Min's. She could feel him through the bond; he was in his room, but was not sleeping. He pushed himself hard and slept too little.

The stone slipped in her fingers, and she nearly stumbled as she rebalanced her weight, hefting it in tired arms. Some of Bashere's soldiers walked past, bemused expressions on their faces, and Aviendha felt herself blush. Although they might not know that she was being punished, she was shamed before them.

How would Elayne reason out this situation? The Wise Ones were angry at Aviendha for not "learning quickly enough." And yet they didn't teach her. They just asked those questions. Questions about what she thought of their

situation, questions about Rand al'Thor or about the way
Rhuarc had handled meeting with the *Car'a'carn*.

Aviendha couldn't help feeling that the questions were
tests. Was she answering incorrectly? If so, why didn't they
instruct her in the proper responses?

The Wise Ones didn't think she was soft. What was left?
What would Elayne say? Aviendha wished for her spears
back so that she could stab something. Attack, test herself
against another, work out her anger.

No, she thought forcefully. *I am going to learn to do this
as a Wise One. I* will *find honor again!*

She reached the manor and dropped her rock. She wiped
her brow; ignoring heat and cold as Elayne had taught her
didn't keep her from sweating when she worked her body
this hard.

"Adrin?" one door guard asked his companion. "Light,
you don't look well. Truly."

Aviendha glanced toward the doorway into the manor.
The guard who had been complaining about the heat was
sagging against the doorway, hand on his forehead. He
really *didn't* look well. Aviendha embraced *saidar.* She
wasn't the best at Healing, but perhaps she could—

The man reached up suddenly, scratching at the skin of
his temples. His eyes rolled up in his head and his fingers
tore gashes in his flesh. Only, instead of blood, the wounds
spat out a black charcoal-like substance. Aviendha could
feel the intense heat even from a distance.

The other guard gaped in horror as his friend ripped
lines of black fire down the sides of his head. A blackish
tar oozed out, boiling and hissing. The man's clothing burst
into flames and his flesh shriveled from the heat.

He didn't utter a sound.

Aviendha shrugged off her shock, immediately weaving
Air in a simple pattern to pull the unaffected guard to safety.
His friend was now just a pulsing mound of black tar which,
in places, sprouted blackened bones. There was no skull.
The heat was so strong that Aviendha had to back away,
pulling the guard with her.

"We . . . we're being attacked!" the man whispered.
"Channelers!"

"No," Aviendha said, "this is something far more evil.
Run for help!"

He seemed too shocked to move, but she shoved him into motion and he began to move. The tar itself didn't seem to be spreading, which was a blessing, but it had already ignited the doorframe of the manor. It could have the entire building in flames before anyone inside was aware of the danger.

Aviendha wove Air and Water, intending to extinguish the flame. However, her weaves frazzled and wavered when they got near the fire. They didn't unweave, but this fire somehow resisted them.

She took another step back from the awesome, burning intensity. Her brow prickled with sweat, and she had to raise her arm to shade her face from the heat. She could barely make out the black char at the center as it began to glow with the deep red and white of extremely hot coals. Soon, only hints of the black remained. The fire spread across the front wall of the building. Aviendha heard screams from inside.

Aviendha shook herself, then growled and wove Earth and Air, pulling chunks of the ground up around her. She hurled these at the fire, seeking to smother it. Her weave could not draw the heat out, but that did not stop her from using weaves to cast items *into* the fire. Chunks of grass-covered earth sizzled and hissed, wan blades flashing to ash before the incredible heat. Aviendha continued to work, sweating from both the exertion and the temperature.

In the distance, she heard people—perhaps the guard among them—calling for buckets.

Buckets? Of course! In the Three-fold Land, water was far too valuable to use in fighting fires. Dirt or sand was used. But here, they *would* use water. Aviendha took several steps backward, searching out the curling river that ran beside the manor. She could just barely make out its surface, reflecting the dancing reds and oranges of the flames. Already, the entire front of the manor was aflame! She felt channeling from inside—Aes Sedai or Wise Ones. Hopefully, they would escape out of the back of the building. The fire had engulfed the inner hallway, and the rooms off of it had no doors out.

Aviendha wove a massive column of Air and Water, pulling a spout of crystalline liquid from the river and drawing it toward her. The column of water undulated in the air like the creature on Rand's banner, a glassy serpentine dragon that slammed against the flames. Steam hissed outward in an explosion, washing over her.

The heat was powerful and the wave of steam scalded her skin, but she did not back down. She pulled more water, hurling a thick column of it at the darkened mound, which she could only just make out through the steam.

That heat was so intense! Aviendha stumbled backward a few steps, gritting her teeth, continuing to work. Then there was a sudden explosion as another column of water burst from the river and slammed into the fire. This, along with her own, diverted nearly the entire flow of the river. Aviendha blinked. The other column was being directed by weaves she could not see, but she did notice a figure standing in a window up on the second floor, hand forward, face concentrating intensely. Naeff, one of Rand's Asha'man. It was said he was particularly strong with Air.

The fires had retreated; only the tarry mound remained, radiating a powerful heat. The wall near it and the entry-way inside had become a gaping, blackened hole. Aviendha continued to pull water and dump it on the charred black mass, though she was beginning to feel extremely tired. Handling so much water required her to channel almost to her capacity.

Soon the water stopped hissing. Aviendha slacked her flow, then let it dribble to a stop. The ground around her was a wet, blackened disarray that smelled heavily of soggy ash. Bits of wood and char floated in the muddy water, and the holes where she had ripped up earth were filled, making pools. She walked forward hesitantly, inspecting the lump that was the remains of the unfortunate soldier. It was glassy and black, like obsidian, and it sparkled wetly. She picked up a length of singed wood—broken from the wall by the force of her water column—and poked at the mass. It was hard and firm.

"Burn you!" a voice bellowed. Aviendha looked up. Rand al'Thor strode through the broken hole that now formed the front of the mansion. He stared at the sky, shaking his fist. "I am the one you want! You will have your war soon enough!"

"Rand," Aviendha said hesitantly. Soldiers were milling about the green, looking concerned, as if expecting a battle.

Bewildered servants peeked out of rooms inside the manor. The entire episode with the flames had taken less than five minutes.

"I will stop you!" Rand roared, causing calls of fright from both servants and soldiers. "Do you hear me! I am coming for you! Don't waste your power! You will need it against me!"

"Rand!" Aviendha called.

He froze, then looked down at her, dazed. She met his eyes, and she could feel his anger, almost as she'd felt the intense flames just a short time before. He turned and stalked away, walking back into the building and up the blackened wooden steps.

"Light!" an anxious voice asked. "Does this sort of thing happen often when *he* is near?"

Aviendha turned to see a young man in an unfamiliar uniform standing and watching. He was lanky, with light brown hair and coppery skin—she didn't remember his name, but she was fairly certain he was one of the officers Rand had brought back after meeting with Rodel Ituralde.

She turned back to the mess, listening to soldiers call orders in the distance. Bashere had arrived and was taking command, telling men to watch the perimeter, though he was likely just giving them something to do. This was not the beginning of an attack. It was just another of the Dark One's touches on the world, like meat spoiling, beetles and rats appearing from nothing, and men dropping dead of strange diseases.

"Yes," Aviendha said in response to the man's question, "it happens often. More often around the *Car'a'carn* than in other places, at least. You have had similar events among your own men?"

"I have heard stories," he said. "Only I dismissed them."

"Not all stories are exaggerations," she said, looking at the blackened remains of the soldier. "The Dark One's prison is weak."

"Bloody ashes," the young man said, turning away. "What have you gotten us into, Rodel?" The man shook his head and stalked off.

Bashere's officers began calling orders, organizing the men to clean up. Would Rand move out of the manor, now? When pockets of evil appeared, people often wanted to leave. And yet, through her bond with Rand, she felt no urgency. In fact . . . it seemed that he had gone back to rest! That man's moods were becoming as erratic as Elayne's during her pregnancy.

Aviendha shook her head and started gathering burned chunks of wood to help clean. As she worked, several Aes Sedai came out of the building and began inspecting the damage. The entire front of the manor was scored with black marks, and the hole where the entryway had been was at least fifteen feet across. One of the women, Merise, eyed Aviendha appreciatively. "A shame," she said.

Aviendha straightened up, lifting a piece of charred wood, her clothing still soaked. With those clouds covering the sun, it would be long before she was dry. "A shame?" she asked. "About the manor?" The portly Lord Tellaen, owner of the place, moaned to himself as he sat on a stool inside the entryway, wiping his brow and shaking his head.

"No," Merise said. "A shame about you, child. Your skill with weaves, it is impressive. If we had you in the White Tower, you'd have been an Aes Sedai by now. Your weaving, it has some roughness to it, but you'd learn to fix that quickly if taught by sisters."

There was an audible sniff, and Aviendha spun. Melaine stood behind her. The golden-haired Wise One had her arms folded beneath her breasts, and her stomach was starting to bulge with child. Her face was not amused. How had Aviendha let the woman walk up behind her without hearing? She was letting her fatigue make her careless.

Melaine and Merise stared at each other for a long moment; then the tall Aes Sedai spun in a flurry of green skirts and moved off to speak with the servants who had been trapped by the flames, asking if any of them needed Healing. Melaine watched her go, then shook her head. "Insufferable woman," she muttered. "To think, how we once regarded them!"

"Wise One?" Aviendha asked.

"I'm stronger than most Aes Sedai, Aviendha, and you're far stronger than I am. You have a control and understanding of weaves that puts most of us to shame. Others have to struggle to learn what comes naturally to you. 'Roughness to your weaves,' she says! I doubt any of the Aes Sedai, save perhaps Cadsuane Sedai, could have managed what you did with that column of water. Moving water that far required you to use the river's own flow and pressure."

"Is that what I did?" Aviendha asked, blinking.

Melaine eyed her, then snorted again, softly to herself. "Yes, that is what you did. You have *such* great talent, child."

Aviendha swelled with the praise; from Wise Ones, it was rare, but always sincere.

"But you refuse to *learn*," Melaine continued. "There isn't much time! Here, I have another question for you. What do you think of Rand al'Thor's plan to kidnap these Domani merchant chiefs?"

Aviendha blinked again, so tired it was hard to think. It defied reason that the Domani used merchants as leaders in the first place. How could a merchant lead people? Did not merchants have to focus on their wares? It was ridiculous. Would the wetlanders ever stop shocking her with their strange ways?

And why was Melaine asking her about this *now* of all times?

"His plan seems a good one, Wise One," Aviendha said. "Yet the spears do not like being used for kidnapping. I think the *Car'a'carn* should have spoken in terms of offering protection—forced protection—for the merchants. The chiefs would have responded better to being told they were protecting rather than kidnapping."

"They would be doing the very same thing, no matter what you call it."

"But what you call a thing is important," Aviendha said. "It is not dishonest if both definitions are true."

Melaine's eyes twinkled, and Aviendha caught a hint of a smile on her lips. "What else do you think of the meeting?"

"Rand al'Thor still seems to think that the *Car'a'carn* can make demands like a wetlander king. This is my shame. I failed to explain the right way."

Melaine waved a hand. "You have no shame there. We all know how bullheaded the *Car'a'carn* is. The Wise Ones have tried as well, and none have been able to train him correctly."

So. That wasn't the reason for her dishonor before the Wise Ones. What was it then? Aviendha ground her teeth in frustration, then forced herself to continue. "Regardless, he needs to be reminded. Again and again. Rhuarc is a wise and patient man, but not all clan chiefs are so. I know that some of the others wonder if their decision to follow Rand al'Thor was an error."

"True," Melaine said. "But look at what happened to the Shaido."

"I did not say they were right, Wise One," Aviendha said. A group of soldiers were hesitantly trying to pry up the glassy black mound. It appeared to have fused to the ground. Aviendha lowered her voice. "They are wrong to question the *Car'a'carn*, but they *are* speaking to one another. Rand al'Thor needs to realize that they will not accept offense after offense from him without end. They may not turn against him like the Shaido, but I would not put it past Timolan—for instance—to simply return to the Three-fold Land and leave the *Car'a'carn* to his arrogance."

Melaine nodded. "Do not worry. We are aware of this . . . possibility."

That meant Wise Ones had been sent to soothe Timolan, who was chief of the Miagoma Aiel. It would not be the first time. Did Rand al'Thor know how hard the Wise Ones worked behind his back to maintain Aiel loyalty? Probably not. He saw them all as one homogeneous group, sworn to him, to be used. That was one of Rand's great weaknesses. He could not see that Aiel, like other people, did not like being used as tools. The clans were far less tightly knit than he believed. Blood feuds had been put aside for him. Couldn't he understand how incredible that was? Couldn't he see how tenuous that alliance continued to be?

But not only was he a wetlander by birth, he was not a Wise One. Few Aiel themselves saw the work the Wise Ones did in a dozen different areas. How simple life had seemed when she had been a Maiden! It would have dazzled her to know how much went on beyond her sight.

Melaine stared blindly at the broken building. "A remnant of a remnant," she said, as if to herself. "And if he leaves us burned and broken, like those boards? What will become of the Aiel then? Do we limp back to the Three-fold Land and continue as we did before? Many will not want to leave. These lands offer too much."

Aviendha blinked at the weight of those words. She

had rarely given thought to what would happen *after* the *Car'a'carn* was finished with them. She was centered on the now, upon regaining her honor and being there to protect Rand al'Thor at the Last Battle. But a Wise One could not just think of the now or the tomorrow. She had to think of the years ahead and the times that would be brought upon the winds.

A remnant of a remnant. He had broken the Aiel as a people. What *would* become of them?

Melaine glanced back at Aviendha, her face softening. "Go to the tents, child, and rest. You look like a *sharadan* that has crawled on his belly across three days of sand."

Aviendha looked down at her arms, seeing the flakes of ash from the burnings. Her clothing was soaked and stained, and she suspected that her face was just as filthy. Her arms ached from carrying the stones all day. Once she acknowledged the fatigue, it seemed to crash upon her like a windstorm. She gritted her teeth and forced herself to remain upright. She would not shame herself by collapsing! But she did turn to leave, as instructed.

"Oh, and Aviendha," Melaine called. "We will discuss your punishment tomorrow."

She turned in shock.

"For not finishing with the stones," Melaine said, surveying the wreckage again. "And for not learning quickly enough. Go."

Aviendha sighed. Another round of questions, and another undeserved punishment. There *was* a correlation of some sort. But what?

She was too exhausted to think about it for now. All she wanted was her bed, and she found herself treacherously recalling the soft, luxurious mattresses back in the palace of Caemlyn. She forced those thoughts out of her mind. Sleep that soundly, muffled in pillows and down comforters, and you'd be too relaxed to wake if someone tried to kill you in the night! How had she let Elayne convince her to sleep in one of those soft-feathered death traps?

Another thought occurred to her as she pushed that one away—a treacherous one. A thought of Rand al'Thor, resting in his room. She could go to him. . . .

No! Not until she had her honor back. She would not go

to him as a beggar. She would go to him as a woman of honor. Assuming that she could ever figure out what she was doing wrong.

She shook her head and trotted toward the Aiel camp at the side of the green.

CHAPTER
12

Unexpected Encounters

Egwene walked the cavernous halls of the White Tower, lost in thought. Her two Red keepers trailed along behind. They seemed a little sullen these days. Elaida ordered them to stay with Egwene more and more often; though the individuals changed, there were almost always two with her. And yet, it seemed that they could sense that Egwene considered them to be attendants rather than guards.

It had been well over a month since Siuan had conveyed her disturbing news in *Tel'aran'rhiod*, but still Egwene thought about it. The events were a reminder that the world was coming apart. This was a time when the White Tower should have been a source of stability. Instead, it divided against itself while Rand al'Thor's men bonded sisters. How could Rand have allowed such a thing? There was obviously little left of the youth with whom she'd grown up. Of course, there was little of the youthful *Egwene* left either. Gone were the days when the two of them had seemed destined to end up married, living on a little farm in the Two Rivers.

That, oddly, led her to thinking of Gawyn. How long had it been since she'd last seen him, stealing kisses in Cairhien? Where was he now? Was he safe?

Keep focused, she told herself. *Clean the patch of floor you're working on first before you move on to the rest of the house.* Gawyn could look after himself; he'd done a competent job of that in the past. Too competent, in some cases.

Siuan and the others would deal with the Asha'man matter. The other news was far more disturbing. One of the

Forsaken, in the camp? A woman, yet channeling *saidin* instead of *saidar*? Egwene would have called it impossible, once. Yet she had seen ghosts in the halls of the White Tower, and the corridors seemed to rearrange on a daily basis. This was just another sign.

She shivered. Halima had *touched* Egwene, supposedly massaging her headaches away. Those headaches disappeared as soon as Egwene had been captured; why hadn't she considered that Halima might have been causing them? What else had the woman been plotting? What hidden knots would the Aes Sedai stumble over, what traps had she laid?

One section of the floor at a time. Clean what you could reach, then move on. Siuan and the others would have to deal with Halima's plots, too.

Egwene's backside hurt, but the pain was growing increasingly irrelevant to her. Sometimes she laughed when beaten, sometimes not. The strap was unimportant. The greater pain—what had been done to Tar Valon—was far more demanding. She nodded to a group of white-clothed novices as they passed her in the hallway, and they bobbed down in curtsies. Egwene frowned, but didn't chastise them—she just hoped that they wouldn't draw penances from the trailing Reds for showing deference to Egwene.

Her goal was the quarters of the Brown Ajah, the section that was now down in the wing. Meidani had taken her time volunteering to train Egwene today. The command had finally come today, weeks after the first dinner with Elaida. Oddly, however, Bennae Nalsad had *also* offered to give her instruction this day. Egwene hadn't spoken to the Shienaran Brown since that first conversation, some weeks before. She'd never repeated lessons with the same woman twice. And yet, the name had been given to her in the morning as the first of the day's visits.

When she reached the east wing, which now held the Brown sector of the Tower, her Red minders reluctantly took up positions in the hallway outside, waiting for her return. Elaida probably would have liked them to stay with Egwene, but after the Reds themselves had been so exacting in protecting their boundary, there was little chance of another Ajah—even the mild Browns—letting a pair of Red sisters infiltrate their quarters. Egwene hurried her pace as she entered the section with brown tiled floors, passing bustling women in nondescript, muted dresses. It was going to be a full day, with her appointments with sisters, her scheduled beatings, and her regular novice load of scrubbing floors or other chores.

She arrived at Bennae's door, but hesitated there. Most sisters agreed to train Egwene only when forced into the duty, and the experience was often unpleasant. Some of Egwene's teachers disliked her because of her affiliation with the rebels, others were annoyed by how easily she could craft weaves, and still others were infuriated to find that she would not show them respect like a novice.

These "lessons," however, had been among Egwene's best chances to sow seeds against Elaida. She'd planted one of those during her first visit with Bennae. Had it begun to sprout?

Egwene knocked, and then entered at the call to come in. The sitting room inside was cluttered with the refuse of scholarship. Stacks and stacks of books—like miniature city towers—leaned against one another. Skeletons of various creatures were mounted in various states of construction; the woman owned enough bones to populate a menagerie. Egwene shivered when she noticed a full human skeleton in the corner, held upright and bound together with threads, some detailed notations written directly on the bones in black ink.

There was barely room to walk and only one clear place to sit—Bennae's own stuffed chair, the armrests worn with a twin set of depressions, doubtless where the Brown's arms had rested during countless late-night reading sessions. The low ceiling felt lower for the several mummified fowl and astronomical contraptions which hung above. Egwene had to duck her head beneath a model of the sun in order to reach the place where Bennae stood rifling through a stack of leather-bound volumes.

"Ah," she said as she noticed Egwene. "Good." Slender in a bony sort of way, she had dark hair that was streaked with gray from age. The hair was in a bun, and she—like many Browns—wore a simple dress that hadn't been fashionable for a century or two.

Bennae moved over to her stuffed sitting chair, ignoring the stiffer chairs by the hearth—both of those had accumulated stacks of papers since Egwene's previous visit. Egwene cleared off a stool, placing the dusty skeleton of a rat on the floor between two stacks of books about the reign of Artur Hawkwing.

"Well, I suppose we should get on with your instruction, then," Bennae said, settling back in her chair.

Egwene kept her face calm. *Had* Bennae requested an opportunity to train Egwene again? Or had she been forced into it? Egwene could see an unsophisticated Brown sister getting repeatedly roped into a duty that nobody else wanted.

At Bennae's request, Egwene performed a number of weaves, work far beyond the skill of most novices but easy for Egwene, even with her power dampened by forkroot. She tried to tease out the Brown's feelings on the relocation of her quarters, but Bennae—like most of the Browns Egwene had spoken to—preferred to avoid that topic.

Egwene did some more weaves. After a time, she wondered just what the point of the meeting was. Hadn't Bennae asked her to demonstrate most of these very same weaves during her previous visit?

"Very well," Bennae said, getting herself a cup of tea from a pot warming on a small coal brazier. She didn't offer any tea to Egwene. "You are skilled enough at that. But I wonder. Do you have the sharpness of mind, the ability to deal with difficult situations, that an Aes Sedai is required to have?"

Egwene said nothing, though she did pointedly pour herself some tea. Bennae did not object.

"Let's see . . ." Bennae mused. "Suppose that you were in a situation where you were in conflict with some members of your own Ajah. You have happened upon information you weren't supposed to know, and your Ajah's leaders are quite upset with you. Suddenly, you find yourself being sentenced to some most unpleasant duties, as if they are trying to sweep you under the rug and forget about you. Tell me, in this situation, how would you react?"

Egwene almost choked on her tea. The Brown wasn't very subtle. She had begun asking about the Thirteenth Depository, had she? And that had landed her in trouble? Few were supposed to know about the secret histories that Egwene had mentioned so casually during her previous visit here.

"Well," Egwene said, sipping her tea, "let me approach it with a clear mind. Best to view it from the perspective of the Ajah's leaders, I should think."

Bennae frowned faintly. "I suppose."

"Now, in this situation you describe, can we assume that these secrets have been entrusted to the Ajah for safekeeping? Ah, good. Well, from their perspective, important and careful plans have been upset. Think of how it must look. Someone has learned secrets they should not. That whispers of a disturbing leak somewhere among your most trusted members."

Bennae paled. "I suppose I could see that."

"Then the best way to handle the situation would be twofold," Egwene said, taking another sip of tea. It tasted terrible. "First, the leaders of the Ajah would have to be reassured. They need to know that it wasn't *their* fault that the information leaked. If I were the hypothetical sister in trouble—and if I'd done nothing wrong—I'd go to them and explain. That way they could stop searching for the one who let information slip."

"But," Bennae said, "that probably won't help the sister—the hypothetical one in trouble—get out of her punishments."

"It couldn't hurt," Egwene said. "Likely, she's being 'punished' to keep her out of the way while the Ajah leaders search for a traitor. When they know there isn't one, they'll be more likely to look at the fallen sister's situation with empathy—particularly after she's offered them a solution."

"Solution?" Bennae asked. Her teacup sat in her fingers, as if forgotten. "And which solution would you offer?"

"The best one: competence. Obviously, *some* people among the Ajah know these secrets. Well, if this sister were to prove her trustworthiness and her capability, perhaps the leaders of her Ajah would realize the best place for her is as one of the caretakers of the secrets. An easy solution, if you consider it."

Bennae sat thoughtfully, a small mummified finch spinning slowly on its cord directly above her. "Yes, but will it work?"

"It is certainly better than serving in some forgotten store-room cataloguing scrolls," Egwene said. "Unjust punishment sometimes cannot be avoided, but it is best never to let others forget that it *is* unjust. If she simply accepts the way people treat her, then it won't be long before they assume she deserves the position they've placed her in." *And thank you, Silviana, for that little bit of advice.*

"Yes," Bennae said, nodding. "Yes, I do suppose that you are correct."

"I am always willing to help, Bennae," Egwene said in a softer voice, turning back to her tea. "In, of course, hypothetical situations."

For a moment, Egwene worried that she'd gone too far in calling the Brown by her name. However, Bennae met her eyes, then actually went so far as to bow her head just slightly in thanks.

If the hour spent with Bennae had been isolated, Egwene would still have found it remarkable. However, she was shocked to discover—upon leaving Bennae's lair of a room—a novice waiting with a message instructing her to attend Nagora, a White sister. Egwene still had time before her meeting with Meidani, so she went. She couldn't ignore a summons from a sister, though she would undoubtedly have to do extra chores later to make up for skipping the floor scrubbing.

At the meeting with Nagora, Egwene found herself being trained in logic—and the "logical puzzles" presented sounded very similar to a request for help in dealing with a Warder who was growing frustrated with his increasing age and inability to fight. Egwene gave what help she could, which Nagora declared to be "logic without flaw" before releasing her. After that, there was another message, this one from Suana, one of the Sitters of the Yellow Ajah.

A Sitter! It was the first time Egwene had been ordered to attend one of them. Egwene hurried to the appointment and was admitted by a maidservant. Suana's quarters looked more like a garden than proper rooms. As a Sitter, Suana could demand quarters with windows, and she made full use of her inset balcony as an herb garden. But beyond that, she had mirrors positioned to reflect light into the room, which was overgrown with small potted trees, shrubs growing in large basins of earth, and even a small garden for carrots and radishes. Egwene noticed with displeasure a small pile of rotted tubers in one container, likely just harvested but somehow already spoiled.

The room smelled strongly of basil, thyme and a dozen other herbs. Despite the problems in the Tower, despite the rotted plants, she was buoyed by the scent of *life* in the room—the freshly turned earth and growing plants. And Nynaeve complained that the sisters in the White Tower ignored the usefulness of herbs! If only she could spend some time with sturdy, square-faced Suana.

Egwene found the woman remarkably pleasant. Suana ran her through a series of weaves, many of them related to Healing, where Egwene had never particularly shone. Still, her skill must have impressed the Sitter, for midway through the lesson—Egwene seated on a cushioned stool between two potted trees, Suana sitting more properly in a stiff leather-covered chair—the tone of the conversation changed.

"We should very much like to have you in the Yellow, I think," the woman said.

Egwene started. "I've never shown particular skill for Healing."

"Being of the Yellow isn't about skill, child," Suana said. "It's about passion. If you love to make things well, to fix that which is broken, there would be a purpose for you here."

"My thanks," Egwene said. "But the Amyrlin has no Ajah."

"Yes, but she's raised from one. Consider it, Egwene. I think you would find a good home here."

It was a shocking conversation. Suana obviously didn't consider Egwene the Amyrlin, but the mere fact that she was recruiting Egwene to her Ajah said something. It meant she accepted Egwene's legitimacy, at least to some degree, as a sister.

"Suana," Egwene said, testing how far she could push that sense of legitimacy, "have the Sitters spoken of what to do about the tensions between the Ajahs?"

"I don't see what *can* be done," Suana replied, glancing toward her overgrown balcony. "If the other Ajahs have decided to see the Yellow as their enemy, then I cannot compel them to be less foolish."

They likely say the same about you, Egwene thought, but said, "Someone must make the first steps. The shell of distrust is growing so thick that soon it will be hard to crack. Perhaps if some of the Sitters of different Ajahs began taking meals together, or were seen traveling the hallways in one another's company, it would prove instructive for the rest of the Tower."

"Perhaps . . ." Suana said.

"They aren't your enemies, Suana," Egwene said, letting her voice grow more firm.

The woman frowned at Egwene, as if realizing suddenly who she was taking advice from. "Well, then, I think it's best that you ran along. I'm certain there is a great deal for you to do today."

Egwene let herself out, carefully avoiding drooping branches and clusters of pots. Once she left the Yellow sector of the Tower and collected her Red Ajah attendants, she realized something. She'd gone through all three meetings without being assigned a single punishment. She wasn't certain what to think of that. She'd even called two of them by name directly to their faces!

They were coming to accept her. Unfortunately, that was only a small part of the battle. The larger part was making certain the White Tower survived the strains Elaida was placing upon it.

Meidani's quarters were surprisingly comfortable and homey. Egwene had always viewed the Grays as similar to the Whites, lacking passion, perfect diplomats who didn't have time for personal emotions or frivolities.

These rooms, however, hinted at a woman who loved to travel. Maps hung within delicate frames, centered on the walls like prized pieces of art. A pair of Aiel spears hung on either side of one map; another was a map of the Sea Folk islands. While many might have opted for the porcelain keepsakes that were so commonly associated with the Sea Folk, Meidani had a small collection of earrings and painted shells, carefully framed and displayed, along with a small plaque beneath listing dates of collection.

The sitting room was like a museum dedicated to one person's journeys. An Altaran marriage knife, set with four

twinkling rubies, hung beside a small Cairhienin banner
and a Shienaran sword. Each had a small plaque explaining
its significance. The marriage knife, for instance, had been
presented to Meidani for her help in settling a dispute between two houses over the death of a particularly important
landowner. His wife had given her the knife as a token of
thanks.

Who would have thought that the cowering woman of the
dinner a few weeks back would have such a proud collection? The rug itself was labeled, the gift of a trader who had
purchased it on the closed docks of Shara, then bestowed
it on Meidani in thanks for Healing his daughter. It was of
strange design, woven from what seemed to be tiny, dyed
reeds, with tufts of an exotic gray fur trimming the edges.
The pattern depicted exotic creatures with long necks.

Meidani herself sat on a curious chair made from woven wicker boughs, crafted to look like a growing thicket
of branches that just happened to take the shape of a chair.
It would have been horribly out of place in any other room
in the Tower, but it fit within these quarters, where each
item was different, none of them related yet somehow all
connected with the common theme of gifts received during
travels.

The Gray's appearance was surprisingly different from
what it had been during the dinner with Elaida. Instead of
the low-cut colorful dress, she wore a high-necked gown
of plain white, long and tapering, cut as if to deemphasize
her bosom. Her deep golden hair was up in a bun, and she
didn't wear a single glimmer of jewelry. Was the contrast
intentional?

"You took your time summoning me," Egwene said.

"I didn't want to appear suspicious before the Amyrlin,"
Meidani said as Egwene crossed the exotic Shara rug. "Besides, I'm still not certain how I regard you."

"I don't care how you regard me," Egwene said evenly,
seating herself on an oversized oak chair, bearing a plaque
that identified it as a gift from a moneylender in Tear. "An
Amyrlin needs not the regard of those who follow her, so
long as she is obeyed."

"You've been captured and overthrown."

Egwene raised an eyebrow, meeting Meidani's gaze.
"Captured, true."

"The Hall among the rebels will have chosen a new Amyrlin by now."

"I happen to know that they have not."

Meidani hesitated. Revealing the existence of contact with the rebel Aes Sedai was a gamble, but if she couldn't secure the loyalty of Meidani and the spies, then she was on shaky ground indeed. Egwene had assumed that it would be easy to gain the woman's support, considering how frightened Meidani had been at supper. But it seemed that the woman was not as easily cowed as it had appeared.

"Well," Meidani said. "Even if that is true, you must know that they picked you to be a figurehead. A puppet to be manipulated."

Egwene held the woman's gaze.

"You have no real authority," Meidani said, voice wavering slightly.

Egwene did not look away. Meidani studied her, brow wrinkling slowly, step by step, furrows appearing across her smooth, ageless Aes Sedai face. She searched Egwene's eyes, like a mason searching a piece of stone for flaws before setting it in place. What she found seemed to confuse her further.

"Now," Egwene said, as if she had not just been questioned, "you will tell me precisely why you have not fled the Tower. While I do believe that your spying on Elaida is valuable, you must know how much danger you are in now that Elaida is aware of your true allegiance. Why not leave?"

"I . . . cannot say," Meidani said, glancing away.

"I'm commanding you as your Amyrlin."

"I still cannot say." Meidani looked down at the floor, as if ashamed.

Curious, Egwene thought, hiding her frustration. "It is obvious that you do not understand the gravity of our situation. Either you accept my authority, or you accept that of Elaida. There is no middle ground, Meidani. And I promise you this: If Elaida retains the Amyrlin Seat, you will find her treatment of those she sees as traitors to be *quite* unpleasant."

Meidani continued to look down. Despite her initial resistance, it seemed that she had little strength of will remaining.

"I see." Egwene rose to her feet. "You've betrayed us,

haven't you? Did you go to Elaida's side before you were exposed or after Beonin's confession?"

Meidani looked up immediately. "What? No! I never betrayed our cause!" She seemed sickened, face pale, mouth a thin line. "How could you *think* that I'd support that horrid woman? I hate what she has done to the Tower."

Well, that was straightforward enough; little room to wiggle around the Three Oaths in those statements. Either Meidani was true or she was Black—though Egwene had difficulty believing that a Black sister would endanger herself by telling a lie that could be exposed with such relative ease.

"Why not run, then?" Egwene asked. "Why stay?"

Meidani shook her head. "I cannot say."

Egwene took a deep breath. Something about the entire conversation irritated her. "Will you at least tell me why you take dinner with Elaida so often? Surely it's not because you enjoy such treatment."

Meidani blushed. "Elaida and I were pillow-friends during our days as novices. The others decided that if I were to renew the relationship, perhaps it would lead to my gaining valuable information."

Egwene folded her arms beneath her breasts. "It seems reckless to assume she would trust you. However, Elaida's thirst for power is guiding her to make reckless moves of her own, so perhaps the plan was not completely ill advised. Regardless, she'll never draw you into her confidence now that she knows of your true allegiances."

"I know. But it was decided that I shouldn't let on that I'm aware of her knowledge. If I were to back away now, it would let on that we've been warned—and that is one of the precious few edges we now hold."

Precious few enough that she should have just run from the Tower. There was nothing to be gained by staying. Why, then? Something was holding the woman back, it seemed. Something strong. A promise?

"Meidani," Egwene said, "I need to know what it is that you aren't telling me."

She shook her head; she almost looked afraid. *Light!* Egwene thought. *I won't do to her what Elaida does those evenings at supper.*

Egwene sat back down. "Straighten your back, Meidani.

You're not some simpering novice. You're Aes Sedai. Start acting like one."

The woman looked up, eyes flashing at the taunt. Egwene nodded approvingly. "We *will* mend the damage that Elaida has done, and I *will* sit in my rightful place as Amyrlin. But we have work to do."

"I can't—"

"Yes," Egwene said. "You can't tell me what is wrong. I suspect that the Three Oaths are involved, though Light knows how. We can work around the problem. You can't tell me why you've remained in the Tower. But can you show me?"

Meidani cocked her head. "I'm not sure. I could take you to—" She cut off abruptly. Yes, one of the Oaths was forcibly preventing her from continuing. "I might be able to show you," Meidani finished lamely. "I'm not certain."

"Then let's find out. How dangerous will it be if those Red handlers of mine follow us?"

Meidani paled. "Dangerous."

"Then we'll have to leave them behind," Egwene said, absently tapping the armrest of her oversized oak chair with one nail as she thought. "We could leave the Gray section of the Tower by another way, but if we are seen, it could raise difficult questions."

"There have been a lot of Reds lurking near the entrances and exits of our quarters," Meidani said. "I suspect all of the Ajahs are watching one another like that. It will be very difficult to get away without being noticed. They wouldn't follow me alone, but if they see you . . ."

Spies, watching the other Ajah quarters? Light! Had it gotten so bad? That was like scouts being sent to watch enemy camps. She couldn't risk being seen leaving with Meidani, but to go alone would draw attention, too—the Reds knew Egwene was supposed to be guarded.

That left a problem, one Egwene could think of only one way to solve. She eyed Meidani. How far to trust her? "You promise that you do not support Elaida, and that you accept my leadership?"

The woman hesitated, then nodded. "I do."

"If I show you something, do you vow not to reveal it to anyone else without my permission first?"

She frowned. "Yes."

Egwene made her decision. Taking a deep breath, she embraced the Source. "Watch closely," she said, weaving threads of Spirit. Dampened by forkroot, she wasn't strong enough to open a gateway, but she could still show Meidani the weaves.

"What is *that*?" Meidani asked.

"It's called a gateway," Egwene said. "Used for Traveling."

"Traveling is impossible!" Meidani said immediately. "The ability has been lost for . . ." She trailed off, eyes opening more widely.

Egwene let the weave dissipate. Immediately, Meidani embraced the Source, looking determined.

"Think of the place you want to go," Egwene said. "You have to know the place you're leaving behind very well to make this work. I assume that you are familiar enough with your own quarters. Pick a destination where nobody is likely to be; gateways can be dangerous if they open in the wrong location."

Meidani nodded, golden bun bobbing as she concentrated. She did an admirable job of imitating Egwene's weave, and a gateway opened directly between the two of them, white line splitting the air and bending upon itself. The hole was on Meidani's side; Egwene saw only a shimmering patch, like a draft of heat warping the air. She rounded the gateway, looking through the hole at a darkened stone hallway beyond. The tiles on the floor were of a subdued white and brown, and there were no windows within sight. In the depths of the Tower, Egwene guessed.

"Quickly," Egwene said. "If I don't return from your quarters after about an hour, my Red minders might begin to wonder what is taking so long. It's already suspicious to have you, of all people, send for me. We can only hope that Elaida isn't careful enough to wonder at the coincidence."

"Yes, Mother," Meidani said, rushing over and taking a bronze lamp from her table, the flame flickering at the spout. Then she hesitated.

"What?" Egwene asked.

"I'm just surprised."

Egwene almost asked what was so surprising, but then she saw it in Meidani's eyes. Meidani was surprised at how quickly she'd found herself obeying. She was surprised by how natural it was to think of Egwene as Amyrlin. This woman hadn't been won over completely, not yet, but she was close.

"Quickly," Egwene said.

Meidani nodded, stepping through the gateway, and Egwene followed. Though the floor beyond was free of dust, the corridor was thick with the musty scent of uncirculated air. The walls were bare of the ornamentations one saw occasionally in the upper corridors, and the only sound was that of a few distant rats scratching. Rats. In the White Tower. Once, that would have been impossible. The failure of the wards was just one more impossibility atop an ever-growing stack.

This was not an area often given attention by the Tower servants. That was probably why Meidani had chosen it to open the gateway. That was well and good, but she was probably erring on the side of safety. This deep within the Tower, it would take precious minutes to return to the main hallways and find whatever it was Meidani wished to show her. And that would present its own problems. What would happen if other sisters took note of Egwene moving through the corridors without her normal complement of Red Ajah guards?

Before Egwene could voice this concern, Meidani began to walk away. Not up the hallway toward the stairwells, but down it, moving deeper. Egwene frowned, but followed.

"I'm not certain if I'll be allowed to show you," Meidani said softly, her skirts swishing, the sound not unlike that of the faint scrambling of the distant rats. "I must warn you, however, that you may be surprised at what you are stepping into. It could be dangerous."

Did Meidani mean physical danger or political danger? It seemed that Egwene was in about as much of the latter as was possible. Still, she nodded and accepted the warning with solemnity. "I understand. But if something dangerous *is* happening in the Tower, I must know of it. It is not only my right, but my duty."

Meidani said no more. She led Egwene through the twisting passage, muttering that she'd have liked to have been able to bring her Warder. He was apparently out in the city on some errand. The hall spiraled not unlike the undulating coils of the Great Serpent itself. Just when Egwene was growing impatient, Meidani stopped beside a closed door. It looked no different from the dozens of other near-forgotten storage rooms that budded off the main corridor. Meidani raised a hesitant hand, then knocked sharply.

The door opened immediately, revealing a keen-eyed Warder with ruddy hair and a square jaw. He eyed Meidani, then turned to Egwene, his expression growing darker. His arm flinched, as if he'd just barely stopped himself from reaching for the sword at his side.

"That will be Meidani," a woman's voice said from inside the room, "come to report on her meeting with the girl. Adsalan?"

The Warder stepped aside, revealing a small chamber set with boxes for chairs. It held four women, all Aes Sedai. And, shockingly, each was of a different Ajah! Egwene hadn't seen women of four different Ajahs so much as walk together in the hallways, let alone hold conference together. Not a single one of them was Red, and each of the four was a Sitter.

Seaine was the stately woman in white robes and silver trim. A Sitter from the White Ajah, she had thick black hair and eyebrows, and watery blue eyes that regarded Egwene with an even expression. Beside her was Doesine, a Sitter of the Yellow Ajah. She was slender and tall for a Cairhienin; her rich rose-colored dress was embroidered with gold. Her hair was adorned with sapphires, matched by the stone at her forehead.

Yukiri was the Gray sister sitting beside Doesine. Yukiri was one of the shortest women that Egwene had ever met, but she had a way of regarding others that always made her seem in control, even when accompanied by very tall Aes Sedai. The last woman was Saerin, an Altaran Sitter for the Brown. Like many Browns, she wore unornamented dresses, this one a nondescript tan. Her olive skin was marred by a scar on her left cheek. Egwene knew very little about her. Of all the sisters in the room, she seemed the least shocked to see Egwene.

"What have you done?" Seaine said to Meidani, aghast.

"Adsalan, bring them in here," Doesine said, rising and gesturing urgently. "If someone were to walk by and see the al'Vere girl there. . . ."

Meidani cringed before the stern words—yes, she would

require a great deal of work before she had the bearing of an Aes Sedai again. Egwene stepped into the room, moving before the brutish Warder could pull her forward. Meidani followed, and Adsalan closed the door with a thump. The room was lit by a pair of lamps that didn't give quite enough light, as if to complement the conspiratorial nature of the women's conference.

The boxes might as well have been thrones for the way the four Sitters occupied them, and so Egwene sat herself on one as well. "You were not given leave to sit, girl," Saerin said coldly. "Meidani, what is the meaning of this outrage? Your oath was to have prevented this sort of lapse!"

"Oath?" Egwene asked. "And which oath would this be?"

"Quiet, girl," Yukiri snapped, slapping Egwene across the back with a switch of Air. It was such a faint punishment that Egwene almost laughed.

"I didn't break my oath!" Meidani said quickly, stepping up beside Egwene. "You ordered me not to tell anyone of these meetings. Well, I have obeyed—I didn't tell her. I showed her." There was a spark of defiance in the woman. That was good.

Egwene wasn't certain what was going on in the room, but four Sitters together presented her with an unequaled opportunity. She'd never thought to get a chance to speak with so many at once, and if these were willing to meet together, then perhaps they were free of the fractures undermining the rest of the Tower.

Or was their meeting a hint of something more dark? Oaths Egwene didn't know about, meetings away from the upper corridors, a Warder guarding the door . . . were these women of four Ajahs, or of one? Had she unwittingly bumbled her way into the center of a nest of Blacks?

Heart beginning to race, Egwene forced herself not to jump to conclusions. If they *were* Black, then she was caught. If they were not, then she had work to do.

"This is very unexpected," calm Seaine was saying to Meidani. "We'll take extra care with the wording of your future orders, Meidani."

Yukiri nodded. "I didn't think that you'd be so childish as to expose us out of spite. We should have realized that you, like all of us, would have experience pushing and bending oaths to suit your needs."

Wait, Egwene thought. *That sounds like. . . .*

"Indeed," Yukiri said. "I think that penance will be in order for this infraction. But what are we to do with this girl she brought? She's not sworn on the Rod, and so it would be—"

"You gave her a *fourth oath*, didn't you?" Egwene interrupted. "What under the Light were you thinking?"

Yukiri glanced at her, and Egwene felt another swish of Air. "You were not given leave to speak."

"The Amyrlin needs no leave to speak," Egwene said, staring the women down. "What have you *done* here, Yukiri? You betray all that we are! The Oaths are not to be used as tools of division. Has this entire Tower gone as insane as Elaida?"

"It's not insanity," Saerin said suddenly, butting into the conversation. The Brown shook her head, more commanding than Egwene would have expected for one of her Ajah. "It was only done out of necessity. This one couldn't be trusted, not after siding with the rebels."

"Do not think we're unaware of your own involvement with that group, Egwene al'Vere," Yukiri said. The haughty Gray was barely in control of her anger. "If we have our way, you will not be treated with such coddling as Elaida has shown you."

Egwene gestured indifferently. "Still me, execute me or beat me, Yukiri, and the Tower will yet be in shambles. The ones you so easily label as rebels are not to blame for that. Secret meetings in the basements, oaths administered without warrant—these are crimes *at least* equal to that of dividing from Elaida."

"You should not question us," Seaine said in a quieter voice. She seemed more timid than the others. "Sometimes, difficult decisions must be made. We cannot have Darkfriends among the Aes Sedai, and measures have been taken to search them out. We here each proved to Meidani that we are not friends of the Shadow, and so there can be no harm in making her give an oath to us. It was a reasonable action to make certain we are all working for the same goals."

Egwene kept her face calm. Seaine had all but admitted to the existence of the Black Ajah! Egwene had never expected to hear that from the mouth of a Sitter, particularly in front of so many witnesses. So these women were using the Oath Rod to search out Black sisters. If you took each sister, removed her oaths and made her reswear them, you could ask her if she were Black. A desperate method, but—Egwene decided—a legitimate one, considering the times.

"I concede that it is a reasonable plan," Egwene said. "But swearing this woman to a new oath is unnecessary!"

"And if the woman is known to have other loyalties?" Saerin demanded. "Just because a woman isn't a Darkfriend doesn't mean she won't betray us in other ways."

And that oath of obedience was probably the reason Meidani couldn't flee the Tower. Egwene felt a stab of sympathy for the poor woman. Sent by the Salidar Aes Sedai to return and spy on the Tower, discovered by these women—presumably—during their search for the Black, then revealed in her true purpose to Elaida. Three different factions, all pushing against her.

"It's still inappropriate," Egwene said. "But we can set that aside for now. What of Elaida herself? Have you determined if she is of the Black? Who gave you this charge, and how did your cabal form?"

"Bah! Why are we *speaking* with her?" Yukiri demanded, standing up and putting her hands on her hips. "We should be deciding what to do with her, not answering her questions!"

"If I am to help in your work," Egwene said, "then I need to be aware of the facts."

"You are *not* here to help, child," Doesine said. The slender Cairhienin Yellow's voice was firm. "Obviously, Meidani brought you to prove that we don't have her completely beneath our thumbs. Like a child throwing a tantrum."

"What of the others?" Seaine said. "We need to gather them and make certain that their orders are worded better. We wouldn't want one of them to go to the Amyrlin before we know where her loyalties lie."

Others? Egwene thought. *Have they sworn all of the spies, then?* It made sense. Discover one, and it would be easy to get the names of the others. "Have you found any actual members of the Black, then?" Egwene asked. "Who are they?"

"You are to remain quiet, child," Yukiri said, focusing green eyes on Egwene. "One more word, and I shall see you taking penance until you run out of tears to weep."

"I doubt you can order me to any more of it than I already have, Yukiri," Egwene said calmly. "Unless I am to be in the Mistress of Novices' study all day each day. Besides, if you sent me to her, what would I tell her? That you personally gave me penance? She'd know that I wasn't scheduled to see you today. That might start raising questions."

"We could just have Meidani order you to penance," said Seaine the White.

"She won't do such a thing," Egwene said. "She accepts my authority as Amyrlin."

The other sisters glanced at Meidani. Egwene held her breath. Meidani managed a nod, though she looked horrified to be defying the others. Egwene released a quiet breath of thanks.

Saerin looked surprised, but curious. Yukiri, still standing with her arms folded, was not so easily dissuaded. "That's meaningless. We'll just *order* her to send you to penance."

"Will you?" Egwene said. "I thought that you told me that the fourth oath was meant to restore unity, to keep her from fleeing to Elaida with your secrets. Now you would use that oath like a cudgel, forcing her to become your tool?"

That brought silence to the room.

"This is why an oath of obedience is a terrible idea," Egwene said. "No woman should have this much power over another. What you have done to these others is only one step shy of Compulsion. I'm still trying to decide if this abomination is in any way justified; the way you treat Meidani and the others will likely sway that decision."

"Must I repeat myself?" Yukiri snapped, turning to the others. "Why are we wasting time clucking with this girl like hens left to the range? We need to make a decision!"

"We're speaking with her because she seems determined to make herself a nuisance," Saerin said curtly, regarding Egwene. "Sit down, Yukiri. I will deal with the child."

Egwene met Saerin's eyes, heart thumping. Yukiri sniffed, then seated herself, finally seeming to remember that she was Aes Sedai as she calmed her expression. This group was under a great deal of pressure. If it became known what they were doing . . .

Egwene kept her eyes on Saerin. She'd assumed that Yukiri was in charge of the group—she and Saerin were near in power, and many Browns were docile. But that had been a mistake; it was too easy to prejudge someone based on their Ajah.

Saerin leaned forward, speaking firmly. "Child, we *must* have your obedience. We cannot swear you to the Oath Rod, and I doubt you'd make an oath of obedience anyway. But you cannot continue this charade of being the Amyrlin Seat. We all know how often you take penance, and we all know what little good it is doing. So let me try something that I assume nobody else has tried with you: reason."

"You may speak your mind," Egwene said.

The Brown sniffed in response. "All right. For one thing, you can't be Amyrlin. With that forkroot, you can barely channel!"

"Is the Amyrlin Seat's authority, then, in her power to channel?" Egwene asked. "Is she nothing more than a bully, obeyed because she can force others to do as she demands?"

"Well, no," Saerin said.

"Then I don't see why my having been given forkroot has anything to do with my authority."

"You've been demoted to novice."

"Only Elaida is foolish enough to assume one can remove an Aes Sedai's rank," Egwene said. "She should never have been allowed to assume she had *that* power in the first place."

"If she didn't assume it," Saerin said, "then you would be dead, girl."

Egwene met Saerin's eyes again. "Sometimes, I feel it would be better to be dead than to see what Elaida has done to the women of this Tower."

That brought silence to the room.

"I must say," Seaine said quietly, "your claims are completely irrational. Elaida is the Amyrlin because she was raised properly by the Hall. Therefore, you *can't* be Amyrlin."

Egwene shook her head. "She was 'raised' after a shameful and unorthodox removal of Siuan Sanche from the seat.

How can you call Elaida's position 'proper' in the face of that?" Something occurred to her, a gamble, but it felt right. "Tell me this. Have you interrogated any women who are currently Sitters? Have you found any Blacks among them?"

While Saerin's eyes remained even, Seaine glanced away, troubled. *There!* Egwene thought.

"You have," Egwene said. "It makes sense. If I were a member of the Black, I'd try very hard to get one of my fellow Darkfriends named as a Sitter. From there they can manipulate the Tower best. Now tell me this. Were any of these Black Sitters among those who raised Elaida? Did any of them stand to depose Siuan?"

There was silence.

"*Answer me*," Egwene said.

"We found a Black among the Sitters," Doesine finally said. "And . . . yes, she was one of those who stood to depose Siuan Sanche." Her voice was somber. She'd realized what Egwene was getting at.

"Siuan was deposed by the bare *minimum* number of Sitters required," Egwene said. "One of them was Black, making her vote invalid. You stilled and deposed your Amyrlin, murdering her Warder, and you did it *unlawfully*."

"By the Light," Seaine whispered. "She's right."

"This is pointless," Yukiri said, standing again. "If we begin second-guessing, trying to confirm which Amyrlins *might* have been raised by members of the Black, then we'd have reason to suspect every Amyrlin who ever held the seat!"

"Oh?" Egwene asked. "And how many of them were raised by a Hall filled by only the exact minimum number of currently sitting members? This is only one reason why it was a grave mistake to unseat Siuan this way. When I was raised, we made certain that every Sitter in Salidar was aware of what was happening."

"False Sitters," Yukiri said, pointing. "Given their places unlawfully!"

Egwene turned toward her, glad they couldn't hear her nervously pounding heart. She had to remain in control. She *had* to. "You call us false, Yukiri? Which Amyrlin would you rather follow? The one who has been making novices and Accepted out of Aes Sedai, banishing an entire Ajah, and causing divisions in the Tower more dangerous than any army that ever assaulted it? A woman who was raised partially through the help of the Black Ajah? Or would you rather serve the Amyrlin who is trying to undo all of that?"

"Surely you're not saying that you think we served the Black in raising Elaida," Doesine said.

"I think we *all* are serving the interests of the Shadow," Egwene said sharply, "so long as we allow ourselves to remain divided. How do you imagine the Black reacted to the near-secret deposing of an Amyrlin Seat, followed by a division among the Aes Sedai? I would not be surprised to find, after some investigation, that this nameless Black sister you discovered was not the only Darkfriend among the group who worked to unseat the rightful Amyrlin."

This brought another round of silence to the room.

Saerin settled back and sighed. "We cannot change the past. Enlightening though your arguments are, Egwene al'Vere, they are ultimately fruitless."

"I agree that we cannot change what has happened," Egwene said, nodding to her. "However, we *can* look to the future. As admirable as I find your work to discover the Black Ajah, I am far more encouraged by your willingness to work together to do it. In the current Tower, cooperation between the Ajahs is rare. I challenge you to take *that* as your main goal, bringing unity to the White Tower. Whatever the cost."

She stood up, and she half-expected a sister to rebuke her, but they almost seemed to have forgotten that they were speaking with a "novice" and a rebel. "Meidani," Egwene said. "You accept me as Amyrlin."

"Yes, Mother," the woman said, bowing her head.

"I charge you, then, to continue your work with these women. They are not our enemies and they never were. Sending you back as a spy was a mistake, one I wish I'd been able to stop. Now that you are here, however, you can be of use. I regret that you must continue your performance before Elaida, but I commend you for your courage in that regard."

"I will serve as needed, Mother," she said, though she looked sick.

Egwene glanced at the others. "Loyalty is better earned than forced. Do you have the Oath Rod here?"

"No," Yukiri said. "It's difficult to sneak away. We can only take it on occasion."

"A pity," Egwene said. "I'd have liked to take the oaths. Regardless, you will promptly take it and release Meidani from the fourth oath."

"We'll consider it," Saerin said.

Egwene raised an eyebrow. "As you wish. But know that once the White Tower is whole again, the Hall will learn of this action you have taken. I would like to be able to inform them that you were being careful, rather than seeking unwarranted power. If you need me in the next few days, you may send for me—but kindly find a way to deal with the two Red sisters who are watching me. I'd rather not use Traveling within the Tower again, lest I unwittingly reveal too much to those who would be better left ignorant."

She left that statement hanging before walking to the door. The Warder didn't stop her, though he did watch with those suspicious eyes of his. She wondered whose Warder he was—she didn't believe any of the sisters inside the room had Warders, though she wasn't certain. Perhaps he belonged to one of the other spies sent from Salidar, and had been drafted by Saerin and the others. That would explain his disposition.

Meidani quickly followed Egwene from the room, glancing over her shoulder, as if expecting argument or censure to fly out behind her. The Warder simply pulled the door shut.

"I can't believe you succeeded," the Gray said. "They should have strung you up by your heels and had you howling!"

"They are too wise for that," Egwene said. "They're the only ones in this blasted Tower—besides maybe Silviana—who have anything resembling heads sitting atop their shoulders."

"Silviana?" Meidani asked with surprise. "Doesn't she beat you every day?"

"Several times a day," Egwene said absently. "She's very dutiful, not to mention thoughtful. If we had more like her, the Tower wouldn't have gotten to this state in the first place."

Meidani regarded Egwene, an odd expression on her face. "You really *are* the Amyrlin," she finally said. It was an odd comment. Hadn't she just sworn that she accepted Egwene's authority?

"Come on," Egwene said, hastening her pace. "I need to get back before those Reds grow suspicious."

CHAPTER
13

An Offer and a Departure

G awyn stood, sword at the ready, facing down two Warders. The barn let in slots of light, air sparkling with dust and bits of straw kicked up from the fighting. Gawyn backed slowly across the packed dirt floor, passing through patches of light. The air was warm on his skin. Trickles of sweat ran down from his temples, but his grip was firm as the two Warders advanced on him.

The one in front was Sleete, a limber, long-armed man with rough-hewn features. In the barn's uneven light, his face looked like an unfinished work one might find in a sculptor's workshop, with long shadows across his eyes, his chin divided by a cleft, his nose crooked from being broken and not Healed. He wore long hair and black sideburns.

Hattori had been quite pleased when her Warder had finally arrived at Dorlan; she'd lost him at Dumai's Wells, and his story was the sort gleemen and bards sang about. Sleete had lain wounded for hours before deliriously managing to grab his horse's reins and pull himself into the saddle. It had loyally carried him, near unconscious, for hours before arriving at a nearby village. The villagers there had been tempted to sell Sleete to a local band of bandits—their leader had visited earlier promising them safety as a reward for revealing any refugees from the nearby battle. However, the mayor's daughter had argued for Sleete's life, convincing them that the bandits must be Darkfriends if they were seeking wounded Warders. The villagers had chosen to hide Sleete instead, and the girl had nursed him to safety.

Sleete had been forced to sneak away once he was well

enough to travel; the girl had apparently taken quite a liking
to him. Whispers among the Younglings said that Sleete's
escape had also come because he had begun feeling affection for the girl himself. Most Warders knew better than to
let themselves grow attached. Sleete had left in the night,
after the girl and her family fell asleep—but in return for
the village's mercy, he'd hunted down the bandits and seen
to it that they would never plague the village again.

It was the marrow of stories and legends—at least,
among regular, lesser men. For a Warder, Sleete's story was
almost commonplace. Men like him attracted legends as ordinary men attracted fleas. In fact, Sleete hadn't wanted to
share his tale; it had come out only owing to a vigorous campaign of questions from the Younglings. He still acted as if
his survival were nothing to brag about. He was a Warder.
Surviving against the odds, riding in delirium over miles
of rough terrain, cutting down an entire band of thieves
with wounds not fully healed—these were just the sorts of
things you did when you were a Warder.

Gawyn respected them. Even the ones he had killed. Especially the ones he had killed. It took a unique kind of
man to show this kind of dedication, this kind of vigilance.
This kind of humility. While Aes Sedai manipulated the
world and monsters like al'Thor got the glory, men like
Sleete quietly did the work of heroes, each and every day.
Without glory or recognition. If they were remembered,
it was usually only by association with their Aes Sedai.
Or it was by other Warders. You didn't forget your own.

Sleete attacked, sword lancing forward in a straight
thrust delivered for maximum speed. The Viper Flicks Its
Tongue, a bold strike, made more effective because Sleete
fought in tandem with the narrow, short man rounding toward Gawyn's left. Marlesh was the only other Warder in
Dorlan—and his arrival had been far less dramatic than
Sleete's. Marlesh had been with the original group of
eleven Aes Sedai who had escaped Dumai's Wells, and he
had stayed with them the entire time. His own Aes Sedai,
a pretty young Domani Green named Vasha, watched idly
from the side of the barn.

Gawyn countered The Viper Flicks Its Tongue with Cat
Dances on the Wall, knocking aside the strike and going
for the legs in one sweep. It wasn't intended to hit, how-

ever; it was a defensive move, meant to enable him to keep
an eye on both opponents. Marlesh tried Leopard's Caress,
but Gawyn moved into Folding the Air, carefully knocking
aside the blow and waiting for another from Sleete, who
was the more dangerous of the two. Sleete repositioned,
taking smooth steps, his blade to the side as he set his back
to the massive piles of hay at the rear of the stuffy barn.

Gawyn moved into Cat on Hot Sand as Marlesh tried
Hummingbird Kisses the Honeyrose. Hummingbird wasn't
the right form to use in such an attack; it was rarely useful
against someone on the defensive, but Marlesh was obviously tired of being parried. He was getting eager. Gawyn
could use that. And would.

Sleete was advancing again. Gawyn brought his sword
back in to guard as the Warders approached in tandem.
Gawyn immediately moved into Apple Blossoms in the
Wind. His blade flashed three times, pushing a wide-eyed
Marlesh back. Marlesh cursed, throwing himself forward,
but Gawyn brought his sword up from the previous form
and moved fluidly into Shake Dew from the Branch. He
stepped forward into a series of six sharp blows, three at
each opponent, knocking Marlesh back and to the ground—
the man had stepped back into the fight too quickly—and
forcing Sleete's blade aside twice, then ending with his
blade against the man's neck.

The two Warders looked at Gawyn, shocked. They had
borne similar expressions the last time Gawyn had defeated
them, and the time before that. Sleete carried a heron-mark
blade and was near-legendary in the White Tower for his
prowess. He was said to have bested even Lan Mandragoran twice out of seven bouts, back when Mandragoran had
been known to spar with other Warders. Marlesh wasn't as
renowned as his companion, but he was still a fully capable
and trained Warder, no easy foe.

But Gawyn had won. Again. Things seemed so simple
when he was sparring. The world contracted down—
compressed like berries squeezed for their juice—into
something smaller and easier to see from up close. All
Gawyn had ever wanted was to protect Elayne. He wanted
to defend Andor. Maybe learn to be a little more like Galad.

Why couldn't life be as simple as a sword match? Opponents clear and arranged before you. The prize obvious:

survival. When men fought, they connected. You became brothers as you traded blows.

Gawyn removed his blade and stepped away, sheathing it. He offered a hand to Marlesh, who took it, shaking his head as he stood. "You are remarkable, Gawyn Trakand. Like a creature of light, color and shadow when you move. I feel like a babe holding a stick when I face you."

Sleete said nothing as he sheathed his own sword, but he did nod his head to Gawyn in respect—just as he had the last two times they'd fought. He was a man of few words. Gawyn appreciated that.

In the corner of the barn there was a half-barrel filled with water, and the men walked to it. Corbet, one of the Younglings, hurriedly dipped a ladleful and handed it to Gawyn. Gawyn gave it to Sleete. The older man nodded again and took a drink while Marlesh took a cup off the dusty windowsill and got himself a drink. "I'm saying, Trakand," the short man continued, "we'll need to find you a blade with some herons on it. No one should have to face you without knowing what they're getting into!"

"I'm not a blademaster," Gawyn said quietly, taking the ladle back from crook-nosed Sleete and having a drink. It was warm, which felt good. Less of a shock, more natural.

"You killed Hammar, didn't you?" Marlesh asked.

Gawyn hesitated. The simplicity he'd felt before, while fighting, was already crumbling. "Yes."

"Well, then you're a blademaster," Marlesh said. "Should have taken his sword when he fell."

"It wasn't respectful," Gawyn said. "Besides, I didn't have time to claim prizes."

Marlesh laughed, as if at a joke, though Gawyn hadn't intended one. He glanced over at Sleete, who was watching him with curious eyes.

A rustle of skirts announced the approach of Vasha. The Green had long black hair and striking green eyes that at times seemed almost catlike. "Are you done playing, Marlesh?" she asked with a faintly Domani accent.

Marlesh chuckled. "You should be happy to see me play, Vasha. I seem to recall my 'playing' saving your neck a couple of times on the battlefield."

She sniffed and raised an eyebrow. Gawyn had rarely seen an Aes Sedai and Warder with as casual a relationship as these two. "Come," she said, turning on her heel and walking toward the open barn doors. "I want to see what has been keeping Narenwin and the others so long indoors. It smells of decisions being made."

Marlesh shrugged and tossed the cup to Corbet. "Whatever they're deciding, I hope it involves moving. I don't like sitting around in this village with those soldiers creeping up on us. If it gets any more tense in camp, I'm likely to run off and join the Tinkers."

Gawyn nodded at that comment. It had been weeks since he'd last dared send the Younglings to raid. Bryne's search parties were getting closer and closer to the village, and that allowed fewer and fewer rides out across the countryside.

Vasha passed out the doors, but Gawyn could still hear her say, "You can sound like such a child at times." Marlesh just shrugged, waving farewell to Gawyn and Sleete before stepping out of the barn.

Gawyn shook his head, refilling the ladle and taking another drink. "Those two remind me of nothing so much as a brother and sister at times."

Sleete smiled.

Gawyn replaced the ladle, nodded to Corbet, then moved to leave. He wanted to check on the Younglings' evening meal and make certain it was being distributed properly. Some of the youths had taken to sparring and practicing when they should have been eating.

As he left, however, Sleete reached out and took his arm. Gawyn looked back in surprise.

"Hattori only has one Warder," the man said in his gravelly, soft voice.

Gawyn nodded. "That's not unheard-of for a Green."

"It isn't because she isn't open to having more," Sleete said. "Years ago, when she bonded me, she said that she would only take another if I judged him worthy. She asked me to search. She doesn't think much on these kinds of things. Too busy with other matters."

All right, Gawyn thought, wondering why he was being told this.

Sleete turned, meeting Gawyn's eyes. "It's been over ten years, but I've found someone worthy. She will bond you this hour, if you wish it."

Gawyn blinked in surprise at Sleete. The lanky man was

shrouded once more in his color-shifting cloak, wearing nondescript brown and green beneath. Others complained that because of his long hair and sideburns, Sleete looked more scruffy than a Warder should. But "scruffy" was the wrong term for this man. Rough, perhaps, but natural. Like uncut stones or a gnarled—yet sturdy—oak.

"I'm honored, Sleete," Gawyn said. "But I came to the White Tower to study because of Andoran traditions, not because I was going to be a Warder. My place is beside my sister." *And if anyone is going to bond me, it will be Egwene.*

"You *came* for those reasons," Sleete said, "but those reasons have passed. You've fought in our war, you've killed Warders and defended the Tower. You are one of us. You belong with us."

Gawyn hesitated.

"You search," Sleete said. "Like a hawk, glancing this way and that, trying to decide whether to perch or to hunt. You'll tire of flying eventually. Join us, and become one of us. You'll find that Hattori is a good Aes Sedai. Wiser than most, far less prone to squabbles or foolishness than many in the Tower."

"I can't, Sleete," Gawyn said, shaking his head. "Andor. . . ."

"Hattori is not regarded as influential by the White Tower," Sleete said. "The others rarely care what she does. To have you, she'd see herself assigned to Andor. You could have both, Gawyn Trakand. Think on it."

Gawyn hesitated again, then nodded. "Very well. I'll think on it."

Sleete released his arm. "As much as a man can ask."

Gawyn moved to leave, but then stopped, looking back toward Sleete in the dusty barn. Then Gawyn gestured toward Corbet and gestured with a curt sign. *Leave and watch,* it meant. The Youngling nodded eagerly—he was one of the youngest among them, always looking for something to do to prove himself. He'd watch the doors and give warning if anyone approached.

Sleete watched with curiosity as Corbet positioned himself, hand on his sword. Gawyn then stepped forward and spoke more quietly, too soft for Corbet to hear. "What do *you* think of what happened in the Tower, Sleete?"

The rough man frowned, then stepped back and leaned against the inside barn wall. With a glance during the casual move, Sleete checked out the window to make certain nobody was listening from that side.

"It's bad," Sleet finally said, tone hushed. "Warder shouldn't fight Warder. Aes Sedai shouldn't fight Aes Sedai. Should never happen. Not now. Not ever."

"But it did," Gawyn said.

Sleete nodded.

"And now we've got two different groups of Aes Sedai," Gawyn continued, "with two different armies, one besieging the other."

"Just keep your head down," Sleete said. "There are hot tempers in the Tower, but there are wise minds as well. They'll do the right thing."

"Which is?"

"End it," Sleete said. "With killing if necessary, other ways if possible. Nothing is worth this division. Nothing."

Gawyn nodded.

Sleete shook his head. "My Aes Sedai, she didn't like the feel of things in the Tower. Wanted to get out. She's wise . . . wise and crafty. But she's also not influential, so the others don't listen to her. Aes Sedai. Sometimes, all they seem to care about is who carries the biggest stick."

Gawyn leaned closer. One rarely heard talk about Aes Sedai ranking and influence. They didn't have ranks, like the military, but they all instinctively knew who among them was in charge. How did it work? Sleete seemed to have some idea, but he didn't talk further on it, so it would have to remain a mystery for now.

"Hattori got out," Sleete continued softly. "Went on this mission to al'Thor, never knowing the depth of what it was about. She just didn't want to be in the Tower. Wise woman." He sighed, standing upright and laying a hand on Gawyn's shoulder. "Hammar was a good man."

"He was," Gawyn said, feeling a twist in his stomach.

"But he would have killed you," Sleete said. "Killed you cleanly and quickly. He was the one on the offensive, not you. He understood why you did what you did. Nobody made any good decisions that day. There weren't any good decisions to be made."

"I . . ." Gawyn just nodded. "Thank you."

Sleete removed his hand and walked toward the entrance. He glanced back, however. "Some say that Hattori should have gone back for me," he said. "Those Younglings of yours, they think she abandoned me at Dumai's Wells. She didn't. She knew I lived. She knew I hurt. But she also trusted me to do my duty while she did hers. *She* needed to get news to the Greens of what had happened at Dumai's Wells, of what the Amyrlin's true orders with al'Thor had entailed. *I* needed to survive. We did our duty. But once that message had been sent, if she hadn't felt me approaching on my own, she would have come for me. No matter what. And we both know it."

With that, he left. Gawyn was left thinking on the curious parting words. Sleete was often an odd one to talk to. As fluid as he was as a swordsman, he didn't make conversation smoothly.

Gawyn shook his head, leaving the barn and waving Corbet free of watch duty. There was no possibility of Gawyn agreeing to become Hattori's Warder. The offer had been tempting for a heartbeat, but only as a way of escaping his problems. He knew that he would not be happy as her Warder, or anyone's Warder save Egwene's.

He'd promised Egwene anything. Anything, as long as it didn't hurt Andor or Elayne. Light, he'd promised her not to kill al'Thor. At least, not until after Gawyn could prove for certain that the Dragon had killed his mother. Why couldn't Egwene see that the man she'd grown up with had turned into a monster, twisted by the One Power? Al'Thor needed to be put down. For the good of them all.

Gawyn clenched and unclenched his fist, stalking across the village center, wishing he could extend the peace and stillness of sword fighting to the rest of his life. The air was pungent with the scent of cows and dung from the barns; he would be glad to get back to a proper city. Dorlan's size and remoteness might make it a good place to hide, but Gawyn strongly wished that Elaida had chosen a less odorous place to house the Younglings. His clothing seemed likely to carry the scent of cattle for the rest of his days—assuming the rebel army didn't discover and slaughter them all in the next few weeks.

Gawyn shook his head as he approached the mayor's house. The two-story building had a peaked roof and sat at the very center of the village. The main body of the Young-lings was camped in the small field out behind the building. Once, that patch had grown blackberries, but the too-hot summer followed by the blizzard of a winter had killed the bushes. They were one of many casualties that were going to lead to an even harsher winter this year.

The field wasn't the best place to camp—the men were constantly grumping about picking blackberry thorns out of their skin—but it was close to the center of the village while yet somewhat secluded. A few thorns were worth the convenience.

To reach the field, Gawyn had to cut across the unpaved village square and pass by the canal that ran past the front of the mayor's house. He nodded to a group of women wash-ing clothes there. The Aes Sedai had recruited them to do the wash for the sisters and for Gawyn's officers. The pay was small for so much work, and Gawyn gave the women what little extra he could afford out of his own pocket, a gesture that had earned him laughter from Narenwin Sedai, but thanks from the village women. Gawyn's mother had always taught that the workers were the spine of a kingdom; break them, and you'd soon find that you could no longer move. This city's people might not be his sister's subjects, but he would not see them taken advantage of by his troops.

He passed the mayor's home, noting the closed shutters on the windows. Marlesh lounged outside, his petite Aes Sedai standing with hands on her hips and scowling at the door. Apparently, she had been refused entry. Why? Vasha didn't have a great deal of rank among the Aes Sedai, but she also wasn't as low as Hattori. If Vasha had been denied entrance . . . well, perhaps there *were* important words being shared inside the building. That made Gawyn curious.

His men would have ignored it—Rajar would have told him that Aes Sedai business was best left to their confer-ences, without unwanted ears flapping to make a mess of things. That was one reason that Gawyn wouldn't make a good Warder. He didn't trust Aes Sedai. His mother had, and look where that had gotten her. And how the White Tower had treated Elayne and Egwene . . . well, he might support the Aes Sedai, but he certainly didn't trust them.

He rounded the back of the building, going about a per-fectly legitimate inspection of the guards. Most of the Aes

Sedai in the village didn't have Warders—either they were Reds or they had left their Warders behind. Some few were old enough to have lost Warders to age and never chosen new ones. Two unfortunate women had lost their Warders at Dumai's Wells. Gawyn and the others did their best to pretend they didn't notice the red eyes or occasional sobs coming from their rooms.

The Aes Sedai, of course, claimed that they didn't need the Youngling guards as protection. They were probably right. But Gawyn had seen dead Aes Sedai at Dumai's Wells; they weren't invincible.

At the back doors, Hal Moir saluted and let Gawyn enter to continue his inspection. Gawyn strode up a short, straight set of stairs and entered the upper hallway. There, he relieved Berden, the dark-skinned Tairen Youngling who was on watch. Berden was an officer, and Gawyn told him to go check on the food distribution in the camp. The man nodded, then left.

Gawyn hesitated in front of Narenwin Sedai's room. If he wanted to hear what was going on between the Aes Sedai, the obvious thing to do would be to eavesdrop. Berden had been the only guard on the second floor, and there were no Warders to protect against unwanted ears. But the thought of listening in left a sour taste in Gawyn's mouth. He shouldn't *have* to eavesdrop. He was the commander of the Younglings, and the Aes Sedai were taking good advantage of his troops. They owed him information. Therefore, rather than trying to listen, he gave a firm knock on the door.

The knock was met by silence. Then the door cracked to show a sliver of Covarla's frowning face. The light-haired Red had been in charge of the sisters in the city before being displaced, but she was still one of the more important women in Dorlan.

"We were not to be interrupted," she snapped through the sliver of open doorway. "Your soldiers had orders to keep everyone out, even other sisters."

"Those rules don't apply to me," Gawyn said, meeting her eyes. "My men are in serious danger in this village. If you won't let me be part of the planning, then I demand at least to be able to listen."

Covarla's impassive face seemed to show annoyance. "Your impudence seems to grow by the day, child," she said. "Perhaps you need to be removed and a more suitable replacement raised to captain that group."

Gawyn clenched his jaw.

"You think they wouldn't set you aside if a sister asked it of them?" Covarla asked, smiling faintly. "A sorry excuse for an army they may be, but they know their place. A pity the same cannot be said for their commander. Go back to your men, Gawyn Trakand."

With that, she shut the door on him.

Gawyn itched to force his way into the room. But that would be satisfying for all of about two breaths, which was how long it would take the Aes Sedai to truss him up with the Power. How would that be for the Younglings' morale? Seeing their commander, the brave Gawyn Trakand, cast out of the building with a gag of Air in his mouth? He ignored his frustration, turning back down the stairs. He went into the kitchen and leaned against the far wall, staring at the steps to the second floor. Now that he'd relieved Berden, he felt he needed to remain on watch himself or send a runner to fetch another man. He wanted to think for a few moments first; if their conference above took long, he'd appoint a replacement.

Aes Sedai. Sensible men stayed away from them when possible, and obeyed them with alacrity when staying away was impossible. Gawyn had trouble doing either; his bloodline prevented staying away, his pride interfered with obeying them. He had supported Elaida in the rebellion not because he liked her—she'd always been cold during her years acting as his mother's advisor. No, he'd supported her because he'd disliked Siuan's treatment of his sister and Egwene.

But would Elaida have treated the girls any better? Would any of them have? Gawyn had made his decision in a moment of passion; it hadn't been the coolheaded act of loyalty that his men assumed.

Where *was* his loyalty, then?

A few minutes later, footsteps on the stairs and faint voices from the hallway above announced that the Aes Sedai had finished their secret conference. Covarla came down the stairs in red and yellow, saying something to the sisters behind her. ". . . can't believe the rebels set up their own Amyrlin."

Narenwin—thin and square-faced—came next, nodding. Then, shockingly, Katerine Alruddin walked out of the stairwell behind them. Gawyn stood up straight, stunned. Katerine had *left* the camp weeks before, the day after Narenwin's arrival. The raven-haired Red had not been part of the original group that was ordered to Dorlan, and had used that as an excuse to return to the White Tower.

When had she come back to Dorlan? *How* had she come back? His men would have reported to Gawyn if they'd seen her. He doubted the watchposts could have missed her arrival.

She eyed Gawyn as the three Aes Sedai passed through the kitchen, smiling slyly. She'd noticed his shock.

"Yes," Katerine said, turning to Covarla. "Imagine it—an Amyrlin without an actual seat to sit upon! They're a group of foolish girls creating a child's puppet show with dolls dressed up like their betters. Of course they would pick a wilder to do the duty, and a mere Accepted at that. They knew how pathetic the decision was."

"But at least she was captured," Narenwin noted, pausing at the doorway as Covarla passed through.

Katerine laughed sharply. "Captured and made to howl half the day. I wouldn't want to be that al'Vere girl right now. Of course, it's no less than she deserves for letting them put the Amyrlin's shawl on her shoulders."

What? Gawyn thought with shock.

The three passed out of the kitchen, voices fading. Gawyn barely noticed. He staggered back, hitting the wall for support. It couldn't be! It sounded like . . . Egwene . . . He *had* to have misheard!

But Aes Sedai couldn't lie. He'd heard rumors that the rebels had their own Hall and Amyrlin . . . but Egwene? It was ridiculous! She was only Accepted!

But who better to set up for a potential fall? Perhaps none of the sisters had been willing to put their necks on the line by taking the title. A younger woman like Egwene would have made a perfect pawn.

Pulling himself together, Gawyn hurried out of the kitchen and after the Aes Sedai. He passed into the late afternoon to find Vasha standing, mouth drooping, as she stared at Katerine. Apparently, Gawyn wasn't the only one shocked by the Red's sudden return.

Gawyn caught Tando, one of the Youngling guards at the front of the building, by the arm. "Did you see her enter the building?"

The young Andoran shook his head. "No, my Lord. One of the men inside reported seeing her meet with the other Aes Sedai—she came down out of the attic suddenly, it seems. But none of the guards knows *how* she got in!"

Gawyn released the soldier and dashed after Katerine. He caught up to the three women in the middle of the dusty town square. All three turned ageless faces toward him, wearing identical thin-mouthed frowns. Covarla's eyes were particular harsh, but Gawyn didn't care if they took the Younglings from him or if they tied him up in air. Humiliation didn't matter. Only one thing mattered.

"Is it true?" he demanded. Then, cringing, he forced respect into his voice. "Please, Katerine Sedai. Is it true what I overheard you saying about the rebels and their Amyrlin?"

She eyed him, measuring him. "I suppose it would be good to pass this news among your soldiers. Yes, the rebel Amyrlin has been captured."

"And her name?" Gawyn asked.

"Egwene al'Vere," Katerine said. "Let the rumors spread truth, for once." She nodded to him with dismissive curtness, then began walking with the other two again. "Put what I have taught you to good use. The Amyrlin insists that the raids be stepped up, and these weaves should lend you unprecedented mobility. Don't be surprised if the rebels anticipate you, however. They know that we have their so-called Amyrlin, and have probably guessed that we have the new weaves as well. It won't be long before Traveling is had by all. Use the edge you've been given before it dulls."

Gawyn was barely listening. A piece of his mind was shocked. Traveling? A thing of legends. Was *that* how Gareth Bryne was keeping his army supplied?

However, the greater part of Gawyn's brain was still numb. Siuan Sanche had been stilled and slated for execution, and she had simply been a deposed Amyrlin. What would they do with a *false* Amyrlin, a leader of a rebel faction?

Made to howl half the day. . . .

Egwene was being tortured. She would be stilled! She probably had been already. After that, she would be executed.

Gawyn watched the three Aes Sedai walk away. Then he turned slowly, strangely calm, laying his hand on the pommel of his sword.

Egwene was in trouble. He blinked deliberately, standing in the square, cattle calling distantly, water bubbling in the canal beside him.

Egwene would be executed.

Where is your loyalty, Gawyn Trakand?

He crossed the village, walking with a strangely sure step. The Younglings would be unreliable in an action against the White Tower. He couldn't use them to mount a rescue. But he was unlikely to be able to manage one on his own. That left him with only one option.

Ten minutes later found him in his tent, carefully packing his saddlebags. Most of his things would have to stay. There were far scout outposts, and he had visited them before in surprise inspections. That would make a good excuse for him to leave the camp.

He couldn't arouse suspicions. Covarla was right. The Younglings followed him. They respected him. But they were not his—they belonged to the White Tower, and would turn on him as quickly as he had turned on Hammar if it were the will of the Amyrlin. If any of them got a *hint* of what he was planning, he wouldn't manage to get a hundred yards away.

He closed and latched his saddlebags. That would have to do. He pushed his way out of the tent, slinging the bags over his shoulder, then made his way toward the horse lines. As he walked, he flagged down Rajar, who was showing a squad of soldiers some advanced swordplay techniques. Rajar set another man in charge, then hurried over to Gawyn, frowning at the saddlebags.

"I'm going to inspect the fourth outpost," Gawyn said.

Rajar glanced at the sky; it was already dimming. "So late?"

"Last time I inspected in the morning," Gawyn said. Odd, how his heart wasn't racing. Calm and even. "Time before that, it was the afternoon. But the most dangerous time to be surprised is evening, when it's still light enough for an attack but late enough that men are tired and full of supper."

Rajar nodded, joining Gawyn as he walked. "Light knows

we need them for watchful scouts now," he agreed. Bryne's own scouts had been investigating villages not half a day's ride from Dorlan. "I'll get you an escort."

"Not needed," Gawyn said. "Last time, Outpost Four saw me coming from a good half a mile. A squad raises too much dust. I want to see how keen their eyes are when it's just one rider."

Rajar frowned again.

"I'll be safe," Gawyn said, forcing out a wry smile. "Rajar, you know I will be. What? Are you afraid I'll be taken by bandits?"

Rajar relaxed, chuckling. "You? They'd sooner catch Sleete. All right, then. But make certain to send a messenger for me when you get back into camp. I'll stay up half the night worrying if you don't return."

Sorry to cost you the sleep then, my friend, Gawyn thought, nodding. Rajar ran back to supervise the sparring, and Gawyn soon found himself just outside the camp, undoing Challenge's hobble as a village boy—doubling as a stablehand—fetched his saddle.

"You have the look of a man who has made up his mind," a quiet voice said suddenly.

Gawyn spun, hand falling to his sword. One of the shadows nearby was moving. Looking closely, he was able to make out the form of a shadowed man with a crooked nose. Curse those Warder cloaks!

Gawyn tried to feign casualness as he had with Rajar. "Happy to have something to do, I suppose," he said, turning from Sleete as the stableboy approached. Gawyn tossed him a copper and took the saddle himself, dismissing the boy.

Sleete continued to watch from the shadow of a massive pine as Gawyn put the saddle on Challenge's back. The Warder knew. Gawyn's act had fooled everyone else, but he could sense that it wouldn't work on this man. Light! Was he going to have to kill another man he respected? *Burn you, Elaida! Burn you, Siuan Sanche, and your entire Tower. Stop using people. Stop using me!*

"When shall I tell your men that you aren't returning?" Sleete asked.

Gawyn pulled the saddle straps tight and waited for his horse to exhale. He looked over Challenge, frowning. "You don't plan to stop me?"

Sleete chuckled. "I fought you thrice today and didn't win a single bout, although I had a good man to lend me aid. You have the look about you of a man who will kill if needed, and I don't thirst for death so eagerly as some might assume."

"You'd fight me," Gawyn said, finally doing up the saddle and lifting the bags into place, tying them on. Challenge snorted. The horse never did like carrying extra weight. "You'd die if you thought it was necessary. If you attacked, even if I killed you, it would raise a ruckus. I'd never be able to explain why I'd killed a Warder. You could stop me."

"True," Sleete said.

"Then why let me go?" Gawyn said, rounding the gelding and taking the reins. He met those shadowed eyes and thought he caught the faintest hint of a smile on the lips beneath them.

"Perhaps I just like to see men care," Sleete said. "Perhaps I hope you'll find a way to help end this. Perhaps I am feeling lazy and sore with a bruised spirit from so many defeats. May you find what you seek, young Trakand." And with a rustle of the cloak, Sleete withdrew, fading into the darkness of oncoming night.

Gawyn slung himself into his saddle. There was only one place he could think to go for help in rescuing Egwene.

With a kick of the heels, he left Dorlan behind.

CHAPTER
14

A Box Opens

S o this is one of the Shadowsouled," Sorilea said. The white-haired Wise One circled around the prisoner, looking thoughtfully at Semirhage. Of course, Cadsuane had not expected fear from one such as Sorilea. The Aiel woman was a rugged creature, like a statue that had weathered storm after storm, patient before the winds. Among the Aiel, this Wise One was a particular specimen of strength. She had arrived at the manor house only recently, coming with those who had brought al'Thor a report from Bandar Eban.

Cadsuane had anticipated finding many things among the Aiel who followed Rand al'Thor: fierce warriors, strange ways, honor and loyalty, inexperience with subtlety and politics. She had been right. One thing she had certainly *not* expected to find, however, was an equal. Certainly not in a Wise One who could barely channel. And yet, oddly, that was how she regarded the leathery-faced Aiel woman.

Not that she trusted Sorilea. The Wise One had her own goals, and they might not completely coincide with Cadsuane's. However, she *did* find Sorilea capable, and there were blessed few people in the world these days who deserved that word.

Semirhage flinched suddenly, and Sorilea cocked her head. The Forsaken was not floating this time; she stood upright, wearing the stiff brown dress, her short, dark hair tangled from lack of brushing. She still projected superiority and control. Just as Cadsuane herself would have in a similar situation.

"What are these weaves?" Sorilea asked, gesturing. The weaves in question were the source of Semirhage's occasional flinching.

"A personal trick of mine," Cadsuane said, undoing the weaves and remaking them to show how they were done. "They ring a sound in your subjects' ears every few minutes and flash a light in their eyes, keeping them from sleep."

"You hope to make her so fatigued that she will talk," Sorilea said, studying the Forsaken again.

Semirhage was warded to keep her from hearing them, of course. Despite two days without decent sleep, the woman wore a serene expression, eyes open but blocked by glowing lights. She had likely mastered some kind of mental trick to help her stave off exhaustion.

"I doubt it will break her," Cadsuane admitted. "Phaw! It barely even makes her flinch." She, Sorilea and Bair—an aged Wise One with no channeling ability—were the only ones in the room. The Aes Sedai maintaining Semirhage's shield sat in their places outside.

Sorilea nodded. "One of the Shadowsouled will not be manipulated so easily. Still, you are wise to try, considering your . . . limitations."

"We could speak to the *Car'a'carn*," Bair said. "Convince him to turn this one over to us for a time. A few days of . . . delicate Aiel questioning and she would speak whatever you wish."

Cadsuane smiled noncommittally. As if she would let another handle the questioning! This woman's secrets were too valuable to risk, even in the hands of allies. "Well, you are welcome to ask," she said, "but I doubt al'Thor will listen. You know how the fool boy can be when it comes to hurting women."

Bair sighed. It was odd to think of this grandmotherly lady engaging in "delicate Aiel questioning."

"Yes," she said. "You are right, I suspect. Rand al'Thor is twice as stubborn as any clan chief I've known. And twice as arrogant too. To presume that women cannot bear pain as well as men!"

Cadsuane snorted at that. "To be honest, I considered having this one strung up and whipped, al'Thor's prohibitions be blackened! But I don't think it would work. Phaw!

We'll need to find something other than pain to break this one."

Sorilea was still regarding Semirhage. "I would speak with her."

Cadsuane made a motion, dismissing the weaves that kept Semirhage from hearing, seeing or speaking. The woman blinked—just once—to clear her vision, then turned to Sorilea and Bair. "Ah," she said. "Aiel. You were such good servants, once. Tell me, how strongly does it bite, knowing how you betrayed your oaths? Your ancestors would cry for punishment if they knew how many deaths lay at the hands of their descendants."

Sorilea gave no reaction. Cadsuane knew some tidbits of what al'Thor had revealed about the Aiel, things that had been said at second or third hand. Al'Thor claimed that the Aiel had once followed the Way of the Leaf, sworn not to do harm, before betraying their oaths. Cadsuane had been interested to learn of these rumors, and she was more interested to hear Semirhage corroborating them.

"She seems so much more human than I had anticipated," Sorilea said to Bair. "Her expressions, her tone, her accent, while strange, are easy to understand. I had not expected that."

Semirhage's eyes narrowed for just a moment at that comment. Odd. That was a stronger reaction than virtually any of the punishments had produced. The flashes of light and sound prompted only slight involuntary twitches. This comment of Sorilea's, however, seemed to affect Semirhage on an emotional level. Would the Wise Ones actually succeed so easily where Cadsuane had long failed?

"I think this is what we need to remember," Bair said. "A woman is just a woman, no matter how old, no matter what secrets she remembers. Flesh can be cut, blood can be spilled, bones can be broken."

"In truth, I feel almost disappointed, Cadsuane Melaidhrin," Sorilea said, shaking a white-haired head. "This monster has very small fangs."

Semirhage reacted no further. Her control was back, her face serene, her eyes imperious. "I have heard some little of you new, oathless Aiel and your interpretations of honor. I will very much enjoy investigating how much pain and suffering it will require before members of your clans will shame themselves. Tell me, how far do you think I would have to push before one of you would kill a blacksmith and dine on his flesh?"

She knew more than "some little" if she understood the near-sacred nature of blacksmiths among the Aiel. Sorilea stiffened at the comment, but let it go. She rewove the ward against listening, then paused, and placed the globes of light in front of Semirhage's eyes as well. Yes, she was weak in the Power, but she was a very quick learner.

"Is it wise to keep her like this?" Sorilea asked, her tone implying that of any other she would have made a demand. For Cadsuane, she softened her words, and it almost brought a smile to Cadsuane's lips. They were like two aged hawks, Sorilea and she, accustomed to roosting and reigning, now forced to nest in neighboring trees. Deference did not come easily to either one of them.

"If I were to choose," Sorilea continued, "I think that I would have her throat slit and her corpse laid out on the dust to dry. Keeping her alive is like keeping a snapwood blacklance as a pet."

"Phaw!" Cadsuane said, grimacing. "You're right about the danger, but killing her now would be worse. Al'Thor cannot—or will not—give me an accurate count of the number of Forsaken he has slain, but he implies that at least half of them still live. They'll be there to fight at the Last Battle, and each weave we learn from Semirhage is one fewer they can use to surprise us."

Sorilea did not seem convinced, but she pressed the issue no further. "And the item?" she asked. "May I see it?"

Cadsuane almost snapped a no. But . . . Sorilea had taught Cadsuane Traveling, an incredibly powerful tool. That had been an offering, a hand extended. Cadsuane needed to work with these women, Sorilea most of all. Al'Thor was a bigger project than one woman could handle.

"Come with me," Cadsuane said, leaving the wooden room. The Wise Ones followed. Outside, Cadsuane instructed the sisters—Daigian and Sarene—to make certain that Semirhage was kept awake, eyes open. It was unlikely to work, but it was the best strategy Cadsuane had at the moment.

Though . . . she *did* also have Semirhage's momentary

look, that hint of anger, displayed at Sorilea's comment. When you could control a person's anger, you could control their other emotions as well. That was why she had focused so hard on teaching al'Thor to rein in his temper.

Control and anger. What was it that Sorilea had said to get the reaction? That Semirhage seemed disappointingly human. It was as if Sorilea had come expecting one of the Forsaken to be as twisted as a Myrddraal or Draghkar. And why not? The Forsaken had been figures of legend for three thousand years, looming shadows of darkness and mystery. It could be disappointing to discover that they were, in many ways, the most human of the Dark One's followers: petty, destructive and argumentative. At least, that was how al'Thor claimed they acted. He was so strangely familiar with them.

Semirhage saw herself as more than human, though. That poise, that control of her surroundings, was a source of strength for her.

Cadsuane shook her head. Too many problems and far too little time. The wooden hallway itself was another reminder of the al'Thor boy's foolishness; Cadsuane could still smell smoke, strong enough to be unpleasant. The gaping hole in the front of the manor—draped only with a cloth—let in chill air during the spring nights. They should have moved, but he claimed that he would not be chased away.

Al'Thor seemed almost eager for the Last Battle. Or perhaps just resigned. To get there he felt he had to force his way through the petty squabbles of people like a midnight traveler pushing through banks of snow to arrive at the inn. The problem was, al'Thor wasn't ready for the Last Battle. Cadsuane could feel it in the way he spoke, the way he acted. The way he regarded the world with that dark, nearly dazed expression. If the man he was now faced the Dark One to decide the fate of the world, Cadsuane feared for all people.

Cadsuane and the two Wise Ones reached her chamber in the manor, a sturdy undamaged room with a good view of the trampled green and camp out front. She made few demands in the way of decoration: a stout bed, a lockable trunk, a mirror and stand. She was too old and impatient to bother with anything else.

The trunk was a decoy; she kept some gold and other

relatively worthless items in it. Her most precious possessions she either wore—in the form of her *ter'angreal* ornaments—or kept locked in a dingy-looking document box that sat on her mirror stand. Of worn oak, the stain uneven, the box had enough dings and dents to look used— but wasn't so shabby as to be out of place with her other things. As Sorilea closed the door behind the three of them, Cadsuane disarmed the box's traps.

It was strange to her how few Aes Sedai learned to innovate with the One Power. They memorized time-tested and traditional weaves, but gave barely a thought for what else they could do. True, experimenting with the One Power could be disastrous, but many simple extrapolations could be made without danger. Her weave for this box was one such. Until recently, she'd used a standard weave of Fire, Spirit and Air to destroy any documents in the box if an intruder opened it. Effective, if a bit unimaginative.

Her new weave was much more versatile. It didn't destroy the items in the box—Cadsuane wasn't certain if they could be destroyed. Instead, the weaves—inverted to be invisible—sprang out in twisting threads of Air and captured anyone in the room when the box was opened. Then another weave set out a large sound, imitating a hundred trumpets playing while lights flashed in the air to give the alarm. The weaves would also go off if anyone opened the box, moved it, or barely touched it with the most delicate thread of the One Power.

Cadsuane flipped up the lid. The extreme precaution was necessary. For inside this box were two items that presented very serious danger.

Sorilea walked over, looking in at the contents. One was a figurine of a wise, bearded man holding aloft a sphere, about a foot tall. The other was a black metallic collar and two bracelets: an *a'dam* made for a man. With this *ter'angreal*, a woman could turn a man who could channel into her slave, controlling his ability to touch the One Power. Perhaps controlling him completely. They had not tested the collar. Al'Thor had forbidden it.

Sorilea hissed quietly, ignoring the statue and focusing on the bracelets and collar. "This thing is evil."

"Yes," Cadsuane said. Rarely would she have called a simple object "evil," but this one was. "Nynaeve al'Meara claims some familiarity with this thing. Though I have not been able to press out of the girl *how* she knows these things, she claims to know that there was only one male *a'dam*, and that she'd arranged for its disposal in the ocean. She also admits, however, that she didn't see it destroyed personally. It may have been used as a pattern by the Seanchan."

"This is unsettling to see," Sorilea said. "If one of the Shadowsouled, or even one of the Seanchan, captured him with this. . . ."

"Light protect us all," Bair whispered.

"And the people who have these are the same people with whom al'Thor wishes to make peace?" Sorilea shook her head. "Creation of these abominations alone should warrant a blood feud. I heard that there were others like it. What of those?"

"Stored elsewhere," Cadsuane said, shutting the lid. "Along with the female *a'dam* we took. Some acquaintances of mine—Aes Sedai who have retired from the world—are testing them trying to discover their weakness." They also had *Callandor*. Cadsuane was loath to let it out of her sight, but she felt that the sword still held secrets that could be teased out.

"I keep this one here because I intend to find a way to test it on a man," she said. "That would be the best way to discover its weaknesses. Al'Thor won't allow any of his Asha'man to be leashed by it, however. Not for the shortest time."

This made Bair uncomfortable. "A little like testing a spear's strength by stabbing it into someone," she muttered.

Sorilea, however, nodded in agreement. She understood.

One of the first things Cadsuane had done after capturing those female *a'dam* was put one on and practice ways to escape from it. She'd done so under carefully controlled circumstances, of course, with women she trusted to help her escape. They'd eventually had to do that. Cadsuane had been able to discover no way out on her own.

But if your enemy was planning to do something to you, you had to discover how to counter it. Even if that meant leashing yourself. Al'Thor couldn't see this. When she asked, he simply muttered about "that bloody box" and being beaten.

"We have to do something about that man," Sorilea said, meeting Cadsuane's eyes. "He has grown worse since we last met."

"He has," Cadsuane said. "He's surprisingly accomplished at ignoring my training."

"Then let us discuss," Sorilea said, pulling over a stool. "A plan must be arranged. For the good of all."

"For the good of all," Cadsuane agreed. "Al'Thor himself most of all."

CHAPTER
15

A Place to Begin

Rand woke on the floor of a hallway. He sat up, listening to the distant sound of water. The stream outside the manor house? No . . . no, that was wrong. The walls and floor here were stone, not wood. No candles or lamps hung from the stonework, and yet there was light, ambient in the air.

He stood, then straightened his red coat, feeling strangely unafraid. He recognized this place from somewhere, distant in his memory. How had he come here? The recent past was clouded, and seemed to slip from him, like fading trails of mist. . . .

No, he thought firmly. His memories obeyed, snapping back into place before the strength of his determination. He had been in the Domani manor house, awaiting a report from Rhuarc about the capture of the first few members of the merchant council. Min had been reading *Each Castle*, a biography, in the deep, green chair of the room they shared.

Rand had been exhausted, as he often was lately. He'd gone to lie down. He was asleep, then. Was this the World of Dreams? Though he had visited it on occasion, he knew very few specifics. Egwene and the Aiel dreamwalkers spoke of it only guardedly.

This place felt different from the dream world, and oddly familiar. He looked down the hallway; it was so long that it vanished into shadows, walls broken by doors at intervals, the wood dry and cracked. *Yes* . . . he thought, seizing at a memory. *I have* been here before, but not in a long time.

He chose one of the doors at random—he knew that it

wouldn't matter which one he picked—and pushed it open. There was a room beyond, of modest size. The far side was a series of gray stone arches, beyond them a little court-yard and a sky of burning red clouds. The clouds grew and sprang from one another like bubbles in boiling water. They were the clouds of an impending storm, unnatural though they were.

He looked more closely, and saw that each new cloud formed the shape of a tormented face, the mouth open in a silent scream. The cloud would swell, expanding upon itself, face distorting, jaw working, cheeks twisting, eyes bulging. Then it would split, other faces swelling out of its surface, yelling and seething. It was transfixing and hor-rifying at the same time.

There was no ground beyond the courtyard. Just that ter-rible sky.

Rand did not want to look toward the left side of the room. The fireplace was there. The stones that formed floor, hearth and columns were warped, as if they had been melted by an extreme heat. At the edges of his vision, they seemed to shift and change. The angles and proportions of the room were wrong. Just as they had been when he'd come here, long ago.

Something was different this time, however. Something about the colors. Many of the stones were black, as if they'd been burned, and cracks laced them. Distant red light glowed from within, as if they had cores of molten lava. There had once been a table here, hadn't there? Polished and of fine wood, its ordinary lines a discomforting con-trast to the distorted angles of the stones?

The table was gone, but two chairs sat before the fire-place, high backed and facing the flames, obscuring whom-ever might be sitting in them. Rand forced himself to walk forward, his boots clicking on stones that burned. He felt no heat, either from them or the fire. His breath caught and his heart pounded as he approached those chairs. He feared what he would find.

He rounded them. A man sat in the chair on the left. Tall and youthful, he had a square face and ancient blue eyes that reflected the hearthfire, turning his irises almost pur-ple. The other chair was empty. Rand walked to it and sat down, calming his heart and watching the dancing flames.

He had seen this man before in visions, not unlike the ones that appeared when he thought of Mat or Perrin.

The colors did not appear on this thought of his friends. That was odd, but somehow not unexpected. The visions he'd seen of the man in the other chair were different from the ones involving Perrin and Mat. They were more visceral, somehow, more real. At times during those visions, Rand had felt almost as if he could reach out and touch this man. He'd been afraid of what would happen if he did.

He had met the man only once. At Shadar Logoth. The stranger had saved Rand's life, and Rand had often wondered who he had been. Now, in this place, Rand finally knew.

"You are dead," Rand whispered. "I killed you."

The man didn't look from the fire as he laughed. It was a rough, low-throated laugh that held little true mirth. Once, Rand had known this man only as Ba'alzamon—a name for the Dark One—and had foolishly thought that in killing him, he had defeated the Shadow for good.

"I watched you die," Rand said. "I stabbed you through the chest with *Callandor*. Isha—"

"That is not my name," the man interrupted, still watching the flames. "I am known as Moridin, now."

"The name is irrelevant," Rand said angrily. "You are dead, and this is just a dream."

"Just a dream," Moridin said, chuckling. "Yes." The man was clad in a black coat and trousers, the darkness relieved only by red embroidery on the sleeves.

Moridin finally looked at him. Flames from the fire cast bright red and orange light across his angular face and unblinking eyes. "Why do you always whine that way? Just a dream. Do you not know that many dreams are more truthful than the waking world?"

"You are dead," Rand repeated stubbornly.

"So are you. I watched *you* die, you know. Lashing out in a tempest, creating an entire mountain to mark your cairn. So arrogant."

Lews Therin had—upon discovering that he'd killed all that he loved—drawn upon the One Power and destroyed himself, creating Dragonmount in the process. Mention of this event always brought on howls of grief and anger in Rand's mind.

But this time, there was silence.

Moridin turned back to watch the heatless flames. To the side, in the stones of the fireplace, Rand saw movement. Flickering bits of shadow, just barely visible through the cracks in the stones. The red-hot heat shone behind, like rock turned molten, and those shadows moved, frantic. Just faintly, Rand could hear scratching. Rats, he realized. There were rats behind the stones, being consumed by the terrible heat trapped on the other side. Their claws scratched, pushing through the cracks, as they tried to escape their burning.

Some of those tiny hands seemed almost human.

Just a dream, Rand told himself forcefully. Just a dream. But he knew the truth of what Moridin had said. Rand's enemy still lived. Light! How many of the others had returned as well? Anger made him grip the armrest of the chair. Perhaps he should have been terrified, but he had stopped running from this creature and his master long ago. Rand had no room left for fear. In fact, it should be Moridin who feared, for the last time they had met, Rand had killed him.

"How?" Rand demanded.

"Long ago, I promised you that the Great Lord could restore your lost love. Do you not think that he can easily recover one who serves him?"

Another name for the Dark One was Lord of the Grave. Yes, it was true, even if Rand wished he could deny it. Why should he be surprised to see his enemies return, when the Dark One could restore the dead to life?

"We are all reborn," Moridin continued, "spun back into the Pattern time and time again. Death is no barrier to my master save for those who have known balefire. They are beyond his grasp. It is a wonder we can remember them."

So some of the others really *were* dead. Balefire was the key. But how had Moridin gotten into Rand's dreams? Rand set wards each night. He glanced at Moridin, noticing something odd about the man's eyes. Small black specks floated about in the whites, crossing back and forth like bits of ash blown on a leisurely wind.

"The Great Lord can grant you sanity, you know," Moridin said.

"Your last gift of sanity brought me no comfort," Rand said, surprising himself with the words. That had been Lews Therin's memory, not his own. Yet Lews Therin was gone

from his mind. Oddly, Rand felt more stable—somehow—
here in this place where all else appeared fluid. The pieces
of himself fit together better. Not perfectly, of course, but
better than they had in recent memory.

Moridin snorted softly, but said nothing. Rand turned
back to the flames, watching them twist and flicker. They
formed shapes, like the clouds, but these were headless
bodies, skeletal, backs arching in pain, writhing for a moment in fire, spasming, before flashing into nothing.

Rand watched that fire for a time, thinking. One might
have thought that they were two old friends, enjoying the
warmth of a winter hearth. Except that the flames gave no
heat, and Rand would someday kill this man again. Or die
at his hands.

Moridin tapped his fingers on the chair. "Why have you
come here?"

Come here? Rand thought, with shock. Hadn't Moridin
brought him?

"I feel so tired," Moridin continued, closing his eyes. "Is
that you, or is it me? I could throttle Semirhage for what
she did."

Rand frowned. Was Moridin mad? Ishamael had certainly seemed crazy, at the end.

"It is not time for us to fight," Moridin said, waving a
hand at Rand. "Go. Leave me in peace. I do not know what
would happen to us if we killed one another. The Great
Lord will have you soon enough. His victory is assured."

"He has failed before and will fail again," Rand said. "I
will defeat him."

Moridin laughed again, the same heartless laugh as before. "Perhaps you will," he said. "But do you think that
matters? Consider it. The Wheel turns, time and time again.
Over and over the Ages turn, and men fight the Great Lord.
But someday, he will win, and when he does, the Wheel
will stop.

"That is why his victory is assured. I think it will be this
Age, but if not, then in another. When you are victorious, it
only leads to another battle. When he is victorious, all things
will end. Can you not see that there is no hope for you?"

"Is that what made you turn to his side?" Rand asked.
"You were always so full of thoughts, Elan. Your logic destroyed you, didn't it?"

"There is no path to victory," Moridin said. "The only path is to follow the Great Lord and rule for a time before all things end. The others are fools. They look for grand rewards in the eternities, but there will be no eternities. Only the now, the last days."

He laughed again, and this time there was joy in it. True pleasure.

Rand stood. Moridin eyed him warily, but did not get up.

"There *is* a way to win, Moridin," Rand said. "I mean to kill him. Slay the Dark One. Let the Wheel turn without his constant taint."

Moridin gave no reaction. He was still staring at the flames. "We are connected," Moridin finally said. "That is how you came here, I suspect, though I do not understand our bond myself. I doubt you can understand the magnitude of the stupidity in your statement."

Rand felt a flash of anger, but fought it down. He would not be goaded. "We shall see."

He reached for the One Power. It was distant, far away. Rand seized it, and felt himself yanked away, as if on a line of *saidin*. The room vanished, and so did the One Power, as Rand entered a deep blackness.

Rand finally stopped thrashing in his sleep, and Min held her breath, hoping that he wouldn't start again. She sat, legs tucked underneath her, wrapped in a blanket as she read in her chair at the corner of the room. A small lamp flickered and danced on the short table beside her, illuminating her stack of musty books. *Falling Shale*, *Marks and Remarks*, *Monuments Past*. Histories, most of them.

Rand sighed softly, but did not move. Min released her breath and settled back into her chair, finger marking her place in a copy of Pelateos's *Ponderings*. With the shutters closed for the night, she could still hear the wind sough in the pines. The room smelled faintly of smoke from the strange fire. Aviendha's quick thinking had made a potential disaster into a mere inconvenience. Not that she was being rewarded for it. The Wise Ones continued to work her as hard as a merchant's last mule.

Min hadn't been able to get close enough to her to have a conversation, despite the fact that they'd been in the camp together for some time now. She didn't know how to think of the other woman. They had become a little more comfortable with one another that evening, sharing *oosquai*. But one day did not friends make, and she was definitely uncomfortable about sharing.

Min glanced again at Rand, lying on his back, eyes closed, breath coming evenly now. His left arm lay across his blankets, the stump exposed. She didn't know how he managed to sleep, with those wounds in his side. As soon as she thought of them, she could feel the pain—it was all part of the rolled-up ball of Rand's emotions in the back of her mind. She had learned to ignore the pain. She'd had to. For him, it would be much, much stronger. How he could stand it, she didn't know.

She wasn't Aes Sedai—thank the Light—but somehow she had bonded him. It was amazing; she could tell where he was, tell if he was distraught. She could mostly keep his emotions from overwhelming her except when they were passionate. But what woman didn't want to be overwhelmed during those moments? It was a particularly . . . exhilarating experience with the bond, which let her feel both her own desire and the raging tempest of fire that was Rand's desire for her.

The thought made her blush, and she pulled open *Ponderings* to distract herself. Rand needed his sleep, and she was going to let him have it. Besides, she needed to study, although she was confronted by conclusions that she didn't like.

These books had belonged to Herid Fel, the kindly old scholar who had joined Rand's school in Cairhien. Min smiled, remembering Fel's distracted way of talking and his confused—yet somehow brilliant—discoveries.

Herid Fel was dead now, murdered, torn apart by Shadowspawn. He'd discovered something in these books, something he'd intended to tell Rand. Something about the Last Battle and the seals on the Dark One's prison. Fel had been killed just before he could pass on the information. Perhaps it was coincidence; perhaps the books had nothing to do with his death. But perhaps they did. Min was determined to find the answers. For Rand, and for Herid himself.

She put down *Ponderings* and picked up *Thoughts Among the Ruins*, a work from over a thousand years ago.

She'd marked a place with a small slip of paper, the very same now-worn note that Herid had sent to Rand shortly before the murder. Min turned it over in her fingers, reading it again.

> Belief and order give strength. Have to clear rubble before you can build. Will explain when see you next. Do not bring girl. Too pretty.

She figured—from reading among his books—that she could trace his thoughts. Rand had wanted information on how to seal the Dark One's prison. Could Fel have discovered what she thought she had?

She shook her head. What was *she* doing trying to solve a scholarly mystery? But who else was there? One of the Brown Ajah might be better suited, but could they be trusted? Even those who had made their oaths to him might decide that it was in Rand's best interests to keep secrets from him. Rand himself was far too busy, and he was too impatient for books lately anyway. That left Min. She was beginning to piece together some of what he would have to do, but there was more—so much more—that was still unknown. She felt she was getting close, but it worried her to reveal what she'd discovered to Rand. How would he respond?

She sighed, scanning the book. She'd never thought that she, of all people, would become a fool for some man. Yet here she was, following him wherever he went, putting his needs before her own. That didn't mean she was his pet, regardless what some of the people in camp said. She followed Rand because she loved him, and she could feel—literally—that he returned her love. Despite the harshness that was invading him bit by bit, despite the anger and the bleakness of his life, he loved her. And so she did what she could to help him.

If she could help solve this one puzzle, the puzzle of sealing the Dark One's prison, she could achieve something not just for Rand, but for the world itself. What did it matter if soldiers in the camp didn't know what her value was? It was probably better if everyone assumed her to be dismissible. Any assassin who came to kill Rand should think that he could ignore Min. The would-be killer would soon discover the knives hidden in Min's sleeves. She wasn't as good with them as Thom Merrilin was, but she knew more than enough to kill.

Rand turned in his sleep, but settled down again. She loved him. She hadn't chosen to do so, but her heart—or the Pattern, or the Creator, or whatever was in charge of these things—had made the decision for her. And now she wouldn't change her feelings if she could. If it meant danger, if it meant suffering the looks of men in the camp, if it meant . . . sharing him with others.

Rand stirred again. This time, he groaned and opened his eyes, sitting up. He raised his hand to his head, somehow managing to look more weary now than he had when he'd gone to sleep. He wore only his smallclothes, and his chest was bare. He sat like that for a long moment, then stood up, walking to the shuttered window.

Min pushed her book closed. "And what do you think you're doing, sheepherder? You barely slept for a couple of hours!"

He opened the shutters and the window, exposing the dark night beyond. A stray curl of wind made her lamp flame shiver.

"Rand?" Min asked.

She could barely hear his voice when he replied. "He's inside my head. He was gone during the dream. But he's back now."

She resisted sinking down in her chair. Light, but she hated hearing about Rand's madness. She'd hoped that when he healed *saidin*, he would be free of the taint's insanities. "He?" she asked, forcing her voice to be steady. "The voice of . . . Lews Therin?"

He turned, clouded night sky outside the window framing his face, the lamp's uneven illumination leaving his features mostly in shadows.

"Rand," she said, setting her book aside and joining him beside the window. "You have to talk to someone. You can't keep it all inside."

"I have to be strong."

She tugged on his arm, turning him toward her. "Keeping me away means you're strong?"

"I'm not—"

"Yes you are. There are things going on in there, behind

those Aiel eyes of yours. Rand, do you think I will stop loving you because of what you hear?"

"You'll be frightened."

"Oh," she said, folding her arms. "So I'm a fragile flower,
am I?"

He opened his mouth, struggling for words, in the way he
once had. Back when he'd been nothing more than a sheepherder on an adventure. "Min, I know you're strong. You
know I do."

"Then trust me to be strong enough to bear what is inside you," she said. "We can't just pretend nothing has happened." She forced herself onward. "The taint left marks on
you. I know it did. But if you can't share it with me, who
can you share it with?"

He ran his hand through his hair, then turned away, beginning to pace. "Burn it all, Min! If my enemies discover
my weaknesses, they will exploit them. I feel blind. I'm
running in the dark on an unfamiliar path. I don't know if
there are breaks in the road, or if the whole cursed thing
ends in a cliff!"

She laid a hand on his arm as he passed, stopping him.
"Tell me."

"You'll think I'm mad."

She snorted. "I *already* think you're a wool-headed fool.
Can it be much worse than that?"

He regarded her, and some of the tension left his face. He
sat down on the edge of the bed, sighing softly. But it *was*
progress.

"Semirhage was right," Rand said. "I hear . . . things. A
voice. The voice of Lews Therin, the Dragon. He speaks to
me and responds to the world around me. Sometimes, he
tries to seize *saidin* from me. And . . . and sometimes he
succeeds. He's wild, Min. Insane. But the things he can do
with the One Power are amazing."

He stared off into the distance. Min shivered. Light! He
let the voice in his head wield the One Power? What did
that mean? That he let the mad part of his brain take control?

He shook his head. "Semirhage claims that this is just insanity, tricks of my mind, but Lews Therin knows things—
things that I don't. Things about history, about the One
Power. You had a viewing of me that showed two people

merging into one. That means that Lews Therin and I are distinct! Two people, Min. He's *real*."

She walked over and sat next to him. "Rand, he's *you*. Or you're him. Spun out into the Pattern again. Those memories and things you can do, they're remnants from who you were before."

"No," Rand said. "Min, he's insane and I'm not. Besides, he failed. I won't. I won't do it, Min. I won't hurt those I love, as he did. And when I defeat the Dark One, I won't leave him able to return a short time later and terrorize us again."

Three thousand years a "short time later"? She put her arms around him. "Does it matter?" she asked. "If there is another person, or if those are just memories from before, the information is useful."

"Yes," Rand said, seeming distant again. "But I'm afraid to use the One Power. When I do, I risk letting *him* take control. He can't be trusted. He didn't mean to kill her, but that doesn't change the fact that he did. Light . . . Ilyena. . . ."

Was this how it happened to all of them? Each one assuming that they were really sane, and that it was the *other* person inside of them who did horrible things?

"It's done now, Rand," she said, holding him close. "Whatever this voice is, it won't grow any worse. *Saidin* is cleansed."

Rand didn't respond, but he did relax. She closed her eyes, enjoying the feeling of his warmth beside her, particularly since he'd left the window open.

"Ishamael lives," Rand said.

She snapped her eyes open. "What?" Just when she was beginning to feel comfortable!

"I visited him in the World of Dreams," Rand said. "And before you ask, no. It wasn't just a nightmare and it wasn't madness. It was real, and I can't explain how I know. You will just have to trust me."

"Ishamael," she whispered. "You killed him!"

"Yes," Rand said. "In the Stone of Tear. He has returned, bearing a new face and a new name, but it is him. We should have realized it would happen; the Dark One won't abandon such useful tools without a fight. He can reach beyond the grave."

"Then how can we win? If everyone we kill just comes back again. . . ."

"Balefire," Rand said. "It will kill them for good."

"Cadsuane said—"

"I don't *care* what Cadsuane said," he snarled. "She is my advisor, and she gives advice. Only advice. *I* am the Dragon Reborn, and *I* will decide how we fight." He stopped, taking a deep breath. "Anyway, it doesn't matter if the Forsaken return, it doesn't matter who or what the Dark One sends at us. In the end, I will destroy him, if possible. If not, then I will at least seal him away so tightly that the world can forget him."

He glanced down at her. "For that . . . I need the voice, Min. Lews Therin knows things. Or . . . or *I* know things. Whichever it is, the knowledge is there. In a way, the Dark One's own taint will destroy him, for it is what gave me access to Lews Therin."

Min glanced at her books. Herid's little slip of paper still peeked from the depths of *Thoughts Among the Ruins*. "Rand," she said. "You have to destroy the seals to the Dark One's prison."

He looked at her, frowning.

"I'm sure of it," she said. "I've been reading Herid's books all this time, and I believe that's what he meant by 'clearing away the rubble.' In order to rebuild the Dark One's prison, you will first need to open it. Clear away the patch made on the Bore."

She had expected him to be incredulous. Shockingly, he just nodded. "Yes," he said. "Yes, that sounds right. I doubt that many will wish to hear it. If those seals are broken, there is no way to tell what will happen. If I fail to contain him . . ."

The prophecies didn't say Rand would win. Only that he would fight. Min shivered again—blasted window!—but met Rand's gaze. "You'll win. You'll defeat him."

He sighed. "Faith in a madman, Min?"

"Faith in you, sheepherder." Suddenly viewings spun around his head. She ignored them most of the time, unless they were new, but now she picked them out. Fireflies consumed in darkness. Three women before a pyre. Flashes of light, darkness, shadow, signs of death, crowns, injuries, pain and hope. A tempest around Rand al'Thor, stronger than any physical storm.

"We still don't know what to do," he said. "The seals are brittle enough that I could break them in my hands, but what then? *How* do I stop him? Does it say anything of that in your books?"

"It's hard to tell," she admitted. "The clues—if that's what they are—are vague. I will keep looking. I promise. I'll find answers for you."

He nodded, and she was surprised to feel his trust through the bond. That was a frighteningly rare emotion from him recently, but he did seem softer than he had during previous days. Still stone, but perhaps with some few cracks, willing to let her inside. It was a beginning.

She tightened her arms around him and closed her eyes again. A place to begin, but with so little time left. It would have to do.

Carefully shielding her burning candle, Aviendha lit the pole-mounted lantern. It flickered alight, illuminating the green around her. Slumbering soldiers snored in rows of tents. The evening was cold, the air crisp, and branches rattled in the distance. A lonely owl hooted. And Aviendha was exhausted.

She'd crossed the grounds fifty times, lighting the lantern, blowing it out, then jogging back across the green and lighting her candle at the manor before walking carefully— shielding the flame—to light the lantern again.

Another month of these punishments and she'd probably go as mad as a wetlander. The Wise Ones would wake one morning and find her going for a swim, or carrying a half-full waterskin, or—even—riding a horse for pleasure! She sighed, too exhausted to think any further, and turned toward the Aiel section of camp to finally sleep.

Someone was standing behind her.

She started, hand going to her dagger, but relaxed as she recognized Amys. Of all the Wise Ones, only she—a former Maiden—could have sneaked up on Aviendha.

The Wise One stood with hands clasped before her, brown shawl and skirt flapping slightly in the wind. Aviendha's skin prickled at the particularly chilly gust. Amys' silver hair seemed almost ghostly in the evening light; a pine needle passing on the breeze had gotten lodged in it. "You approach your punishments with such . . . dedication, child," Amys said.

Aviendha looked down. Pointing out her activities was to shame her. Was she running out of time? Had the Wise Ones finally decided to give up on her? "Please, Wise One. I only do as duty demands."

"Yes, you do," Amys said. She reached up, running her hand through her hair, and found the pine needle, then let it drop to the dead grass. "And, also, you do not. Sometimes, Aviendha, we are so concerned with the things we have done that we do not stop to consider the things we have not."

Aviendha was glad for the darkness, which hid her shameful blush. In the distance, a soldier rang the evening bell to chime the hour, the soft metal ringing with eleven melancholy peals. How did she respond to Amys' comments? There didn't seem to be any proper response.

Aviendha was saved by a flash of light just beyond the camp. It was faint, but in the darkness, the flicker was easy to notice.

"What?" the Wise One asked, noticing Aviendha's gaze and turning to follow it.

"Light," Aviendha said. "From the Traveling grounds."

Amys frowned, then the two of them moved toward the grounds. Soon they encountered Damer Flinn, Davram Bashere, a small guard of Saldaeans and Aiel walking into the camp. What did one think of a creature such as Flinn? The taint had been cleansed, but this man—and many of the others—had come, asking to learn, before that had happened. Aviendha herself would have sooner embraced Sightblinder himself as done that, but they *had* proven to be powerful weapons.

Amys and Aviendha moved to the side as the small party hurried toward the manor house, lit only by the distant flickering torches and the cloud-covered sky above. Though most of the force sent to meet the Seanchan had been made up of Bashere's soldiers, there were several Maidens in the group. Amys locked eyes with one of them, an older woman named Corana. She hung back, and though it was difficult to tell in the darkness, she looked concerned. Perhaps angry.

"What news?" Amys asked.

"The invaders, these Seanchan," Corana nearly spat the word, "they have agreed to another meeting with the *Car'a'carn*."

Amys nodded. Corana, however, sniffed audibly, short hair ruffling in the chill breeze.

"Speak," Amys said.

"The *Car'a'carn* sues too hard for peace," Corana replied. "These Seanchan have given him reason to declare a blood feud, but he simpers and panders to them. I feel like a trained dog, sent to lick the feet of a stranger."

Amys glanced at Aviendha. "What do you say to this, Aviendha?"

"My heart agrees with her words, Wise One. But, while the *Car'a'carn* is a fool in some things, he is not being one now. My mind agrees with him, and in this case, it is the mind I would follow."

"How can you say that?" Corana snapped. She emphasized the *you*, as if to imply that Aviendha—recently a Maiden— should understand.

"Which is more important, Corana?" Aviendha replied raising her chin. "The argument you have with another Maiden, or the feud your clan has with its enemy?"

"The clan comes first, of course. But what does that matter?"

"The Seanchan deserve to be fought," Aviendha said, "and you are right that it pains to ask them for peace. But you forget that we have a greater enemy. Sightblinder himself has a feud with all men, and our duty is larger than feuds between nations."

Amys nodded. "There will be time enough to show the Seanchan the weight of our spears at another date."

Corana shook her head. "Wise One, you sound like a wetlander. What care have we for their prophecies and stories? Rand al'Thor's duty as *Car'a'carn* is much greater than his duty to the wetlanders. He *must* lead us to glory."

Amys stared harshly at the blond Maiden. "You speak like a Shaido."

Corana locked her stare for a moment, then wilted, turning away. "Pardon, Wise One," she finally said. "I have *toh*. But you should know that the Seanchan had Aiel in their camp."

"What?" Aviendha asked.

"They were leashed," Corana said, "like their tame Aes Sedai. They were being shown off like prizes for our arrival, I suspect. I recognized many Shaido among them."

Amys hissed softly. Shaido or not, Aiel being held as *da-mane* was a grave insult. And the Seanchan were flaunting their captives. She gripped her dagger.

"What do you say now?" Amys glanced at Aviendha.

Aviendha gritted her teeth. "The same, Wise One, though I'd almost rather cut out my tongue than admit it."

Amys nodded, looking back at Corana. "Do not think that we will ignore this insult, Corana. Vengeance *will* come. Once this war is done, the Seanchan will feel the storm of our arrows and the tips of our spears. But not until *after.* Go tell the two clan chiefs what you have told me."

Corana nodded—she would meet her *toh* later, in private, with Amys—and left. Damer Flinn and the others had already reached the manor house; would they wake Rand? He was sleeping now, though Aviendha had been forced to mute her bond in the middle of her night's punishment, lest she endure sensations that she'd rather have avoided. At least, she'd rather have avoided them secondhand.

"There will be dangerous words of this among the spears," Amys said thoughtfully. "There will be calls to attack, demands that the *Car'a'carn* give up his attempts to make peace."

"Will they stay with him when he refuses?" Aviendha asked.

"Of course they will," Amys said. "They're Aiel." She glanced at Aviendha. "We haven't much time, child. Perhaps it is time to stop coddling you. I will think up better punishments for you starting tomorrow."

Coddling me? Aviendha watched Amys stalk away. *They couldn't possibly come up with anything more useless or demeaning!*

But she'd learned long ago not to underestimate Amys. With a sigh, Aviendha broke into a trot, heading back toward her tent.

CHAPTER
16

In the White Tower

I'm curious to hear the novice speak. Tell me, Egwene al'Vere, how would *you* have handled the situation?"

Egwene looked up from the bowl of shells, two-legged steel nutcracker in one hand, a bulbous walnut in the other. It was the first time any of the Aes Sedai present had addressed her. She had begun to think that attending the three Whites would turn out to be another waste of time.

The afternoon's location was a small inset balcony on the third level of the White Tower. Sitters could demand rooms with not only full windows, but balconies as well, something that was uncommon—though not unheard-of—for regular sisters. This one was shaped like a small turret, with a sturdy stone wall running around the rim in a curve, a similar stone hanging from the outcropping above. There was generous space between the two and the view was quite beautiful, eastward across the rising hills that eventually climbed to Kinslayer's Dagger. The Dagger itself might have been distantly visible on a clear day.

A cool breeze blew across the balcony, and this high up it was fresh and unsullied by the stink of the city below. A sinuous pair of sticklesharps—with their three-pronged leaves and clinging vines—grew on each side of the balcony, their creeping tendrils covering the inside of the stonework and making it look almost like a deep forest ruin. The plants were more ornamentation than Egwene would have expected in the quarters of a White, but Ferane was reported to be a shade on the vain side. She probably liked it that her balcony was so distinctive, even if protocol required her to

keep the vines pruned as to not mar the gleaming profile of
the Tower itself.

The three Whites sat in wicker chairs at a low table.
Egwene sat before them on a wicker stool, back to the open
air, denied the view as she cracked nuts for the others. Any
number of servants or kitchen workers could have done the
work. But this was the sort of thing that sisters found to fill
the time of novices whom they thought might be lounging
about too much.

Egwene had thought that cracking the walnuts was just a
pretense. After being ignored for the better part of an hour,
she had begun to wonder, but all three were looking at her
now. She shouldn't have doubted her instincts.

Ferane had the coppery skin of a Domani, and a temperament to match, odd for a White. She was short, with an
apple-shaped face and dark, lustrous hair. Her auburn dress
was filmy but decent with a wide white sash at the waist
to match her shawl, which she was currently wearing. The
dress didn't lack for embroidery, and the fabric did seem
an indication, perhaps intentional, of her Domani heritage.

The other two, Miyasi and Tesan, both wore white, as if
they feared that dresses of any other colors were a betrayal
of their Ajah. That notion was becoming more and more
common among all of the Aes Sedai. Tesan was a Taraboner, with her dark hair in beaded braids. The beads were
white and gold, and they framed a narrow face that looked
as if it had been pinched at top and bottom and pulled. She
always looked worried about something. Though perhaps
that was just the times. Light knew they all had a great deal
to worry over.

Miyasi was more calm, her head topped by iron-gray hair
in a bun. Her Aes Sedai face betrayed none of the many
years that she must have seen for her hair to silver so fully.
She was tall and plump, and she preferred her walnuts
shelled very particularly. No fragments or broken pieces of
nut for her, only full halves. Egwene carefully pried one
from the shell she had cracked, then handed it over; the
small brown lump was wrinkled and ridged, like the brain
of a tiny animal.

"What was it you asked, Ferane?" Egwene asked, cracking another walnut and discarding the shell in a pail at her
feet.

The White barely frowned at Egwene's improper response. They were all growing accustomed to the fact that this "novice" seldom acted her presumed station. "I asked," Ferane said coolly, "what *you* would have done in the Amyrlin's place. Consider this part of your instruction. You know that the Dragon has been reborn and you know that the Tower *must* control him in order for the Last Battle to proceed. How would you handle him?"

A curious question. It didn't sound much like "instruction." But Ferane's tone didn't make it sound like an offer to complain about Elaida either. There was too much contempt for Egwene in that voice.

The other two Whites remained quiet. Ferane was a Sitter, and they deferred to her.

She's heard how often I mention Elaida's failure with Rand, Egwene thought, looking into Ferane's steely black eyes. *So. A test, is it?* This would have to be handled very carefully.

Egwene reached for another walnut. "First, I would send a group of sisters to his home village."

Ferane raised an eyebrow. "To intimidate his family?"

"Of course not," Egwene said. "To interrogate them. Who is this Dragon Reborn? Is he a man of temper, a man of passions? Or is he a calm man, careful and cautious? Was he the type to spend time alone in the fields, or did he make quick friends of the other youths? Would you be more likely to find him in a tavern or a workshop?"

"But *you* already know him," Tesan piped in.

"I do," Egwene said, cracking the walnut. "But we were speaking of a hypothetical situation." *Best you remember that in the real world, I know the Dragon Reborn personally. As nobody else in this Tower does.*

"Let us assume that you are you," Ferane said. "And that he is Rand al'Thor, your childhood friend."

"Very well."

"Tell me," Ferane said, leaning forward. "Of the types of men you listed just before, which best fits this Rand al'Thor?"

Egwene hesitated. "All of them," she said, dropping a fragmented walnut into a small bowl with others. Miyasi wouldn't touch it, but the other two weren't so picky. "If I were me and the Dragon were Rand, I'd know him to be a rational person, for a man—if somewhat bullheaded at times. Well, most of the time. More importantly, I'd know him to be a good man at heart. And so, my next step would be to send sisters to him to offer guidance."

"And if he rejected them?" Ferane asked.

"Then I'd send spies," Egwene said, "and watch to see if he has changed from the man I once knew."

"And while you waited and spied, he would terrorize the countryside, wreaking havoc and bringing armies to his banner."

"And is that not what we want him to do?" Egwene asked. "I don't believe he could have been prevented from taking *Callandor*, should we have wanted him to be. He has managed to restore order to Cairhien, unite Tear and Illian beneath one ruler, and presumably has gained the favor of Andor as well."

"Not to mention subjugating those Aiel," Miyasi said, reaching for a handful of nuts.

Egwene caught her with a sharp gaze. "Nobody *subjugates* the Aiel. Rand gained their respect. I was with him at the time."

Miyasi froze, hand partway to the bowl of nutmeats. She shook herself, breaking Egwene's gaze, grabbing the bowl and retreating back to her chair. A cool breeze blew across the balcony, rustling the vines, which Ferane had complained were not greening this spring like they should. Egwene returned to shelling walnuts.

"It seems," Ferane said, "that you would simply let him sow chaos as he saw fit."

"Rand al'Thor is like a river," Egwene said. "Calm and placid when not agitated, but a furious and deadly current when squeezed too tightly. What Elaida did to him was the equivalent of trying to force the Manetherendrelle through a canyon only two feet wide. Waiting to discover a man's temperament is not foolish, nor is it a sign of weakness. Acting without information is lunacy, and the White Tower deserved the tempest it riled up."

"Perhaps," Ferane said. "But you have still not told me how *you* would deal with the situation, once your information was collected and the time for waiting had passed." Ferane was known for her temper, but at the moment her voice held the coldness common among Whites. It was the coldness of one who spoke without emotion, thinking about logic without tolerating outside influences.

It was not the best way to approach problems. People were much more complex than a set of rules or numbers. There was a time for logic, true, but there was also a time for emotion.

Rand was a problem she hadn't allowed herself to dwell on—she needed to deal with one problem at a time. But there was also much to be said for planning ahead. If she *didn't* consider how to deal with the Dragon Reborn, she'd eventually find herself in as bad a situation as Elaida.

He *had* changed from the man she had known. And yet the seeds of personality within him must be the same. She'd seen his rage during their months traveling together into the Aiel Waste. That hadn't often come out during his childhood, but she could see now that it must have been lurking. It wasn't that he had suddenly developed a temper; it was simply that nothing in the Two Rivers had upset him.

During the months she'd traveled with him, he'd seemed to harden with each step. He was under extraordinary pressures. How did one deal with such a man? She frankly had no idea.

But this conversation wasn't about what to do with Rand, not really. It was about Ferane trying to determine what kind of woman Egwene was.

"Rand al'Thor sees himself as an emperor," Egwene said. "And I suppose he is one, now. He will react poorly if he thinks he is being pushed or shoved in any particular direction. If I were to deal with him, I would send a delegation to honor him."

"A lavish procession?" Ferane asked.

"No," Egwene said. "But not a threadbare one either. A group of three Aes Sedai, led by a Gray, accompanied by a Green and a Blue. He views the Blue favorably because of past associations, and Greens are often perceived as the opposites to Reds, a subtle indication that we are willing to work with him rather than gentle him. A Gray because it would be expected, but also because if a Gray is sent, then it means negotiations, not armies, will follow."

"Good logic," Tesan said, nodding.

Ferane was not so easily convinced. "Delegations like

this one have failed in the past. I believe that Elaida's own delegation was led by a Gray."

"Yes, but Elaida's delegation was fundamentally flawed," Egwene said.

"And why is that?"

"Why, because it was sent by a *Red*, of course," Egwene said, cracking a nut. "I have trouble seeing the logic in raising a member of the Red Ajah to Amyrlin during the days of the Dragon Reborn. Doesn't that seem destined to create animosity between him and the Tower?"

"One might say," Ferane countered, "that a Red is needed during these troubled times, for the Red are the most experienced at dealing with men who can channel."

"'Dealing' with is different from 'working' with," Egwene said. "The Dragon Reborn should *not* have been left to run free, but since when has the White Tower been in the business of *kidnapping* and forcing people to our will? Are we not known as the most subtle and careful of all people? Do we not pride ourselves on being able to make others do as they should, all the while letting them think it was *their* idea? When in the past have we locked kings in boxes and beaten them for disobedience? Why now—of all the times under the Light—have we forsaken our fine practice and become simple footpads instead?"

Ferane selected a walnut. The other two Whites were sharing an unsettled look. "There is sense in what you say," the Sitter finally admitted.

Egwene set aside the nutcracker. "Rand al'Thor is a good man, in his heart, but he needs guidance. These days are when we should have been at our most subtle. He should have been led to trust Aes Sedai above all others, to rely on our counsel. He should have been shown the wisdom in listening. Instead, he has been shown that we will treat him like an unruly child. If he *is* one, he cannot be allowed to think we regard him in such a way. Because of our bungling, he has taken some Aes Sedai captive, and has allowed still others to be *bonded* to those Asha'man of his."

Ferane sat up stiffly. "Best not to mention that atrocity."

"What is this?" Tesan said, shocked, hand raised to her breast. Some Whites never seemed to pay attention to the world around them. "Ferane? Did you know of this?"

Ferane didn't respond.

"I've . . . heard this rumor," said stout Miyasi. "If it is true, then something must be done."

"Yes," Egwene said. "Unfortunately, we cannot focus on al'Thor right now."

"He is the greatest problem facing the world," pinch-faced Tesan said, leaning forward. "We must deal with him first."

"No," Egwene said. "There are other issues."

Miyasi frowned. "With the Last Battle impending, I can't see any other issues of importance."

Egwene shook her head. "In dealing with Rand now, we'd be like a farmer, looking at his wagon and worrying that there aren't any goods in the bed for him to sell—but ignoring the fact that his axle is cracked. Fill the bed before it is time, and you'll just break the wagon and be worse off than when you started."

"And what, exactly, are you implying?" Tesan demanded.

Egwene looked back at Ferane.

"I see," Ferane said. "You are referring to the division in the White Tower."

"Can a cracked stone be a good foundation for a building?" Egwene asked. "Can a frayed rope hold a panicky horse? How can *we*, in our current state, hope to manage the Dragon Reborn himself?"

Ferane said, "Why, then, do you continue to enforce the division by insisting that you are the Amyrlin Seat? You defy your own logic."

"And renouncing my claim on the Amyrlin Seat would mend the Tower?" Egwene asked.

"It would help."

Egwene raised an eyebrow. "Let us assume, for a moment, that by renouncing my claim, I could persuade the rebel faction to rejoin the White Tower and accept Elaida's leadership." She raised the eyebrow further, indicating how likely she thought *that* was. "Would the divisions be healed?"

"You just said they would be," Tesan said, frowning.

"Oh?" Egwene said. "Would sisters stop scurrying through the hallways, frightened to be alone? Would groups of women from different Ajahs stop regarding each other with hostility when they pass in the hallways? With all due respect, would we no longer feel the need to wear our shawls at all times to reinforce who we are and where our allegiance is?"

Ferane glanced down, briefly, at her white-fringed shawl.

Egwene leaned forward, continuing. "Surely you, of all women in the White Tower, can see the importance of the Ajahs working together. We need women with different skills and interests to gather into Ajahs. But does it make sense for us to refuse to work together?"

"The White has not caused this . . . regrettable tension," Miyasi said with a little snort. "The others acting with such abundance of emotion have created it."

"The present leadership has caused it," Egwene said, "a leadership which teaches that it's all right to still fellow sisters in secret, to execute Warders before their Aes Sedai are even brought to trial. That there's nothing wrong with removing a sister's shawl and reducing her to an Accepted, that there's nothing wrong with *disbanding* an entire Ajah. And what of acting without the counsel of the Hall in something as dangerous as kidnapping and imprisoning the Dragon Reborn? Is it unexpected that the sisters would be so frightened and worried? Is it not all completely *logical*, what has happened to us?"

The three Whites were quiet.

"I will not submit," Egwene said. "Not while doing so leaves us fractured. I will continue to assert that Elaida is *not* the Amyrlin. Her actions have proven it. You want to help battle the Dark One? Well, your first step is not to deal with the Dragon Reborn. Your first step should be to reach out to sisters of the other Ajahs."

"Why us?" Tesan said. "The actions of others are not our responsibility."

"And you are not to blame at all?" Egwene asked, letting a little of her anger seep through. Would *none* of her sisters accept a modicum of responsibility? "You, of the White, should have seen where this road would lead. Yes, Siuan and the Blue were not without their flaws—but *you* should have seen the flaw in pulling her down, then allowing Elaida to disband the Blue. Besides, I believe that several members of your own Ajah were integral to the act of setting up Elaida as Amyrlin."

Miyasi recoiled slightly. The Whites did not like to be reminded of Alviarin and her failure as Elaida's Keeper. Instead of turning against Elaida for ousting the White, they seemed to have turned against their own member for the shame she had caused them.

"I still think that this is work for the Grays," Tesan said, but she sounded less convinced than she had just moments before. "You should speak with them."

"I have," Egwene said. Her patience was beginning to fray. "Some will not speak with me and continue to send me to penance. Others say these rifts are not their fault, but with some coaxing have agreed to do what they can. The Yellows have been very reasonable, and I think they're beginning to see the problems in the Tower as a wound to be healed. I'm still working with several Brown sisters—they seem more fascinated by the problems than worried about them. I've sent several of them looking through the histories for examples of division, hoping they'll run across the story of Renala Merlon. The connection should be easy to make, and perhaps they will begin to see that our problems here can be solved.

"The Greens have, ironically, been the most stubborn. They can be very like Reds in many ways, which is infuriating as they really should be willing to accept me as one who would have been among them. That only leaves the Blue, who have been banished, and the Red. I doubt that sisters of that last Ajah are going to be very receptive to my suggestions."

Ferane sat back, thoughtful, and Tesan sat with three forgotten walnuts in her hand, staring at Egwene. Miyasi scratched at her iron-gray hair, eyes wide with surprise.

Had Egwene given away too much? Aes Sedai were remarkably like Rand al'Thor; they did not like to know when they were being maneuvered.

"You are shocked," she said. "What, do you think I should simply sit—like most—and do nothing while the Tower crumbles? This white dress has been forced upon me, and I do not accept what it represents, but I *will* use it. A woman in novice white is one of the few who can pass from one Ajah quarter to another these days. Someone has to work to mend the Tower, and I am the best choice. Besides, it is my duty."

"How very . . . reasonable of you," Ferane said, her ageless brow furrowed.

"Thank you," Egwene said. Were they worried that she'd overstepped her bounds? Angered that she'd been manipulating Aes Sedai? Coldly determined to see her punished yet again?

Ferane leaned forward. "Let us say that we wished to work toward mending the Tower. What path would you recommend?"

Egwene felt a surge of excitement. She'd had nothing but setbacks during the last few days. Idiot Greens! They would feel foolish indeed once she was accepted as Amyrlin.

"Suana, of the Yellow Ajah, will soon be inviting you three to share a meal with her," Egwene said. At least, Suana would make the offer, once Egwene prodded her. "Accept and take your meal in a public place, perhaps one of the Tower gardens. Be seen enjoying one another's company. I will try to get a Brown sister to invite you next. Let yourself be seen by the other sisters mixing among the Ajahs."

"Simple enough," Miyasi said. "Very little effort required, but excellent potential for gain."

"We shall see," Ferane said. "You may withdraw, Egwene."

She didn't like being dismissed so, but there was no helping it. Still, the woman had shown Egwene respect by using her name. Egwene stood up, and then—very carefully—nodded her head to Ferane. Though Tesan and Miyasi gave no strong reactions, both pairs of eyes widened slightly. By now, it was well known in the Tower that Egwene never curtsied. And, shockingly, Ferane bowed her head, just a degree, returning the gesture.

"Should you decide to choose the White, Egwene al'Vere," the woman said, "know that you will find a welcome here. Your logic this day was remarkable for one so young."

Egwene hid a smile. Just four days back, Bennae Nalsad had all but offered Egwene a place in the Brown, and Egwene was still surprised at how vigilantly Suana recommended the Yellow to her. Almost they made her change her mind—but that was mostly her frustration with the Green at the moment. "Thank you," she said. "But you must remember that the Amyrlin must represent all Ajahs. Our discussion was enjoyable, however. I hope that you will allow me to join you again in the future."

With that, Egwene withdrew, letting herself smile broadly as she nodded to Ferane's sturdy, bowlegged Warder standing guard just inside the balcony. Her smile lasted right up until she left the White sector of the Tower and found Katerine waiting in the hallway. The Red was not one of the two assigned to Egwene earlier in the day, and talk about the Tower said that Elaida was relying on Katerine more and more now that her Keeper had vanished on a mysterious mission.

Katerine's sharp face bore a smile of its own. That was not a good sign. "Here," the woman said, offering a wooden cup holding a clear liquid. It was time for Egwene's afternoon dose of forkroot.

Egwene grimaced, but took the cup and drank the contents. She wiped her mouth with her handkerchief, then began to walk down the hallway.

"And where are you going?" Katerine asked.

The smugness in her tone made Egwene hesitate. Egwene turned, frowning. "My next lesson—"

"You will have no further lessons," Katerine said. "At least, not of the kind you have been receiving. All agree that your skill with weaves is impressive, for a novice."

Egwene frowned. Were they going to raise her to Accepted again? She doubted that Elaida would allow her any more freedom, and she rarely spent any time in her quarters, so the extra space would be unimportant.

"No," Katerine said, toying idly with the fringe on her shawl. "What you need to learn, it has been decided, is humility. The Amyrlin has heard of your foolish refusal to curtsy to sisters. In her opinion, it's the last symbol of your defiant nature, and so you are to receive a new form of instruction."

Egwene felt a moment of fear. "What kind of instruction?" she said, keeping her voice even.

"Chores and work," Katerine said.

"I already do chores, just like the novices."

"You mistake me," Katerine said. "From now on, *all* you will do is chores. You are to report to the kitchens immediately—you will spend every afternoon working there. In the evenings, you will scrub floors. In the mornings you will report to the groundsmaster and work the gardens. This will be your life, those same three activities every day—five hours at each one—until you give up your foolish pride and learn to curtsy to your betters."

It was an end to Egwene's freedom, what little she had. There was glee in Katerine's eyes.

"Ah, so you understand," Katerine said. "No more visiting sisters in their quarters, wasting their time as you practice weaves that you have already mastered. No more laziness; now you will work instead. What think you of that?"

It wasn't the difficulty of the work that worried Egwene— she didn't mind the chores she did each day. It was the lack of contact with other sisters that would ruin her. How would she mend the White Tower? Light! It was a disaster.

She gritted her teeth and forced down her emotion. She met Katerine's eyes, saying, "Very well. Let us go."

Katerine blinked. She'd obviously expected a tantrum, or at least a fight. But this was not the time. Egwene turned her step toward the kitchens, leaving the quarters of the Whites behind. She couldn't let them know how effective this punishment was.

She forced down her panic as she walked, the cavernous hallways of the inner Tower lined with bracketed lamps, long and sinuous, like the heads of serpents spouting tiny flames up toward the stone ceiling. She could deal with this. She *would* deal with this. They would not break her.

Perhaps she should work for a few days, then pretend that she had been humbled. Should she give the curtsy Elaida demanded? It was a simple thing, really. One curtsy, and she could go back to her more important duties.

No, she thought. *No, that would not be the end of it. I'd lose the moment I gave that first curtsy.* Giving in would prove to Elaida that Egwene could be broken. Curtsying would begin a descent into destruction. Soon, Elaida would decide that Egwene needed to start using honorifics for the Aes Sedai. The false Amyrlin would send Egwene back to work detail, knowing it had been effective before. Would Egwene bend there too? How long before any credibility she had ended up forgotten, trampled into the tiles of the Tower hallways?

She could not bend. The beatings had not changed her behavior; work detail must not change her either.

Three hours of working the kitchens did little to improve

her mood. Laras, the hefty Mistress of Kitchens, had set Egwene at scrubbing out one of the ovenlike fireplaces. It was dirty, grimy work, not conducive to thinking. Not that there were many ways out of her situation.

Egwene knelt back on her heels, raising an arm and wiping her brow. The arm came away smeared with soot. Egwene sighed softly, her mouth and nose protected by a damp cloth to keep her from breathing too much ash. Her breath was hot and stuffy against her face, and her skin was sticky with sweat. The drops that fell from her face were stained with black soot; through the cloth she could smell the dull, crusty scent of ash that had been burned over and over and over again.

The fireplace was a large square construction of burned red bricks. It was open on both sides and more than large enough to crawl into—which was exactly what Egwene had to do. Dark crusts built up on the inside of the flue and chimney, and they needed to be scrubbed free lest they clog the chimney or break free and fall into the food. Outside in the dining room, Egwene could hear Katerine and Lirene chatting and laughing with each other. The Reds periodically poked heads in to check on her, but her real supervisor was Laras, who was scrubbing pots on the other side of the room.

Egwene had changed into a work dress for the duty. While it had once been white, it had been repeatedly used by novices cleaning the fireplaces, and the soot had been ground into the fibers. Patches of gray stained the cloth, like shadows.

She rubbed the small of her back, got back on her hands and knees, and crawled farther into the fireplace. Using a small wooden scrape, she worked clumps of ash free from seams between the bricks, then gathered it up and deposited it in brass buckets, the rims of which were powdered white and gray with ash. Her first task had been to dig out all of the loose soot and pile it into the buckets. Her hands were so blackened from the work she worried that the most furious scrubbing wouldn't get them clean. Her knees ached, and they seemed a strange counterpart to her backside, which still stung from her regular morning beating.

She continued, scratching with her scrape at a blackened section of brick, dimly lit by the lantern she'd left burning

in a corner inside the fireplace. She itched to use the One
Power; but the Reds outside would sense her channeling, and
she'd discovered that her afternoon dose of forkroot had been
uncharacteristically strong, leaving her unable to channel as
much as a trickle. In fact, it had been strong enough to leave
her drowsy, which made the work even harder.

Was this to be her life? Trapped inside a fireplace, scrubbing at bricks nobody saw, locked away from the world?
She couldn't stand up to Elaida if everyone forgot about her.
She coughed quietly, the sound echoing against the inside
of the fireplace.

She needed a plan. Her only recourse seemed to be to use
the sisters who were trying to root out the Black Ajah. But
how to visit them? Without being trained by sisters, she had
no way to escape her Red handlers by entering the domains
of other Ajahs. Could she sneak away somehow while doing labor? If her absence were discovered, she'd probably
end up in an even *worse* situation.

But she couldn't let her life be dominated by this menial
labor! The Last Battle was approaching, the Dragon Reborn
ran free, and the Amyrlin Seat was on her hands and knees
cleaning fireplaces! She gritted her teeth, scrubbing furiously. The soot had been baked on for so long that it formed
a glossy black patina on the stone. She'd never get it all off.
She just needed to make sure it was clean enough that none
would break free.

Reflected in that glossy patina, she saw a shadow move
across the opening of the far side of the fireplace. Egwene
immediately reached for the Source—but, of course, she
found nothing. Not with forkroot clouding her mind. But
there was *definitely* someone outside the fireplace, crouching down, moving quietly. . . .

Egwene gripped the scrape in one hand, slowly reaching
down with the other to grab the brush she'd been using to
scoop up ash. Then she spun.

Laras froze, peeking into the fireplace. The Mistress of
Kitchens wore a large white apron, stained with a few soot
marks itself. Her pudgy round face had seen its share of
winters; her hair was starting to gray, and lines creased the
sides of her eyes. Leaning over as she was, her jowls formed
a second, third and fourth chin, and she gripped the side of
the fireplace opening with a thick-fingered hand.

Egwene relaxed. Why had she been so certain that someone had been sneaking up on her? It was just Laras coming
to check on her.

Yet why had the woman moved so silently? Laras glanced
to the side, eyes narrowing. Then she raised a finger to her
lips. Egwene felt herself tense again. What was going on?

Laras backed out of the fireplace, waving for Egwene to
follow. The Mistress of Kitchens moved on light feet, far
quieter than Egwene would have thought possible. Assistant cooks and scullions clanged away in other parts of the
kitchen, but none were directly visible. Egwene crept free
of the fireplace, tucking the scrape into her belt and wiping
her hands on her dress. She pulled the cloth free from her
face, breathing sweet, soot-free air. She took a deep breath,
and received a harsh glare from Laras, followed by another
finger to the lips.

Egwene nodded, following Laras through the kitchens.
In a few moments she and Egwene stood in a pantry, thick
with the scent of dried grains and aging cheeses. The tiles
gave way to more durable brickwork here. Laras shoved
aside a few sacks, then pulled open a piece of the floor. It
was a wooden trapdoor, capped with shaved brickwork on
the top to make it seem part of the floor. It revealed a small,
rock-walled chamber underneath the pantry, large enough
to hold a person, though a tall man would be cramped.

"You wait here until night," Laras said in a low voice. "I
can't get you out right now, not with the Tower fluttery as
a yard full of hens when the fox is about. But the garbage
goes out late at night, and I'll hide you among the girls who
unload it. A dockworker will take you to a small boat and
row you across the river. I have some friends among the
guard; they'll turn the other way. Once you reach the other
side, it's up to you what you do. I'd advise against going
back to those fools who made you their puppet. Find some
place to lie low until this all blows over, then come back
and see if whoever's in charge will take you in. Isn't likely it
will be Elaida, the way things are going. . . ."

Egwene blinked in surprise.

"Well," the heavyset woman said. "In you go."

"I—"

"No time for jabbering!" Laras said, as if she weren't the
one doing all of the talking. She was obviously nervous,

the way she kept glancing about and tapping her foot. But she'd obviously *also* done this sort of thing before. Why was the simple cook in the White Tower so skilled at sneaking, so handy with a plan to get Egwene out of the fortified and besieged city? And why did she have a bolt-hole in the kitchens in the first place? Light! How had she created it?

"Don't worry about me," Laras said, eyeing Egwene. "I can handle myself. I'll keep all of the kitchen servants away from where you were working. Those Aes Sedai only check on you every half-hour or so—and since they just checked a minute ago, it will be a while before they look in again. When they *do* check, I can plead ignorance and everyone will assume you slipped out of the kitchens. We'll soon have you out of the city and nobody will be the wiser."

"Yes," Egwene said, finally finding her tongue, "but *why?*" She had assumed that, after helping Min and Siuan, Laras wouldn't be eager to help another fugitive.

Laras looked back at her, in the woman's eyes a determination as hard as any Aes Sedai's. Egwene certainly had overlooked this woman! Who was she really?

"I won't be a party to the breaking of a girl's spirit," Laras said sternly. "Those beatings are shameful! Fool Aes Sedai. I've served loyally these years, I have, but now they've told me that you're to be worked as hard as I can push you, indefinitely. Well, I can see when a girl has moved away from being instructed and into being beaten down. I won't have it, not in my kitchens. Light burn Elaida for thinking she could do such a thing! Execute you or make you a novice, I don't care. But this breaking is unacceptable!"

The woman stood, setting hands on hips, a puff of flour rising from her apron. Oddly, Egwene found herself considering the offer. She'd denied Siuan's offer to save her, but if she fled now, she would return to the rebel camp having freed herself. That would be far superior to being rescued. She could get away from all this, away from the beatings, away from the drudgery.

To do what? To sit on the outside and watch the Tower collapse?

"No," she said to Laras. "Your offer is very kind, but I can't take it. I'm sorry."

Laras frowned. "Now, you listen—"

"Laras," Egwene interrupted, "one does not take that

tone with an Aes Sedai, no matter that one is the Mistress of Kitchens."

Laras hesitated. "Fool girl. You ain't Aes Sedai."

"Accept it or not, I still can't go. Unless you intend to try stuffing me into that hole yourself—gagging and tying me to keep me from crying out, followed by escorting me across the river in person—then I suggest letting me return to my work."

"But why?"

"Because," Egwene said, glancing back at the fireplace. "Someone has to fight her."

"You can't fight like this," Laras said.

"Each day is a battle," Egwene said. "Each day I refuse to bend means something. Even if Elaida and her Reds are the only ones who know it, that's something. A small something, but more than I could do from the outside. Come. I've still got two hours of work left."

She turned and began to walk back toward the fireplace. A reluctant Laras closed the hatch on her hidden chamber, then joined her. The woman made much more noise now as she walked, brushing against counters, her footfalls sounding on the bricks. Curious how she'd been able to be so quiet when she wanted to.

A flash of red cloth, like the blood of a dead rabbit in the snow, moved through the kitchens. Egwene froze as Katerine, wearing a dress with crimson skirts and yellow trim, spotted her. The Red's mouth was thin-lipped, her eyes narrow. Had she seen Egwene and Laras walk off?

Laras froze.

"I see now what I was doing wrong," Egwene quickly said to the Mistress of Kitchens, eyeing a second hearth, which lay near where they had been standing in the pantry. "Thank you for showing it to me. I'll be more careful now."

"See that you are," Laras said, shaking out of her shock. "Otherwise, you'll see what a *real* punishment is like, not those halfhearted paddlings the Mistress of Novices gives. Now back to work with you."

Egwene nodded, hurrying back toward the fireplace. Katerine held up a hand to forestall her. Egwene's heart thumped traitorously.

"No need," Katerine said. "The Amyrlin has demanded that the novice attend her tonight at dinner. I told the Amyrlin that one day of work would hardly break someone as fool-ishly stubborn as this child, but she is insistent. I guess you are to be given your first chance to prove your humility, child. I suggest you take it."

Egwene glanced down at her blackened hands and soiled dress.

"Go, run," Katerine said. "Wash up and clean yourself. The Amyrlin will not be kept waiting."

Washing up proved to be nearly as difficult as cleaning the fireplace. The soot had stained her hands much in the way it had the work dress. Egwene spent the better part of an hour washing in a tub full of lukewarm water, trying to make herself presentable. Her fingernails were ragged from scraping the bricks, and it seemed that each time she rinsed her hair, she washed out an entire bucket's worth of soot flakes.

However, she was glad for the chance. She rarely had much time for bathing; usually she could not stop for more than a quick scrub. As she rinsed and scrubbed in the small, gray-tiled bathing chamber, she considered her next step.

She had turned down the opportunity to flee. That meant she had to work with Elaida and her Reds, the only sisters she saw. But could they be made to see their errors? She wished she could send the whole lot of them for penance and be rid of them.

But no. She was Amyrlin; she represented all Ajahs, including the Red. She couldn't treat them as Elaida had treated the Blues. They were the most antagonistic toward her, but that meant a greater challenge. She seemed to be making some headway with Silviana, and hadn't Lirene Doirellin admitted that Elaida had made serious mistakes?

Maybe the Reds weren't the only ones she could influ-ence. There were always chance meetings with other sisters in the hallways. If one of them approached her to speak, the Reds couldn't very well tow her away. They would show some decorum, and that would give Egwene a chance to interact a bit with other sisters.

But how to treat Elaida herself? Was it wise to let the false Amyrlin continue to think that Egwene was nearly cowed? Or was it time to make a stand?

By the end of her bath, Egwene felt a great deal cleaner

and a great deal more confident. Her war had taken a serious turn for the worse, but she could still fight. She ran a hurried brush through her wet hair, threw on a new novice dress—my, how good it felt to have the soft, clean fabric on her skin!—and left to join her handlers.

They escorted her up to the Amyrlin's chambers. Egwene passed several groups of sisters, and she held herself carefully erect for their benefit. The handlers took her through the Red sector of the Tower, the tiles on the floor shifting to a pattern of red and charcoal. There were more people walking about here, women in their shawls, servants bearing the Flame of Tar Valon on their chests. Never any Warders; that always felt strange to Egwene, since they were so common in other parts of the Tower.

A long climb and a few twists later, they arrived at Elaida's quarters. Egwene checked her skirts unconsciously. She had determined during the walk that she needed to approach Elaida with silence, just as she had last time. Riling her further would only lead to more restrictions. Egwene would not debase herself, but neither would she go out of her way to insult Elaida. Let the woman think as she wished.

A servant opened the door, leading Egwene in, and into the dining chamber. There, she was shocked by what she found. She had assumed she'd attend Elaida alone, or maybe with Meidani. Egwene hadn't for a moment considered that the dining room would be filled with women. There were five, one from each Ajah save the Red and the Blue. And each woman was a Sitter. Yukiri was there, as was Doesine, both from the clandestine hunters of the Black Ajah. Ferane was there, though she seemed surprised to see Egwene; had the White not known about this dinner earlier, or had she simply not mentioned it?

Rubinde, of the Green Ajah, sat beside Shevan of the Brown, a sister whom Egwene had been wanting to meet. Shevan was one of those who supported negotiating with the rebel Aes Sedai, and Egwene hoped to be able to nudge her more toward helping unify the White Tower from within.

There wasn't a Red sister at the table other than Elaida. Was that because the Red Sitters were all out of the Tower?

Perhaps Elaida thought the room balanced with her there, as she still thought of herself as Red, although she wasn't supposed to.

It was a long table, crystal goblets sparkling and reflecting light from the ornate bronze standlamps, running along the walls painted a rusty red-yellow in color. Each woman wore a fine gown in the color of her Ajah. The room smelled of succulent meats and steamed carrots. The women chatted. Amicable, but forced. Tense. They didn't want to be there.

Across the room, Doesine nodded to Egwene, almost in respect. It was an indication of something. "I'm here because you said that this sort of thing was important," it seemed to say. Elaida sat at the head of the table, wearing a red dress with full sleeves, uncut garnets trimming them and the bodice, her face bearing a satisfied smile. Servants bustled back and forth, pouring wine and bringing food. Why had Elaida called a dinner of Sitters? Was this an attempt to heal the rifts in the White Tower? Had Egwene misjudged her?

"Ah, good," Elaida said, noticing Egwene. "You've finally arrived. Come here, child."

Egwene did so, walking through the room, the last few Sitters catching notice of her. Some seemed confused, others made curious, by her presence. As she walked, Egwene realized something.

This one evening could easily undo all that she'd worked for.

If the Aes Sedai here saw her subserviently waiting on Elaida, Egwene would lose integrity in their eyes. Elaida had declared that Egwene was cowed—but Egwene had proven otherwise. If she bent to Elaida's will here, even a little, it would be seen as proof.

Light burn the woman! Why had she invited so many of the women that Egwene had been working to influence? Was it simple happenstance? Egwene joined the false Amyrlin at the head of the table, and a servant handed her a crystal pitcher of glistening red wine. "You are to keep my cup full," Elaida said. "Wait there, but don't come too close. I'd rather not have to smell the soot on you from your punishments this afternoon."

Egwene clenched her jaw. Smell the soot? After an hour

of scrubbing? Doubtful. From the side, she could see the satisfaction in Elaida's eyes as she sipped her wine. Then Elaida turned to Shevan, who sat in the chair to Elaida's right. The Brown was a lanky woman, with knobbed arms and an angular face, like a person made of gnarled sticks. Her eyes were thoughtful as she studied her hostess.

"Tell me, Shevan," Elaida said. "Do you still insist on those foolish talks with the rebels?"

Shevan responded. "The sisters must be given a chance to reconcile."

"They've had their chance," Elaida said. "Honestly, I expected more of a Brown. You're behaving doggedly, without a whit of understanding how the real world works. Why, even Meidani agrees with me, and she's a Gray! You know how *they* are."

Shevan turned away, seeming more disturbed than before. Why did Elaida invite them to dinner, if only to insult them and their Ajahs? As Egwene watched, the Red turned her attention to Ferane, and complained to her about Rubinde, a Sitter from the Green who also resisted Elaida's efforts to end the talks. As she spoke, she raised her cup to Egwene, tapping it. Elaida had barely taken a few sips.

Egwene ground her teeth, filling the cup. The others had seen her do labor before—why, she'd cracked walnuts for Ferane. This wouldn't ruin her reputation, not unless Elaida forced her to abase herself somehow.

But what was the point of this dinner? Elaida didn't seem to be making any attempt to bring the Ajahs together. If anything, she was prying those rifts wider, the way she was dismissing those who disagreed with her. Occasionally, she would have Egwene refill her cup, but it never had room for more than a sip or two.

Slowly, Egwene began to understand. This dinner wasn't about working with the Ajahs. It was about bullying the Sitters into doing as Elaida felt they should. And Egwene was simply there to be shown off! This was all about proving to the others how much power Elaida had—she could take someone that others had named Amyrlin, put a novice dress on her and send her to penance every day.

Egwene felt herself grow angry again. Why could Elaida always stir her emotions? Soup bowls were removed and plates of steamed, buttered carrots were brought, a hint of cinnamon striking the air. Egwene had not been given dinner, but she felt too sick to care about eating.

No, she thought, steeling herself. *I will not end this early, like last time. I will endure. I am stronger than Elaida. I'm stronger than her madness.*

The conversation continued, Elaida making insulting comments to the others, sometimes with intent, sometimes with apparent unawareness. The others steered the talk away from the rebels and toward the strangely overcast skies. Eventually, Shevan mentioned a rumor about the Seanchan working with Aiel far to the south.

"The Seanchan again?" Elaida said with a sigh. "You needn't worry about them."

"My sources say otherwise, Mother," Shevan said stiffly. "I think we need to pay close attention to what they are doing. I have had some sisters ask this child about her experience with them, which has been extensive. You should hear the things they do to Aes Sedai."

Elaida laughed a tinkling, melodic laugh. "Surely you know how the child is prone to exaggerate!" She glanced at Egwene. "Have you been spreading lies for your friend, the fool al'Thor? What did he tell you to say about these invaders? They are working for him, are they not?"

Egwene didn't respond.

"Speak," Elaida said, gesturing with her cup. "Tell these women you have been speaking lies. Confess or I'll have you in penance again, girl."

The penance she would take for not speaking would be better than suffering Elaida's rage at contradicting her. Silence was the path to victory.

And yet, as Egwene glanced down the long mahogany table, set with bright white Sea Folk porcelain and flickering red candles, she saw five pairs of eyes studying her. She could see their questions. Egwene had spoken boldly to them when alone, but would she hold to her assertions now, faced by the most powerful woman in the world? A woman who held Egwene's life in her hands?

Was Egwene the Amyrlin? Or was she just a girl who liked to pretend?

Light burn you, Elaida, she thought, gritting her teeth, seeing that she had been wrong. Silence wouldn't lead to victory, not in front of these women. *You are* not *going to like how this proceeds.*

"The Seanchan are not working for Rand," Egwene said. "And they are a severe danger to the White Tower. I have spread no lies. To say otherwise would be to betray the Three Oaths."

"You haven't taken the Three Oaths," Elaida said sternly, turning toward her.

"I have," Egwene said. "I've held no Oath Rod, but it isn't the Rod that makes my words true. I have spoken the words of the oaths in my heart, and to me they are more dear, for I have nothing forcing me to hold to them. And by that oath holding me, I tell you again. I am a Dreamer, and I have Dreamed that the Seanchan will attack the White Tower."

Elaida's eyes flared for a moment, and she gripped her fork until her knuckles whitened. Egwene held her eyes, and finally Elaida laughed again. "Ah, stubborn as ever, I see. I shall have to tell Katerine that she was right. You'll have penance for your exaggerations, child."

"These women know I don't speak lies," Egwene said calmly. "And each time you insist that I do, you lower yourself in their eyes. Even if you disbelieve my Dream, you *must* admit that the Seanchan are a threat. They leash women who can channel, using them as weapons with a kind of twisted *ter'angreal*. I have felt the collar on my neck. I still feel it, sometimes. In my dreams. My nightmares."

The room fell still.

"You *are* a foolish child," Elaida said, obviously trying to pretend that Egwene was no threat. She should have turned to look at the eyes of the others. If she had, she'd have seen the truth. "Well, you have forced my hand. You will kneel before me, child, and beg forgiveness. Right now. Otherwise, I will lock you away alone. Is that what you want? Don't think that the beatings will stop, however. You'll still get your daily penance, you'll just be thrown back into your cell after each one. Now, kneel and beg forgiveness."

The Sitters glanced at one another. There was no backing down now. Egwene *wished* it hadn't come to this. But it had, and Elaida had demanded a fight.

It was time to give her one. "And if I do not bow before

you?" Egwene asked, meeting the woman's eyes. "What then?"

"You *will* kneel, one way or another," Elaida growled, embracing the Source.

"You'll use the Power on me?" Egwene asked calmly. "Do you have to resort to that? Have you no authority without channeling?"

Elaida paused. "It is within my rights to discipline one who isn't showing proper respect."

"And so you will *make* me obey," Egwene said. "Is this what you will do to everyone in the Tower, Elaida? An Ajah opposes you, and it is disbanded. Someone displeases you, and you try to destroy her right to be Aes Sedai. You will have every sister bowing down before you by the end of this."

"Nonsense!"

"Oh?" Egwene asked. "And have you told them about your idea for a new oath? Sworn on the Oath Rod by every sister, an oath to obey the Amyrlin and support her?"

"I—"

"Deny it," Egwene said. "Deny that you made the statement. Will the Oaths let you?"

Elaida froze. If she were Black, she *could* deny it, Oath Rod or not. But either way, Meidani could substantiate what Egwene had said.

"It was idle talk," Elaida said. "Just speculation, thoughts spoken out loud."

"There is often truth in speculation," Egwene said. "You locked the Dragon Reborn himself in a box; you just threatened to do the same to me, in front of all of these witnesses. People call him a tyrant, but you are the one destroying our laws and ruling by fear."

Elaida's eyes opened wide, her anger visible. She seemed . . . shocked. As if she couldn't understand how she'd gone from disciplining an unruly novice into debating an equal. Egwene saw the woman begin to weave a thread of Air. That had to be stopped. A gag of Air would end this debate.

"Go ahead," Egwene said calmly. "Use the Power to silence me. As Amyrlin, shouldn't you be able to *talk* an opponent into obedience, rather than resorting to force?"

Out of the corner of her eye, Egwene saw diminutive Yukiri, of the Gray, nod at that comment.

Elaida's eyes flared in anger as she dropped the thread of

Air. "I don't need to rebut a mere novice," Elaida snapped. "The Amyrlin doesn't explain herself to one such as you."

"'The Amyrlin understands the most complex of creeds and debates,'" Egwene said, quoting from memory. "'Yet in the end, she is the servant of all, even the lowest of laborers.'" That had been said by Balladare Arandaille, the first Amyrlin to be raised from the Brown Ajah. She'd used the words in her last writings before her death; those writings had been an explanation of her reign and what she had done during the Kavarthen wars. Arandaille had felt that once a crisis was passed, it was the moral duty of an Amyrlin to explain herself to the common people.

Sitting beside Elaida, Shevan nodded appreciatively. The quote was somewhat obscure; Egwene blessed Siuan's quiet training in the wisdom of the former Amyrlins. Much of what she'd said had come from the secret histories, but there had been a number of nuggets from women such as Balladare as well.

"What is this nonsense you're sputtering?" Elaida spat.

"What did you intend to do with Rand al'Thor once you captured him?" Egwene said, ignoring the comment.

"I don't—"

"You're not answering *me*," Egwene said, nodding to the table of women, "but *them*. Have you explained yourself, Elaida? What were your plans? Or will you dodge this question just as you have the others I've asked?"

Elaida's face was turning red, but she calmed herself with some effort. "I would have kept him secure, and well shielded, here in the Tower until it was time for the Last Battle. That would have prevented him from causing the suffering and chaos he's created in many nations. It was worth the risk of angering him."

"'As the plow breaks the earth shall he break the lives of men, and all that was shall be consumed in the fire of his eyes,'" Egwene said. "'The trumpets of war shall sound at his footsteps, the ravens feed at his voice, and he shall wear a crown of swords.'"

Elaida frowned, taken aback.

"*The Karaethon Cycle*, Elaida," Egwene said. "When you had Rand locked away to be kept 'secure,' had he yet taken Illian? Had he yet worn what he was to name the Crown of Swords?"

"Well, no."

"And how did you expect him to fulfill the prophecies if he was hidden away in the White Tower?" Egwene said. "How was he to cause war, as the prophecies say he must? How was he to break the nations and bind them to him? How could he 'slay his people with the sword of peace' or 'bind the nine moons to serve him' if he was locked away? Do the prophecies say that he will be 'unfettered'? Do they not speak of the 'chaos of his passing'? How can anything pass at all if he is kept in chains?"

"I. . . ."

"Your logic is astounding, Elaida," Egwene said coldly. At that, Ferane smiled slyly; she was probably thinking yet again that Egwene would fit well in the White Ajah.

"Bah," Elaida said, "you ask meaningless questions. The prophecies would *have* to have been fulfilled. There was no other way."

"So you're saying that your attempt to bind him was destined to fail."

"No, not at all," Elaida said, red-faced again. "We shouldn't be bothering with this—it's not for you to decide upon. No, we should be talking about your rebels, and what *they've* done to the White Tower!"

A good turn of the conversation, an attempt to put Egwene on the defensive. Elaida wasn't completely incompetent. Just arrogant.

"I see *them* trying to heal the rift between us," Egwene said. "We cannot change what has happened. We can't change what you did to Siuan, even if those with me did discover a method of Healing her stilling. We can only move forward and try our best to smooth the scars. What are you doing, Elaida? Refusing talks, trying to bully the Sitters into withdrawing? Insulting Ajahs that are not your own?"

Doesine, of the Yellow, gave a quiet murmur of agreement. That drew Elaida's eyes, and she fell silent for a moment, as if realizing that she had lost control of the debate. "Enough of this."

"Coward," Egwene said.

Elaida's eyes flared wide. "How *dare* you!"

"I dare the truth, Elaida," Egwene said quietly. "You are a coward and a tyrant. I'd name you Darkfriend as well, but

I suspect that the Dark One would perhaps be embarrassed to associate with you."

Elaida screeched, weaving in a flash of Power, slamming Egwene back against the wall, toppling the pitcher of wine from her hands. It shattered on a patch of wooden floor beside the rug, throwing a spray of bloodlike liquid across the table and half of its occupants, staining the white tablecloth with a smear of red.

"You name *me* Darkfriend?" Elaida screamed. "You are the Darkfriend. You and those rebels outside, who seek to distract me from doing what must be done."

A blast of woven Air slammed Egwene against the wall again, and she dropped to the ground, hitting shards of the broken pitcher that sliced open her arms. A dozen switches beat her, ripping her clothing. Blood seeped from her arms, and it began to splash into the air, smirching the wall as Elaida beat her.

"Elaida, stop it!" Rubinde said, standing, green dress swishing. "Are you mad?"

Elaida turned, panting. "Do *not* tempt me, Green!"

The switches continuing to beat Egwene. She bore it silently. With effort, she stood up. She could feel her face and arms swelling already. But she maintained a calm gaze at Elaida.

"Elaida!" Ferane yelled, standing. "You violate Tower law! You *cannot* use the Power to punish an initiate!"

"I *am* Tower law!" Elaida raved. She pointed at the sisters. "You mock me. I know you do it. Behind my back. You show me deference when you see me, but I know what you say, what you whisper. You ungrateful fools! After what I've done for you! Do you think I'll suffer you forever? Take this one as an example!"

She spun, pointing at Egwene, then stumbled back in shock to find Egwene calmly watching her. Elaida gasped softly, raising a hand to her breast as the switches beat. They could all see the weaves, and they could all see that Egwene did not scream, although her mouth was not gagged with Air. Her arms dripped blood, her body was beaten before them, and yet she found no reason to scream. Instead, she quietly blessed the Aiel Wise Ones for their wisdom.

"And what," Egwene said evenly, "am I to be an example of, Elaida?"

The beating continued. Oh, how it hurt! Tears formed in the corners of Egwene's eyes, but she had felt worse. Far worse. She felt it each time she thought of what this woman was doing to the institution she loved. Her true pain was not from the wounds, but from how Elaida had acted before the Sitters.

"By the Light," Rubinde whispered.

"I wish I weren't needed here, Elaida," Egwene said softly. "I wish that the Tower had a grand Amyrlin in you. I wish I could step down and accept your rule. I wish you deserved it. I would willingly accept execution, if it would mean leaving a competent Amyrlin. The White Tower is more important than I am. Can you say the same?"

"You want execution!" Elaida bellowed, recovering her tongue. "Well, you shall not have it! Death is too good for you, Darkfriend! I shall see you beaten—everyone shall see you beaten—until I am *through* with you. Only then will you die!" She turned to the servants, who stood, gaping, at the sides of the room. "Send for soldiers! I want this one cast into the deepest cell this Tower can provide! Let it be voiced through the city that Egwene al'Vere is a Darkfriend who has rejected the Amyrlin's grace!"

Servants ran to do as she demanded. The switches continued to beat, but Egwene was growing numb. She closed her eyes, feeling faint—she had lost much blood from her left arm, which bore the deepest of her gashes.

It had come to a head, as she'd feared that it would. She had cast her lot.

But she didn't fear for her life. Instead, she feared for the White Tower. As she leaned back against the wall, thoughts fading, she was overcome with sorrow.

Her battle from within the Tower was at an end, one way or another.

CHAPTER
17

Questions of Control

"Y ou should be more careful," Sarene said from inside the room. "The Amyrlin Seat, we have much
influence with her. Your punishments, we may be
able to persuade her to lessen them, if you are helpful."

Semirhage's sniff of disdain was quite audible to Cadsuane, listening from the hallway outside the interrogation
room, sitting in a comfortable log chair. Cadsuane sipped at
a cup of warm sweetleaf. The hallway was of simple wood,
carpeted with a long maroon and white rug, prismlike
lamps on the walls flickering with light.

There were several others in the hallway with her—
Daigian, Erian, Elza—whose turn it was to maintain Semirhage's shield. Aside from Cadsuane, each Aes Sedai in the
camp took turns. It was too dangerous to risk forcing the
duty only on the Aes Sedai of lesser stature, lest they grow
weary. The shield had to remain strong. Light only knew
what would happen if Semirhage got free.

Cadsuane sipped her tea, her back to the wall. Al'Thor
had insisted that "his" Aes Sedai be allowed opportunities
to interrogate Semirhage, instead of just those Cadsuane
had chosen. She wasn't certain if this was some attempt at
asserting his authority or if he genuinely thought that they
might succeed where she—so far—had failed.

Anyway, that was why Sarene was doing the questioning today. The Taraboner White was a thoughtful person,
completely unaware that she was one of the most beautiful
women to gain the shawl in years. Her nonchalance was
not unexpected, as she was of the White Ajah, who could
often be as oblivious as Browns. Sarene also didn't know

that Cadsuane was outside eavesdropping, through the use of a weave of Air and Fire. It was a simple trick, one often learned by novices. Mixing it with this newly found trick of inverting one's weaves meant that Cadsuane could listen in without anyone inside knowing that she was there.

The Aes Sedai outside saw what she was doing, of course, but none said anything. Even though two of them—Elza and Erian—were among the group of fools who had sworn fealty to the al'Thor boy, they stepped lightly around her; they knew how she regarded them. Idiot women. At times, it seemed that half of her allies were only determined to make her job harder.

Sarene continued her interrogation inside. Most of the Aes Sedai in the manor had now given questioning a try. Brown, Green, White and Yellow—all had failed. Cadsuane herself had yet to address any questions to the Forsaken personally. The other Aes Sedai looked at her as an almost mythic figure, a reputation she had nurtured. She'd stayed away from the White Tower for many decades at a time, ensuring that many would assume she was dead. When she reappeared, it made a stir. She'd gone hunting false Dragons, both because it was necessary and because each man she captured added to her reputation with the other Aes Sedai.

All of her work pointed at these final days. Light blind her if she was going to let that al'Thor boy ruin it all now!

She covered her scowl by taking a sip of her tea. She was slowly losing control, thread by thread. Once, something as dramatic as the squabbles at the White Tower would have drawn her immediate attention. But she couldn't begin to work on that problem. Creation itself was unraveling, and her only way to fight that was to turn all her efforts on al'Thor.

And he resisted her every attempt to aid him. Step by step he was becoming a man with insides like stone, unmoving and unable to adapt. A statue with no feelings could *not* face the Dark One.

Blasted boy! And now there was Semirhage, continuing to defy her. Cadsuane itched to go in and confront the woman, but Merise had asked the very questions Cadsuane would have, and she had failed. How long would Cadsuane's image remain intact if she proved herself as impotent as the others?

Sarene began to talk again.

"The Aes Sedai, you should not treat them so," Sarene said, voice calm.

"Aes Sedai?" Semirhage responded, chuckling. "Don't you feel ashamed, using that term to describe yourselves? Like a puppy calling itself a wolf!"

"We may not know everything, I admit, but—"

"You know nothing," Semirhage replied. "You are children playing with your parents' toys."

Cadsuane tapped the side of her tea cup with her index finger. Again, she was struck by the similarities between herself and Semirhage—and again, those similarities made her insides itch.

Out of the corner of her eye, she saw a slender serving woman climb the steps carrying a plate of beans and steamed radishes for Semirhage's midday meal. Time already? Sarene had been interrogating the Forsaken for three hours, and she had been talked neatly in circles the entire time. The serving woman approached and Cadsuane waved for her to enter.

A moment later, the tray crashed to the floor. At the sound, Cadsuane leaped to her feet, embracing *saidar*, quite nearly rushing into the room. Semirhage's voice made Cadsuane hesitate.

"I will not eat that," the Forsaken said, in control, as always. "I have grown tired of your swill. You will bring me something appropriate."

"If we do," Sarene's voice said, obviously snatching for any advantage, "will you answer our questions?"

"Perhaps," Semirhage replied. "We shall see if it fits my mood."

There was a silence. Cadsuane glanced at the other women in the hall, all of whom had leaped to their feet at the sound, although they couldn't hear the voices. She motioned them to sit down.

"Go and fetch her something else," Sarene said, speaking inside the room to the serving woman. "And send someone to clean this up." The door opened, then shut quickly as the servant hurried away.

Sarene continued, "This next question, it will determine if you actually get to eat that meal or not." Despite the firm voice, Cadsuane could hear a quickness to Sarene's words.

The sudden drop of the tray of food had startled her. They were all so jumpy around the Forsaken. They weren't deferential, but they *did* treat Semirhage with a measure of respect. How could they not? She was a legend. One did not enter the presence of such a creature—one of the most evil beings ever to live—and *not* feel at least a measure of awe.

Measure of awe. . . .

"That's our mistake," Cadsuane whispered. She blinked, then turned and opened the door into the room.

Semirhage stood in the center of the small chamber. She had been retied in Air, the weaves likely woven the moment that she'd dropped her tray. The brass platter lay discarded, the beans soaking juice into the aged wooden boards. This room had no window; it had been a storage chamber at one point, converted into a "cell" to hold the Forsaken. Sarene—dark hair in beaded braids, beautiful face surprised at the intrusion—sat in a chair before Semirhage. Her Warder, Vitalien, broad-shouldered and ashen-faced, stood in the corner.

Semirhage's head was not bound, and her eyes flicked toward Cadsuane.

Cadsuane had committed herself; she had to confront the woman now. Fortunately, what she planned didn't require much delicacy. It all came back to a single question. How would Cadsuane break herself? The solution was easy, now that it occurred to her.

"Ah," Cadsuane said with a no-nonsense attitude. "I see that the child has refused her meal. Sarene, release your weaves."

Semirhage raised her eyebrows and opened her mouth to scoff, but as Sarene released her weaves of Air, Cadsuane grabbed Semirhage by the hair and—with a casual sweep of her foot—knocked the woman's legs out from beneath her, dropping her to the floor.

Perhaps she could have used the Power, but it felt *right* to use her hands for this. She prepared a few weaves, though she probably wouldn't need them. Semirhage, though tall, was a woman of willowy build, and Cadsuane herself had always been more stout than she was slim. Plus, the Forsaken seemed utterly dumbfounded at how she was being treated.

Cadsuane knelt down with one knee on the woman's

back, then shoved her face forward into the spilled food. "Eat," she said. "I don't approve of wasted food, child, particularly during these times."

Semirhage sputtered, releasing a few phrases that Cadsuane could only assume were oaths, though she didn't recognize any of them. The meanings were likely lost in time. Soon, the oaths subsided and Semirhage grew still. She didn't fight back. Cadsuane wouldn't have either; that would only hurt her image. Semirhage's power as a captive came from the fear and respect that the Aes Sedai gave her. Cadsuane needed to change that.

"Your chair, please," she said to Sarene.

The White stood, looking shocked. They had tried all measure of torture available to them under al'Thor's requirements, but each of those had betrayed esteem. They were treating Semirhage as a dangerous force and a worthy enemy. That would only bolster her ego.

"Are you going to eat?" Cadsuane asked.

"I will kill you," Semirhage said calmly. "First, before all of the others. I will make them listen to you scream."

"I see," Cadsuane replied. "Sarene, go tell the three Sisters outside to come in." Cadsuane paused, thoughtful. "Also, I saw some maids cleaning rooms on the other side of the hallway. Fetch them for me as well."

Sarene nodded, rushing from the room. Cadsuane sat in the chair, then wove threads of Air and picked Semirhage up. Elza and Erian glanced into the room, looking very curious. Then they entered, Sarene following. A few moments later, Daigian entered with five servants: three Domani women in aprons, one spindly man, his fingers brown with stain from recoating logs, and a single serving boy. Excellent.

As they entered, Cadsuane used her threads of Air to turn Semirhage around across her knee. And then she proceeded to spank the Forsaken.

Semirhage held out at first. Then she began to curse. Then she began to sputter out threats. Cadsuane continued, her hand beginning to hurt. Semirhage's threats turned to howls of outrage and pain. The serving girl with the food returned in the middle of it, adding even more to Semirhage's shame. The Aes Sedai watched with slack jaws.

"Now," Cadsuane said after a few moments, breaking into one of Semirhage's howls of pain. "Will you eat?"

"I'll find everyone you've ever loved," the Forsaken said, tears in her eyes, "I'll feed them to each other while you watch. I'll—"

Cadsuane "tsk"ed and began again. The crowd in the room watched in amazed silence. Semirhage began to cry—not from the pain, but from the humiliation. That was the key. Semirhage could not be defeated by pain or by persuasion—but destroying her image, that would be more terrible in her mind than any other punishment. Just as it would have been for Cadsuane.

Cadsuane stilled her hand after a few more minutes, releasing the weaves that held Semirhage motionless. "Will you eat?" she asked.

"I—"

Cadsuane raised her hand, and Semirhage practically leaped off of her lap and scrambled onto the floor, eating the beans.

"She is a person," Cadsuane said, looking at the others. "Just a person, like any of us. She has secrets, but any young boy can have a secret that he refuses to tell. Remember that."

Cadsuane stood and walked to the door. She hesitated beside Sarene, who watched with fascination as the Forsaken ate beans off of the floor. "You may want to begin carrying a hairbrush with you," Cadsuane added. "That can be quite hard on your hands."

Sarene smiled. "Yes, Cadsuane Sedai."

Now, Cadsuane thought, leaving the room, *what to do about al'Thor?*

"My Lord," Grady said, rubbing his weathered face, "I don't think you understand."

"Then explain it to me," Perrin said. He stood on a hillside, looking down over the huge gathering of refugees and soldiers. Mismatched tents of many different designs—tan, single-peaked Aiel structures; colorful large Cairhienin ones; two-tipped tents of basic design—sprang up as the people prepared for the night.

The Shaido Aiel, as hoped, had not given chase. They had let Perrin's army withdraw, though his scouts said that they had now moved in to investigate the city. Either way, it meant Perrin had time. Time to rest, time to limp away, time—he'd hoped—to use gateways to transport away most of these refugees.

Light, but it was a big group. Thousands upon thousands of people, a nightmare to coordinate and administer to. His last few days had been filled with an endless stream of complaints, objections, judgments and papers. Where did Balwer find so much paper? It seemed to satisfy many of the people who came to Perrin. Judgments and the settlement of disputes seemed so much more official to them when a piece of paper outlined them. Balwer said Perrin would need a seal.

The work had been distracting, which was good. But Perrin knew he couldn't push aside his problems for long. Rand pulled him northward. Perrin *had* to march for the Last Battle. Nothing else mattered.

And yet, that very single-mindedness in him—ignoring everything but his objective—had been the source of much trouble during his hunt for Faile. He had to find a balance, somehow. He needed to decide for himself if he wanted to lead these people. He needed to make peace with the wolf inside himself, the beast that raged when he went into battle.

But before he could do any of that, he needed to get the refugees home. That was proving a problem. "You've had time to rest now, Grady," Perrin said.

"The fatigue is only one part of it, my Lord," Grady said. "Though, honestly, I *still* feel as if I could sleep a week's time."

He *did* look tired. Grady was a stalwart man, with the face of a farmer and the temperament of one, too. Perrin would trust this man to do his duty before most lords he'd known. But Grady could be pushed only so far. What did it do to a man, to have to channel so much? Grady had bags beneath his eyes, and his face was pale despite his tanned skin. Though he was still a young man, he'd started to go gray.

Light, but I used this man too hard, Perrin thought. *Him and Neald both.* That had been another effect of Perrin's single-mindedness, as he was beginning to see. What he'd

done to Aram, how he'd allowed those around him to go
without leadership. . . . *I have to fix this. I have to find a
way to deal with it all.*

' If he didn't, he might not *get* to the Last Battle.

"Here's the thing, my Lord." Grady rubbed his chin again,
surveying the camp. The various contingents—Mayeners,
Alliandre's guard, the Two Rivers men, the Aiel, the refugees from various cities—all camped separately, in their
own rings. "There are some hundred thousand people who
need to get home. The ones that will leave, anyway. Many
say they feel safer here, with you."

"They can give over wanting that," Perrin said. "They
belong with their families."

"And the ones whose families are in Seanchan lands?"
Grady shrugged. "Before the invaders came, many of these
people would be happy to return. But now . . . Well, they
keep talking about staying where there's food and protection."

"We can still send the ones who want to go," Perrin said.
"We'll travel lighter without them."

Grady shook his head. "That's the thing, my Lord. Your
man, Balwer, he gave us a count. I can make a gateway big
enough for about two men to walk through at once. If you
figure them taking one second to go through . . . Well, it
would take hours and hours to send them all. I don't know
the number, but he claimed it would be days' worth of work.
And he said that his estimates were probably too optimistic.
My Lord, I could barely keep a gateway open an hour, with
how tired I am."

Perrin gritted his teeth. He'd have to get those numbers
from Balwer himself, but he had a sinking feeling that Balwer would be right.

"We'll keep marching, then," Perrin said. "Moving
north. Each day, we'll have you and Neald make gateways
and return some of the people to their homes. But don't tire
yourselves."

Grady nodded, eyes hollow from fatigue. Perhaps it
would be best to wait a few more days before starting the
process. Perrin nodded a dismissal to the Dedicated, and
Grady jogged back down into camp. Perrin remained on the
hillside, inspecting the various sections of the camp as the
people prepared for the evening meal. The wagons sat at

the center of the camp, laden with food that—he feared—would run out before he could reach Andor. Or should he go around to Cairhien? That was where he had last seen Rand, though his visions of the man made it seem he wasn't in either country. He doubted the Queen of Andor would welcome him with open arms, after the rumors about him and that blasted Red Eagle banner.

Perrin left that problem alone for the moment. The camp seemed to be settling in. Each ring of tents sent representatives to the central food depot to claim their evening rations. Each group was in charge of its own meals; Perrin just oversaw the distribution of materials. He made out the quartermaster—a Cairhienin named Bavin Rockshaw—standing on the back of a wagon, dealing with each representative in turn.

Satisfied with his inspection, Perrin walked down into the camp, passing through the Cairhienin tents on the way to his own tents, which were with the Two Rivers men.

He took his enhanced senses for granted, now. They had come along with the yellowing of his eyes. Most people around him didn't seem to notice those anymore, but he was starkly reminded of the contrast when he met anyone new. Many of the Cairhienin refugees, for instance, paused in their labors setting up tents. They watched him as he passed, whispering, "Goldeneyes."

He didn't much care for the name. Aybara was the name of his family, and he bore it proudly. He was one of the few who could pass it on. Trollocs had seen to that.

He shot a glance at a nearby group of the refugees, and they hastily turned back to pounding in tent stakes. As they did, Perrin passed a couple of Two Rivers men—Tod al'Caar and Jori Congar. They saw him and saluted, fists to hearts. To them, Perrin Goldeneyes wasn't a person to fear, but one to respect, although they did still whisper about that night he'd spent in Berelain's tent. Perrin wished he could escape the shadow of *that* event. The men were still enthusiastic and energized by their defeat of the Shaido, but it hadn't been too long ago that Perrin had felt he wasn't welcome among them.

Still, for the moment, these two seemed to have set aside that displeasure. Instead, they saluted. Had they forgotten that Perrin had grown up with them? What of the times when Jori had made sport of Perrin's slow tongue, or the times when he'd stopped by the forge to brag about which girls he'd managed to steal a kiss from?

Perrin just nodded back. No use in digging up the past, not when their allegiance to "Perrin Goldeneyes" had helped rescue Faile. Though, as he left them, his too-keen ears caught the two of them chatting about the battle, just a few days past, and their part of it. One of them still smelled like blood; he hadn't cleaned his boots. He probably didn't even notice the bloodstained mud.

Sometimes, Perrin wondered if his senses weren't actually any better than anyone else's. He took the time to notice things that others ignored. How could they miss that scent of blood? And the crisp air of the mountains to the north? It smelled of home, though they were many leagues from the Two Rivers. If other men took the time to close their eyes and pay attention, would they be able to smell what he did? If they opened those eyes and looked closer at the world around them, would men call their eyes "keen" as they did Perrin's?

No. That was just fancy. His senses *were* better; his kinship with the wolves had changed him. He hadn't thought of that kinship in a while—he'd been too focused on Faile. But he'd stopped feeling so self-conscious about his eyes. They were part of him. No use grumbling about them.

And yet, that rage he felt when he fought . . . that loss of control. It worried him, more and more. The first time he'd felt it had been that night, so long ago, fighting Whitecloaks. For a time, Perrin hadn't known if he was a wolf or a man.

And now—during one of his recent visits to the wolf dream—he'd tried to kill Hopper. In the wolf dream, death was final. Perrin had almost lost himself that day. Thinking of it awakened old fears, fears he'd shoved aside. Fears relating to a man, behaving like a wolf, locked in a cage.

He continued down the pathway to his tent, making some decisions. He'd pursued Faile with determination, avoiding the wolf dream as he'd avoided all of his responsibilities. He'd claimed that nothing else had mattered. But he knew that the truth was much more difficult. He'd focused on Faile because he loved her so much, but—in addition—he'd done so because it had been convenient. Her rescue had been an excuse to avoid things like his discomfort with leadership and the blurred truce between himself and the wolf inside of himself.

He had rescued Faile, but so many things were still wrong. The answers might lie in his dreams.

It was time to return.

CHAPTER 18

A Message in Haste

Siuan froze—basket of dirty laundry on her hip—the moment she walked into the Aes Sedai camp. It was her own laundry, this time. She'd finally realized that she didn't need to do both hers and Bryne's. Why not let the novices put in some time on her washing? There were certainly enough of them these days.

And every one of them crowded the walkway around the pavilion at the center of camp. They stood arm-to-arm, a wall of white topped by heads of hair in every natural hue. No ordinary meeting of the Hall would have drawn such attention. Something must be going on.

Siuan set the wicker laundry basket on a stump, then pulled a towel over it. She didn't trust that sky, although it hadn't rained more than the occasional drizzle in the past week. Don't trust a dockmaster's sky. Words to live by. Even if the consequence only meant a basket of wet clothing, soiled at that.

She hurried across the dirt road and stepped up onto one of the wooden walkways. The rough boards shifted slightly underfoot and creaked with her footfalls as she hurried towards the pavilion. There was talk of replacing the walkways with something more permanent, perhaps as expensive as paving stones.

She reached the backs of the gathered women. The last meeting of the Hall that had drawn this level of attention had revealed that Asha'man had bonded sisters and that the taint itself had been cleansed. Light send that there weren't any surprises of *that* size waiting! Her nerves were taut enough, dealing with Gareth bloody Bryne. Suggesting that she let him teach her how to hold a sword, just in case. She'd never thought that swords were much use. Besides, who ever heard of an Aes Sedai with a weapon, fighting like a crazed Aiel? Honestly, that man.

She bullied her way through the novices, annoyed that she had to get their attention in order to make them let her pass. They gave way as soon as they saw a sister passing through them, of course, but they were so distracted that it took work to move them out of the way. She chided a few of them for not being about their duties. Where was Tiana? She should have had these girls back to their chores. If Rand al'Thor himself bloody appeared in camp, the novices should continue their lessons!

Finally, near the pavilion flaps, she found the woman she'd expected. Sheriam, as Egwene's Keeper, couldn't enter the Hall without the Amyrlin. And so she was reduced to waiting outside. It was probably better than stewing back in her tent.

The fire-haired woman had lost a fair bit of her plumpness over the previous weeks. She really needed to commission new dresses; her old ones were beginning to hang on her. Still, she seemed to have regained some calm recently, to be less erratic. Perhaps whatever had been ailing her had passed. She'd always insisted that nothing was wrong in the first place.

"Fish guts," Siuan grumbled as a novice accidentally elbowed her. Siuan glared at the girl, who wilted and scurried away, her family of novices reluctantly following. Siuan turned back to Sheriam. "So what is it? Did one of the stable boys turn out to be the King of Tear?"

Sheriam raised an eyebrow. "Elaida has Traveling."

"*What?*" Siuan asked, glancing into the tent. The seats were filled with Aes Sedai, and lanky Ashmanaille—of the Gray—was addressing them. Why hadn't this meeting been Sealed to the Hall?

Sheriam nodded. "We found out when Ashmanaille was sent to collect from Kandor." Tributes were one of the main sources of income for Egwene's Aes Sedai. For many centuries, each kingdom had sent such donations to Tar Valon. The White Tower no longer relied on that income—it had far better means of sustaining itself, ones that didn't rely on outside generosity. Still, tributes were never turned away,

and many of the Borderland kingdoms still held to the old
ways.

Before the White Tower broke, one of Ashmanaille's
duties had been to keep track of these donations and send
monthly thanks on behalf of the Amyrlin. The split of the
White Tower, and the discovery of Traveling, had made it
very easy for Egwene's Aes Sedai to send a delegation and
collect tributes in person. The Kandori chief clerk hadn't
cared which of the two White Tower sides he supported, so
long as the tribute was sent, and had been happy to deliver
the money to Ashmanaille directly.

The siege of Tar Valon had made it simple to siphon this
coin away from tributes that might have gone to Elaida, instead using them to pay Bryne's soldiers. A very neat twist
of fate. But no sea remained calm forever.

"The chief clerk was quite livid," Ashmanaille said in
her no-nonsense voice. "'I already paid your money this
month,' he told me. 'I gave it to a woman who came not one
day gone. The woman bore a letter from the Amyrlin herself, sealed properly, which told me to give the money *only*
to a member of the Red Ajah.'"

"This doesn't say for certain Elaida has Traveling," Romanda noted from inside the tent. "The Red sister could
have gotten to Kandor by other means."

Ashmanaille shook her head. "They saw a gateway made.
The chief clerk discovered an accounting error and sent a
scribe out after Elaida's delegation to give them a few extra
coins. The man described what he saw *perfectly*. The horses
were riding through a black hole in the air. It stunned him
so deeply that he called for the guard—but by then Elaida's
people were already gone. I interrogated him myself."

"I dislike trusting the word of one man," said Moria, sitting near the front of the group.

"The chief clerk described in detail the woman who took
the money from him," Ashmanaille said. "I am confident
that it was Nesita. Perhaps we could discover if she is in the
Tower? That would give us further proof."

Others raised objections, but Siuan ceased to listen
closely. Perhaps this was a very clever ruse intended to distract them, but they couldn't take that chance. Light! Was
she the only one with a head on her shoulders?

She grabbed the nearest novice, a mousy girl who was

probably older than she looked—she'd have to be, since she looked no older than nine. "I need a courier," Siuan informed her. "Fetch one of the messengers Lord Bryne left at the camp for running news to him. *Quickly.*"

The girl yelped, dashing away.

"What was that about?" Sheriam asked.

"Saving our lives," Siuan said, glaring at the crowding novices. "All right!" she growled. "Enough gawking! If your classes are postponed because of this fiasco, then find some work to do. Any novice still standing on this walkway in ten seconds will find herself doing penance until she can't count straight!"

That initiated a mass exodus of white, the families of women bustling away with hurried steps. In moments, only the small group of Accepted remained, along with Sheriam and Siuan. The Accepted cringed when Siuan glanced at them, but she said nothing. Part of the privilege of being an Accepted was increased freedom. Besides, as long as Siuan could move without bumping someone, she was satisfied.

"Why wasn't this meeting Sealed to the Hall in the first place?" she asked Sheriam.

"I don't know," Sheriam admitted, glancing into the large tent. "It's daunting news, if it's true."

"This was bound to occur eventually," Siuan said, though she was nowhere near that calm on the inside. "News of Traveling has to be spreading."

What happened? she thought. *They didn't break Egwene, did they? Light send it wasn't her or Leane who was forced to give up this secret. Beonin. It had to be her. Burn it all!*

She shook her head. "Light send that we can keep Traveling secret from the Seanchan. When they *do* assault the White Tower, we'll want at least that advantage."

Sheriam eyed her, skepticism showing. Most of the sisters didn't believe Egwene's Dreaming of the attack. Fools—they wanted to catch the fish, but didn't want to gut it. You didn't raise a woman to Amyrlin, then treat her warnings lightly.

Siuan waited impatiently, tapping her foot, listening to the conversation inside the tent. Just as she was beginning to wonder if she'd need to send another novice, one of Bryne's couriers trotted up to the tent on horseback. The ill-tempered brute he was riding was midnight black with white just above the hooves, and it snorted at Siuan as the rider pulled up short, wearing a neat uniform and close-cropped brown hair. Did he *have* to bring that creature with him?

"Aes Sedai?" the man asked, bowing to her from horseback. "You have a message for Lord Bryne?"

"Yes," Siuan said. "And you'll see it delivered with *all haste*. You understand me? All of our lives could depend on it."

The soldier nodded sharply.

"Tell Lord Bryne . . ." Siuan began. "Tell him to watch his flanks. Our enemy has been taught the method we used to get here."

"It shall be done."

"Repeat it back to me," Siuan said.

"Of course, Aes Sedai," the slender man said, bowing again. "Just so you know, I have been a messenger in the general's command for over a decade. My memory—"

"Stop," Siuan interrupted. "I don't care how *long* you've been doing this. I don't care how good your memory is. I don't care if, by some twist of fate, you've been asked to run this *very same message* a thousand times before. You *will* repeat it back to me."

"Um, yes, Aes Sedai. I'm to tell the Lord General to watch his flanks. Our enemy has been taught the method we used to get here."

"Good. Go."

The man nodded.

"Now!"

He reared that awful horse and galloped out of the camp, cloak flapping behind him.

"What was *that* about?" Sheriam asked, glancing away from the proceedings inside the Hall.

"Making certain we don't wake up with Elaida's army surrounding us," Siuan said. "I'll bet I'm the only one who thought to warn our general that the enemy may have just undone our biggest tactical advantage. So much for a siege."

Sheriam frowned, as if she hadn't considered that. She wouldn't be alone. Oh, some would think of Bryne, and would be planning to send word to the general eventually. But for many, the catastrophe here *wasn't* the fact that Elaida could now move her armies to flank them, or that now Bryne's siege was useless. The catastrophe would be more personal for them: the knowledge they'd worked to keep secret had fallen into the hands of others. Traveling was *theirs*, and now Elaida had it! Very Aes Sedai. Indignation first, implication second.

Or perhaps Siuan was just feeling bitter. Someone inside the tent finally thought to call for the meeting to be Sealed to the Hall, and so Siuan withdrew, stepping off the walkway and onto the hard-packed earth. Novices scuttled this way and that, heads bowed to avoid her eyes, though they were quick to curtsy. *I haven't been doing a very good job of acting weak today,* Siuan thought with a grimace.

The White Tower was crumbling. The Ajahs weakened one another with petty infighting. Even here, in Egwene's camp, more time was spent politicking than preparing for the coming storm.

And Siuan was partially responsible for those failures.

Elaida and her Ajah certainly bore the lionfish's share of the blame. But would the Tower have split in the first place if Siuan had fostered cooperation between the Ajahs? Elaida hadn't had *that* long to work. Every rift that appeared in the Tower could likely be traced back to tiny cracks during Siuan's tenure as Amyrlin. If she'd been more of a mediator among the factions of the White Tower, could she have pounded strength into the bones of these women? Could she have kept them from turning on one another like razorfish in a blood frenzy?

The Dragon Reborn was important. But he was only one figure in the weaving of these final days. It was too easy to forget that, too easy to watch the dramatic figure of legend and forget everyone else.

She sighed, picking up her laundry and—out of habit—checking to make certain everything was there. As she did so, a figure in white approached her from one of the branching pathways. "Siuan Sedai?"

Siuan looked up, frowning. The novice before her was one of the strangest in the camp. Nearly seventy years old, Sharina had the weathered, creased face of a grandmother. She kept her silver hair up in a bun, and while she walked without a stoop, there was a certain distinct *weight* to her. She had seen so much, done so much, passed so many years.

And unlike an Aes Sedai, Sharina had *lived* all of those years. Working, raising a family, even burying children.

She was strong in the power. Remarkably so; she would wear the shawl for certain, and as soon as she did, she'd be far above Siuan. For now, though, Sharina curtsied deeply. She gave an almost perfect show of deference. Of all of the novices, she was known to complain the least, make the least trouble, and study the most assiduously. As a novice, she understood things that most Aes Sedai had never learned—or had forgotten the moment they took the shawl. How to be humble when necessary, how to take a punishment, how to know when you needed to learn rather than pretend you already knew. *If only we had a few score more of her,* Siuan thought, *and a few score less Elaidas and Romandas.*

"Yes, child?" Siuan asked. "What is it?"

"I saw you picking up that wash, Siuan Sedai," Sharina said. "And I thought that perhaps I should carry it for you."

Siuan hesitated. "I wouldn't want you to tire yourself."

Sharina raised an eyebrow in a very un-novice-like expression. "These old arms carried loads twice that heavy back and forth from the river just last year, Siuan Sedai, juggling three grandchildren all the way. I think I'll be all right." There was something in her eyes, a hint that her offer was not all it seemed to be. This one was adept at more than just Healing weaves, it appeared.

Curious, Siuan let the aged woman take the basket. They began to walk down the pathway toward the novices' tents.

"It's curious," Sharina said, "that such a large disturbance could be caused by such a seemingly simple revelation, wouldn't you say, Siuan Sedai?"

"Elaida's discovery of Traveling *is* an important revelation."

"And yet nowhere near as important as the ones rumored to have come during the meeting a few months back, when that man who can channel visited. Odd that this should create such a scene."

Siuan shook her head. "The thinking of crowds is often odd at first consideration, Sharina. Everyone is still talking about that Asha'man visit, and they're thirsty for more. So they react with excitement at the chance to hear something else. In that way, the great revelations can come in secret, but then cause lesser ones to be received in an explosion of anxiety."

"One could put that observation to good use, I should think." Sharina nodded to a group of novices as they passed. "If one wanted to cause worry, that is."

"What are you saying?" Siuan asked, eyes narrowing.

"Ashmanaille reported first to Lelaine Sedai," Sharina said softly. "I've heard that Lelaine was the one who let the news slip. She spoke it out loud in the hearing of a family of novices while calling for the Hall to meet. She also deflected several early calls for the meeting to be Sealed to the Hall."

"Ah," Siuan said. "So *that's* why!"

"I relate only hearsay, of course," Sharina explained, pausing in the shade of a scraggly blackwood tree. "It is probably just foolishness. Why, an Aes Sedai of Lelaine's stature would *know* that if she let information slip in the hearing of novices, it would soon pass to all willing ears."

"And in the Tower, every ear is willing."

"Exactly, Siuan Sedai," Sharina said, smiling.

Lelaine had wanted to create a menagerie of a meeting— she'd wanted novices listening in, and every sister in the camp joining in the discussion. Why? And why was Sharina confiding her very un-novice-like opinions?

The answer was obvious. The more threatened the women in the camp felt—the more danger they saw from Elaida—the easier it would be for a firm hand to seize control. Though the sisters were indignant now over the mere loss of a closely guarded secret, they would soon realize the danger that Siuan had already seen. Soon there would be fear. Worry. Anxiety. The siege would never work, not now that the Aes Sedai inside it could Travel wherever and whenever they wished. Bryne's army at the bridges had become useless.

Unless Siuan missed her guess, Lelaine would be making certain that everyone else noticed the implications, too.

"She wants us scared," Siuan said. "She wants a crisis." It was clever. Siuan should have seen this coming. The fact that she hadn't—and the fact that she'd gotten no wind of Lelaine's plans—also whispered an important fact. The woman might not trust Siuan as deeply as she seemed to. Blast!

She focused on Sharina. The gray-haired woman stood patiently, waiting as Siuan worked through what she'd revealed.

"Why did you tell me this?" Siuan asked. "For all you know, I'm Lelaine's lackey."

Sharina raised her eyebrows. "Please, Siuan Sedai. These eyes aren't blind, and they see a woman working very hard to keep the Amyrlin's enemies occupied."

"Fine," Siuan said. "But you are still exposing yourself for very little reward."

"Little reward?" Sharina asked. "Excuse me, Siuan Sedai, but what do you suppose my fate will be if the Amyrlin doesn't return? No matter what she says now, we can sense Lelaine Sedai's true opinions."

Siuan hesitated. Though Lelaine now played the part of Egwene's pious advocate, not too long ago she had been as displeased as everyone else over the too-old novices. Few liked it when traditions changed.

Now that the new novices had been entered into the novice book, it would be very difficult to put them out of the Tower. But that didn't mean the Aes Sedai would continue to let older women in. Beyond that, there was a good chance that Lelaine—or whoever ended up with the Amyrlin Seat—would find a way to delay or disrupt the progression of the women who had been accepted against tradition. That would certainly include Sharina.

"I will let the Amyrlin know of your actions here," Siuan said. "You will be rewarded."

"My reward will be Egwene Sedai's return, Siuan Sedai. Pray it be swift. She entangled our fate with her own the moment she took us in. After what I've seen, and what I've felt, I have no intention of stopping my training." The woman hefted the basket. "I assume you wish these washed and returned to you?"

"Yes. Thank you."

"I am a novice, Siuan Sedai. It is my duty and my pleasure." The elderly woman bowed in respect and continued on down the path, walking with a step younger than her years.

Siuan watched her go, then stopped another novice. Another messenger to Bryne. Just in case. *Hurry up, girl,*

Siuan thought to Egwene, glancing toward the spire of the White Tower. *Sharina isn't the only one whose fate is entangled with yours. You've got us all wound up in that net of yours.*

CHAPTER
19

Gambits

C haos. The entire world was chaos.

Tuon stood on the balcony of her audience hall in the palace of Ebou Dar, hands clasped behind her back. In the palace grounds—flagstones washed white, like so many surfaces in the city—a group of Altaran armsmen in gold and black practiced formations beneath the watchful eyes of a pair of her own officers. Beyond them, the city proper rose, white domes banded with colors spreading alongside tall, white spires.

Order. Here in Ebou Dar, there was order, even in the fields of tents and wagons outside the city. Seanchan soldiers patrolled and kept the peace; there were plans to clean out the Rahad. Just because one was poor was not a reason—or an excuse—to live without law.

But this city was just a tiny, tiny pocket of order in a world of tempest. Seanchan itself was broken by civil war, now that the Empress had died. The Corenne had come, but recapturing these lands of Artur Hawkwing progressed slowly, stalled by the Dragon Reborn in the east and Domani armies in the north. She still waited to hear news of Lieutenant-General Turan, but the signs were not good. Galgan maintained that they might be surprised at the outcome, but Tuon had seen a black dove the hour she was informed of Turan's predicament. The omen had been clear. He would not return alive.

Chaos. She glanced to the side, where faithful Karede stood in his thick armor, colored blood-red and a deep green, nearly black. He was a tall man, square face nearly as solid as the armor he wore. He had fully two dozen Deathwatch

Guards with him this day—the day after Tuon's return to
Ebou Dar—along with six Ogier Gardeners, all standing
along the walls. They lined the sides of the high-ceilinged,
white-pillared room. Karede sensed the chaos, and did
not intend to let her be taken again. Chaos was the most
deadly when you made assumptions about what it could and
couldn't infect. Here in Ebou Dar, it manifested in the form
of a faction intent on taking Tuon's own life.

She had been dodging assassinations since she could
walk, and she had survived them all. She anticipated them.
In a way, she thrived because of them. How were you to
know that you were powerful unless assassins were sent to
kill you?

Suroth's betrayal, however . . . Chaos, indeed, when the
leader of the Forerunners herself turned traitor. Bringing
the world back into order was going to be very, very difficult. Perhaps impossible.

Tuon straightened her back. She had not thought to become Empress for many years yet. But she would do her
duty.

She turned away from the balcony and walked back into
the audience chamber to face the crowd awaiting her. Like
the others of the Blood, she wore ashes on her cheeks to
mourn the loss of the Empress. Tuon had little affection for
her mother, but affection was not needed for an empress.
She provided order and stability. Tuon had only begun to
understand the importance of these things as the weight
had settled on her shoulders.

The chamber was wide and rectangular, lit with candelabras between the pillars and the radiant glow of sunlight
through the wide balcony behind. Tuon had ordered the
room's rugs removed, preferring the bright white tiles. The
ceiling bore a painted mural of fishers at sea, with gulls in
the clear air, and the walls were a soft blue. A group of ten
da'covale knelt before the candelabras to Tuon's right. They
wore filmy costumes, waiting for a command. Suroth was
not among them. The Deathwatch Guard saw to her, at least
until her hair grew out.

As soon as Tuon entered the room, all of the commoners
bowed on knees with foreheads to the ground. Those of the
Blood knelt, bowing their heads.

Across from the *da'covale*, on the other side of the hall,

Lanelle and Melitene knelt in dresses emblazoned with silver lightning bolts in red panels on their skirts. Their leashed *damane* knelt facedown. Tuon's kidnapping had been unbearable to several of the *damane*; they had taken to inconsolable weeping during her absence.

Her audience chair was relatively simple. A wooden seat with black velvet on the arms and back. She sat down, wearing a pleated gown of the deepest sea blue, a white cape fluttering behind her. As soon as she did, the people in the room rose from their positions of adulation—all save the *da'covale*, who remained kneeling. Selucia stood and stepped up beside the chair, her golden hair in a braid down her right side, the left side of her head shaven. She did not wear the ashes, since she was not of the Blood, but the white band on her arm indicated that she—like the entire Empire—mourned the loss of the Empress.

Yuril, Tuon's secretary and secretly her Hand, stepped up to the other side of the chair. The Deathwatch Guards moved in subtly around her, dark armor glittering faintly in the sunlight. They had been particularly protective of her lately. She didn't blame them, recent events considered.

Here I am, Tuon thought, *surrounded by my might,* da-mane *on one side and Deathwatch Guard on the other. And yet I feel no safer than I did with Matrim.* How odd, that she should have felt safe with him.

Directly in front of her, lit by indirect sunlight from the open balcony behind, was a collection of the Blood, Captain-General Galgan highest of them. He wore armor this day, the breastplate painted a deep blue, nearly dark enough to be black. His powdery white hair ran in a crest with the sides of his head shaven, and was plaited to his shoulders, for he was of the High Blood. With him were two members of the low Blood—Banner-General Najirah and Banner-General Yamada—and several commoner officers. They waited patiently, carefully not meeting Tuon's eyes.

A gathering of other members of the Blood stood several steps behind, to witness her acts. Wiry Faverde Noth-ish and long-faced Amenar Shumada led them. They were both important—important enough to be dangerous. Sur-oth wouldn't be the only one who saw opportunity in these times. If Tuon were to fall, practically anyone could become Empress. Or Emperor.

The war in Seanchan would not end quickly; but when it did, the victor would undoubtedly raise him- or herself to the Crystal Throne as well. And then there would be two leaders of the Seanchan Empire, divided by an ocean, united in desire to conquer one another. Neither could allow the other to live.

Order, Tuon thought, tapping the black wood of her armrest with a blue-lacquered fingernail. *Order must emanate from me. I will bring the calm airs to those beset by storms.*

"Selucia is my Truthspeaker," she announced to the room. "Let it be published among the Blood."

The statement was expected. Selucia bowed her head in acceptance, though she had no desire for any appointment other than to serve and protect Tuon. She would not welcome this position. But she was also honest and straightforward; she would make an excellent Truthspeaker.

At least this time, Tuon could be certain that her Truthspeaker wasn't one of the Forsaken.

Did she believe Falendre's story, then? It stretched plausibility; it sounded like one of Matrim's fanciful tales of imaginary creatures that lurked in the dark. And yet, the other *sul'dam* and *damane* had corroborated Falendre's tale.

Some facts, at least, seemed straightforward. Anath had been working with Suroth. Suroth—after some persuasion— had admitted that she had met with one of the Forsaken. Or, at least, she thought she had. She hadn't known that the Forsaken was the same as Anath, but she seemed to find the revelation believable.

Whether or not she really was Forsaken, Anath had met with the Dragon Reborn, imitating Tuon. And had then tried to kill him. *Order,* Tuon thought, keeping her face still. *I represent order.*

Tuon gestured rapidly to Selucia, who was still Tuon's Voice—and her shadow—even with the added responsibility of Truthspeaker. When ordering those far beneath herself, Tuon would first pass the words to Selucia, who would speak them.

"You are required to send him in," Selucia said to a *da'covale* beside the throne. He bowed himself to the ground, touching head to the floor, then hurried to the other end of the large room and opened the door.

Beslan, King of Altara and High Seat of House Mitsobar, was a slender youth with black eyes and hair. He had the olive skin common to the Altaran people, but he had taken to wearing clothing like that favored by the Blood. Loose trousers of yellow and a high-collared coat that came down only to the middle of his chest, a yellow shirt underneath. The Blood had left a clear passage down the middle of the room, and Beslan walked through it, eyes lowered. Upon reaching the supplication space before the throne, he went down on his knees, then bowed low. The perfect image of a loyal subject, except for the thin golden crown on his head.

Tuon gestured to Selucia.

"You are bidden to rise," Selucia said.

Beslan rose, though he kept his gaze averted. He was a fine actor.

"The Daughter of the Nine Moons expresses her condolences to you for your loss," Selucia said to him.

"I give the same to her for her loss," he said. "My grief is but a candle to the great fire felt by the Seanchan people."

He was *too* servile. He was a king; he was not required to bow himself so far. He was the equal of many of the Blood.

She could almost have believed he was just being submissive before the woman who would soon become Empress. But she knew too much of his temperament, through both spies and hearsay.

"The Daughter of the Nine Moons wishes to know the reason you have ceased holding court," Selucia said, watching Tuon's hands move. "She finds it distressing that your people cannot have audience with their king. Your mother's death was as tragic as it was shocking, but your kingdom needs you."

Beslan bowed. "Please have her know that I did not think it appropriate to elevate myself above her. I am uncertain how to act. I meant no insult."

"Are you certain that is the true reason?" Selucia Voiced. "It is not, perhaps, because you are planning a rebellion against us, and do not have time for your other duties?"

Beslan looked up sharply, eyes wide. "Your Majesty, I—"

"You need not speak any further lies, child of Tylin," Tuon said directly to him, causing gasps of surprise from the assembled Blood. "I know of the things you have said to General Habiger and your friend, Lord Malalin. I know of your quiet meetings in the basement of The Three Stars. I know of it all, King Beslan."

The room fell silent, Beslan bowed his head for a moment. Then, surprisingly, he rose to his feet and stared her directly in the eyes. She wouldn't have thought the soft-spoken youth had it in him. "I will not allow my people to—"

"I would still my tongue if I were you," Tuon interrupted. "You stand on sand as it is."

Beslan hesitated. She could see the question in his eyes. Wasn't she going to execute him? *If I intended to kill you,* she thought, *you would be dead already, and you would never have seen the knife.*

"Seanchan is in upheaval," Tuon said, regarding him. He appeared shocked at the words. "Oh, did you think I would ignore it, Beslan? I am not content to stare at the stars while my empire collapses around me. The truth must be acknowledged. My mother is dead. There is no empress.

"However, the forces of the Corenne are *more* than sufficient to maintain our positions here on this side of the ocean, Altara included." She leaned forward, trying to project a sense of *control*, of *firmness*. Her mother had been able to do so at all times. Tuon did not have her mother's height, but she would need that aura. Others had to feel safer, more secure, simply by entering her presence.

"In times such as these," Tuon continued, "threats of rebellion cannot be tolerated. Many will see opportunity in the Empire's weakness, and their divisive squabbling—if left unchecked—would prove the end of us all. Therefore, I must be firm. Very firm. With those who defy me."

"Then why," Beslan said, "am I still alive?"

"You started planning your rebellion *before* events in the Empire were made known."

He frowned, dumbfounded.

"You began your rebellion when Suroth led here," Tuon said, "and when your mother was still queen. Much has changed since then, Beslan. Very much. In times like these, there is potential for great accomplishment."

"You must know I have no thirst for power," Beslan said. "The freedom of my people is all I desire."

"I do know it," Tuon said, clasping her hands before her, lacquered nails curling, elbows on the armrests of her chair.

"And that is the other reason you are still alive. You rebel not out of lust for station, but out of sheer ignorance. You are misguided, and that means you can change, should you receive the proper knowledge."

He looked at her, confused. *Lower your eyes, fool. Don't make me have you strapped for insolence!* As if he had heard her thoughts, he averted his eyes, then lowered them. Yes, she had judged correctly regarding this one.

How precarious her position was! True, she had armies—but so many of them had been thrown away by Suroth's aggression.

All kingdoms on this side of the ocean would need to bow before the Crystal Throne, eventually. Each *marath'damane* would be leashed, each king or queen would swear the oaths. But Suroth had pushed too hard, particularly in the fiasco with Turan. A hundred thousand men, lost in one battle. Madness.

Tuon *needed* Altara. She needed Ebou Dar. Beslan was well loved by the people. Putting his head on a pike after the mysterious death of his mother. . . . Well, Tuon *would* have stability in Ebou Dar, but she would rather not have to leave battlefronts unmanned to accomplish it.

"Your mother's death is a loss," Tuon said. "She was a good woman. A good queen."

Beslan's lips tightened.

"You may speak," Tuon said.

"Her death . . . is unexplained," he said. The implication was obvious.

"I do not know if Suroth caused her to be killed," Tuon said, softening her voice. "She claims that she did not. But the matter is being investigated. If it turns out that Suroth was behind the death, you and Altara will have an apology from the throne itself."

Another gasp from the Blood. She silenced them with a glance, then turned back to Beslan. "Your mother's loss *is* a great one. You must know that she was loyal to her oaths."

"Yes," he said, voice bitter. "And she gave up the throne."

"No," Tuon said curtly. "The throne belongs to you. This is the ignorance of which I spoke. You *must* lead your people. They *must* have a king. I have neither time nor desire to do your duty for you.

"You assume that the Seanchan dominance of your

homeland will mean your people lack freedom. That is false. They will be more free, more protected, and more powerful when they accept our rule.

"I sit above you. But is this so undesirable? With the might of the empire, you will be able to hold your borders and patrol your lands outside of Ebou Dar. You speak of your people? Well, I have ordered something prepared for you." She nodded to the side, where a willowy-limbed *da'covale* stepped forward with a leather satchel.

"Inside," Tuon said, "you will find numbers gathered by my scouts and guard forces. You can see directly the reports of crimes during our occupation here. You will have reports and manifests, comparing how the people were *before* the Return and *after* it.

"I believe you know what you will find. The Empire is a resource to you, Beslan. A powerful, powerful ally. I will not insult you by offering you thrones you do not want. I will entice you by promising stability, food, and protection for your people. All for the simple price of your loyalty."

He hesitantly accepted the satchel.

"I offer you a choice, Beslan," Tuon said. "You may choose execution, if you wish. I will not make you *da'covale*. I will let you die with honor, and it will be published that you died because you rejected the oaths and chose not to accept the Seanchan. If you wish it, I will allow it. Your people will know that you died in defiance.

"Or, you may choose to serve them better. You may choose to live. If you do so, you will be raised to the High Blood. You will step forward and reign as your people need you to do. I promise you that I will *not* direct the affairs of your people. I will demand resources and men for my armies, as is proper, and your word cannot countermand my own. Aside from that, your power in Altara will be absolute. No Blood will have the right to command, harm, or imprison your people without your permission.

"I will accept and review a list of noble families you feel should be raised to the low Blood, and I will raise no fewer than twenty of them. Altara will become the permanent seat of the Empress on this side of the ocean. As such, it will be the most powerful kingdom here. You may choose."

She leaned forward, unlacing her fingers. "But understand this. If you decide to join with us, you *will* give me your heart, and not just your words. I will not allow you to ignore your oaths. I have given you this chance because I believe you can be a strong ally, and I think that you were misguided, perhaps by Suroth's twisted webs.

"You have one day to make your decision. Think well. Your mother thought this to be the best course, and she was a wise woman. The Empire means stability. A rebellion would mean only suffering, starvation and obscurity. These are not times to be alone, Beslan."

She sat back as Beslan regarded the satchel in his hands. He bowed in supplication to withdraw, though the motion was jerky, as if he were distracted.

"You may go," she said to him.

He rose, but did not turn to leave. The room fell still as he stared down at his hands and the satchel. She could read his struggle in his expression. A *da'covale* approached to hasten him on his way, as he had been dismissed, but Tuon raised her hand, stilling the servant.

She leaned forward, several members of the Blood shuffling their feet as they waited. Beslan just stared at that satchel. Finally, he looked up, eyes determined. And then, surprisingly, he got back down on his knees.

"I, Beslan of House Mitsobar, pledge my fealty and service to the Daughter of the Nine Moons and through her to the Seanchan Empire, now and for all time, save that she chooses to release me of her own will. My lands and throne are hers, and I yield them to her hand. So I do swear before the Light."

Tuon let herself smile. Behind Beslan, Captain-General Galgan stepped forward, addressing the King. "That is not the proper way to—"

Tuon silenced him with a gesture. "We demand that this people adopt our ways, General," she said. "It is fitting that we accept some of theirs." Not too many of those ways, of course. But she could thank her long conversations with Mistress Anan for allowing her to understand this. The Seanchan had, perhaps, made a mistake with this people in making them swear Seanchan oaths of obedience. Matrim had sworn those oaths, but ignored them handily when the time came—yet he had been certain to keep his word to her, and his men had assured her he was a man of honor.

How strange that they would be willing to elevate one

oath over another. These people were odd. But she would
have to understand them in order to rule them—and she
would have to rule them to gather strength for her return to
Seanchan.

"Your oath is pleasing to me, King Beslan. I raise you to
the High Blood and give you and your House dominance
over the kingdom of Altara, for now and all time, your will
for the administration and governance of it second only to
that of the Imperial Throne itself. Rise."

He stood, legs looking shaky. "Are you certain you're not
ta'veren, my Lady?" he asked. "Because I certainly wasn't
expecting to do *that* when I walked in here."

Ta'veren. These people and their foolish superstitions! "I
am pleased with you," she said to him. "I knew your mother
for only a short time, but I did find her quite capable. I
would not have enjoyed being forced to execute her only
remaining son."

He nodded in appreciation. To the side, Selucia covertly
signed, *That was well handled. Unconventional, perhaps,
but very delicately done.*

Tuon felt a warm sense of pride. She turned to the white-
haired General Galgan. "General. I realize you have been
waiting to speak with me, and your patience is to be commended. You may now speak your thoughts. King Beslan,
you may withdraw or remain. It is your right to attend any
public conferences I have in your kingdom, and you need
no permission or invitation to attend."

Beslan nodded, bowing but retreating to the side of the
room to watch.

"Thank you, Highest Daughter," Galgan said reverently,
stepping forward. He waved to his *so'jhin*, who stood in the
hallway outside. They entered—first prostrating themselves
before Tuon—then quickly set up a table and several maps.
One servant brought Galgan a bundle, which he carried,
approaching Tuon. Karede was at her right shoulder in a
moment, Selucia at her left, but Galgan kept a respectful
distance. He bowed and unrolled the item on the ground. It
was a banner of red, bearing a circle in the center, split by
a sinuous line. One half of the circle was black, the other
white.

"What is it?" Tuon asked, leaning forward.

"The banner of the Dragon Reborn," Galgan said. "He

sent it with a messenger, asking yet again for a meeting." He glanced up—not meeting her eyes, but showing a thoughtful, concerned face.

"This morning when I arose," Tuon said, "I saw a pattern like three towers in the sky and a hawk, high in the air, passing between them."

The various members of the Blood in the room nodded appreciatively. Only Beslan seemed confused. How did these people live, not knowing the omens? Had they no desire to understand the visions of fate the Pattern was giving them? The hawk and three towers were an omen of difficult choices to come. They indicated that boldness would be needed.

"What are your thoughts on the Dragon Reborn's request for a meeting?" Tuon asked Galgan.

"Perhaps it would be unwise to meet with this man, Highest Daughter. I am not certain of his claims to his title. Beyond this question, does the Empire not have other concerns at this time?"

"You wonder why our forces have not retreated," Tuon said. "Why we have not struck out for Seanchan to secure the throne."

He bowed his head. "I trust your wisdom, Highest Daughter."

"This *is* the Dragon Reborn," Tuon said. "And not just an impostor. I am convinced of it. He must bow before the Crystal Throne before the Last Battle can begin. And so we must stay. It is not an accident that the Return happened now. We are needed here. More than we are needed, unfortunately, in our homeland."

Galgan nodded slowly. He agreed with her on not retreating to Seanchan; he had simply assumed it would be what she wished. In declaring they would stay, she had earned his respect. Not that he wouldn't still consider seizing the throne for himself. A man could not hold his position without a great deal of ambition.

However, he was known to be a prudent man as well as an ambitious one. He would not strike unless he was convinced it was for the best. He would have to believe that he had a strong potential for success and that removing Tuon would be better for the Empire. That was the difference between an ambitious fool and an ambitious wise man. The latter understood that killing someone was only the beginning. Taking Tuon's life and assuming the throne himself would gain him nothing if it alienated the rest of the Blood.

He walked to his table with maps. "If you wish to continue to prosecute the war, Highest Daughter, permit me to explain the condition of your army. One of our most ambitious plans is being organized by Lieutenant-General Yulan."

Galgan gestured to the assembled officers and a short, dark-skinned man of the low Blood stepped forward. He wore a black wig to hide his baldness, and he approached and knelt before Tuon, bowing.

"You are commanded to rise and speak, General," Selucia Voiced.

"The Highest Daughter should know my thanks," Yulan said, rising. At the map table, he gestured for several aides to hold up a map so that Tuon could see. "Aside from setbacks in Arad Doman, the process of reclaiming these lands has proceeded as expected. More slowly than we would wish, but not without great victories. The people of these kingdoms do not rally to the defense of their neighboring nations. We have had great success seizing them one at a time. Only two issues cause us worry. The first is this Rand al'Thor, the Dragon Reborn, who has been pursuing an aggressive war of unification to the north and east. The Highest Daughter's wisdom will be needed in teaching us to subdue him.

"The other concern has been the large number of *marath'damane* concentrated in the place known as Tar Valon. I believe the Highest Daughter has heard of the great weapon they used to destroy a large patch of land north of Ebou Dar."

Tuon nodded.

"The *sul'dam* have never seen its like," Yulan continued. "We assume it is a thing of *damane*, which can be taught to them, if the right *marath'damane* are taken. This wondrous ability they have to transport instantly from one place to another—if true—will prove a second technique of great tactical advantage that we *must* capture."

Tuon nodded again, studying the map, which showed the place called Tar Valon. Selucia Voiced, "The Highest Daughter is curious as to your plans. You will proceed."

"My thanks are expressed deeply," Yulan said, bowing. "As Captain of the Air, I have the honor of commanding the *raken* and *to'raken* serving the Return. I believe that a strike at the very heart of our enemy's lands would not only be possible, but highly advantageous. We have not yet had to fight many of these *marath'damane* in combat, but as we advance into lands controlled by the Dragon Reborn, we will undoubtedly face them in great numbers.

"They assume that they are safe from us at this time. A strike now could have great impact on the future. Each *marath'damane* we leash is not only a powerful tool gained by our forces, but one lost by the enemy. Preliminary reports claim that there are hundreds upon hundreds of *marath'damane* congregated in this place called the White Tower."

That many? Tuon thought. A force like that could turn the war entirely. True, those *marath'damane* who had traveled with Matrim had said that they would not take part in wars. Indeed, *marath'damane* who had once been Aes Sedai had—so far—proven useless as weapons. But could there be some way to twist their supposed vows? Something Matrim had said in passing made her suspect they could. Her fingers flew.

"The Daughter of the Nine Moons wonders how a strike against them could be feasible," Selucia Voiced. "The distance is great. Hundreds of leagues."

"We would use a force of mostly *to'raken*," General Yulan said. "With some *raken* for scouting. Our captured maps show large grasslands with very few inhabitants, which could be used as resting points along the way. We could strike across Murandy here," he pointed at a second map, which aides held up, "and come at Tar Valon from the south. If it pleases the Highest Daughter, we could raid at night, while the *marath'damane* are asleep. Our objective would be to capture as many of them as possible."

"It is wondered if this really could be accomplished," Selucia Voiced. Tuon was intrigued. "What numbers would we be able to use for such a raid?"

"If we were fully committed?" Yulan asked. "I believe I could gather up between eighty and a hundred *to'raken* for the assault."

Eighty to a hundred *to'raken*. So, perhaps around three

hundred soldiers, with equipment, leaving room to bring
back captured *marath'damane*. Three hundred would be a
considerable force for a raid like this, but they would have
to move quickly and lightly, so as to not be trapped.

"If it pleases the Highest Daughter," General Galgan said,
stepping forward again. "I believe General Yulan's plan has
much merit. It is not without potential for great loss, but we
will never have another such opportunity. If brought to bear
in our conflict, those *marath'damane* could disable us. And
if we could gain access to this weapon of theirs, or even
their ability to travel great distances. . . . Well, I believe that
the risk of every *to'raken* in our army is worth the gains."

"If it pleases the Highest Daughter," General Yulan
continued. "Our plan calls for the use of twenty squads of
the Fists of Heaven—two hundred troops total—and fifty
linked *sul'dam*. We think that, perhaps, a small group of
Bloodknives would be appropriate as well."

Bloodknives, the most elite members of the Fists of
Heaven, itself an exclusive group. Yulan and Galgan *were*
dedicated to this action! One never committed Bloodknives
unless one was very serious, for they did not return from their
missions. Their duty was to stay behind after the Fists withdrew and cause damage—as much damage as possible—to
the enemy. If they could place some of them in Tar Valon,
with orders to kill as many *marath'damane* as possible. . . .

"The Dragon Reborn will not react well to this raid,"
Tuon said to Galgan. "Is he not connected to these
marath'damane?"

"By some reports," Galgan said. "Others say he is opposed to them. Still others say they are his pawns. Our poor
intelligence in this area lowers my eyes, Highest Daughter.
I have not been able to sort the lies from the truths. Until
we have better information, we must assume the worst, that
this raid will anger him greatly."

"And you still think it worthwhile?"

"Yes," Galgan said without hesitation. "If these
marath'damane are connected to the Dragon Reborn, then
we have greater reason to strike now, before he can use
them against us. Perhaps the raid will enrage him—but it
will also weaken him, which will place you in a better position for negotiating with him."

Tuon nodded thoughtfully. Undoubtedly, this was the

difficult decision of the omen. But her choice seemed
very obvious. Not a difficult decision at all. All of the
marath'damane in Tar Valon *must* be collared, and this was
an excellent way to weaken resistance to the Ever Victorious Army with a single, powerful blow.

But the omen spoke of a difficult decision. She gestured
to Selucia. "Are there any in the room who disapprove of
this plan?" the Voice asked. "Any who would offer objection to what General Yulan and his men have advanced?"

The Blood in the room regarded one another. Beslan
might have stirred, but he remained silent. The Altarans
had not made any objections to their *marath'damane* being
collared; it seemed they had little trust for those who could
channel. They had not been as prudent as Amadicia in out-
lawing these Aes Sedai, but neither were they welcoming.
Beslan would not object to a strike against the White Tower.

She sat back, waiting . . . For what? Perhaps this wasn't
the decision the omen had referred to. She opened her
mouth to give the order to go forward with the raid, but at
that moment the opening of the doors made her pause.

The Deathwatch Guards who guarded the door stepped
aside a moment later, admitting a *so'jhin* who served in the
hallway. The strong-armed man, Ma'combe, bowed himself
low to the ground, the black braid over his right shoulder
dropping to the side and hitting the tiled floor. "May it
please the Daughter of the Nine Moons, Lieutenant-General
Tylee Khirgan would like an audience."

Galgan looked shocked.

"What is it?" Tuon asked him.

"I had not realized that she had returned, Highest Daughter," he said. "I suggest in humility that she be given leave
to speak. She is one of my finest officers."

"She may enter," Selucia Voiced.

A male *da'covale* in a white robe entered, preceding a
woman in armor, her helm under her arm. Dark of skin,
with short black hair worn in tight curls against her scalp,
she was tall and lean. Her hair was sprinkled with white
at the temples. The overlapping plates of her armor were
striped with red, yellow and blue lacquer, and creaked as
she walked. She was only of the low Blood—recently raised
by General Galgan's order—but she had been informed of

this via *raken*. She wore her hair barely shaved a finger's width up the sides of her head.

Tylee's eyes were red with fatigue. Judging by the scent of sweat and the stink of horse she gave off, she had come straight to Tuon upon arriving in the city. She was followed into the room by several younger soldiers, also exhausted, one bearing a large brown sack. Upon reaching the supplication space—a red square of cloth—all went down on their knees. The common soldiers proceeded to touch foreheads to the floor, and Tylee jerked as if to follow, but stopped herself. She was not yet accustomed to being one of the Blood.

"It is obvious that you are tired, warrior," Selucia Voiced. Tuon leaned forward. "It is presumed that you have news of great import?"

Tylee rose to one knee, then gestured to the side. One of her soldiers rose to his knees and lifted up his brown sack. It was stained on the bottom with a dark, crusted liquid. Blood.

"If it pleases the Highest Daughter," Tylee said, voice betraying exhaustion. She nodded to her man, and he opened his sack, dumping things onto the floor. The heads of several animals. A boar, a wolf, and . . . a hawk? Tuon felt a chill. That hawk's head was as large as a person's. Perhaps larger. But they were not . . . right. The heads were horribly deformed.

She could swear that the hawk's head, which rolled so that she could see the face clearly, had *human* eyes. And . . . the other heads had . . . human features as well. Tuon suppressed a shiver. What foul omen was this?

"What is the meaning of this?" Galgan demanded.

"I presume that the Highest Daughter knows of my military venture against the Aiel," Tylee said, still on one knee. Tylee had captured *damane* during that engagement, though Tuon didn't know much more than that. General Galgan had been awaiting her return with some curiosity to receive the full story.

"In my venture," Tylee continued, "I was joined by men of various nationalities, none of whom had sworn the oaths. I will give a full report on them when there is time." She hesitated, then glanced at the heads. "These . . . creatures . . .

attacked my company during our return ride, ten leagues from Ebou Dar. We took heavy casualties. We brought several full bodies as well as these heads. They walked on two feet, like men, but had much the appearance of animals." She hesitated again. "I believe them to be what some on this side of the ocean speak of as Trollocs. I believe them to be coming here."

Chaos. The Blood began to argue about the implausibility of it. General Galgan immediately ordered his officers to organize patrols and send runners to warn of a potential attack on the city. The *sul'dam* at the side of the room hurried forward to inspect the heads while the Deathwatch Guards quietly surrounded Tuon, to give an extra layer of defense, watching everyone—Blood, servants, and soldiers—with equal care.

Tuon felt she should be shocked. But, oddly, she wasn't. *So Matrim was not mistaken about this,* she signed covertly to Selucia. And she had assumed Trollocs to be nothing more than superstition. She glanced at the heads again. Revolting.

Selucia seemed troubled. *Are there other things he said that we discounted, I wonder?*

Tuon hesitated. *We shall have to ask him. I should very much like to have him back.* She froze; she hadn't meant to admit so much. She found her own emotions curious, however. She *had* felt safe with him, ridiculous though it seemed. And she wished he were with her now.

These heads were yet another proof that she knew very little of him. She reasserted control of the chattering crowd. Selucia Voiced, "You will silence yourselves."

The room fell still, though the Blood and the *sul'dam* still looked very disturbed. Tylee still knelt, head bowed, the soldier who had borne the heads kneeling beside her. Yes, she would have to be *thoroughly* questioned.

"This news changes little," Selucia Voiced. "We were already aware that the Last Battle approaches. We appreciate Lieutenant-General Tylee's revelations. She is to be commended. But this only makes it *more* urgent that we subdue the Dragon Reborn."

There were several nods from those in the room, including General Galgan. Beslan did not seem so quickly persuaded. He just looked troubled.

"If it pleases the Highest Daughter," Tylee said, bowing.

"You are allowed to speak."

"These last few weeks, I have seen many things that have given me thought," Tylee said. "Even before my troops were attacked, I was worried. The wisdom and grace of the Highest Daughter undoubtedly let her see further than one such as I, but I believe that our conquests so far in this land have been easy compared to what might come. If I may be so bold . . . I believe that the Dragon Reborn and those associated with him may make better allies than enemies."

It *was* a bold statement. Tuon leaned forward, lacquered nails clicking on the armrests of her chair. Many of the low Blood would be so in awe at meeting one of the Empress's household, much less the Highest Daughter, that they would not dare speak. Yet this woman offered suggestions? In direct opposition to Tuon's published will?

"A difficult decision is not always a decision where both sides are equally matched, Tuon," Selucia said suddenly. "Perhaps, in this case, a difficult decision is one that is right, but requires an implication of fault as well."

Tuon blinked in surprise. *Yes,* she realized. *Selucia is my Truthspeaker now.* It would take time to accustom herself to the woman in that role. It had been years since Selucia had corrected or reproved her in public.

And yet, meeting with the Dragon Reborn, in person? She *did* need to contact him, and had planned to. But would it not be better to go to him in strength, his armies defeated, the White Tower torn down? She needed him brought to the Crystal Throne under very controlled circumstances, with the understanding that he was to submit to her authority.

And yet . . . with Seanchan in rebellion . . . with her position here in Altara barely stabilized . . . Well, perhaps some time to think—some time to take a few deep breaths and secure what she already had—would be worth delaying her strike on the White Tower.

"General Galgan, send *raken* to our forces in Almoth Plain and eastern Altara," she said firmly. "Tell them to hold our interests, but avoid confrontation with the Dragon Reborn. And reply to his request for a meeting. The Daughter of the Nine Moons will meet with him."

General Galgan nodded, bowing.

Order must be brought to the world. If she had to do that

by lowering her eyes slightly and meeting with the Dragon Reborn, then so be it.

Oddly, she felt herself wishing—once again—that Matrim were still with her. She could have put his knowledge of this Rand al'Thor to good use in preparing for the meeting. *Stay well, you curious man,* she thought, glancing back at the balcony, northward. *Do not dig yourself into trouble deeper than you can climb to freedom. You are Prince of the Ravens now. Remember to act appropriately.*

Wherever it is you are.

CHAPTER
20

On a Broken Road

"**W**omen," Mat declared as he rode Pips down the dusty, little-used road, "are like mules." He frowned. "Wait. No. Goats. Women are like *goats*. Except every flaming one thinks she's a horse instead, and a prize racing mare to boot. Do you understand me, Talmanes?"

"Pure poetry, Mat," Talmanes said, tamping the tabac down into his pipe.

Mat flicked his reins, Pips continuing to plod along. Tall three-needle pines lined the sides of the stone roadway. They'd been lucky to find this ancient road, which must have been made before the Breaking. It was mostly overgrown, the stones shattered in many places, large sections of the roadway just . . . well, just gone.

Sapling pines had begun to sprout at the sides of the roadway and between rocks, miniature versions of their towering fathers above. The path was wide, if very rough, which was good. Mat had seven thousand men with him, all mounted, and they'd been riding hard in the little under a week they'd spent traveling since sending Tuon back to Ebou Dar.

"Reasoning with a woman is impossible," Mat continued, eyes forward. "It's like . . . Well, reasoning with a woman is like sitting down to a friendly game of dice. Only the woman refuses to acknowledge the basic bloody rules of the game. A man, he'll cheat you—but he'll do it honestly. He'll use loaded dice, so that you think you're losing by chance. And if you aren't clever enough to spot what he's doing, then maybe he deserves to take your coin. And that's that.

"A woman, though, she'll sit down to that same game and she'll smile, and act like she's going to play. Only when it's her turn to throw, she'll toss a pair of her *own* dice that are *blank* on all six sides. Not a single pip showing. She'll inspect her throw, then she'll look up at you and say, 'Clearly I just won.'

"Now, you'll scratch your head and look at the dice. Then you'll look up at her, then down at the dice again. 'But there aren't any pips on these dice,' you'll say.

"'Yes there are,' she'll say. 'And both dice rolled a one.'

"'That's exactly the number you need to win,' you'll say.

"'What a coincidence,' she'll reply, then begin to scoop up your coins. And you'll sit there, trying to wrap your head 'bout what just happened. And you'll realize something. A pair of ones *isn't* the winning throw! Not when you threw a six on your turn. That means she needed a pair of twos instead! Excitedly, you'll explain what you've discovered. Only then, do you know what she'll do?"

"No idea, Mat," Talmanes replied, chewing on his pipe, a thin wisp of smoke curling out of the bowl.

"Then she'll reach over," Mat said, "and rub the blank faces of her dice. And then, with a perfectly straight face, she'll say, 'I'm sorry. There was a spot of dirt on the dice. Clearly you can see that they *actually* came up as twos!' And she'll believe it. She'll bloody believe it!"

"Incredible," Talmanes said.

"Only that's not the end of it!"

"I had presumed that it wouldn't be, Mat."

"She scoops up all of your coins," Mat said, gesturing with one hand, the other steadying his *ashandarei* across his saddle. "And then every other woman in the room will come over and congratulate her on throwing that pair of twos! The more you complain, the more of those bloody women will join the argument. You'll be outnumbered in a moment, and each of those women will explain to you how those dice *clearly* read twos, and how you really need to stop behaving like a child. Every single *flaming* one of them will see the twos! Even the prudish woman who has hated your woman from birth—since your woman's granny stole the other woman's granny's honeycake recipe when they were both maids— *that* woman will side against you."

"They are nefarious creatures indeed," Talmanes said, voice flat and even. Talmanes rarely smiled.

"By the time they're done," Mat continued, almost more to himself, "you'll be left with no coin, several lists' worth of errands to run and what clothing to wear and a splitting headache. You'll sit there and stare at the table and begin to wonder, just maybe, if those dice didn't read twos after all. If only to preserve what's left of your sanity. *That's* what it's like to reason with a woman, I tell you."

"And you did so. At length."

"You aren't making sport of me, are you?"

"Why, Mat!" the Cairhienin said. "You know I'd never do such a thing."

"Too bad," Mat muttered, glancing at him suspiciously. "I could use a laugh." He looked over his shoulder. "Vanin! Where on the Dark One's blistered backside are we?"

The fat former horsethief looked up. He rode a short distance behind Mat, and he carried a map of the area unrolled and folded across a board so he could read it in the saddle. He'd been poring over the bloody thing the better half of the morning. Mat had asked him to get them through Murandy quietly, not get them lost in the mountains for months!

"That's Blinder's Peak," Vanin said, gesturing with a pudgy finger toward a flat-topped mountain just barely visible over the tips of the pines. "At least, I think it is. It might be Mount Sardlen."

The squat hill didn't look like much of a mountain; it barely had any snow atop it. Of course, few "mountains" in this area were impressive, not compared to the Mountains of Mist, back near the Two Rivers. Here, northeast of the Damona range, the landscape fell into a grouping of low foothills. It was difficult terrain, but navigable, if one were determined. And Mat *was* determined. Determined not to be pinned in by the Seanchan again, determined not to be seen by any who didn't *have* to know he was there. He'd paid the butcher too much so far. He wanted out of this hangman's noose of a country.

"Well," Mat said, reining Pips back to ride beside Vanin, "which of those mountains is it? Maybe we should go ask Master Roidelle again."

The map belonged to the master mapmaker; it was only

because of his presence that they'd been able to find this roadway in the first place. But Vanin insisted on being the one to guide the troop—a mapmaker wasn't the same thing as a scout. You didn't have a dusty cartographer ride out and lead the way for you, Vanin insisted.

In truth, Master Roidelle didn't have a lot of experience being a guide. He was a scholar, an academic. He could explain a map for you perfectly, but he had as much trouble as Vanin making sense of where they were, since this roadway was so disjointed and broken, the pines high enough to obscure landmarks, the hilltops all nearly identical.

Of course, there was also the fact that Vanin seemed threatened by the presence of the mapmaker, as if he were worried about being unseated from his position guiding Mat and the Band. Mat had never expected such an emotion from the overweight horsethief. It might have been enough to make him amused if they weren't lost so much of the flaming time.

Vanin scowled. "I think that *has* to be Mount Sardlen. Yes. It's got to be."

"Which means . . . ?"

"Which means we keep heading along the roadway," Vanin said. "The same thing I told you an hour ago. We can't bloody march an army through a forest this thick, now can we? That means staying on the stones."

"I'm just asking," Mat said, pulling down the brim of his hat against the sun. "A commander's got to ask things like this."

"I should ride ahead," Vanin said, scowling again. He was fond of scowls. "If that *is* Mount Sardlen, there should be a village of fair size an hour or two further along. I might be able to spot it from the next rise."

"Go, then," Mat said. They had advance scouts out, of course, but none of them were as good as Vanin. Despite his size, the man could sneak close enough to an enemy fortification to count the whiskers in the camp guards' beards and never be seen. He'd probably make off with their stew, too.

Vanin shook his head as he regarded the map again. "Actually," he muttered, "now that I think about it, maybe that's Favlend Mountain. . . ." He set off at a trot before Mat could object.

Mat sighed, heeling Pips to catch up to Talmanes. The Cairhienin shook his head. He could be an intense one, Talmanes. Early in their association, Mat had assumed him to be stern, unable to have fun. He was learning better. Talmanes wasn't stern, he was just reserved. But at times, there seemed to be a twinkle to the nobleman's eyes, as if he were laughing at the world, despite that set jaw and his unsmiling lips.

Today, he wore a red coat, trimmed with gold, and his forehead was shaved and powdered after Cairhienin fashion. It looked bloody ridiculous, but who was Mat to judge? Talmanes might have terrible fashion sense, but he was a loyal officer and a good man. Besides, he had excellent taste in wine.

"Don't look so glum, Mat," Talmanes said, puffing on his gold-rimmed pipe. Where'd he gotten that, anyway? Mat didn't remember him having it before. "Your men have full bellies, full pockets, and they just won a great victory. Not much more than that a soldier can ask for."

"We buried a thousand men," Mat said. "That's no victory." The memories in his head—the ones that weren't his—said he should be proud. The battle *had* gone well. But there were still those dead who had depended on him.

"There are always losses," Talmanes said. "You can't let them eat you up, Mat. It happens."

"There aren't losses when you don't fight in the first place."

"Then why ride to battle so often?"

"I only fight when I can't avoid it!" Mat snapped. Blood and bloody ashes, he *only* fought when he had to. When they trapped him! Why did that seem to happen every time he turned around?

"Whatever you say, Mat," Talmanes said, taking out his pipe and pointing it at Mat knowingly. "But something's got you on edge. And it isn't the men we lost."

Flaming noblemen. Even the ones you could stand, like Talmanes, always thought they knew so much.

Of course, Mat was now a nobleman himself. *Don't think about that,* he told himself. Talmanes had spent a few days calling Mat "Your Highness" until Mat had lost his temper and yelled at the man—Cairhienin could be such sticklers for rank.

When Mat had first realized what his marriage to Tuon meant, he'd laughed, but it had been the laughter of incredulous pain. And men called him lucky. Well why couldn't his luck have helped him avoid *this* fate! Bloody Prince of the Ravens? What did *that* mean?

Well, right now he had to worry about his men. He glanced over his shoulder, looking along the ranks of cavalrymen, with crossbowmen riding behind. There were thousands of both, though Mat had ordered their banners stowed. They weren't likely to pass many travelers on this backwater path, but if anyone *did* see them, he didn't want their tongues wagging.

Would the Seanchan chase him? He and Tuon both knew they were on opposing sides now, and she'd seen what his army could do.

Did she love him? He was married to her, but Seanchan didn't think like regular people. She'd stayed in his possession, enduring captivity, never running. But he had little doubt that she'd move against him if she thought it best for her empire.

Yes, she'd send men after him, though potential pursuit didn't trouble him half as much as the worry that she might not make it back to Ebou Dar safely. Someone had offered a very large pile of coin for Tuon's head. That Seanchan traitor, the leader of the army Mat had destroyed. Had he been working alone? Were there others? What had Mat released Tuon into?

The questions haunted him. "Should I have let her go, do you think?" Mat found himself asking.

Talmanes shrugged. "You gave your word, Mat, and I think that rather large Seanchan fellow with the determined eyes and the black armor wouldn't have reacted well if you'd tried to keep her."

"She could still be in danger," Mat said, almost to himself, still looking backward. "I shouldn't have let her out of my sight. Fool woman."

"Mat," Talmanes said, pointing at him with the pipe again. "I'm surprised at you. Why, you're starting to sound downright husbandly."

That gave Mat a start. He twisted around in Pips' saddle. "What was that? What does that mean?"

"Nothing, Mat," Talmanes said hurriedly. "Just that, the way you're mooning after her, I—"

"I'm *not* mooning," Mat snapped, pulling the lip of his hat down, then adjusting his scarf. His medallion was a comfortable weight around his neck. "I'm just worried. That's all. She knows a lot about the Band, and she could give away our strengths."

Talmanes shrugged, puffing his pipe. They rode for a time in silence. The pine needles soughed in the wind, and Mat occasionally heard women's laughter from behind, where the Aes Sedai rode in a little cluster. For all the fact that they didn't like one another, they usually got along just fine when others could see them. But, as he'd said to Talmanes, women were only enemies with one another as long as there wasn't a man around to gang up on.

The sun was marked by a blazing patch of clouds; Mat hadn't seen pure sunlight in days. He hadn't seen Tuon in as long either. The two events seemed paired in his head. Was there a connection?

Bloody fool, he thought to himself. *Next you'll start thinking like her, reading portents into every little thing, looking for symbols and meaning every time a rabbit runs across your path or a horse lets wind.*

That kind of fortunetelling was all nonsense. Though he had to admit, he now cringed every time he heard an owl hoot twice.

"Have you ever loved a woman, Talmanes?" Mat found himself asking.

"Several," the short man replied, riding with pipe smoke curling behind him.

"Ever consider marrying one of them?"

"No, thank the Light," Talmanes said. Then, apparently, he thought better of what he'd just said. "I mean, it wasn't right for me at the time, Mat. But I'm certain it will work out fine for you."

Mat scowled. If Tuon was going to bloody finally decide to go through with the marriage, couldn't she have picked a time when others couldn't hear?

But no. She'd gone and spoken in front of everyone, including the Aes Sedai. That meant Mat had been doomed. Aes Sedai were great at keeping secrets unless those secrets could in any way embarrass or inconvenience Matrim Cauthon. *Then* you could be certain the news would spread through the entire camp in a day's time, and likely be known three villages down the road as well. His own bloody *mother*— leagues and leagues away—had probably heard the news by now.

"I'm not giving up gambling," Mat muttered. "Or drinking."

"So I believe you've told me," Talmanes said. "Three or four times so far. I half believe that if I were to peek into your tent at night, I'd find you mumbling it in your sleep. 'I'm going to keep bloody gambling! Bloody, bloody gambling and drinking! Where's my bloody drink? Anyone want to gamble for it?'" He said it with a perfectly straight face, but once again, there was that hint of a smile in his eyes, if you knew just where to look.

"I just want to make sure everyone knows," Mat said. "I don't want anyone to start thinking I'm getting soft just because of . . . you know."

Talmanes shot him a consoling look. "You won't go soft just because you got married, Mat. Why, some of the Great Captains themselves are married, I believe. Davram Bashere is for certain, and Rodel Ituralde. No, you won't go soft because you're married."

Mat nodded sharply. Good that was settled.

"You might go *boring* though," Talmanes noted.

"All right, that's it," Mat declared. "Next village we find, we're going to go dicing at the tavern. You and me."

Talmanes grimaced. "With the kind of third-rate wine these little mountain villages have? Please, Mat. Next you'll be wanting me to drink ale."

"No arguing." Mat glanced over his shoulder as he heard familiar voices. Olver—ears sticking out to the sides, diminutive face as ugly as any Mat had seen—sat astride Wind, chatting with Noal, who rode beside him on a bony gelding. The gnarled old man was nodding appreciatively to what Olver was saying. The little boy looked astonishingly solemn, and was undoubtedly explaining yet another of his theories on how to best sneak into the Tower of Ghenjei.

"Ho, now," Talmanes said. "There's Vanin."

Mat turned to spot a rider approaching along the rocky path ahead. Vanin always looked so ridiculous, perched like a melon atop the back of his horse, his feet sticking out to the sides. But the man could ride, there was no doubting that.

"It *is* Mount Sardlen," Vanin proclaimed as he rode up to them, wiping his sweaty, balding brow. "The village is just ahead; it's called Hinderstap on the map. These *are* bloody good maps," he added grudgingly.

Mat exhaled in relief. He'd begun to think that they might end up wandering these mountains until the Last Battle came and went. "Great," he began, "we can—"

"A village?" a curt female voice demanded.

Mat turned with a sigh as three riders forced their way up to the front of the column. Talmanes reluctantly raised a hand to the soldiers behind, halting the march as the Aes Sedai descended on poor Vanin. The rotund man squatted down in his saddle, looking for all the world as though he'd rather have been discovered stealing horses—and therefore on his way to execution—than have to sit there and be interrogated by Aes Sedai.

Joline led the pack. Once, Mat might have described her as a pretty girl, with her slender figure and large, inviting brown eyes. But that ageless Aes Sedai face was an instant warning for him now. No, he wouldn't dare *think* of the Green as pretty now. Begin letting yourself think of Aes Sedai as pretty, and in two clicks of the tongue you'd find yourself wrapped around her finger and hopping at her command. Why, Joline had already hinted that she'd like to have Mat as a Warder!

Was she still sore at him because he'd paddled her? She couldn't hurt him with the Power, of course—even without his medallion, since Aes Sedai were sworn not to use the Power to kill except in very specific instances. But he was no fool. He'd noticed that those oaths of theirs didn't say anything about using knives.

The two with Joline were Edesina, of the Yellow Ajah, and Teslyn, of the Red. Edesina was pleasant enough to look at, save for that ageless face, but Teslyn was about as appetizing as a stick. Sharp of face, the Illianer woman was bony and scrappy, like an aged cat left too long on its own. But she seemed to have a good head on her shoulders, from what Mat had seen, and he'd found her treating him with some measure of respect sometimes. Respect from a Red. Imagine that.

Still, from the way each of those Aes Sedai looked at Mat in turn as they reached the front of the line, you'd never know that they owed him their lives. That was the way of it with women. Save her life, and she'd inevitably claim that she'd been about to escape on her own, and therefore owed you nothing. Half the time, she'd berate you for messing up her supposed plans.

Why did he bother? One of these days, burn him, he was going to get smart and leave the next lot crying in their chains.

"What was this?" Joline demanded of Vanin. "You've finally determined where we are?"

"Bloody well have," Vanin said, then unabashedly scratched himself. Good man, Vanin. Mat smiled. Treated all people the same, Vanin did. Aes Sedai and all.

Joline stared Vanin straight in the eyes, looming like a gargoyle atop some lord's mansion stonework. Vanin actually cringed, then wilted, then finally looked downward, abashed. "I mean, I have indeed, Joline Sedai."

Mat felt his smile fade. *Burn it all, Vanin!*

"Excellent," Joline said. "And there is a village ahead, I heard? Finally, perhaps, we'll find a decent inn. I could use something other than the 'fare' these ruffians of Cauthon's call food."

"Here now," Mat said, "that isn't—"

"How far do we be from Caemlyn, Master Cauthon?" Teslyn cut in. She did her best to ignore Joline. The two of them seemed at one another's throats lately—in the most cool-faced and outwardly amiable of ways, of course. Aes Sedai didn't squabble. He'd gotten a talking to once for calling their "discussions" "squabbles." Never mind that Mat had sisters, and knew what a good squabble sounded like.

"What did you say earlier, Vanin?" Mat asked, looking at him. "That we're about two hundred leagues from Caemlyn?"

Vanin nodded. The plan was to head for Caemlyn first, as he needed to meet up with Estean and Daerid and secure needed information and supplies. After that, he could make good on his promise to Thom. The Tower of Ghenjei would have to wait a few more weeks.

"Two hundred leagues," Teslyn said. "How long until we arrive, then?"

"Well, I guess that depends," Vanin said. "I could probably make two hundred leagues in a little over a week, if I were going alone, with a couple of good horses to ride in shifts and was crossing familiar terrain. The whole army, though, through these hills using a broken roadway? Twenty days, I'd say. Maybe longer."

Joline glanced at Mat.

"We *aren't* leaving the Band behind," Mat said. "Not an option, Joline."

She looked away, her expression dissatisfied.

"You're welcome to go on your own," Mat said. "That goes for each of you. You Aes Sedai aren't my prisoners; leave any time you want, so long as you head north. I won't risk you heading back to be taken by Seanchan."

What would it be like, traveling with just the Band again, not an Aes Sedai in sight? Ah, if only.

Teslyn looked thoughtful. Joline glanced at her, but the Red didn't give any indication if she'd be willing to leave or not. Edesina, however, hesitated, then nodded to Joline. She was willing.

"Very well," Joline said to Mat with a haughty air. "It would be good to be away from your crudeness, Cauthon. Prepare for us, say, twenty-four mounts and we shall be off."

"*Twenty-four?*" Mat asked.

"Yes," Joline said. "Your man here mentioned that he'd need two horses to make the trip in a reasonable amount of time. So that he could remount, presumably, when one of the beasts grew tired."

"I count two of you," Mat said, his anger rising. "That means *four* horses. I figured you'd be smart enough to do *that* math, Joline." And then, softer, he added, "If just barely."

Joline's eyes opened wide, and Edesina's expression was painted with shock. Teslyn gave him a shocked glance, seeming disappointed. To the side, Talmanes just lowered his pipe and whistled quietly.

"That medallion of yours makes you impudent, Matrim Cauthon," Joline said coldly.

"My mouth makes me impudent, Joline," Mat replied with a sigh, fingering the medallion hidden beneath his loosely tied shirt. "The medallion just makes me truthful.

I believe you were going to explain why you need to take twenty-four of my horses when I barely have enough for my men as it is?"

"Two each for Edesina, me, and my Warders," Joline said stiffly. "Two each for the former *sul'dam*. You don't presume that I'm going to leave them behind to be corrupted by your little band here?"

"Two Warders and two *sul'dam*," Mat said. "That's twelve horses."

"Two for Setalle. I assume she'll want to be away from all of this with us."

"Fourteen."

"Two more for Teslyn," Joline said. "She will undoubtedly want to go with us, though she currently has nothing to say on the matter. And we'll need about four pack animals' worth to carry our things. They'll have to trade their burdens too, so four more for that. Twenty-four."

"Which you'll feed how?" Mat asked. "If you're riding that hard, you won't have time to graze your horses. There's barely anything for them to eat these days anyway." That had proven a big problem; the spring grass wasn't coming in. The meadows they passed were brown with fallen leaves, the dead winter weeds pressed flat by snow, barely a new shoot of grass or weed. Horses could feed on the dead leaves and winter grass, of course, but wild deer and other animals had been active, eating down whatever they could find.

If the land didn't decide to start blooming soon . . . well, they were in for a difficult summer. But that was another problem entirely.

"We will need you to give us feed, of course," Joline said. "And some coin for inns. . . ."

"And who is going to take care of all those horses? You going to brush them down each night, check their hooves, see that their feed is properly measured?"

"I suppose we should take a handful of your soldiers with us," Joline said, sounding dissatisfied. "A necessary inconvenience."

"The only thing that is *necessary*," Mat said flatly. "Is for my men to stay where they're wanted, not where they're an *inconvenience*. No, they stay—and you'll have no coin from me. If you want to go, you can take one horse each and a single packhorse to carry your things. I'll give you some feed for the poor beasts, and giving you that much is generous."

"But with only one horse each, we'll barely be faster than the army!" Joline said.

"Imagine that," Mat said. He turned away from her. "Vanin, go and tell Mandevwin to pass the word. We'll be camping soon. I know it's barely afternoon, but I want the Band far enough from that village not to be threatening, but close enough that a few of us can go down to feel things out."

"All right," Vanin said, with none of the respect he'd shown the bloody Aes Sedai. He turned his horse and began to ride down the line.

"And Vanin," Mat called. "Make sure Mandevwin is aware that when I say 'a few of us' will go down, I mean a very small group, led by myself and Talmanes. I won't have that village invaded by seven thousand soldiers looking for fun! I'll buy a cart in the town and what ale I can find, then send it back for the men. There is to be strict order in camp, with no one accidentally wandering down to visit, now. Understand?"

Vanin nodded, looking grim. It was never fun to be the one who had to inform the men that they weren't going to be getting leave. Mat turned back to the Aes Sedai. "Well?" he asked. "You taking my kind offer or not?"

Joline just sniffed, then trotted her horse back down the ranks, obviously turning down the chance to go alone. Pity, that. It would have made him smile each step of the way to think of it. Though, it probably would have taken Joline all of three days to find some sap in a village somewhere to give her his horses so that her crew could ride faster.

Edesina rode away, and Teslyn trailed after, regarding Mat with a curious expression. She still looked disappointed in him too. He glanced away, then felt annoyed at himself. What did *he* care what she thought?

Talmanes was looking at him. "That was odd of you, Mat," the man said.

"What?" Mat said. "The restriction on the men? They're a good lot, the Band, but I've never known a group of soldiers

who weren't likely to get themselves in a little trouble now
and then, particularly where there's ale to be found."

"I wasn't talking about the men, Mat," Talmanes said,
bending to tap out his pipe against his stirrup, dottle falling
to flutter back onto the stony roadway beside his horse. "I'm
talking about how you treated the Aes Sedai. Light, Mat, we
could have been rid of them! I'd count twenty-four horses and
some coin a bargain to be free of two Aes Sedai."

"I won't be shoved around," Mat said stubbornly, waving
for the Band to begin its march again. "Not even to get rid
of Joline. If she wants something from me, let her ask with
a grain of politeness, rather than trying to bully me into
giving her whatever she wants. I'm no lap dog." Burn it, he
wasn't! And he *wasn't* husbandly either, whatever that
meant.

"You really do miss her," Talmanes said, sounding a little
surprised as their horses fell into pace beside one another.

"What are you blathering about now?"

"Mat, you are not always the most refined of men, I'll
admit. Sometimes your humor is indeed a bit ripe and your
tone on the brusque side. But you are rarely downright rude,
nor *intentionally* insulting. You really are on edge, aren't
you?"

Mat said nothing, just pulled the brim of his hat down
again.

"I'm sure that she will be fine, Mat," Talmanes said, tone
gentler. "She is royalty. They know how to take care of
themselves. And she's got those soldiers watching after her.
Not to mention Ogier. Ogier warriors! Who would think of
such a thing? She'll be all right."

"We're done with this conversation," Mat said, shifting
his spear to hold it upright, curved blade toward the unseen
sun above, butt in the lancer's strap at the side of his saddle.

"I just—"

"Over," Mat said. "You don't have any more of that tabac,
do you?"

Talmanes sighed. "It was the last pinch. Good tabac—
Two Rivers grown. The only pouch of it I've seen in some
time. It was a gift from King Roedran, along with the pipe."

"He must have valued you."

"It was good, honest work," Talmanes said. "And terribly

boring. Not like riding with you, Mat. It's good to have you back, crust and all. But your talk of feed with the Aes Sedai does have me worried."

Mat nodded. "How are we on rations?"

"Low," Talmanes said.

"We'll buy what we can at the village," Mat said. "We've got coin coming out our ears, after what Roedran gave you."

A small village wasn't likely to have enough to supply the whole army. But, according to the maps, they'd soon be entering more populated lands. You'd pass a village or two every day in those areas, traveling with a quick force like the Band. To stay afloat, you scavenged and bought whatever little bit you could at each village you passed. A wagon-load here, a cartful there, a bucket or two of apples from a passing farmstead. Seven thousand men was a lot to feed, but a good commander knew not to turn down even a handful of grain. It added up.

"Yes, but will the villagers sell?" Talmanes asked. "On our way down to meet you, we had a savage time getting anyone to sell us food. Seems there isn't much to be found these days. Food is getting scarce, no matter where you go and no matter how much money you have."

Bloody perfect. Mat ground his teeth, then grew annoyed at himself for doing so. Well, maybe he *was* a little on edge. Not because of Tuon, though.

Either way, he needed to relax. And that village ahead— what had Vanin called it? Hinderstap? "How much coin do you have on you?"

Talmanes frowned. "Couple of gold marks, pouch full of silver crowns. Why?"

"Not enough," Mat said, rubbing his chin. "We'll have to dig some more out of my personal chest first. Maybe bring the whole thing." He turned Pips around. "Come on."

"Wait, Mat," Talmanes said, reining in and following. "What are we doing?"

"You're going to kindly take me up on my offer to go enjoy ourselves at the tavern," Mat said. "And while we're at it, we're going to resupply. If my luck's with me, we'll do it for free."

If Egwene or Nynaeve had been there, they'd have boxed his ears and told him he was going to do no such thing.

Tuon probably would have looked at him curiously and then said something that made him feel his shame right down into his boots.

The good thing about Talmanes, however, was that he simply spurred his horse forward, face stoic, eyes betraying just a hint of amusement. "Well, I've *got* to see this, then!"

CHAPTER
21

Embers and Ash

P errin opened his eyes and found himself hanging in
the air.

He felt a spike of terror, floundering in the sky.
Black clouds boiled overhead, dark and ominous. Below, a
plain of wild brown grasses rolled in the wind, no signs of
humans. No tents, no roads, not even any footprints.

Perrin wasn't falling. He just hung there. He waved his
arms reflexively, as if to swim, panicking as his mind tried
to make sense of the disorientation.

The wolf dream, he thought. *I'm in the wolf dream. I
went to sleep, hoping to come here.*

He forced himself to breathe in and out and still his flail-
ing, though it was difficult to be calm while hanging hundreds of feet up in the sky. Suddenly, a gray-furred form
shot past him, leaping through the air. The wolf soared
down to the field below, landing easily.

"Hopper!"

Jump down, Young Bull. Jump. It is safe. As always, the
Sending from the wolf came as a mixture of scents and
images. Perrin was getting better and better at interpret-
ing those—the soft earth as a representation of the ground,
rushing wind as an image of jumping, the scent of relaxation and calmness to indicate there was no need to fear.

"But how?"

*Times before, you always rushed ahead, like a pup newly
weaned. Jump. Jump down!* Far below, Hopper sat on his
haunches in the field, grinning up at Perrin.

Perrin ground his teeth and muttered a curse or two for
stubborn wolves. It seemed to him that the dead ones were

particularly bullheaded. Though Hopper did have a point. Perrin had leaped before in this place, if never from the sky itself.

He took a deep breath, then closed his eyes and imagined himself jumping. Air rushed around him in a sudden burst, but then his feet hit soft ground. He opened his eyes. A large gray wolf, scarred from many fights, was sitting on the ground beside him, and wild millet spread out in a broad plain around him, heavily mixed with stands of long, thin grasses that reached high in the air. Scratchy stalks rubbed against Perrin's arms in the wind, making him itch. The grasses smelled too dry, like cut hay left in a barn over the winter.

Some things were transitory here in the Wolf Dream; leaves lay in a pile by his feet at one moment, but then were gone the next. Everything smelled just faintly stale, as if it weren't quite there.

He looked up. The sky was stormy. Normally, clouds in this place were as transitory as other things. It could be completely overcast; then, in a blink, it would suddenly be clear. This time, those dark storm clouds remained. They boiled, spun, and shot lines of lightning between different thunderheads. Yet the lightning never struck the ground, and it made no noise.

The plain was oddly silent. The clouds shrouded the entire sky, ominous. And they did not leave.

The Last Hunt comes. Hopper looked up at the sky. *We will run together, then. Unless we sleep instead.*

"Sleep?" Perrin said. "What of the Last Hunt?"

It comes, Hopper agreed. *If Shadowkiller falls to the storm, all will sleep forever. If he lives, then we will hunt together. You and us.*

Perrin rubbed his chin, trying to sort through the Sending of images, smells, sounds, feelings. It made little sense to him.

But, well, he was here now. He'd wanted to come, and he'd decided that he'd get some answers from Hopper, if he could. It was good to see Hopper again.

Run, Hopper sent. His Sending was not alarmed. It was an offer. Let us run together.

Perrin nodded, and began to jog through the grasses. Hopper loped beside him, sending amusement. *Two legs,*

Young Bull? Two legs are slow! That Sending was an image of men stumbling over themselves, tripping because of their elongated, silly legs.

Perrin hesitated. "I have to keep control, Hopper," he said. "When I let the wolf take control . . . well, I do dangerous things."

The wolf cocked his head, trotting beside Perrin across the grassy field. The stalks crunched and scraped as the two of them passed through, finding a small game trail, turning along it.

Run, Hopper urged, obviously confused at Perrin's reluctance.

"I can't," Perrin said, stopping. Hopper turned and took a few bounds back to him. He smelled confused.

"Hopper, I frighten myself," Perrin said, "when I lose control. The first time it happened to me was just after I met the wolves. You need to help me understand."

Hopper simply continued to stare at him, tongue hanging out the front of his mouth just slightly, jaws parted.

Why am I doing this? Perrin thought, shaking his head. Wolves didn't think like men. What did it matter what Hopper thought of it all?

We will hunt together, Hopper sent.

"What if I don't want to hunt with you?" Perrin said. Saying the words made his heart twist. He *did* like this place, the wolf dream, dangerous though it could be. There were wonderful things about what had happened to him since leaving the Two Rivers.

But he couldn't continue to lose control. He had to find a balance. Throwing away the axe had made a difference. The axe and the hammer were different weapons—one could be used *only* for killing, while the other gave him a choice.

But he had to make good on that choice. He had to control himself. And the first step seemed to be learning to control the wolf within him.

Run with me, Young Bull, Hopper sent. *Forget these thoughts. Run like a wolf.*

"I can't," Perrin replied. He turned, scanning the plains. "But I need to know this place, Hopper. I need to learn how to use it, control it."

Men, Hopper thought, Sending the smells of dismissiveness and anger. *Control. Always control.*

"I want you to teach me," Perrin said, turning back to the wolf. "I want to master this place. Will you show me how?"

Hopper sat back on his haunches.

"Fine," Perrin said. "I will search out other wolves who will."

He turned, striking down the game trail. He didn't recognize this place, but he'd learned that the wolf dream was unpredictable. This meadow with the waist-high grass and its stands of yew could be anywhere. Where would he find wolves? He quested out with his mind, and found that it was much more difficult to do here.

You don't want to run. But you look for wolves. Why are you so difficult, cub? Hopper sat in front of him in the grass.

Perrin grumbled, then took a leap that launched him through the air a hundred yards. He landed with his foot falling to the grass as if it had been a normal step.

And there Hopper was ahead of him. Perrin hadn't seen the wolf leap. He had been in one place, and now in another. Perrin gritted his teeth, questing out again. For other wolves. He felt something, distant. He needed to push harder. He concentrated, drew more strength into himself, somehow, and managed to push his mind farther.

This is dangerous, Young Bull, Hopper sent. *You come here too strongly. You will die.*

"You always say that," Perrin replied. "Tell me what I want to know. Show me how to learn."

Stubborn pup, Hopper Sent. *Return when you aren't determined to poke your snout into a fireasp's den.*

With that, something slammed against Perrin, a weight against his mind. Everything vanished, and he was tossed— like a leaf before a storm—out of the wolf dream.

Faile felt her husband stir next to her as he slept. She glanced at him in the dark tent; though she lay beside him on the pallet, she hadn't been sleeping. She'd been waiting, listening to his breaths. He turned onto his back, muttering drowsily.

Of all the nights for him to be restless . . . she thought with annoyance.

They were a week out of Malden. The refugees had made

camp—or, well, camps—near a waterway that led straight to the Jehannah Road, which was only a short distance away.

Things had gone smoothly these last few days, though Perrin had judged the Asha'man too tired still to make gateways. She had spent the evening with her husband, reminding him of several important reasons why he'd married her in the first place. He'd certainly been enthusiastic, though there *was* that odd edge to his eyes. Not a dangerous edge, just a sorrowful one. He had grown haunted while they were apart. She could understand that. She had a few ghosts of her own. One could not expect everything to remain the same, and she could tell that he still loved her—loved her fiercely. That was enough, and so she didn't worry on it further.

But she *was* planning an argument that would pull his secrets from him. She would wait a few more days for that. It was good to remind a husband that one would not sit content with everything he did, but it wouldn't do to make him think she was unappreciative to have him back.

Quite the opposite. She smiled, rolling over and laying her hand on his chest, furred with hair, her head on his bare shoulder. She loved this burly, tumbling avalanche of a man. Being back with him was sweeter, even, than the victory of her escape from the Shaido.

His eyes fluttered open and she sighed. Love him or not, she wished he'd remain asleep this night! Hadn't she tired him out enough?

He looked at her; his golden eyes seemed to glow just faintly in the darkness, though she knew it was a trick of the light. Then he pulled her a little closer. "I didn't sleep with Berelain," he said, voice gruff. "No matter what the rumors say."

Dear, sweet, *blunt* Perrin. "I know you didn't," she said consolingly. She'd heard the rumors. Virtually every woman she'd talked to in the camp, from Aes Sedai to servant, had pretended she was trying to hold her tongue, yet spilled the same news. Perrin, spending a night in the First of Mayene's tent.

"No, really," Perrin said, a pleading tone entering his voice. "I didn't, Faile. Please."

"I said I believed you."

"You sounded . . . I don't know. Burn it, woman, you sounded jealous."

Would he never learn? "Perrin," she said flatly. "It took me the better part of a *year*—not to mention considerable trouble—to seduce you, and then it only worked because there was a marriage involved! Berelain hasn't the skill to handle you."

He reached his right hand up, scratching his beard, seeming confused. Then he just smiled.

"Besides," she added, snuggling closer, "you spoke the words. And I trust you."

"So you're not jealous?"

"Of course I am," she said, swatting his chest. "Perrin, haven't I explained this? A husband *needs* to know his wife is jealous, otherwise he won't realize how much she cares for him. You guard that which you find most precious. Honestly, if you keep making me spell things out like this, then I won't have any secrets left!"

He snorted softly at that last comment. "I doubt that's possible."

He grew quiet, and she closed her eyes, hoping he'd go back to sleep. Outside the tent, she could hear the distant voices of guards chatting on patrol and the sound of one of the farriers—Jerasid, Aemin or Falton—working late into the night, pounding out a shoe or nail to ready one of the horses for the next day's march. It was good to hear that sound again. The Aiel were useless when it came to horses, and the Shaido had either released the ones they captured or turned them into workhorses. She had seen many fine saddle mares pulling carts during her days in Malden.

Should it feel strange to be back? She had spent less than two months as a captive, but it had seemed like years. Years spent running errands for Sevanna, being punished arbitrarily. But that time had not broken her. Strangely, she'd felt more like a noblewoman during those days than she had before.

It was as if she hadn't quite understood what it was to be a lady until Malden. Oh, she'd had her share of victories. *Cha Faile*, the people of the Two Rivers, Alliandre and Perrin's camp members. She'd put her training to use, helping Perrin learn to be a leader. All of this had been important, had required her to use what her mother and father had trained her to be.

But Malden had opened her eyes. There, she had found people who had needed her more than she'd ever been needed before. Beneath Sevanna's cruel dictatorship, there had been no time for games, no room for mistakes. She had been humiliated, beaten and nearly killed. And that had given her a true understanding of what it was to be a liege lady. She actually felt a stab of guilt for the times she had lorded over Perrin, trying to force him—or others—to bend to her will. Being a noblewoman meant going first. It meant being beaten so others were not. It meant sacrificing, risking death, to protect those who depended upon you.

No, it didn't feel strange to be back, for she'd taken Malden—the parts that mattered—with her. Hundreds had sworn allegiance to her among the *gai'shain*, and she had saved them. She had done it through Perrin, but she had made plans, and one way or another, she would have escaped and brought back an army to free those who had sworn to her.

There *had* been costs. But she would deal with those later tonight, Light willing. She opened an eye and peeked at Perrin. He seemed to be sleeping, but was his breath even? She slipped her arm free.

"I don't care what happened to you," he said.

She sighed. No, not asleep. "What happened to me?" she asked with confusion.

He opened his eyes, staring up at the tent. "The Shaido, the man who was with you when I saved you. Whatever he did . . . whatever you did to survive. It's all right."

Was that what was bothering him? Light! "You big ox," she said, thumping a fist on his chest, causing him to grunt. "What are you saying? That it would be all right for me to be unfaithful? Just after you were so concerned to tell me that you *hadn't* been?"

"What? No, it's different, Faile. You were a prisoner, and—"

"And I can't care for myself? You *are* an ox. No one touched me. They're Aiel. You *know* they wouldn't dare harm a *gai'shain*." It wasn't quite true; women had often been abused in the Shaido camp, for the Shaido had stopped acting like Aiel.

But there had been others in the camp, Aiel who hadn't

been Shaido. Men who had refused to accept Rand as their *Car'a'carn*, but who also had trouble accepting Shaido authority. The Brotherless had been men of honor; though they'd called themselves cast off, they had been the only ones in Malden who had maintained the old ways. When the *gai'shain* women had started to be in danger, the Brotherless had chosen and protected those they could. They hadn't asked anything for their efforts.

Well . . . that wasn't true. They had *asked* for much, but had *demanded* nothing. Rolan had always been an Aiel to her in action, if not in word. But, like Masema's death, her relationship with Rolan was not something Perrin needed to know about. She had never so much as kissed Rolan, but she *had* used his desire for her as an advantage. And she suspected that he'd known what she was doing.

Perrin had killed Rolan. That was another reason that her husband didn't need to know about the Brotherless man's kindness. It would tear Perrin apart inside if he knew what he'd done.

Perrin relaxed, closing his eyes. He had changed during these two months, perhaps as much as she had. That was good. In the Borderlands, her people had a saying: "Only the Dark One stays the same." Men grew and progressed; the Shadow just remained as it was. Evil.

"We'll have to do some planning tomorrow," Perrin said, yawning. "Once gateways are available, we will have to decide whether to force the people to leave, and decide who goes first. Has anyone discovered what happened to Masema?"

"Not that I know of," she said carefully. "But with so many of his possessions gone from his tent. . . ."

"Masema doesn't care about possessions," Perrin mumbled quietly, eyes still closed. "Though maybe he would have taken them to rebuild. I guess he *might* have run off, though it's strange that nobody knows where or how."

"He probably slipped away during the confusion after the battle."

"Probably," Perrin agreed. "I wonder . . ." He yawned. "I wonder what Rand will say. Masema was the point of this whole trip. I was to fetch him and bring him back, and I guess I've failed."

"You destroyed the men who were murdering and rob-bing in the Dragon's name," Faile said, "and you cut out the heart of the Shaido leadership, not to mention all you've learned about the Seanchan. I think the Dragon will find that what you've accomplished here far outweighs not bringing Masema back."

"Maybe you're right," Perrin mumbled sleepily. "Blasted colors. . . . I don't want to watch you sleeping, Rand. What happened to your hand? Light-blinded fool, take better care of yourself. . . . You're all we have. . . . Last Hunt coming. . . ."

She could barely make out that last part. Why was he talking about Rand's hand going hunting? Was he actually falling asleep this time?

Sure enough, he soon started snoring softly. She smiled, shaking her head fondly. He *was* an ox, sometimes. But he was her ox. She climbed off of the pallet and moved through their tent, pulling on a robe and tying its belt. A pair of sandals followed, and then she slipped out through the tent flaps. Arrela and Lacile guarded there, along with two Maidens. The Maidens nodded to her; they would keep her secret.

Faile left the Maiden guards, but took Arrela and Lacile with her as she walked out into the darkness. Arrela was a dark-haired Tairen woman who was taller than most Maidens, with a brusque way about her. Lacile was short, pale, and very slender, and she walked with a graceful sway. They were as different as women could get, perhaps, though their captivity had united them all. Both members of *Cha Faile* had been captured with her and gone to Malden as *gai'shain*.

After traveling a short distance, they picked up two other Maidens—Bain and Chiad had spoken with them, likely. They passed out of the camp, moving to a spot where a pair of willow trees stood side by side. There, Faile was met by a pair of women who still wore *gai'shain* white. Bain and Chiad were Maidens themselves, first-sisters and dear to Faile. They were more loyal—even—than those who had sworn to her. Loyal to her, yet free of oaths to her. A contradiction only Aiel could pull off.

Unlike Faile and the others, Bain and Chiad would not put off the white just because their captors had been defeated. They would wear the clothing for a year and a day. In fact, coming here this night—acknowledging their lives from before they had been taken—stretched what their honor would allow. However, they admitted that being *gai'shain* in the Shaido camp had been anything but standard.

Faile met them with a smile, but did not shame them by calling them by name or by using Maiden handtalk. However, she couldn't keep herself from asking, "You are well?" as she accepted a small bundle from Chiad.

Chiad was a beautiful woman with gray eyes and short, reddish blond hair hidden beneath the hood of her *gai'shain* robe. She grimaced at the question. "Gaul searched the entire Shaido camp to find me, and reports say he defeated twelve *algai'd'siswai* with his spear. Perhaps I shall have to make a bridal wreath for him after all, once this is all through."

Faile smiled.

Chiad smiled back. "He did not expect that one of the men he killed would turn out to be the one to whom Bain was *gai'shain*. I do not think Gaul is happy to have both of us serving him."

"Foolish man," Bain—the taller of the two—said. "Very like him to not watch where he jabbed his spear. He couldn't kill the right man without accidentally slaying a few others." Both women chuckled.

Faile smiled and nodded; Aiel humor was beyond her. "Thank you very much for fetching these," she said, holding up the small, cloth-wrapped bundle.

"It was nothing," Chiad said. "There were too many hands working that day, so it was easy. Alliandre Maritha Kigarin already waits for you at the trees. We should return to the camp."

"Yes," Bain added. "Perhaps Gaul would like his back rubbed again, or water fetched for him. He grows so angry when we ask, but *gai'shain* gain honor only through service. What else are we to do?"

The women laughed again, and Faile shook her head as they ran back toward the camp, white robes swishing. She cringed at the thought of having to wear such clothing again, if only because it made her think about her days of service to Sevanna.

Lanky Arrela and graceful Lacile joined her at the base of the two willows. The Maiden guards stayed behind, watching from afar. A third Maiden joined those two, moving out of the shadows, likely sent by Bain and Chiad to protect Alliandre. Faile found the dark-haired queen standing at the base of the trees, looking like a lady again in a rich red gown with golden chains lacing her hair. It was an extravagant display, as if she were determined to disprove the days she'd spent acting as a servant. Alliandre's gown made Faile more aware of her simple robe. But there wasn't much she could have done without waking Perrin. Arrela and Lacile wore only the embroidered breeches and shirts common to those in *Cha Faile*.

Alliandre carried a small lantern with the shutters drawn, letting out only a crack of light that illuminated her youthful face, topped by dark hair. "Did they find anything?" she asked. "Please tell me that they did." She had always been impressively grounded, for a queen, if somewhat demanding. Her time in Malden seemed to have tempered the latter feature.

"Yes." Faile hefted the bundle. The four women huddled around her as she knelt on the ground, the tips of the short grass lit by the lantern, shining like tongues of flame. Faile unwrapped the bundle. The contents weren't anything extraordinary. A small handkerchief of yellow silk. A belt of worked leather which had a pattern of bird feathers pressed into its sides. A black veil. And a thin leather band with a stone tied at the center.

"That belt belonged to Kinhuin," Alliandre said, pointing to it. "I saw him wearing it, before. . . ." She trailed off, then knelt and picked it up.

"The veil is that of a Maiden," Arrela said.

"They're different?" Alliandre asked with surprise.

"Of course they are," Arrela said, picking up the veil. Faile had never met the Maiden who had become Arrela's protector, but the woman had fallen in the battle, though not as dramatically as Rolan and the others.

The piece of silk was Jhoradin's; Lacile hesitated, then took it in her hands, turning it over and revealing that there was a spot of blood on it. That left only the leather cord. Rolan had worn it at his neck, on occasion, beneath his *cadin'sor*. Faile wondered what it had meant to him, and if there was any significance to the single bit of stone, a rough-cut chunk of turquoise. She picked it up, then glanced at

Lacile. Surprisingly, the slender woman seemed to be crying. Because Lacile had gone so quickly to the hefty Brotherless's bed, Faile had assumed that her relationship with him had been one of necessity, not affection.

"Four people are dead," Faile said, mouth suddenly dry. She spoke formally, for that was the best way to keep the emotion from her voice. "They protected us, even cared for us. Though they were the enemy, we mourn them. Remember, though, that they were Aiel. For an Aiel, there are far worse ends than death in combat."

The others nodded, but Lacile met Faile's eyes. For the two of them, it was different. When Perrin had barreled out of that alleyway—roaring in anger at seeing Faile and Lacile apparently being manhandled by Shaido—many things had happened very quickly. In the fray, Faile had distracted Rolan at just the right moment, making him hesitate. He'd done so out of concern for her, but that pause had allowed Perrin to kill him.

Had Faile done it intentionally? She still didn't know. So much had been going through her mind, so many emotions at seeing Perrin. She'd cried out, and . . . she could not decide if she'd been trying to distract Rolan to let him die by Perrin's hand.

For Lacile, there was no such wavering. Jhoradin had leaped in front of her, putting her behind him and raising his weapon against the intruder. She'd put a knife in his back, killing a man for the first time in her life. And it had been a man whose bed she'd shared.

Faile had killed Kinhuin, the other member of the Brotherless who had protected them. He wasn't the first man whose life she had taken—nor the first one she'd taken from behind. But he *was* the first man she'd killed who had seen her as a friend.

There was nothing else that could have been done. Perrin had seen only Shaido, and the Brotherless had seen only an invading enemy. That conflict could not have ended without Perrin or the Brotherless dead. No amount of screaming would have stopped any of the men.

But that made it more tragic. Faile steeled herself to keep her eyes from tearing up like Lacile's. She hadn't loved Rolan, and she was glad that Perrin was the one who had survived the conflict. But Rolan *had* been an honorable man,

and she felt . . . dirtied, somehow, that his death had been
her fault.

This shouldn't have had to be. But it was. Her father had
often spoken of situations like this, when you had to kill
people you liked just because you met them on the wrong
side of the battlefield. She'd never understood. If she had
to go back and do it again, she would take the very same
actions. She wouldn't be able to risk Perrin. Rolan had had
to die.

But the world seemed a sadder place to her for the necessity of it.

Lacile turned away, sniffling softly. Faile knelt, taking a
small flask of oil from the bundle Chiad had left. She took
the leather strap and pulled off the stone, then set the strap
in the center of the cloth bundle. She poured the oil on it,
then used a tinder stick, lit at the lantern, to set the strap
afire.

She watched it burn, tiny little flames of blue and green,
topped by orange. The scent of burning leather was shockingly similar to that of burning human flesh. The night was
still, no wind to shake the flames, and so they danced freely.

Alliandre doused the belt and put it on to the miniature
fire. Arrela did the same with the veil. Finally, Lacile added
the handkerchief. She was still crying.

This was all they could do. There hadn't been a way to
see to the bodies in the chaos of leaving Malden. Chiad had
said there was no dishonor in leaving them, but Faile had
needed to do something. Some small way of honoring Rolan and the others.

"Dead by our hand," Faile said, "or simply dead from
battle, these four showed us honor. As the Aiel would say,
we have great *toh* to them. I don't think it can be repaid. But
we can remember them. The Brotherless and one Maiden
showed us kindness when they didn't need to. They kept
their honor when others had abandoned it. If there is a redemption to be found for them, and for us, this will be it."

"There's a Brotherless in Perrin's camp," Lacile said, eyes
reflecting the flames of their pyre. "Niagen is his name; he
is *gai'shain* to Sulin, the Maiden. I went to tell him of what
the others did for us. He is a kind man."

Faile closed her eyes. Lacile probably meant that she had
gone to the bed of this Niagen. That wasn't forbidden of

gai'shain. "You can't replace Jhoradin like that," she said, opening her eyes. "Or undo what you did."

"I know," Lacile said defensively. "But they were so full of humor, despite the terrible situation. There was something about them. Jhoradin wanted to take me back to the Three-fold Land, make me his wife."

And you'd never have done it, Faile thought. *I know you wouldn't have. But now that he's dead, you realize the opportunity you lost.*

Well, who was she to chastise? Let Lacile do as she wished. If this Niagen was half the man that Rolan or the others had been, then perhaps Lacile would do well with him.

"Kinhuin had only just started looking out for me," Alliandre said. "I know what he wished for, but he never demanded it. I think he was planning to leave the Shaido, and would have helped us escape. Even if I turned him down, he would have helped us."

"Marthea hated what the other Shaido did," Arrela said. "But she stayed with them for her clan. She died for that loyalty. There are worse things to die for."

Faile watched the last embers of the miniature pyre flicker out. "I think Rolan actually loved me," she said. And that was all.

The four rose and returned to the camp. The past was a field of embers and ash, an old Saldaean proverb said, the remnants of the fire that was the present. Those embers blew away behind her. But she kept Rolan's turquoise stone. Not for regret, but for remembrance.

Perrin lay awake in the still night, smelling the canvas of his tent and the unique scent of Faile. She wasn't there, though she had been recently. He'd dozed off, and now she was gone. Perhaps to the privy.

He stared up in the darkness, trying to make sense of Hopper and the wolf dream. The more he thought about it, the more determined he grew. He would march to the Last Battle—and when he did, he wanted to be able to control the wolf inside of him. He wanted either to be free of all of these people who followed him, or to learn how to accept their loyalty.

He had some decisions to make. They wouldn't be easy, but he'd make them. A man had to do hard things. That was the way of life. That was what had gone wrong with the way he'd handled Faile's capture. Instead of making decisions, he'd avoided them. Master Luhhan would have been disappointed in him.

And that led Perrin to another decision, the hardest of all. He was going to have to let Faile ride into danger, perhaps risk her again. Was that a decision? Could he *make* such a decision? The mere thought of her in danger made him want to sick up. But he would have to do something.

Three problems. He would face them and he would decide. But he would consider them first, because that was what he did. A man was a fool to make decisions without thinking first.

But the decision to face his problems brought him a measure of peace, and he rolled over and drifted back to sleep.

CHAPTER
22

The Last That Could Be Done

Semirhage sat alone in the small room. They had taken away her chair and given her no lantern or candle.

Blast this cursed Age and its cursed people! What she would have given for glowbulbs on the walls. During *her* days, prisoners hadn't been denied light. Of course, she had locked several of her experiments away in total darkness, but that was different. It had been important to discover what effect the lack of light would have on them. These so-called Aes Sedai who held her, they had no rational reason for leaving her in darkness. They just did it to humiliate her.

She pulled her arms closer, huddling against the wooden wall. She did *not* cry. She was of the Chosen! So what if she had been forced to abase herself? She was not broken.

But . . . the fool Aes Sedai no longer regarded her as they had. Semirhage hadn't changed, but they had. Somehow, in one swoop, that cursed woman with the paralis-net in her hair had unraveled Semirhage's authority with the entire lot of them.

How? How had she lost control so quickly? She shuddered as she remembered being turned over the woman's knees and spanked. And the nonchalance of it. The only emotion in the woman's voice had been a slight annoyance. She'd treated Semirhage—one of the Chosen!—as if she were barely worthy of notice. That had galled more than the blows.

It would not happen again. Semirhage would be ready for the blows next time, and she would give them no weight. Yes, that would work. Wouldn't it?

She shuddered again. She had tortured hundreds, perhaps thousands, in the name of understanding and reason. Torture made sense. You truly saw what a person was made of, in more ways than one, when you began to slice into them. That was a phrase she'd used on numerous occasions. It usually made her smile.

This time it did not.

Why couldn't they have given her pain? Broken fingers, cuts into her flesh, coals in the pits of her elbows. She had steeled her mind to each of these things, preparing for them. A small, eager part of herself had looked forward to them.

But this? Being forced to eat food off the floor? Being treated like a child in front of those who had regarded her with such awe?

I will kill her, she thought, not for the first time. *I will remove her tendons, one at a time, using the Power to heal her so that she lives to experience the pain. No. No, I'll do something* new *to her. I will show her agony that hasn't been known to anyone in any Age!*

"Semirhage." A whisper.

She froze, looking up in the darkness. That voice had been soft, like a chill wind, yet still sharp and biting. Had she imagined it? *He* couldn't be there, could he?

"You have failed greatly, Semirhage," the voice continued, so soft. A faint light shone underneath the door, but the voice came from *inside* her cell. The light seemed to grow brighter, and it flushed a deep red, illuminating the hem of a figure in a black cloak standing before her. She looked up. The ruddy light revealed a face of white, the color of dead skin. The face had no eyes.

She immediately knelt to the floor, prostrating herself on the aged wood. Though the figure before her looked like a Myrddraal, it was much taller and much, *much* more important. She shivered as she remembered the voice of the Great Lord himself, speaking to her.

When you obey Shaidar Haran, you obey me. When you disobey. . . .

"You were to capture the boy, not kill him," the figure whispered in a hiss, like steam escaping through cracks between pot and lid. "You took his hand and nearly his life. You have revealed yourself and have lost valuable pawns. You have been captured by our enemies, and now they have broken you." She could hear the smile on its lips. Shaidar Haran was the only Myrddraal she had ever seen bear a smile. But, then, she did not think this thing was truly a Myrddraal.

She did not reply to its charges. One did not lie, or even make excuses, before this figure.

Suddenly, the shield blocking her vanished. Her breath caught. *Saidar* had returned! Sweet power. However, as she reached for it, she hesitated. Those imitation Aes Sedai outside would feel it if she channeled.

A cold, long-nailed hand touched her chin. The flesh of it felt like dead leather. It rotated her face upward to meet the eyeless gaze. "You have been given one last chance," the maggotlike lips whispered. "Do. Not. Fail."

The light faded. The hand at her chin withdrew. She continued to kneel, fighting down terror. One last chance. The Great Lord always rewarded failure in . . . imaginative ways. She had given such rewards before, and had no desire to receive them. They would make any torture or punishment these Aes Sedai could imagine look childish.

She forced herself to her feet, feeling her way around the room. She reached the door and, holding her breath, tried it.

The door opened. She slipped out of the room without letting the hinges creak. Outside, three corpses lay on the ground, slumped free of their chairs. The women who had been maintaining her shield. There was someone else there, kneeling on the floor before the three of them. One of the Aes Sedai. A woman in green, with brown hair, pulled back into a tail, her head bowed.

"I live to serve, Great Mistress," the woman whispered. "I am instructed to tell you that there is Compulsion in my mind you are to remove."

Semirhage raised an eyebrow; she hadn't realized there were any of the Black among those Aes Sedai here. Removing Compulsion could have a very . . . nasty effect on a person. Even if the Compulsion were weak or subtle, the brain could be harmed seriously by removing it. If the Compulsion were strong . . . well, it was quite interesting to watch.

"Also," the woman said, handing something forward, wrapped in cloth. "I am to give you this." She removed the cloth, revealing a dull-colored metallic collar, and two bracelets. The Domination Band. Crafted during the Breaking, strikingly similar to the *a'dam* Semirhage had spent so much time working with.

With this *ter'angreal*, a male channeler could be controlled. A smile finally broke through Semirhage's fear.

Rand had only visited the Blight on a single occasion, though he could faintly remember having come to this area on several occasions, before the Blight infected the land. Lews Therin's memories. Not his own.

The madman took to hissing and muttering angrily as they rode through the Saldaean scrub. Even Tai'daishar grew skittish as they moved northward.

Saldaea was a brown landscape of brushland and dark soil, nowhere near as barren as the Aiel Waste, but hardly a soft or lush land. Homesteads were common, but they had nearly the look of forts, and young children held themselves like trained warriors. Lan had once told him that among Borderlanders, a boy became a man when he earned the right to carry a sword.

"Has it occurred to you," Ituralde said, riding on Rand's left, "that what we are doing here could constitute an invasion?"

Rand nodded toward Bashere, who rode through the brush at Rand's right. "I bring with me troops of their own blood," he said. "The Saldaeans are my allies."

Bashere laughed. "I doubt that the Queen will see it that way, my friend! It's been many months since I last asked her for orders. Why, I wouldn't be surprised to find that she's demanded my head by now."

Rand turned his eyes forward. "I am the Dragon Reborn. It is not an invasion to march against the forces of the Dark One." Ahead of them rose the foothills of the Mountains of Dhoom. They had a dark cast, as if their slopes were coated with soot.

What would he himself do if another monarch used a gateway to deposit nearly fifty thousand troops within his borders? It *was* an act of war, but the Borderlanders' forces were away doing Light only knew what, and he would not leave these lands undefended. Just an hour's ride to the south, Ituralde's Domani had set up a fortified camp beside a river that had its source up in the highlands of World's

End. Rand had inspected their camp and ranks. After that, Bashere had suggested that Rand ride up to inspect the Blight. The scouts had been surprised at how quickly the Blight was advancing, and Bashere thought it important that Ituralde and Rand see for themselves. Rand agreed. Maps sometimes couldn't convey the truth eyes could see.

The sun was dipping toward the horizon like a drooping eye longing for sleep. Tai'daishar stamped a hoof, tossing his head. Rand raised a hand, halting his group—two generals, fifty soldiers and an equal number of Maidens, with Narishma at the back to weave gateways.

Northward, on the shallow slope, a scrub of broad-bladed grasses and squat brush swayed like waves in the wind. There was no specific line where the Blight began. A spot on a blade there, a sickly cast to a stem there. Each individual speck was innocent, yet there were too many, far too many. At the top of the hillside, not a single plant was free of the spots. The pox seemed to fester even as he watched.

There was an oily sense of death to the Blight, of plants barely surviving, kept alive like prisoners starved to the very edge of mortality. If Rand had seen anything like this back in a field in the Two Rivers, he would have burnt the entire crop, and would have been surprised that it hadn't been done already.

To his side, Bashere knuckled his long, dark mustaches. "I remember when it didn't start for another few leagues," he noted. "That wasn't so long ago."

"I have patrols running the length of it already," Ituralde said. He stared out at the sickly landscape. "All the reports are the same. It's quiet out there."

"That should be enough warning that something is wrong," Bashere said. "There are always patrols or raids of Trollocs to fight. If not that, then something worse, to scare them away. Worms or bloodwrasps."

Ituralde leaned one arm on his saddle, shaking his head as he continued staring at the Blight. "I've no experience with fighting such things. I know how men think, but Trolloc raiding parties keep no supply lines, and I've only heard *stories* of what worms can do."

"I will leave some of Bashere's officers with you as advisors," Rand said.

"That would help," Ituralde said, "but I wonder if it

wouldn't be better to just leave *him* here. His soldiers could patrol this area, and you could use my troops in Arad Doman. No offense, my Lord, but don't you think it's odd to have us working in each other's kingdoms?"

"No," Rand said. It wasn't odd, it was bitter sense. He trusted Bashere, and the Saldaeans had served Rand well, but it would be dangerous to leave them in their own homelands. Bashere was uncle to the Queen herself, and what of his men? How would they react when their own people asked why they had become Dragonsworn? Strange as it was, Rand knew that he would cause a much smaller conflagration by leaving foreigners on Saldaean soil.

His reasoning with Ituralde was equally brutal. The man had sworn to him, but allegiances could change. Out here, near the Blight, Ituralde and his troops would have very little opportunity to turn against Rand. They were in hostile territory, and Rand's Asha'man would be their only quick means of getting back to Arad Doman. If left in his homeland, however, Ituralde could marshal troops and perhaps decide he didn't need the Dragon Reborn's protection.

It was much safer to keep the armies in hostile territory. Rand hated thinking that way, but that was one of the main differences between the man he had been and the man he had become. Only one of those men could do what needed to be done, no matter that he hated it.

"Narishma," Rand called. "Gateway."

He didn't have to turn to feel Narishma seize the One Power and begin weaving. The sensation prickled at Rand, enticing, but he fought it off. It was becoming more and more difficult for him to seize the Power without emptying his stomach, and he did *not* intend to sick up in front of Ituralde.

"You shall have a hundred Asha'man by the end of the week," Rand said, speaking to Ituralde. "I suspect you will make good use of them."

"Yes, I think I can do just that."

"I want daily reports, even if nothing happens," Rand replied. "Send the messengers through a gateway. I'll be breaking camp and moving to Bandar Eban in four days."

Bashere grunted; this was the first Rand had said of the move. Rand turned his horse toward the large, open gateway behind them. Some of the Maidens had already ducked through, going first, as always. Narishma stood to the side, his hair in its two dark braids set with bells. He had been a Borderlander, too, before he had become Asha'man. Too many clouded loyalties. Which would come first for Narishma? His homeland? Rand? The Aes Sedai to whom he was a Warder? Rand was fairly certain the man was loyal; he was one of those who had come to him at Dumai's Wells. But the most dangerous enemies were those you assumed you could trust.

None of them can be trusted! Lews Therin said. *We should never have let them get so close to us. They'll turn on us!*

The madman always had trouble with other men who could channel. Rand nudged Tai'daishar forward, ignoring Lews Therin's ramblings, though hearing the voice did take him back to that night. The night where he had dreamed of Moridin, and there had been no Lews Therin in his mind. It twisted Rand's belly to know that his dreams were no longer safe. He had come to rely on them as a refuge. Nightmares could take him, true, but they were his own nightmares.

Why had Moridin come to help Rand in Shadar Logoth, back during the fight with Sammael? What twisted webs was he weaving? He had claimed that Rand had invaded *his* dream, but was that just another lie?

I have to destroy them, he thought. *All of the Forsaken, and I must do it for good this time. I must be hard.*

Except that Min didn't want him to be hard. He didn't want to frighten her, of all people. There were no games with Min; she might call him a fool, but she did not lie, and that made him want to be the man *she* wished him to be. But did he dare? Could a man who could laugh also be the man who could face what needed to be done at Shayol Ghul?

To live you must die, the answer to one of his three questions. If he succeeded, his memory—his legacy—would live on after he died. It was not very comforting. He didn't want to die. Who did? The Aiel claimed they did not seek death, though they embraced it when it came.

He entered the gateway, Traveling back to the manor house in Arad Doman, with the ring of pines surrounding the trampled brown grounds and the long ranks of tents. It would take a hard man to face his own death, to fight the Dark One while his blood spilled on the rocks. Who could laugh in the face of that?

He shook his head. Having Lews Therin in his mind didn't help.

She's right, Lews Therin said suddenly.

She? Rand asked.

The pretty one. With the short hair. She says we need to break the seals. She's right.

Rand froze, pulling Tai'daishar up short, ignoring the groom who had come to take the horse. To hear Lews Therin agreeing. . . .

What do we do after that? Rand asked.

We die. You promised we could die!

Only if we defeat the Dark One, Rand said. *You know that if he wins, there will be nothing for us. Not even death.*

Yes . . . nothing, Lews Therin said. *That would be nice. No pain, no regret. Nothing.*

Rand felt a chill. If Lews Therin began to think that way . . . *No,* Rand said, *it wouldn't be nothing. He would have our soul. The pain would be worse, far worse.*

Lews Therin began to weep.

Lews Therin! Rand snapped in his mind. *What do we do? How did you seal the Bore last time?*

It didn't work, Lews Therin whispered. *We used* saidin, *but we touched it to the Dark One. It was the only way! Something has to touch him, something to close the gap, but he was able to taint it. The seal was weak!*

Yes, but what do we do differently? Rand thought.

Silence. Rand sat for a moment, then slid off of Tai'daishar and let the nervous groom lead him away. The rest of the Maidens were coming through the large gateway, Bashere and Narishma taking the rear. Rand didn't wait for them, though he noticed Deira Bashere—Davram Bashere's wife—standing outside the Traveling ground. The tall, statuesque woman had dark hair with lines of white at the temples. She gave Rand a measuring look. What would she do if Bashere died in Rand's service? Would she continue to follow, or would she lead the troops away, back to Saldaea? She was as strong of will as her husband. Perhaps more so.

Rand passed her with a nod and a smile and walked through the evening camp toward the manor house. So

Lews Therin did not know how to seal the Dark One's prison. What good was the voice then? Burn him, but he had been one of Rand's few hopes!

Most people here were wise enough to move away when they saw him stalking across the grounds. Rand could remember when such moods hadn't struck him, when he had been a simple sheepherder. Rand the Dragon Reborn was a different man altogether. He was a man of responsibility and duty. He had to be.

Duty. Duty was like a mountain. Well, Rand felt as if he was trapped between a good dozen different mountains, all moving to destroy him. Among those forces, his emotions seemed to boil under pressure. Was it any wonder when they burst free?

He shook his head, approaching the manor. To the east lay the Mountains of Mist. The sun was near to setting, and the mountains were bathed in a red light. Beyond them and to the south, so strangely close, lay Emond's Field and the Two Rivers. A home he would never see again, for a visit would only alert his enemies to his affection for it. He had worked hard to make them think he was a man without affection. At times, he feared that his ruse had become reality.

Mountains. Mountains like duty. The duty of solitude in this case, for somewhere southward along those too-near mountains was his father. Tam. Rand hadn't seen him in so long. Tam *was* his father. Rand had decided that. He had never known his birth father, the Aiel clan chief named Janduin, and while he had obviously been a man of honor, Rand had no desire to call him father.

At times, Rand longed for Tam's voice, his wisdom. Those were the times when Rand knew he had to be the most hard, for a moment of weakness—a moment running to his father for succor—would destroy nearly everything he had worked for. And it would likely mean the end of Tam's life as well.

Rand entered the manor house through the burned hole in the front, pushing aside the thick canvas that now formed an entry, and kept his back to the Mountains of Mist. He was alone. He *needed* to be alone. Relying on anyone would risk being weak when he reached Shayol Ghul. At the Last Battle, he would not be able to lean on anyone other than himself.

Duty. How many mountains must one man carry?

It still smelled of smoke inside the manor house. Lord Tellaen had complained about the fire hesitantly—yet persistently—until Rand had ordered compensation for the man, although the bubble of evil hadn't been Rand's fault. Or had it? Being *ta'veren* had many strange effects, from making people say things they wouldn't normally to bringing him the allegiance of those who had been wavering. He was a focus for trouble, bubbles of evil included. He hadn't chosen to be that focus, but he *had* chosen to stay in the manor house.

Either way, Tellaen had been compensated. It was a pittance compared with the amount of money Rand was spending to fund his armies, and even that was small compared with the funds he'd dedicated to bring food to Arad Doman and other troubled areas. At this rate, his stewards worried that he would soon bankrupt his assets in Illian, Tear and Cairhien. Rand had not told them that he didn't care.

He would see the world to the Last Battle.

And will you have no legacy other than that? a voice whispered in the back of his mind. Not Lews Therin, but his own thought, a small voice, the part of him that had prompted him to found schools in Cairhien and Andor. *You wish to live after you die? Will you leave all of those who follow you to war, famine and chaos? Will the destruction be how you live on?*

Rand shook his head. He couldn't fix everything! He was just one man. Looking beyond the Last Battle was foolish. He couldn't worry about the world then, he *couldn't*. To do so would be to take his eye off the goal.

And what is the goal? that voice seemed to say. *Is it to survive, or is it to thrive? Will you set the groundwork for another Breaking or for another Age of Legends?*

He had no answers. Lews Therin roused slightly, babbling incoherently. Rand climbed the stairs to the second floor of the manor. Light, he was tired.

What was it the madman had said? When he'd sealed the Bore into the Dark One's prison, he'd used *saidin*. That was because so many of the Aes Sedai at the time had turned against him, and he'd been left only with the Hundred Companions—the most powerful male Aes Sedai of his time. No women. The female Aes Sedai had called his plan too risky.

Eerily, Rand felt as if he could almost remember those events—not what had happened, but the anger, the desperation, the decision. Was the mistake, then, not using the female half of the power as well as the male? Was that what had allowed the Dark One to counterstrike and taint *saidin*, driving Lews Therin and the remaining men of the Hundred Companions insane?

Could it be that simple? How many Aes Sedai would he need? Would he need *any*? Plenty of Wise Ones could channel. Surely there was more to it than that.

There was a game children played, Snakes and Foxes. It was said that the only way to win was to break the rules. What of his other plan, then? Could he break the rules by slaying the Dark One? Was that something that even he, the Dragon Reborn, dared contemplate?

He crossed the creaking wood floor of the hallway and pushed open the door to his room. Min lay propped up by pillows on the log bed, wearing her embroidered green trousers and a linen shirt, as she leafed through yet another book by the light of a lamp. An elderly serving woman bustled about, collecting dishes from Min's evening meal. Rand threw off his coat, sighing to himself and flexing his hand.

He sat down on the side of the bed as Min set aside her book, a volume called *A Comprehensive Discussion of Pre-Breaking Relics*. She sat up and rubbed the back of his neck with one hand. Bowls clinked as the serving woman gathered them, and she bowed in apology, moving with extra speed as she placed them in her carrying basket.

"You're pushing yourself too hard again, sheepherder," Min said.

"I have to."

She pinched his neck hard, and he flinched, grunting. "No you don't," she said, her voice close to his ear. "Haven't you been listening to me? What good will you be if you wear yourself out before you reach the Last Battle? Light, Rand, I haven't heard you laugh in months!"

"Is this really a time for laughter?" he asked. "You would have me be happy while children starve and men slaughter one another? I should *laugh* to hear that Trollocs are still getting through the Ways? I should be happy that the majority of the Forsaken are still out there somewhere, plotting how best to kill me?"

"Well, no," Min said. "Of course not. But we can't let the troubles in the world destroy us. Cadsuane says that—"

"Wait," he snapped, twisting around so that he was facing her. She knelt on the bed, short dark hair curling down beneath her chin. She looked shocked by his tone.

"What does Cadsuane have to do with this?" he asked.

Min frowned. "Nothing."

"She's been telling you what to say," Rand said. "She's been using you to get to me!"

"Don't be an idiot," Min said.

"What has she said about me?"

Min shrugged. "She worries about how harsh you've become. Rand, what is this?"

"She's trying to get to me, manipulate me," he said. "She's using you. What have you told her, Min?"

Min pinched him again sharply. "I don't like that tone, looby. I thought Cadsuane was your counselor. Why should I need to watch what I say around her?"

The serving woman continued to clink dishes. Why couldn't she just leave! This wasn't the kind of discussion he wanted to have in front of strangers.

Min couldn't be working *with* Cadsuane, could she? Rand didn't trust Cadsuane by any measure. If she'd gotten to Min. . . .

Rand felt his heart twist. He wasn't suspicious of *Min*, was he? She'd always been the one he could look to for honesty, the one who played no games with him. What would he do if he lost her? *Burn me!* he thought. *She's right. I've grown too harsh. What will become of me if I begin to grow suspicious of those that I* know *love me? I'll be no better than mad Lews Therin.*

"Min," he said, softening his voice. "Maybe you're right. Perhaps I've gone too far."

She turned to look at him, relaxing. Then she stiffened, eyes widening in shock.

Something cold clicked around Rand's neck.

Rand immediately raised his hand to his neck, spinning. The serving woman stood behind him, but her form was shimmering. She vanished and was replaced by a woman with dark skin and black eyes, her sharp face triumphant. Semirhage.

Rand's hand touched metal. Too-cold metal that felt like ice, pressed against his skin. In a rage, he tried to pull free his sword from its black, dragon-painted sheath, but found that he could not do so. His legs strained as if against some incredible weight. He scratched at the collar—his fingers could still move—but the metal seemed to be a single solid piece.

At that moment, Rand felt terror. He met Semirhage's eyes anyway, and she smiled deeply. "I've been waiting for quite a long time to get a Domination Band on you, Lews Therin. Odd, how circumstances occur, isn't—"

Something flashed in the air, and Semirhage barely had time to cry out before something deflected the blade just barely—a weave of Air, Rand could only assume, though he could not see weaves made from *saidar*. Still, Min's knife had left a gash on the side of Semirhage's face before passing by and burying itself in the wood of the door.

"Guards!" Min cried. "Maidens, to arms! The *Car'a'carn* is in danger!"

Semirhage cursed, waving a hand, and Min cut off. Rand twisted anxiously, trying—and failing—to seize *saidin*. Something blocked him. Min was tossed off the bed by weaves of Air, her mouth locked shut. Rand tried to run to her, but again found that he could not. His legs simply refused to move.

At that moment, the door to his room opened. Another woman entered with a hurried step. She glanced out of the doorway, as if watching for something, then closed it behind her. Elza. Rand felt a surge of hope, but then the small woman joined Semirhage, taking up the other bracelet that controlled the *a'dam* around Rand's neck. She looked up at Rand, her eyes red, looking dazed—as if something had hit her soundly on the head. However, when she saw him kneeling, she smiled. "And so you finally come to your destiny, Rand al'Thor. You will face the Great Lord. And you will lose."

Elza. Elza was Black, burn her! Rand's skin prickled as he felt her embrace *saidar*, standing beside her mistress. They both confronted him, each one wearing a bracelet, and Semirhage looked supremely confident.

Rand growled, turning to Semirhage. He would *not* be trapped like this!

The Forsaken touched the bleeding gash on her cheek, then *tsked* to herself. She wore a drab brown dress. How had she escaped captivity? And where had she gotten this cursed collar? Rand had given that to Cadsuane for safe-keeping. She had *vowed* that it would be safe!

"No guards will come, Lews Therin," Semirhage said absently, holding up her braceleted hand; the bracelet matched the collar on his neck. "I've warded the room against listeners. You will find that you cannot so much as move unless I allow it. You've tried already, and you must see how futile it is."

Desperate, Rand reached for *saidin* again, but found nothing. In his head, Lews Therin began to snarl and weep, and Rand felt almost as if he would join the man. Min! He had to get to her. He had to be strong enough!

He forced himself toward Semirhage and Elza, but it was as if he were trying to move someone else's legs. He was trapped in his own head, like Lews Therin. He opened his mouth to curse, but nothing came out beyond a croak.

"Yes," Semirhage said, "you cannot speak without permission either. And I would suggest that you not reach for *saidin* again. You will find the experience unpleasant. When I tested the Domination Band before, I found it to be a far more elegant tool than those Seanchan *a'dam*. Their *a'dam* allow some small measure of freedom, relying on nausea as an inhibitor. The Domination Band demands far more obedience. You will act exactly as I desire. For instance. . . ."

Rand stood up off the bed, his legs moving against his will. Then, his own hand whipped up and began to squeeze his throat just above the neck band. He gasped, stumbling. Frantic, he reached again for *saidin*.

He found pain. It was as if he'd reached into a burning vat of oil, then drawn the fiery liquid into his own veins. He screamed in shock and agony, collapsing to the wooden floor. The pain made him writhe, his vision growing black.

"You see." Semirhage's voice sounded distant. "Ah, I had forgotten how satisfying that is."

The pain was like a million ants burrowing through his skin and down to the bone. He twisted, muscles spasming.

We're in the box again! Lews Therin cried.

And suddenly, he was. He could see it, the black con-
fines, crushing him. His body sore from repeated beatings,
his mind frantic to remain sane. Lews Therin had been his
only companion. It was one of the first times Rand could
remember communicating with the madman; Lews Therin
had started to respond to him only shortly before that day.

Rand hadn't been willing to see Lews Therin as part of
himself. The mad part of himself, the part that could deal
with the torture, if only because it was already so tortured.
More pain and suffering was meaningless. You could not
fill a cup that had already begun to overflow.

He stopped screaming. The pain was still there, it made
his eyes water, but the screams would not come. All fell
still.

Semirhage looked down at him, frowning, blood dripping from her chin. Another wave of pain washed across
him. Whoever he was.

He stared up at her. Silent.

"What are you doing?" she said, compelling him.
"Speak."

"No more can be done to me," he whispered.

Another wave of pain. It shocked him, and something inside of him whimpered, but he gave no outward reaction.
Not because he held the screams in, but because he *couldn't*
feel anything. The box, the two wounds in his side cor-
rupting his own blood, beatings, humiliation, sorrows and
his own suicide. Killing himself. He could suddenly and
starkly remember that. After all of these things, what more
could Semirhage do to him?

"Great Mistress," Elza said, turning to Semirhage, eyes
still seeming faintly dazed by something. "Perhaps now we
should—"

"Quiet, worm," Semirhage spat at her, wiping the blood
from her chin. She looked at it. "That's twice now those
knives have tasted my blood." She shook her head, then
turned and smiled at Rand. "You say nothing more can be
done to you? You forget, Lews Therin, to whom you speak.
Pain is my specialty, and you are still little more than a boy.
I've broken men ten times as strong as you. Stand."

He did. The pain had not gone away. She obviously intended to keep using it against him until she got a reaction.

He turned around, obeying her wordless command, and found Min hanging above the floor, tied by invisible ropes of Air. Her eyes were wild with fear, her arms bound behind her back, her mouth blocked by a woven Air gag.

Semirhage chuckled. "There is nothing more that I can do, you say?"

Rand seized *saidin*—not of his choice, but of hers. The roar of power slammed into him, bringing with it the strange nausea that he'd never been able to explain. He fell to his hand and knees, emptying his stomach with a groan as the room shook and spun around him.

"How odd," he heard Semirhage say, as if distant. He shook his head, still holding the One Power—wrestling with it as he always had to with *saidin*, forcing that powerful, twisting flow of energy to his will. It was like chaining a tempest of wind, and was difficult even when he was strong and healthy. Now it was nearly impossible.

Use it, Lews Therin whispered. *Kill her while we can!*

I will not kill a woman, Rand thought stubbornly, a figment of a memory from the back of his mind. *That is the line I will not cross. . . .*

Lews Therin roared, trying to take *saidin* from Rand, but without success. In fact, Rand found that he couldn't channel willfully any more than he could step without Semirhage's permission.

He righted himself by her command, the room growing more steady, the nausea retreating. And then he began to form weaves, complicated ones of Spirit and Fire.

"Yes," Semirhage said, almost to herself. "Now, if I can remember. . . . The male way of doing this is so odd, sometimes."

Rand made the weaves, then pushed them toward Min. "No!" he screamed as he did so. "Not that!"

"Ah, so you see," Semirhage said. "You weren't so difficult to break after all."

The weaves touched Min and she writhed in pain. Rand continued to channel, tears springing to his eyes as he was forced to send the complex weaves through her body. They brought agony only, but they did it very well. Semirhage must have released Min's gag, for she began to scream, weeping.

"Please, Rand!" she begged. "Please!"

Rand roared in anger, trying to stop, unable to. He could *feel* Min's pain through the bond, feel it as he caused it.

"Stop this!" he bellowed.

"Beg," Semirhage said.

"Please," he said, weeping. "Please, I beg you."

Suddenly, he stopped, the torturing weaves unraveling. Min hung in the air, whimpering, eyes dazed from the shock of pain. Rand turned around, facing Semirhage and the smaller figure of Elza beside her. The Black looked terrified, as if she'd gotten herself into something she hadn't been prepared for.

"Now," the Forsaken said, "you see that you have always been intended to serve the Great Lord. We will leave this room and will deal with those so-called Aes Sedai who imprisoned me. We will Travel to Shayol Ghul and present you to the Great Lord, and then this can all be finished."

He bowed his head. There had to be a way out! He imagined her using him to tear through the ranks of his own men. He imagined them afraid to attack, lest they harm him. He saw the blood, death and destruction he would cause. And it chilled him, turned him to ice inside.

They have won.

Semirhage glanced at the door, then turned back to him and smiled. "But I'm afraid we must deal with her first. Let us be about it, then."

Rand turned and began to walk toward Min. "No!" he said. "You promised if I begged—"

"I promised nothing," Semirhage said with a laugh. "You begged quite prettily, Lews Therin, but I have chosen to ignore your pleas. You can release *saidin*, however. This needs to be somewhat more personal."

Saidin winked away, and Rand felt the withdrawal of power with regret. The world seemed more dull around him. He stepped up to Min, her pleading eyes meeting his. Then he pressed his hand to her throat, gripping it, and began to squeeze.

"No. . . ." he whispered in horror as his hand, against his will, cut off her air. Min stumbled, and he unwillingly forced her down to the ground, easily ignoring her struggles. He loomed above her, pressing his hand against her throat, gripping it and choking her. She looked at him, eyes beginning to bulge.

This can't be happening.

Semirhage laughed.

Ilyena! Lews Therin wailed. *Oh, Light! I've killed her!*

Rand squeezed harder, leaning down for leverage, his fingers squeezing Min's skin and pushing down on her throat. It was as if he gripped his own heart, and the world became black around him, everything darkened except for Min. He could feel her pulse throbbing beneath his fingers.

Those beautiful dark eyes of hers watched him, loving him even as he killed her.

This can't be happening!

I've killed her!

I'm mad!

Ilyena!

There had to be a way out! Had to be! Rand wanted to close his eyes, but he couldn't. She wouldn't let him—not Semirhage, but Min. She held his eyes with her own, tears lining her cheeks, dark, curled hair disheveled. So beautiful.

He scrambled for *saidin*, but could not take it. He tried with every bit of will he had to relax his fingers, but they just continued to squeeze. He felt horror, he *felt* her pain. Min's face grew purple, her eyes fluttered.

Rand wailed. *THIS CAN'T BE HAPPENING! I WILL NOT DO THIS AGAIN!*

Something snapped inside of him. He grew cold; then that coldness vanished, and he could feel nothing. No emotion. No anger.

At that moment he grew aware of a strange force. It was like a reservoir of water, boiling and churning just beyond his view. He reached toward it with his mind.

A clouded face flashed before Rand's own, one whose features he couldn't quite make out. It was gone in a moment.

And Rand found himself filled with an alien power. Not *saidin*, not *saidar*, but something else. Something he'd never felt before.

Oh, Light, Lews Therin suddenly screamed. *That's impossible! We can't use it! Cast it away! That is death we hold, death and betrayal.*

It is HIM.

Rand closed his eyes as he knelt above Min, then he

channeled the strange, unknown force. Energy and life surged through him, a torrent of power like *saidin*, only ten times as sweet and a hundred times as violent. It made him alive, made him realize that he'd never *been* alive before. It gave him such strength as he'd never imagined. It rivaled, even, the power he'd held when drawing from the Choedan Kal.

He screamed, in both rapture and rage, and wove enormous spears of Fire and Air. He slammed the weaves against the collar at his neck, and the room exploded with flames and bits of molten metal, each one distinct to Rand. He could feel each shard of metal blast away from his neck, warping the air with its heat, trailing smoke as it hit a wall or the floor. He opened his eyes and released Min. She gasped and sobbed.

Rand stood and turned, white-hot magma in his veins—as when Semirhage had tortured him, yet somehow opposite. As painful as this was, it was also pure ecstasy.

Semirhage looked utterly shocked. "But . . . that's impossible . . ." she said. "I felt nothing. You can't—" She looked up, staring at him with wide eyes. "The True Power. Why have you betrayed me, Great Lord? Why?"

Rand raised a hand and, filled with the power he did not understand, wove a single weave. A bar of pure white light, a cleansing fire, burst from his hand and struck Semirhage in the chest. She flashed and vanished, leaving a faint afterimage to Rand's vision. Her bracelet dropped to the floor.

Elza ran toward the door. She vanished before another bar of light, her entire figure becoming light for a moment. Her bracelet dropped to the floor, as well, the women who had held them burned completely from the Pattern.

What have you done? Lews Therin asked. *Oh, Light. Better to have killed again than to do this. . . . Oh, Light. We are doomed.*

Rand savored the power for a moment longer, then—regretfully—let it drop away. He would have held on, but he was simply too exhausted. The vanishing of it left him numb.

Or . . . no. That numbness had nothing to do with the power he'd held. He turned around, looking down at Min, who coughed quietly and rubbed her neck. She looked up at him, and seemed afraid. He doubted that she would ever see him the same way again.

He had been wrong; there *had* indeed been something more that Semirhage could do to him. He had felt himself killing one he loved dearly. Before, when he'd done it as Lews Therin, he had been mad and unable to control himself. He could barely remember slaying Ilyena, as if through a clouded dream. He'd realized what he had done only after Ishamael had awakened him.

Finally, now, he knew precisely what it was like to watch as he killed those he loved.

"It is done," Rand whispered.

"What?" Min asked, coughing again.

"The last that could be done to me," he said, surprised at his own calmness. "They have taken everything from me now."

"What are you saying, Rand?" Min asked. She rubbed her neck again. Bruises were beginning to show.

He shook his head as—finally—voices sounded in the hallway outside. Perhaps the Asha'man had sensed him channeling when he'd tortured Min.

"I have made my choice, Min," he said, turning toward the door. "You have asked for flexibility and laughter from me, but such things are no longer mine to give. I am sorry."

Once, weeks ago, he had decided that he must become stronger—where he had been iron, he had decided to become steel. It appeared that steel was too weak.

He would be harder, now. He understood how. Where he had once been steel, he became something else. From now on, he was *cuendillar*. He had entered a place like the void that Tam had trained him to seek, so long ago. But within this void he had no emotion. None at all.

They could not break or bend him.

It was done.

CHAPTER
23

A Warp in the Air

W hat of the sisters who were guarding her cell?"
Cadsuane asked, stomping up the wooden steps
beside Merise.

"Corele and Nesune are alive, thankfully, though they
were left extremely weak," Merise said, holding her skirt up
as she hurried along. Narishma followed them, the bells at
the end of his braids ringing softly. "Daigian is dead. We're
not certain why the other two were left alive."

"Warders," Cadsuane said. "Kill the Aes Sedai, and their
Warders would know immediately—and we would have
learned that something was wrong." The Warders should
have noticed that something was wrong anyway—they'd
have to interrogate the men to see what they had felt. But
there was likely a correlation.

Daigian had no living Warder. Cadsuane felt a stab of
regret for the pleasant sister, but shoved it aside. No time
for it now.

"The other two were placed in some kind of trance,"
Merise said. "I could see no remnants of weaves, nor could
Narishma. We discovered the sisters just before the alarm
was sounded, then went for you as soon as we were assured that al'Thor was alive and our enemies had been dealt
with."

Cadsuane nodded crossly. Of all the nights to be out visiting the Wise Ones in their tents! Sorilea and a small group
of them followed behind Narishma, and Cadsuane didn't
dare slow her pace, lest the Aiel women trample her in their
haste to see al'Thor.

They reached the top of the stairs, then sped down the

hallway toward al'Thor's room. How could he have gotten himself into this much trouble, *again*! And how had that blasted Forsaken gotten free of her cell? Someone must have helped her, but that meant a Darkfriend in their camp. It wasn't unlikely—if Darkfriends existed in the White Tower, then they could undoubtedly be found here. But what Darkfriend could incapacitate three Aes Sedai? Surely channeling on that level should have been felt by every sister or Asha'man in the camp.

"Was the tea involved?" Cadsuane asked Merise quietly.

"Not that we can tell," the Green replied. "We'll know more when the other two wake. They fell unconscious as soon as we brought them out of their trance."

Cadsuane nodded. Al'Thor's door was open, and Maidens swarmed outside it like wasps who had just discovered their nest was gone. Cadsuane couldn't say that she blamed them. Apparently, al'Thor had said little of what had happened. The fool boy was lucky to still be alive! *What a Light-cursed mess,* Cadsuane thought, passing the Maidens and entering the chamber.

A small knot of Aes Sedai clustered on the far side of the room, speaking quietly. Sarene, Erian, Beldeine—all of those in the camp who weren't either dead or incapacitated. Except Elza. Where was Elza?

The three nodded to Cadsuane as she entered, but she spared them barely a glance. Min sat on the bed, rubbing her neck, eyes red, short hair disheveled, face pale. Al'Thor stood beside the open far window, looking out at the night, his hand clasping his stump behind him. His coat lay rumpled on the floor, and he stood in white shirtsleeves, a cool wind blowing in and ruffling his red-gold hair. Nynaeve watched him, frowning.

Cadsuane surveyed the room; behind her, in the hall, the Wise Ones began to interrogate the Maidens. "Well?" Cadsuane said. "What happened?"

Min looked up. There were red marks on her neck, the beginnings of bruises. Rand did not turn from the window. *Insolent boy,* Cadsuane thought, coming farther into the room. "Speak up, boy!" she said. "We need to know if the camp is in danger."

"The danger has been dealt with," he said softly. Something in his voice made her hesitate. She had been expecting anger, or perhaps satisfaction, from him. Fatigue at the very least. Instead, his voice sounded cool.

"Will you explain what that means?" Cadsuane demanded.

Finally, he turned, looking at her. She took an involuntary step backward, though she couldn't say why. He was still the same foolish boy. Too tall, too self-confident, and too blunt-headed. There was a strange serenity about him now, but it had a dark edge. Like the serenity one saw in the eyes of a condemned man the moment before he stepped up to the hangman's noose.

"Narishma," Rand said, looking past Cadsuane. "I have a weave for you. Memorize it; I will show it to you only once." With that, al'Thor put his hand out to the side and a bar of brilliant white fire shot from between his fingers and struck his coat, which lay on the floor. It vanished in a burst of light.

Cadsuane hissed. "I told you never to use that weave, boy! You will *never* do so again. Do you hear me! This is not—"

"That is the weave we must use when fighting Forsaken, Narishma," al'Thor said, his quiet voice cutting straight through Cadsuane's. "If we kill them with anything else, they can be reborn. It is a dangerous tool, but still just a tool. Like any other."

"It is forbidden," Cadsuane said.

"I have decided that it is not," al'Thor said calmly.

"You don't have any idea what that weave can do! You're a child playing with—"

"I have seen balefire destroy cities," al'Thor said, eyes growing haunted. "I have seen thousands burned from the Pattern by its purifying flames. If you call me a child, Cadsuane, then what are those of you who are thousands of years my juniors?"

He met her gaze. Light! What had happened to him? She struggled to collect her thoughts. "So Semirhage is dead?"

"Worse than dead," al'Thor said. "And far better off, in many ways, I should think."

"Well, then. I suppose we can get on with—"

"Do you recognize that, Cadsuane?" al'Thor said, nodding toward something metallic sitting on the bed, mostly hidden by the sheets.

Hesitantly she walked forward. Sorilea looked over, expression unreadable. Apparently, she didn't wish to be drawn into the conversation when al'Thor was in such a mood. Cadsuane didn't blame her.

Cadsuane pulled back the sheets, revealing a familiar pair of bracelets. There was no collar.

"Impossible," she whispered.

"That is what I assumed," al'Thor said in that terribly calm voice of his. "I told myself that it obviously *couldn't* be one of the same *ter'angreal* I relinquished to you. You promised they would be protected and hidden."

"Well, then," Cadsuane said, unnerved. She covered the things back up. "That is settled then."

"It is. I sent people to your room. Tell me, is this box where you were keeping the bracelets? We found it open on the floor of your quarters."

A Maiden brought out a familiar oak box. It was the same one, obviously. Cadsuane turned toward him in anger. "You searched my room!"

"I was unaware that you were visiting the Wise Ones," al'Thor said. He gave a small nod of respect to Sorilea and Amys, which they hesitantly returned. "I sent servants to check on you, as I feared that Semirhage might have tried for revenge on you."

"They shouldn't have touched this," Cadsuane said, taking the box from the Maiden. "It was prepared with very intricate wards."

"Not intricate enough," al'Thor said, turning away from her. He still stood by that darkened window, looking out over the camp.

The room fell silent. Narishma had been asking quietly after Min's health, but he fell silent when al'Thor stopped speaking. Rand obviously felt that Cadsuane was responsible for the male *a'dam* being stolen, but that was preposterous. She had prepared the best ward she knew, but who knew what knowledge the Forsaken had for getting past wards?

How *had* al'Thor survived? And what of the other contents of that box? Did al'Thor now have the access key, or had the statuette been taken by Semirhage? Did Cadsuane dare ask? The silence continued. "What are you waiting for?" she finally asked with all the bravado she could summon. "Do you expect an apology from me?"

"From you?" al'Thor asked. There was no humor in his voice, just the same cold evenness. "No, I suspect that I could sooner extract an apology from a stone than from you."

"Then—"

"You are exiled from my sight, Cadsuane," he said softly. "If I see your face again after tonight, I will kill you."

"Rand, no!" Min said, standing up beside the bed. He didn't turn toward her.

Cadsuane felt an immediate stab of panic, but shoved it aside with her anger. "What?" she demanded. "This is foolishness, boy. I. . . ."

He turned, and again that gaze of his made her trail off. There was a danger to it, a shadowy cast to his eyes that struck her with more fear than she'd thought her aging heart could summon. As she watched, the air around him seemed to *warp*, and she could almost think that the room had grown darker.

"But. . . ." She found herself stuttering. "But you don't kill women. Everyone knows it. You can hardly put the Maidens into danger for fear of them getting hurt!"

"I have been forced to revise that particular inclination," al'Thor said. "As of tonight."

"But—"

"Cadsuane," he said softly, "do you believe that I could kill you? Right here, right now, without using a sword or the Power? Do you believe that if I simply willed it, the Pattern would bend around me and stop your heart? By . . . coincidence?"

Being *ta'veren* didn't work that way. Light! It didn't, did it? He couldn't bend the very *Pattern* to his will, could he?

And yet, meeting his eyes, she *did* believe. Against all logic, she looked in those eyes and knew that if she didn't leave, she would die.

She nodded slowly, hating herself, strangely weak.

He turned away from her, looking back out the window. "Be certain that I do not see your face. Ever again, Cadsuane. You may go now."

Dazed, she turned—and from the corner of her eye, she saw a deep darkness emanating from al'Thor, warping the air even further. When she glanced back, it was gone. With gritted teeth, she left.

"Prepare yourselves and your armies," al'Thor said to those who remained, voice echoing in the room behind. "I intend to be gone by week's end."

Cadsuane raised a hand to her head and leaned against the hallway wall outside, heart thumping, hand sweating. Before, she had been working against a stubborn but good-hearted boy. Someone had taken that child and replaced him with this man, a man more dangerous than any she had ever met. Day by day, he was slipping away from them.

And at the moment, she hadn't a blasted clue what to do about it.

CHAPTER
24

A New Commitment

Exhausted from days of hard travel, Gawyn sat atop Challenge on a low hill southwest of Tar Valon.

This countryside should have been green with spring's arrival, but the hillside before him bore only scraggly dead weeds, slain by the winter snows. Tufts of yew and blackwood poked up here and there, breaking the brown landscape. He counted more than a few stands that were now populated only by stumps. A war camp devoured trees like hungry woodgnarls, using them for arrows, fires, buildings and siege equipment.

Gawyn yawned—he'd pushed hard through the night. Bryne's war camp was well dug in here, and was a bustle of motion and activity. An army this large spawned organized chaos at best. A small band of mounted cavalry could travel light, as Gawyn's Younglings had; a force like that could grow to several thousand and remain lean. Expert horsemen, like the Saldaeans, were said to manage larger bands of seven or eight thousand while keeping their mobility.

But a force like the one below was a different beast entirely. It was an enormous, sprawling thing, in the shape of an enormous bubble with a smaller camp at its center; that probably held the Aes Sedai. Bryne also had forces occupying all of the bridge towns on both sides of the River Erinin, effectively cutting off the island from ground supply.

The army squatted near Tar Valon like a spider eyeing a butterfly hovering just outside of its web. Lines of troops rode in and out patrolling, purchasing food, running messages. Dozens upon dozens of squads, some mounted, others walking. Like bees leaving the hive while others swarmed back in. The eastern side of the main camp was crowded with a mishmash of shanties and tents, the normal riffraff of camp followers that collected around an army. Near by, just inside the main war-camp boundary, a wooden palisade—perhaps fifty yards across—rose in a tall ring. Probably a command post.

Gawyn knew he had been seen by Bryne's scouts as he approached, yet none had stopped him. They probably wouldn't unless he tried to ride away. A single man—wearing a decent gray cloak and trousers, with a lacing shirt of white—wasn't of much interest. He could be a sell-sword, coming to ask for a place in the ranks. He could be a messenger from a local lord, sent to complain about a group of scouts. He could even be a member of the army. While many of those in Bryne's force wore uniforms, many others just wore a simple yellow band on their coatsleeves, not yet able to pay for proper insignia to be sewn on.

No, a single man approaching the army was not a danger. A single man riding *away* from it, however, was cause for alarm. A man coming to the camp could be friend, foe or neither. A man who inspected the camp then rode away was almost certainly a spy. So long as Gawyn didn't leave before making his intentions known, Bryne's outriders would be unlikely to bother him.

Light, but he could use a bed. He'd spent a restless two nights, sleeping only a couple of hours during each one, wrapped in his cloak. He felt irritable and cranky, partially just at himself for refusing to go to an inn, lest he be chased by the Younglings. He blinked bleary eyes, and spurred Challenge down the incline. He was committed now.

No. He'd been committed the moment he'd left Sleete behind in Dorlan. By now, the Younglings knew of their leader's betrayal. Sleete wouldn't allow them to waste time searching. He'd tell them what he knew. Gawyn wished he could convince himself that they'd be surprised, but he'd received more than one frown or look of confusion regarding the way he spoke of Elaida and the Aes Sedai.

The White Tower didn't deserve his allegiance, but the Younglings—he could never go back to them, now. It itched at him; this was the first time his wavering had been revealed to a large group. Nobody knew that he'd helped Siuan escape, nor was it widespread knowledge that he'd dallied with Egwene.

Yet leaving had been the right thing to do. For the first time in months, his actions matched his heart. Saving Egwene. *That* was something he could believe in.

He approached the outskirts of camp, keeping his face impassive. He hated the idea of working with the rebel Aes Sedai almost as much as he had hated abandoning his men. These rebels were no better than Elaida. They were the ones who had propped Egwene up as an Amyrlin, as a target. Egwene! A mere Accepted. A pawn. If they failed in their bid for the Tower, they themselves might be able to escape punishment. Egwene would be executed.

I'll get in, Gawyn thought. *I'll save her somehow. Then I'll talk some sense into her and bring her away from all of the Aes Sedai. Perhaps even talk sense into Bryne. We can all get back to Andor, to help Elayne.*

He rode forward with renewed determination, banishing some of his exhaustion. To reach the command post, he had to ride through the camp followers, who outnumbered the actual troops. Cooks to fix the food. Women to serve the food and wash the soiled dishes. Wagon drivers to carry the food. Wheelwrights to fix the wagons that carried the food. Blacksmiths to make horseshoes for the horses that pulled the wagons that carried the food. Merchants to buy the food, and quartermasters to organize it. Less reputable merchants who sought to profit off of the soldiers and their battle pay, and women who sought to do the same. Boys to run messages, hoping to someday carry a sword themselves.

It was a complete mess. A half-shanty conglomeration of tents and shacks, each of a different hue, design and state of disrepair. Even a capable general like Bryne could impose only so much order on camp followers. His men would keep the peace, more or less, but they couldn't force followers to keep military discipline.

Gawyn passed through the middle of it all, ignoring those who called to him offering to shine his sword or sell him a sweetbun. The prices would be low—this was a place that fed off of soldiers—but with his warhorse and finer clothing, he'd be marked as an officer. If he bought from one, the others would smell coin, and he could end up surrounded by all who hoped to sell to him.

He ignored the calls, eyes forward, toward the army itself ahead. Its tents were generally organized in neat rows, grouped by squad and banner, though sometimes in smaller clusters. Gawyn could have guessed the layout without seeing it. Bryne liked organization, but also believed strongly in delegation. Bryne would allow officers to run their camps as they wished, and that led to a setup that was less uniform, yet was far better at running itself.

He headed directly for the palisade. The camp followers around him weren't easy to ignore, however. Their calls to him lingered in the air, together with the scents of cooking, privies, horses and cheap perfume. The camp wasn't as crowded as a city, but it also wasn't as well maintained. Sweat mixed with burning cook fires mixed with stagnant water mixed with unwashed bodies. It made him want to hold a handkerchief to his face, though he refrained. It would make him look like a spoiled noble, turning his nose up at the common people.

The stink, the confusion and the yells didn't help his mood any. He had to grit his teeth to keep himself from cursing at each hawker. A figure stumbled onto the pathway in front of him—he reined in. The woman wore a brown skirt and a white blouse, her hands grimy. "Out of the way," Gawyn snapped. His mother would have been outraged to hear him speaking with such anger. Well, his mother was dead now, by al'Thor's hand.

The woman in front of him looked up and ran back out of the pathway. She had light hair tied in a yellow kerchief and a faintly plump body. Gawyn caught just a glimpse of her face as she turned.

Gawyn froze. That was an Aes Sedai face! It was unmistakable. He sat, shocked, as the woman pulled her kerchief down and hurried away.

"Wait!" he called, turning his horse. But the woman did not stop. He hesitated, lowering his arm as he saw the woman join a line of washwomen working between several wooden troughs a short distance away. If she was pretending to be a common woman, then she likely had her own blasted Aes Sedai reasons, and she wouldn't appreciate him exposing her. Very well. Gawyn forced down his annoyance. Egwene. He had to focus on Egwene.

When he reached the command palisade, the air improved measurably. A quartet of soldiers stood on guard, halberds held at their sides, steel caps gleaming and matched by breastplates emblazoned with Bryne's three stars. A banner bearing the flame of Tar Valon flapped beside the gateway.

"Recruit?" asked one of the soldiers as Gawyn rode up. The heavyset man bore a red stripe on his left shoulder, marking him as a watch sergeant. He carried a sword instead of a halberd. His breastplate barely fit his girth, and his chin bristled with red hairs. "You'll have to meet with Captain Aldan," the man said with a grunt. "Big blue tent about a quarter of the way around the outside of the camp. You've got your own horse and sword; that'll get you good pay." The man pointed toward a distant point in the main body of the army, outside the palisade. That wouldn't do. He could see Bryne's banner flying inside.

"I'm not a recruit," Gawyn said, turning Challenge to get a better look at the men. "My name is Gawyn Trakand. I need to speak with Gareth Bryne immediately about a matter of some urgency."

The soldier raised an eyebrow. Then he chuckled to himself.

"You don't believe me," Gawyn said flatly.

"You should go speak to Captain Aldan," the man said lazily, pointing toward the distant tent again.

Gawyn took a calming breath, trying to force down his irritation. "If you'd just send for Bryne, you'd find that—"

"Are you going to be trouble?" the soldier asked, puffing himself up. The other men readied their halberds.

"No trouble," Gawyn said evenly. "I just need—"

"If you're going to be in our camp," the soldier interrupted, stepping forward, "you're going to have to learn how to do what you're told."

Gawyn met the man's eyes. "Very well. We can do it this way. It will probably be faster anyway."

The sergeant laid a hand on his sword.

Gawyn kicked his feet free of the stirrups and pushed himself out of the saddle. It would be too hard to keep from killing the man from horseback. He slid his blade free as his feet hit the muddy ground, the sheath rasping like an inhaled breath. Gawyn fell into Oak Shakes Its Branches, a form that wielded nonlethal blows, often used by masters for training their students. It was also very effective against a large group all using different weapons.

Before the sergeant had his sword free, Gawyn slammed into him, ramming an elbow into his gut just beneath the poorly fitting breastplate. The man grunted and bent, then Gawyn knocked him on the side of the head with the hilt of his sword—the man should have known better than to wear his cap askew like that. Then Gawyn fell into Parting the Silk to deal with the first halberdier. As another of the men screamed for help, Gawyn's blade slashed across the first halberdier's breastplate with a ringing sound, forcing the man back. Gawyn finished by sweeping the man's feet from under him, then fell into Twisting the Wind to block a pair of blows from the other two men.

It was unfortunate, but he had to resort to striking the thighs of the two standing halberdiers. He'd have preferred to avoid wounding them, but fights—even one such as this, against far less skilled opponents—became unpredictable the longer they lasted. One had to control the battlefield quickly and soundly, and that meant dropping the two soldiers—clutching their bleeding thighs. The sergeant was out cold from the rap to the head, but the first halberdier was rising shakily. Gawyn kicked the man's halberd aside, then planted a boot in his face, knocking him back and bloodying his nose.

Challenge whinnied from behind, snorting and stamping the ground. The warhorse sensed a fight, but was well trained. He knew that when his reins were dropped, he was to remain still. Gawyn wiped his blade on his trouser leg, then slid it back into its sheath, the wounded soldiers groaning on the ground. He patted Challenge on the nose and took up the reins again. Behind Gawyn, nearby camp followers backed away, then ran. A group of soldiers from inside the palisade approached with bows drawn. That was not good. Gawyn turned to face them, pulling his still-sheathed sword free from his belt and tossing it to the ground in front of the men.

"I am unarmed," he said over the sounds of the wounded. "And none of these four will die this day. Go and tell your general that a lone blademaster just felled a squad of his guards in under ten heartbeats. I'm an old student of his. He'll want to see me."

One of the men scrambled forward to take Gawyn's fallen sword while another signaled to a runner. The others kept their bows raised. One of the fallen halberdiers began to crawl away. Gawyn turned Challenge at an angle, making ready to duck behind the horse if the soldiers moved to draw. He'd much prefer it not come to that, but of the two of them, Challenge was far more likely to survive a few short-bow shafts than Gawyn.

Several of the soldiers risked coming forward to help their fallen friends. The heavyset watch sergeant was stirring, and he sat up, cursing under his breath. Gawyn made no threatening motions.

Perhaps it had been a mistake to fight the men, but he had already wasted too much time. Egwene could be dead by now! When a man like that sergeant tried to assert his authority, you really only had two options. You could talk your way up through the ranks of the bureaucracy, convincing each soldier each step of the way that you *were* important. Or you could make a disturbance. The second was faster, and the camp obviously had enough Aes Sedai support to Heal a few injured soldiers.

Eventually, a small group of men strode out from inside the palisade. Their uniforms were sharp, their postures dangerous, their faces worn. At their head came a square-faced man with graying temples and a strong, stocky build. Gawyn smiled. Bryne himself. The gamble had worked.

The Captain-General surveyed Gawyn, then moved on to a quick inspection of his fallen soldiers. At last, he shook his head. "Stand down," he said to his men. "Sergeant Cords."

The stocky sergeant stood up. "Sir!"

Bryne glanced back at Gawyn. "Next time a man comes to the gate claiming to be nobility and asking for me, send for an officer. Immediately. I don't care if the man has two months of scruffy beard and reeks of cheap ale. Understood?"

"Yes, sir," the sergeant said, blushing. "Understood, sir."

"See your men to the infirmary, Sergeant," Bryne said, still looking at Gawyn. "*You*, come with me."

Gawyn clenched his jaw. He hadn't received such an address from Gareth Bryne since before he'd started shaving. Still, he couldn't really expect the man to be pleased. Just inside the palisade, Gawyn spotted a young boy who was likely a stablehand or messenger boy. He handed Challenge to the wide-eyed youth, instructing him to see the horse cared for. Then Gawyn retrieved his sword from the man holding it and hurried after Bryne.

"Gareth," Gawyn said, catching up, "I—"

"Hold your tongue, young man," Bryne said, not turning toward him. "I haven't decided what I'm going to do with you."

Gawyn snapped his mouth closed. That was uncalled for! Gawyn was still brother to the rightful Queen of Andor, and would be First Prince of the Sword should Elayne take and hold the throne! Bryne should show him respect.

But Bryne could be stubborn as a boar. Gawyn held his tongue. They reached a tall, peaked tent with two guards at the front. Bryne ducked inside and Gawyn followed. The inside was neat and clean, more so than Gawyn had expected. The desk was stacked with rolled maps and orderly sheets of paper, and the pallets in the corner were rolled carefully, blankets folded with sharp angles. Bryne was obviously relying on someone meticulous to tidy up for him.

Bryne clasped his hands behind his back, breastplate reflecting Gawyn's face as he turned around. "All right. Explain what you're doing here."

Gawyn drew himself up. "General," he said, "I think you mistake yourself. I'm no longer your student."

"I know," Bryne said curtly. "The boy *I* trained would never have pulled a childish stunt like that one to get my attention."

"The watch sergeant was belligerent, and I had no patience for the posturing of a fool. This seemed the best way."

"The best way to *what*?" Bryne asked. "Outrage me?"

"Look," Gawyn said, "perhaps I was hasty, but I have an important task. You need to listen to me."

"And if I don't?" Bryne asked. "If I instead throw you out of my camp for being a spoiled princeling with too much pride and not enough sense?"

Gawyn frowned. "Be careful, Gareth. I've learned a great deal since we last met. I think you'll find that your sword can no longer best mine as easily as it once did."

"I have no doubt of that," Bryne said. "Light, boy! You

always were a talented one. But you think that just because you're skilled with the sword, your words hold more weight? I should listen because you'll kill me if I don't? I thought I taught you far better than that."

Bryne had aged since Gawyn had last seen him. But that age didn't bow Bryne down—it rested comfortably on his shoulders. A few more traces of white at his temples, a few more wrinkles around the eyes, yet strong and lean enough of body that he looked years younger than he was. One couldn't look at Gareth Bryne and see anything other than a man in—certainly not past—his prime.

Gawyn locked eyes with the general, trying to keep the anger from boiling out. Bryne held his gaze, calm. Solid. As a general should be. As Gawyn should be.

Gawyn looked away, suddenly feeling ashamed of himself. "Light," he whispered, releasing his sword and raising a hand to his head. He suddenly felt very, very tired. "I'm sorry, Gareth. You're right. I've been a fool."

Bryne grunted. "Good to hear you say that. I was beginning to wonder what had happened to you."

Gawyn sighed, wiping his brow, wishing for something cool to drink. His anger melted away, and he felt exhausted. "It has been a difficult year," he said, "and I rode myself too hard getting here. I'm at the edge of my mind."

"You aren't the only one, lad," Bryne said. He took a deep breath and walked to a small serving table, poured a cup of something for Gawyn. It was only warm tea, but Gawyn took it thankfully and sipped.

"These are times to test men," Bryne said, pouring himself a cup. He took a sip and grimaced.

"What?" Gawyn asked, glancing down at his cup.

"It's nothing. I despise this stuff."

"Then why drink it?" Gawyn asked.

"It's supposed to improve my health," Bryne grumbled. Before Gawyn could ask further, the large general continued, "So are you going to make me throw you in the stocks before you'll tell me why you decided to fight your way into my command post?"

Gawyn stepped forward. "Gareth. It's Egwene. They have her."

"The White Tower Aes Sedai?"

Gawyn nodded urgently.

"I know." Bryne took another drink, then grimaced again.

"We have to go for her!" Gawyn said. "I came to ask you for help. I intend to mount a rescue."

Bryne snorted softly. "A rescue? And how do you intend to get into the White Tower? Even the Aiel couldn't break into that city."

"They didn't want to," Gawyn said. "But I don't need to take the city, I just need to sneak a small force in, then get one person out. Every rock has its cracks. I'll find a way."

Bryne set his cup aside. He looked at Gawyn, firm, weathered face an icon of nobility. "But tell me this, lad. How are you going to get her to come out with you?"

Gawyn started. "Why, she'll be happy to come. Why wouldn't she?"

"Because she's forbidden us to rescue her," Bryne said, clasping his hands behind his back again. "Or so I've been able to gather. The Aes Sedai tell me little. One would think they'd be more trusting toward a man they depend on to run this siege of theirs. Anyway, the Amyrlin can communicate with them somehow, and she's instructed them to leave her be."

What? That was ridiculous! Obviously, the Aes Sedai in camp were fudging the facts. "Bryne, she's imprisoned! The Aes Sedai I heard talking said that she's being beaten daily. They'll execute her!"

"I don't know," Bryne said. "She's been with them for weeks now and they haven't killed her yet."

"They'll kill her," Gawyn said urgently. "You know they will. Perhaps you parade a fallen enemy before your soldiers for a time, but eventually you have to mount his head on a pike to let them know he's dead and gone. You know I'm right."

Bryne regarded him, then nodded. "Perhaps I do. But there's still nothing I can do. I'm bound by oaths, Gawyn. I can't do anything unless that girl instructs me to."

"You'd let her die?"

"If that's what it takes to keep my oath, then yes."

If Bryne was bound by oath . . . well, he'd sooner hear an Aes Sedai tell a lie than see Gareth Bryne break his word. But Egwene! There had to be something he could do!

"I'll try to get you an audience with some of the Aes Sedai I serve," Bryne said. "Perhaps they can do something.

If you persuade them that a rescue is needed, and that the Amyrlin would want it, then we'll see."

Gawyn nodded. It was something at least. "Thank you."

Bryne waved indifferently. "Though I *should* see you in the stocks. For wounding three of my men, if nothing else."

"Have an Aes Sedai Heal them," Gawyn said. "From what I've heard, you've no lack of sisters to bully you."

"Bah," Bryne said. "I can rarely get them to Heal anyone unless the soldier's life is threatened. I had a man take a bad spill while riding the other day, and I was told that Healing would only teach him to be reckless. 'Pain is its own lesson,' the blasted woman said. 'Perhaps next time he won't see fit to make sport for his friends while riding.'"

Gawyn grimaced. "But surely they'll make an exception for those men. After all, an enemy did do the wounding."

"We'll see," Bryne said. "The sisters rarely visit the soldiers. They've their own business to be about."

"There's one in the outer camp now," Gawyn said absently, glancing over his shoulder.

"Younger girl? Dark hair, without the ageless face?"

"No, this was an Aes Sedai. I could tell *because* of the face. She was kind of plump, with lighter hair."

"Probably just scouting for Warders," Bryne said, sighing. "They do that."

"I don't think so," Gawyn said, glancing over his shoulder. "She was hiding among the washwomen." As he thought about it, he realized that she could very well be a spy for the White Tower loyalists.

Bryne's frown deepened. Perhaps he had the same thoughts. "Show me," he said, striding toward the tent flaps. He threw them aside, walking back out into the morning light, Gawyn following.

"You never did explain what you are doing here, Gawyn," Bryne said as they walked through the orderly camp, soldiers saluting their general as he passed.

"I told you," Gawyn said, hand resting comfortably on the pommel of his sword. "I *am* going to find a way to get Egwene out of that death trap."

"I didn't mean what you're doing in my camp. I meant why you were in the area in the first place. Why aren't you back in Caemlyn, helping your sister?"

"You have news of Elayne," Gawyn said, stopping. Light!

He should have asked earlier. He really *was* tired. "I heard that she was in your camp earlier. She's gone back to Caemlyn? Is she safe?"

"She hasn't been with us for a long while," Bryne said. "But she seems to be doing well." He stopped, glancing at Gawyn. "You mean you don't know?"

"What?"

"Well, rumors are unreliable," Bryne said. "But I have confirmed many of them with the Aes Sedai, who have been Traveling to Caemlyn to listen for news. Your sister holds the Lion Throne. It seems that she's undone much of the mess your mother left for her."

Gawyn took a deep breath. *Thank the Light,* he thought, closing his eyes. Elayne lived. Elayne held the throne. He opened his eyes, and the overcast sky seemed a little more bright. He continued walking, Bryne falling into step beside him.

"You really didn't know," Bryne said. "Where have you been, lad? You're the First Prince of the Sword now, or you will be once you return to Caemlyn! Your place is at your sister's side."

"Egwene first."

"You made an oath," Bryne said sternly. "Before me. Have you forgotten?"

"No," Gawyn said. "But if Elayne has the throne, then she's safe for now. I'll get Egwene and tow her back to Caemlyn where I can keep an eye on her. Where I can keep an eye on both of them."

Bryne snorted. "I think I'd like to watch you trying that first part," he noted. "But regardless, why weren't you there when Elayne was trying to take the throne? What have you been doing that is more important than that?"

"I . . . grew entangled," Gawyn said, eyes forward.

"Entangled?" Bryne asked. "You were at the White Tower when all of this—" He cut off, falling silent. The two walked side by side for a moment.

"Where did you hear sisters talking about Egwene's capture?" Bryne asked. "How would you know she's being punished?"

Gawyn said nothing.

"Blood and bloody ashes!" Bryne exclaimed. The general rarely cursed. "I *knew* that the person leading those raids against me was too well informed. And here I was, looking for a leak among my officers!"

"It doesn't matter now."

"I'll judge that," Bryne said. "You've been killing my men. Leading raids against me!"

"Leading raids against the rebels," Gawyn said, turning hard eyes on Bryne. "You may blame me for bullying my way into your camp, but do you honestly expect me to feel guilty for helping the White Tower against the force *besieging* it?"

Bryne fell silent. Then he nodded curtly. "Very well. But that makes you an enemy commander."

"No longer," Gawyn said. "I've left that command."

"But—"

"I helped them," Gawyn said. "I no longer do. Nothing I see here will return to your enemies, Bryne. I swear it on the Light."

Bryne didn't respond immediately. They passed tents, likely for the high officers, approaching the palisade wall. "Very well," Bryne said. "I can trust you haven't changed enough to break your word."

"I wouldn't turn against that oath," Gawyn said harshly. "How could you think that I would?"

"I've had experience with unexpected renunciations of oaths lately," Bryne said. "I said I believe you, lad. And I do. But you *still* haven't explained why you didn't return to Caemlyn."

"Egwene was with the Aes Sedai," Gawyn said. "As far as I knew, Elayne was as well. This seemed a good place to be, although I wasn't certain I liked Elaida's authority."

"And what is Egwene to you?" Bryne asked softly.

Gawyn met his eyes. "I don't know," he admitted. "I wish I did."

Strangely, Bryne chuckled. "I see. And I understand. Come, let's find this Aes Sedai you think you saw."

"I *did* see her, Gareth," Gawyn said, nodding to the guards as they passed out the gates. The men saluted Bryne, but watched Gawyn as they would a blacklance. As well they should.

"We shall see what we find," Bryne said. "Regardless, once I get you a meeting with the Aes Sedai leaders, I want your word that you'll go back to Caemlyn. Leave Egwene to us. You need to help Elayne. It's your place to be in Andor."

"I could say the same of you." Gawyn surveyed the teeming followers' camp. Where had the woman been?

"You could," Bryne said gruffly. "But it wouldn't be true. Your mother saw to that."

Gawyn glanced at him.

"She put me out to pasture, Gawyn. Banished me and threatened me with death."

"Impossible!"

Bryne looked grim. "I felt the same way. But it is true nonetheless. The things she said . . . they stung, Gawyn. That they did indeed."

That was all Bryne said, but from him, it spoke volumes. Gawyn had never heard the man offer a word of discontent about his station or his orders. He had been loyal to Morgase—loyal with the kind of steadfastness a ruler could only hope for. Gawyn had never known a man more sure, or a man less likely to complain.

"It must have been part of some scheme," Gawyn said. "You know Mother. If she hurt you, there was a reason."

Bryne shook his head. "No reason other than foolish love for that fop Gaebril. She nearly let her clouded head ruin Andor."

"She'd never!" Gawyn snapped. "Gareth, you of all people should know that!"

"I should," Bryne said, lowering his voice. "And I wish I did."

"She had another motive," Gawyn said stubbornly. He felt the heat of anger rise within him again. Around them, peddlers glanced at the two, but said nothing. They probably knew not to approach Bryne. "But now we'll never know it. Not now that she's dead. *Curse* al'Thor! The day can't come soon enough when I can run him through."

Bryne looked at Gawyn sharply. "Al'Thor saved Andor, son. Or as near to it as a man could."

"How could you say that?" Gawyn said. "How could you speak well of that monster? He *killed* my mother!"

"I don't know if I believe those rumors or not," Bryne said, rubbing his chin. "But if I do, lad, then perhaps he did Andor a favor. You don't know how bad it got, there at the end."

"I can't believe I'm hearing this," Gawyn said, lowering his hand to his sword. "I won't hear her name soiled like that, Bryne. I mean it."

Bryne looked him directly in the eyes. His gaze was so *solid*. Like eyes carved of granite. "I'll always speak truth, Gawyn. No matter who challenges me on it. It's hard to hear? Well, it was harder to live. No good comes of spreading complaints. But her son needs to know. In the end, Gawyn, your mother turned against Andor by embracing Gaebril. She *needed* to be removed. If al'Thor did that for us, then we have need to thank him."

Gawyn shook his head, rage and shock fighting one another. This was Gareth Bryne?

"These aren't the words of a spurned lover," Bryne said, face set, as if shoving aside emotions. He spoke softly as he and Gawyn walked, camp followers giving them a wide berth. "I can accept that a woman could lose affection for a man and bestow it on another. Yes, Morgase the woman I can forgive. But Morgase the Queen? She gave the kingdom to that snake. She sent her allies to be beaten and imprisoned. She wasn't right in her mind. Sometimes, when a soldier's arm festers, it needs to be cut free to save the man's life. I'm pleased at Elayne's success, and it is a wound to speak these words. But you have to bury that hatred of al'Thor. He wasn't the problem. Your mother was."

Gawyn kept his teeth clenched. *Never,* he thought. *I will never forgive al'Thor. Not for this.*

"I can see the intent behind that look," Bryne said. "All the more reason to get you back to Andor. You'll see. If you don't trust me, ask your sister. See what she says of it."

Gawyn nodded sharply. Enough of that. Ahead, he noted the place where he'd seen the woman. He glanced toward the distant lines of washwomen, then turned and strode toward them, edging between two merchants with pungent pens full of chickens, selling eggs. "This way," he said, perhaps too sharply.

He didn't look to see if Bryne followed. Soon the general caught up to him, looking displeased, but he kept his peace. They walked down a crowded, twisting pathway among people in browns and dull grays, and soon reached the line of women kneeling before two long wooden troughs of slowly flowing water. Men stood at the far end, pouring water down the troughs, and the line of women washed clothing in the sudsy one, then rinsed them off in the cleaner trough. No wonder the ground was so wet! At least here it smelled of suds and cleanliness.

The women had their sleeves rolled up to their upper arms, and most of them chatted idly as they worked, rubbing clothing against boards in the troughs. They were all dressed in those same brown skirts he had seen on the Aes Sedai. Gawyn rested his hand idly on his pommel, inspecting the women from behind.

"Which one?" Bryne asked.

"Just a moment," Gawyn said. There were dozens of women. Had he really seen what he'd thought? Why would an Aes Sedai be in this camp, of all places? Surely Elaida wouldn't send an Aes Sedai out to spy; their faces made them too easy to recognize.

Of course, if they were that easy to recognize, why couldn't he spot her now?

And then he saw her. She was one of the only women who wasn't chatting with those around her. She knelt with her head bowed, the yellow kerchief tied around her head, shading her face, a few locks of light hair sticking out from under the cloth. Her posture was so subservient that he almost missed her, but the shape of her body stood out. She was plump, and that kerchief was the only yellow one in the line.

Gawyn strode down the line of working women, several of whom stood up, hands on hips as they explained in no uncertain terms that "Soldiers with their big feet and awkward elbows" should stay out of the way of women at work. Gawyn ignored them, pressing on until he stood beside the yellow kerchief.

This is insane, Gawyn thought. *There's never in all of history been an Aes Sedai who could force herself to adopt that kind of posture.*

Bryne stepped up beside him. Gawyn stooped down, trying to get a look at the woman's face. She bowed down further, scrubbing more furiously at the shirt in the trough before her.

"Woman," Gawyn said. "May I see your face?"

She didn't respond. Gawyn looked up at Bryne. Hesitantly, the general reached down and pushed back the plump woman's kerchief. The face underneath was *distinctly* Aes Sedai, with that unmistakable ageless quality. She didn't look up. She just kept working.

"I said it wouldn't work," said a hefty woman nearby. The woman rose and waddled down the line, wearing a tentlike dress of green and brown. "'My Lady,' I told her, 'you can do as you wish, I ain't one to refuse such as you, but someone's going to notice you.'"

"You're in charge of the washwomen," Bryne said.

The large woman nodded firmly, her red curls bouncing. "Indeed I am, General." She turned to the Aes Sedai, curtsying. "Lady Tagren, I did warn you. Light burn me, but I did. I'm right sorry."

The woman called Tagren bowed her head. Were those tears on her cheeks? Was that even *possible*? What was going on?

"My Lady," Bryne said, squatting down beside her. "Are you Aes Sedai? If you are, and you command me to leave, I will do so without question."

A good way to approach it. If she really was Aes Sedai, she couldn't lie.

"I'm not Aes Sedai," the woman whispered.

Bryne looked up at Gawyn, frowning. What did it mean if she said that? An Aes Sedai couldn't lie. So. . . .

The woman softly said, "My name is Shemerin. I *was* Aes Sedai, once. But no more. Not since. . . ." She looked down again. "Please. Just leave me to work in my shame."

"I will," Bryne said. Then he hesitated. "But I'll need you to talk to some sisters from the camp first. They'd have my ears if I don't bring you in to speak with them."

The woman, Shemerin, sighed but stood up.

"Come on," Bryne said to Gawyn. "I have no doubt that they'll also want to talk to you. Best to get this over with quickly."

CHAPTER
25

In Darkness

Sheriam peeked into her dark tent, hesitant, but saw nothing inside. Allowing herself a smile of satisfaction, she stepped in and drew the flaps closed. Things were going quite well, for once.

Of course, she still checked her tent before she entered, searching for the one who had sometimes lurked inside. The one whom she'd never been able to sense, yet always felt as though she should. Yes, Sheriam still checked, and probably would for months yet—but there was no need, now. No phantom waited to punish her.

The square little tent was large enough to stand up in, with a cot along one side and a trunk along the other. There was just room for a desk, but it would so crowd the space that she'd barely be able to move. Besides, there was a perfectly acceptable desk nearby, in Egwene's unused tent.

There had been talk of giving that tent to someone else—most sisters had to share, though more tents were being brought in each week. However, the Amyrlin's tent was a symbol. As long as there was hope of Egwene's return, her tent should wait for her. It was kept neat by the inconsolable Chesa, whom Sheriam *still* caught crying about her mistress's captivity. Well, so long as Egwene was away, that tent was functionally Sheriam's for all but sleeping. After all, an Amyrlin's Keeper was expected to look after her affairs.

Sheriam smiled again, sitting down on her cot. Not long ago, her life had been a perpetual cycle of frustration and pain. Now that was over. Bless Romanda. Whatever else Sheriam thought of the fool woman, Romanda had been the one to chase Halima—and Sheriam's punishments—out of the camp.

Pain would come again. There was always agony and punishment involved in the service she gave. But she had learned to take the times of peace and cherish them.

At times, she wished she'd kept her mouth closed, not asked questions. But she had, and here she was. Her allegiances had brought her power, as promised. But nobody had warned her of the pain. Not infrequently she wished she'd chosen the Brown and hidden herself away in a library somewhere, never to see others. But now she was where she was. There was no use wondering about what could have happened.

She sighed, then removed her dress and changed her shift. She did so in the dark; candles and oil were both rationed, and with the rebels' funds drying up, she'd need to hide away what she had for later use.

She climbed onto the cot, pulling up the blanket. She wasn't so naive as to feel *guilty* about the things she'd done. Every sister in the White Tower tried to get ahead; that's what life was about! There wasn't an Aes Sedai who wouldn't stab her sisters in the back if she thought it would give her advantage. Sheriam's friends were just a little more . . . practiced at it.

But why had the end of days had to come *now* of all times? Others in her association spoke of the glory and great honor of being alive at this time, but Sheriam didn't agree. She'd joined to rise in White Tower politics, to have the power to punish those who spited her. She'd never wanted to participate in some final reckoning with the Dragon Reborn, and she'd certainly never desired to have *anything* to do with the Chosen!

But nothing could be done now. Best to enjoy the peace of being free of both the beatings and Egwene's self-righteous pratings. Yes indeed. . . .

There was a woman with great strength in the Power standing outside her tent.

Sheriam snapped her eyes open. She could sense other women who could channel, just like any other sister. *Bloody ashes!* she thought nervously, squeezing her eyes shut. *Not again!*

The tent flaps rippled. Sheriam opened her eyes to find a

jet-black figure standing above her cot; slivers of moonlight passing through the fluttering tent flaps were just enough to outline the figure's form. It was clothed in an unnatural darkness, ribbons of black cloth fluttering behind it, the face obscured by a deep blackness. Sheriam gasped and threw herself from the cot, making obeisance on the canvas tent bottom. There was barely room enough for her to kneel. She cringed, expecting the pain to come upon her again.

"Ah . . ." a rasping voice said. "Very good. You are obedient. I am pleased."

It wasn't Halima. Sheriam had never been able to sense Halima, who it appeared had been channeling *saidin* all along. Also, Halima had never come in such a . . . dramatic way.

Such strength! It seemed likely that this was one of the Chosen. Either that, or at least a very powerful servant of the Great Lord, far above Sheriam. That worried her to the bone, and she trembled as she bowed. "I live to serve, Great Mistress," Sheriam said quickly. "I, who am blessed to bow before you, to live during these times, to—"

"Stop your babbling," the voice growled. "You are well placed in this camp, I understand?"

"Yes, Great Mistress," Sheriam said. "I am the Keeper of the Chronicles."

The figure sniffed. "Keeper to a ragged bunch of would-be Aes Sedai rebels. But that is no matter. I have need of you."

"I live to serve, Great Mistress," Sheriam repeated, growing more worried. What did this creature want of her?

"Egwene al'Vere. She must be deposed."

"What?" Sheriam asked, startled. A switch of Air cracked against her back, and it burned. Fool! Did she want to get herself killed? "My apologies, Great Mistress," she said quickly. "Forgive my outburst. But it was by orders from one of the Chosen that I helped raise her as Amyrlin in the first place!"

"Yes, but she has proven to have been a . . . poor choice. We needed a child, not a woman with merely the face of a child. She must be removed. You will make certain this group of foolish rebels stops supporting her. And end those blasted meetings in *Tel'aran'rhiod*. How is it so many of you get there?"

"We have *ter'angreal*," Sheriam said, hesitantly. "Several in the shape of an amber plaque, several others in the shape of an iron disc. Then a handful of rings."

"Ah, sleepweavers," the figure said. "Yes, those could be useful. How many?"

Sheriam hesitated. Her first instinct was to lie or hedge—this seemed like information she could hold over the figure. But lying to one of the Chosen? A poor choice. "We had twenty," Sheriam said truthfully. "But one was with the woman Leane, who was captured. That leaves us with nineteen." Just enough for Egwene's meetings in the World of Dreams—one for each of the Sitters and one for Sheriam herself.

"Yes," the figure hissed, shrouded in darkness. "Useful indeed. Steal the sleepweavers, then give them to me. This rabble has no business treading where the Chosen walk."

"I. . . ." Steal the *ter'angreal*? How was she going to manage *that*? "I live to serve, Great Mistress."

"Yes you do. Do these things for me, and you will find yourself greatly rewarded. Fail me. . . ." The figure contemplated for a moment. "You have three days. Each of the sleepweavers you fail to acquire in that time will cost you a finger or a toe." With that, the Chosen opened a gateway right in the middle of the room, then vanished through it. Sheriam caught a glimpse of the familiar tiled hallways of the White Tower on the other side.

Steal the sleepweavers! All nineteen of them? In three days? *Darkness above!* Sheriam thought. *I should have lied about the number we had! Why didn't I lie?*

She remained kneeling, breathing in and out, for a long time, thinking about her predicament. Her period of peace was at an end, it appeared.

It had been brief.

"She will be tried, of course," Seaine said. The soft-spoken White sat on a chair provided for her by the two Reds guarding Egwene's cell.

The cell door was open, and Egwene sat on a stool inside—also provided by the Reds. Those two guards, plump Cariandre and stern Patrinda, watched carefully from the hallway, both holding the Source and maintaining Egwene's shield. They looked as if they expected her to dart away, scrambling for freedom.

Egwene ignored them. Her two days of imprisonment had not been pleasant, but she would suffer them with dignity. Even if they locked her away in a tiny room with a door that wouldn't let in light. Even if they refused to let her change from the bloodied novice dress. Even if they beat her each day for how she had treated Elaida. Egwene would *not* bow.

The Reds reluctantly allowed her visitors, as stipulated by Tower law. Egwene was surprised she *had* visitors, but Seaine wasn't the only one who had come to her. Several had been Sitters. Curious. Nevertheless, Egwene was starved for news. How was the Tower reacting to Egwene's imprisonment? Were the rifts between the Ajahs still deep and wide, or had her work started to bridge them?

"Elaida broke Tower law quite explicitly," Seaine explained. "And it was witnessed by five Sitters of five different Ajahs. She has tried to forestall a trial, but was unsuccessful. However, there were some who listened to her argument."

"Which was?" Egwene asked.

"That you are a Darkfriend," Seaine said. "And, because of it, she expelled you from the Tower, and *then* beat you."

Egwene felt a chill. If Elaida was able to get enough support for that argument. . . .

"It will not stand," Seaine said, consolingly. "This is not some backward village, where the Dragon's Fang scrawled on someone's door is enough to convict."

Egwene raised an eyebrow. She'd been raised in "some backward village," and they'd had enough sense to look for more than rumors in convicting someone, no matter what the crime. But she said nothing.

"Proving that accusation is difficult by Tower standards," Seaine said. "And so I suspect that she will not try to prove it in trial—partially because doing so would require her to let you speak for yourself, and I suspect that she'll want to keep you hidden."

"Yes," Egwene said, eyeing the Reds lounging nearby. "You are probably right. But if she can't prove I'm a Darkfriend and she couldn't stop this from going to trial . . ."

"It is not an offense worthy of deposing her," Seaine said. "The maximum punishment is formal censure from the Hall and penance for a month. She would retain the stole."

But would lose a great deal of credibility, Egwene thought. It was encouraging. But how to make certain that Elaida didn't just hide her away? She had to keep the pressure on Elaida—Light-cursed difficult while locked away in her tiny cell each day! It had been only a short time so far, but already the lost opportunities grated on her.

"You will attend the trial?" Egwene asked.

"Of course," Seaine said, even-tempered, as Egwene had come to expect from the White. Some Whites were all coolness and logic. Seaine was much warmer than that, but was still very reserved. "I *am* a Sitter, Egwene."

"I assume that you're still seeing the effects of the Dark One's stirring?" Egwene shivered and glanced at her cell floor, remembering what had happened to Leane. Her own cell was far more austere than Leane's, perhaps because of the accusations of her being a Darkfriend.

"Yes." Seaine's voice grew softer. "They seem to be getting worse. Servants dying. Food spoiling. Entire sections of the Tower rearranging at random. The second kitchen moved to the sixth level last night, moving an entire section of the Yellow Ajah quarters into the basement. It's like what happened with the Browns earlier, and that one *still* hasn't been worked out."

Egwene nodded. With the way the rooms had shifted, those few novices whose rooms hadn't moved suddenly now had assigned accommodations on the twenty-first and twenty-second levels, where Brown Ajah quarters had been. The Browns were, reluctantly, all moving down to the wing. Would it be a permanent change? Always before, the sisters had lived in the Tower proper, the novices and Accepted living in the wing.

"You have to bring these things up, Seaine," Egwene said softly. "Keep reminding the sisters that the Dark One stirs and that the Last Battle approaches. Keep their attention on working together, not dividing."

Behind Seaine, one of the Red sisters checked the candle on the table. The time allotted for Egwene to receive visitors was ending. She'd soon be locked away again; she could smell the dusty, unchanged straw behind her.

"You *must* work hard, Seaine," Egwene said, rising as the Reds approached. "Do what I cannot. Ask the others to do so as well."

"I will try," Seaine said. She stood and watched as the Reds took Egwene's stool, then gestured her back into the cell. The ceiling was too low for her to stand without stooping.

Egwene moved reluctantly, bending down. "The Last Battle comes, Seaine. Remember."

The White nodded, and the door shut, locking Egwene into darkness. Egwene sat down. She felt so blind! What would happen at the trial? Even if Elaida was punished, what would be done with Egwene?

Elaida would try to have her executed. And she still had grounds, as Egwene had—by the White Tower's definition—impersonated the Amyrlin Seat.

I must stay firm, Egwene told herself in the darkness. *I warmed this pot myself, and now I must boil in it, if that is what will protect the Tower.* They knew she continued to resist. That was all she could give them.

CHAPTER
26

A Crack in the Stone

A viendha surveyed the manor grounds, swarming with people preparing to depart. Bashere's men and women were well trained for wetlanders, and they worked efficiently to stow their tents and prepare their gear. However, compared to the Aiel, the other wetlanders—those who weren't actual soldiers—were a mess. Camp women skittered this way and that, as if sure they would leave some task undone or some item unpacked. The messenger boys ran with their friends, trying to *look* busy so that they wouldn't have to do anything. The civilians' tents and equipment were only slowly being packed and stowed, and they would need horses, wagons and teams of drivers to get them all where they needed to go.

Aviendha shook her head. The Aiel brought only what they could carry, and their war band included only spears and Wise Ones. And when more than just spears were required for an extended campaign, all workers and craftspeople knew how to prepare themselves for departure with speed and efficiency. There was honor in that. Honor which demanded that each person be able to care for themselves and their own, not slowing the clan down.

She shook her head, turning back to her task. The only ones who truly lacked honor on a day like this were those who did not work. She dipped a finger into the pail of water on the ground in front of her, then raised her hand and let it hover over a second pail. A drop of water dripped free. She moved her hand and did it again.

It was the type of punishment in which no wetlander could have seen significance. They would have thought it easy work, sitting on the ground, leaning with her back against the wooden logs of the manor house. Moving her hand back and forth, emptying one pail and filling the other, one drop at a time. To them it would have been barely a punishment at all.

That was because wetlanders were often lazy. They would rather drip water into pails than carry rocks. Carrying rocks, however, involved activity—and activity was good for the mind and the body. Moving water was meaningless. Useless. It didn't allow her to stretch her legs or work her muscles. And she did it while the rest of the camp gathered tents for the march. That made the punishment ten times as shameful! She earned *toh* for every moment she did not help, and there was not a thing she could do about it.

Except move water. Drip, by drip, by drip.

It made her angry. Then that anger made her ashamed. The Wise Ones never let their emotions dominate them in such a way. She had to remain patient and try to understand why she was being punished.

Even trying to approach the problem made her want to scream. How many times could she go over the same conclusions in her mind? Perhaps she was too dense to sort it out. Perhaps she didn't deserve to be a Wise One.

She stuck her hand back in the bucket, then moved another drop of water. She didn't like what these punishments were doing to her. She was a warrior, even if she no longer carried the spear. She did not fear punishment, nor did she fear pain. But, more and more, she *did* fear that she would lose heart and become as useless as one who sandstared.

She *wanted* to become a Wise One, wanted it desperately. She was surprised to find that, for she'd never thought that she could desire anything with as much passion as she'd long ago wanted the spears. Yet as she had studied the Wise Ones during these last months, and her respect for them had grown, she had accepted herself as their equal, to help shepherd the Aiel in this most dangerous of days.

The Last Battle would be a test unlike any her people had ever known. Amys and the others were working to protect the Aiel, and Aviendha sat and moved drops of water!

"Are you all right?" a voice asked.

Aviendha started, looking up, reaching for her knife so abruptly that she nearly spilled the pails of water. A woman with short, dark hair stood in the shade of the building a short distance away. Min Farshaw's arms were folded and she wore a coat the color of cobalt with silver embroidery. She wore a scarf at her neck.

Aviendha settled back down, releasing her knife. Now she was letting wetlanders sneak up on her? "I am well," she said, struggling to keep from blushing.

Her tone and actions should have indicated that she didn't wish to be shamed by conversation, but Min didn't seem to notice that. The woman turned and looked out over the camp. "Don't . . . you have anything to be doing?"

Aviendha could not suppress the blush this time. "I am doing what I should."

Min nodded, and Aviendha forced herself to still her breathing. She could not afford to grow angry at this woman. Her first-sister had asked her to be kind to Min. She decided not to take offense. Min didn't know what she was saying.

"I thought that I could talk to you," Min said, still looking out at the camp. "I'm not sure who else I could approach. I don't trust the Aes Sedai, and neither does he. I'm not sure he trusts anyone, now. Maybe not even me."

Aviendha glanced to the side, and saw that Min was watching Rand al'Thor as he moved through the camp, wearing a coat of black, gold-red hair ablaze in the afternoon light. He seemed to tower over the Saldaeans who attended him.

Aviendha had heard about the events the night before, when he had been attacked by Semirhage. One of the Shadowsouled themselves; Aviendha wished she had seen the creature before she was killed. She shuddered.

Rand al'Thor had fought and won. Though he acted the fool much of the time, he was a skilled—and lucky— warrior. Who else alive could claim to have personally defeated as many of the Shadowsouled as he had? There was much honor in him.

His fight had left him scarred in ways she did not yet understand. She could feel his pain. She'd felt it during Semirhage's attack, too, though at first she'd mistakenly thought it to be a nightmare. She'd quickly realized that she was wrong. No nightmare could be that terrible. She could still feel echoes of that incredible pain, those waves of agony, the frenzy inside of him.

Aviendha had raised the alarm, but not quickly enough. She had *toh* to him for her mistake; she would deal with that once she was finished with her punishments. If she ever *did* finish.

"Rand al'Thor will deal with his problems," she said, dripping more water.

"How can you say that?" Min asked, glancing at her. "Can't you feel his pain?"

"I feel each and every moment of it," Aviendha said through gritted teeth. "But he must face his own trials, just as I face mine. Perhaps there will be a day when he and I can face ours together, but that time is not now."

I must be his equal, first, she added in her head. *I will not stand beside him as his inferior.*

Min studied her, and Aviendha felt a chill, wondering what visions the woman saw. Her predictions of the future were said always to come true.

"You are not what I expected," Min finally said.

"I have deceived you?" Aviendha said, frowning.

"No, not that," Min said with a small laugh. "I mean, I was wrong about you, I guess. I wasn't certain what to think, after that night in Caemlyn when . . . well, that night when we bonded Rand together. I feel close to you, yet distant from you at the same time." She shrugged. "I guess I expected you to come looking for me the moment you got into camp. We had things to discuss. When you didn't, I worried. I thought perhaps I had offended you."

"You have no *toh* to me," Aviendha said.

"Good," Min said. "I still worry sometimes that we'll . . . come to a confrontation."

"And what good would a confrontation serve?"

"I don't know," Min said with a shrug. "I figured it would be the Aiel way. Challenge me to a fight of honor. For him."

Aviendha snorted. "Fight over a man? Who would do such a thing? If you had *toh* toward me, perhaps I could demand that we dance the spears—but only if you were a Maiden. And only if I were still one too. I suppose that we could fight with knives, but it would hardly be a fair fight. What honor would there to be gained in fighting one with no skill?"

Min flushed, as if Aviendha had offered her an insult. What a curious reaction. "I don't know about that," Min said, flipping a knife from her sleeve and spinning it across her knuckles. "I'm hardly defenseless." She made the knife vanish up her other sleeve. Why was it that the wetlanders always showed off such flourishes with their knives? Thom Merrilin had been prone to that as well. Didn't Min understand that Aviendha could have slit the woman's throat thrice over during the time it took to flash that knife like a street performer? Aviendha said nothing, however. Min was obviously proud of the skill, and there was no need to embarrass the woman.

"It is unimportant," Aviendha said, continuing her work. "I would not fight with you unless you gave me grave insult. My first-sister considers you a friend, and I would like to do so as well."

"All right," Min said, folding her arms and looking back at Rand. "Well, I guess that's a good thing. I have to admit, I don't much like the idea of sharing."

Aviendha hesitated, then dipped her finger into the pail. "Neither do I." At least, she didn't like the idea of sharing with a woman she didn't know very well.

"Then what do we do?"

"We continue as we have," Aviendha said. "You have what you wish, and I am occupied by other matters. When it becomes a different time, I will inform you."

"That's . . . straightforward of you," Min said, looking confused. "You have other matters to occupy you? Like dipping your finger in buckets of water?"

Aviendha blushed again. "Yes," she snapped. "Just like that. You will excuse me." She stood and strode away, leaving the buckets. She knew that she should not have lost her temper, but she could not help it. Min, repeatedly pointing out her punishment. Her inability to decipher what the Wise Ones wished of her. Rand al'Thor, constantly putting himself into danger, and Aviendha unable to lift a finger to help him.

She could stand it no longer. She crossed the brown thatch of the manor green, clenching and unclenching her fists, keeping her distance from Rand. The way this day was going, he'd notice her wrinkled finger and ask why she had been soaking it! If he discovered that the Wise Ones had been punishing her, he would probably do something rash and make a fool of himself. Men were like that, Rand al'Thor most of all.

She stalked across the springy ground, the brown thatch patterned with square impressions where tents had stood, threading her way through wetlanders scurrying this way and that. She passed a line of soldiers tossing sacks of grain to the next and loading them in a wagon hitched to two thick-hoofed draft horses.

She kept moving, trying to keep herself from exploding. The truth was, she felt just as likely to do something "rash" as Rand al'Thor would be. Why? Why couldn't she decipher what she was doing wrong? The other Aiel in the camp seemed as ignorant as she, though of course they had not spoken to her of the punishments. She remembered well seeing similar punishments when she'd been a Maiden, and had always known to stay out of Wise Ones' business.

She rounded the wagon, and found herself heading toward Rand al'Thor again. He was talking with three of Davram Bashere's quartermasters, taller than each of them by a head. One of them, a man with a long black mustache, pointed toward the horselines and said something. Rand caught sight of Aviendha and raised his hand toward her, but she turned away quickly, moving toward the Aiel campsite at the north side of the green.

She ground her teeth, trying—unsuccessfully—to tame her anger. Did she not have a right to anger, if only at herself? The world was close to ending and she spent her days being punished! Ahead, she spotted a small cluster of Wise Ones—Amys, Bair and Melaine—standing beside a pile of brown tent packs. The tight, oblong bundles had straps for ease of carrying over the shoulder.

Aviendha should have returned to her pails and redoubled her efforts. But she did not. Like a child with a stick charging a narshcat, she stalked up to the Wise Ones, fuming.

"Aviendha?" Bair asked. "Have you finished your punishment already?"

"No I have not," Aviendha said, stopping in front of them, hands fists at her sides. Wind tugged at her shirt, but she let it flap. Hurrying camp workers—both Aiel and Saldaean—gave the group a wide berth.

"Well?" Bair asked.

"You are not learning quickly enough," Amys added, shaking her white-haired head.

"Not learning quickly enough?" Aviendha demanded. "I have learned everything you have asked of me! I have memorized every lesson, repeated every fact, performed every duty. I have answered all your questions and have seen you nod in approval at each answer!"

She stared them down before continuing. "I can channel better than any Aiel woman alive," she said. "I have left behind the spears, and I welcome my place among you. I have done my duty and sought honor on each occasion. Yet you continue to give me punishments! I will have no more of it. Either tell me what it is you wish of me or send me away."

She expected anger from them. She expected disappointment. She expected them to explain that a mere apprentice was not to question full Wise Ones. She expected, at least, to be given greater punishment for her temerity.

Amys glanced at Melaine and Bair. "It is not we who punish you, child," she said, seeming to choose her words with care. "These punishments come by your own hand."

"Whatever I have done," Aviendha said, "I cannot see that it would have you make me *da'tsang*. You shame yourselves by treating me so."

"Child," Amys said, meeting her eyes. "Are you *rejecting* our punishments?"

"Yes," she said, heart thumping. "I am."

"You think your stakes as strong as ours, do you?" Bair asked, shading her aged face with her hand. "You presume to be our equal?"

Their equal? Aviendha thought, panic setting in. *I'm not their equal! I have years left to study. What am I doing?*

Could she back down now? Beg forgiveness, meet her *toh* somehow? She should hurry back to her punishment and move the waters. Yes! That is what she needed to do. She had to go and—

"I see no more reason to study," she found herself saying instead. "If these punishments are all you have left to teach me, then I must assume that I have learned all that I must. I am ready to join you."

She gritted her teeth, waiting for an explosion of furious incredulity. What was she thinking? She shouldn't have let Min's foolish talk rile her so.

And then Bair started to laugh.

It was a full-bellied sound, incongruous coming from the small woman. Melaine joined her, the sun-haired Wise One holding her stomach, slightly bulging from her pregnancy. "She took even longer than you, Amys!" Melaine exclaimed. "As stubborn a girl as I've ever seen."

Amys' expression was uncharacteristically soft. "Welcome, sister," she said to Aviendha.

Aviendha blinked. "What?"

"You are one of us now, girl!" Bair said. "Or soon will be."

"But I defied you!"

"A Wise One cannot allow others to step upon her," Amys said. "If she comes into the shade of our sisterhood thinking like an apprentice, then she will never see herself as one of us."

Bair glanced at Rand al'Thor, who stood in the distance talking to Sarene. "I never realized how important our ways were until I studied these Aes Sedai. Those at the bottom simper and beg like hounds, and are ignored by those who consider themselves their betters. It is a wonder they achieve anything!"

"But there is rank among Wise Ones," Aviendha said. "Is there not?"

"Rank?" Amys looked puzzled. "Some of us have more honor than others, earned by wisdom, actions and experience."

Melaine held up a finger. "But it is important—*vital*, even—that each Wise One be willing to defend her own well. If she believes that she is right, she cannot let herself be shoved aside, even by other Wise Ones, no matter how aged or wise."

"No woman is ready to join us until she has declared herself ready," Amys continued. "She must present herself as our equal."

"A punishment is not a true punishment unless you accept it, Aviendha," Bair said, still smiling. "We thought you ready weeks ago, but you stubbornly continued to obey."

"Almost, I began to think you prideful, girl," Melaine added with a fond smile.

"Girl no longer," Amys said.

"Oh, she's still a girl," Bair said. "Until one more thing is done."

Aviendha felt dazed. They'd said she wasn't learning quickly enough. Learning to stand up for herself! Aviendha had never allowed others to push her around, but these weren't "others"—they were Wise Ones, and she the apprentice. What would have happened if Min hadn't riled her? She would have to thank the woman, although Min didn't realize what she'd done.

Until one more thing is done . . . "What must I still do?" Aviendha asked.

"Rhuidean," Bair said.

Of course. A Wise One visited that most sacred city twice in her life. Once when she became an apprentice, once when she became a full Wise One.

"Things will be different, now," Melaine said. "Rhuidean is no longer what it once was."

"That is no reason to abandon the old ways," Bair replied. "The city may be open, but nobody will be foolish enough to walk through the pillars. Aviendha, you must—"

"Bair," Amys cut in, "if it is well with you, I would prefer to tell her."

Bair hesitated, then nodded. "Yes, of course. It is only right. We turn our backs on you now, Aviendha. We will not see you again until you return to us as a sister returning from a long journey."

"A sister we had forgotten that we knew," Melaine said, smiling. The two turned from her, then Amys began to walk toward the Traveling ground. Aviendha hurried to catch up.

"You may wear your clothing this time," Amys said, "as it is the mark of your station. Normally, I would suggest that you travel to the city by foot, even though we know of Traveling now, but I think that custom is best bent in this case. Still, you should not Travel directly to the city. I suggest Traveling to Cold Rocks Hold and walk from there. You must spend time in the Three-fold Land to contemplate your journey."

Aviendha nodded. "I will need a waterskin and supplies there."

"Ready and waiting for you at the hold," Amys said. "We've been expecting you to leap this chasm soon. You should have leapt it days ago, considering all the hints we gave you." She eyed Aviendha, who glanced down at the ground.

"You have no reason for shame," Amys said. "That burden is upon us. Despite Bair's joking, you did well. Some women spend months and months being punished before deciding that they have had enough. We had to be hard on you, child—harder than I've ever seen a ready apprentice treated. There is just so little time!"

"I understand," Aviendha said. "And . . . thank you."

Amys snorted. "You forced us to be *very* creative. Remember this time you spent and the shame you felt, for it is the shame any *da'tsang* will know, should you consign them to their fate. And they cannot escape it simply by demanding release."

"What do you do if an apprentice declares herself ready to be a Wise One during her first few months of training?"

"Strap her a few times and set her digging holes, I suspect," Amys said. "I don't know of that ever happening. The closest was Sevanna."

Aviendha had wondered why the Wise Ones had accepted the Shaido woman without complaint. Her declaration had been enough: and so Amys and the others had been forced to accept her.

Amys pulled her shawl close. "There is a bundle for you with the Maidens guarding the Traveling ground. Once you reach Rhuidean, travel to the center of the city. You will find the pillars of glass. Pass through the center of them, then return here. Spend well your days running to the city. We pushed you hard so that you would have this time for contemplation. It is likely the last you will have for some while."

Aviendha nodded. "The battle comes."

"Yes. Return quickly once you pass through the pillars. We will need to discuss how to best handle the *Car'a'carn*. He has . . . changed since last night."

"I understand," Aviendha said, taking a deep breath.

"Go," Amys said, "and return." She put emphasis on the final word. Some women did not survive Rhuidean.

Aviendha met Amys' eyes, and nodded. Amys had been a second mother to her in many ways. She was rewarded by a rare smile. Then Amys turned her back to Aviendha, just as the other two had.

Aviendha took another deep breath, glancing back across the trampled grass before the manor house to where Rand spoke with the quartermasters, his expression stern, the arm missing a hand held folded behind his back, the other arm gesturing animatedly. She smiled at him, though he wasn't looking in her direction.

I will be back for you, she thought.

Then she trotted to the Traveling ground, collected the pack and wove a gateway that would deposit her a safe distance from Cold Rocks Hold, beside a rock formation known as the Maiden's Spear, from which she could run to the hold and prepare herself. The gateway opened to the familiar, dry air of the Waste.

She ducked through the gateway, exulting—finally—in what had just happened.

Her honor had returned.

"I came out through a small watergate, Aes Sedai," Shemerin said, bowing her head before the others in the tent. "In truth, it wasn't so difficult, once I left the Tower and got into the city. I didn't dare leave by one of the bridges. I couldn't let the Amyrlin know what I was doing."

Romanda watched, arms folded. Her tent was lit by two brass lamps, flames dancing at the tips. Six women listened to the runaway's story. Lelaine was there, for all that Romanda had tried to keep her from hearing about the meeting. Romanda had hoped that the slender Blue would be too busy basking in her status in camp to bother with such a seemingly trivial event.

Beside her was Siuan. The former Amyrlin had latched herself on to Lelaine with the strength of a barnacle. Romanda was well enough pleased with the newfound ability to Heal a stilling—she *was* Yellow after all—but a part of her wished it hadn't happened to Siuan. As if Lelaine weren't bad enough to deal with. Romanda had not forgotten Siuan's crafty nature, even if so many others in camp seemed to have done so. Lesser strength in the Power did not mean decreased capacity for scheming.

Sheriam was there, of course. The red-haired Keeper sat beside Lelaine. Sheriam had been withdrawn lately, and barely maintained the dignity of an Aes Sedai. Foolish woman. She needed to be removed from her place; everyone could see that. If Egwene ever returned—and Romanda prayed that she did, if only because it would upset Lelaine's plans—then there would be an opportunity. A new Keeper.

The other person in the tent was Magla. Romanda and Lelaine had argued—with control, of course—over who would be first to interrogate Shemerin. They'd decided that the only fair way was to do it together. Because Shemerin was Yellow, Romanda had been able to call the meeting in her own tent. It had been a shock when Lelaine had shown up with not just Siuan but Sheriam in tow. But they'd never said how many attendants they could bring. And so Romanda was left with only Magla. The thick-shouldered woman sat beside Romanda, listening quietly to the confession. Should Romanda have sent for someone else? It would have looked very obvious, delaying the meeting for that.

It wasn't really an interrogation, however. Shemerin spoke freely, without resisting questions. She sat on a small stool before them. She'd refused a cushion for it. Romanda had rarely seen a woman as determined to punish herself as this poor child.

Not a child, Romanda thought. *A full Aes Sedai, whatever she says. Burn you, Elaida, for turning one of* us *into this!*

Shemerin had been Yellow. Burn it, she *was* Yellow. She'd been talking to them for the better part of an hour now, answering questions about the status of the White Tower. Siuan had been the first to ask how the woman had come to escape.

"Please forgive me for seeking work in the camp without coming to you, Aes Sedai," Shemerin said, head bowed. "But I have fled the Tower against the law. As an Accepted leaving without permission, I am a runaway. I knew I would be punished if discovered.

"I have stayed in this area because it is so familiar, and I cannot let it go. When your army came, I saw a chance for work, and I took it. But please, do not force me to go back. I will not be a danger. I will seek a life as a normal woman, careful not to use my abilities."

"You are Aes Sedai," Romanda said, trying to keep the edge out of her voice. This woman's attitude lent much credence to the things Egwene said about Elaida's power-hungry reign in the Tower. "No matter what Elaida says."

"I. . . ." Shemerin just shook her head. Light! She never

had been the most poised of Aes Sedai, but it was shocking to see her fallen so far.

"Tell me about this watergate," Siuan said, leaning forward in her chair. "Where could we find it?"

"On the southwestern side of the city, Aes Sedai," Shemerin said. "About five minutes' walk eastward from where the ancient statues of Eleyan al'Landerin and her Warders stand." She hesitated, suddenly seeming anxious. "But it is a small gate. You couldn't take an army through it. I only know of it because I had the duty of caring for the beggars who live there."

"I want a map anyway," Siuan said, then she glanced at Lelaine. "At least, I think we should have one."

"It is a wise idea," Lelaine said in a nauseatingly magnanimous tone.

"I do want to know more of your . . . situation," Magla said. "How is it Elaida could *think* that demoting a sister was wise? Egwene did speak of this event, and I did find it incredible then, too. What was Elaida's thought?"

"I . . . cannot speak for the Amyrlin's thought," Shemerin said. She cringed as the women in the room gave her a set of not-so-subtle glares at calling Elaida the Amyrlin. Romanda didn't join in. Something small was creeping beneath the canvas floor of the tent, moving from one corner toward the center of the room. Light! Was that a mouse? No, it was too small. Perhaps a cricket. She shifted uncomfortably.

"But surely you did do something to earn her ire," Magla said. "Something worthy of such treatment?"

"I. . . ." Shemerin said. She kept glancing at Siuan for some reason.

Fool woman. Romanda almost thought Elaida had made the right move. Shemerin should never have been given the shawl. Of course, demoting her to Accepted was no way to handle the situation either. The Amyrlin couldn't be given that much power.

Yes, that was definitely something under the canvas, determinedly pushing its way to the center of the tent, a tiny lump moving in jerks and starts.

"I was weak before her," Shemerin finally said. "We were speaking of . . . events in the world. I could not stomach them. I did not show poise befitting an Aes Sedai."

"That's it?" Lelaine asked. "You didn't plot against her? You didn't contradict her?"

Shemerin shook her head. "I was loyal."

"I find that hard to believe," Lelaine said.

"I believe her," Siuan said dryly. "Shemerin showed well enough she was in Elaida's pocket on several occasions."

"This do be a dangerous precedent," Magla noted. "Burn my soul, but it do."

"Yes," Romanda agreed, watching the canvas-covered whatever-it-was inch along before her. "I suspect she used poor Shemerin as an example, acclimating the White Tower to the concept of demotion. That will let her use it on those who are actually her enemies."

The conversation hit a lull. The Sitters who supported Egwene would likely head the list of those to be demoted, if Elaida retained her power and the Aes Sedai reconciled.

"Is that a mouse?" Siuan asked, looking down.

"It's too small," Romanda said. "And it's not important."

"Small?" Lelaine said, leaning down.

Romanda frowned, glancing at the spot again. It *did* seem to have grown larger. In fact—

The bump jerked suddenly, pushing upward. The canvas floor split, and a thick-bodied cockroach—as wide as a fig—scrambled through. Romanda pulled back in revulsion.

The roach skittered across the canvas, antennae twitching. Siuan took off her shoe to swat it. But the bottom of the tent bubbled up near the rip, and a second cockroach climbed through. Then a third. And then a wave of them, pouring through the split like too-hot tea sprayed from a mouth. A black and brown carpet of scrambling, scratching, scurrying creatures, pushing over one another in their hurry to get out.

The women screeched in revulsion, throwing back stools and chairs as they stood. Warders were in the room a moment later; broad-shouldered Rorik bonded to Magla, and that coppery-skinned stone of a man was Burin Shaeren, bonded to Lelaine. They had swords drawn at the screams, but the cockroaches seemed to stump them. They stood, staring at the stream of filthy insects.

Sheriam hopped up on her chair. Siuan channeled and began to squash the creatures closest to her. Romanda hated to use the One Power for death, even on such vile creatures, but she too found herself channeling Air and smashing the insects in swaths, but the creatures were pouring in too quickly. Soon the ground was swarming with them, and the Aes Sedai were forced to scramble out of the tent and into the quiet darkness of the camp. Rorik pulled the flaps shut, though that wouldn't stop the insects from squeezing out.

Outside, Romanda couldn't stop herself from running her fingers through her hair, just in case, to make certain none of the creatures had gotten into it. She shivered as she imagined the creatures scrambling over her body.

"Is there anything in the tent that is dear to you?" Lelaine asked, looking back at the tent. Through the lamplight, she could see the shadowy insects scurrying up the walls.

Romanda spared a thought for her journal, but knew that she'd never be able to touch those pages after her tent had been infested this way. "Nothing that I'd care to keep now," she said, weaving Fire. "And nothing I can't replace."

The others joined her, and the tent burst into flames, Rorik jumping back as they channeled. Romanda thought she heard the insects popping and sizzling inside. The Aes Sedai moved back from the sudden heat. In moments, the entire tent was an inferno. Women rushed out of nearby tents to look.

"I do no think that was natural," Magla said softly. "Those did be four-spine roaches. Sailors do see them on ships that visit Shara."

"Well, it isn't the worst we've seen from the Dark One," Siuan said, folding her arms. "And we'll see worse yet, mark my words." She eyed Shemerin. "Come, I want that map from you."

They left with Rorik and the others, who would alert the camp that the Dark One had touched it this night. Romanda stood watching the tent burn. Soon it was only smoldering coals.

Light, she thought. *Egwene is right. It* is *coming. Fast.* And the girl was imprisoned now; she'd met with the Hall the night before in the World of Dreams, informing them of her disastrous dinner with Elaida and the aftermath of insulting the false Amyrlin. And yet Egwene still refused rescue.

Torches were lit and Warders roused as a precaution

against more evil. She smelled smoke. That was the remains of all she had owned in the world.

The Tower needed to be whole. Whatever it took. Would she be willing to bow before Elaida to make that happen? Would she put on an Accepted dress again if it would bring unity for the Last Battle?

She couldn't decide. And that disturbed her nearly as much as those scuttling roaches had.

CHAPTER
27

The Tipsy Gelding

M at didn't escape the camp without the Aes Sedai, of course. Bloody women.

He rode down the ancient stone roadway, no longer followed by the Band. He was, however, accompanied by the three Aes Sedai, two Warders, five soldiers, Talmanes, a pack animal and Thom. At least Aludra, Amathera and Egeanin hadn't insisted on coming. This group was too big as it was.

The three-needle pines guarded the road, smelling of pine sap, and the air was melodic with mountain finches' calls. It was still several hours until sundown; he'd halted the Band near noon. He rode slightly ahead of the clustered Aes Sedai and Warders. After he'd refused Joline horses and funds, they hadn't been *about* to let him win another point. Not when they could force him to take them down to the village, where they could spend at least one night in an inn with soft beds and warm baths.

He didn't argue too loudly. He hated to have more tongues wagging about the Band, and women *did* gossip, even Aes Sedai. But there was little chance of the Band passing without causing a stir in the village anyway. If any Seanchan patrols made it through these twisting mountain paths. . . . Well, Mat would just have to keep the Band on a steady pace northward and that was that. No use crying about it.

Besides, he was beginning to feel right again, riding Pips down that road, spring breeze crisp in the air. He'd taken to wearing one of his older coats, red with brown trim, unbuttoned to show his old tan shirt beneath.

This was what it was about. Traveling to new villages,

throwing dice in the inns, pinching a few barmaids. He would *not* think of Tuon. Flaming Seanchan. She'd be all right, wouldn't she?

No. His hands almost itched to be at the dicing. It had been far too long since he'd sat down in a corner somewhere and thrown with the ordinary sort. They'd be a little dirtier of face and coarser of language, but as good of heart as any man. Better than most lords.

Talmanes rode just ahead. He'd probably wish for a nicer tavern than Mat, a place to join a game of cards rather than throwing dice. But they might not have much of a choice. The village was of decent size, probably worthy of being called a town, but was unlikely to have more than three or four inns. Their choices would be limited.

Decent size, Mat thought, grinning to himself as he took off his hat and scratched at the back of his head. Hinderstap would *only* have three or four inns, and that made it a "small" town. Why, Mat could remember when he'd thought Baerlon a large city, and it probably wasn't much larger than this Hinderstap!

A horse pulled up beside him. Thom was looking at that blasted letter again. The lanky gleeman's face was thoughtful, his white hair stirring in the breeze, as he stared down at the words. As if he hadn't read them a thousand times already.

"Why don't you put that away?" Mat said. Thom looked up. It had taken some talking to get the gleeman to come down to the village, but Thom needed it, needed some distraction.

"I mean it, Thom," Mat said. "I know you're eager to go for Moiraine. But it'll be weeks before we can break away, and reading over those words won't do anything but make you anxious."

Thom nodded and folded the paper with reverent fingers. "You're right, Mat. But I'd been carrying this letter for months. Now that I've shared it, I feel. . . . Well, I just want to be on with it."

"I know," Mat said, looking up toward the horizon. Moiraine. The Tower of Ghenjei. Mat almost felt as if he could see the building out there, looming. That's where his path pointed, and Caemlyn was just a stepping-stone along the way. If Moiraine was still alive . . . Light, what would that mean? How would Rand react?

The rescue was another reason Mat felt he needed a good night dicing. Why had he agreed to go with Thom into the tower? Those burning snakes and foxes—he had no desire to see *them* again.

But . . . he also couldn't let Thom go alone. There was an inevitability to it. As if a part of Mat had known all along that he had to go back and face those creatures again. They'd gotten the better of him twice now, and the Eelfinn had tied strings around his brain with those memories in his head. He had a debt to settle with them, that was for certain.

Mat had little love for Moiraine, but he wouldn't leave her to them, no matter that she was Aes Sedai. Bloody ashes. He'd probably be tempted to ride in and save one of the Forsaken themselves if they were trapped there.

And . . . maybe one was. Lanfear had fallen through that same portal. Burn him, what would he do if he found her there? Would he really rescue her as well?

You're a fool, Matrim Cauthon. Not a hero. Just a fool.

"We'll get to Moiraine, Thom," Mat said. "You have my word, burn me. We'll find her. But we have to see the Band someplace safe, and we *need* information. Bayle Domon says he knows where the tower is, but I won't be comfortable until we can go to some large city and sniff for rumors and stories about this tower. Someone has to know something. Besides, we'll need supplies, and I doubt we'll find what we need in these mountain villages. We need to reach Caemlyn if possible, though maybe we'll stop at Four Kings on the way."

Thom nodded, though Mat could see he chafed at leaving Moiraine trapped, being tortured or who knows what. Thom's brilliant blue eyes got a far-off look to them. Why did he care so much? What was Moiraine to him but another Aes Sedai, one of those who had cost the life of Thom's nephew?

"Burn it," Mat said. "We're not supposed to be thinking about things like this, Thom! We're going to have a good night of dice and laughter. There'll probably be some time for a song or two as well."

Thom nodded, face growing lighter. He had his harp case strapped to the back of his horse; it would be good to see him open it again. "You plan to try juggling for your supper again, apprentice?" Thom asked, eyes twinkling.

"Better than trying to play that blasted flute," Mat grumbled. "Never was very good at that. Rand took to it right fine, though, didn't he?"

Colors swirled in Mat's head, resolving to an image of Rand, sitting alone in a room by himself. He sat splay-legged in a richly embroidered shirt, a coat of black and red tossed aside and crumpled next to the log wall beside him. Rand had one hand to his forehead as if trying to squeeze away the pain of a headache. His other was . . .

That arm ended in a stump. The first time Mat had seen that—a few weeks back—it had shocked him. How had Rand lost the hand? The man barely seemed alive, propped up like that, unmoving. Though his lips did seem to be moving, mumbling or muttering. *Light!* Mat thought. *Burn you, what are you doing to yourself?*

Well, at least Mat wasn't near him. *Count your fortunes in that,* Mat told himself. Life hadn't been so easy lately, but he *could* have been stuck near Rand. Sure, Rand was a friend. But Mat didn't mean to be there when Rand went insane and killed everyone he knew. There was friendship, and then there was stupidity. They'd fight together at the Last Battle, of course, no helping that. Mat just hoped to be on the other side of that battlefield from any *saidin*-wielding madmen.

"Ah, Rand," Thom said. "That boy could have made a life for himself as a gleeman, I warrant. Maybe even a proper bard, if he'd started when he was younger."

Mat shook his head, dispelling the vision. *Burn you, Rand. Leave me alone.*

"Those were better days, weren't they, Mat?" Thom smiled. "The three of us, traveling down the river Arinelle."

"Myrddraal chasing us for reasons unknown," Mat added grimly. Those days hadn't been so easy either. "Dark-friends trying to stab us in the back every time we turned around."

"Better than *gholam* and Forsaken trying to kill us."

"That's like saying you're grateful to have a noose around your neck instead of a sword in your gut."

"At least you can escape the noose, Mat." Thom knuckled his long, white mustache. "Once the sword is stuck into you, there's not much you can do about it."

Mat hesitated, then found himself laughing. He rubbed

at the scarf around his neck. "I suppose you're right at that, Thom. I suppose you're right. Well, for today why don't we forget about all of that? We'll go back and pretend things are like they once were!"

"I don't know if that's possible, lad."

"Sure it is," Mat said stubbornly.

"Oh?" Thom asked, amused. "You're going to go back to thinking that old Thom Merrilin is the wisest, most well traveled man you've ever known? You'll play the gawking peasant again, clinging to my coat every time we pass a village with more than one inn in it?"

"Here now. I wasn't so bad as all that."

"I hasten to differ, Mat," Thom said, chuckling.

"I don't remember much." Mat scratched at his head again. "But I do recall that Rand and I did right well for ourselves after we split up with you. We made it to Caemlyn, at least. Brought your flaming harp back to you unharmed, didn't we?"

"I noticed a few nicks in the frame. . . ."

"Burn you, none of that!" Mat said, pointing at him. "Rand practically *slept* with that harp. Wouldn't *think* of selling it, even when we were so hungry we'd have gnawed on our own boots if we hadn't needed them to get to the next town." Those days were fuzzy to Mat, full of holes, like an iron bucket left too long to rust. But he had pieced together some things.

Thom chuckled. "We can't go back, Mat. The Wheel has turned, for better or worse. And it will keep on turning, as lights die and forests dim, storms call and skies break. Turn it will. The Wheel is not hope, and the Wheel does not care, the Wheel simply *is*. But so long as it turns, *folk* may hope, folk may care. For with light that fades, another will eventually grow, and each storm that rages must eventually die. As long as the Wheel turns. As long as it turns. . . ."

Mat guided Pips around a particularly deep cleft in the broken roadway. Ahead, Talmanes chatted with several of their guards. "That has the sound of a song about it, Thom."

"Aye," Thom said, almost with a sigh. "An old one, forgotten by most. I've discovered three versions of it, all with the same words, set to different tunes. I guess the area has me thinking of it; it's said that Doreille herself penned the original poem."

"The area?" Mat said with surprise, glancing at the three-needle pines.

Thom nodded, thoughtful. "This road is old, Mat. Ancient. Probably was here before the Breaking. Landmarks like this have a tendency to find their way into songs and stories. I think this area is what was once called the Splintered Hills. If that's true, then we're in what was once Coremanda, right near the Eagle's Reaches. I bet you if we climbed a few of those taller hills, we'd find old fortifications."

"And what does that have to do with Doreille?" Mat asked, uncomfortably. She'd been Queen of Aridhol.

"She visited here," Thom said. "Penned several of her finest poems in the Eagle's Reaches."

Burn me, Mat thought. *I remember.* He remembered standing on the walls of a high fort, cold on the mountaintop, looking down at a long, twisting roadway, broken and shattered, and an army of men with violet pennants charging up the hillside into a rain of arrows. The Splintered Hills. A woman on the balcony. The Queen herself.

He shivered, banishing the memory. Aridhol had been one of the ancient nations that had stood long ago, when Manetheren had been a power. The capital of Aridhol had another name. Shadar Logoth.

Mat hadn't felt the pull of the ruby dagger in a very long time. He was nearly beginning to forget what it had been like to be tied to it, if it was possible to forget such a thing. But sometimes he remembered that ruby, red like his own blood. And the old lust, the old desire, would seep into him again . . .

Mat shook his head, forcing down those memories. Burn it, he was supposed to be enjoying himself!

"What a time we've had," Thom said idly. "I feel old these days, Mat, like a faded rug, hung out to dry in the wind, hinting of the colors it once showed so vibrantly. Sometimes, I wonder if I'm any use to you anymore. You hardly seem to need me."

"What? Of course I need you, Thom!"

The aging gleeman eyed him. "The trouble with you, Mat, is that you're actually *good* at lying. Unlike those other two boys."

"I mean it! Burn me, but I do. I suppose you could run off and tell stories and travel like you used to. But things around here might run a lot less smoothly, and I sure would miss your wisdom. Burn me, but I would. A man needs friends he can trust, and I'd trust you with my life any day."

"Why Matrim," Thom said, looking up, eyes glimmering with mirth, "bolstering a man's spirits when he's down? Convincing him to stay and do what is important, rather than running off to seek adventure? That sounds downright *responsible*. What's gotten into you?"

Mat grimaced. "Marriage, I guess. Burn me, but I'm not going to stop drinking or gambling!" Ahead, Talmanes turned around and glanced at Mat, then rolled his eyes.

Thom laughed, watching Talmanes. "Well, lad, I didn't mean to get your spirits down. Just idle talk. I still have a few things I can show this world. If I really can free Moiraine . . . well, we'll see. Besides, somebody needs to be here to watch, then put this all to song, someday. There will be more than one ballad that comes from all of this."

He turned, rifling through his saddlebags. "Ah!" he said, pulling out his patchwork gleeman's cloak. He threw it on with a flourish.

"Well," Mat said, "when you write about us, you might find a few gold marks in it if you saw your way to include a nice verse about Talmanes. You know, something about how he has one eye that stares in strange directions, and how he often carries this scent about him which reminds one of a goat pen."

"I heard that!" Talmanes called from ahead.

"I meant you to!" Mat called back.

Thom just laughed, plucking at his cloak, arranging it for best display. "I can't promise anything." He chuckled some more. "Though, if you don't mind, Mat, I think I'll separate from the rest of you once we get into the village. A gleeman's ears may pick up information that won't be spoken in the presence of soldiers."

"Information would be nice," Mat said, rubbing his chin. The trail turned up ahead; Vanin said they'd find the village just beyond the turn. "I feel as though I've been traveling through a tunnel for months now, with no sight or sound of the outside world. Burn me, but it would be nice to know where Rand is, if only to know where *not* to go." The colors spun, showing him Rand—but the man was standing in a room with no view of the outside, giving Mat no clue as to where he might be.

"Life's that tunnel most times, I'm afraid," Thom said. "People expect a gleeman to bring information, so we pull it out and brush it off for display—but much of the 'news' we tell is just another batch of stories, in many cases less true than the ballads from a thousand years ago."

Mat nodded.

"And," Thom added, "I'll see if I can dig up hints for the incursion."

The Tower of Ghenjei. Mat shrugged. "We're more likely to find what we need in Four Kings or Caemlyn."

"Yes, I know. But Olver made me promise to check. If you hadn't set Noal to keeping the boy distracted, I'd expect to open our saddlebags and find him in there. He really wanted to come."

"A night dancing and gambling is no place for a boy," Mat muttered. "I just wish I could trust the men back at camp not to corrupt him worse than a tavern would."

"Well, he stayed back quietly enough once Noal got out the board." Olver was convinced that if he played Snakes and Foxes enough, he'd pick out some secret strategy for defeating the Aelfinn and Eelfinn. "The lad still thinks he's coming with us into the tower," Thom said more quietly. "He knows he can't be one of the three, but he plans to wait outside for us. Maybe burst in to save us if we don't come back soon enough. I don't want to be there when he discovers the truth."

"I don't intend to be there myself," Mat said. Ahead, the trees broke wide into a small valley with green pastures rising high along the hills to the sides. A town of several hundred buildings was nestled between the slopes, a mountain stream running down the middle. The houses were of a deep gray stone, each with a prominent chimney, most of which curled with smoke. The roofs were sloped to deal with what were probably very snowy winters, though the only white still visible now was on distant peaks. Workers were already busy on several of the roofs replacing winter-damaged shingles, and goats and sheep grazed the hillsides, watched over by shepherd boys.

There were a few hours of light remaining, and other men worked on shopfronts and fences. Others strolled through the streets of the village, no urgency in their gait. Overall, the little town had a relaxing air of mixed industry and laziness.

Mat pulled up beside Talmanes and the soldiers. "That's a nice sight," Talmanes noted. "I was beginning to think every town in the world was either falling apart, packed with refugees or under the thumb of invaders. At least this one doesn't seem likely to vanish on us . . ."

"Light send it so," Mat said, shivering, thinking of the town in Altara that had vanished. "Anyway, let's hope they don't mind dealing with a few strangers." He eyed the soldiers; all five were Redarms, among the best he had. "Three of you five, go with the Aes Sedai. I suspect that they'll want to stay at a different inn from myself. We'll meet up in the morning."

The soldiers saluted, and Joline sniffed as she passed on her horse, pointedly not looking at Mat. She and the others headed down the incline in a little cluster, three of Mat's soldiers following.

"That looks like an inn there," Thom said, pointing toward a larger building on the eastern side of the village. "You'll find me there." He waved, then kicked his mount into a trot and rode on ahead, gleeman's cloak streaming. Arriving first would give him the best chance at a dramatic entrance.

Mat glanced at Talmanes, who shrugged. The two of them made their way down the slope with two soldiers as an escort. Because of the bend in the road, they were approaching from the southwest. To the northeast of the village, the ancient roadway continued. It looked strange to have such a large road leading past a village like this, even if that road was old and broken. Master Roidelle claimed that it would lead them straight up into Andor. It was too uneven to be used as a major highway, and the direction it led no longer passed major cities, so it had been forgotten. Mat blessed their luck in finding it, though. The main passages into Murandy had been crowded with Seanchan.

According to Roidelle's maps, Hinderstap specialized in producing goat's cheese and mutton for the various towns and manor lands in the region. The villagers should be used to outsiders. Indeed, several boys came running from the fields the moment they spotted Thom and his gleeman's cloak. He'd make a stir, but a familiar one. The Aes Sedai, though, would be memorable.

Ah, well, he thought as he and Talmanes rode down the

grass-lined road. He would retain his good humor; this time, he would *not* let the Aes Sedai ruin it.

By the time Mat and Talmanes reached the village, Thom had already gathered a small crowd. He stood upright on his saddle and juggled three colored balls in his right hand while talking of his travels in the south. The villagers here wore vests and green cloaks of a deep, velvety cloth. They looked warm, though upon closer inspection, Mat noticed that many of them—cloaks, vests and trousers—had been torn, and carefully mended.

Another group of people, mostly women, had gathered around the Aes Sedai. Good; Mat had half-expected the villagers to be frightened. One of those standing at the side of Thom's group eyed Mat and Talmanes appraisingly. He was a sturdy fellow, with thick arms and linen sleeves that were rolled to the elbows despite the chill spring air. His arms curled with dark hair that matched his beard and the locks on his head.

"You have the look of a lord about you," the man said, approaching Mat.

"He's a pr—" Talmanes began before Mat cut him off hastily.

"I suppose I do at that," Mat said, keeping an eye on Talmanes.

"I'm Barlden, the mayor here," the man said, folding his arms. "You're welcome to come and trade. Be aware that we don't have much to spare."

"Surely you at least have some cheese," Talmanes said. "That's what you produce, isn't it?"

"All that hasn't molded or spoiled is needed for our custom," Mayor Barlden said. "That's just the way of things, these days." He hesitated. "But if you have cloth or clothing you'll trade, we might be able to scrape something up to feed you for the day."

Feed us for a day? Mat thought. *All thirteen of us?* He'd need to bring a wagonload back at least, not to mention the ale he'd promised his men.

"You still need to hear about the curfew. Trade, warm yourselves by the hearths for a time, but know that all outsiders *must* be out of the town by nightfall."

Mat glanced up at the cloud-covered sky. "But that's barely three hours away!"

"Those are our rules," Barlden said curtly.

"It's ridiculous," Joline said, turning away from the village women. She nudged her horse a little closer to Mat and Talmanes, her Warders—as always—shadowing her. "Master Barlden, we *cannot* agree to this foolish prohibition. I understand your hesitation during these dangerous times, but surely you can see that your rules should not apply here."

The man kept his arms folded and said nothing.

Joline pursed her lips, rearranging her hands on her reins so that her great serpent ring was prominently visible. "Does the symbol of the White Tower mean so little these days?"

"We respect the White Tower." Barlden looked at Mat. He *was* wise. Meeting the gaze of an Aes Sedai tended to make one's resolve weaken. "But our rules are strict, my Lady. I'm sorry."

Joline sniffed. "I suspect that your innkeepers are less than satisfied with this requirement. How are they to make ends meet if they can't rent rooms to travelers?"

"The inns are compensated," the mayor said gruffly. "Three hours. Do your business and be on your way. We mean to be friendly to all who pass our way, but we can't see our rules broken." With that, he turned and left. As he walked away, he was joined by a small group of burly men, several carrying axes. Not threateningly. Casually, as if they'd been out chopping wood, and just happened to be walking through town. Together. In the same direction as the mayor.

"I should say this is quite the welcome," Talmanes muttered.

Mat nodded. At that moment, the dice started rattling in his head. *Burn it!* He decided to ignore them. They were never any help anyway. "Let's go find a tavern," he said, heeling Pips forward.

"Still determined to make a night of it, eh?" Talmanes said, smiling as he joined Mat.

"We'll see," Mat said, listening to those dice despite himself. "We'll see."

Mat spotted three inns on his initial ride through the village. There was one at the end of the main thoroughfare, and it had two bright lanterns burning out front, even though night hadn't yet fallen. Those whitewashed walls and clean glass windows would draw the Aes Sedai like moths to a flame. That would be the inn for traveling merchants and dignitaries unfortunate enough to find themselves in these hills.

But outsiders couldn't stay the night now. How long had that prohibition been in place? How did these inns maintain themselves? They could still provide a bath and meal, but without renting rooms. . . .

Mat didn't buy the mayor's comment about inns being "compensated." If they weren't doing anything useful for the village, why pay them? It was just plain odd.

Anyway, Mat didn't head for the nice inn, nor the one Thom had chosen. That one wasn't on the main road, but was on a wide street just to the northeast. It would serve the average visitor, respectable men and women who didn't like to spend what they didn't have to. The building was well cared for; the beds would be clean, and the meals satisfactory. The locals would visit for drinks on occasion, mostly when they felt that their wives were keeping a close eye on them.

The last inn would have been the most difficult to find, had Mat not known where to look for it. It was three streets out from the center, in the back west corner of the village. No sign hung out front; just a wooden board carved with what looked like a drunken horse that sat inside one of the windows. None of those windows had glass.

Light and laughter came from inside. Most outsiders would have been made uncomfortable by the lack of an inviting sign and street lanterns near this inn. It was really more of a tavern than an inn; Mat doubted if it had ever held anything other than a few pallets in the back that one could rent for a copper. This was the place for working locals to relax. With evening approaching, many would have already made their way here. It was a place for community and for relaxation, a place for smoking a pinch of tabac with your friends. And for throwing a few games of dice.

Mat smiled and dismounted, then hitched Pips to the post outside.

Talmanes sighed. "You realize that they probably water their drinks."

"Then we'll have to order twice as many," Mat said, undoing a few bags of coins from his saddle and stuffing them in pockets inside his coat. He gestured for his soldiers to stay and guard the horses. The pack animal carried a coin chest. It contained Mat's personal stash: he wouldn't risk the Band's wages on gambling.

"All right, then," Talmanes said. "But you realize that I'm going to make *certain* that you and I go to a proper tavern once we reach Four Kings. I'll have you educated yet, Mat. You're a prince now. You'll need—"

Mat held up a hand, cutting Talmanes off. Then he pointed at the post. Talmanes sighed again and slid free of the saddle, then hitched his horse. Mat stepped up to the tavern door, took a deep breath, and entered.

Men crowded around tables, their cloaks draped over chairs or hung on pegs, their ripped and resewn vests unbuttoned, their sleeves rolled up. Why *did* people here wear clothing that was once so nice, yet now torn and patched? They had plenty of sheep, and should therefore have wool to spare.

Mat ignored the oddity for the moment. The men in this place played at dice, drank mugs of ale off of sticky tables, and slapped at the backsides of passing barmaids. They seemed exhausted, many of their eyes drooping with fatigue. But that was to be expected after a day's work. Despite the tired eyes, there was an almost palpable chatter in the room, voices overlapping one another in low, rumbling murmurs. A few people looked up as Mat entered, and some of them frowned at his nice clothing, but most people paid him no heed.

Talmanes followed reluctantly, but he wasn't the type of nobleman who minded rubbing shoulders with those of lower station. He'd visited his share of seedy taverns in his time, even if he had taken to complaining about Mat's choices. And so Talmanes was as quick as Mat to pull a chair up to a table where a few men already sat. Mat smiled broadly and flashed gold, tossing it to the passing barmaid and demanding some drinks. *That* got some attention, both from those around the table and from Talmanes.

"What are you doing," Talmanes hissed, leaning toward Mat. "You want to see us slit open the moment we stumble out of here?"

Mat just smiled. One of the nearby tables had a dice game going. Looked like Cat's Paw—or, at least, that's what it had been called the night Mat had first been taught it. They called it Third Gem in Ebou Dar, and he'd heard it called Feathers Aloft in Cairhien. It was the perfect game for his purposes. There was only one dicer in the game, with the crowd of onlookers betting against or for his tosses.

Mat took a deep breath, then pulled his chair over to the table, snapping a gold crown onto the wood directly in the center of a wet ring of ale made by the bottom of a mug, now held by a short fellow who'd lost most of his mousy hair, but what he did have hung long down around his collar. He almost choked on his ale.

"Care if I make a throw?" Mat said to the table's occupants.

"I . . . don't know if we can match that," said a man with a short black beard. "M'lord," he added belatedly.

"My gold against your silver," Mat said lightly. "I haven't had a good game of dice in ages."

Talmanes pulled his chair over, interested. He'd seen Mat do this before, putting down gold coins and winning silvers. Mat's luck made up for the difference, and he always came out far ahead. Sometimes he could come out ahead playing gold for coppers. That didn't make him much money. It only took so long before the men involved either ran out of coin or decided to stop playing. And Mat would be left with a handful of silvers and nobody to dice with.

That wouldn't help. The army had plenty of coin. It needed food, and so it was time to try something different. Several of the men set down silver coins. Mat shook the dice in his hands, then tossed. Blessedly, the dice came up with one showing a single pip and the other showing two. An instant loss.

Talmanes blinked, and the men around the table glanced at Mat, looking chagrined—as if embarrassed to have bet against a lord who obviously wasn't expecting to lose. That was an easy way to get oneself in trouble.

"Well, look at that," Mat said. "Guess you win. It's yours." He rolled the gold crown to the center of the table, to be split among the men who had bet against him, as per the rules.

"How about another?" Mat said, slapping down two gold crowns. There were more takers this time. Again, he threw and lost, nearly sending Talmanes into a choking fit. Mat had lost throws before—it happened, even to him. But two throws in a row?

He sent the two crowns rolling, and then he pulled out four. Talmanes placed a hand on his arm. "No offense, Mat," the man said in a quiet voice. "But maybe you should stop. Everyone has an off night. Let's finish our drinks and go buy what supplies we can before night falls."

Mat just smiled and watched as the bets piled up against his four coins. He had to lay down a fifth, since so many people wanted in on the toss. He ignored Talmanes and threw, losing yet again. Talmanes groaned, then reached over and took a mug from the serving girl, who had finally arrived to fill Mat's order.

"Don't look so grim," Mat said softly, hefting the pouch in his hand as he reached for his own mug. "This is what I wanted."

Talmanes raised an eyebrow, lowering his mug.

Mat said, "I can lose when I want to, if it's for the best."

"How can losing be for the best?" Talmanes asked, watching the men argue about how to divide Mat's gold.

"Wait." Mat took a slurp of ale. It was as watered-down as Talmanes had feared. Mat turned back to the table, counting out a few more gold coins.

As the time passed, more and more people began gathering around the table. Mat made sure to win a few tosses—just as he had to lose a bit when spending a night winning, he didn't want to arouse any suspicions about his losing streak. Yet bit by bit, the coins in his pouches ended up in the hands of the men playing against him. Before long, all was silent in the tavern, men crowding around Mat and waiting their turn to bet against him. Sons and friends had run to grab their fathers and cousins, dragging them to The Tipsy Gelding—as the inn was called.

At one point—during a break in the throws while Mat was waiting for another mug of ale—Talmanes pulled him aside. "I don't like this, Mat," the wiry man said in a low voice, leaning in. Sweat had long since streaked the powder on his shaved forehead, and he'd wiped it away, leaving the skin bare.

"I told you." Mat took a swig of watery ale. "I know what I'm doing." Men cheered to the side as one of them drank three mugs, one after another. The air smelt of sweat and muddy ale, spilled to the wood floor then trampled by the boots of those arriving from the pastures.

"Not that," Talmanes said, glancing at the cheering men. "You can waste your coin if you want, so long as you spare a few coins to buy me a drink now and then. That's not what's bothering me, not anymore."

Mat frowned. "What?"

"Something feels wrong about these folk, Mat." Talmanes spoke very softly, glancing over his shoulder. "While you've been playing, I've been talking to them. They don't care about the world. The Dragon Reborn, the Seanchan, nothing. Not a care."

"So?" Mat said. "They're simple folk."

"Simple folk should worry even *more*," Talmanes said. "They're trapped here between gathering armies. But these just shrug when I talk, then drink some more. It's as if they're . . . they're *too* focused on their revelry. As if it's all that matters to them."

"Then they're perfect," Mat said.

"It'll be dark soon," Talmanes said, glancing at the window. "We've used an hour, probably more. Maybe we should—"

At that moment, the door of the inn slammed open and the burly mayor entered, accompanied by the men who had joined him earlier, although they'd left their axes behind. They didn't look pleased to find half the village inside the tavern gambling with Mat.

"Mat," Talmanes began again.

Mat raised a hand, cutting him off. "This is what we've been waiting for."

"It is?" Talmanes asked.

Mat turned back to the dicing table, smiling. He'd gone through most of his bags of coins, but he had enough for a few more throws—not counting what he'd brought along outside, of course. He picked up the dice and counted out some gold crowns, and the crowd began to throw down coins of their own—many of which, by now, were gold ones they'd won from Mat.

He tossed and lost, causing a roar of excitement from those watching. Barlden looked as if he wanted to toss Mat out—it *was* getting late, and sunset couldn't be far off—but the man hesitated when he saw Mat pull out another handful of gold coins. Greed nibbled every man, and strict "rules" could be bent if opportunity walked past and winked suggestively enough.

Mat tossed again, and lost. More roars. The mayor folded his arms.

Mat reached into his pouch and found nothing but air. The men around him looked crestfallen, and one called for a round of drinks to "help the poor young lord forget about his luck."

Not bloody likely, Mat thought, covering a smile. He stood up, raising his hands. "I see it's getting late," he said to the room.

"Too late," Barlden interjected, pushing past a few smelly goatherds with fur-collared cloaks. "You should be going, outlander. Don't be thinking I'll make these men give back what you lost to them fairly, either."

"I wouldn't dream of it," Mat said, slurring his words just a tad. "Harnan and Delarn!" he bellowed. "Bring in the chest!"

The two soldiers from outside hurried in a moment later, bearing the small wooden chest from the packhorse. The tavern grew silent as the soldier carried it over to the table and set it down. Mat fished out the key, wobbling slightly, then unlocked the lid and revealed the contents.

Gold. A lot of it. Practically all he had left of his personal coin. "There's time for one more throw," Mat said to a stunned room. "Any takers?"

Men began to toss down coins until the pile contained most of what Mat had lost. It wasn't nearly enough to match what was in his chest. He looked it over, tapping his chin. "That's not going to be enough, friends. I'll take a bad bet, but if I've only got one more throw tonight, I want a chance of walking out of here with something."

"It's all we've got," one of the men said, amid a few calls for Mat to go ahead and toss anyway.

Mat sighed, then closed the lid to the chest. "No," he said. Even Barlden was watching with a gleam in his eyes. "Unless." Mat paused. "I came here for supplies. I guess I'd take barter. You can keep the coins you won, but I'll bet this chest for supplies. Foodstuffs for my men, a few casks of ale. A cart to carry it on."

"There isn't enough time." Barlden glanced at the darkening windows.

"Surely there is," Mat said, leaning forward. "I'll leave after this toss. You have my word on it."

"We don't bend rules here," the mayor said. "The price is too high."

Mat expected calls from the betting men, challenging the mayor, begging him to make an exception. But there were none. Mat felt a sudden spike of fear. After all of that losing . . . if they kicked him out anyway. . . .

Desperate, he pulled open the top of the chest again, revealing the gold coins inside.

"I'll give you the ale," the innkeeper said suddenly. "And Mardry, you've got a wagon and team. It's only a street down."

"Yes," said Mardry, a bluff-faced man with short dark hair. "I'll bet that."

Men began to call that they could offer food—grain from their pantries, potatoes from their cellars. Mat looked to the mayor. "There's still got to be what, half an hour until nightfall? Why don't we see what they can gather? The village store can have a piece of this too, if I lose. I'll bet you could use the extra coin, what with the winter we had."

Barlden hesitated, then nodded, still watching the chest of coins. Men whooped and ran about, fetching the wagon, rolling out the ale. More than a few galloped off for their homes or the village store. Mat watched them go, waiting in the quickly emptying tavern room.

"I see what you're doing," the mayor said to Mat. He didn't seem to be in a rush to gather anything.

Mat turned toward him, questioningly.

"I won't have you cheating us with a miracle win at the end of the evening." Barlden folded his arms. "You'll use my dice. And you'll move nice and slow as you toss. I know you lost many games here as the men report, but I suspect that if we search you, we'll find a couple of sets of dice hidden on your person."

"You're welcome to give me a search," Mat said, raising his arms to the side.

Barlden hesitated. "You will have thrown them away, of course," he finally said. "It's a fine scheme, dressing like a lord, loading dice so they make you lose instead of win. Never heard of a man bold enough to throw away gold like that on fake dice."

"If you're so certain that I'm cheating," Mat said, "then why go through with this?"

"Because I know how to stop you," the mayor replied. "Like I said, you'll use my dice on this throw." He hesitated, then smiled, grabbing a pair of dice off the table that Mat had been using. He tossed them. They came up a one and a two. He tossed them again, and got the same result.

"Better yet." The mayor smiled deeply. "You'll use these. In fact . . . I'll make the throw for you." Barlden's face in the dim light took on a decidedly sinister cast.

Mat felt a stab of panic.

Talmanes took his arm. "All right, Mat," he said. "I think we should go."

Mat held up a hand. Would his luck work if someone else threw? Sometimes it worked to prevent him from being wounded in combat. He was sure of that. Wasn't he?

"Go ahead," he said to Barlden.

The man looked shocked.

"You can make the throw," Mat said. "But it counts the same as if I'd tossed. A winning toss, and I walk away with everything. A losing toss, and I'll be on my way with my hat and my horse, and you can keep the bloody chest. Agreed?"

"Agreed."

Mat stuck out his hand for a shake, but the mayor turned away, holding the dice in his hand. "No," he said. "You'll get no chance to swap these dice, traveler. Let's just go out front and wait. And you keep your distance."

They did as he said, leaving the muggy, ale-soaked stench of the tavern for the clear street outside. Mat's soldiers brought the chest. Barlden demanded that the chest remain open so that it couldn't be switched. One of his thugs poked around inside it, biting the coins, making certain that it really was full and that the coins were authentic. Mat waited, leaning against the door as a wagon rolled up, and men from inside the tavern began rolling casks of ale onto its bed.

The sun was barely a haze of light on the horizon, behind those blasted clouds. As Mat waited, he saw the mayor grow more and more anxious. Blood and bloody ashes, the man was a stickler for his rules! Well, Mat would show him, and all of them. He'd show them. . . .

Show them what? That he couldn't be beaten? What did that prove? As Mat waited, the cart piled higher and higher with foodstuffs, and he began to feel a strange sense of guilt.

I'm not doing anything wrong, he thought. *I've got to feed my men, don't I? These men are betting fair, and I'm betting fair. No loaded dice. No cheating.*

Except his luck. Well, his luck was his own—just as every man's luck was his own. Some men were born with a talent for music, and they became bards and gleemen. Who begrudged them earning coin with what the Creator gave them? Mat had luck, and so he used it. There was nothing wrong with that.

Still, as the men came back into the inn, he started to see what it was that Talmanes had noticed. There was an edge of desperation to these men. *Had* they been too eager to gamble? *Had* they been foolhardy with their betting? What *was* that look in their eyes, a look that Mat had mistaken for weariness? Had they been drinking to celebrate the end of the day, or had they been drinking to banish that haunted cast in their eyes?

"Maybe you were right," Mat said to Talmanes, who was watching the sun with almost as much anxiety as the mayor. Its last light was dusting the tops of the peaked homes, coloring the tan tile a deeper orange. The sunset was a blaze behind the clouds.

"We can go, then?" Talmanes asked.

"No," Mat said. "We're staying."

And the dice stopped rattling in his head. It was so sudden, the silence so unexpected, that he froze. It was enough to make him think he'd made the wrong decision.

"Burn me, we're staying," he repeated. "I've never backed down from a bet before, and I don't plan to now."

A group of riders returned, bearing sacks of grain on their horses. It was amazing what a little coin could do for motivation. As more riders arrived, a young boy came trotting up the road. "Mayor," he said, tugging on Barlden's purple vest. That vest bore a crisscross of patched rips across the front. "Mother says that the outlander women aren't done bathing. She's trying to hurry them, but. . . ."

The mayor tensed. He glanced at Mat angrily.

Mat snorted. "Don't think I can do anything to hurry *that*

lot," he said. "If I were to go rush them, they'd likely dig in like mules and take twice as long. Let someone else bloody have a turn dealing with them."

Talmanes kept glancing at the lengthening shadows along the road. "Burn me," he muttered. "If those ghosts start appearing again, Mat. . . ."

"This is something else," Mat said as the newcomers threw their grain onto the wagon. "It *feels* different."

The wagon was already loaded high with foodstuffs; a good haul to have purchased from a village this size. It was just what the Band needed, enough to nudge them along, keep them fed until they reached the next town. That food wasn't worth the gold in the coffer, of course, but it was about equal to what he'd lost dicing inside, particularly with the wagon and horses thrown in. They were good draft animals, sturdy, well cared for from the look of coat and hoof.

Mat opened his mouth to say it was enough, then hesitated as he noticed that the mayor was talking quietly with a group of men. There were six of them, their vests drab and ragged, their black hair unkempt. One was gesturing toward Mat and holding what looked to be a sheet of paper in his hand. Barlden shook his head, but the man with the paper gestured more insistently.

"Here now," Mat said softly. "What's this?"

"Mat, the sun . . ." Talmanes said.

The mayor pointed sharply, and the ragged men sidled away. The men who had brought the food were crowding around the dimming street, keeping to the center of it. Most were looking toward the horizon.

"Mayor," Mat called. "That's good enough. Make the throw!"

Barlden hesitated, glancing at him, then looked down at the dice in his hand almost as if he'd forgotten them. The men around him nodded anxiously, and so he raised his hand in a fist, rattling the dice. The mayor looked across the street to meet Mat's eyes, then threw the dice onto the ground between them. They seemed too loud, a tiny rattling thunderstorm, like bones cracking against one another.

Mat held his breath. It had been a long while since he'd had reason to worry about a toss of the dice. He leaned down, watching the white cubes tumble against the dirt. How would his luck react to someone *else* throwing?

The dice came to a stop. A pair of fours. An outright winning throw. Mat released a long, relieved breath, though he felt a trickle of sweat down his temple.

"Mat . . ." Talmanes said softly, making him look up. The men standing on the road didn't look so pleased. Several of them cheered in excitement until their friends explained that a winning throw from the mayor meant that Mat would take the prize. The crowd grew tense. Mat met Barlden's eyes.

"Go," the burly man said, gesturing in disgust toward Mat and turning away. "Take your spoils and leave this place. Never return."

"Well," Mat said, relaxing. "Thank you kindly for the game, then. We—"

"GO!" the mayor bellowed. He looked at the last slivers of sunlight on the horizon, then cursed and began waving for the men to enter The Tipsy Gelding. Some lingered, glancing at Mat with shock or hostility, but the mayor's urgings soon bullied them into the low-roofed inn. He pulled the door shut and left Mat, Talmanes and the two soldiers standing alone on the street.

It suddenly seemed eerily quiet. There wasn't a villager on the street. Shouldn't there be some noise from inside the tavern, at least? Some clinking of mugs, some grumbling about the lost wager?

"Well," Mat said, voice echoing against silent housefronts, "I guess that's that." He walked over to Pips, calming the horse, who had begun to shuffle nervously. "Now, see, I told you, Talmanes. Nothing to be worried about at all."

And that's when the screaming began.

CHAPTER
28

Night in Hinderstap

B urn you, Mat!" Talmanes said, yanking his sword
free from the gut of a twitching villager. Talmanes
almost *never* swore. "Burn you twice over and once
again!"

"*Me?*" Mat snapped, spinning, his *ashandarei* flashing
as he neatly hamstrung two men in bright green vests. They
fell to the packed earthen street, eyes wide with rage as they
sputtered and growled. "Me? I'm not the one trying to kill
you, Talmanes. Blame *them*!"

Talmanes managed to pull himself into his saddle. "They
told us to leave!"

"Yes," Mat said, grabbing Pips' reins and pulling the
horse away from The Tipsy Gelding. "And *now* they're trying to kill us. I can't rightly be blamed for their unsociable
behavior!" Howls, screams, and yells rose from all across
the village. Some were angry, some were terrified, others
were agonized.

More and more men piled out of the tavern, each one
grunting and yelling, each one trying his best to kill every
person around him. Some of them came for Mat, Talmanes
or Mat's Redarms. But many just attacked their companions, hands ripping at skin, nails tearing gouges in faces.
They fought with a primal lack of skill, and only a few
thought to pick up rocks, mugs or lengths of wood as weapons.

This was far more than a simple bar fight. These men
were trying to kill each other. Already there were a half-
dozen corpses or near-corpses on the street, and from what

Mat could see of the inside of the inn, the fighting was equally brutal inside.

Mat tried to edge closer to the wagon with its load of food, Pips clopping alongside him. His chest of gold still lay on the street. The fighting men ignored both food and coin, concentrating on one another.

Talmanes, as well as Harnan and Delarn—his two soldiers—backed away with him, nervously pulling their own mounts. A group of raving men soon descended on the two villagers Mat had hamstrung, beating their heads against the ground over and over until they stopped moving. Then the pack looked up at Mat and his men, bloodlust clouding their eyes. It was an incongruous expression on the clean faces of men in neat vests and combed hair.

"Blood and bloody ashes," Mat said, swinging into his saddle. "Mount up!"

Harnan and Delarn needed no further instruction. They cursed, sheathing swords and swinging into saddles. The pack of villagers surged forward, but Mat and Talmanes cut off the attack. Mat tried to go for wounding blows only, but the villagers were deceptively strong and fast, and he found himself fighting just to keep them from pulling him out of the saddle. He cursed, reluctantly beginning to wield killing blows, taking two of the men with sweeps to the neck. Pips kicked out and knocked another to the ground with a hoof to the head. In a few moments, Harnan and Delarn joined the fight.

The villagers didn't back away. They kept fighting in a frenzy until the entire pack of eight had dropped. Mat's soldiers fought with wide-eyed terror, and Mat didn't blame them. It was flaming eerie, seeing common villagers react like this! There didn't seem to be an ounce of humanity left in them. They spoke only in grunts, hisses, and screams, their faces painted with anger and bloodlust. Now the other villagers—those not directly attacking Mat's men—started forming into packs, slaughtering the groups smaller than themselves by bludgeoning them, clawing them, biting them. It was unnerving.

As Mat watched, a body broke through one of the tavern window frames. The corpse rolled to the ground, neck broken. On the other side, Barlden stood with wild, nearly inhuman eyes. He screamed into the night, then saw Mat and—for just a moment—seemed to show a hint of recognition. Then it was gone, and the mayor bellowed again, running forward to leap through the broken window and attack a pair of men whose backs were turned.

"Move!" Mat said, rearing Pips as another pack of villagers saw him.

"The gold!" Talmanes said.

"Burn the gold!" Mat said. "We can win more, and that food isn't worth our lives. Go!"

Talmanes and the soldiers turned their mounts and galloped down the street, Mat kicking Pips to join them, leaving the gold and wagon behind. It *wasn't* worth their lives—if possible, he'd bring the army in on the morrow to recover it. But they had to survive first.

They galloped for a short time, and Mat slowed them at the next corner, holding up a hand. He glanced over his shoulder. The villagers were still coming, but the gallop had left them behind for now.

"I'm still blaming you," Talmanes said.

"I thought you *liked* fighting," Mat said.

"I like *some* fights," Talmanes said. "On the battlefield or a nice bar fight. This . . . this is insane." The pack of villagers behind had fallen to all fours and were moving in a strange lope. Talmanes shivered visibly.

There was barely enough light to see by. Now that the sun had set, those mountains and the gray clouds blocked what light remained. Lanterns lined many of the streets, but it didn't look as if anyone would be lighting them.

"Mat, they're gaining," Talmanes said, sword held at the ready.

"This isn't just about our wager," Mat said, listening to the screams and shouts. They came from all around the village. Down a side road, a couple of struggling bodies burst through the upper window of a house. They were women, clawing at each other as they fell, crashing to the ground with a sickening thud. They stopped moving.

"Come on," Mat said, turning Pips. "We've got to find Thom and the women." They galloped down a side street that would intersect with the main thoroughfare, passing packs of men and women fighting in the gutters. A fat man with bloodied cheeks stumbled into the road, and Mat reluctantly rode him down. There were too many people fighting at the sides for him to risk leading his men around the poor fool. Mat even saw *children* fighting, biting at the legs of those larger than they, throttling those their own age.

"The entire bloody town has gone insane," Mat muttered grimly as the four of them barreled onto the main street and turned toward the fine inn. They'd pick up the Aes Sedai, then swing out eastward for Thom, as his inn was the most distant.

Unfortunately, the main street was worse than the one Mat had left. It was almost completely dark now. Indeed, it seemed to him that the darkness had come *too* quickly here. Unnaturally swift. The road's length squirmed with shadows, figures battling, screeching, struggling in the deepening gloom. In that darkness, the fights looked at times to be solid, single creatures—horrific monstrosities with a dozen waving limbs and a hundred mouths to scream from the blackness.

Mat spurred Pips forward. There was nothing to do but charge down the middle of it.

"Light," Talmanes yelled as they galloped toward the inn. "Light!"

Mat gritted his teeth and leaned forward on Pips, spear held close to his side as he rode through the nightmare. Roars shook the darkness and bodies rolled across the street. Mat shivered at the horror of it, cursing under his breath. The night itself seemed to be trying to smother them, to strangle them, and to spawn beasts of blackness and murder.

Pips and the other horses were well trained, and the four of them charged straight down the street. Mat narrowly avoided being pulled from the saddle as dark forms leapt for his legs, trying to yank him free. They screamed and hissed, like legions of the drowned trying to pull him down into a deep, unearthly sea.

Beside Mat, Delarn's horse suddenly pulled to a halt, then, as a mass of black figures leaped in front of it, the gelding reared in panic, throwing Delarn from his saddle.

Mat reined in Pips, turning at the man's scream, which was somehow more distinct and more *human* than the howls around them.

"Mat!" Talmanes yelled, charging past. "Keep going! We can't stop!"

No, Mat thought, shoving down his panic. *No, I'm not leaving someone to this.* He took a deep breath and ignored Talmanes, kicking Pips back toward the black clot of bodies where Delarn had fallen. Sweat sprayed from his forehead, chilled by the wind of the gallop. Moans, screams, and hisses all around him seemed to descend on him.

Mat roared and threw himself from Pips' back—he couldn't bring his mount in without risking trampling the man he wanted to save. He hated fighting in darkness, he bloody *hated* it. He attacked those dark figures, whose faces he couldn't see save for an occasional flash of teeth or insane eyes reflecting the dying light. It reminded him, briefly, of another night, killing Shadowspawn in the dark. Save these figures he fought didn't have the grace of a Myrddraal. They didn't even have the coordination of Trollocs.

For a moment, it seemed Mat fought the shadows themselves—shadows made by sputtering firelight, random and uncoordinated, yet all the more deadly for his inability to anticipate them. He narrowly escaped getting his skull crushed by attacks that made no sense. During the day, those attacks would have been laughable, but from this darkened pack of men—and women—who didn't care what they hit or who they hurt, the attacks were overwhelming. Mat found himself fighting just to stay alive, spinning his *ashandarei* in wide arcs, using it to trip as often as he used it to kill. If something moved in the darkness, he struck. How in the light was he going to find Delarn in this!

A shadow moved just a short distance away, and Mat instantly recognized a sword-form. Rat Gnawing the Grain? A villager wouldn't know that. Good man!

Mat spun toward that shadow, slashing two other shadows across the chest, earning grunts and howls of pain. Delarn's figure fell beneath a pile of several others, and Mat bellowed in denial, leaping across a fallen body and landing with his spear descending in a broad sweep. Shadows bled where he struck, the blood just another patch of darkness, and Mat used the butt of his weapon to beat back another. He reached down, pulling one of the shadows to its feet, and heard a muttered curse. It was Delarn.

"Come on," Mat said, pulling the man toward Pips, who stood firm, snorting, in the darkness. The attacking men seemed to ignore animals, which was fortunate. Mat shoved the stumbling Delarn toward the horse, then turned and engaged the pack he'd known would chase after him. Again, Mat danced with the darkness, striking again and again, trying to disengage so that he could climb into the saddle. He risked a glance over his shoulder, and found that Delarn had managed to get onto Pips' back—but the soldier sat slumped, a huddled mound. How badly was he wounded? He barely seemed able to keep himself upright. Blood and bloody ashes!

Mat turned back to the attackers, spinning his spear, trying to force them back. But they didn't care about being wounded, they didn't care how dangerous Mat was. They just kept coming! Surrounding him. Coming at him from every side. Bloody ashes! He twisted just in time to see a dark shape rush him from behind.

Something flashed in the night, reflecting some very distant light. The dark figure behind Mat slumped to the ground. Another flash, and one of the ones in front of Mat fell. Suddenly, a figure on a white horse rushed past, and another knife flashed in the air, dropping a third man.

"Thom!" Mat called, recognizing the cloak.

"Get on your horse!" Thom's voice called back. "I'm running out of knives!"

Mat swept out with his spear, dropping two more villagers, then dashed forward and leaped into his saddle, trusting Thom to cover his retreat. Indeed, he heard a few cries of pain from behind. A moment later, a thundering sound on the road announced the imminent approach of horses. Mat pulled himself into his saddle as the creatures tore through the black morass, scattering the villagers.

"Mat, you fool!" Talmanes shouted from one of the horses, barely visible as a silhouette against the night.

Mat smiled gratefully at Talmanes, turning Pips, and caught Delarn as the man almost slid free. The Redarm was alive, for he struggled weakly, but there was a slick wet patch at his side. Mat held the man in front of him, ignoring the reins in the darkness and controlling Pips with a quick twist of the knees. He didn't know horseback battle commands himself, but those blasted memories did, and so he'd trained Pips to obey.

Thom galloped past, and Mat turned Pips to follow, steadying Delarn with one hand and carrying his spear in the other. Talmanes and Harnan rode to either side of him, charging down the corridor of madness toward the inn at the end.

"Come on, man," Mat whispered to Delarn. "Hang on. The Aes Sedai are just ahead. They'll fix you up."

Delarn whispered something back.

Mat leaned forward. "What was that?"

". . . and toss the dice until we fly," Delarn whispered. "To dance with Jak o' the Shadows. . . ."

"Great," Mat muttered. There were lights ahead, and he could see they were coming from the inn. Perhaps they'd find one place in this flaming village where the people's brains hadn't turned inside out.

But no. Those bursts of light were familiar. Balls of fire, flashing in the upper-story windows of the inn.

"Well," Talmanes noted from his left, "looks like the Aes Sedai still live. That's something, at least."

Figures clustered around the front of the inn, fighting in the darkness, their forms periodically lit from above by the flashes in the windows.

"Round to the back," Thom suggested.

"Go," Mat said to them, charging past the fighting figures. Talmanes, Thom and Harnan followed close on Pips' hooves. Mat blessed his luck that they didn't hit a hole or rut in the ground as they crossed the softer earth coming around behind the inn. The horses could easily have tripped and broken a leg, throwing all of them into disaster.

The back of the inn was silent, and Mat reined in. Thom leaped from his horse, his agility defying his earlier complaints about his age. He took up position watching the side of the building to see that they weren't followed.

"Harnan!" Mat said, thrusting his spear toward the stables. "Get the women's horses out and ready them. Saddle them if you can, but be ready to go without those if we have to. Light willing, we won't have to ride far, just a mile or so to get out of the village and away from this insanity."

Harnan saluted in the darkness, then dismounted and dashed over to the stables. Mat waited long enough to determine that nobody was going to jump out at him from the darkness, then spoke to Delarn, still held in front of him. "You still conscious?"

Delarn nodded weakly. "Yes, Mat. But I've taken a gut wound. I. . . ."

"We'll get the Aes Sedai," Mat said. "All you need to do is sit right here. Stay in the saddle, all right?"

Delarn nodded again. Mat hesitated at the weakness in the man's motions, but Delarn took Pips' reins, and seemed determined. So Mat slid out of the saddle, holding his *ashandarei* at the ready.

"Mat," Delarn said from the saddle.

Mat turned back.

"Thank you. For coming back for me."

"I wasn't going to leave a man to that," Mat said, shivering. "Dying on the battlefield is one thing, but to die out there, in that darkness. . . . Well, I wasn't going to let it happen. Talmanes! See if you can find some light."

"Working on it," the Cairhienin said from beside the inn's back door. He had found a lantern hanging there. A few strikes of flint and steel later, and a small, soft glow lit the backyard of the inn. Talmanes quickly closed the shield, keeping the light mostly hidden.

Thom trotted back to them. "No one following, Mat," he said.

Mat nodded. By the lanternlight, he could see that Delarn was in bad shape. Not just the gut wound, but scrapes across the face, rips in his uniform, one eye swollen shut.

Mat whipped out a handkerchief and pressed it against the gut wound, standing beside Pips and reaching up to the man in the saddle. "Hold this tight. How'd the wound happen? They don't use weapons."

"One got my own sword away from me," Delarn said with a grunt. "He used it well enough once he had it."

Talmanes had opened the back door of the inn. He looked to Mat and nodded. The way inside was clear.

"We'll be back soon," Mat promised Delarn. Holding his *ashandarei* in a loose grip, he crossed the short distance to the door and nodded to Talmanes and Thom. The three of them ducked inside.

The door led to the kitchens. Mat scanned the dark room, and Talmanes nudged him, pointing at several lumps on the floor. The sliver of lantern light revealed a pair of kitchen boys, barely ten years old, dead on the ground, their necks twisted. Mat glanced away, steeling himself, and inched into the room. Light! Only lads, and now dead by this insanity.

Thom shook his head grimly, and the three of them crept forward. They found the cook in the next hallway, grunting as he beat on the head of what appeared to be the innkeeper. It was a man in a white apron, at least. He was already dead. The fat cook turned toward Mat and Talmanes the moment they entered the hallway, feral rage in his eyes. Mat reluctantly struck, silencing him before he could howl and bring more people against them.

"There's fighting on the stairs," Talmanes said, nodding forward.

"I'll bet there's a servants' stairwell," Thom noted. "This looks like a nice enough place for it."

Sure enough, by cutting through two hallways in the back, they found a narrow, rickety stairwell leading up into darkness. Mat took a deep breath, then started up the stairs, holding his *ashandarei* at the ready. The inn was only two stories high, and the flashes had been coming from the second floor, near the front.

They entered the second floor, pushing open the door to the acrid scent of burned flesh. The hallways here were of wood, the grain obscured by thick white paint. The floor lay under a deep chestnut carpet. Mat nodded to Talmanes and Thom, and—weapons at the ready—they burst out of the stairwell and into the hallway.

Immediately, a ball of fire whooshed in their direction. Mat cursed, throwing himself backward and into Talmanes, narrowly avoiding the fire. Thom flattened himself with a gleeman's agility, getting under the fire. Mat and Talmanes almost tumbled back down the stairs.

"Bloody ashes!" Mat yelled into the hallway. "What do you think you're doing?"

There was silence. Followed, finally, by Joline's voice. "Cauthon?" she called.

"Who do you bloody think it is!" he shouted back.

"I don't know!" she said. "You came around so quickly, weapons out. Are you *trying* to get killed?"

"We're *trying* to rescue you!" Mat yelled.

"Do we look like we need rescuing?" came the response.

"Well, you're still here, aren't you?" Mat called back.

That was met with silence.

"Oh, for Light's sake," Joline finally called back. "Will you come out here?"

"You're not going to throw another fireball at me, are you?" Mat muttered, stepping out into the hallway as Thom climbed to his feet, Talmanes following. He found the three Aes Sedai standing at the head of the wide, handsome stairs at the other end of the hallway. Teslyn and Edesina continued to throw fireballs down at unseen villagers below, their hair wet, their dresses disheveled as if they'd been donned hastily. Joline wore only an enveloping white dressing robe, her pretty face calm, her dark hair slick and wet and hanging down over the front of her right shoulder. The robe was parted slightly at the top, giving a hint of what hid inside. Talmanes whistled softly.

"She's not a woman, Talmanes," Mat whispered warningly. "She's an Aes Sedai. Don't think of her as a woman."

"I'm trying, Mat," Talmanes said. "But it's hard." He hesitated, then added, "Burn me."

"Be careful or she will," Mat said, tugging his hat down slightly in the front. "In fact, she nearly did that just a moment ago."

Talmanes sighed, and the three of them crossed the hallway to the women. Joline's two Warders and the three Redarms, who had their weapons out, stood just inside the bathing chamber. A dozen or so servants were tied up in the corner: a pair of young girls—probably bathing attendants—and several men in vests and trousers. Apparently Joline's dress had been cut to strips and used for bonds. The silk would work far better than wool towels. Near the top of the stairs, just below the Aes Sedai, Mat could barely make out a cluster of corpses that had fallen to swords, not fire.

Joline eyed Mat as he approached, a look implying that she considered all this to be *his* fault somehow. She folded her arms, closing up the top of the robe, though he wasn't sure if that was because of Talmanes' gawking or if the move was coincidental.

"We need to move," Mat told the women. "The whole city has gone mad."

"We can't go," Joline said. "Not and leave those servants to the mob. Besides, we need to find Master Tobrad and make certain he is safe."

"Master Tobrad is the innkeeper?" Mat asked. A fireball whooshed down the stairs.

"Yes," Joline said.

"Too late," Mat said. "His brains are already decorating the walls downstairs. Look, like I said, the *entire village* is crazy. Those servants tried to kill you, didn't they?"

Joline hesitated. "Yes."

"Leave them," Mat said. "We can't do anything for them."

"But if we wait until dawn . . ." Joline said hesitantly.

"And what?" Mat said. "Burn to ash every person who tries to climb those stairs? You're making a ruckus here, and it's drawing more and more people. You're going to have to kill them all to stop them."

Joline glanced at the other two women.

"Look," Mat said. "I have a wounded Redarm down below, and I intend to get him out of this alive. You can't do any good for these people here. I suspect the men had to kill that group at the top of the stairs before you all felt threatened enough to use the Power. You know how determined they are."

"All right," Joline said. "I'll come. But we're bringing the two serving girls. Blaeric and Fen can carry them."

Mat sighed—he'd have liked the Warders' blades free to help in case they ran into trouble—but said nothing more. He nodded to Talmanes and Thom, and waited impatiently as the Warders picked up the two bound serving girls and slung them over shoulders. After that, the whole group hustled back down the servants' stairwell, Talmanes leading and Mat and the Redarms at the rear. He could hear screams that sounded half angry, half joyous as the villagers at the base of the stairs realized no more fire would fall. There were thumps and shouts, followed by doors opening, and Mat cringed, imagining the other servants—left tied up in the bathing chamber—falling to the crowd.

Mat and the others burst out into the backyard of the inn, only to find Delarn on the ground beside Pips. Harnan knelt beside him, and the bearded soldier looked up with anxiety. "Mat!" he said. "He fell from the saddle. I—"

Edesina cut him off, rushing over and kneeling beside Delarn. She closed her eyes, and Mat felt a chill from his medallion. It made him shiver as he imagined the One Power leaking out of her and into the man. That was almost as bad as dying, bloody ashes but it was! He gripped the medallion beneath his shirt.

Delarn stiffened, but then gasped, eyes fluttering open.

"It is done," Edesina said, standing up. "He will be weak from the Healing, but I reached him in time."

Harnan had gathered and saddled all of their horses, Light bless him. Good man. The women mounted, and spared several glances over their shoulders at the inn.

"It's as if the darkness itself intoxicates them," Thom said while Mat helped Delarn into his saddle. "As if Light itself has forsaken them, leaving them only to the Shadow. . . ."

"Nothing we can do," Mat said, pulling himself into his saddle behind Delarn. The soldier was too weak to ride on his own, after that Healing. Mat eyed the serving girls that the Warders had slung over the fronts of their horses. They struggled against their bonds, hate in their eyes. He turned and nodded to Talmanes, who had affixed the lantern to a saddle pole. The Cairhienin opened the shield, bathing the inn's stableyard in light. A path led northward, out of the yard into the dark. Away from the army, but also directly out of the village, toward the hills. That was good enough for Mat.

"Ride," he said, kicking Pips into motion. The group fell in beside him.

"I told you we should leave," Talmanes noted, looking over his shoulder, riding at Mat's left. "But you had to stay for one more toss."

Mat didn't look back. "Not my fault, Talmanes. How was I to know that staying would cause them all to start tearing each other's throats out?"

"What?" Talmanes asked, glancing at him. "Isn't this *usually* how people react when you tell them you're going to spend the night?"

Mat rolled his eyes, but didn't feel much like laughing as he led the group out of the village.

Hours later, Mat sat on a rock outcropping on a dark hillside, looking down at Hinderstap. The village was dark. Not a light burned. It was impossible to tell what was going on, but still he watched. How could a man sleep, after what they'd been through?

Well, the soldiers *did* sleep. He didn't blame Delarn. An Aes Sedai Healing could drain a man. Mat had felt that icy chill himself on occasion, and he didn't intend to repeat the experience. Talmanes and the other Redarms hadn't the excuse of a Healing, but they were soldiers. Soldiers learned to sleep when they could, and the night's experience didn't seem to have disturbed them nearly as much as it had Mat. Oh, they'd been worried while in the thick of it, but now it was just another battle passed. Another battle survived. That had led stout Harnan to joking and smiling as they bedded down.

Not Mat. There was an odd *wrongness* about the entire experience. Was the curfew intended to keep this from happening, somehow? Had Mat, by staying, *caused* all of these deaths? Blood and bloody ashes. Did no place in the world make sense anymore?

"Mat, lad," Thom said, joining him, walking with his familiar limp. He'd had a fractured arm, though he hadn't mentioned it until Edesina had noticed him flinching and insisted on Healing him. "You should sleep." Now that the moon had risen—hidden behind the clouds—there was enough light for Mat to see Thom's concern.

The group had stopped in a small hollow off one side of the trail. It gave a good view back toward the village, and—more importantly—it overlooked the path that Mat and the others had used to escape. The hollow lay on a steep hillside, the only approach from below. One person on watch could keep a good eye out for anyone trying to sneak into the camp.

The Aes Sedai had bedded down near the back of the hollow, though Mat didn't think they were actually sleeping. Joline's Warders had thought to bring bedrolls, just in case. Warders were like that. Mat's men only had their cloaks, but that hadn't deterred them from sleeping. Talmanes was even snoring softly, despite the spring chill. Mat had forbidden a fire. It wasn't so cold that they needed one, and it would just signal anyone looking for them.

"I'm fine, Thom," Mat said, making room on his rock as the gleeman settled down. "You're the one who should get some sleep."

Thom shook his head. "One nice thing I've noticed about

getting older is that your body doesn't seem to need its sleep as much anymore. Dying doesn't take as much energy as growing, I guess."

"Don't start that again," Mat said. "Do I need to remind you about how you hauled my skinny backside out of trouble back there? What was that you were worried about earlier? That I didn't *need* you anymore? If you hadn't been with me today, if you hadn't come looking for me, I'd be dead in that village. Delarn too."

Thom grinned, eyes bright in the moonlight. "All right, Mat," he said. "No more. I promise."

Mat nodded. The two of them sat for a time on their rock, looking out at the city. "It's not going to leave me alone, Thom," Mat finally said.

"What?"

"All of this," Mat said tiredly. "The bloody Dark One and his spawn. They've been chasing me since that night in the Two Rivers, and nothing has stopped them."

"You think this was him?"

"What else could it have been?" Mat asked. "Quiet village folk, turning into violent madmen? It's the Dark One's own work, and you know it."

Thom was silent. "Yes," he finally said. "I suppose it is at that."

"They're still coming for me," Mat said angrily. "That bloody *gholam* is out there, I know it is, but that's just part of it. Myrddraal and Darkfriends, monsters and ghosts. Chasing me and hunting me. I've stumbled from one disaster to another, barely keeping my neck above water, ever since this began. I keep saying I just need to find a hole somewhere to dice and drink, but that won't stop it. Nothing will."

"You're *ta'veren*, lad," Thom said.

"I didn't ask to be. Burn me, I wish they'd all just go bother Rand. He likes it." He shook his head, dispelling the image that formed, showing Rand asleep in his bed, Min curled up beside him.

"You really think that?" Thom asked.

Mat hesitated. "I wish I did," he admitted. "It would make things easier."

"Lies never make things easier in the long run. Unless

they're to exactly the right person—usually a woman—at exactly the right time. When you tell them to yourself, you just bring more trouble."

"I brought those people trouble. In the village." He glanced toward the back of the camp, where the two Warders sat, guarding the still-bound serving girls. They continued to struggle. Light! Where did they get the strength? It was inhuman.

"I don't think this was you, Mat," Thom said thoughtfully. "Oh, I don't disagree that trouble hunts you—the Dark One himself seems to do so. But Hinderstap . . . well, when I was singing in that common room, I heard some tidbits. They seemed like nothing. But looking back, it strikes me that the people were *expecting* this. Or something like it."

"How could they have been?" Mat said. "If this had happened before, they'd all be dead."

"Don't know," Thom said thoughtfully. Then something seemed to strike him. He began fishing inside his cloak. "Oh, I forgot. Maybe there *is* some connection between you and what happened. I managed to take this away from a man who was too drunk for his own good." The gleeman pulled out a folded piece of paper and handed it to Mat.

Mat took the paper, frowning, and unfolded it. He squinted in the diffuse moonlight, leaning close, and grunted when he made out what the paper contained—not words, but a very accurate drawing of Mat's face, hat atop his head. It even had the foxhead medallion drawn in around his neck. Bloody ashes.

He contained his annoyance. "Handsome fellow. Good nose, straight teeth, dashing hat."

Thom snorted.

"I saw some men showing a paper to the mayor," Mat said, refolding the drawing. "I didn't see what was on it, but I'll bet it was the same as this. What did the man you took this from say about it?"

"An outlander woman in some village north of here is giving them out and offering a reward to anyone who has seen you. The man got the paper from a friend, so he didn't have a description of her or the town's name. Either his friend kept him ignorant, wanting the reward for himself, or he was just too drunk to remember."

Mat tucked the paper into his coat pocket. The light of

false dawn was beginning to glow to the east. He'd sat up all night, but he didn't feel tired. Just . . . drained. "I'm going back," he said.

"What?" Thom asked, surprised. "To Hinderstap?"

Mat nodded, rising. "As soon as it's light. I need to—"

A muffled curse interrupted him. He spun, reaching for his *ashandarei*. Thom had a pair of knives in his hands in the blink of an eye. Fen, Joline's Saldaean Warder, was the one who had cursed. He stood, hand on his sword, searching the ground around him. Blaeric stood by the Aes Sedai, sword out, alert and on guard.

"What?" Mat asked tersely.

"The prisoners," Fen said.

Mat started, realizing that the lumps that had lain near the Warders were gone. He dashed over, cursing. Talmanes' snores stopped as the sounds woke him and he sat up. The bonds made from strips of Joline's dress lay on the ground, but the serving girls were gone.

"What happened?" Mat asked, looking up.

"I . . ." The dark-haired Warder looked dumbfounded. "I have no idea. They were here just a moment ago!"

"Did you doze off?" Mat demanded.

"Fen wouldn't have done such a thing," Joline said, sitting up in her bedroll, her voice calm. She still wore only that dressing robe.

"Lad," Thom said, "we both saw those girls here barely a minute ago."

Talmanes cursed and woke the five Redarms. Delarn was looking a great deal better, his weakness from the Healing barely seeming to bother him as he climbed to his feet. The Warders called for a search, but Mat just turned back to the village below. "The answers are there," Mat said. "Thom, you're with me. Talmanes, watch the women."

"We have little need of being 'watched,' Matrim," Joline said grumpily.

"Fine," he snapped. "Thom, you're with me. Joline, you watch the soldiers. Either way, you all stay here. I can't worry about a whole group right now."

He didn't give them a chance to argue. Within minutes, Mat and Thom were on their horses, riding down the path back toward Hinderstap.

"Lad," Thom said, "what is it you expect to find?"

"I don't know," Mat replied. "If I did, I wouldn't be so keen to look."

"Fair enough," Thom said softly.

Mat spotted the oddities almost immediately. Those goats out on the western pasture. He couldn't tell for certain in the dawn light, but it looked like someone was herding them. And were those lights winking on in the village? There hadn't been a single one of those all night long! He hastened Pips' pace, Thom following silently.

It took the better part of an hour to arrive—Mat hadn't wanted to risk camping too close, though he'd also been disinclined to hunt a way around and back to the army in the dark. It was fully light, if still very early, by the time they rode back into the inn's yard. A couple of men in dun coats were working on the back door, which had apparently been broken off its hinges sometime after Mat and the others left. The men looked up as Mat and Thom rode into the yard, and one of them pulled off his cap, looking anxious. Neither one made a threatening move.

Mat slowed Pips to a halt. One of the men whispered to the other, who ran inside. A moment later, a balding man with a white apron stepped out through the doorway. Mat felt himself go pale.

"The innkeeper," Mat said. "Burn me, I saw you dead!"

"Best go get the mayor, son," the innkeeper said to one of the working men. He glanced back at Mat. "*Quickly.*"

"What in the bloody name of Hawkwing's left hand is going on here?" Mat demanded. "Was it all some kind of twisted show? You—"

A head stuck out of the inn door, peeking around the innkeeper toward Mat. The pudgy face had curly blond hair. Last time he'd seen this man, the cook, Mat had been forced to gut the man and slit his throat.

"You!" he said, pointing. "I *killed* you!"

"Calm down, now, son," the innkeeper said. "Come in, we'll get you some tea, and—"

"I'm not going anywhere with you, spirit," Mat said. "Thom, you seeing this?"

The gleeman rubbed his chin. "Perhaps we should hear the man out, Mat."

"Ghosts and spirits," Mat muttered, turning Pips. "Come on." He urged Pips forward, charging around to the front of the inn, Thom following. Here he caught a glimpse of many workers inside, carrying buckets of white paint. To fix the places where Aes Sedai fire had scored the building, likely.

Thom pulled up beside Mat. "I've never seen anything like this, Mat," he said. "Why would spirits need to paint walls and repair doors?"

Mat shook his head. He'd spotted the place where he'd fought the villagers to save Delarn. He pulled Pips to a halt suddenly, making Thom curse and round his own mount around to come back.

"What?" Thom asked.

Mat pointed. There was a stain of blood on the ground and across several rocks beside the road. "Where they stabbed Delarn," he said.

"All right," Thom said. Around them, men passed on the street, gazes averted. They gave Mat and Thom a wide berth.

Blood and bloody ashes, Mat thought. *I've gotten us surrounded again. What if they attack? Bloody fool!*

"So there's blood," Thom said. "What did you expect?"

"Where's the rest of the blood, Thom?" Mat growled. "I killed a good dozen men here, and I saw them bleed. You dropped three with your knives. Where's the *blood*?"

"It vanishes," a voice said.

Mat spun Pips to find the burly, hairy-armed mayor standing on the road a short distance away. He must have been near already; there was no way the workers could have fetched him that quickly. Of course, the way things seemed to be going in this village, who could tell that for certain? Barlden wore a cloak and shirt with several fresh rips in them.

"The blood vanishes," he said, sounding exhausted. "None of us have seen it. We just wake up and it's gone."

Mat hesitated, looking around the village. Women peeked out of houses, holding children. Men left for the fields, carrying crooks or hoes. Save for the air of anxiety at Mat and Thom's presence, one would never know anything had gone wrong in the village.

"We won't hurt you," the mayor said, turning away from Mat. "So you needn't look so worried. At least, not until the sun sets. I'll give you an explanation, if you want one. Either come and listen or be gone with you. I don't really

care, so long as you stop disturbing my town. We've work
to do. Much more than usual, thanks to you."

Mat glanced at Thom, who shrugged. "It never hurts to
listen," Thom said.

"I don't know," Mat said, eyeing Barlden. "Not unless
you think it could hurt to end up surrounded by *crazy, hom-
icidal mountainfolk*."

"We leave, then?"

Mat shook his head slowly. "No. Burn me, they've still
got my gold. Come on, let's see what he has to say."

"It started several months back," the mayor said, standing
beside the window. They were in a neat—yet simple—
sitting room in his manor. The curtains and carpet were of a
soft pale green, almost the color of oxeye leaves, with light
tan wood paneling. The mayor's wife had brought tea made
from dried sweetberries. Mat hadn't chosen to drink any,
and he had made certain to lean against the wall near the
street door. His spear rested beside him.

Barlden's wife was a short, brown-haired woman, faintly
pudgy, with a motherly air. She returned from the kitchen,
carrying a bowl of honey for the tea, then hesitated as she
saw Mat leaning by the wall. She eyed the spear, then put
the bowl on the table and retreated.

"What happened?" Mat asked, glancing at Thom, who
had also declined a seat. The old gleeman stood with arms
crossed beside the door from the kitchens. He nodded to
Mat; the woman wasn't listening at the door. He'd make a
motion if he heard someone approach.

"We aren't sure if it was something *we* did, or just a cruel
curse by the Dark One himself," the mayor said. "It was a
normal day, early this year, just before the Feast of Abram.
Nothing really special about it that I can remember. The
weather had broken by then, though the snows hadn't come
yet. A lot of us went about our normal activities the next
morning, thinking nothing of it.

"The oddities were small, you see. A broken door here,
a rip in someone's clothing they didn't remember. And the
nightmares. We all shared them, nightmares of death and
killing. A few of the women started talking, and they realized that they couldn't remember turning in the previous

evening. They could remember waking, safe and comfortable in their beds, but only a few remembered actually *getting into* bed. Those who could remember had gone to sleep early, before sunset. For the rest of us, the late evening was just a blur."

He fell silent. Mat glanced at Thom, who did not respond. Mat could see in those blue eyes of his that he was memorizing the tale. *He'd better get it* right *if he puts me in any ballads,* Mat thought, folding his arms. *And he'd better include my hat. This is a good bloody hat.*

"I was in the pastures that night," the mayor continued. "I was helping old man Garken with a broken strip of fencing. And then . . . nothing. A fuzzing. I awoke the next morning in my own bed, next to my wife. We felt tired, as if we hadn't slept well." He stopped, then more softly, he added, "And I had the nightmares. They're vague, and they fade. But I can remember one vivid image. Old man Garken, dead at my feet. Killed as if by a wild beast."

Barlden stood next to a window in the eastern wall, opposite Mat, staring out. "But I went to see Garken the next day, and he was fine. We finished fixing the fence. It wasn't until I got back to town that I heard the chattering. The shared nightmares, the missing hours just after sunset. We gathered, talking it through, and then it happened again. The sun set, and when it rose I woke up in bed again, tired, mind full of nightmares." He shivered, then walked over to the table and poured himself a cup of tea.

"We don't know what happens at night," the mayor said, stirring in a spoonful of honey.

"You don't know?" Mat demanded. "I can bloody *tell* you what happens at night. You—"

"We *don't* know what happens," the mayor interrupted, looking up sharply. "And have no care to know."

"But—"

"We have no *need* to know, outlander," the mayor said harshly. "We want to live our lives as best we can. Many of us turn in early, lying down before sunset. There are no holes in our memories that way. We go to bed, we wake up in that same bed. There are nightmares, perhaps some damage to the house, but nothing that can't be fixed. Others prefer to visit a tavern and drink to the setting of the sun. There's a blessing in that, I suppose. Drink all you want, and you never have to worry about getting home. You always wake safe and sound in bed."

"You can't avoid this entirely," Thom said softly. "You can't pretend nothing is different."

"We don't." Barlden took a drink of tea. "We have the rules. Rules that *you* ignored. No fires lit after sunset—we can't have a blaze starting in the night, without anyone to fight it. And we forbid outsiders inside the town after sunset. We learned that lesson quickly. The first people trapped here after nightfall were relatives of Sammrie the cooper. We found blood on the walls of his home the next morning. But his sister and her family were safely asleep in the beds he'd given them." The mayor paused. "Now they have the same nightmares we do."

"So just leave," Mat said. "Leave this bloody place and go somewhere else!"

"We've tried," the mayor said. "We always wake up back here, no matter how far we go. Some have tried ending their lives. We buried the bodies. They woke up the next morning in their beds."

The room fell silent.

"Blood and bloody ashes," Mat whispered. He felt chilled.

"You survived the night," the mayor said, stirring his tea again. "I assumed that you hadn't, after seeing that bloodstain. We were curious to see where you'd wake up. Most of the rooms in the inns are permanently taken by travelers who are now, for better or worse, part of our village. We aren't able to choose where someone awakens. It just happens. An empty bed gets a new occupant, and from then on they wake up there each morning.

"Anyway, when I heard you talking to one another about what you'd seen, I realized that you must have escaped. You remember the night too vividly. Anyone who . . . joins us simply has the nightmares. Count yourselves lucky. I suggest you move on and forget Hinderstap."

"We have Aes Sedai with us," Thom said. "They might be able to do something to help you. We could tell the White Tower, have them send—"

"No!" Barlden said sharply. "Our lives aren't so bad, now that we know how to deal with our situation. We don't want Aes Sedai eyes on us." He turned away. "We nearly turned your group away flat. We do that, sometimes, if we sense that the travelers won't obey our rules. But you had Aes Sedai with you. They ask questions, they get curious. We worried that if we turned you away, they'd get suspicious and force entrance."

"Forcing them to leave at sunset made them even more curious," Mat said. "And having their bathing attendants bloody try to *kill* them isn't a good way to keep the secret either."

The mayor looked wan. "Some wished . . . well, that you'd be trapped here. They thought that if Aes Sedai were bound here, they'd find a way out for all of us. We don't all agree. Either way, it's *our* problem. Please, just. . . . Just go."

"Fine." Mat stood up straight and picked up his spear. "But first, tell me where *these* came from." He pulled the paper from his pocket, the one that bore a drawing of his face.

Barlden glanced at it. "You'll find those spread around the nearby villages," he said. "Someone's looking for you. As I told Ledron last night, I'm not in the business of selling out guests. I wasn't about to kidnap you and risk keeping you here overnight just for some reward."

"Who's looking for me?" Mat repeated.

"About twenty leagues to the northeast, there's a small town called Trustair. Rumor says that if you want a little coin, you can bring news about a man who looks like the one in this picture, or the other one. Visit an inn in Trustair called The Shaken Fist to find the one looking for you."

"Other picture?" Mat asked, frowning.

"Yes. A burly fellow with a beard. A note at the bottom says he has golden eyes."

Mat glanced at Thom, who'd raised a bushy eyebrow.

"Blood and bloody ashes," Mat muttered and pulled the side of his hat down. Who was looking for him and Perrin, and what did they want? "We'll be going, I suppose," he said. He glanced at Barlden. Poor fellow. That went for the entire village. But what was Mat to do about it? There were fights you could win, and others you just had to leave for someone else.

"Your gold is on the wagon outside," the mayor said. "We didn't take any from your winnings. The food is there too." He met Mat's eyes. "We hold to our word, here. Other things are out of our control, particularly for those who don't listen to the rules. But we aren't going to rob a man just because he's an outsider."

"Mighty tolerant of you," Mat said flatly, pulling open the door. "Have a good day, then, and when night comes, try not to kill anyone I wouldn't kill. Thom, you coming?"

The gleeman joined him, limping slightly from his old wound. Mat glanced back at Barlden, who stood with sleeves rolled up in the center of the room, looking down at his teacup. He seemed like he was wishing that cup held something a little stronger.

"Poor fellow," Mat said, then stepped out into the morning light after Thom and pulled the door shut behind him.

"I assume we're going after that person spreading around pictures of you?" Thom asked.

"Right as Light, we are," Mat said, tying his *ashandarei* to Pips' saddle. "It's on the way to Four Kings anyway. I'll lead your horse if you can drive the wagon."

Thom nodded. He was studying the mayor's home.

"What?" Mat asked.

"Nothing, lad," the gleeman said. "It's just . . . well, it's a sad tale. Something's wrong in the world. There's a snag in the Pattern here. The town unravels at night, and then the world tries to reset it each morning to make things right again."

"Well, they should be more forthcoming," Mat said. The villagers had pulled the food-filled wagon up while Mat and Thom had been chatting with the mayor. It was hitched to two strong draft horses, tan of coloring and wide of hoof.

"More forthcoming?" Thom asked. "How? The mayor is right, they *did* try to warn us."

Mat grunted, walking over to open the chest and check on his gold. It was there, as the mayor had said. "I don't know," he said. "They could put up a warning sign or something. Hello. Welcome to Hinderstap. We will murder you in the night and eat your *bloody* face if you stay past sunset. Try the pies. Martna Baily makes them fresh daily."

Thom didn't chuckle. "Poor taste, lad. There's too much tragedy in this town for levity."

"Funny," Mat said. He counted out about as much gold as he figured would be a good price for the food and the wagon. Then, after a moment, he added ten more silver crowns. He set all of this in a pile on the mayor's doorstep, then closed the chest. "The more tragic things get, the more *I* feel like laughing."

"Are we really going to take this wagon?"

"We need the food," Mat said, lashing the chest to the back of the wagon. Several large wheels of white cheese and a half dozen legs of mutton lay prominently alongside the casks of ale. The food smelled good, and his stomach rumbled. "I won it fair." He glanced at the villagers passing on the street. When he'd first seen them the day before, he'd thought the slowness of their pace was due to the lazy nature of the mountain villagers. Now it struck him that there was another reason entirely.

He turned back to his work, checking the horses' harness. "And I don't feel a bit bad taking the wagon and horses. I doubt these villagers are going to be doing much traveling in the future. . . ."

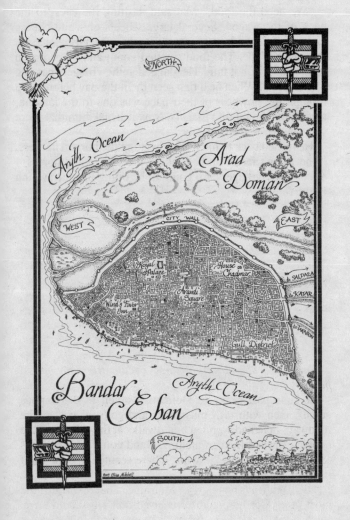

CHAPTER
29

Into Bandar Eban

*M*oiraine Damodred, who died because of my
weakness.

Rand slowed Tai'daishar to a walk as he
passed through the massive gateway to Bandar Eban, his
entourage following, ranks of Aiel leading him. The gates
were said to be carved with the city's seal, but swung open
as they were, Rand couldn't see them.

*The nameless Darkfriend I beheaded in those Muran-
dian hills. I've forgotten the looks of the others with her,
but I will never forget her face.*

The list ran through his head. Almost a daily ritual now,
the name of every woman who had died by his hand or because of his actions. The street inside the city was of packed
earth, lined with ruts that crisscrossed at the intersections.
The dirt was lighter here than he was used to.

*Colavaere Saighan, who died because I made her a
pauper.*

He rode past ranks of Domani, women in diaphanous
gowns, men with thin mustaches and colorful coats. The
roadways here had wooden boardwalks at the sides, and the
people crowded them, watching. Rand could hear banners
and flags flapping in the wind. There seemed to be a lot of
them in the city.

The list always began with Moiraine. That name hurt the
most of all, for he could have saved her. He should have.
He hated himself for allowing her to sacrifice herself for
him.

A child stepped off the boardwalk and started to run out
into the street, but his father caught him by the hand and

hauled him back into the press of people. Some coughed and muttered, but most were silent. The sounds of Rand's troops marching on the packed earth seemed a thunder by comparison.

Was Lanfear alive again? If Ishamael could be returned, what about her? In that case, Moiraine's death had been for naught, and his cowardice was even more galling. Never again. The list would remain, but he would never again be too weak to do what must be done.

There were no cheers from the people on those board-walks. Well, he had not come to liberate. He had come to do what must be done. Perhaps he would find Graendal here; Asmodean said she had been in the country, but that had been so long ago. If he found her, perhaps that would assuage his conscience at invading.

Did he have one of those anymore? He could not decide.

Liah, of the Cosaida Chareen, whom I killed, telling myself it was for her own good. Oddly, Lews Therin started to chant with him, reading off the names, a strange, echoing chant inside his head.

Ahead, a large group of Aiel stood waiting for him in a city square set with copper fountains in the shape of horses leaping from a frothy wave. A man on horseback waited before the fountain, an honor guard around him. He was a solid, square-faced man with furrowed skin and gray hair. His forehead was shaved and powdered, after the fashion of Cairhienin soldiers. Dobraine was trustworthy, as much as any Cairhienin was, at least.

Sendara of the Iron Mountain Taardad, Lamelle of the Smoke Water Miagoma, Andhilin of the Red Salt Goshien.

Ilyena Therin Moerelle, Lews Therin said, slipping the name in between two others. Rand let it stand. At least the madman didn't scream again.

"Lord Dragon," Dobraine said smoothly, bowing to Rand as he approached. "I deliver to you the city of Bandar Eban. Order has been restored, as you commanded."

"I asked you to restore order to the entire country, Dobraine," Rand said softly. "Not just one city."

The nobleman wilted slightly.

"You have one of the merchant council for me?" Rand asked.

"Yes," Dobraine said. "Milisair Chadmar, last to flee the city's chaos." His eyes were eager. He had always been stalwart, but was that a ruse? Rand had trouble trusting anyone lately. The ones who seemed most trustworthy were the ones you needed to watch the most. And Dobraine was Cairhienin. Dared Rand trust anyone from Cairhien, with their games?

Moiraine was Cairhienin. I trusted her. Mostly.

Perhaps Dobraine hoped that Rand would choose him as king in Arad Doman. He had been steward of Cairhien, but he—like most others—knew that Rand intended Elayne for the Sun Throne.

Well, Rand might give this kingdom to Dobraine at that. He was better than most. Rand nodded for him to lead the way, and he did so, turning with the group of Aiel to march down a large side street. Rand continued, list still running through his mind.

The buildings here were tall and square, with the shape of boxes stacked atop one another. Many of them had balconies, packed with people, like the boardwalks beneath.

Each name on Rand's list pained him, but that pain was a strange, distant thing now. His feelings were . . . different since the day he had killed Semirhage. She had taught him how to bury his guilt and his hurt. She had thought to chain him, but instead had given him strength.

He added her name and Elza's name to the list. They didn't have any right to be there. Semirhage was less a woman and more a monster. Elza had betrayed him, serving the Shadow all along. But he added the names. They had as much claim on him for killing them as any. More, even. He had been unwilling to kill Lanfear to save Moiraine, but he had used balefire to burn Semirhage out of existence rather than allow himself to be captured again.

He fingered the object he carried in a pouch on his saddle. It was a smooth figurine. He had not told Cadsuane that his servants had recovered it from her room. Now that Cadsuane was exiled from his presence, he never would. He knew that she tagged along still with his entourage, pushing the limits of his command to never let him see her face. But she did as ordered, and so he let it be. He would not speak to her, and she would not speak to him.

Cadsuane had been a tool, and that tool had proven ineffective. He did not regret casting it aside.

Jendhilin, Maiden of the Cold Peak Miagoma, he thought, Lews Therin muttering alongside him. The list was so long. It would grow before he died.

Death no longer worried him. Finally, he understood Lews Therin's cries to let it end. Rand deserved to die. Was there a death so strong that a man would never have to be reborn? He reached the end of the list, finally. Once, he'd repeated it to keep himself from forgetting the names. That was not possible now; he could not forget them if he wished. He repeated them as a reminder of what he was.

But Lews Therin had one more name to add. *Elmindreda Farshaw,* he whispered.

Rand pulled Tai'daishar up short, stopping his column of Aiel, Saldaean cavalry, and camp attendants in the middle of the street. Dobraine turned back questioningly on his white stallion.

I did not kill her! Rand thought. *Lews Therin, she lives on. We didn't kill her! That was Semirhage who was to blame, in any case.*

Silence. He could still feel his fingers on her flesh, squeezing, impotent yet incredibly strong. Even if Semirhage had been behind the actions, Rand was the one who had been too weak to send Min away and protect her.

He hadn't sent her away. Not because he was too weak, but because something in him had stopped caring. Not about her—he loved her fiercely, and always would. But he knew that death, pain and destruction came in his wake, and he dragged them behind him like a cloak. Min might die here, but if he sent her away, she would be in just as much danger. His enemies likely suspected that he loved her.

There was no safety. If she died, he would add her to the list and suffer for it.

He started moving again before question could be called to his actions. Tai'daishar's hooves thumped on the earthen streets, made soft by the humidity. Rains came often here; Bandar Eban was the prime port city of the northwest. If it wasn't a great city like those in the south, it was still impressive. Row upon row of square houses, built of wood, ridged at the second and third stories. They looked like children's blocks, stacked on top of one another, so perfectly square with the stories divided. They filled the city, rolling down a gentle incline to the massive port.

The city was widest at the port, making it seem like the head of a man opening his mouth wide, as if to drink in the ocean itself. The docks were nearly empty; the only ships moored were a cluster of Sea Folk vessels—three-masted rakers—and some fishing trawlers. The massive size of the port only made it look more desolate for the lack of ships.

That was the first sign that all was not well in Bandar Eban.

Other than the virtually unoccupied harbor, the most distinctive aspect of the city was the banners. They flew above—or hung from—every building, no matter how humble. Many of those banners proclaimed the trade practiced in a given building—much as a simple wooden sign would in Caemlyn. The banners were far more extravagant than most, bright-colored and fluttering in the wind above the buildings. Matching tapestry-like banners hung from the sides of most buildings, announcing in bright lettering the owner, master craftsman and merchant of each shop. Even homes bore banners with the names of the families who lived therein.

Copper-skinned and dark-haired, the Domani favored bright clothing. Domani women were infamous for their dresses, which were filmy enough to be scandalous. It was said that very young Domani girls practiced the art of manipulating men, preparing for the day when they would be of age.

The sight of them all standing along the roads, watching, was nearly spectacle enough to draw Rand out of his brooding. Perhaps a year ago, he would have gawked, but now he barely gave them a glance. In fact, it came to him that Domani people were far less striking when gathered together like this. A flower in a field of weeds was always a sight, but if you passed cultivated flower beds every day, none of them drew your notice.

Distracted though he was, he did pick out the signs of

starvation. There was no mistaking that haunted cast to the children, that lean look to the faces of the adults. This city had been in chaos just weeks ago, though Dobraine and the Aiel had restored the law. Some of the buildings bore poorly mended windows or broken boards, and some of the banners had obviously been ripped recently and shoddily mended. Law had been restored, but the lack of it was still a fresh memory.

Rand's group reached a central crossroads, proclaimed by large flapping banners to be Arandi Square, and Dobraine turned the procession to the east. Many of the Aiel with the Cairhienin wore the red headband marking them as *siswai'aman*. Spears of the Dragon. Rhuarc had some twenty thousand Aiel camped around the city and in the nearby towns; by now most Domani would know that these Aiel followed the Dragon Reborn.

Rand was glad to find that the Sea Folk rakers had arrived— finally—with grain from the south. Hopefully, that would do as much to restore order as Dobraine and the Aiel had.

The procession turned into the wealthy section of the city. He knew where they'd find it long before the homes started looking more lavish: as far from the docks as possible, while still remaining a comfortable distance from the city walls. Rand could have found the rich even without looking at a map. The city's landscape all but demanded their location.

A horse clopped up beside Rand. At first, he assumed it would be Min—but no, she was riding behind, with the Wise Ones. Did she look at him differently now, or was he just imagining it? Did she remember his fingers at her throat every time she saw his face?

It was Merise who had moved up beside him, riding a placid dun mare. The Aes Sedai was infuriated by Rand's exile of Cadsuane. Unsurprising. Aes Sedai liked to maintain a very calm and controlled front, but Merise and the others had pandered to Cadsuane much like a village innkeeper simpering over a visiting king.

The Taraboner woman had chosen to wear her shawl today, proclaiming her affiliation to the Green Ajah. She wore it, perhaps, in an effort to reinforce her authority. Inwardly, Rand sighed. He had been expecting a confrontation, but he had hoped that the business of the move would delay it until tempers subsided. He respected Cadsuane, after a fashion, but he had never trusted her. There had to be consequences for failure, and he felt a great relief from having dealt with her. There would be no more of her strings wrapping themselves around him.

Or, at least, fewer of them.

"This exile, it is foolish, Rand al'Thor," Merise said dismissively. Was she intentionally trying to rile him, perhaps to make him easier to bully? After months of dealing with Cadsuane herself, this woman's pale imitation was almost amusing.

"You should beg for her forgiveness," Merise continued. "She has condescended to continue with us, though your inane restriction has forced her to wear a cloak with the hood up, despite the warmth of the day. You should be ashamed."

Cadsuane again. He shouldn't have left her room to wiggle around his command.

"Well?" Merise asked.

Rand turned his head and looked Merise in the eyes. He had discovered something shocking during the last few hours. By bottling up the seething fury within him—by becoming *cuendillar*—he had gained an understanding that had long eluded him.

People did not respond to anger. They did not respond to demands. Silence and questions, these were far more effective. Indeed, Merise—a fully trained Aes Sedai—wilted before that stare.

He put no emotion into it. His rage, his anger, his passion—it was all still there, buried within. But he had surrounded it with ice, cold and immobilizing. It was the ice of the place Semirhage had taught him to go, the place that was like the void, but far more dangerous.

Perhaps Merise could sense frozen rage within him. Or perhaps she could sense the other thing, the fact that he'd used that . . . power. Distantly, Lews Therin began to cry. The madman did that whenever Rand thought of what he had done to escape Semirhage's collar.

"What you did, it was a foolish move," Merise continued. "You should—"

"Do you think me a fool, then?" Rand asked softly.

Respond to demands with silence, respond to challenges with questions. It was amazing how it worked. Merise cut off, then shivered visibly. She glanced down, to the pouch on his saddle where he carried the small statue of a man holding aloft a sphere. Rand fingered it, holding his reins loosely.

He did not flaunt the statuette. He simply carried it, but Merise and most of the others knew the nearly unlimited power he could tap if he wished. It was a weapon greater than any other ever known. With it, he might be able to annihilate the world itself. And it sat innocently on his saddle. That had an effect on people.

"I . . . No, I don't," she admitted. "Not always."

"Do you think that failures should be unpunished?" Rand asked, voice still soft. Why had he lost his temper? These little annoyances were not worth his passion, his fury. If one bothered him too much, all he needed do was snuff it out, like a candle.

A dangerous thought. Had that been his? Had it been Lews Therin's? Or . . . had the thought come from . . . elsewhere?

"Surely you have been too harsh," Merise said.

"Too harsh?" he asked. "Do you realize her mistake, Merise? Have you considered what could have happened? What *should* have happened?"

"I—"

"The end of all things, Merise," he whispered. "The Dark One with control of the Dragon Reborn. The two of us, fighting on the same side."

She fell silent, then said, "Yes. But mistakes, you yourself have made them. They might have ended in similar disaster."

"I pay for my mistakes," he said, turning away. "I pay for them each day. Each hour. Each breath."

"I—"

"Enough." He did not yell the word. He spoke firmly, but quietly. He made her feel the full force of his displeasure, his gaze seizing her own. She suddenly slumped in her saddle, looking up at him with wide eyes.

There was a loud cracking noise from the side, followed by a sudden crash. Screams broke the air. Rand turned with alarm. A balcony filled with onlookers had broken free of its supports and fallen to the street, smashing like a barrel hit by a boulder. People groaned in pain, others called out for help. But the sounds had come from both sides of the street. Rand frowned and turned; a *second* balcony—directly across from the first—had fallen as well.

Merise paled, then turned her horse hastily, heading to help the wounded. Other Aes Sedai were already hurrying to Heal those who had fallen.

Rand kneed Tai'daishar forward. That had not been caused by the Power, but by his *ta'veren* nature changing probability. Wherever he visited, remarkable and random events occurred. Large numbers of births, deaths, weddings and accidents. He had learned to ignore them.

He had rarely seen an occurrence quite so . . . violent, however. Could he be sure it wasn't due to some interaction with the new force? That unseen yet tempting well of power Rand had tapped, used and enjoyed? Lews Therin thought what happened should have been impossible.

The original reason mankind had bored into the Dark One's prison had been power. A new source of energy for channeling, like the One Power, but different. Unknown and strange, and potentially vast. That source of power had turned out to be the Dark One himself.

Lews Therin whimpered.

Rand carried the access key with him for a reason. It linked him to one of the greatest *sa'angreal* ever created. With that power and the aid of Nynaeve, Rand had cleansed *saidin*. The access key had allowed him to tap an unimaginable river, a tempest as vast as the ocean. It had been the greatest thing he had ever experienced.

Until the moment when he had used the unnamed power.

That other force called to him, sang to him, tempted him. So much power, so much divine wonder. But it terrified him. He didn't dare touch it, not again.

And so he carried the key. He was not certain which of the two sources of energy was more dangerous, but as long as both called to him, he was able to resist both. Like two people, both yelling for his attention, they drowned one another out. For the moment.

Besides, he would *not* be collared again. The access key wouldn't have helped him against Semirhage—no amount of the One Power would aid a man if he were caught unaware—but perhaps it would in the future. Once, he hadn't dared carry it for fear of what it offered. He no longer had room to indulge such weakness.

The destination was easy to pick out; about five hundred Cairhienin armsmen were camped on the grounds of a spacious, stately mansion. Aiel also had tents on the grounds—but they had also claimed nearby buildings, and several nearby roofs. For the Aiel, camping in a place was essentially the same thing as guarding it, as an Aiel resting was about twice as alert as a regular soldier on patrol. Rand had left the larger bulk of his force outside the city; he would leave it to Dobraine and his stewards to find quarters for Rand's men within the walls.

Rand halted Tai'daishar, then surveyed his new home.

We have no home, Lews Therin whispered. *We destroyed it. Burned it away, melted to slag, like sand in a fire.*

The mansion was certainly a step up from the mostly log manor. Its large grounds were bordered by iron gates. The flower beds were empty—flowers were hesitant to bloom this spring—but the lawn was greener than most he had seen. Oh, it was mostly yellow and brown, but there were patches of green. The groundskeepers were trying very hard, their efforts also manifest in the rows of Aryth yews cut in the shapes of fanciful animals at the sides of the lawn.

The mansion itself was nearly a palace; there was one of those in the city, of course, belonging to the king. But it was said to be inferior to the homes of the Council of Merchants. The banner flapping tall atop the manor was of brilliant gold and black, and it proclaimed this to be the seat of House Chadmar. Perhaps this Milisair had seen the departure of the others as an opportunity. If so, the only real opportunity she'd gained was the chance to be taken by Rand.

The gates to the mansion grounds were open, and the Aiel in his entourage were already hurrying in, joining clusters of society or clan members. It was irksome that they rarely waited on Rand's commands or orders, but Aiel were Aiel. Any suggestion that they should wait was simply met with laughter, as if he had made a grand joke. It would be easier to tame the wind itself than to get them to behave like wetlanders.

That made him think of Aviendha. Where *had* she gone, so suddenly? He could feel her through the bond, but it was faint—she was very far away. To the east. What business was there for her in the Waste?

He shook his head. All women were difficult to understand, and an Aiel woman was tenfold more incomprehensible. He had hoped that he would be able to spend some time with her, but she'd pointedly avoided him. Well, perhaps it was Min's presence that kept her away. Perhaps he would be able to keep himself from hurting her before death came. Better that Aviendha fled. His enemies didn't know of her yet.

He urged Tai'daishar through the gates, riding up the drive to the manor house itself. He dismounted, plucking the statuette from its strap and sliding it into the oversized pocket of his coat, which had been quickly tailored to hold it. He handed his mount off to a groom—one of the manor house's own servants, wearing a coat of green with a bright white shirt beneath, the collar and cuffs ruffled. The manor's servants had already been apprised that Rand would be using the place as his own, now that its former occupant had been . . . given his protection.

Dobraine joined him as he strode up the steps to the building. It was washed a crisp white, with wooden pillars lining the front landing. He stepped inside the front doors. After living in several palaces, he was still impressed. And disgusted. The opulence he found beyond the manor's front doors would never have indicated that the people of the city starved. A line of very nervous servants stood in a row along the back of the entryway. He could sense their fear. It was not every day that one's dwelling was annexed by the Dragon Reborn himself.

Rand pulled off his riding glove by tucking his hand between his arm and his side, then slipped the glove in his belt. "Where is she?" he asked, turning to the pair of Maidens—Beralna and Riallin—who were keeping an eye on the servants.

"Second floor," one of the Maidens said. "Sipping tea while her hand shakes so much it threatens to break the porcelain."

"We keep telling her she's not a prisoner," the other Maiden said. "She just can't leave."

Both of them found that amusing. Rand glanced to the side as Rhuarc joined him in the entryway. The tall, fire-haired clan chief inspected the room, with its twinkling chandelier and ornamented vases. Rand knew what he was thinking. "You may take the fifth," he said. "But only from the rich who live in this district."

That wasn't how it was done; the Aiel should have been allowed the fifth from everyone. But Rhuarc did not argue. What the Aiel had done in taking Bandar Eban hadn't really been a true conquest, though they had fought gangs and thugs. Perhaps he shouldn't have given them anything. But considering the mansions like this one, there was wealth to spare for the Aiel here, among the wealthy at least.

The Maidens nodded, as if they had expected it, then loped off, probably to begin selecting their share. Dobraine watched them with consternation. Cairhien had suffered the Aiel fifth on several occasions.

"I never can understand why you let them plunder like highwaymen who find the caravan guards asleep," Corele said, sweeping into the room with a smile. She raised an eyebrow at the impressive furnishings. "And such a pretty place as this. Like letting soldiers trample spring buds, isn't it?"

Had she been sent to deal with him now that he'd shaken Merise? She met Rand's gaze in her pleasant way, but he held it until she broke and turned away. He could remember a time when that had never worked with Aes Sedai.

He turned to Dobraine. "You have done well here," he said to the lord. "Even if you haven't brought order as widely as I wish. Gather your armsmen. Narishma has been instructed to provide a gateway for you to Tear."

"Tear, my Lord?" Dobraine asked, surprised.

"Yes," Rand said. "Tell Darlin to stop pestering me with messengers. He is to keep gathering his forces; I'll bring him to Arad Doman when I decide the time is right." That would be after he met with the Daughter of the Nine Moons, which meeting would determine much.

Dobraine looked faintly crestfallen. Or was that just Rand's interpretation? Dobraine's expression rarely changed. Was he imagining his hopes of this kingdom withering away? Was he plotting against Rand? "Yes, my Lord. I assume I'm to leave immediately?"

Dobraine has never given us reason to doubt him. He even gathered support for Elayne to take the Sun Throne!

Rand had been away from him too long. Too long to trust him. But best to get him out for now; he'd had too much time to get a foothold here, and Rand didn't trust any Cairhienin to avoid games with politics.

"Yes, you leave within the hour," Rand said, turning to walk up the graceful white stairs.

Dobraine saluted, stoic as always, and left out the front doorway. He obeyed immediately. No word of complaint. He *was* a good man. Rand knew he was.

Light, what is happening to me? Rand thought. *I need to trust some people. Don't I?*

Trust . . . ? Lews Therin whispered. *Yes, perhaps we can trust him. He cannot channel. Light, the one we can't trust at all is ourselves. . . .*

Rand clenched his jaw. He would reward Dobraine with the kingdom if Alsalam couldn't be found. Ituralde didn't want it.

The stairs rose straight and broad to a landing, then split and twisted up to the second floor, touching the landing there on two separate sides. "I need an audience chamber," Rand said to the servants below, "and a throne. Quickly."

Less than ten minutes later, Rand sat in a plushly decorated sitting room on the second floor, waiting for the merchant Milisair Chadmar to be brought to him. His ornately carved white wood chair wasn't quite a throne, but it would do. Perhaps Milisair had used it for audiences herself. The room did seem laid out like a throne room, with a shallowly raised dais for him to sit on. Both dais and floor below were covered in a textured green and red rug of fanciful design which matched the Sea Folk porcelain on pedestals at the corner. Four broad windows behind him—each large enough to walk through—ushered overcast sunlight into the room, and it fell on his back as he sat in the chair and leaned forward, one arm resting across his knees. The figurine sat on the floor just before him.

Shortly, Milisair Chadmar walked through the doorway past the Aiel guards. She wore one of those famous Domani dresses. It covered her body from neck to toe but was barely opaque and clung to every curve—of which she had more than her fair share. The dress was of deep green, and she wore pearls at her neck. Her dark hair, in tight

curls, hung down past her shoulders, several locks framing
her face. He hadn't expected her to be so young, barely into
her thirties.

It would be a shame to execute her.

Just one day, he thought to himself, *and already I think
of executing a woman for not agreeing to follow me. There
was a time when I could barely stand to execute deserving
criminals.* But he would do what must be done.

Milisair's deep curtsy seemed to imply that she accepted his authority. Or perhaps it was simply a means of
allowing him a better view of what the dress accentuated.
A very Domani thing to do. Unfortunately for her, he already had more problems with women than he knew how
to handle.

"My Lord Dragon," Milisair said, rising from her curtsy.
"How may I serve you?"

"When was the last communication you had from King
Alsalam?" Rand asked. He pointedly didn't give her leave
to sit in one of the room's chairs.

"The King?" she asked, surprised. "It has been weeks
now."

"I will need to speak to the messenger who brought the
latest message," Rand said.

"I am not certain he can be found." The woman sounded
flustered. "I do not keep track of the coming and going of
every messenger in the city, my Lord."

Rand leaned forward. "Do you lie to me?" he asked
softly.

Her mouth opened, perhaps in shock at his bluntness.
The Domani were no Cairhienin—who had a seemingly
inborn political craftiness—but they *were* a subtle people.
Particularly the women.

Rand was neither subtle nor crafty. He was a sheepherder
turned conqueror, and his heart was that of a Two Rivers
man, even if his blood was Aiel. Whatever politicking she
was used to playing, it wouldn't work on him. He had no
patience for games.

"I . . ?" Milisair said, staring at him. "My Lord Dragon. . . ."

What was she hiding? "What did you do with him?"
Rand asked, making a guess. "The messenger?"

"He knew nothing of the King's location," Milisair said

quickly, the words seeming to spill from her. "My questioners were quite thorough."

"He is dead?"

"I. . . . No, my Lord Dragon."

"Then you will have him brought to me."

She paled further, and glanced to one side, perhaps reflexively seeking escape. "My Lord Dragon," she said hesitantly, bringing her eyes back to him. "Now that you are here, perhaps the King will remain . . . hidden. Perhaps there is no need to seek him out further."

She thinks he's dead too, Rand thought. *It has made her take risks.*

"There *is* need to find Alsalam," Rand said, "or at least discover what happened to him. We need to know his fate so that you can choose a new king. That is how it happens, correct?"

"I'm certain you can be crowned quickly, my Lord Dragon," she said smoothly.

"I will not be king here," Rand said. "Bring me the messenger, Milisair, and perhaps you will live to see a new king crowned. You are dismissed."

She hesitated, then curtsied again and withdrew. Rand caught a glimpse of Min standing outside with the Aiel, watching the merchant depart. He caught her eyes, and she looked troubled. Had she seen any viewings about Milisair? He almost called to her, but she vanished, walking away with a quick step. To the side, Alivia watched her go with curiosity. The former *damane* had stayed aloof recently, as if biding her time, waiting until she could fulfill her destiny in helping Rand die.

He found himself standing. That look in Min's eyes. Was she angry with him? Was she remembering his hand at her neck, his knee pressing her against the floor?

He sat back down. Min could wait. "All right," he said, addressing the Aiel. "Bring me my scribes and stewards, along with Rhuarc, Bael and whatever city worthies haven't fled the city or been killed in riots. We need to go over the grain distribution plans."

The Aiel sent runners and Rand settled back into his chair. He would see the people fed, restore order and gather the Council of Merchants. He would even see that a new king was chosen.

But he would *also* find out where Alsalam had gone. For there, his instincts said, was the best place to find Graendal. It was his best lead.

If he did find her, he would see that she died by balefire, just like Semirhage. He would do what must be done.

CHAPTER
30

Old Advice

Gawyn remembered very little of his father—the man had never been much of a father, to him at least—but he did have a strong memory of a day in the Caemlyn palace gardens. Gawyn had been standing beside a small pond, pitching pebbles into it. Taringail had walked past down the Rose March, young Galad at his side.

The scene was still vivid in Gawyn's mind. The heavy scent of the roses in full bloom. The silver ripples on the pond, the minnows scattering away from the miniature boulder he'd just tossed at them. He could picture his father well. Tall, handsome, hair with a slight wave to it. Galad had been straight-backed and somber even then. A few months later, Galad would rescue Gawyn from drowning in that very pond.

Gawyn could hear his father speak words that he'd never forgotten. Whatever else one thought of Taringail Damodred, this bit of advice rang true. "There are two groups of people you should *never* trust," the man had been saying to Galad as they passed. "The first are pretty women. The second are Aes Sedai. Light help you, son, if you ever have to face someone who is both."

Light help you, son.

"I simply cannot see disobeying the Amyrlin's express will in this matter," Lelaine said primly, stirring ink in the small jar on her desk. No man trusted beautiful women, for all their fascination with them. But few realized what Taringail had said—that a pretty girl, like a coal that had cooled just enough to no longer look hot, could be far, far more dangerous.

Lelaine wasn't beautiful, but she *was* pretty, particularly when she smiled. Slender and graceful, without a speck of gray in her dark hair, an almond face with full lips. She looked up at him with eyes that were far too comely to belong to a woman of her craftiness. And she seemed to know. She understood that she was just attractive enough to draw attention, but not stunning enough to make men wary.

She was a woman of the most dangerous type. One who felt real, who made men think they might be able to hold her attention. She wasn't pretty like Egwene, who made you want to spend time with her. This woman's smile made you want to count the knives on your belt and in your boot, just to make sure none of them had found their way into your back while you were distracted.

Gawyn stood beside her writing table, shaded by the straight-topped blue tent. He hadn't been invited to sit, and he had not asked for the privilege. Talking to an Aes Sedai, particularly an important one, required wits and sobriety. He'd rather stand. Perhaps it would keep him more alert.

"Egwene is trying to protect you," Gawyn said, controlling his frustration. "That's why she commanded you to forgo a rescue. She obviously doesn't want you to risk yourselves. She is self-sacrificing to a fault." *If she weren't,* he added in his mind, *she'd never have let you all bully her into pretending to be the Amyrlin Seat.*

"She seems very confident of her safety," Lelaine said, dipping her pen into the ink. She began to write on a piece of parchment; a note to someone. Gawyn politely didn't read over her shoulder, though he did notice the calculated move on her part. He was unimportant enough that he couldn't demand her full attention. He chose not to acknowledge the insult. Trying to bully Bryne hadn't worked; it would be even less effective with this woman.

"She's trying to put your worries at ease, Lelaine Sedai," he said instead.

"I am a fair judge of people, young Trakand. I do not think she feels she is in danger." She shook her head. Her perfume smelled of apple blossoms.

"I do not doubt you," he replied. "But perhaps if I knew *how* it is you communicate with her, I could judge better. If I could—"

"You have been warned not to ask about that, child," Lelaine said in her soft, melodious voice. "Leave things of the Aes Sedai to the Aes Sedai."

Virtually the same answer each sister gave when he asked how they communicated with Egwene. He clenched his jaw in frustration. What had he expected? It involved using the One Power. After all his time in the White Tower, he still had little idea of what the Power could and couldn't do.

"Regardless," Lelaine continued, "the Amyrlin thinks herself quite safe. What we've discovered in Shemerin's story only reinforces and corroborates what Egwene has told us. Elaida is so mad with power that she doesn't consider the rightful Amyrlin a threat."

There was more she wasn't saying. Gawyn could tell it. He could never get a straight answer from them regarding what Egwene's status was currently. He'd heard rumors that she'd been imprisoned, no longer allowed to roam free as a novice. But getting information from an Aes Sedai was about as easy as churning rocks into butter!

Gawyn took a breath. He couldn't lose his temper. If he did that, he'd *never* get Lelaine to listen. And he needed her. Bryne wouldn't move without Aes Sedai authorization, and as far as Gawyn had been able to tell, his best chances of gaining it came from Lelaine or Romanda. Everyone seemed to listen to one of the two or the other.

Fortunately, Gawyn had found that he could play them off one another. A visit to Romanda almost always prompted an invitation from Lelaine. Of course, the reason they were eager to see him in the first place had very little to do with Egwene. No doubt the conversation would move in that direction very soon.

"Perhaps you are right, Lelaine Sedai," he said, trying a different tack. "Perhaps Egwene *does* believe herself to be safe. But isn't there a possibility that she is wrong? You can't honestly believe that Elaida will let a woman who claimed to be *Amyrlin* wander around the White Tower free? This is obviously just a means of showing off a captured rival before executing her."

"Perhaps," Lelaine said, continuing to write. She had a flowing, ornate hand. "But must I not uphold the Amyrlin, even if she is misguided?"

Gawyn gave no response. Of course she could disobey the will of the Amyrlin. He knew enough of Aes Sedai politics to understand it was done all the time. But saying that would accomplish nothing.

"Still," Lelaine said absently. "Perhaps I can bring a motion before the Hall. We might be able to persuade the Amyrlin to listen to a new kind of plea. We shall see if I can formulate a new argument."

"We shall see" or "Perhaps we can" or "I will consider what to do." Never a firm commitment; every half-offer came smeared liberally with goose grease for easy escape. Light, but he was growing weary of Aes Sedai answers!

Lelaine looked up at him, favoring him with a smile. "Now, as I have agreed to do something for you, perhaps you will be willing to offer me something. Great deeds are rarely accomplished without the aid of many partners, you may know."

Gawyn sighed. "Speak your needs, Aes Sedai."

"Your sister has, by all reports, made a very admirable showing for herself in Andor," Lelaine said, as if she hadn't said nearly the exact same thing the last three times she'd met with Gawyn. "She *did* have to step on a few toes to secure her throne, however. What do you think her policy will be regarding House Traemane's fruit orchards? Under your mother, the tax assessments on the land were *very* favorable toward Traemane. Will Elayne revoke this special privilege, or will she try to use it as honey to soothe those who stood against her?"

Gawyn stifled another sigh. It always came back to Elayne. He was convinced that neither Lelaine nor Romanda had any real interest in rescuing Egwene—they were too pleased with their increased power in her absence. No, they met with Gawyn because of the new queen on the Lion Throne.

He had no idea why an Aes Sedai of the Blue Ajah would care about apple orchard taxation rates. Lelaine wouldn't be looking for monetary gain; that wasn't the Aes Sedai way. But she would want leverage, a means of securing a favorable connection with the Andoran noble houses. Gawyn resisted answering. Why help this woman? What good was it doing?

But yet . . . could he be *certain* she wouldn't work for Egwene's release? If he stopped making these meetings useful to Lelaine, would she discontinue them? Would he find himself shut out of his one source of influence—no matter how small—in the camp?

"Well," he said, "I think that my sister will be more strict than my mother was. She always has thought that the favorable position of the orchard growers was no longer justified."

He could see that Lelaine subtly began taking notes on what he said at the bottom of her parchment. Was that the real reason for getting out the ink and quill?

He had no choice but to answer as honestly as he could, though he had to be careful not to let himself get pressed for *too* much information. His connection to Elayne was the only thing he had with which to bargain, and he had to ration his usefulness to stretch it long. It irked him. Elayne wasn't a bargaining chip, she was his sister!

But it was all he had.

"I see," Lelaine said, "and what of the northern cherry orchards? They haven't been particularly productive lately, and. . . ."

Shaking his head, Gawyn left the tent. Lelaine had prodded him about Andoran taxation rates for the better part of an hour. And, once again, Gawyn was uncertain if he'd achieved anything useful in his visit. He'd never get Egwene free at this rate!

As always, a novice in white waited outside the tent to escort him from the inner camp. This time the novice was a short, plump woman who looked more than a few years too old to have taken up the white.

Gawyn allowed the woman to lead him through the Aes Sedai camp, trying to pretend that she was just a guide, rather than a guard to see that he left as instructed. Bryne was right; the women did *not* like unnecessary bodies— soldiers in particular—wandering around their neat little imitation White Tower of a village. He passed bustling groups of white-clad women crossing walkways, watching him with the faint distrust the friendliest of people often gave an outsider. He passed Aes Sedai, universally self-assured whether they wore rich silk or stiff wool. He passed some groups of worker women, far more neat than those out in the soldier camp. They walked with an almost Aes Sedai air themselves, as if they gained a measure of authority by being allowed into the *real* camp.

All these groups crisscrossed through an open square of

trampled weeds that formed the common area. The most confusing thing he had discovered in this camp had to do with Egwene. More and more, he was coming to realize that the people here really *did* see her as Amyrlin. She wasn't simply a decoy set up to draw ire, nor was she a calculated insult, meant to rile Elaida. Egwene *was* Amyrlin to them.

Obviously, she had been chosen because the rebels wanted someone easy to control. But they didn't treat her as a puppet—both Lelaine and Romanda spoke of her with respect. There was an advantage to Egwene's absence, since it created a void of power. Therefore, they accepted Egwene as a source of authority. Was he the only one who remembered that she'd been an Accepted just months ago?

She *was* in over her head. However, she'd also impressed the people in this camp. It was like his mother's own rise to power in Andor many years before.

But why did she refuse to allow a rescue? Traveling had been rediscovered—from what he'd heard, Egwene herself had rediscovered it! He needed to talk to her. Then he could judge if her unwillingness to escape came from a fear of putting others in danger, or if it was something else.

He unhobbled Challenge from the post at the border between Aes Sedai and army camps, nodded farewell to his novice handler, then swung into the saddle, checking the position of the sun. He turned his mount east along a pathway between army tents, and set out in a quick trot. He hadn't been lying when he'd told Lelaine he had another appointment; he'd promised to meet Bryne. Of course, Gawyn had set up the meeting because he'd known he might need a means of escaping Lelaine. Bryne had taught him that: It didn't show fear to prepare your retreat ahead of time. It was just plain good strategy.

Well over an hour's ride later, Gawyn found his old teacher where they'd planned to meet: one of the outlying guard posts. Bryne was conducting an inspection not unlike the one Gawyn had used to mask his escape from the Younglings. The general was just mounting his big-nosed bay gelding as Gawyn trotted up, crossing the scrub grass and wan spring weeds. The guard post sat in a hollow on the side of a gentle incline, with a good view of the approach from the north. The soldiers stood respectfully in their general's presence, and they veiled their hostility to-

ward Gawyn. It had gotten around that he'd led the force
which had raided them so successfully. A strategist like
Bryne could respect Gawyn for his skill, no matter that they
had been on opposite sides, but these men had seen colleagues killed by Gawyn's troops.

Bryne turned his horse to the side, nodding to Gawyn.
"You're later than you said you'd be, son."

"But not later than you expected?" Gawyn said, pulling
Challenge up.

"Not at all," the sturdy man said, smiling. "You were visiting Aes Sedai."

Gawyn grinned at that, and the two turned their mounts
and began to cross the open hills toward the north. Bryne
planned to inspect all of the guard posts on the western side
of Tar Valon, a duty that would involve a lot of riding, so
Gawyn had offered to accompany him. There was blessed
little else to do with his time; few of the soldiers would spar
with him, and those who would tried just a little too hard
to cause an "accident." The Aes Sedai would only suffer so
much of his prodding, and Gawyn didn't have a mind for the
game of stones lately. He was too on edge, worried about
Egwene and frustrated at his lack of progress. The truth was,
he'd never been very good at the game in the first place—not
like his mother. Bryne had insisted that Gawyn practice it
anyway as a method of learning battlefield strategy.

The hillsides were scraggly with yellow weeds and larks-
brush, with its tiny, faintly blue leaves and gnarled branches.
There should have been wildflowers coating the hills in
patches, but not a single one bloomed. The landscape felt
sickly—yellow in patches, whitish blue in others, with generous helpings of dead brown scrub that hadn't regrown after the harsh winter.

"And are you going to tell me how the meeting went?"
Bryne asked as they rode, a squad of soldiers following behind as an honor guard.

"I'll bet you have guessed that already as well."

"Oh, I don't know," Bryne said. "It is an unusual time,
and strange events are common. Perhaps Lelaine decided to
forgo scheming for a time and actually listen to your pleas."

Gawyn grimaced. "I think you'd sooner find a Trolloc
who has taken up weaving than an Aes Sedai who has given
up scheming."

"I do believe that you were warned," Bryne said.

There was no argument that Gawyn could make, so they simply rode in silence for a short time, passing the distant river to the right. Beyond that, the tower and roofs of Tar Valon. A prison.

"We'll eventually need to discuss that group of soldiers you left behind, Gawyn," Bryne said suddenly, eyes forward.

"I don't see what there is to discuss," Gawyn said, which wasn't completely truthful. He had suspicions of what Bryne would ask, and he didn't look forward to the conversation.

Bryne shook his head. "I'll need information, lad. Locations, troop counts, equipment lists. I know you were staging from one of the villages to the east, but which one? How many are in your force, and what kind of support are Elaida's Aes Sedai giving them?"

Gawyn kept his eyes forward. "I came to help Egwene. Not to betray those who trusted me."

"You already betrayed them."

"No," Gawyn said firmly. "I abandoned them, but I have not betrayed them. And I do not intend to."

"And you expect me to let a potential advantage die untaken?" Bryne asked, turning to him. "What you have in that brain of yours could save lives."

"Or *cost* lives," Gawyn said, "if you look at it from the other side."

"Don't make this difficult, Gawyn."

"Or what?" Gawyn asked. "You'll put me to the question?"

"You'd suffer for them?"

"They are my men," Gawyn said simply. *Or, at least, they were.* Either way, he had had enough of being pushed around by circumstances and wars. He would give no loyalty to the White Tower, but neither would he offer it to these rebels. Egwene and Elayne held his heart and his honor. And if he couldn't give it to them, he would give it to Andor—and the entire world—by hunting down Rand al'Thor and seeing him dead.

Rand al'Thor. Gawyn didn't believe Bryne's defense of the man. Oh, he believed that Bryne meant what he said— but he was mistaken. It could happen to the best of people, taken in by the charisma of a creature like al'Thor. He had fooled Elayne herself. The only way to help any of them would be to expose this Dragon and dispose of him.

He looked over at Bryne, who turned away. He was still thinking about the Younglings, likely. It was unlikely that Bryne would put Gawyn to the question. Gawyn knew the general, and his sense of honor, too well. It wouldn't happen. But Bryne *might* decide to imprison Gawyn. Perhaps it would be wise to offer him something.

"They are youths, Bryne," Gawyn said.

Bryne frowned.

"Youths," Gawyn repeated. "Barely past their training. They belong on the sparring field, not on the battlefield. Their hearts are good, and their skills sound, but they are much less a threat to you now that I am gone. I was the one who knew your strategy. Without me, they will have a much harder time of their raids. I suspect that if they continue to strike, they shall have their day with the butcher soon enough. No need for me to hasten them along."

"Very well," Bryne replied. "I will wait. But if their raids continue to be effective, you will hear this question from me again."

Gawyn nodded. The best thing he could do for the Younglings would be to help end this division between the rebels and the loyalists. But that seemed far beyond the scope of what he could accomplish. Perhaps after he freed Egwene he could think of some way to help. Light! They couldn't really be intending to go to blows, could they? The skirmish following Siuan Sanche's fall had been bad enough. What would happen if armies met here, just outside of Tar Valon? Aes Sedai against Aes Sedai, Warder fighting Warder on a battlefield? A disaster.

"It can't come to that," he found himself saying.

Bryne looked at Gawyn as their horses continued across the field.

"You can't attack, Bryne," Gawyn said. "A siege is one thing. But what will you do if they order you to mount an assault?"

"What I always do," Bryne said. "Obey."

"But—"

"I gave my word, Gawyn."

"And how many deaths is that word worth? Assaulting the White Tower would be a disaster. No matter how slighted these rebel Aes Sedai may feel, there will be no reconciliation if it happens by the sword."

"That's not our decision," Bryne said. He glanced at Gawyn, a thoughtful expression on his face.

"What?" Gawyn asked.

"I'm wondering why it matters to you. I thought you were just here for Egwene."

"I. . . ." Gawyn floundered.

"Who are you, Gawyn Trakand?" Bryne asked, prodding further. "What are your allegiances, really?"

"You know me better than most, Gareth."

"I know who you were *supposed* to be," Bryne said. "First Prince of the Sword, trained by Warders but bonded to no woman."

"And that's not what I am?" Gawyn asked testily.

"Peace, son," Bryne said. "This wasn't meant to be an insult. Just an observation. I know you were never as single-minded as your brother. I suppose I should have seen this in you."

Gawyn turned toward the aging general. What was the man talking about?

Bryne sighed. "It's a thing most soldiers never face, Gawyn. Oh, they may consider it, but they don't let it torment them. This question is for someone else, someone higher up."

"What question?" Gawyn asked, perplexed.

"Choosing a side," Bryne said. "And, once you've picked one, deciding if you made the right decision. The foot soldiers don't have to make this choice, but those of us who lead . . . yes, I can see it in you. That skill of yours with the sword is no small gift. Where do you use it?"

"For Elayne," Gawyn said quickly.

"As you do now?" Bryne asked with amusement.

"Well, once I save Egwene."

"And if Egwene won't go?" Bryne asked. "I know that look in your eyes, lad. I also know some small bit about Egwene al'Vere. She won't leave this battlefield until a victor has been chosen."

"I'll take her away," Gawyn said. "Back to Andor."

"And will you *force* her to go?" Bryne asked. "As you forced your way into my camp? Will you become a bully and a footpad, remarkable only because of your ability to kill or punish those who disagree with you?"

Gawyn didn't answer.

"Whom to serve?" Bryne said, thoughtful. "Our own skill frightens us, sometimes. What is the ability to kill if one has no outlet for it? A wasted talent? The pathway to becoming a murderer? The power to protect and preserve is daunting. So you look for someone to give the skill to, someone who will use it wisely. The need to make a decision chews at you, even after you've made it. I see the question more in younger men. We old hounds, we're just happy to have a place by the hearth. If someone tells us to fight, we don't want to shake things up too much. But the young men . . . they wonder."

"Did you question, once?" Gawyn asked.

"Yes," Bryne said. "More than once. I wasn't Captain-General during the Aiel War, but I *was* a rank-captain. I wondered then, many times."

"How could you question your side during the Aiel war, of all things?" Gawyn said, frowning. "They came to slaughter."

"They didn't come for us," Bryne said. "They just wanted the Cairhienin. Of course, that wasn't so easy to see at first, but truth be told, some of us wondered. Laman deserved his death. Why should we die to stand in the way of it? Maybe more of us should have asked the question."

"Then what's the answer?" Gawyn asked. "Where do you put your trust? Whom do I serve?"

"I don't know," Bryne said frankly.

"Then why ask in the first place?" Gawyn snapped, pulling his horse up short.

Bryne reined in his animal, turning back. "I don't know the answer because there isn't one. At least, each person's answer is their own. When I was young, I fought for honor. Eventually, I realized that there was little honor to be found in killing, and I found that I had changed. Then I fought because I served your mother. I trusted her. When she failed me, I began to wonder again. What of all those years of service? What of the men I'd killed in her name? What did any of that mean?"

He turned and flicked his reins, moving again. Gawyn hasted Challenge to catch up.

"You wonder why I'm here, instead of in Andor?" Bryne asked. "It's because I can't let go. It's because the world is changing, and I need to be part of it. It's because once everything in Andor was taken from me, I needed a new place for my loyalty. The Pattern brought me this opportunity."

"And you chose it just because it was there?"

"No," Bryne said. "I picked it because I'm a fool." He met Gawyn's eyes. "But I *stayed* because it was right. That which has been broken must be made whole, and I've seen what a terrible leader can do to a kingdom. Elaida can't be allowed to pull this world down with her."

Gawyn started.

"Yes," Bryne said. "I've actually come to believe them. Fool women. But by the Light, Gawyn, they're right. What I'm doing is right. She's right."

"Who?"

Bryne shook his head, muttering. "Bloody woman."

Egwene? Gawyn wondered.

"My motives aren't important to you, son," Bryne said. "You're not one of my soldiers. But you need to make some decisions. In the days coming, you'll need to have a side and you'll need to know why you've chosen it. That's all I'll say on the matter."

He kicked his horse into a faster gait. In the distance, Gawyn could pick out another guard post. He hung back as Bryne and his soldiers approached it.

Pick a side. What if Egwene *wouldn't* go with him?

Bryne was right. Something *was* coming. You could smell it in the air, feel it in the weak sunlight that managed to shoulder its way through the clouds. You could sense it, distantly, in the north, crackling like unseen energy on that dark horizon.

War, battles, conflicts, changes. Gawyn felt as if he didn't know what the different sides were. Let alone which one to pick for himself.

CHAPTER
31

A Promise to Lews Therin

Cadsuane kept her cloak on, hood up, despite the mugginess that strained her ability to "ignore" the heat. She dared not lower the hood or remove the cloak. Al'Thor's words had been specific; if he saw her face, she would be executed. She wouldn't risk her life to prevent a few hours of discomfort, even if she thought al'Thor was safely back in his newly appropriated mansion. The boy often appeared where he wasn't expected or wanted.

She wasn't about to let him exile her, of course. The more power a man held, the more likely he was to be an idiot with it. Give a man one cow, and he'd care for it with concern, using its milk to feed his family. Give a man ten cows, and he was likely to think himself rich—then let all ten starve for lack of attention.

She clomped down the boardwalk, passing bannered buildings like boxes stacked atop one another. She wasn't particularly pleased to be in Bandar Eban again. She had nothing against the Domani; she just preferred cities that weren't so crowded. And with the problems in the countryside, the place was more packed than normal. Refugees continued to trickle in despite the rumors regarding al'Thor's arrival in the city. She passed a cluster of them in the alley to her left, a family, faces darkened by dirt.

Al'Thor promised food. That brought hungry mouths, none eager to return to their farms, even after they were given food. The countryside was still too chaotic, and the food here too new. The refugees couldn't be certain the grain wouldn't just spoil, as so much did recently. No, they stayed, packing the city, crowding it.

Cadsuane shook her head, continuing down the board-walk, those wretched clogs clattering against the wood. The city was famous for these long, sturdy walkways, which allowed foot traffic to avoid the mud of the streets. Cobbles would have fixed that, but the Domani often prided themselves on being *different* from the rest of the world. Indigestibly spicy food with dreadful eating utensils. A capital filled with frivolous banners, set on a huge port. Scandalous dresses on the women; long, thin mustaches on the men and an almost Sea Folk–like fondness for earrings.

Hundreds of those banners flapped in the wind as Cadsuane passed, and she gritted her teeth against the temptation to pull off her hood and feel the wind on her face. Light-cursed ocean air. Normally, Bandar Eban was chilly and rainy. Rarely had she felt it this warm. The humidity was dreadful either way. Rational people stayed inland!

She made her way down several streets, crossing through the mud at intersections. That was the irredeemable flaw of boardwalks, in her opinion. The locals knew which streets to cut across and which ones were deep in mud, but Cadsuane had to just tramp across wherever she could. That's why she'd hunted out these clogs, built after the Tairen style, to go over her shoes. It had been surprisingly hard to find a merchant selling them; the Domani obviously had little interest in them, and most people she passed either went barefoot in the mud or knew where to cross and keep from soiling their shoes.

Halfway down to the docks, she finally reached her destination. The fine banner flapping out front proclaimed the inn's name as The Wind's Favor, beating against an inlaid wood front. Cadsuane made her way inside and took off the clogs in the muddy entryway before stepping up into the inn proper. There, finally, she allowed herself to lower her hood. If al'Thor randomly happened to visit this particular inn, then he'd just have to hang her.

The inn's common room was decorated more like a king's dining hall than a tavern. White tablecloths coated the tables, and the varnished wooden floor was mopped to a shine. The walls were hung with tasteful still-life paintings—a bowl of fruit on the wall behind the bar, a vase of flowers on the wall opposite it. The bottles on the ledge behind the bar were almost all wine, very few bottles of brandy or other liquors.

The slender innkeeper, Quillin Tasil, was a tall, oval-faced Andoran man. Thinning on top with dark, short hair at the sides of his head, he wore a full beard, trimmed short, which was almost all gray. His fine lavender coat had white ruffled cuffs peeking out from the sleeves, but he wore an innkeeper's apron over the front. He generally had had good information, but was also willing to look into inquiries for her among his associates. A very useful man indeed.

He smiled at Cadsuane as she entered, wiping his hands on a towel. He gestured her toward a table, then went back to the bar to fetch some wine. Cadsuane settled herself as two men on the other side of the room began to argue loudly. The other patrons—only four, two women at a table on the far side, two more men at the bar—paid the argument no heed. One couldn't spend much time in Arad Doman without learning to ignore the frequent flares in temper. Domani men were as hotheaded as volcanoes, and most people agreed that Domani women were the reason. These two men did not turn to a duel, as would have been common in Ebou Dar. Instead, they shouted for a few moments, then began to agree with each other, then insisted on buying one another wine. Fights were common; bloodshed infrequent. Injuries were bad for business.

Quillin approached, bearing a cup of wine—it would be one of his finest vintages. She never requested such from him, but never complained either.

"Mistress Shore," he said with his affable voice, "I wish I'd known earlier that you were back in town! The first I heard of it was your letter!"

Cadsuane took the offered cup. "I am not accustomed to giving reports on my whereabouts to every acquaintance, Master Tasil."

"Of course not, of course not," he said, and seemed completely unoffended at her sharp response. She'd never been able to get a rise out of him. That had always made her curious.

"The inn seems to be doing well," she said politely, causing him to turn and look over his few patrons. They seemed uncomfortable to be sitting at immaculate tables atop a gleaming floor. Cadsuane wasn't certain if it was the intimidating cleanliness that kept people away from The Wind's Favor, or if it was Quillin's insistence on never hiring gleemen or musicians to perform. He claimed they spoiled the atmosphere. As she watched, he noticed that a new patron entered, tracking in mud. She could see Quillin's fingers itching to go scrub the floor.

"You there," Quillin called to the man. "Scrape your shoes before coming in, if you please."

The man froze, frowning, but went back to do as instructed. Quillin sighed and moved over to sit at her table. "Frankly, Mistress Shore, it gets a little too busy here lately for my tastes. Can't keep track of all my patrons sometimes! People go without drink, waiting for me to get to them."

"You could hire help," she noted. "A serving girl or two."

"What? And let them have all the fun?" He said it in all seriousness.

Cadsuane took a sip of her wine. An excellent vintage indeed, perhaps expensive enough that an inn—no matter how splendid—shouldn't have had it readily available behind the bar. She sighed. Quillin's Domani wife was one of the most accomplished silk merchants in the city; many Sea Folk vessels sought her out personally to trade with her. Quillin had kept accounts for his wife's business for some twenty years before he had retired, both of them wealthy.

And what did he do with it? Open an inn. It had apparently always been a dream of his. Cadsuane had learned long ago to stop questioning the odd penchants of people with too much free time.

"What news of the city, Quillin?" she asked, sliding a small bag of coins across the table toward him.

"Mistress, you offend," he said, raising his hands. "I couldn't take your coin!"

She raised an eyebrow. "I have little patience for games today, Master Tasil. If you don't want it yourself, then give it to the poor. Light knows there are enough of those in the city these days."

He sighed, but reluctantly pocketed the purse. Perhaps that was why his common room was often empty; an innkeeper who had no regard for money was a strange beast. Many of the common men would find Quillin as discomforting as the immaculate floor and tasteful decorations.

Quillin was, however, *very* good for information. His wife shared her gossip with him. With her face, he obviously knew she was Aes Sedai. Namine—his eldest daughter—had gone to the White Tower, eventually choosing the Brown and settling into the library there. A Domani librarian was nothing unusual—the Terhana library in Bandar Eban was one of the greatest in the world. However, Namine's casual, yet keen, understanding of current events had been enough of a curiosity that Cadsuane had followed the connection, hoping to discover well-placed parents. Ties such as a daughter in the White Tower often made people amiable toward other Aes Sedai. That had led her to Quillin. Cadsuane didn't trust him entirely, but she *was* fond of him.

"What news of the city?" Quillin asked. Honestly, what innkeeper wore a silk embroidered vest beneath his apron? No wonder people found the inn strange. "Where should I start? There has almost been too much to keep track of lately!"

"Start with Alsalam," Cadsuane said, sipping her wine. "When was he last seen?"

"By credible witnesses, or by hearsay?"

"Tell me both."

"There have been lesser windborn and merchants who claim to have received personal communication from the King as recently as a week ago, my Lady, but I regard such claims with skepticism. Very soon after the King's . . . hiatus began you could find forged letters claiming to dictate his wishes. I have seen some few sets of orders with my own eyes that I trust—or, at least, I trust the seal on them—but the King himself? I'd say it has been almost half a year since anyone I can vouch for has seen him."

"His whereabouts, then?"

The innkeeper shrugged, looking apologetic. "For a while, we were certain that the Council of Merchants was behind the disappearance. They rarely let the King out of their sight, and with the troubles to the south, we all assumed they'd taken His Majesty to safety."

"But?"

"But my sources," that meant his wife, "aren't convinced any longer. The Council of Merchants has been too disorganized lately, each member trying to keep their own chunk of Arad Doman from unraveling. If they'd had the King, they'd have revealed him by now."

Cadsuane tapped the side of her cup with a fingernail, annoyed. Could there be truth, then, to the al'Thor boy's belief that one of the Forsaken had Alsalam? "What else?"

"There are Aiel in the city, Lady," Quillin said, scrubbing at an invisible spot on the tabletop.

She gave him a flat stare. "I hadn't noticed."

He chuckled. "Yes, yes, obvious, I suppose. But the exact number in the area is twenty-four thousand. Some say the Dragon Reborn has them here just to prove his power and authority. After all, who ever heard of *Aiel* distributing food? Half the poor in the city are too frightened to go to the handouts, for fear the Aiel have used some of their poisons on the grain."

"Aiel *poisons*?" She'd never heard that particular rumor before.

Quillin nodded. "Some claim that as the reason for the food spoilages, my Lady."

"But food was spoiling in the country long before the Aiel arrived, wasn't it?"

"Yes, yes, of course," Quillin said. "But it can be hard to remember things like that in the face of so much bad grain. Besides, spoilage *has* grown much worse since the Lord Dragon arrived."

Cadsuane covered her frown by taking a sip of wine. It had grown worse with al'Thor's arrival? Was that just rumor, or was it the truth? She lowered her cup. "And the other strange occurrences in the city?" she asked carefully, to see what she could discover.

"You've heard of those, then?" Quillin said, leaning in. "People don't like to speak of them, of course, but my sources hear things. Stillborn children, men dying from falls that should barely have caused a bruise, stones toppling from buildings and striking women dead as they trade. Dangerous times, my Lady. I hate to pass on mere hearsay, but I've seen the numbers myself!"

The events were not, in themselves, unexpected. "Of course, there are the balances."

"Balances?"

"Marriages on the rise," she said, waving a hand, "children who encounter wild beasts but escape unharmed, unexpected fortunes discovered beneath the floorboards of a pauper's home. That sort of thing."

"That certainly *would* be nice," Quillin said, chuckling. "We can wish and hope, my Lady."

"You've heard no such stories?" Cadsuane asked with surprise.

"No, my Lady. I can ask around, if you wish."

"Do so." Al'Thor was *ta'veren*, but the Pattern was a thing of balance. For every accidental death caused by Rand's presence in a city, there was always a miraculous survival.

What did it mean if that was breaking down?

She went on to specific questions for Quillin, the whereabouts of the members of the merchant council at the top of the list. She knew that the al'Thor boy wanted to capture them all; if she could get information about their locations that he didn't have, it could be very useful. She also asked Quillin to find out the economic situation of the other major Domani cities and supply any news of rebel factions or Taraboners striking across the border.

As she left the inn—reluctantly raising her hood and stepping back into the muggy afternoon—she found that Quillin's words had left her with more questions than she'd had when she'd come.

It looked like rain. Of course, that was always the way it looked lately. Overcast and dreary, with a gray sky and clouds that bled together in a uniform haze. At least it had actually rained the previous night; for some reason, that made the overcast sky more bearable. As if it were more natural, allowing her to pretend that the perpetual gloom wasn't another sign of the Dark One's stirring. He had withered the people with a drought, he had frozen them with a sudden winter, and now he seemed determined to destroy them through sheer melancholy.

Cadsuane shook her head, tapping her clogs to make sure they were sturdily affixed, then walked onto the muddied boardwalk and made her way down toward the docks. She would see just how accurate these rumors about spoilage were. Had the strange events surrounding al'Thor really grown more destructive, or was she just allowing herself to find what she feared?

Al'Thor. She had to face the truth: she had bungled her handling of him. Of course, she hadn't made any mistakes with the male *a'dam*, whatever al'Thor claimed. Whoever had stolen the collar had been exceedingly powerful and crafty. Anyone capable of such a feat could just as easily have fetched another male *a'dam* from the Seanchan. They were likely to have plenty of them.

No, the *a'dam* had been taken from her own room in an effort to sow distrust; of that she was certain. Perhaps, even, the theft had been intended to mask something else: the returning of the figurine to al'Thor. His temperament had become so dark, there was no telling what destruction he could cause with that.

The poor, foolish boy. He should never have had to suffer collaring at the hands of one of the Forsaken; that would only remind him of the times he had been beaten and caged by Aes Sedai. It would make her job more difficult. If not impossible.

That was the question she had to face now. Was he beyond saving? Was it too late to change him? And if it was, what—if anything—could she do? The Dragon Reborn *had* to meet the Dark One at Shayol Ghul. If he did not, all was lost. But what if allowing him to meet the Dark One would be equally disastrous?

No. She refused to believe that their battle had already been lost. There *had* to be something that could be done to change al'Thor's direction. But what?

Al'Thor hadn't reacted like most peasants suddenly granted power; he hadn't grown selfish or petty. He hadn't hoarded wealth, nor had he struck with childish vengeance against any who had slighted him in his youth. Indeed, there had actually been a wisdom to many of his decisions—the ones that didn't involve gallivanting into danger.

Cadsuane continued down the boardwalk, passing Domani refugees in their incongruously bright clothing. She occasionally had to step around clusters of them sitting on the damp logs, an impromptu camp growing up around the mouth to an alleyway or the unused side door of a building. None made way for her. What good was an Aes Sedai face if you covered it up? This city was just too packed.

Cadsuane slowed near a row of pennants which spelled out the name of the dock registrar. The docks themselves were just ahead, lined by twice as many Sea Folk ships as before, many of them rakers, the largest of Sea Folk vessels. More than a few were converted Seanchan ships, likely stolen from Ebou Dar during the mass escape a short while back.

The docks were crowded with people eager for grain. The crowds jostled and yelled, not looking at all worried about the "poisons" Quillin had mentioned. Of course, starvation could overcome a great number of fears. Dock workers controlled the crowds; among them were Aiel in brown *cadin'sor*, holding their spears and glaring as only Aiel could. There also appeared to be a fair number of merchants on the docks, probably hoping to secure some of the handouts for storage and later sale.

The docks looked much as they had every day since al'Thor's arrival. What had made her pause? There seemed to be a prickling sensation on her back, as if. . . .

She spun to find a procession riding down the muddy street. Al'Thor sat proudly on his dark gelding, his clothing colored to match, with only a little red embroidery. As usual, he led a score of soldiers, advisors and a growing number of Domani sycophants.

She seemed to encounter him very frequently traveling the streets. She forced herself to hold her ground, not shying away into an alley, though she did pull her hood down a little lower to shade her face. Al'Thor gave no sign that he recognized her as he rode just in front of her. He seemed troubled by his own thoughts, as he often was. She wanted to yell at him that he needed to move more quickly, secure the crown of Arad Doman and move on, but she held her tongue. She would *not* let her nearly three hundred years of life end with an execution at the hands of the Dragon Reborn!

His retinue passed. As before, when she turned away from him, she thought she saw . . . from the corner of her eye . . . darkness around him, like too much shade from the clouds above. Whenever she looked directly at him, it vanished—in fact, whenever she *tried* to see it, she couldn't make it out. It only appeared when she saw him indirectly, and by happenstance.

She had never read or heard of such a thing in all of her years. To see it around the Dragon Reborn terrified her. This had grown bigger than her pride, much larger than her failures. No. It had *always* been larger than she was. Guiding al'Thor wasn't like guiding a galloping horse, it was like trying to guide a deep sea tempest itself!

She would *never* be able to change his course. He didn't trust Aes Sedai, and with good reason. He didn't seem to trust anyone, save perhaps for Min—but Min had resisted every attempt that Cadsuane had made at involving her. The girl was almost as bad as al'Thor.

Visiting the docks was useless. Talking to her informants was useless. If she didn't do something *soon*, they were all doomed. But what? She leaned back against the building behind her, triangular banners blowing in front of her, pointing north. Toward the Blight and al'Thor's ultimate destiny.

An idea struck her. She seized it like a drowning woman in the churning waves. She didn't know what it was attached to, but it was her only hope.

She spun on her heels and hurried back the way she had come, her head bowed, barely daring to think about her plan. It could fail so easily. If al'Thor really was as dominated by his rage as she feared, then even this would not help him.

But if he really was that far gone, then there wasn't *anything* that would help him. That meant she had nothing to lose. Nothing but the world itself.

Pushing her way through crowds and occasionally taking to the muddy street to avoid them, she arrived at the mansion. Some Aiel had taken the camp where Dobraine's armsmen had staged until his withdrawal. They camped all about, some on the grounds, some in a wing of the mansion, others in nearby buildings.

Cadsuane made her way to the wing that belonged to the Aiel, and she was not stopped. She enjoyed privileges among the Aiel that none of the other sisters had been given. She found Sorilea and the other Wise Ones in conference in one of the libraries. They were sitting on the floor, of course. Sorilea nodded to Cadsuane as she entered. She was all bone, thin and leathery, yet never could a person think her frail. Not with those eyes, set into a face that, despite being worn by wind and sun, was too young for her age. How was it that the Wise Ones could live so long, yet not obtain the Aes Sedai agelessness? That was a question Cadsuane had not been able to answer.

She lowered her hood and joined the Wise Ones, seating

herself on the floor, eschewing cushions. She looked Sorilea in the eyes. "I have failed," she said.

The Wise One nodded, as if she had thought this same thing. Cadsuane forced herself not to show her annoyance.

"There is no shame in failure," Bair said, "when that failure was the fault of another."

Amys nodded. "The *Car'a'carn* is stubborn beyond all men, Cadsuane Sedai. You have no *toh* toward us."

"Shame or *toh*," Cadsuane said, "it will all be irrelevant soon. But I have a plan. Will you help me?"

The Wise Ones shared a look among them.

"What is this plan?" Sorilea asked.

Cadsuane smiled, then began to explain.

Rand glanced over his shoulder, watching Cadsuane scuttle away. She probably thought that he hadn't noticed her hiding there at the side of the street. The cloak hid her face, but nothing could conceal that self-assured posture, not even the clumsy footgear. Even as she hurried, she seemed in control, and others moved out of her way reflexively.

She flirted with his prohibition, following him through the town like this. However, she had not shown him her face, and so he let her go. It had probably been a poor move to exile her in the first place, but there was no going back now. He would just have to control his temper in the future. Keep it wrapped in ice, steaming deep inside his chest, pulsing like a second heart.

He turned back to the docks. Perhaps there was no reason for him to check on the food distribution directly. However, he had found that the grain had a distinctly higher chance of getting to those who needed it if everyone knew they were being watched. This was a people who had been without a king for too long; they deserved to see that someone was in control.

Upon reaching the wharf, he turned Tai'daishar to angle along the back of the docks, moving at an unhurried pace. He glanced at the Asha'man riding beside him. Naeff had a strong, rectangular face and the lean build of a warrior; he'd been a soldier in the Queen's Guard of Andor before resigning in disgust during the reign of "Lord Gaebril." Naeff had found his way to the Black Tower, and now wore both the Sword and Dragon.

Eventually, Rand would probably have to either let Naeff return to his Aes Sedai—he had been among the first ones bonded—or bring her to him. He was loath to have another Aes Sedai nearby, although Nelavaire Demasiellin, a Green, was relatively pleasant as Aes Sedai went.

"Continue," Rand said to Naeff as they rode. The Asha'man had been running messages and meeting with the Seanchan with Bashere.

"Well, my Lord," Naeff said, "it's just my gut feeling, but I don't think they'll accept Katar for the meeting place. They always grow difficult when Lord Bashere or I mention it, claiming they will have to seek further instructions from the Daughter of the Nine Moons. Their tones imply that the 'instructions' will be that the location is unacceptable."

Rand spoke softly. "Katar is neutral ground, neither in Arad Doman nor deep within Seanchan lands."

"I know, my Lord. We've tried. I promise that we have."

"Very well," Rand said. "If they continue to be bullheaded about this, I will choose another location. Return to them and say we will meet at Falme."

From behind, Flinn whistled quietly.

"My Lord," Naeff said. "That's *well* within the Seanchan border."

"I know," Rand said, glancing at Flinn. "But it has a . . . certain historic significance. We will be safe; these Seanchan are bound rigidly by their honor. They will not attack if we arrive under a banner of truce."

"Are you certain?" Naeff asked quietly. "I don't like the way they look at me, my Lord. There's contempt in their eyes, every one of them. Contempt and pity, as if I'm some lost hound, searching for scraps behind the inn. Burn me, but it makes me sick."

"They've got those collars of theirs handy, my Lord," Flinn said. "Flag of truce or not, they'll be itching to bind us all."

Rand closed his eyes, keeping the rage inside, feeling the salty sea air blow across him. He opened his eyes to a sky bounded by dark clouds. He would not think of the collar at his neck, his hand strangling Min. That was the past.

He was harder than steel. He could not be broken.

"We *must* have peace with the Seanchan," he said. "Differences notwithstanding."

"Differences?" Flinn asked. "I don't rightly think I'd call that a difference, my Lord. They want to enslave every one of us, maybe execute us. They think it's a *favor* to do either!"

Rand held the man's gaze. Flinn was not rebellious; he was as loyal as they came. But still Rand made him wilt and bow his head. Dissension could not be tolerated. Dissension and lies had brought him to the collar. No more.

"I'm sorry, my Lord," Flinn finally said. "Burn me if Falme isn't a fine choice! You'll have them watching the skies with fear, you will."

"Go with the message now, Naeff," Rand said. "I want this settled."

Naeff nodded, turning his horse and trotting away from the column, a small group of Aiel guards joining him. One could only Travel from a place one knew well, and so he couldn't simply leave from dockside. Rand continued his ride, troubled by Lews Therin's silence. The madman had been unusually distant lately. That should have pleased Rand, but it disturbed him instead. It had to do with the unnamed power that Rand had touched. He still often heard the madman weeping, whispering to himself, terrified.

"Rand?"

He turned, not having heard Nynaeve's horse approach. She wore a bold green dress, modest by Domani standards, but still far more revealing than she'd ever have considered during her days in the Two Rivers. *She has a right to change,* Rand thought. *What is a loosening of dress compared to the fact that I have ordered exiles and executions?*

"What did you decide?" she asked.

"We will meet them at Falme," he said.

She muttered quietly.

"What was that?" he asked.

"Oh, just something about you being a wool-headed fool," she said, looking at him with defiant eyes.

"Falme will be agreeable to them," he said.

"Yes," she said. "It puts you perfectly within their hands."

"I cannot afford to wait, Nynaeve," he said. "This is a risk we must take. But I doubt they will attack."

"Did you doubt it last time too?" she asked. "The time when they took your hand?"

He glanced down at his stump. "They are unlikely to have one of the Forsaken with them this time."

"You can be sure?"

He met her eyes, and she held them, something few people could seem to manage these days. Finally, he shook his head. "I cannot be sure."

She sniffed in response, indicating that she'd won that argument. "Well, we'll just have to be extra careful. Perhaps memories of the *last* time you visited Falme will make them uncomfortable."

"I hope so," he said.

She muttered something else to herself, but he didn't catch it. Nynaeve would never make an ideal Aes Sedai; she was far too free with her emotions, particularly her temper. Rand did not find it a fault; at least he always knew where he stood with Nynaeve. She was terrible at games, and that made her valuable. He trusted her. She was one of the few.

We do trust her, don't we? Lews Therin asked. *Can we?*

Rand didn't answer. He completed his review of the docks. Nynaeve stayed at his side. She seemed to be in a dark mood, though Rand couldn't see why. With Cadsuane's banishment, Nynaeve could fill the role as his primary advisor. Didn't that please her?

Perhaps she was worried about Lan. As Rand turned his procession back toward the center of town, he asked, "Have you heard from him?"

Nynaeve glanced at him, eyes narrowing. "Who?"

"You know who," Rand said, riding past a row of bright red banners waving atop a line of homes, each holding scions of the same family.

"His actions are none of your concern," Nynaeve said.

"The entire world is my concern, Nynaeve." He looked at her. "Would you not agree?"

She opened her mouth, no doubt to snap at him, but faltered as she met his eyes. *Light,* he thought, seeing the apprehension in her face. *I can do it to Nynaeve, now. What is it that they see when they look at me?* That look in her eyes almost made him frightened of himself.

"Lan will be well," Nynaeve said, looking away.

"He has ridden to Malkier, hasn't he?"

She flushed.

"How long?" Rand asked. "He hasn't gotten to the Blight already, has he?" Turned loose to follow what he saw as both his duty and destiny, Lan would ride straight to Malkier alone. The kingdom—his kingdom—had been consumed by the Blight decades ago, when he'd been a babe.

"Two or three more months," she said. "Perhaps a little longer. He rides to Shienar to stand at the Gap, even if he has to do so alone."

"He seeks vengeance," Rand said softly. "'To avenge what cannot be defended.'"

"He does his duty!" Nynaeve said. "But . . . I do worry at his brashness. He insisted that I take him to the Borderlands, so I did, but I left him in Saldaea. I wanted him as far from the Gap as possible. He'll have to cross some difficult terrain to get where he's going."

Rand felt an icy coldness as he considered Lan riding to the Gap. To his death, essentially. But there was nothing to be done about that. "I am sorry, Nynaeve," he said, though he did not feel it. He had trouble feeling anything lately.

"You think I'd send him alone?" she snapped. "Woolheaded, both of you! I've seen that he'll have his own army, although he doesn't want one."

And she was perfectly capable of it. Perhaps she'd sent warning to the remnants of the Malkieri in Lan's name. Lan was a strange mixture; he refused to raise the banner of Malkier or claim his place as its king, for he feared leading the last of his countrymen to their deaths. Yet he would be perfectly willing to ride to that same death himself in the name of honor.

Is that what I do? Rand thought. *Ride to my death in the name of honor? But no, it's different. Lan has a choice.* There were no prophecies saying that Lan would die, whatever the man's assumptions about his own fate.

"He could use some help regardless," Nynaeve said uncomfortably. Asking for help always made her uncomfortable. "His army will be small. I doubt they'll stand long against the Trollocs."

"Will he attack?" Rand asked.

Nynaeve hesitated. "He didn't say," she said. "But yes, I think he will. He thinks you are wasting time here, Rand. If he arrives and gathers an army, and finds Trollocs gathered at Tarwin's Gap . . . yes, I think he'll attack."

"Then he deserves what he will get, for riding without the rest of us," Rand said.

Nynaeve scowled at him. "How can you say that?"

"I must," Rand replied softly. "The Last Battle is imminent. Perhaps my own attack on the Blight will happen at the same time as Lan's. Perhaps not." He paused thoughtfully. If Lan and whatever army he brought engaged at the Gap . . . perhaps that would draw attention. If Rand *didn't* attack there, it would throw off the Shadow. He could strike them where they didn't expect it while their eyes were on Lan.

"Yes," Rand said thoughtfully. "His death could serve me well indeed."

Nynaeve's eyes widened in fury, but Rand ignored her. A very quiet place, deep inside of him, was struck with worry over his friend. He had to ignore that worry, silence it. But that voice whispered to him.

He named you friend. Do not abandon him. . . .

Nynaeve controlled her anger, which impressed Rand. "We will speak of this again," she said to him, voice curt. "Perhaps after you've had a chance to think on exactly what abandoning Lan would mean."

He liked to think of Nynaeve as the same belligerent Wisdom who had bullied him back in the Two Rivers. She'd always seemed as if she tried *too* hard, as if she had worried that others would ignore her title because of her youth. But she had grown a lot since then.

They reached the mansion, where fifty of Bashere's soldiers stood guard before the gates. They saluted in unison as Rand passed through them. He passed Aiel camped outside, dismounted at the stables and transferred the access key from its loop on his saddle to the oversized pocket of his coat—more of a pouch, buttoned into his coat—designed for the statuette. The hand holding its globe aloft reached out of its depths.

He went to his throne room. He couldn't call it anything other than that, now that the King's throne had been brought to him. It was oversized, with gilding and gemstones affixed to the wood at the arms and to the back, above the head. They protruded like budding eyes, giving the throne an ornate richness that Rand disliked. It hadn't been in the palace. One of the local merchants had been "protecting" it from the riots. Perhaps he had considered seizing the seat in a more figurative sense as well.

Rand sat on the throne, despite its gaudiness, shifting so that the access key in his pocket didn't jab him in the side. The powerful in the city weren't certain what to think of him, and he preferred it that way. He didn't name himself king, yet his armies secured the capital. He spoke of restoring Alsalam's place to him, yet sat on the throne as if he had a right to it. He had not moved into the palace. He wanted them to wonder.

In truth, he hadn't made a decision. A lot would depend on this day's reports. He nodded to Rhuarc as he entered; the muscular Aielman returned the gesture. Then Rand stepped down from the throne and he and Rhuarc sat down on the circular rug of spiraling colors which lay on the floor in front of the green-carpeted dais. The first time they'd done this, it had caused a quiet stir among the Domani attendants and functionaries of Rand's growing court.

"We have located and taken another of them, Rand al'Thor," Rhuarc said. "Alamindra Cutren was hiding on her cousin's lands near the northern border; what we learned on her estate led us directly to her."

That made four members of the merchant council in his custody. "What of Meashan Dubaris? You said you might have her as well."

"Dead," Rhuarc said. "By the hands of a mob a week gone."

"You are certain of this? It could be a lie to set you off her track."

"I have not seen the body myself," Rhuarc said, "but men I trust have, and they say it matches her description. I am reasonably assured that the trail was genuine."

Four captured, and two dead, then. That left four more to locate before he had enough members to order a new vote for king. It would not be the most ethical council election in Domani history; why did he bother? He could *appoint* a king, or name himself to the throne. Why did he care what the Domani thought proper?

Rhuarc watched him; the Aiel chief's eyes were thoughtful. He likely wondered the same things.

"Keep searching," Rand said. "I do not intend to take Arad Doman for myself; we will find the rightful king or

we will see the Council of Merchants assembled so that
they can choose a new one. I will not care who it is, so long
as he is not a Darkfriend."

"As you say, *Car'a'carn*," Rhuarc said, moving to rise.

"Order is important, Rhuarc," Rand said. "I don't have
time to secure this kingdom myself. We don't have long
before the Last Battle." He glanced at Nynaeve, who had
joined several Maidens at the back of the small room. "I
want four more members of the merchant council in our
possession by the end of the month."

"You set a demanding pace, Rand al'Thor," Rhuarc said.

Rand stood up. "Just find me those merchants. These
people deserve leaders."

"And the king?"

Rand glanced to the side, to where Milisair Chadmar
stood, carefully watched by Aiel guards. She seemed . . .
haggard. Her once-luxurious raven hair had been pulled up
into a bun, obviously because it was easier to care for that
way. Her dress was still rich, but now wrinkled, as if she'd
been wearing it for too long. Her eyes were red. She was
still beautiful, but much in the way that a painting would
still be beautiful if it were crumpled up, then smoothed out
on a table.

"May you find water and shade, Rhuarc," Rand said in
dismissal.

"May you find water and shade, Rand al'Thor." The tall
Aiel withdrew, some of his spears following him. Rand
took a deep breath, then stepped up to the gaudy throne and
sat. Rhuarc he treated with the respect he deserved. The
others . . . well, *they* would get the respect they deserved as
well.

He leaned forward, motioning Milisair to approach. One
of the Maidens nudged her in the back, forcing her forward.
The woman looked far more apprehensive than she had the
last time she had come before Rand.

"Well?" he asked her.

"My Lord Dragon . . ." she began, glancing around, as if
seeking aid from the Domani stewards and attendants who
stood there. They ignored her; even the fop Lord Ramshalan looked the other way.

"Speak, woman," Rand demanded.

"The messenger you asked after," she said. "He is dead."

Rand took in a deep breath. "And how did this happen?"

"The men I assigned to watch after him," she said quickly, "I hadn't realized how poorly they were treating the messenger! Why, they hadn't given him water for days, and the fevers struck. . . ."

"In other words," Rand said, "you failed to extract information from him, so you left him in a dungeon to rot, only remembering where he was when I demanded he be produced."

"*Car'a'carn*," one of the Maidens—a very young woman named Jalani—said, stepping forward. "We found this one packing her things, as if she were planning to escape the city."

Milisair paled visibly. "Lord Dragon," she said. "A moment of weakness! I—"

Rand waved for silence. "What am I to do with you now?"

"She should be executed, my Lord!" Ramshalan said, stepping forward eagerly.

Rand looked up with a frown. He hadn't been asking for a response. Lanky, with one of the thin black Domani mustaches, Ramshalan had a prominent nose that might have indicated some Saldaean forebear. He wore an outrageous coat of blue, orange and yellow, with ruffled white cuffs peeking out underneath. Apparently, such things passed for fashionable among some segments of the Domani upper crust. His earrings bore the mark of his house, and he had a black beauty mark in the shape of a bird in flight affixed to his check.

Rand had known many like him, courtiers with too few brains but too many family connections. Noble life seemed to breed them, much as the Two Rivers bred sheep. Ramshalan was particularly annoying because of his nasal voice and eager willingness to betray others in his desire to curry favor with Rand.

Still, men like him had their uses. Occasionally. "What do you think, Milisair?" Rand said musingly. "Should I have you executed for treason, as this man suggests?"

She did not weep, but she was obviously terrified, her hands shaking as she held them out, her eyes wide, unblinking.

"No," Rand said finally. "I need you to help choose a new

king. What good would it do to search the countryside for
your colleagues if I began to execute the Council members
I've already found?"

She let out the breath she had been holding, and tension
left her shoulders

"Lock her in the same dungeon where she imprisoned
the King's messenger," Rand said to the Maidens. "Make
sure she doesn't suffer the same fate—at least, not until after I'm finished with her."

Milisair cried out in despair. Aiel Maidens pulled her
from the room screaming, but Rand had already put her
from his head. Ramshalan watched her go with satisfaction;
apparently, she'd insulted him several times in public. That
was one point in her favor.

"The other members of the merchant council," Rand said
to the functionaries. "Have any of them had contact with
the King?"

"None more recently than four or five months ago, my
Lord," said one of them, a stumpy, large-bellied Domani
man named Noreladim. "Though we don't know about Alamindra, as she was just recently . . . discovered."

Perhaps she would have news, though he couldn't see her
having a better lead than a messenger who claimed to have
come from Alsalam himself. Burn that woman for letting
him die!

If Graendal sent the messenger, Lews Therin said suddenly, *I'd have never been able to break him. She's too
good with Compulsion. Crafty, so crafty.*

Rand hesitated. It was a good point. If the messenger
had been subject to Graendal's Compulsion, there would
have been little chance of him being able to betray her location. Not unless the web of Compulsion had been lifted,
which would have required a Healing beyond Rand's skill.
Graendal had always covered her tracks well.

But he wasn't sure she was in the country. If he could find
a messenger and Compulsion was there, he'd have enough.
"I need to speak with anyone else who claims to have a
message from the King," he said. "Others in the city who
might have had contact."

"They will be found, Lord Dragon," said the prim Ramshalan.

Rand nodded absently. If Naeff set up the meeting with

the Seanchan as hoped, then Rand could leave Arad Doman soon after. He hoped to leave them with a king, hoped to find and kill Graendal. But he would settle for peace with the Seanchan and food for these people. He could not solve everyone's problems. He could just force them into abeyance long enough for him to die at Shayol Ghul.

And thereby leave the world to break again once he was gone. He gritted his teeth. He had already wasted too much time worrying about things he could not fix.

Is that why I resist naming a Domani king? he thought. *Once I die, that man would lose his authority, and Arad Doman would be back where it began. If I don't leave a king who has the support of the merchants, then I'm essentially offering the kingdom up to the Seanchan the moment I die.*

So many things to balance. So many problems. He couldn't fix them all. He *couldn't*.

"I don't approve of this, Rand," Nynaeve said, standing beside the door, arms folded. "And we're not done talking about Lan, either."

Rand waved a dismissive hand.

"He's your *friend*, Rand," Nynaeve said. "Light! And what of Perrin and Mat? Do you know where they are? What has happened to them?"

The colors swirled before his eyes, revealing an image of Perrin standing by a tent with Galad. Why was Perrin with *Galad* of all people? And when had Elayne's half-brother joined the Whitecloaks? The colors changed to Mat, riding through the streets of a familiar city. Caemlyn? Thom was there, with him.

Rand frowned to himself. He could feel a pull from Perrin and Mat, both distant. It was their *ta'veren* natures, trying to draw them together. They both needed to be with him for the Last Battle.

"Rand?" Nynaeve asked. "Aren't you going to respond?"

"About Perrin and Mat?" Rand asked. "They live."

"How do you know?"

"I simply do." He sighed, shaking his head. "And they had better remain alive. I'll have need of them both before this is over."

"Rand!" she said. "They're your friends!"

"They're threads in the Pattern, Nynaeve," he said, rising.

"I barely know them anymore, and I suspect they would say the same thing of me."

"Don't you care about them?"

"Care?" Rand walked down the steps of the raised platform that held his throne. "What I care about is the Last Battle. What I care about is making peace with the Light-cursed Seanchan so that I can stop bothering with their squabble and get to the real battle. Beside those cares, a pair of boys from my little village are meaningless."

He looked at her, challenging. Ramshalan and the other attendants backed away quietly, not wanting to be caught between his gaze and Nynaeve.

She was silent, although her face took on a profound sadness. "Oh, Rand," she finally said. "You can't go on like this. This hardness within you, it will break you."

"I do what I must," he said, anger creeping into him. Would he never hear the end of complaints about his choices?

"This isn't what you must do, Rand," she said. "You're going to destroy yourself. You'll—"

Rand's anger surged. He spun, pointing at her. "Would you end up exiled like Cadsuane, Nynaeve?" he bellowed. "I will *not* be played with! I am done with that. Give advice when it is asked for, and the rest of the time *do not patronize me!*"

She recoiled, and Rand gritted his teeth, forcing the anger back down. He lowered his hand, but realized it had begun to reach reflexively for the access key in the pocket at his side. Nynaeve's eyes fixed on it, opening wide, and he slowly forced his hand away from the statuette.

The explosion surprised him. He had thought his temper controlled. He forced it down, and had a surprisingly difficult time of it. He turned and stalked from the room, throwing open the door, his Maidens following him. "I will have no more audiences today," he told the attendants who tried to follow him. "Go and do as I have told you! I need the other members of the merchant council. Go!"

They scattered. Only the Aiel remained, guarding him as he made his way to the rooms he had claimed in the mansion.

A short time longer. He only had to keep things balanced a short time longer. Then it could end. And he found that he was beginning to look forward to that end as much as Lews Therin did.

You promised we could die, Lews Therin said between distant sobs.

I did, Rand said. *And we will.*

CHAPTER
32

Rivers of Shadow

Nynaeve stood on the broad wall around Bandar Eban, looking down over the darkened city. The wall was on the inland side of the city, but Bandar Eban was built on a slope, so she could see out over it, past the city, toward the ocean beyond. The night fog rolled in across the waters, hanging above a crisp black mirror sea. It seemed like a reflection of the clouds high above. Those clouds glowed with a phantom pearl light, cast by a moon she could not see.

The fog did not reach the city; it rarely did. It hung over the ocean, churning. Like the ghost of a forest fire, stopped by some unseen barrier.

She could still feel the storm to the north. It called on her to ride through the streets, shouting warning. Flee to the cellars! Store up food, for a disaster will strike! Unfortunately, packing earth or reinforcing walls would not help against this tempest. It was of a different sort entirely.

The ocean fog was often herald to winds, and this night was no exception. She pulled her shawl close, smelling brine on the air. It mixed with the inevitable scents of an overcrowded city. Refuse, packed bodies, soot and smoke from fires and stoves. She missed the Two Rivers. The winds there were cold in the winters, but they were always fresh. Bandar Eban's winds always felt slightly *used*.

There would never again be a place for her in the Two Rivers. She knew this, though it hurt her. She was Aes Sedai now; it had become who she was, more important to her now than being Wisdom had once been. With the One Power, she could Heal people in a way that still seemed a marvel. And with the authority of the White Tower behind her, she was one of the most powerful individuals in the world, matched only by other sisters and the occasional monarch.

And in regard to monarchs, she herself was married to a king. He might not have a kingdom, but Lan *was* a king. To her, if nobody else. Life in the Two Rivers would not suit him. And, truthfully, it wouldn't suit her either. That simple life—once all she had been able to imagine—would now seem dull and unfulfilling.

Still, it was difficult not to feel wistful, particularly when watching the night fogs.

"There," Merise said, voice edged with tension. She, along with Cadsuane and Corele, stood looking in the other direction—not southwest over the city and ocean, but east. Nynaeve had almost decided against accompanying the group, as she had little doubt that Cadsuane partly blamed Nynaeve for her exile. However, the prospect of seeing the apparitions had been too enticing.

Nynaeve turned from the city and crossed the top of the wall, joining the others. Corele glanced at her, but Merise and Cadsuane ignored her. That suited Nynaeve. Though it did continue to irk her that Corele—of the Yellow Ajah— was so guarded in her acceptance of Nynaeve. Corele was pleasant, consoling, yet sternly unwilling to admit that Nynaeve was also a member of the Yellow. Well, the woman would have to change ruts eventually, once Egwene secured the White Tower.

Nynaeve peered through the crenellations atop the wall, scanning the dark landscape outside the city. She could faintly make out the remnants of the shanties that had crowded up against the walls until recently. The dangers— some real, others exaggerated—in the countryside had caused most of the refugees to crowd into the city's streets. Dealing with them, and the disease and hunger they brought with them, still demanded a lot of Rand's time.

Out beyond that trampled-down shantytown there were only shrubs, stunted trees, a shadowed bit of broken timber that might have been a wagon wheel. The nearby fields were barren. Plowed, seeded, yet still barren. Light! Why didn't crops grow anymore? Where would they find food this winter?

Anyway, that wasn't what she was looking for at the moment. What was it Merise had seen? Where—

Then Nynaeve saw it. Like a wisp of the ocean fog, a tiny patch of glowing light was blowing across the ground. It grew, bulging like a tiny storm cloud, glowing with a pearly light not unlike that of the clouds above. It resolved into the shape of a man, walking. Then that luminescent fog sprouted more figures. Within moments, an entire glowing procession strode across the dark ground, moving at a mournful pace.

Nynaeve shivered, then sternly reprimanded herself. Spirits from the dead they might be, but they were no danger so far away. But try as she might, she could not banish the goose bumps from her arms.

The procession was too distant for her to make out many details. There were both men and women in the line, clad in glowing clothing that flowed and shimmered like the city's banners. There was no color to the apparitions, just paleness, unlike most of the ghosts that had been appearing lately.

These were composed completely of a strange, otherworldly light. Several figures in the group—which was now about two hundred strong—were carrying a large object. Some kind of palanquin? Or . . . no. It was a coffin. Was this a funeral procession from long ago, then? What had happened to these people, and why had they been drawn back to the world of the living?

Rumors in the city said the procession had first appeared the night after Rand arrived in Bandar Eban. The wall's guards, who were likely the most reliable, had confirmed that to her in uneasy voices.

"I do not see the reason for so much fuss," Merise said with her Taraboner accent, folding her arms. "Ghosts, we are all accustomed to them by now, are we not? At least these aren't causing people to melt or burst into flames."

Reports in the city indicated that "incidents" were growing more and more frequent. Just in the last few days, Nynaeve had investigated three credible reports of people who had had insects burrow out of their skin, killing them. There had also been the man who had been found in his bed one morning, completely changed into burned charcoal. His linens hadn't been singed. She had seen that body herself.

These incidents weren't caused by the ghosts, but the people had begun to blame the apparitions. Better than them blaming Rand, she supposed.

"This waiting in the city, it is frustrating," Merise continued.

"Our time in this city *does* seem to lack fruit," Corele agreed. "We should be moving on. You've heard that he is proclaiming that the Last Battle will begin soon."

Nynaeve felt a stab of worry for Lan, then anger toward Rand. He still thought that if he could stage his assault at the same time as Lan's attack on Tarwin's Gap, he could confuse his enemies. Lan's attack could very well be the beginning of the Last Battle. Why, then, wouldn't Rand commit troops to help?

"Yes," Cadsuane said, musingly, "he is probably right." Why did she keep that hood up? Rand obviously wasn't around.

"Then we have all the greater reason to move on," Merise said sternly. "Rand al'Thor, he is a fool! And Arad Doman, it is irrelevant. A king or no king? What does it matter?"

"The Seanchan are not irrelevant," Nynaeve said, sniffing. "What of them? You would have us march to the Blight and leave our kingdoms open to invasion?"

Merise didn't react. Corele smiled and shrugged, then looked toward Damer Flinn, who leaned against the wall behind them, his arms folded. The leathery old man's casual posture suggested that he saw the procession of ghosts as nothing special. And these days, he might be right.

Nynaeve looked back out at the ghost procession, who were walking in an arc, rounding the city wall. The other Aes Sedai resumed their conversation, Merise and Corele taking further opportunity to voice their displeasure with Rand in their separate ways—one dour, the other congenial.

It made Nynaeve want to defend him. Though he had been difficult and erratic lately, there *was* important work for him to do in Arad Doman. The meeting with the Seanchan in Falme was only a short time away. Beyond that, Rand was right to worry about filling the Domani throne. And what if Graendal really was here, as he seemed to think? The others thought he must be mistaken about the Forsaken, but Rand had discovered Forsaken in nearly every other kingdom. Why not Arad Doman? A missing king, a land seething with confusion, famine and strife? These things sounded exactly like the kinds of trouble one would discover near one of the Forsaken.

The others continued to talk. Nynaeve started to leave, and as she did so she noticed that Cadsuane was watching her. Nynaeve hesitated, turning toward the cloaked woman. Cadsuane's face was barely visible by torchlight, but Nynaeve caught a grimace in the shadows, as if Cadsuane were displeased with Merise's and Corele's complaints. Nynaeve and Cadsuane stared at each other for a moment; then Cadsuane nodded curtly. The aged Aes Sedai turned and began to walk away, right in the middle of one of Merise's tirades about Rand.

The other Aes Sedai bustled to catch up. What had that look been for? Cadsuane had a habit of treating other Aes Sedai as if they were less worthy of respect than a common mule. It was as if all the rest of them were mere children in her eyes.

But, well, considering the way many Aes Sedai had been acting lately. . . .

Frowning to herself, Nynaeve left in the other direction, nodding to the wall guards. That nod of Cadsuane's couldn't possibly have been given out of respect. Cadsuane was *far* too self-righteous and arrogant for that.

What to do about Rand, then? He didn't want Nynaeve's help—or anyone's help—but that was nothing new. He'd been just as stubborn as a sheepherder back in the Two Rivers, and his father had been nearly as bad. That had never stopped Nynaeve the Wisdom, so it certainly wouldn't stop Nynaeve the Aes Sedai. She'd wrangled Coplins and Congars; she could do the same for trumped-up Rand al'Thor. She had half a mind to stride to his new "palace" and give him an earful.

Except . . . Rand al'Thor wasn't just any Coplin or Congar. Stubborn folks back in the Two Rivers hadn't had Rand's strangely menacing aura.

She'd dealt with dangerous men before. Her own Lan was as dangerous as a wolf on the prowl, and could be as prickly, too, even if he was good at hiding it from most people. But as threatening and as intimidating as Lan could be, he'd sooner chop off his own hand than raise it to harm her.

Rand was different. Nynaeve reached the steps leading off the wall into the city and headed down them, waving away a guard's suggestion that she take one of them in escort. It was night and there were a lot of refugees about, but she was hardly helpless. She did accept a lantern from another guard, however. Using the One Power to craft light would make the passersby uncomfortable.

Rand. Once, she'd thought him as gentle as Lan. His devotion to protecting women had been almost laughable in its innocence. That Rand was gone. Nynaeve saw again the moment when he had exiled Cadsuane. She'd believed that he *would* kill Cadsuane if he saw her face again, and thinking of the moment still gave her shivers. Surely it had been her imagination, but the room had seemed to *darken* distinctly at that moment, as if a cloud had passed over the sun.

Rand al'Thor *had* grown unpredictable. His explosion of temper at Nynaeve herself a few days ago was just another example. Of course, he would never exile or threaten *her*, despite what he had said. He wasn't that hard. Was he?

She reached the bottom of the stone steps, walking out onto a boardwalk stained with the mud of evening traffic. She pulled her shawl close. Huddled people clustered on the other side of the street. The shop entrances and alleyways there offered protection from the wind.

She heard a child cough among a distant group. She froze, then heard the cough again. It was not an easy sound. Muttering, she crossed the street, then forced her way through the refugees, holding up her lantern to illuminate one group of drowsy people after another. Many had the coppery skin of the Domani, but there were a fair number of Taraboners as well. And . . . were those Saldaeans? That was unexpected.

Most of the refugees lay in ragged blankets next to their meager possessions. A pot here, a quilt there. One young girl had a small cloth doll that might have once been fine, but had now lost one of its arms. Rand certainly was effective at subduing countries, but his kingdoms needed more than just handouts of grain. They needed stability, and they needed something—someone—they could believe in. Rand was getting increasingly bad at offering either one.

Where was the source of that cough? Few of the refugees spoke to her, and they were hesitant to answer her questions.

When she finally found the boy, she was more than a little annoyed. His parents had made their beds in a hollow between two wooden shops, and as Nynaeve approached, the father stood up to confront her. He was a scruffy Domani with a dark, ragged beard and a thick mustache that might have once been trimmed to Domani fashion. He wore no coat, and his shirt was nearly in tatters.

Nynaeve stared him down with a look she had learned long before her days as an Aes Sedai. Honestly, men could be so foolish! His son was likely dying, and yet he confronted one of the few people in the city who could help. The wife had more sense, which was usually the case. She laid a hand on her husband's leg, causing him to glance down. He finally turned away with a quiet mutter.

The wife's features were difficult to see through the grime on her face. The dirt was streaked with tear lines on her cheeks; she had obviously had a difficult couple of nights.

Nynaeve knelt—ignoring the looming father—then pulled back the blanket from the face of the child in the woman's arms. Sure enough, he was gaunt and pale, and his eyes fluttered open in some delusion.

"How long has he been coughing?" Nynaeve said, pulling a few packets of herbs out of the pouch at her side. She didn't have much, but they would have to do.

"A week now, Lady," the woman replied.

Nynaeve tsked in annoyance, pointing toward a nearby tin cup. "Fill that," she snapped at the father. "You are lucky the boy has survived this long with the white shakes; he likely wouldn't live the night without intervention."

Despite his earlier reluctance, the father hastened to obey, filling the cup from a nearby barrel. At least there wasn't a lack of water here, with the frequent rains.

Nynaeve took the cup and mixed the acem and feverbane in it, then wove a thread of Fire and heated the water. It started steaming faintly, and the father muttered some more. Nynaeve shook her head; she'd always heard that the Domani were pragmatic people when it came to use of the One Power. The unrest in the city must really be getting to them.

"Drink," she said to the boy, kneeling down and using all five Powers in a complex weave of Healing that she used instinctively. Her ability had awed some of the other Aes Sedai, but had earned her scorn from others. Either way, her method worked, even if she couldn't explain how she did what she did. That was one of the blessings and the curses of being a wilder; she could do things by instinct that other Aes Sedai struggled to learn. However, it was difficult for Nynaeve to unlearn some of the bad habits she'd learned.

The boy, though dazed, responded to the cup pressed to his lips. Her Healing weave lay across him as he drank, and he stiffened, inhaling sharply. The herbs weren't needed, but they would help give him strength following the rigorous Healing. She'd gotten over her habit of always using herbs when Healing, but she still felt they had their place and usefulness.

The father knelt down threateningly, but Nynaeve pressed the tips of her fingers to his chest and forced him back. "Give the child air."

The boy blinked, and Nynaeve could see sense flood back into his eyes. He shivered weakly. Nynaeve Delved him to determine how well the Healing had worked. "The fever has broken," she said with a nod, standing and releasing the One Power. "He will need to eat well over the next few days; I will give your descriptions to the dockmasters, and you will receive extra rations. Do *not* sell the food, or I will find out, and I will be angry. Do you understand?"

The woman looked down, ashamed. "We would never. . . ."

"I don't take anything for granted anymore," Nynaeve said. "Anyway, he should live, if you do as I say. Feed him the rest of that draught tonight, by sips if you have to. If the fever starts again, bring him to me at the Dragon's palace."

"Yes, my Lady," the woman said as the husband knelt, taking the boy and smiling.

Nynaeve picked up her lantern and rose.

"Lady," the woman said. "Thank you."

Nynaeve turned back. "You should have brought him to me days ago. I don't care what foolish superstitions people are spreading, the Aes Sedai are not your enemies. If you know any who are sick, encourage them to visit us."

The woman nodded, and the husband seemed cowed. Nynaeve stalked out of the alleyway and back onto the dark street, passing folk who watched her with a mixture of awe and horror. Foolish people! Would they let their own children die rather than get them Healed?

Back on the street, Nynaeve calmed herself. The diversion really hadn't taken much of her time, and—tonight at least—time was one of the things she had plenty of. She wasn't having much luck dealing with Rand. Her only consolation was that Cadsuane had done worse as his advisor.

How did one handle a creature like the Dragon Reborn? Nynaeve knew that the old Rand was there, within him somewhere. He had simply been beaten and kicked so many times that he'd gone into hiding, letting this harsher version rule. As much as it galled her to admit it, bullying him was just not going to work. But how was she to get him to do what he should, since he was too bullheaded to respond to ordinary prodding?

Nynaeve halted, lantern light illuminating an empty street before her. There was one person who *had* managed to work with Rand while at the same time teaching and training him. It hadn't been Cadsuane, nor had it been any of the Aes Sedai who tried to capture him, trick him or bully him.

It had been Moiraine.

Nynaeve continued on her way. During the last months of her life, the Blue had all but fawned over Rand. In order to get him to take her as his advisor, she'd agreed to obey his commands and offer advice only when it was wanted. What good was advice when it was given only when it was wanted? People needed most to hear the advice they didn't want!

But Moiraine *had* been successful. Through her, Rand had begun to overcome his aversion to Aes Sedai. Without Rand's eventual acceptance for Moiraine, it was doubtful that Cadsuane would ever have made headway in becoming his counselor.

Well, Nynaeve wasn't about to act the same way for Rand al'Thor, no matter how many fancy titles he had. However, she did have something to learn from Moiraine's success. Perhaps Rand had listened to Moiraine because her subservience had flattered him, or maybe he had simply been tired of people pushing him around. Rand *did* have many people trying to control him. They must frustrate him, and they made Nynaeve's own job a lot more difficult, since she was the one that he *actually* needed to listen to.

Did he, perhaps, see her simply as another of those irrelevant manipulators? She wouldn't put it past him.

She needed to show him that they were working for the same goals. She didn't want to tell him what to do; she just wanted him to stop acting like a fool. And, beyond that, she just wanted him to be safe. She'd also like him to be a leader that people respected, not one that people feared. He seemed incapable of seeing that the path he was on was that of a tyrant.

Being a king really wasn't all that different from being mayor in the Two Rivers. The mayor needed to be respected and liked. The Wisdom and the Women's Circle could do the difficult tasks, such as punishing those who overstepped their bounds. The mayor, however, needed to be loved. That led to a civil and a safe town.

But how to show that to Rand? She couldn't force him; she needed to get him to listen to her in another way. A plan began to take root in her head. By the time she reached the mansion, she had an idea of what to do.

The gate to the mansion grounds was guarded by Saldaeans; the Aiel preferred to stay closer to Rand, watching the rooms and the hallways of the mansion itself. Haster Nalmat, the officer on duty, gave Nynaeve a bow as she approached; some people still knew how to treat Aes Sedai. The grounds beyond the gate were ornamental and cultivated. Nynaeve's lantern cast strange shadows on the grass as its light shone through the trees trained and trimmed in the shapes of fanciful animals. The shadows moved in concert with her lantern, the phantom shapes lengthening and merging with the greater blackness of the night around her. Like rivers of shadow.

A larger group of Saldaean soldiers stood guard at the front of the mansion; far more than were necessary. Whenever men stood on guard, their friends tended to gather, no doubt to gossip. Nynaeve strode up to the group, causing several of them to stop leaning lazily against the mansion's gallery of pillars.

"Who of you are not on duty right now?" she asked.

Sure enough, three of the nine soldiers raised their hands, looking somewhat sheepish.

"Excellent," Nynaeve said, handing her lantern to one of

them. "You three, come with me." She strode into the mansion, the three soldiers scrambling in behind.

It was late—the ghost procession appeared only at midnight—and the mansion slumbered. The intricate chandelier in the entryway had been extinguished, and the hallways were dark. Testing her memory, she picked a direction and walked down it. The whitewashed walls were as immaculate here as they were in other sections of the mansion, but they were unornamented. Her instinct proved correct as she soon entered a small pantry, where servants would prepare platters of food before taking them to the dining room. The hallway she had chosen led out to the mansion sitting rooms; another hallway at the back led to the kitchens. The room was furnished with a big sturdy wooden table and some tall stools. Those were occupied by a group of men playing a game of dice, wearing green and white linen shirts—the livery of Milisair's house—with thick work trousers.

They looked up with shock as Nynaeve strode into the room; one of the men actually leaped to his feet, his stool toppling to the floor behind him. He pulled off his hat—a lopsided brown thing that even Mat would have been embarrassed to wear—looking like a child caught poking his finger into the pie before dinner.

Nynaeve didn't care what they were doing; she had found some servants of the mansion, and that was all that mattered. "I must see the dosun," she said, using the local term for the head housekeeper. "Fetch her for me."

Her soldiers entered the room behind her. All three were Saldaeans, and if they were somewhat oafish, they walked with the swaggers of men who intimately understood fighting. She doubted that these simple servants needed any more intimidation than an Aes Sedai, but the soldiers would likely prove useful later.

"The dosun?" the worker with the hat finally said. "Are you sure you wouldn't rather see the steward or—"

"The dosun," Nynaeve said. "Bring her to me *now*. Give her time to throw on a robe, but no more." She pointed at one of her soldiers. "You, go with him. Make sure he doesn't speak to anyone else or give the woman a chance to escape."

"Escape?" the worker yelped. "Why would Loral want to do that? What did she do, my Lady?"

"Nothing, I hope. Go!"

The two men—one worker, one soldier—hurried off, and the other three workers remained at the table, looking uncomfortable. Nynaeve folded her arms beneath her breasts, considering her plan. Rand had determined that his hunt for the Domani king had hit a wall with the death of the messenger. Nynaeve wasn't so certain. There were others involved, and a few well-placed questions might be very illuminating.

It was unlikely the dosun had done anything wrong. But Nynaeve did *not* want the worker who fetched her letting his tongue wag to the people he might meet along the way; better to instill into him a sense of danger and use the soldier to keep him quiet. Not to mention punctual.

Her foresight proved effective. Within minutes, the worker hurried back into the room, towing a disheveled, elderly woman in a blue evening robe. Gray hair poked out from beneath her hastily wrapped red kerchief, and her aging Domani face was absolutely white with apprehension. Nynaeve felt guilty. How this woman must feel, awoken at night by a terrified servant claiming that one of the Aes Sedai wanted her immediately!

The Saldaean soldier followed, then stood guard beside the doorway. He was bowlegged and squat, and he wore one of those long Saldaean mustaches. The other two lounged beside the doorway Nynaeve had come through, their casual air only serving to make the room more tense. They had picked up on something of her intent, it seemed.

"Peace, goodwoman," Nynaeve said, nodding to the table. "You may sit. You others, go to the main entryway and stay there. Don't speak to anyone."

The four workers needed no further prodding. Nynaeve told one of the soldiers to follow them and make certain they did as she said. The late hour was working to her advantage; with so many of the servants and Rand's attendants asleep, she could investigate without alerting those who might be guilty.

The departure of the workers only made the dosun more nervous. Nynaeve sat at the table on one of the vacated stools. The men had left their dice behind in their haste, but had—of course—made sure to take their coins. The room was lit by a small lamp, burning with an open flame on the windowsill. The Saldaean had taken her lantern with him when following the workers.

"Your name is Loral, is it not?" Nynaeve asked.

The dosun nodded warily.

"You are aware that Aes Sedai do not lie?"

The housekeeper nodded again. Most Aes Sedai *couldn't* lie, though Nynaeve technically could, since she hadn't held the Oath Rod. That was part of what earned her a lesser status in the eyes of the others. Undeservedly so. The Oath Rod was only a formality; Two Rivers folk needed no *ter'angreal* to make them honest. "Then you will believe me when I tell you that I do not suspect you personally of having done anything wrong. I just need your help."

The woman seemed to relax a bit. "What help do you need, Nynaeve Sedai?"

"It has been my experience that the head housekeeper knows more of a house's workings than the stewards, or even the owners of the property. Have you been employed here for long?"

"I have served the Chadmar family through three generations," the old woman said with no small measure of pride. "And had hoped to serve another, if Her Ladyship had—" The housekeeper cut off. Rand had imprisoned "Her Ladyship" in her own dungeons. That didn't bode well for there being another generation to serve.

"Yes, well," Nynaeve said, covering the uncomfortable silence. "The unfortunate circumstances involving your lady are part of my task this evening."

"Nynaeve Sedai," the aged woman said, growing eager, "do you suppose you can see her to freedom? Restore her to the Lord Dragon's good graces?"

"Perhaps." *Doubtful,* Nynaeve added in her mind, *but anything is possible.* "My activities tonight may help. Did you ever see this messenger, the one your mistress imprisoned?"

"The one sent by the King?" Loral asked. "I never spoke with him, Aes Sedai, but I *did* see him. Tall, handsome fellow, curiously clean-shaven for a Domani man. I passed him in the hallway. Had one of the most beautiful faces I rightly think I've ever seen on a man."

"And then?" Nynaeve asked.

"Well, he went directly to speak with Lady Chadmar,

and then. . . ." Loral trailed off. "Nynaeve Sedai, I don't mean to be getting my lady into any more trouble, and—"

"He was sent for questioning," Nynaeve said shortly. "I have little time for foolishness, Loral. I am *not* here looking for evidence against your mistress, and I don't really care what your loyalties are. There are much larger issues at stake. Answer my question."

"Yes, Lady," Loral said, paling. "We all knew what had happened, of course. Didn't seem right, sending one of the King's men to a questioner like that. Particularly that man. Shame to mar a face so beautiful, and all."

"You know the location of the questioner and the dungeon?"

Loral hesitated, then nodded reluctantly. Good. She didn't intend to withhold information.

"Let us go, then," Nynaeve said, rising.

"My Lady?"

"To the dungeon," Nynaeve said. "I assume it isn't on the property anywhere, not if Milisair Chadmar was as careful as I think."

"It's a modest distance away, in the Gull's Feast," Loral said. "You wish to go *tonight*?"

"Yes," Nynaeve said, then hesitated. "Unless I decide to visit the questioner at his home instead."

"They are the same place, my Lady."

"Excellent. Come."

Loral didn't have much choice. Nynaeve allowed her—guarded by a soldier—to return to her rooms for a dress.

A short time later, Nynaeve and her soldiers marched the dosun—along with the four workers, to keep them from accidentally giving warning of what was happening—from the building. All five looked decidedly displeased. They probably believed the superstitious rumors that the night was not safe. Nynaeve knew better. The night might not be safe, but it wasn't any worse than other times. In fact, it might be safer. If there were fewer people about, there were fewer chances of someone nearby suddenly growing thorns out of their skin, bursting into flame or dying in some other horribly random way.

They left the mansion grounds, Nynaeve walking with a firm step, hoping to keep the others from feeling too nervous. She nodded to the soldiers at the gate, and went in the direction Loral indicated. Their feet thumped against the wood of the boardwalk, the clouded night sky glowing just faintly from moonlight above.

Nynaeve didn't give herself the luxury of questioning her plan. She'd decided on a course, and so far it was going well. True, Rand might grow angry at her for appropriating soldiers and stirring up trouble. But sometimes, to see what was at the bottom of a cloudy rain barrel, you *needed* to stir the water to bring up what was at the bottom. It was just too coincidental. Milisair Chadmar had taken the messenger captive months ago, but he had died only a short time before Rand wanted him. He was the only person in the city with a clue to the King's location.

Coincidences did happen. Sometimes, when two farmers were feuding and one of their cows died in the night, it was just an accident. And sometimes, a little searching uncovered the opposite.

Loral led the group toward the Gull's Feast, also known as the Gull District, a part of town close to where the fishermen dumped waste from their hauls. Like most sensible people, Nynaeve avoided that section of town, and her nose reminded her just why as they approached. Fish guts might make excellent fertilizer, but Nynaeve could smell the composting heaps from several streets away. Even the refugees avoided this dark area.

The walk was a fairly long one—understandably, the rich sector of town was distant from the Gull's Feast. Nynaeve stalked along, paying no heed to the shadowed alleyways and buildings, though her entourage—soldiers excepted—clustered around her apprehensively. The Saldaeans instead kept their hands on their serpentine swords, trying to look in all directions at once.

She wished she had news from the White Tower. How long had it been since she'd had news from Egwene or one of the others? She felt blind. It was her own fault for insisting that she go with Rand. *Someone* had needed to keep an eye on him, but that meant being unable to keep any eyes on everyone else. Was the Tower still divided? Was Egwene still Amyrlin? News on the streets was little help. As always, for every rumor she heard, there were two more contradicting it. The White Tower was fighting itself. No, it fought the Asha'man. No, the Aes Sedai had been destroyed by the Seanchan. Or by the Dragon Reborn. No, those rumors were all lies spread by the Tower to bait its enemies into striking.

Very little was said about Elaida or Egwene specifically, though garbled news of two Amyrlins was spreading. That was problematic. Neither group of Aes Sedai would like spreading the news of a second Amyrlin. Tales of squabbles among the Aes Sedai would only end up hurting all of them.

Eventually, Loral stopped walking. The four workers stopped behind her, bundling together with worried expressions. Nynaeve glanced at Loral. "Well?"

"There, Lady." The woman pointed a bony finger to the building across the street.

"The chandler's shop?" Nynaeve asked.

Loral nodded.

Nynaeve summoned one of the bowlegged Saldaean soldiers. "You, watch these five and make sure they don't get into trouble. You other two, come with me."

She started across the street, but when she didn't hear footsteps leave the boardwalk, she turned with a frown. The three guards stood together, looking at the single lantern, likely cursing themselves for not thinking to bring another.

"Oh, for the Light's sake," Nynaeve snapped, raising her hand and embracing the Source. She wove a globe of light above her fingers, casting a cool, even illumination across the ground around her. "Leave the lantern."

The two Saldaeans complied, hurrying after her. She stepped up to the chandler's door, then wove a ward against eavesdropping and placed it in the air around herself, the door and the two soldiers.

She looked at one of the soldiers. "What's your name?"

"Triben, my Lady," he said. He was a hawk-faced man with a short, trimmed mustache and a scar across his forehead. "That's Lurts," he said, pointing at the other soldier, a massive wall of a man who Nynaeve had been surprised to see was uniformed as a cavalryman.

"All right, Triben," Nynaeve said. "Kick the door open."

Triben didn't question her; he just raised a booted foot and kicked. The frame cracked easily and the door slammed open, but if her ward had been placed correctly, nobody in the building would be able to hear. She peeked in. The room smelled of wax and perfumes, and the wooden floor was marked by numerous spots. Drip marks; wax that had been cleaned up often left a mark.

"Quickly," she said to the soldiers, releasing the ward but maintaining the globe of light. "Lurts, go to the back of the shop and watch the alley; make certain nobody escapes. Triben, with me."

Lurts moved with surprising speed for his bulk, taking his position in the back room of the shop. Her globe illuminated barrels for dipping candles and a pile of burned nubs in the corner, bought for pennies to be re-melted. A staircase mounted to the right. A small alcove in the front of the shop was the storefront, and it contained various sizes and shapes of candles, from the standard white rod to the perfumed and decorated brick. If Loral was wrong about this being the place. . . .

But any good secret operation would have a working front. Nynaeve hurried up the stairs, wood creaking beneath her weight. The building was narrow. On the upper floor, she and Triben found two rooms. One door was open a crack, so Nynaeve dimmed her globe of light and wove a ward against listeners into the room. Then she burst in, hawk-faced Triben following, his sword scraping against its scabbard as he pulled it free.

There was only one person in the room, an overweight man sleeping on a mattress on the floor, blankets in a heap around his feet. Nynaeve wove a few threads of Air, tying him up in one smooth motion. His eyes bulged open, and he opened his mouth to scream, but Nynaeve stuffed Air between his lips, gagging him.

She turned to Triben and nodded, tying off her weaves. They left the bound man there, struggling against his bonds, and crossed to the other door. She wove another weave against eavesdropping into the room before entering, and it was a good thing she did—for the two younger men in this room roused much more quickly. One sat bolt upright, letting out a yelp just as Triben headed across the floorboards. Triben punched him in the stomach, knocking the air out of his lungs.

Nynaeve bound him with a thread of Air, then did the same for the other young man, who was rousing drowsily in his bunk. She towed the two toward her, brightening her globe of light, hanging the men up in the air a few inches.

They were both Domani, with dark hair and crude faces, thin mustaches above their lips. Both wore only their smallclothes. They seemed too old to be apprentices.

"I think we have the right place, Nynaeve Sedai," Triben said, walking around the pair to stand beside her.

She raised an eyebrow at him.

"Those are no chandler's apprentices," Triben continued. He slid his sword back into its sheath. "Calluses on the palms, but no burns on their hands? Muscled arms? And they're far too old. That fellow on the left has had his nose broken at least once."

She looked closer; Triben was right. *I should have seen that.* Still, she had noticed the age. "Which one do you think I should ungag," she asked casually, "and which one should I kill?"

Both men began to squirm, eyes wide. They should have known that an Aes Sedai would never do anything of the sort. In fact, she probably shouldn't have implied it, but private jailers like these riled her anger.

"The one on the left seems most eager to talk, Lady," Triben said. "Perhaps he will tell you what you wish to know."

She nodded, releasing the man's gag. He began to speak immediately. "I will do whatever you say! Please, don't fill my stomach with insects! I haven't done anything wrong, I promise you, I—"

She stuffed the Air gag back in.

"Too much complaining," she said. "Perhaps the other will know to hush and speak when spoken to." She released his gag.

This man remained dangling in the air, obviously terrified, but saying nothing. The One Power could unnerve the most hardened of killers.

"How do I get into the dungeon?" she asked this man.

He looked sick, but he had probably already guessed that she'd want the dungeon. It was unlikely that an Aes Sedai would burst into the shop after midnight because she'd been sold a bad candle.

"Trapdoor," the man said, "under the rug in the shop front."

"Excellent," Nynaeve said. She tied off the weaves binding the men's hands, then replaced the gag on the one who had spoken. She didn't leave them hanging in the air—she didn't want to have to pull them along behind her—and instead let them walk on their own feet.

She had Triben fetch the overweight man from the other room, then herded all three down the stairs. Below, they met the muscular Lurts keeping careful watch on the alley out back. A youth sat on the floor in front of him, and Nynaeve's globe of light illuminated his face, a frightened Domani one with uncharacteristically light hair and hands spotted with burns.

"Now, *that's* a chandler's apprentice," Triben said, scratching his forehead scar. "They probably have him doing all of the work for the front."

"He was asleep under those blankets over there." Lurts nodded to a shadowed pile in the corner as he joined Nynaeve. "Tried to scramble out the front door after you went up the stairs."

"Bring him," Nynaeve said. In the small storefront, Triben pulled back the rug, then used the edge of his sword to prod through the slats until he knocked against something underneath—hinges, Nynaeve assumed. After a little careful prying, he got the trapdoor open. A ladder reached down into the darkness below.

Nynaeve stepped forward, but Triben held up a hand. "Lord Bashere would hang me up by my own stirrups if I let you go first, Lady," he said. "No telling what might be down there." He leaped into the hole, sliding down the ladder with one hand, his sword in the other. He thumped to the ground below, and Nynaeve rolled her eyes. Men! She gestured for Lurts to watch the jailers, then released their bonds so they could climb down. She gave each of them a stern look; then she proceeded down the ladder without Triben's ridiculous flair, leaving Lurts to herd the jailers after.

She raised her globe of light and surveyed the cellar. The walls were stone, which made her feel much less nervous about the weight of the building above. The floor was packed dirt, and there was a wooden doorway built into the wall across from her. Triben was listening at it.

She nodded, and he pulled it open, darting inside eagerly. The Saldaeans seemed to be picking up some habits from the Aiel. Nynaeve followed, preparing weaves of Air, just

in case. Behind her, the sullen jailers began to climb down
the ladder, followed by Lurts.

There wasn't much to see in the other room. Two dungeon cells with thick wooden doors, a table with some
stools beside it, and a large wooden trunk. Nynaeve sent her
globe of light to the corner as hawk-faced Triben inspected
the trunk. He lifted the lid, then raised an eyebrow, pulling
out several glittering knives. Aids for questioning. Nynaeve
shivered. She turned harsh eyes on the jailers behind her.

She untied the gag on the one who had spoken. "Keys?"
she asked.

"Bottom of the trunk," said the thug. The overweight
jailer—the leader of the group, no doubt, as he didn't share
a room—shot him a furious glance. Nynaeve jerked the
leader into the air. "Don't provoke me," she growled. "It's
already far too late at night for reasonable people to be
awake."

She nodded to Triben, and he dug out the keys and
opened the cell doors. The first cell was empty; the second
one held a disheveled woman, still wearing a fine Domani
dress, though it was soiled. Lady Chadmar was dirty and
ragged and she curled against the wall, drowsy, barely even
noticing that the door was open. Nynaeve caught a whiff of
a stench that, up until that moment, had been covered by the
scent of rotting fish. Human excrement and an unwashed
body. Likely, that was one reason for locating the dungeon
here in the Gull's Feast.

Nynaeve inhaled sharply at seeing how the woman was
being treated. How could Rand allow this? The woman herself had done this very thing to others, but that didn't make
it right for him to stoop to her level.

She waved for Triben to close the door; then she sat down
on one of the room's stools, regarding the three jailers. Behind, Lurts guarded the way out, keeping an eye on the
poor apprentice. The overweight jailer still hung in the air.

She needed information. She could have asked Rand for
permission to visit the jail in the morning, but in doing so,
she would have risked alerting these men that they were
going to be visited. She was depending on surprise and intimidation to reveal what had been hidden.

"Now," she said to the three, "I am going to ask some
questions. You are going to answer. I'm not certain what

I'm going to do with you yet, so realize it's best to be *very* honest with me."

The two on the ground looked up at the other man, floating in the invisible weaves of Air. They nodded.

"The man who was brought to you," she said. "The messenger of the King. When did he first arrive?"

"Two months ago," one of the toughs said—the one with the large chin and the broken nose. "Arrived in a sack with the candle nubs from Lady Chadmar's mansion, just like all the prisoners."

"Your instructions?"

"Hold him," the other tough said. "Keep him alive. We didn't know much, er, Lady Aes Sedai. Jorgin is the one who does all the questioning."

She looked up at the fat man. "You're Jorgin?"

He nodded reluctantly.

"And what were your instructions?"

Jorgin didn't respond.

Nynaeve sighed. "Look," she said to him. "I am Aes Sedai, and am bound by my word. If you tell me what I want to know, I will see that you are not suspected in the death. The Dragon doesn't care about you three, otherwise you wouldn't still be here in charge of this little . . . stopover of yours."

"If we talk, we go free?" the fat man said, eyeing her. "Your word?"

Nynaeve glanced about the tiny room with a dissatisfied eye. They had left Lady Chadmar in the dark, and the door was packed with cloth to muffle screams. The cell would be dark, stuffy and cramped. Men who would work a place like this barely deserved life, let alone freedom.

But there was a much larger sickness to deal with. "Yes," Nynaeve said, the word bitter in her mouth. "And you know that's better than you deserve."

Jorgin hesitated, then nodded. "Let me down, Aes Sedai, and I'll answer your questions."

She did so. The man might not know it, but she had very little authority to stand on; she wouldn't resort to his methods of extracting answers, and she was acting without Rand's knowledge. The Dragon probably wouldn't react well when he discovered that she'd been prying—not unless she could present him with discoveries.

Jorgin said to the broken-nosed thug, "Mord, fetch me a stool."

Mord glanced at Nynaeve for approval, which she gave with a curt nod. As Jorgin settled his bulk onto the stool, he leaned forward, hands clasped before him. He resembled a hulking beetle tipped up on its side.

"I don't see what you need from me," the man said. "You seem to know everything already. You know about my facility and about the people it has held. What more is there to know?"

Facility? Some word for it. "That is my own business," Nynaeve said, giving him a stare which she hoped implied that the concerns of the Aes Sedai were not to be questioned. "Tell me, how did the messenger die?"

"Without dignity," Jorgin replied. "Like all men, in my experience."

"Give me specifics, or you'll go back to hanging in the air."

"I opened the cell door a few days back to feed him. He was dead."

"How long had it been since you'd fed him, then?"

Jorgin snorted. "I don't starve my guests, Lady Aes Sedai. I just . . . encourage them to be free with what they know."

"And how much encouragement did you give the messenger?"

"Not enough to kill him," the jailer said defensively.

"Oh, come now," Nynaeve said. "The man remained for months in your possession, presumably healthy all that time. Then, the *day* before he is to be brought before the Dragon Reborn, he suddenly dies? You already have my promise of amnesty. Tell me who bribed you to kill him and I'll see that you're protected."

The jailer shook his head. "It wasn't like that. I'm telling you, he just died. It happens sometimes."

"I tire of your games."

"It's not a game, burn you!" Jorgin snarled. "You think a man could get far in my profession if it were known that he'd accept a bribe to kill one of his guests? You couldn't trust him any further than you could a lying Aiel!"

She let that last comment slide, though a man like this one could *never* be "trusted."

"Look," Jorgin said, "that wasn't the type of prisoner you kill, anyway. *Everybody* wants to know where the King is. Who'd kill the only one with information about it? That man was worth good money."

"So he's not dead," Nynaeve surmised. "Who did you sell him to?"

"Oh, he's dead," the jailer said with a chuckle. "If I *had* sold him, I wouldn't have lived long afterward. You learn that sort of thing quickly, doing what I do."

She turned to the other two thugs. "Is he lying?" she asked of them. "A hundred gold marks to the one of you who can give me proof that he is."

Mord glanced at his boss, then grimaced. "For a hundred in gold, I'd sell you my own mother, Lady. Burn me, but I would. Jorgin's telling the truth, though. That body was good and dead. The Dragon's men checked when they brought the lady to us."

So Rand had considered that possibility. But she still had no proof that these men were telling her the truth. If there *was* something to hide, they'd work hard to bury it deep. She decided to try a different path.

"What did you discover, then," she said, "about the King's location?"

Jorgin just sighed. "Like I told the Lord Dragon's men, and like I told Lady Chadmar before she landed here in the dungeons herself. That man knew something, but he wouldn't speak it."

"Come now," Nynaeve said, shooting a glance at the chest with its sharp equipment. She had to look away again before it angered her. "A man of your . . . skill? And you couldn't pry one simple fact out of him?"

"Dark One take me if I'm lying!" The jailer's face flushed as if this were a matter of pride for him. "I've never *seen* a man resist like that one did! A pretty feather of a man like him should have broken without much encouragement at all. But he didn't. He would speak on anything other than the things we wanted!" Jorgin leaned forward. "I don't know how he did it, Lady. Burn me, but I don't! It's like some . . . force had ahold of his tongue. It was like he *couldn't* talk. Even if he'd wanted to!"

The two thugs muttered to themselves, looking appre-

hensive. It seemed that Nynaeve's questioning had hit a
nerve.

"So you pushed him too hard," Nynaeve guessed. "And
that's how he died."

"Take it all, woman!" the jailer growled. "Blood and
bloody ashes! I *didn't* kill him! Sometimes, people just die."

Unfortunately, she was coming to believe him. Jorgin
was a wretch of a man who could use a decade doing chores
beneath the eyes of a Wisdom. But he wasn't lying.

So much for her grand plans. She sighed, standing up,
realizing just how tired she really was. Light! This scheme
was more likely to make Rand explode at her than persuade him to listen to her counsel. She needed to return
to the mansion for some sleep. Perhaps tomorrow she'd be
able to think up a better way to show Rand that she was on
his side.

She waved for the guards to take the jailer and his men
back up above. After that, she wove Air to shut the cell door
on Milisair Chadmar. Nynaeve *would* see that the woman's
conditions were improved. Despicable human being or not,
she should not be treated this way. Rand would have to understand that when she explained it to him. Why, Milisair
looked so pale she might be coming down with the shakes!
Absently, Nynaeve walked to the viewing slit at the top of
the cell door, then wove a Delving of Spirit to make certain
the woman was not ill.

As soon as she began the Delving, Nynaeve froze. She
had expected to find Milisair's body taxed by exhaustion.
She had expected to find disease, perhaps hunger.

She had not expected to find poison.

Cursing, suddenly alert, Nynaeve threw open the cell
door and rushed inside. Yes, she could see it easily through
the Delving. Tarchrot leaf. Nynaeve herself had given that
to a hound who had needed to be put down. It was a common enough plant, and had a very bitter flavor. Not the best
poison, as it had such an unpleasant taste, and yet had to be
ingested.

Yes, it was a bad poison—unless the person you were
poisoning was already captive and had no choice but to eat
the food you gave her. Nynaeve began a Healing, weaving
all five Powers, strangling the poison and strengthening

Milisair's body. It was a relatively easy Healing, as tarchrot leaf wasn't particularly strong. You either had to use a lot of it—as she had with the hound—or you had to administer it several times for it to take effect. But if you did it slowly like that, the person you killed with it would seem to die naturally.

Once Milisair was safe, Nynaeve burst from the cell. "Stop!" she bellowed at the men. "Jorgin!"

Lurts, at the back, turned with surprise. He grabbed the jailer Jorgin by the arm and spun him around.

"Who prepares the prisoner's food?" Nynaeve demanded, stalking toward him.

"The food?" Jorgin asked, looking confused. "That's one of Kerb's jobs. Why?"

"Kerb?"

"The lad," Jorgin said. "Nobody important. An apprentice we found among the refugees a few months back. Quite a lucky find—our last apprentice ran off on us, and this one was already trained in—"

Nynaeve hushed him with a raised hand, suddenly anxious. "The boy! Where is he?"

"He was just here . . ." Lurts said, glancing up. "Went with—"

There was a sudden scrambling from above. Nynaeve cursed, calling for Triben to catch the boy. She shoved her way to the ladder and began climbing. She darted out into the shop above, her glowing light following. The two thugs stood cowering in the center room, looking confused, and a Saldaean guard stood with a sword pulled on them. He looked at her questioningly.

"The boy!" she said.

Triben glanced toward the shop door. It was open. Preparing weaves of Air, Nynaeve dashed out onto the street.

There, she found the boy, Kerb, in the muddy street, held down by the four dice-playing workers she'd brought from the mansion. Even as she stepped off the boardwalk onto the street, they pulled the struggling, frantic boy to his feet. The last Saldaean stood at the doorway, sword out, as if he'd been rushing in to see if she was in danger.

"He bolted out of the door, Aes Sedai," one of the workers said, "as if the Dark One himself was chasing him. Your soldier ran over to see if you were in danger, but we figured it'd be best to snatch this lad before he could get away. Just in case."

Nynaeve let out a breath to calm herself. "You did well," she said. The youth struggled, weakly. "You did well indeed."

CHAPTER
33

A Conversation with the Dragon

T his," Rand declared, "had better be important."

Nynaeve turned to find the Dragon Reborn standing in the doorway to the sitting room. He wore a dark red robe with black dragons embroidered up the arms. His stump was hidden in the folds of the left sleeve. Though his hair was tousled from sleep, his eyes were alert.

He strode into the sitting room, ever the king—even now, long after midnight and just awakened, he walked as if he were absolutely certain of himself. Some servants had brought a pot of hot tea, and he filled a cup as Min followed him into the room. She also wore a sleeping robe; the robes were one of the fashions of the Domani, and hers was of yellow silk, the weave far thinner than Rand's. Aiel maidens took up positions by the door, lounging in their strangely dangerous way.

Rand took a gulp from his cup. It was getting harder and harder to see in him the boy Nynaeve had known in the Two Rivers. Had his jaw always been set with those lines of determination? When had his step grown so sure, his posture so demanding? This man almost seemed an . . . interpretation of the Rand she'd once known. Like a statue, carved from rock to look like him, but exaggerated in heroic lines.

"Well?" Rand demanded. "Who is this?"

The young apprentice, Kerb, sat tied in Air upon one of the room's cushioned benches. Nynaeve glanced at him, then embraced the Source and wove a ward against eavesdropping. Rand looked at her sharply. "You channeled?" he asked. He could sense when she did so without taking precautions; he felt goose bumps on the flesh, according to Egwene and Elayne's investigations.

"A ward," she said, refusing to be cowed. "Last I checked, I didn't need your *permission* to channel. You've grown high and mighty, Rand al'Thor, but don't forget that I paddled your backside when you were barely as tall as a man's shins."

Once that would have gotten a reaction from him, if only a huff of annoyance. Now he just looked at her. Those eyes of his seemed, at times, the part of him that had changed the most.

He sighed. "Why have you wakened me, Nynaeve? Who is this spindly, terrified youth? If it had been anyone else who sent that message this time of night, I'd have sent them to Bashere for a flogging."

Nynaeve nodded at Kerb. "I think this 'spindly, terrified youth' knows where the King is."

That got Rand's attention, and Min's as well. She'd poured herself a cup of tea and was leaning against a wall. Why weren't they *married*?

"The King?" Rand asked. "Graendal too, then. How do you know this, Nynaeve? Where did you find him?"

"At the dungeon where you sent Milisair Chadmar," Nynaeve said, eyeing him. "It is terrible, Rand al'Thor. You have no right to treat a person in such a manner."

He didn't rise to that comment either. Instead, he simply walked over to Kerb. "He heard something from the interrogation?"

"No," Nynaeve said. "But I think he killed the messenger. I know for a fact that he tried to poison Milisair. She'd have been dead by the end of the week if I hadn't Healed her."

Rand glanced at Nynaeve, and she could almost *feel* him connecting the comments to figure out what she had been doing. "You Aes Sedai," he finally said, "share much with rats, I have come to realize. You are always in places where you are not wanted."

Nynaeve snorted. "If I'd stayed away, then Milisair would be dying and Kerb would be free."

"I assume you've asked him who ordered him to kill the messenger."

"Not yet," Nynaeve said. "I did find the poison among his things, however, and confirmed that he had prepared food both for Milisair and for the messenger." She hesitated before continuing. "Rand, I'm not certain that he'll be *able* to answer our questions. I Delved him, and while he's not sick physically, there's . . . something there. In his mind."

"What do you mean?" Rand asked softly.

"A block of some sort," Nynaeve said. "The jailer seemed frustrated—even surprised—that the messenger had been able to resist his 'questioning.' I think there must have been some block on that man too, something to keep him from revealing too much."

"Compulsion," Rand said. He spoke offhandedly, raising his tea to his lips.

Compulsion was dark, evil. She'd felt it herself; she still shivered when she considered what Moghedien had done to her. And that had been only a small thing, removing some memories.

"Few are as skilled with Compulsion as Graendal," Rand said musingly. "Perhaps this is the confirmation I've been looking for. Yes . . . this could be a great discovery indeed, Nynaeve. Great enough to make me forget how you obtained it."

Rand rounded the bench and leaned down to meet the young man's eyes.

"Release him," Rand commanded her.

She complied.

"Tell me," Rand said to Kerb, "who told you to poison those people?"

"I don't know anything!" the boy squeaked. "I just—"

"Stop," Rand said softly. "Do you believe that I can kill you?"

The boy fell silent and—though Nynaeve wouldn't have thought it possible—his blue eyes opened wider.

"Do you believe that if I simply said the word," Rand continued in his eerie, quiet voice, "your heart would stop beating? I am the Dragon Reborn. Do you believe that I can take your life, or your soul itself, if I so much as will it to happen?"

Nynaeve saw it again, the patina of darkness around Rand, that aura that she couldn't *quite* be certain was there.

She raised her tea to her lips—and found that it had suddenly grown bitter and stale, as if it had been left to sit too
long.

Kerb slouched down and began to cry.

"Speak," Rand commanded.

The youth opened his mouth, but only a groan came
out. He was so transfixed by Rand that he didn't—or
couldn't—blink the sweat from his eyes.

"Yes," Rand said thoughtfully. "This is Compulsion,
Nynaeve. She's here! I was *right*." He looked at Nynaeve.
"You will have to unravel the web of Compulsion, wipe it
from his mind, before he can tell us what he knows."

"What?" she asked incredulously.

"I have little skill with this kind of weaving," Rand said
with a wave of his hand. "I suspect that you can remove
Compulsion, if you try. It is similar to Healing, in a way.
Use the same weave that creates Compulsion, but reverse it."

She frowned. Healing the poor boy sounded like a fine
idea—every wound *should* be Healed, after all. But trying
something she'd never done before, and doing so in front
of Rand, was not appealing. What if she did it wrong and
somehow hurt the boy?

Rand sat down on the cushioned bench seat across from
the youth, Min walking over to sit beside him. She was regarding her tea with a grimace; apparently, hers had spoiled
as suddenly as Nynaeve's had.

Rand watched Nynaeve, waiting.

"Rand, I—"

"Just try it," Rand said. "I can't tell you how it is done
specifically, not for a woman, but you are clever. I'm certain
you can manage."

His unintentionally patronizing tone sent her back into
a rage. Being as tired as she was didn't help. She gritted
her teeth, turning toward Kerb, and wove all five Powers.
His eyes darted back and forth, though he couldn't see the
weaves.

Nynaeve laid a very light Healing across him, causing
him to stiffen. She wove a separate line of Spirit, Delving into
his head as delicately as she could, prodding at the weaves
that clumped across his mind. Yes, she could see it now, a
complex web made from lines of Spirit, Air and Water. It was

horrible, looking at it with her mind's eye, crisscrossing the youth's brain. Bits of the weave touched here and there, like tiny hooks, jutting deep into the brain itself.

Reverse the weave, Rand had said. That was far from easy. She'd have to pull the web of Compulsion off layer by layer, and if she made a mistake, she could very easily kill him. She almost backed away.

But who else was there? Compulsion was a forbidden weave, and she doubted that Corele or the others had any experience with it. If Nynaeve stopped now, Rand would just send for the others and ask them to do it. They'd obey him, laughing behind their hands at Nynaeve, the Accepted who thought herself a full Aes Sedai.

Well, she had discovered new ways of Healing! She had helped cleanse the taint from the One Power itself! She had Healed stilling and gentling!

She could do this.

She worked quickly, weaving a mirror image of the first layer of Compulsion. Each use of the Power was exact, but reversed from the pattern already woven in the boy's mind. Nynaeve laid her weave down carefully, hesitantly, and as Rand had said, both puffed away and vanished.

How had he known? She shivered, thinking of what Semirhage had said about him. Memories from another life, memories he had no right to. There was a reason the Creator allowed them to forget their past lives. No man should have to remember the failures of Lews Therin Telamon.

She continued, layer after layer, stripping away the Compulsion's weaves like a hedge-doctor removing bandages from a wounded leg. It was exhausting work, but fulfilling. Each weave fixed a wrong, healed the youth a little more, made something just a hair more *right* in the world.

It took the better part of an hour, and was a grueling experience. But she did it. As the last layer of Compulsion vanished, she let out an exhausted sigh and released the One Power, convinced that she couldn't channel a single thread more if it were to save her life. She wobbled over to a chair and slumped down. Min, she noticed, had curled up on the bench seat beside Rand and had fallen asleep.

But he did not sleep. The Dragon Reborn watched, as if seeing things Nynaeve could not. He stood up and walked to Kerb. In her dizzied state, Nynaeve hadn't noticed the young chandler's face. It was oddly blank, like that of a person dazed from a strong blow to the head.

Rand lowered himself to one knee, cradling the youth's chin in his hand, staring into his eyes. "Where?" he asked softly. "Where is she?"

The youth opened his mouth, and a line of drool leaked out the side of it.

"*Where is she?*" Rand repeated.

Kerb moaned, eyes still blank, tongue parting his lips just slightly.

"Rand!" Nynaeve said. "Stop it! What are you doing to him?"

"I have done nothing," Rand said quietly, not looking toward her. "This is what you did, Nynaeve, in unraveling those weaves. Graendal's Compulsions are powerful—but crude, in some ways. She fills a mind with Compulsion to such an extent as to erase personality and intellect, leaving behind a puppet who works only according to her direct commands."

"But he was able to interact just moments ago!"

Rand shook his head. "If you ask the men at the jail, they'll tell you this one was slow of thought and rarely spoke to them. There was no real person in this head, only layered weaves of Compulsion. Instructions cleverly designed to wipe whatever personality this poor wretch had and replace it with a creature who would act exactly as Graendal wished. I've seen it dozens of times."

Dozens of times? Nynaeve thought with a shiver. *You've seen it, or Lews Therin saw it? Which memories rule you right now?*

She looked at Kerb, sick to her stomach. His eyes weren't blank from being dazed as she'd thought; they were more empty than that. When Nynaeve had been younger, new to her role as Wisdom, a woman had been brought to her who had fallen off of her wagon. The woman had slept for days, and when she'd finally awoken, she'd had a stare like this one. No hint that she recognized anyone, no clue that there was any soul left in the husk that was her body.

She'd died about a week later.

Rand spoke to Kerb again. "I need a location," Rand said. "Something. If there is any vestige within you that resisted, any scrap that fought her, I promise you revenge. A location. Where is she?"

Spittle dripped from the boy's lips. They seemed to quiver. Rand stood up, looming, still holding the youth's eyes with his own. Kerb shivered, then whispered two words.

"Natrin's Barrow."

Rand exhaled softly, then released Kerb with an almost reverent motion. The youth slipped from the bench to the floor, spittle drooling from his lips onto the rug. Nynaeve cursed, leaping from her seat, then wobbling slightly as the room spun. Light, she was exhausted! She steadied herself, closed her eyes and took a few deep breaths. Then she knelt at the boy's side.

"You needn't bother," Rand said. "He is dead."

Nynaeve confirmed the death for herself. Then she snapped her head up, looking at Rand. What right did he have to look as exhausted as she felt? He had done barely anything! "What did you—"

"I did nothing, Nynaeve. I suspect that once you removed that Compulsion, the only thing keeping him alive was his anger at Graendal, buried deeply. Whatever bit of himself remained, it knew the only help it could give were those two words. After that, he just let go. There was nothing more we could do for him."

"I don't accept that," Nynaeve said, frustrated. "He could have been Healed!" She should have been able to help him! Undoing Graendal's Compulsion had felt so good, so *right*. It shouldn't have ended this way!

She shuddered, feeling dirtied. Used. How was she better than the jailer who had done such horrible things for information? She glared at Rand. He could have told her what removing Compulsion would do!

"Don't look at me like that, Nynaeve." He walked to the door and gestured for the Maidens there to collect Kerb's body. They did so, carrying it away as Rand called softly for a new pot of tea.

He returned, sitting down on the bench beside the sleeping Min; she'd tucked one of the bench's pillows under her head. One of the two lamps in the room was burning low, and that left his face half in shadow. "This was the only way it could have happened," he continued. "The Wheel weaves as the Wheel wills. You are Aes Sedai. Is that not one of your creeds?"

"I don't know what it is," Nynaeve snapped, "but it's not an excuse for your actions."

"What actions?" he asked. "You brought this man to me. Graendal used Compulsion on him. Now I will kill her for it—that action will be my sole responsibility. Now, let me be. I shall try to go back to sleep."

"Don't you feel any guilt at all?" she demanded.

They locked eyes, Nynaeve frustrated and helpless, Rand. . . . Who could guess what Rand felt these days!

"Should I suffer for them all, Nynaeve?" he asked quietly, rising, face still half in the darkness. "Lay this death at my feet, if you wish. It will just be one of many. How many stones can you pile on a man's body before the weight stops mattering? How far can you burn a lump of flesh until further heat is irrelevant? If I let myself feel guilt for this boy, then I would need to feel guilt for the others. And it would crush me."

She regarded him in the half light. A king, certainly. A soldier, though he had only occasionally seen war. She forced down her anger. Hadn't this all been about proving to him that he could trust her?

"Oh, Rand," she said, turning away. "This thing you have become, the heart without any emotion but anger. It will destroy you."

"Yes," he said softly.

She looked back at him, shocked.

"I continue to wonder," he said, glancing down at Min, "why you all assume that I am too dense to see what you find so obvious. Yes, Nynaeve. Yes, this hardness will destroy me. I know."

"Then why?" she asked. "Why won't you let us help you?"

He looked up—not at her, but staring off at nothing. A servant knocked quietly, wearing the white and forest green of Milisair's house. She entered and deposited the new pot of tea, picked up the old one, then withdrew.

"When I was much younger," he said, voice soft, "Tam told me of a story he'd heard while traveling the world. He spoke of Dragonmount. I didn't know at the time that he'd actually seen it, nor that he had found me there. I was just a shepherd boy, and Dragonmount, Tar Valon and Caemlyn were almost mythical places to me.

"He told me of it, though, a mountain so high it made even Twinhorn's Peak back home seem a dwarf. Tam's stories claimed no man had ever climbed to Dragonmount's peak. Not because it was impossible—but because reaching the top would take every last ounce of strength a man had. So tall was the mountain that besting it would be a struggle that drained a man completely."

He fell silent.

"So?" Nynaeve finally asked.

He looked at her. "Don't you see? The stories claimed no man had climbed the mountain because in doing so, he would be without strength to return. A mountaineer could best it, reach the top, see what no man had ever seen. But then he would die. The strongest and wisest explorers knew this. So they never climbed it. They always wanted to, but they waited, reserving that trip for another day. For they knew it would be their last."

"But that's just a story," Nynaeve said. "A legend."

"That's what I am," Rand said. "A story. A legend. To be told to children years from now, spoken of in whispers." He shook his head. "Sometimes, you can't turn back. You have to keep pressing on. And sometimes, you know this climb is your last.

"You all claim that I have grown too hard, that I will inevitably shatter and break if I continue on. But you assume that there needs to be something left of me to continue on. That I need to climb back down the mountain once I've reached the top.

"That's the key, Nynaeve. I see it now. I will not live through this, and so I don't need to worry about what might happen to me after the Last Battle. I don't need to hold back, don't need to salvage anything of this beaten up soul of mine. I know that I must die. Those who wish for me to be softer, willing to bend, are those who cannot accept what will happen to me." He looked down at Min again. Many times before, Nynaeve had seen affection in his eyes when he regarded her, but this time they were blank. Set in that same, emotionless face.

"We can find a way, Rand," Nynaeve said. "Surely there is a way to win but also let you live."

"No," he growled softly. "Do not tempt me down that path again. It only leads to pain, Nynaeve. I . . . I used to think about leaving something behind to help the world survive once I died, but that was a struggle to keep living. I can't indulge myself. I'll climb this bloody mountain and face the sun. You all will deal with what comes next. That is how it must be."

She opened her mouth to object again, but he gave her a sharp glance. "That is how it *must* be, Nynaeve."

She closed her mouth.

"You did well tonight," Rand said. "You have saved us all a lot of trouble."

"I did it because I want you to trust me," Nynaeve said, then immediately cursed herself. Why had she said that? Was she really so tired that she blabbed the first thing that came to her mind?

Rand just nodded. "I do trust you, Nynaeve. As much as I trust anyone; more than I trust most. You think you know what is best for me, even against my wishes, but that is something I can accept. The difference between you and Cadsuane is that you actually care about me. She only cares about my place in her plans. She wants me to be part of the Last Battle. You want me to live. For that, you have my thanks. Dream on my behalf, Nynaeve. Dream for things I no longer can."

He leaned down to pick up Min; he managed it despite his missing hand, snaking one arm underneath her and gripping with his hand as he lifted her up. She stirred, then snuggled in close to him, waking and murmuring a complaint that she could walk. He didn't put her down; perhaps because of the exhaustion in her voice. Nynaeve knew she stayed up with her books most nights, pushing herself almost as hard as Rand did.

Carrying Min, he walked toward the door. "We will deal with the Seanchan first," he said. "Be well prepared for that meeting. I will take care of Graendal soon after."

He left her then. The flickering lamp finally gave out, leaving only the one on the table.

Rand had surprised her again. He was still a wool-headed fool, but he was a surprisingly self-aware one. How could a man understand so much, yet still be so ignorant?

And why couldn't she come up with an argument against what he'd said? Why couldn't she make herself yell at him that he was wrong? There was *always* hope. By surrendering that most important emotion, he might make himself strong—but risked losing all reason he might have to care about the outcome of his battles.

For some reason, she couldn't find words for the argument.

CHAPTER

34

Legends

A ll right," Mat said, unrolling one of Roidelle's best maps on his table. Talmanes, Thom, Noal, Juilin and Mandevwin had arranged their chairs around the table. Beside the map of the area, Mat unrolled a sketch of the layout of a medium-sized town. It had taken some doing to find a merchant willing to sketch them a map of Trustair, but after Hinderstap, Mat didn't like to go into a town without knowing what they were up against.

Mat's pavilion was shaded by the pine forest outside, and the day was cool. Occasionally, the wind would blow, and a small sprinkle of dead pine needles would shake free from the boughs above and fall to the ground, some scratching the top of the tent as they fell. Outside, soldiers called to one another and pots clanged as the midday meal was distributed.

Mat studied the town map. It was time to stop being a fool. The whole world had decided to turn against him— even rural mountain towns were death traps, these days. Next he knew, the daisies on the sides of the road would be ganging up to try and eat him.

That thought gave him pause as he remembered the poor peddler, sinking into the phantom Shiotan town. When that ghostly place had vanished, it had left behind a meadow with butterflies and flowers. Including daisies. *Burn me,* he thought.

Well, Matrim Cauthon wasn't about to end up dead on some random backwater road. This time he would *plan* and he would be *ready*. He nodded to himself in satisfaction.

"The inn is here," Mat said, pointing at the town map.

"The Shaken Fist. Two separate travelers agreed that it was a fine inn, the nicest of the three in the town. The woman looking for me hasn't made any effort to hide her whereabouts, so that means she thinks that she is well protected. We can expect guards."

Mat pulled out another of Roidelle's maps, one that better showed the geography around Trustair. The town sat in a small hollow, surrounded by gently rolling hills beside a small lake fed by highland springs. The lake reportedly produced some fine trout, the salting of which was the town's main trade.

"I want three squads of light cavalry here," Mat said, pointing at an upper slope. "They'll be hidden by the trees, but will have full view of the skies. If a red nightflower goes up, they're to come in directly along the main road here for a rescue. We'll have a hundred crossbowmen sequestered on either side of the town as a backup to the cavalry. If the nightflower is green instead, the cavalry is to march in and secure the main roads to the town, here, here and here."

Mat looked up, pointing at Thom. "Thom, you'll take Harnan, Fergin and Mandevwin as 'apprentices' and Noal can be your footman."

"Footman?" Noal asked. He was a gnarled man, missing teeth, with a hooked beak of a nose. But he was tough as an old, battle-scored sword passed down from father to son. "Why does a gleeman need a footman?"

"All right," Mat said. "You can be his brother then, who doubles as a manservant. Juilin, you—"

"Wait, Mat," Mandevwin said, scratching his face near his eye patch. "I'm to be an apprentice gleeman? I'm not certain my voice is suited to fine singing. You've heard me, I warrant. And with only one eye, I doubt I'll fare well at juggling."

"You're a new apprentice," Mat said. "Thom knows you don't have any talent, but he took pity on you because your great-aunt—with whom you've lived since your parents died in a tragic oxen stampede—took sick of the clover pox and went crazy. She started feeding you table scraps and treated you like the family hound, Marks, who'd run away when you were just seven."

Mandevwin scratched his head. His hair was streaked with gray. "Aren't I a little old to be an apprentice, though?"

"Nonsense," Mat said. "You're young at heart, and since you never married—the only woman you ever loved ran away with the tanner's son—Thom's arrival offered you an opportunity to start fresh."

"But I don't want to leave my great-aunt," Mandevwin protested. "She's cared for me since I was a child! It's not honest of a man to abandon an elderly woman just because she gets a little confused."

"There *is* no great-aunt," Mat said with exasperation. "This is just a legend, a story to go with your false name."

"Can't I have a story that makes me more honorable?" Mandevwin asked.

"Too late," Mat said, rifling through a stack on his desk, searching out a cluster of five pages covered in scrawled handwriting. "You can't change now. I spent half the night working on your story. It's the best out of the lot. Here, memorize this." He handed it over to Mandevwin, then got out another stack of papers and began looking through them.

"Are you sure we're not taking this a little too far, lad?" Thom asked.

"I'm *not* going to be surprised again, Thom," Mat said. "Burn me, but I'm not going to let it happen. I'm tired of walking into traps unprepared. I plan to take command of my own destiny, stop running from problem to problem. It's time to be in charge."

"And you do that with . . ." Julin said.

"Elaborate aliases with backstories," Mat said, handing Thom and Noal their sheets. "Bloody right I do."

"What about me?" Talmanes asked. That twinkle to his eyes was back, though he spoke with a completely earnest voice. "Let me guess, Mat. I'm a traveling merchant who once trained with the Aiel and who has come to the village because he's heard there's a trout that lives in the lake who insulted his father."

"Nonsense," Mat said, handing him his sheets. "You're a Warder."

"That's rather suspicious," Talmanes noted.

"You're *supposed* to be suspicious," Mat said. "It's always easier to beat a man in cards when he's thinking about something else. Well, you'll be our 'something else.' A Warder passing through town on mysterious business won't be so grand an event that it will draw too much attention, but to those who know what to look for, it will be a good distraction. You can use Fen's cloak. He said he'd let me borrow it; he still feels guilty for letting those serving women get away."

"Of course, you didn't tell him that they simply *vanished*," Thom added. "And that there was no way for him to keep it from happening."

"Didn't see the point of telling him," Mat said. "No use dwelling on the past, I say."

"A Warder, is it?" Talmanes said, flipping through his stack of papers. "I'll have to practice scowling."

Mat regarded him with a flat expression. "You're not taking this seriously."

"What did you ask? Is there someone who *is* taking this seriously?" Burn that twinkle. Had Mat really ever thought this man was slow to laugh? He just did it on the inside. That was the most infuriating way.

"Light, Talmanes," Mat said. "A woman in that town is looking for Perrin and me. She knows what we look like so well that she can produce a drawing more accurate than my own mother could have made. That gives me a chill, like the Dark One himself standing over my shoulder. And I can't go into the flaming place myself, since every bloody man, woman and child has a picture with my face on it and a promise of gold for information!

"Now maybe I went a little far with the preparations, but I intend to find this person before they can order a flock of Darkfriends—or worse—to cut my throat in the night. Understood?"

Mat looked each of the five men in the eyes, nodded, and started toward the tent flap, but paused beside Talmanes's chair. Mat cleared his throat, then half mumbled, "You secretly harbor a love of painting, and you wish you could escape this life of death you've committed yourself to. You came through Trustair on your way south, rather than taking a more direct route, because you love the mountains. You're hoping to hear word of your younger brother, whom you haven't seen in years, and who disappeared on a hunting trip in southern Andor. You have a very tortured past. Read page four."

Mat hurried on, pushing his way out into the shaded

noon, though he did catch a glimpse of Talmanes rolling his eyes. Burn the man! There was good drama in those pages!

Through the pine trees he could see that the sky was cloudy. Again. When *was* that going to end? Mat shook his head as he walked through camp, nodding to the groups of soldiers who offered him salutes or calls of greeting to "Lord Mat." The Band were staying here for the day—camped on a secluded, wooded hillside a half-day march from the town—while they made final preparations for the assault. The three-needle pines here were tall, and their limbs spread wide, the shade keeping underbrush to a minimum. Tents clustered in groups around the pines, and the air was cool and shaded, smelling of sap and loam.

He went about the camp, checking into the workings of his men and seeing that everything was being handled efficiently. Those old memories, the ones that the Eelfinn had given him, had begun to blend so evenly with his own that he could hardly tell which instincts came from them and which were his own.

It was good to be among the Band again; he hadn't realized how much he'd missed them. It would be nice to reunite with the rest of the men, the troops led by Estean and Daerid. Hopefully, they'd had an easier time of it than Mat's force had.

The cavalry banners came first in his rounds. They were separate from the rest of the camp—horsemen always considered themselves superior to foot. Today, as all too often, the men were worried about feed for their horses. To a good cavalryman, his horse always came first. Their trip from Hinderstap had been hard on the animals, particularly since there wasn't much to graze on. Little was growing this spring, and the winter's leavings were strangely sparse. Horses would refuse patches of thatch, almost as if it had gone bad, like other food stores. They didn't have much grain; they had hoped to live off the land, as they were moving too quickly for grain wagons.

Well, he'd just have to find something to do about that. Mat assured the cavalrymen he was working on the problem, and they took him at his word. Lord Mat hadn't let them down yet. Of course, the ones he *had* let down were rotting in their graves. He denied a request to fly the banner. Perhaps after the raid on Trustair.

He didn't have any true foot with him at the moment; they were all with Estean and Daerid. Talmanes had wisely understood that they'd need mobility, and had brought the three banners of horse and nearly four thousand mounted crossbowmen. Mat checked on the crossbowmen next, pausing to watch a couple of squads drilling in firing ranks at the back of the camp.

Mat stopped beside a tall pine, its lowest branches a good two feet above his head, leaning against the trunk. The line of crossbowmen weren't practicing their aim so much as their coordination. You didn't really aim in most battles, which was why the crossbows worked so well. They required a tenth the training of a longbow. Sure, the latter could fire faster and farther, but if you didn't have a lifetime to spare practicing, then these crossbows were a fine substitute.

Besides, the crossbow reloading process made it easier to train the ranks to fire together. The squad's captain stood on the far side, slapping a rod against the side of a tree once every two seconds to give a beat. Each crack of the wood was an order. Raise crossbows to the shoulder on the first. Fire on the second. Lower on the third. Crank on the fourth. Up to the shoulder again on the fifth. The men were getting good—firing in coordinated waves made for more consistent killing. Each fourth crack let loose a wave of bolts into the trees.

We'll need more of those, Mat thought, noticing how many of the bolts splintered during the training shots. You wasted more ammunition practicing than you did fighting, but each bolt now could be worth two or three in combat. The men were getting good indeed. If he'd had a few banners worth of *these* when he'd fought at Bloodwash Falls, perhaps Nashif would have learned his lesson a lot sooner.

Of course, they'd be *more* useful if they could fire faster. The cranking was the slow point. Not the turn of the crank itself, but the necessity of lowering the crossbow each time. It cost four seconds just to move the weapon about. These new cranks and boxes that Talmanes had learned to make from that mechanic in Murandy sped things up greatly. But the mechanic had been on his way to sell the cranks in Caemlyn, and who knew who else had bought them along the way? Before too long, everyone might have them. An advantage was negated if both you and your enemies had it.

Those boxes had given a lot to Mat's success in Altara against the Seanchan. He was loath to surrender the advantage. Could he find a way to make the bows fire even faster?

Thoughtful, he checked on a few more things in the camp—the Altarans they'd recruited into the Band were settling in well, and other than feed for the horses and perhaps crossbow bolts, supplies looked good. Satisfied, he went looking for Aludra.

She had established herself near the back of the camp, alongside a little cleft in the rocky hillside. Though this spot was much smaller than the glade of trees the Aes Sedai and their attendants used, it was noticeably more secluded. Mat had to weave around three separate cloth sheets hanging between trees—placed carefully to block any view into Aludra's workspace—before he reached her. And he had to stop when Bayle Domon held out a hand, holding Mat back until Aludra gave leave for him to enter.

The slender, dark-haired Illuminator sat on a stump in the center of her little camp, powders, rolls of paper, a writing board for notes and tools neatly arranged on strips of cloth on the ground around her. She no longer wore her braids, and her long hair fell loose around her shoulders. That made her look odd to Mat. Still pretty, though.

Burn it, Mat. You're married now, he told himself. Aludra *was* pretty, though.

Egeanin was there, holding a nightflower shell upright for Aludra to work on. Aludra's full-lipped face frowned in concentration as she tapped lightly on the shell. Egeanin's dark hair was growing out, making her look less and less like one of the Seanchan nobility. Mat still had trouble trying to decide what to call the woman. She wanted to be known as Leilwin, and sometimes he thought of her like that. It was foolish to go about changing your name just because someone said you had to, but he didn't really blame her for not wanting to rile Tuon. She was a bloody stubborn one, Tuon was. He found himself glancing to the south again, but caught himself. Blood and ashes! She'd be just fine.

Anyway, Tuon was gone now. So why did Egeanin continue the charade of calling herself Leilwin? Mat had actually called her by her old name once or twice after Tuon's departure, but had received a curt reprimand. Women! They made no sense, and Seanchan women least of all.

Mat glanced at Bayle Domon. The muscular, bearded Illianer leaned against a tree near the entrance to Aludra's camp, two flapping white sheets of cloth extending in either direction near him. He still held out a warning hand. As if this entire camp weren't Mat's in the first place!

Mat didn't push his way past, though. He couldn't afford to offend Aludra. She was flaming close to being done with those dragon designs of hers, and he meant to have those. But Light, if it didn't smart to have to pass a checkpoint in his own camp!

Aludra looked up from her work, tucking a stray lock of hair behind her ear. She noted Mat, then looked back to her nightflower and began tapping with the hammer again. Bloody ashes! Seeing that reminded him why he visited Aludra so infrequently. The checkpoint was bad enough, but did the woman have to pound on something explosive with a hammer? Had she no sense at all? The entire lot of Illuminators were that way, though. Short a few foals of a full herd, as Mat's father might say.

"He may enter," Aludra said. "Thank you, Master Domon."

"It do be a pleasure, Mistress Aludra," Bayle said, lowering his hand and nodding amiably to Mat. Mat straightened his coat and walked forward, intent on asking about crossbows. Something immediately caught his eye, however. Spread out on the ground behind Aludra were a series of neat pages with detailed drawings, along with a list of notations with numbers beside them.

"Are these the plans for the dragons?" Mat asked eagerly. He knelt down on one knee to inspect the sheets, without touching them. Aludra could be particular about that kind of thing.

"Yes." She was still tapping with her hammer. She eyed him, looking just faintly uncomfortable. Because of Tuon, he suspected.

"And these figures?" Mat tried to ignore the awkwardness.

"Supply requirements," she said. She put down her hammer and inspected the cylindrical nightflower from all sides. She nodded to Leilwin.

Bloody ashes, but the figures were large! A mountain of charcoal, sulphur and . . . bat guano? The notes claimed there was a city specializing in producing it over in the northern reaches of the Mountains of Mist. What city specialized in gathering *bat guano*, of all things? There were requirements for copper and tin as well, though for some reason there were no numbers beside those. Just a little star notation.

Mat shook his head. How would the common people react if they knew that the majestic nightflowers were just a paper, powder and—of all things—bat dung? No wonder Illuminators were so secretive with their craft. It wasn't just about preventing competition. The more you knew about the process, the less wondrous and more ordinary it became.

"This is a lot of material," Mat said.

"A miracle, that is what you asked me for, Matrim Cauthon," she replied, handing her nightflower to Leilwin and picking up her writing board. She made some notations on the sheet strapped to the front. "That miracle, I have broken down into a list of ingredients. A feat which is in itself miraculous, yes? Do not complain of the heat when someone offers you the sun in the palm of her hands."

"Doesn't seem so manageable to me," Mat muttered, mostly to himself. "Is this figure the costs?"

"I am not a scribe," Aludra said. "Those are estimates only. The calculations, I have taken them as far as I can go, but the rest will have to be figured by those more proficient. The Dragon Reborn, he can afford such costs." Leilwin watched Mat with a curious expression. Things had changed with her, too, because of Tuon. But not in the way he'd expected.

Mention of Rand brought the colors swirling into Mat's vision, and he suppressed a sigh as he shook them away. Maybe Rand could manage costs like these, but *Mat* certainly couldn't. Why, he'd have to dice with the queen of Andor herself to find this kind of coin!

But that was Rand's problem. Burn him, he'd better appreciate what Mat was going through for him. "This doesn't include a manpower estimate," Mat noticed, scanning the sheets again. "How many bellfounders are you going to need for this project?"

"Every one you can get," Aludra said curtly. "Is that not what you promised me? Every bellfounder from Andor to Tear."

"I suppose," Mat said. He hadn't actually expected her to take him literally on that. "What about copper and tin? You don't have an estimate of those."

"I need all of it."

"All of. . . . What do you mean, *all* of it?"

"All of it," she repeated, as simply and calmly as if she were asking for more cloudberry jam for her porridge. "Every scrap of copper and tin you can scrounge up this side of the Spine of the World." She paused. "Perhaps that does seem too ambitious."

"Bloody right it's ambitious," Mat muttered.

"Yes," Aludra said. "Let us assume the Dragon has control of Caemlyn, Cairhien, Illian and Tear. If he were to provide me with access to each and every mine and metal store of copper and tin in those four cities, I suppose it would be sufficient."

"Every metal store," Mat said flatly.

"Yes."

"In four of the world's largest cities."

"Yes."

"And you 'suppose' that would be sufficient."

"I believe that is what I said, Matrim Cauthon."

"Great. I'll see what I can do about that. Would you like the bloody Dark One to come polish your shoes while you're at it? Maybe we could dig up Artur Hawkwing and get him to do a dance for you."

Leilwin gave Mat a glare at the mention of Artur Hawkwing. After a moment, Aludra finished her annotations, then turned to regard Mat. She spoke flatly, just vaguely hostile. "My dragons, they will be a great power for a man of war. You claim what I have given you is extravagant. It is only needed." She eyed him. "I will not lie and say I didn't expect this *dismissiveness* from you, Master Cauthon. Pessimism, she is a fond friend of yours, yes?"

"That's uncalled for," Mat grumbled, glancing back down at the drawings. "I barely know her. Mere acquaintances, at best. You've got my oath on it."

That earned a snort from Bayle. Whether it was one of amusement or derision was impossible to tell without looking back to judge his face. Mat didn't glance at him. Aludra was staring at him. Their eyes met for a moment, and Mat realized he'd probably been too curt with her. Maybe he was uncomfortable around her. A little. They'd been getting close before Tuon. And was that pain, hidden in Aludra's eyes?

"I'm sorry, Aludra," he said. "I shouldn't have talked like that."

She shrugged.

He took a deep breath. "Look, I know that . . . well, it's odd how Tuon—"

She waved a hand, cutting him off. "It is nothing. I have my dragons. You have brought me the chance to create them. Other matters are no longer of concern. I wish you happiness."

"Well," he said. He rubbed his chin, then sighed. Best to just let it pass. "Anyway, I hope I can get this done. You ask for a *lot* of resources."

"These bellfounders and materials," she said, "they are what I need. No more and no less. I have done what I can here, without resources. I will still need to spend weeks testing—we will need to make a single dragon first, to check. So you have some time to gather all of this. But it will take much time, and yet you refuse to tell me when the dragons will be needed."

"Can't tell you things I don't know myself, Aludra," Mat said, glancing northward. He felt a strange tugging, as if someone had hooked a fisherman's line about his insides and was softly—but insistently—pulling on it. *Rand, is that you, burn you?* Colors swirled. "Soon, Aludra," he found himself saying. "Time is short. So short."

She hesitated, as if sensing something in his voice. "Well," she said. "If that be the case, then my requests are not so extravagant, yes? If the world goes to war, the forges will soon be needed for arrowheads and horseshoes. Better to put them to work now on my dragons. Let me assure you, each one we finish will be worth a thousand swords in battle."

Mat sighed, stood up and tipped his hat to her. "All right, then," he said. "Fair enough. Assuming Rand doesn't bloody burn me to a crisp the moment I suggest this, I'll see what I can do."

"You would be wise to show Mistress Aludra respect," Leilwin said, eyeing Mat, speaking with that slow Seanchan drawl. "Rather than being so flippant toward her."

"That was sincere!" Mat said. "That last part was, at least. Burn me, woman. Can't you tell when a man's being sincere?"

She eyed him, as if trying to decide if that very pronouncement were some kind of mockery. Mat rolled his eyes. Women!

"Mistress Aludra is brilliant," Leilwin said sternly. "You don't understand the gift she is giving you in these plans. Why, if the Empire had these weapons. . . ."

"Well, see that you don't give them to it, Leilwin," Mat said. "I don't want to wake up one morning and find that you've run off with these plans in an attempt at retrieving your title!"

She looked insulted that he'd suggest such a thing, though it seemed like the logical thing to do. Seanchan had an odd sense of honor—Tuon hadn't tried once to flee from him, though she'd had ample opportunity.

Of course, Tuon had suspected from near the beginning that she'd marry him. She'd had that *damane*'s Foretelling. Burn him, he *wouldn't* look southward again. He wouldn't!

"My ship is being driven by different winds now, Master Cauthon," Leilwin said simply, turning from him and glancing at Bayle.

"But you wouldn't help us fight the Seanchan," Mat protested. "It seems that you'd—"

"You do be swimming in deep water right now, lad," Bayle interjected in a soft voice. "Aye, deep water, filled with lionfish. It may be time to stop splashing so loudly."

Mat closed his mouth. "All right then," he said. Shouldn't the two of them be treating him with more respect? Wasn't he some kind of high Seanchan prince or something? He should have known that wouldn't help him with Leilwin or the bearded sailor.

Anyway, he *had* been sincere. Aludra's words made sense, crazy though they sounded at first. They *would* need to dedicate a lot of foundries to the work. The weeks it was going to take him to reach Caemlyn seemed even more galling now. Those weeks spent on the road should be spent building dragons! A wise man learned that there was no use fretting over long marches—but Mat felt far from wise lately.

"All right," he said again. He looked back at Aludra. "Though—for completely different reasons—I'd like to take these plans with me and keep them safe."

"Completely different reasons?" Leilwin asked in a flat tone, as if searching for another insult.

"Yes," Mat said. "Those reasons being that I don't want them here when Aludra taps one of those nightflowers the wrong way and blows herself halfway to Tarwin's Gap!"

Aludra chuckled at that, though Leilwin looked offended again. It was hard *not* to offend a Seanchan. Them and the bloody Aiel. Strange how opposite they could be in many ways, yet the same in so many others.

"You may take the plans, Mat," Aludra said. "So long as you keep them in that trunk with your gold. That is one object in this camp that will receive the greatest attention from you."

"Thank you kindly," he said, stooping to gather up the pages, ignoring the veiled insult. Hadn't they just made up? Bloody woman. "By the way, I nearly forgot. Do you know anything about crossbows, Aludra?"

"Crossbows?" she asked.

"Yes," Mat said, stacking the papers. "I figure there should be a way to make them load faster. You know, like those new cranks, only maybe with some kind of spring or something. Maybe a crank you could twist without having to lower the weapon first."

"This is hardly my area of expertise, Mat," Aludra said.

"I know. But you're smart about things like this, and maybe. . . ."

"You will have to find someone else," Aludra said, turning to pick up another half-finished nightflower. "I am far too busy."

Mat reached up under his hat, scratching his head. "That—"

"Mat!" a voice called. "Mat, you've got to come with me!" Mat turned as Olver ran into Aludra's camp. Bayle held out a warning hand, but of course Olver just ran right beneath it.

Mat straightened up. "What?" he asked.

"Someone's come to the camp," Olver said, excitement painting his features. And those features were a sight. Ears that were too big for his head, nose that was squashed down, mouth that was too wide. On a child his age, the ugliness was endearing. He'd have no such luck when he grew older. Maybe the men in camp were right to be teaching him weapons. With a face like that, he'd better know how to defend himself.

"Wait, slow down," Mat said, tucking Aludra's plans into his belt. "Someone's come? Who? Why do you need me?"

"Talmanes sent me to fetch you," Olver said. "He thinks she's someone important. Said to tell you she's got some pages with your picture on them, and that she's got a 'distinctive face,' whatever that means. That. . . ."

Olver continued, but Mat had stopped listening. He nodded to Aludra and the others, then trotted out of her camp, past the sheets and out into the woods proper. Olver tagged along behind as Mat hurried to the front of the camp.

There, sitting on a short-legged white mare, was a pudgy woman with a grandmotherly air, a brown dress, and streaks of gray in her hair, which was pulled back in a bun. She was surrounded by a group of soldiers, Talmanes and Mandevwin standing directly in front of her, like two stone pillars barring entrance to a harbor.

The woman had an Aes Sedai face, and an aging Warder stood beside her horse. Though he had graying hair, the stocky man exuded that sense of danger that all Warders had. He studied the Band's soldiers with unyielding eyes, arms folded.

The Aes Sedai smiled at Mat as he trotted up. "Ah, very nice," she said primly. "You've grown prompt since we last parted, Matrim Cauthon."

"Verin," Mat said, panting slightly from the run. He glanced at Talmanes who held up a sheet of paper, one of those imprinted with Mat's face. "You've discovered that someone's been distributing pictures of me in Trustair?"

She laughed. "You could say that."

He looked at her, meeting those dark brown Aes Sedai

eyes. "Blood and bloody ashes," he muttered. "It was *you*, wasn't it? You're the one who's been looking for me!"

"For some time, I might add," Verin said lightly. "And rather against my will."

Mat closed his eyes. So much for his intricate plan for the raid. Burn it! And it was a good plan, too. "How'd you find I was here?" he asked, opening his eyes.

"A kind merchant came to me in Trustair an hour ago and explained that he'd just had a nice meeting with you, and that you'd paid him handsomely for a sketch of Trustair. I figured that I'd spare the poor town an assault by your . . . associates and just come to you myself."

"An hour ago?" Mat said, frowning. "But Trustair is still half a day's march away!"

"Indeed it is." Verin smiled.

"Burn me," he said. "You've got Traveling, don't you?"

Her smile deepened. "I surmise that you're trying to get to Andor with this army, Master Cauthon."

"That depends," Mat said. "Can you take us there?"

"In a very short time," Verin said. "I could have your men in Caemlyn by evening."

Light! Twenty days shaved off his march? Maybe he *could* get Aludra's dragons into production soon! He hesitated, eyeing Verin, forcing himself to contain his excitement. There was always a cost when Aes Sedai were involved.

"What do you want?" he asked.

"Frankly," she replied, sighing slightly. "What I *want*, Matrim Cauthon, is to be cut free from your *ta'veren* web! Do you know how long you've forced me to wait in these mountains?"

"*Forced?*"

"Yes," she said. "Come, we have much to discuss." She flicked her reins, moving her horse into camp, and Talmanes and Mandevwin reluctantly stepped aside, letting her in. Mat joined the two of them, watching as she made straight for the cook fires.

"I guess there won't be a raid," Talmanes said. He didn't sound sad.

Mandevwin fingered his eye patch. "Does this mean I can go back to my poor aged aunt?"

"You *have* no poor aged aunt," Mat growled. "Come on, let's hear what the woman has to say."

"Fine," Mandevwin said. "But next time, I get to be the Warder, all right, Mat?"

Mat just sighed, hurrying after Verin.

CHAPTER
35

A Halo of Blackness

The cool sea breeze washed across Rand the moment
he rode through the gateway. That soft, featherlike
wind carried with it the scents of a thousand cook
fires scattered through the city of Falme, heating morning
stews.

Rand reined in Tai'daishar, unprepared for the memories
those scents would carry with them. Memories of a time
when he'd still been uncertain about his role in the world.
Memories of a time when Mat had constantly ribbed him
for wearing fine coats, despite the fact that Rand tried to
avoid them. Memories of a time when he had been ashamed
of the banners that now flapped behind him. He had once
insisted on keeping them hidden, as if in doing so he could
hide from his own fate.

The procession waited for him, buckles creaking, horses
snorting. Rand had visited Falme once, briefly. Back in
those days, he hadn't been able to stay anywhere for long.
He'd spent those months either chasing or being chased.
Fain had led him to Falme, bearing the Horn of Valere and
the ruby dagger to which Mat had been bound. The colors
flashed again, as he thought of Mat, but Rand ignored them.
For these few moments, he wasn't in the present.

Falme marked a turning point in Rand's life as profound
as the one that had later occurred in the barren lands of the
Aiel, when he had proven himself to be the *Car'a'carn*. After Falme, there had been no more hiding, no more fighting
what he was. This was the place where he'd first acknowledged himself as a killer, the place where he'd first realized

what a danger he was to those around him. He'd tried to leave them all behind. They'd come after him.

At Falme, the shepherd boy had burned, his ashes scattered and blown away by those ocean winds. From those ashes, the Dragon Reborn had risen.

Rand kneed Tai'daishar forward, and the procession began again. He had ordered the gateway opened a short ride from the city, hopefully out of eyesight of *damane*. Of course he had Asha'man creating it—thereby hiding the weaves from women—but he didn't want to give them any clues about Traveling. The Seanchan inability to Travel was one of his greatest advantages.

Falme itself stood on a small spit of land—Toman Head—jutting out into the Aryth Ocean. High cliffs along both sides broke the waves, creating a soft, distant roar. The city's dark stone buildings covered the peninsula like rocks on the bed of a river. Most were squat, one-story buildings—built wide, as if the inhabitants expected the waves to wash up over the cliffs and crash against their homes. The grasslands here didn't show as much withering as the land did to the north, but the new spring grass was starting to look yellow and wan, as if the blades regretted poking their heads out of the soil.

The peninsula sloped down to a natural harbor, and numerous Seanchan ships lay at anchor there. Seanchan flags flew, proclaiming this city a part of their empire; the banner that fluttered highest above the city displayed a golden hawk in flight, clutching three bolts of lightning. It was fringed with blue.

The strange creatures the Seanchan had brought from their side of the ocean moved through distant streets, too far off for Rand to make out details. *Raken* flew in the sky; the Seanchan apparently had a large stable of them here. Toman Head was just south of Arad Doman, and this city was no doubt a major staging area for the Seanchan campaign to the north.

That conquest would end today. Rand *had* to make peace, had to convince the Daughter of the Nine Moons to call off her armies. That peace would be the calm before a storm. He wouldn't be protecting his people from war; just preserving them so that they could die for him elsewhere. But he would do what had to be done.

.t was to shield them. If the *damane* tried to capture him, they would be shocked by his resilience. He might be able to resist a full circle.

"I will *not* be captured again," he whispered. "Never again. They will not take me by surprise."

"Maybe we should turn back," Nynaeve said. "Rand, we don't have to meet them on their terms. It—"

"We stay," Rand said softly. "We deal with them here and now." Ahead, he could see a figure sitting in the pavilion at a table on a dais. There was a chair across from the figure, on an equal level. That surprised him; from what he knew of the Seanchan, he had expected to have to argue for equal footing with one of the Blood.

Was this the Daughter of the Nine Moons? This child? Rand frowned as they approached, but realized that she wasn't actually a child, just a very small woman. Dressed in black clothing, she had dark skin, like one of the Sea Folk. There were gray-white ashes on the cheeks of her calm, round face. Upon close inspection, she appeared to be near his own age.

Rand took a deep breath and dismounted. It was time for the war to end.

The Dragon Reborn was a young man. Tuon had been told that, but something about it still surprised her.

Why should she be surprised by this youth? Conquering heroes were often young. Artur Hawkwing himself, the Empire's great progenitor, had been a young man when he'd begun his conquest.

Those who conquered, those who dominated the world, burned themselves out quickly, like lamps with untrimmed wicks. He wore gold and red on black, the buttons on his coat sparkling as he dismounted from his large black gelding and approached the pavilion. The black coat had red and gold embroidery on the cuffs—the missing hand was quite obvious, looking at those cuffs—but his clothing was otherwise unadorned. As if he saw no need to distract from his face with finery.

His hair was the color of a deep sunset, a dark red. He had a regal bearing to him—a stride that was firm, each step confident, eyes straight ahead. Tuon had been trained

Nynaeve rode up beside him as they continued toward Falme. Her neat dress of blue and white was cut after the Domani fashion, but made of a much thicker—and far more modest—material. She seemed to be adopting fashions from around the world, wearing dresses from the cities she visited, but imposing her own sense of what was proper upon them. Once, perhaps, Rand would have found this amusing. That emotion no longer seemed possible for him. He could only feel the cold stillness inside, the stillness that capped a fountain of frozen rage.

He would keep the rage and stillness balanced long enough. He *had* to.

"And so we return," Nynaeve said. Her multicolor *ter'angreal* jewelry somewhat spoiled the look of her neatly tailored dress.

"Yes," Rand said.

"I remember the last time we were here," she said idly. "Such chaos, such madness. And at the end of it all, we found you with that wound in your side."

"Yes," Rand whispered. He had earned that first of his unhealable wounds here, fighting Ishamael in the skies above the city. The wound grew warm as he thought of it. Warm, and painful. He had started regarding that pain as an old friend, a reminder that he was alive.

"I saw you up in the air," Nynaeve said. "I didn't believe it. I . . . tried to Heal that wound, but I was still blocked then, and couldn't summon the anger. Min wouldn't leave your side."

Min hadn't come with him this day. She remained close to him, but something had changed between them. Just as he had always feared that it would. When she looked at him, he knew she saw him killing her.

Just a few weeks before, he wouldn't have been able to keep her from accompanying him, no matter what. Now she remained behind without a single protest.

Coldness. It would be over soon. No room for regret or sorrow.

The Aiel ran ahead to check for an ambush. Many of them wore the red headbands. Rand wasn't worried about an ambush. The Seanchan would not betray him, not unless there was another Forsaken in their midst.

Rand reached down, touching the sword he wore at his

waist. It was the curved one, with the scabbard of black, painted with the twisting dragon, red and gold. For more reasons than one, it made him think of the last time he had been in Falme.

"I killed a man with a sword for the first time in this city," Rand said softly. "I've never spoken of it. He was a Seanchan lord, a blademaster. Verin had told me not to channel in the city, so I faced him with the sword only. I beat him. Killed him."

Nynaeve raised an eyebrow. "So you *do* have a right to carry a heron-mark blade."

Rand shook his head. "There were no witnesses. Mat and Hurin were fighting elsewhere. They saw me right after the fight, but did not witness the killing blow."

"What do witnesses matter?" she scoffed. "You defeated a blademaster, so you are one. Whether or not it was seen by others is immaterial."

He looked at her. "Why carry the heron mark if not to be seen by others, Nynaeve?"

She didn't respond. Ahead, just outside of the city, the Seanchan had erected a striped pavilion of black and white. There appeared to be hundreds of *sul'dam* and *damane* pairs surrounding the open-sided tent, *damane* wearing the distinctive gray dress, *sul'dam* wearing their dresses of red and blue with the lightning bolt on the breast. Rand had brought only a few channelers: Nynaeve, three Wise Ones, Corele, Narishma, Flinn. A fraction of what he could access, even without turning to his forces stationed in the east.

But no, it was better to bring only a token guard, to look as though he came in peace. If this meeting turned into a battle, Rand's only hope would be a quick escape via gateway. Either that . . . or do something to end the fight himself.

The figurine of the man holding aloft the sphere hung from the saddle before him. With it, he might be able to stand against a hundred *damane*. Two hundred. He could remember the Power he'd held when cleansing *saidin*. It had been the Power to level cities, to destroy any who stood against him.

No. It wouldn't turn to that. He couldn't *afford* to let it turn to that. Surely the Seanchan knew that attacking him would lead to disaster. Rand had come to meet with them

again, aware that a traitor in their ranks had tried to c̶ or kill him. They would have to see his sincerity.

But if they didn't. . . . He reached down and grasped access key, just in case, and slipped it into his oversi͟ outer coat pocket. Then, taking a deep breath, he stea͟ ied himself and sought the void. There, he seized the One Power.

Nausea and dizziness threatened to toss him to the ground. He wobbled, legs gripping Tai'daishar, hand clutching the access key in its pocket. He gritted his teeth. In the back of his mind, Lews Therin roused. The madman scrambled for the One Power. It was a desperate fight, and when Rand finally won, he found that he'd slumped in his saddle.

And he was muttering to himself again.

"Rand?" Nynaeve asked.

Rand straightened his back. He *was* Rand, wasn't he? Sometimes, after a battle like this, he had trouble recalling who he was. Had he finally pushed Rand, the intruder, into seclusion and become Lews Therin? The previous day, he had woken at midday, huddled in the corner of his rooms, crying and whispering to himself about Ilyena. He could *feel* the soft texture of her long golden hair in his hands, and could remember holding her close. He could remember seeing her dead at his feet, slain by the One Power.

Who was he?

Did it really matter?

"Are you all right?" Nynaeve asked again.

"We are fine." Rand did not realize he'd used the plural until the words were out of his mouth. His vision was recovering, though it still seemed just a little bit fuzzy. Everything was distorted a fraction, as it had been since the battle where Semirhage had taken his hand. He barely noticed it anymore.

He straightened, then drew a little extra power through the access key, filling himself with *saidin*. It was so sweet, despite the nausea that it caused. He longed to take in more, but held himself back. He already held more of the Power than any man could unaided. It would be enough.

Nynaeve glanced at the figurine at his side. The globe at the top glowed faintly. "Rand. . . ."

"I'm only holding a little extra, as a precaution." The more of the One Power a person held, the more difficult

to walk that way, to give no quarter, in the way she stepped. Who had trained him, she wondered. Likely, he had the finest of teachers to prepare him in the ways of kings and leaders. Yet reports said he had grown up as a farmer in a rural village. A story, carefully spread to bring him credibility with the common people, perhaps?

He strode up to the pavilion, a *marath'damane* on his left. The woman wore a dress colored like the sky on a clear day, set with trim like clouds. She wore her hair in a single dark braid and adorned herself with a set of gaudy jewelry. She seemed displeased by something, her brow furrowed, her mouth a tight line. Her presence made Tuon shiver. One would think she'd have grown more accustomed to *marath'damane*, after traveling with Matrim. But not so. They were unnatural. Dangerous. Tuon could no more grow comfortable around an unleashed *damane* than she could tolerate having a grassfang twisted around her ankle, its tongue tickling her skin.

Of course, if the *marath'damane* was unsettling, then the two men who walked to the right of the Dragon were more so. One, little more than a youth, wore his hair in braids tied with bells. The other was an older man with white hair and a tanned face. Despite the difference in their ages, both walked with the casual swagger of men well acquainted with battle. And both wore black coats, sparkling pins on the high collars. Asha'man, they were called. Men who could channel. Abominations best killed quickly. In Seanchan, there had been a very few who—in their lust for an unanticipated edge—had tried to train these *Tsorov'ande Doon*, these Black-Souled Tempests. The fools had fallen quickly, often destroyed by the very tools that they sought to control.

Tuon steeled herself. Karede and the Deathwatch Guards around her grew tense. It was subtle—fists tightening at their sides, breaths inhaled and released slowly. Tuon didn't turn toward them, though she made a covert gesture to Selucia.

"You are to maintain your calm," the Voice said softly to the men.

They would do so—they were Deathwatch Guard. Tuon hated to make the comment, as it would lower their eyes. But she would *not* have a mishap. Meeting with the Dragon

Reborn would be dangerous. There was no avoiding that. Even with twenty *damane* and *sul'dam* on each side of the pavilion. Even with Karede at her back and Captain Musenge and a force of archers watching from a covered rooftop just within bowshot. Even with Selucia at her right, tense and ready to pounce, like a jagwin on the high rocks. Even with all of that, Tuon was exposed. The Dragon Reborn was a bonfire inexplicably lit inside a house. You could not prevent it from damaging the room. You just hoped to save the building.

He walked directly to the chair opposite Tuon and sat down, never once questioning that she had set him as her equal. She knew that the others wondered why she still wore the ashes of mourning, why she hadn't proclaimed herself Empress. The mourning period was over, but Tuon had not taken her throne.

It was because of this man. The Empress could not meet anyone, not even the Dragon Reborn, as an equal. The Daughter of the Nine Moons, however . . . this one man could be *her* equal. And so she had hesitated. The Dragon Reborn would not likely respond well to another setting herself above him, no matter if that other had a perfectly legitimate reason for doing so.

As he sat down, a distant flare of lightning arced between two clouds, though Malai—one of the *damane* who could tell fortunes of the weather—had insisted that no rain was near. Lightning on a day without rain. *Tread very lightly,* she thought, reading the omen, *and be careful what you speak.* Not the most illuminating of omens. If she trod any *more* carefully, she would have to take flight into the air!

"You are the Daughter of the Nine Moons," the Dragon Reborn said. It was a statement, not a question.

"You are the Dragon Reborn," she replied. Looking into those slatelike eyes, she realized that she had been wrong in her first impression. He was *not* a young man. Yes, his body might be that of a youth. But those eyes . . . those were old eyes.

He leaned forward slightly. Her Deathwatch Guards tensed, leather creaking. "We will make peace," al'Thor said. "Today. Here."

Selucia hissed softly. His words sounded a great deal like a demand. Tuon had shown him great respect by placing him at her level, but one did *not* give orders to the Imperial family.

Al'Thor glanced at Selucia. "You can tell your body-guard that she can relax," he said dryly. "This meeting will not turn to conflict. I will not allow it."

"She is my Voice," Tuon said carefully, "and my Truth-speaker. My bodyguard is the man behind my chair."

Al'Thor snorted softly. So he was an observant man. Or a lucky one. Few had correctly guessed Selucia's nature.

"You wish for peace," Tuon said. "Have you terms for your . . . offer?"

"It is not an offer, but a necessity," al'Thor said. He spoke with softness. All of these people spoke with such quick words, yet al'Thor's had a *weight* to them. He reminded her of her mother. "The Last Battle comes. Surely your people remember the prophecies. By prosecuting this war of yours, you endanger us all. My forces—*everyone's forces*—are needed in the struggle against the Shadow."

The Last Battle would be between the Empire and the forces of the Dark One. Everybody knew that. The proph-ecies clearly showed that the Empress would defeat those who served the Shadow, and then she would send the Dragon Reborn in to duel with Lighteater.

How much had he fulfilled? He didn't seem blinded yet, so that had yet to happen. The Essanik Cycle said that he would stand on his own grave and weep. Or did that proph-ecy refer to the dead walking, as they did already? Cer-tainly, some of those spirits had walked across their own graves. The writings were unclear, sometimes.

This people seemed to have forgotten many of the proph-ecies, just as they forgot their oaths to watch for the Return. But she did not say this. *Watch your words carefully. . . .*

"You believe the Last Battle is close, then?" she asked.

"Close?" al'Thor asked. "It is as close as an assassin, breathing his foul breath upon your neck as he slides his knife across your skin. It is close like the last chime of mid-night, after the other eleven have struck. Close? Yes, it is close. Horribly close."

Had the madness taken him already? If it had, that would make things much more difficult. She studied him, searching for signs of insanity. He seemed in control of himself.

A sea breeze blew through the canopy, ruffling the canvas and carrying with it the scent of rotten fish. Many things seemed to be rotting these days.

Those creatures, she thought. *The Trollocs.* What did their appearance foretell? Tylee had destroyed them, and the scouts had found no others. Looking at the intensity of this man, she hesitated. Yes, the Last Battle was close, perhaps as close as he said. That made it all the more important that she unify these lands beneath her banner.

"You *must* see why this is so important," the Dragon Reborn said. "Why do you fight me?"

"We are the Return," Tuon said. "The omens said it was time for us to come, and we expected to find a united kingdom, ready to praise us and lend us armies for the Last Battle. Instead, we found a fractured land that had forgotten its oaths and prepared for nothing. How can you not see that we must fight? It does not bring us pleasure to kill you, no more than it brings a parent joy to discipline a child who has gone astray."

Al'Thor seemed incredulous. "We are *children* to you?"

"It was a metaphor only," Tuon said.

He sat for a moment, then rubbed his chin with his hand. Did he blame her for the loss of the other one? Falendre had spoken of it.

"A metaphor," he said. "An apt one, perhaps. Yes, the land *did* lack unity. But I have forged it together. The solder is weak, perhaps, but it will hold long enough. If not for me, then your war of unification would be commendable. As it is, you are a distraction. We must have peace. Our alliance need last only until my life ends." He met her eyes. "I assure you that will not be overly long."

She sat at the wide table, arms folded before her. If al'Thor stretched out his arm, he would not be able to reach her. That was intentional, though the precaution was laughable, in hindsight. He would not need his hand should he decide to kill her. Best not to think of that.

"If you see the value of unification," she said, "then perhaps you should unite your lands beneath the Seanchan banner, have your people take the oaths and—" The woman standing behind al'Thor, the *marath'damane,* opened eyes wide as Tuon spoke.

"No," al'Thor said, interrupting Tuon.

"But surely you can see that one ruler, with—"

"No," he said, softly, yet more firmly. More dangerous. "I will not see another person chained by your foul leashes."

"Foul? They are the only way to deal with those who can channel!"

"We have survived without them for centuries."

"And you have—"

"This is not a point I will concede," al'Thor said.

Tuon's guards—Selucia included—gritted their teeth, and the guards dropped hands to sword hilts. He had interrupted her twice in a row. The Daughter of the Nine Moons. How could he be so bold?

He was the Dragon Reborn, that was how. But his words were foolishness. He *would* bow before her, once she was Empress. The prophecies demanded it. Surely that meant that his kingdoms would join with the Empire.

She had let the conversation slip out of her control. The *marath'damane* were a touchy subject to many on this side of the ocean. They likely understood the logic in leashing the women, but their traditions were difficult to relinquish. That was no doubt why they were so disturbed by talking about these things.

She needed to nudge the conversation in other directions. Into a realm that would throw the Dragon Reborn off guard. She studied him. "Is this all our conversation is to be about?" she said. "We sit across from one another and speak only of our differences?"

"What else would we talk about?" al'Thor said.

"Perhaps something we have in common."

"I doubt there is much in that area that is relevant."

"Oh?" Tuon said. "And what of Matrim Cauthon?"

Yes, *that* shocked him. The Dragon Reborn blinked, mouth opening slightly. "Mat?" he said. "You know Mat? How . . ."

"He kidnapped me," Tuon said. "And dragged me most of the way across Altara."

The Dragon Reborn gaped, then shut his mouth. "I remember now," he said softly. "I saw you. With him. I did not connect you to that face. Mat . . . what have you been doing?"

You saw *us?* Tuon thought skeptically. So the madness *had* manifested itself. Would that make him easier to manipulate, or more difficult? Probably the latter, unfortunately.

"Well," al'Thor finally said, "I trust that Mat had his reasons. He always does. And they seem so *logical* to him at the time. . . ."

So, Matrim *did* know the Dragon Reborn; he would be an excellent resource to her. Perhaps that was why he had been brought to her, so she would have a means of learning about the Dragon Reborn. She would have to recover him before he could help her in that area.

Matrim would not like that, but he would have to see reason. He was First Prince of the Ravens. He needed to be raised to the High Blood, shave his head and learn the *proper* way of living. That all seemed a shame to her—for reasons she could not explain to herself.

She couldn't help asking after him a little more. Partly because the topic appeared to unbalance al'Thor, and partly because she was curious. "What type of man is he, this Matrim Cauthon? I must admit, I found him to be something of an indolent scoundrel, too quick to find excuses to avoid oaths he'd taken."

"Don't speak of him that way!" Surprisingly, the words came from the *marath'damane* standing beside al'Thor's chair.

"Nynaeve . . ." al'Thor began.

"Don't hush me, Rand al'Thor," the woman said, folding her arms. "He's your friend too." The woman looked back at Tuon, meeting her eyes. *Meeting* them. A *marath'damane*!

She continued, "Matrim Cauthon is one of the finest men you will ever know, Your Highness, and I won't listen to ill speech of him. What's right is right."

"Nynaeve is right," al'Thor said reluctantly. "He is a good man. Mat may seem a little rough at times, but he is as solid a friend as one could hope for. Though he *does* grumble about what his conscience makes him do."

"He saved my life," the *marath'damane* said. "Rescued me at great cost and personal danger when no other thought to come for me." Her eyes were afire with anger. "Yes, he drinks and gambles far too much. But don't speak of him as if you know him, because you don't. His heart is golden, under it all. If you've hurt him. . . ."

"Hurt him?" Tuon said. "*He* kidnapped *me!*"

"If he did so, then there was cause," Rand al'Thor said.

Such loyalty! Once again, she was forced to reassess her view of Matrim Cauthon.

"But this is irrelevant," al'Thor said, standing up suddenly. One of the Deathwatch Guards drew his sword. Al'Thor glared at the guard, and Karede quickly motioned at the man, who replaced his sword, ashamed, his eyes lowered.

Al'Thor placed his hand on the table, palm down. He leaned forward, trapping Tuon's eyes with his own. Who could look away from those intense gray eyes, like steel? "None of this matters. Mat doesn't matter. Our similarities and our differences do not matter. All that matters is need. And I *need* you."

He leaned forward further, looming. His form didn't change, but he suddenly seemed a hundred feet tall. He spoke in that same calm, piercing voice, but there was a threat to it now. An edge.

"You *must* call off your attacks," he said, nearly a whisper. "You must sign a treaty with me. These are not requests. They are my will."

Tuon found herself longing, suddenly, to obey him. To please him. A treaty. A treaty would be excellent, it would give her a chance to stabilize her hold on the lands here. She could plan how to restore order back in Seanchan. She could recruit and train. So many possibilities opened to her, as if her mind were suddenly determined to see every advantage of the alliance and none of the flaws.

She reached for those flaws, scrambling to see the problems in uniting herself with this man. But they became liquid in her mind and slipped away. She couldn't snatch them up and form objections. The pavilion grew silent, the breeze falling still.

What was happening to her? She felt short of breath, as though a weight constricted her chest. She felt as if she couldn't help but bend before the will of this man!

His expression was grim. Despite the afternoon light, his face was shadowed, far more so than everything else beneath the pavilion. He held her eyes still, and her breaths came quick and short. In the corners of her vision, she thought she saw something around him. A dark haze, a halo of blackness, emanating from him. It warped the air like a great heat. Her throat constricted, and words were forming. Yes. Yes. I will do as you ask. Yes. I must. I must.

"No," she said, the word barely a whisper.

His expression grew darker, and she saw fury in the way he pressed his hand down, fingers trembling with the force. The way he clenched his jaw. The way his eyes opened wider. Such intensity.

"I need—" he began.

"No," she repeated, confidence growing. "You will bow before me, Rand al'Thor. It will *not* happen the other way around." Such darkness! How could one man contain it? He seemed to throw a shadow the size of a mountain.

She could not ally with this creature. That seething hatred, it terrified her, and terror was an emotion with which she was unfamiliar. This man could *not* be allowed freedom to do as he wished. He had to be contained.

He watched her for a moment longer. "Very well," he said. His voice was ice.

He spun, stalking away from the pavilion, not looking back. His entourage followed; they all, including the *marath'damane* with the braid, looked disturbed. As if they themselves weren't certain what—or who—they followed in this man.

Tuon watched him go, panting. She could not let the others see how rattled she was. They couldn't know that, in that last moment, she'd feared him. She watched until his mounted figure had passed beyond the hillsides. And still her hands shook. She did not trust herself to speak.

Nobody spoke in the time it took her to calm herself. Perhaps they were as shaken as she. Perhaps they sensed her worry. Finally, long after al'Thor had gone, Tuon stood. She turned and regarded the collected Blood, generals, soldiers and guards. "I am the Empress," she said in a soft voice.

As one, they fell to their knees, even the High Blood prostrating themselves.

That was the only ceremony needed. Oh, there would be a formal crowning back in Ebou Dar, with processions and parades and audiences. She would accept the personal oaths of allegiance from each member of the Blood, and would have the chance—by tradition—to execute any of them by her own hand, without reason, who she felt had opposed her ascent to the throne.

There would be all of that and more. But her declaration was the *true* coronation. Spoken by the Daughter of the Nine Moons after the period of mourning.

Festivities began the moment she bade them all rise. There would be a week of jubilation. A necessary distraction. The world needed her. It needed an empress. From this moment on, everything would change.

As the *da'covale* rose and began to sing the praises of her coronation, Tuon stepped up to General Galgan. "Pass the word to General Yulan," she said softly. "Tell him to prepare his attack against the *marath'damane* of Tar Valon. We must strike against the Dragon Reborn, and quickly. This man cannot be allowed to gain any more strength than he already has."

CHAPTER 36

The Death of Tuon

I began my journey in Tear," Verin said, sitting down on Mat's best chair, made of dark walnut with a nice tan pillow. Tomas took up position behind her, hand on the pommel of his sword. "My goal was to make my way to Tar Valon."

"Then how did you end up *here*?" Mat asked, still suspicious as he seated himself on the pillowed bench. He hated the thing; it was completely impossible to sit on it in any way that was comfortable. Pillows didn't help. Somehow, they made the seat *more* awkward. Bloody thing must have been designed by insane, cross-eyed Trollocs and built from the bones of the damned. That was the only reasonable explanation.

He shifted on the bench, and nearly called for another chair, but Verin was continuing. Mandevwin and Talmanes were just inside the tent, the former standing with folded arms, the latter settling himself on the floor. Thom sat on the floor on the other side of the room, watching Verin with calculating eyes. They were all in Mat's smaller audience tent, which was intended only for short conferences between officers. Mat hadn't wanted to bring Verin to his actual sitting tent, as it was still spread out with his plans for raiding Trustair.

"I ask myself the same question, Master Cauthon," Verin said, smiling, her aging Warder standing behind her chair. "How did I end up here? It certainly wasn't my intention. And yet here I am."

"You say it almost as if it were an accident, Verin Sedai,"

Mandevwin said. "But we're speaking of a distance of several hundred leagues!"

"Plus," Mat added, "you can Travel. So if you intended to go to the White Tower, then why not just bloody Travel there and be done with it?"

"Good questions," Verin said. "Indeed. Might I have some tea?"

Mat sighed, shifting on the devil bench again, and waved for Talmanes to give the order. Talmanes rose and ducked outside for a moment to pass the word, then returned and sat down again.

"Thank you," Verin said. "I find myself quite parched." She projected that familiar distracted air that was so common to sisters from the Brown Ajah. Because of the holes in his memory, Mat's first meeting with Verin was fuzzy to him. In fact, his memory of her at *all* was fuzzy. But he did seem to remember thinking she had the temperament of a scholar.

This time, studying her, her mannerisms seemed too exaggerated to him. As if she were leaning on the preconceptions about Browns, using them. Fooling people, like a street performer taking in country boys with a clever game of three-card shuffle.

She eyed him. That smile on the corner of her lips? That was the smile of a jackleg who didn't care that you were on to her con. Now that you understood, you could both enjoy the game, and perhaps together you could dupe someone else.

"Do you realize how strongly *ta'veren* you are, young man?" Verin asked.

Mat shrugged. "Rand's the one you want for that sort of thing. Honestly, I'm barely anything compared to him." Blasted colors!

"Oh, I wouldn't consider downplaying the Dragon's importance," Verin said, chuckling. "But you can't hide your light in his shadow, Matrim Cauthon. Not in the presence of any but the blind, at least. In any other time, you'd undoubtedly be the most powerfully *ta'veren* individual alive. Probably the most powerful to have lived in centuries."

Mat shifted on the bench. Bloody ashes, he hated the way that made him look as if he was squirming. Maybe he should just stand up. "What are you talking about, Verin?" he said instead. He folded his arms and tried to at least *pretend* that he was comfortable.

"I'm talking about how you yanked me halfway across the continent." Her smile widened as a soldier entered with a steaming cup of mint tea. She took it gratefully, and the soldier retreated.

"Yanked you?" Mat said. "*You* were looking for *me*."

"Only after I determined that the Pattern was tugging me somewhere." Verin blew on her tea. "That meant you or Perrin. It couldn't have been Rand's fault, since I'd been able to leave that one easily."

"Rand?" Mat asked, dismissing yet another flash of colors. "You were with him?"

Verin nodded.

"How . . . did he seem?" Mat said. "Is he . . . you know. . . ."

"Mad?" Verin asked.

Mat nodded.

"I'm afraid so," Verin said, lips downturning slightly. "I think he's still in control of himself, however."

"Bloody One Power," Mat said, reaching beneath his shirt to touch the comforting foxhead medallion.

Verin looked up. "Oh, I'm not convinced young al'Thor's problems are completely due to the Power, Matrim. Many would like to blame his temperament on *saidin*, but to do that is to ignore the incredible stresses that we've settled on that poor boy's shoulders."

Mat raised an eyebrow, glancing at Thom.

"Either way," Verin sipped her tea, "one cannot blame *too* much on the taint, as it will no longer affect him."

"It won't?" Mat asked. "He's decided to stop channeling?"

She laughed. "A fish would sooner stop swimming. No, the taint will no longer affect him because the taint is no more. Al'Thor cleansed *saidin*."

"What?" Mat asked sharply, sitting up.

Verin sipped her tea.

"Are you serious?" Mat asked.

"Quite," she replied.

Mat glanced at Thom again. Then he plucked at his coat and ran a hand through his hair.

"What are you doing?" Verin asked with amusement.

"I don't know," Mat said, feeling sheepish. "I guess I just think I should feel different, or something. The whole world up and changed on us, didn't it?"

"You could say that," Verin said, "though I would argue that the cleansing itself is more like a pebble thrown into a pond. The ripples will take some time to reach the shore."

"A pebble?" Mat asked. "A *pebble*?"

"Well, perhaps more of a boulder."

"A bloody mountain if you ask me," Mat muttered. He settled back on the awful bench.

Verin chuckled. Flaming Aes Sedai. Did they *have* to be like that? It was probably another oath they took and told nobody about, something to do with acting mysterious. He stared at her. "What was that chuckle for?" he finally demanded.

"Nothing," she said. "I merely suspect that you will soon feel a little of what *I* did this last month."

"Which was?"

"Well," she said. "I believe I was talking about that before we got sidetracked on irrelevant topics."

"On the flaming *cleansing of the True Source*," Mat muttered. "Honestly."

"I experienced the most curious of events," Verin continued. Ignoring Mat, of course. "You may not be aware of this, but in order to Travel from a location, you need to spend time in it. Usually, stopping in a place for an evening is enough. Consequently, after parting from the Dragon, I made my way to a nearby village and took a room at the inn. I settled down, learning the room and preparing to open a Gateway in the morning.

"In the middle of the night, however, the innkeeper arrived. He explained with chagrin that I needed to be moved to another room. It appeared that a leak had been discovered in the roof above my room, and it would soon seep through my ceiling. I protested, but he was insistent.

"And so I moved across the hall and began learning *that* room. Just when I was feeling I knew it well enough to open a gateway, I was interrupted again. This time, the innkeeper—more embarrassed—explained that his wife had lost her ring in that room during early morning cleaning. The woman awoke in the night and was very upset. The innkeeper—looking quite tired—apologetically wanted to move me again."

"And?" Mat asked. "Coincidence, Verin."

She raised an eyebrow at him, then smiled as he shifted on the bench again. Burn it all, he wasn't squirming!

"I refused to be moved, Matrim," she said. "I told the innkeeper he was quite welcome to search the room *after* I left, and promised that I would *not* take any rings I discovered with me. Then I firmly shut the door on him." She sipped her drink. "A few minutes later, the inn caught fire—a coal from the hearth rolled to the floor and ended up burning the entire place to the ground. Everyone escaped, fortunately, but the inn was a loss. Tired and bleary-eyed, Tomas and I had to move on to the next village and find rooms there instead."

"So?" Mat said. "Still sounds like a coincidence."

"This continued for three days," Verin said. "I was interrupted even when I tried to learn a place outside a building. Random passersby asking to share the fire, a falling tree crashing down in camp, a flock of sheep wandering by, an isolated storm. Various random events always contrived to keep me from learning the area."

Talmanes whistled softly. Verin nodded. "Each time I tried to learn an area, something went wrong. I was inevitably moved for some reason. However, when I decided I *wasn't* going to do anything to learn a location and wasn't planning to make a gateway, nothing happened. Another person might have simply moved on and given up on Traveling for the time, but my nature asserted itself, and I found myself studying the phenomenon. It was quite regular."

Bloody ashes. That was the sort of thing Rand was supposed to do to people. Not Mat. "By your account, you should still be in Tear."

"Yes," she said, "but I soon started to feel a tugging on me. Something pulling me, yanking me. As if. . . ."

Mat shifted again. "As if someone's got a bloody fishhook inside of you? And is standing far away, pulling gently—but insistently—on it?"

"Yes," Verin said. She smiled. "What a clever description."

Mat didn't respond.

"I decided to use more mundane means to make my voyage. I thought that maybe my inability to Travel had something to do with al'Thor's proximity, or perhaps the gradual unraveling of the Pattern due to the Dark One's influence. I secured a place in a merchant caravan traveling northward toward Cairhien. They had an empty wagon they were willing to rent for a reasonable rate. I was quite fatigued from my days spent staying up all hours because of fires, crying babies and constant moves from one inn room to another. As such, I fear I slept much longer than I should have. Tomas napped as well.

"When we awoke, we were surprised to discover that the caravan had taken a turn to the northwest instead of heading toward Cairhien. I spoke with the caravan master, and he explained that he'd received a last-minute tip that his goods would fetch a much better price in Murandy than in Cairhien. As he considered it, he mentioned that he really should have told me about the change, but it had slipped his mind."

She took another sip of tea. "It was then that I knew for certain that I was being directed. Most wouldn't have noticed it, I suspect, but I have made a study of the nature of *ta'veren*. The caravan hadn't moved far toward Murandy— only one day—but mixed with the tugging, it was enough. I spoke with Tomas, and we determined to avoid going where we were being pulled. Skimming is an inferior substitute for Traveling, but does not have the same limitation of knowing the area. I opened a gateway, but when we reached the end of our journey, we stepped not into Tar Valon, but a small village in northern Murandy!

"That shouldn't have been possible. However, as we considered it, Tomas and I realized he had been speaking fondly of a hunting trip he'd gone on once in the village of Trustair, and I'd opened the gateway at that moment. I must have let myself focus on the wrong location."

"And here we are," Tomas said, arms folded, looking dissatisfied as he stood behind his Aes Sedai's chair.

"Indeed," Verin said. "Curious, wouldn't you say, young Matrim? I accidentally end up here, in your path, right when you have great need of someone to create a gateway for your army?"

"Still could be coincidence."

"And the tugging?"

He didn't know what to say to that.

"Coincidence is how being *ta'veren* works," Verin said. "You find a discarded object that is of great use to you, or happen to meet an individual at just the right time. Random chance randomly works in your favor. Or haven't you noticed?" She smiled. "Care to throw some dice on it?"

"No," he said reluctantly.

"One thing bothers me, however," Verin said. "Was there no *other* person who could have happened into your path? Al'Thor has those Asha'man scouring the countryside looking for men who can channel, and I suspect rural areas like this are top on their list, as it is more likely that channelers could stay unnoticed in such places. One of them could have happened into your path and given you a gateway."

"Not bloody likely," Mat said, shivering. "I'm not trusting the Band to the likes of them."

"Not to get to Andor in a heartbeat?" Verin asked.

Mat hesitated. Well, maybe.

"*I* had to be here for some reason," she said thoughtfully.

"I still think you're reading too much into this," he replied, shifting yet again on the burning bench.

"Perhaps. Perhaps not. First, we should negotiate my price for taking you to Andor. I assume you want to reach Caemlyn?"

"Price?" Mat said. "But you think the Pattern forced you here! Why demand a price of me?"

"Because," she said, raising a finger, "while I waited to find you—I honestly didn't know if it would be you or young Perrin—I realized that there were several things I could provide you that no other could." She reached into a pocket of her dress, pulling out several pieces of paper. One was the picture of Mat. "You didn't ask where I got this."

"You're Aes Sedai," Mat said, shrugging. "I figured you . . . you know, *saidar*ed it."

"*Saidar*ed it?" she asked flatly.

He shrugged.

"I received this paper, Matrim—"

"Call me Mat," he said.

"I received this paper, *Matrim*, from a Darkfriend," she said, "who told me—thinking me a servant of the Shadow— that one of the Forsaken had commanded that the men in these pictures be killed. You and Perrin are in grave danger."

"I'm not surprised," he said, hiding the chill her announcement made him feel. "Verin, Darkfriends have been trying to kill me since the day I left the Two Rivers." He paused. "Burn me. Since the day *before* I left the Two Rivers. What does it change?"

"This is different," Verin said, growing stern. "The level of danger you are in . . . I . . . Well, let us simply agree that you are in great, great danger. I suggest that you be *very* careful during the next few weeks."

"I'm always careful," Mat said.

"Well, be more so," she said. "Go into hiding. Don't take chances. You will be essential before this is through."

He shrugged. Go into hiding? He could do that. With Thom's help, he could probably do himself up so that even his sisters wouldn't recognize him. "I can do that," he said. "Bloody simple cost. How long will it take you to get us to Caemlyn?"

"That wasn't my cost, Matrim," she said, amused. "That was a suggestion. One I think you should listen to with great prejudice." She slipped a small folded piece of paper out from under the picture. It was sealed with a drop of blood-red wax.

Mat took it hesitantly. "It is?"

"Instructions," Verin said. "Which you will follow on the tenth day after I leave you in Caemlyn."

He scratched his neck, frowning, then moved to break the seal.

"You aren't to open them until that day," Verin said.

"What?" Mat demanded. "But—"

"That is my cost," Verin said simply.

"Bloody woman," he said, looking back at the paper. "I'm not going to swear to something unless I know what it is."

"I doubt you will find my instructions harsh, Matrim," she noted.

Mat scowled at the seal for a moment, then stood up. "I pass on it."

She pursed her lips. "Matrim, you—"

"Call me Mat," he said, grabbing his hat off the top of a cushion. "And I said there's no deal. I'll be in Caemlyn in twenty days of marching, anyway." He pushed open the tent flaps, gesturing out. "I'm not going to have you tying strings around me, woman."

She didn't move, though she did frown. "I had forgotten how difficult you can be."

"And proud of it," Mat said.

"And if we have a compromise?" Verin asked.

"You'll tell me what is in that bloody paper?"

"No," Verin said. "Because I might not need you to go through with the contents. I hope to be able to return to you and relieve you of the letter and send you on your way. But if I cannot. . . ."

"The compromise, then?" Mat said.

"You may choose not to open the letter," Verin said. "Burn it. But if you do so, you wait fifty days in Caemlyn, just in case it takes me longer to return than I had expected."

That gave him pause. Fifty days was a long time to wait. But if he could do it in Caemlyn, rather than traveling on his own. . . .

Was Elayne in the city? He'd worried about her, since her escape from Ebou Dar. If she was there, he might at least be able to get production started quickly on Aludra's dragons.

But fifty days? Waiting? Either that, or open the bloody letter and do what it said? He didn't like either option. "Twenty days," he said.

"Thirty days," she said, rising, then raised a finger to cut off his objection. "A *compromise*, Mat. Among Aes Sedai, I think you shall find me to be far more amenable to those than most." She held out her hand.

Thirty days. He could wait thirty days. He looked at the letter in his hands. He could resist opening it, and thirty days of waiting didn't really lose him any time. It was only a little longer than he'd take to reach Caemlyn on his own. In fact, this was a bloody bargain! He needed a few weeks to get the dragons going, and he wanted time to find out more about the Tower of Ghenjei and the snakes and foxes. Thom couldn't complain—when it would take them two weeks to reach Caemlyn anyway.

Verin eyed him, a hint of worry on her face. He couldn't let her know how pleased he was. Let a woman know that, and she'd find some way to make you pay her back.

"Thirty days," Mat said reluctantly, taking her hand, "but at the end of them, I can go."

"Or you can open the letter after ten days," Verin said, "and do what it says. One of the two, Matrim. I have your word?"

"You do," he said. "But I'm not going to open the bloody letter. I'm going to wait thirty days, then be off on my business."

"We shall see," she said, smiling to herself and releasing his hand. She folded up the picture of him, then took a small leather-bound satchel from her pocket. She opened it, sliding the picture inside, and as she did, he noticed that she had a small stack of folded, sealed pieces of paper inside just like the one he was holding. What was the purpose of those?

Once the letters were safely tucked in her pocket, she took out a carved piece of translucent stone—a brooch, shaped like a lily. "Begin breaking down your camp, Matrim. I need to make your gateway as soon as possible. I myself need to Travel shortly."

"Fine." Mat looked down at the sealed, folded paper in his hands. Why was Verin being so cryptic?

Burn it! he thought. *I'm not going to open it. I'm not.* "Mandevwin," he said. "Get Verin Sedai her own tent to wait in as we break camp and assign a couple of soldiers to fetch for her anything she needs. Also, inform the other Aes Sedai that she's here. They'll probably be interested to hear of her arrival, Aes Sedai being Aes Sedai."

Mat tucked the folded paper into his belt, then started to leave. "And have somebody *burn* that bloody bench. I can't believe we carted the thing this far."

Tuon was dead. Gone, cast aside, forgotten. Tuon had been the Daughter of the Nine Moons. She was now just a notation in the histories.

Fortuona was Empress.

Fortuona Athaem Devi Paendrag kissed the soldier lightly on the forehead as he knelt, head bowed, on the short grass. The muggy Altaran heat made it feel as if summer had already arrived, but the grass—which had seemed lush and full of life just weeks before—had grown stunted and was beginning to yellow. Where were the weeds and thistles? Recently seeds didn't sprout as they should. Like grain, they were going bad, dying before they truly came alive.

The soldier before Fortuona was one of five. Behind those five stood two hundred members of the Fists of Heaven—the most elite of her attack forces. They wore dark leather breastplates and helms of light wood and leather, shaped like insects. Both helms and breastplates were emblazoned with the sign of the clenched fist. Fifty *sul'dam* and *damane* pairs, including Dali and her *sul'dam* Malahavana, whom Fortuona had given to the cause. She had felt the need to sacrifice something personal to this most important of missions.

Hundreds of *to'raken* milled in the pens behind, walked by their handlers, who were preparing them for the flight to come. Already, a flock of *raken* circled above, graceful.

Fortuona looked down at the soldier before her, laying her fingers on his forehead, where she had kissed him. "May your death bring victory," she said softly, speaking the ritual words. "May your knife draw blood. May your children sing your praises until the final dawn."

He bowed his head further. Like the four others in the row, he wore black leather. Three knives hung from his belt, and he had no cloak or helm. He was a small man—all members of the Fists of Heaven were small and compact, and over half in this group were women. Weight was always an issue for those facing missions using *to'raken.* In a raid, two small, well-trained soldiers were preferable to one lumbering hulk in heavy armor.

It was early evening, the sun just setting. Lieutenant-General Yulan—who would lead the strike force personally—felt it best to take flight late in the day. Their assault would begin in darkness, shrouding it from those who might be watching the horizon in Ebou Dar. Once, the caution would have been unnecessary. What matter if people in Ebou Dar saw hundreds of *to'raken* take to the skies? News could never travel as quickly as *raken* wings.

But their enemies could travel far more quickly than they should be able to. Be it *ter'angreal*, weave or something else that gave the power, it was a distinct danger. Better to use all stealth. The flight to Tar Valon would take several days.

Fortuona moved to the next soldier in the line of five. The woman's black hair was braided. Fortuona kissed her on the forehead, saying the same ritual words. These five were Bloodknives. The pure black stone ring each one wore was a specialized *ter'angreal* that would grant them strength and speed, and would shroud them in darkness, allowing them to blend into shadows.

The incredible abilities came at a cost, however, for the rings leeched life from their hosts, killing them in a matter of days. Removing the ring would slow that process slightly, but once activated—done by touching a drop of one's own blood to the stone ring while wearing it—the process was irreversible.

These five would not return. They would stay behind, whatever the results of the raid, to kill as many *marath'damane* as they could. It was a terrible waste—those *damane* should be leashed—but better to kill them than leave them in the hands of the Dragon Reborn.

Fortuona moved to the next soldier in the short line, giving him the kiss and the blessing.

So much had changed in the days since her meeting with the Dragon Reborn. Her new name was only one of the manifestations. Now even the High Blood often prostrated themselves before her. Her *so'jhin*—Selucia included—had shaved the hair from their heads. From now on, they would leave the right side of their heads shaved and grow hair down the left side, braiding it as it grew. For now, they wore caps on the left.

The common people walked more confidently, more proudly. They had an empress again. With all that was wrong in the world, this one thing was right again.

Fortuona kissed the last of the five Bloodknives, speaking the words condemning them to death, but also to heroism. She stepped back, Selucia standing at her side. General Yulan came forward and bowed himself low. "Let it be known by the Empress, may she live forever, that we shall *not* fail her."

"It is known," Selucia said. "Light follow you. Know that Her Majesty, may she live forever, saw a new spring rose drop three petals in the garden today. The omen of your victory has been given. Fulfill it, General, and your reward shall be great."

Yulan stood, saluting, fist to breast, metal snapping against metal. He led the soldiers to the *to'raken* pens, the five Bloodknives first. Within moments, the first creature ran down a long pasture outside the back of the pen, marked with poles and streamers, then launched itself into the air. Others followed, a fleet, more than Fortuona had ever seen in the sky at once. As the final light of sunset died, they struck northward.

Raken and *to'raken* were not normally used in this manner. Most raids would be accomplished by dropping the soldiers off at a staging point, where the *to'raken* would wait while the soldiers attacked and returned. But this raid was too vital. Yulan's plan called for a more daring assault, the likes of which had rarely been contemplated. *To'raken* with *damane* and *sul'dam* on their backs, attacking from the air. It could be the beginning of a bold new tactic. Or it could lead to a disaster.

"We have changed everything," Fortuona said softly. "General Galgan is wrong; this will not give the Dragon Reborn a worse bargaining position. It will turn him against us."

"And was he not against us before?" Selucia asked.

"No," Fortuona said. "We were against him."

"And there is a difference?"

"Yes," Fortuona said, watching the cloud of *to'raken*, just barely visible in the sky. "There is. I fear we shall soon see just how big a difference that is."

CHAPTER
37

A Force of Light

Min sat quietly, watching Rand dress. His motions were tense and careful, like the steps of a performer walking the high rope at a menagerie. He did up the left cuff on his crisp white shirt with slow, deliberate fingers. The right cuff was already done up; his servants saw to that.

It was approaching evening outside. Not quite dark yet, though the shutters were closed in preparation. Rand reached for a gold and black coat, sliding on one sleeve, then the other. Then did the buttons one after another. He had no trouble with these; he was growing practiced at working with only one hand. Button after button. First, second, third, fourth. . . .

Min felt like screaming.

"Do you want to talk about it?" she asked.

Rand did not turn from the mirror. "About what?"

"The Seanchan."

"There will be no peace," he said, straightening his coat collar. "I have failed." His tone was emotionless, yet somehow taut.

"It's all right to be frustrated, Rand."

"Frustration is pointless," he said. "Anger is pointless. Neither emotion will change facts, and the fact is that I have no more time to waste on the Seanchan. We will have to risk an attack from behind by riding to the Last Battle without stability in Arad Doman. It is not ideal, but it is what must happen."

The air shimmered above Rand, and a mountain appeared there. Viewings were so common around Rand that

Min usually forced herself to ignore them unless they were new—though she did spend time some days trying to pick them all out and sort through them. This one was new, and it caught her attention. The towering mountain was blasted out on one side, making a jagged hole down the slope. Dragonmount? It was cloaked in dark shadows, as if shaded by clouds high above. That was odd; whenever she'd seen the mountain, it had reached higher than the clouds themselves.

Dragonmount in shadows. It would be important to Rand in the future. Was that a tiny prick of light shining from the heavens down onto the point of the mountain?

The viewing vanished. Though Min knew what some of them meant, this one baffled her. She sighed, leaning back in the red-cushioned chair. Her books lay scattered on the floor; she'd been dedicating more and more time to her studies, partly because she felt Rand's sense of urgency, and partly because she didn't know what else to do. She liked to think that she was capable of taking care of herself. And she'd begun to think of herself as a last defense for Rand.

Min had discovered just how useful she was as a "line of defense." She'd been about as useful as a child! In fact, she'd been a hindrance, a tool for Semirhage to use against him. She'd been indignant when Rand had suggested sending her away, giving him a tongue-lashing for even suggesting it. Send her away! To keep her safe? That was foolishness! She could take care of herself.

So she had thought. Now she saw that he'd been right.

That made her sick. So she studied and tried to stay out of his way. He'd changed on that day, as if something bright had turned off inside of him. A lamp flickering out, its oil gone, leaving only the casing. He looked at her differently, now. When those eyes of his studied her, did they see only a liability?

She shivered, trying to shove that thought from her mind.

Rand put on his boots, then did up their buckles.

He stood, reaching for the sword which leaned against his clothing chest. The black scabbard, with its lacquered red and gold dragon, sparkled in the light. Such a strange weapon those scholars had found beneath the submerged statue. The sword felt so *old*. Was Rand wearing it today as a symbol of something? A sign, perhaps, that he was riding to battle?

"You're going after *her*, aren't you?" Min found herself asking. "Graendal."

"I have to fix what problems I can," Rand said, pulling the ancient sword from the sheath and checking the blade. There was no heron mark, but the fine steel blade glistened in the lamplight, showing the undulating lines of its folded metal. It had been Power-forged, he claimed. He seemed to know things about it he did not share.

Rand snapped the blade into the black scabbard, looking at her. "Fix the problems you can, don't fret over the ones you cannot. It was something Tam once told me. Arad Doman will have to survive against the Seanchan on its own. The last thing I can do for the people here is remove one of the Forsaken from their soil."

"She might be waiting for you, Rand," Min said. "Did it occur to you that the boy Nynaeve found was a plant? Intended to be discovered, to lead you into a trap?"

He hesitated, then shook his head. "He was genuine, Min. Moghedien might have considered a trick like that, but not Graendal. She'd be too worried about being traced. We have to move quickly, before word reaches her that she has been compromised. I must strike now."

Min stood.

"Are you coming, then?" Rand asked, looking surprised.

She flushed. *What if things go as poorly with Graendal as they did with Semirhage? What if I become a tool against him again?*

"Yes," she said, just to prove to herself that she wasn't giving up. "Of course I'm coming. Don't think you can leave me behind!"

"I wouldn't dream of it," he said flatly. "Come."

She'd expected more of an argument.

From the night stand he picked up the statuette of a man holding aloft a globe. He turned the *ter'angreal* in his hand, inspecting it, then looked up at Min, as if in challenge. She said nothing.

He tucked the statuette into the oversized pocket of his coat, then strode from the room, ancient, Power-forged sword belted to his waist.

Min hurried after Rand. He glanced at the pair of Maidens guarding the door. "I go to battle," he said to them. "Bring no more than twenty."

The Maidens exchanged a brief moment of handtalk; then one loped ahead and the other tailed Rand as he marched down the hallway. Min hurried up beside him, heart thumping, her boots loud on the floorboards. He had rushed off like this to fight Forsaken before, but usually he took more time to plan. He'd maneuvered Sammael for months before striking at Illian. He'd had barely a single day to decide what do with Graendal!

Min checked her knives, making certain they were secure in her sleeves, but it was just a nervous habit. Rand reached the end of the hallway, then strode down the stairs, his face still calm, his step quick but not hurried. Yet he seemed like a thunderstorm, contained and wrapped up, somehow bound and channeled toward a single goal. How she wished he'd just explode and lose his temper, the way he used to! He'd exasperated her then, but he'd never frightened her. Not as he did now, with those icy eyes she couldn't read, that aura of danger. Since the incident with Semirhage, he spoke of doing "whatever he had to" regardless of cost, and she knew that he must seethe at having failed to convince the Seanchan to ally with him. What would that combination of failure and determination lead him to do?

At the bottom of the wide staircase, Rand spoke to a servant. "Fetch for me Nynaeve Sedai and Lord Ramshalan. Bring them to the sitting room."

Lord Ramshalan? The overstuffed man from Lady Chadmar's former circle? "Rand," Min said quietly, reaching the bottom of the stairs, "what are you planning?"

He said nothing. He strode through the white marble entryway, entering the sitting room, which was decorated in deep reds to contrast with the white floor. He did not sit, but remained standing with his arms behind his back, studying the map of Arad Doman he'd ordered placed on the wall. The aged map hung where a fine oil painting once had, and seemed completely out of place in the room.

On the map, there was a black ink mark at the edge of a small lake to the southeast. Rand had placed it there the morning after Kerb died. It marked Natrin's Barrow.

"It was a fort, once," Rand said absently.

"The city where Graendal is hiding?" Min said, walking up beside him.

He shook his head. "It's not a city. I've sent scouts. It's just a solitary structure, built long ago to watch the Mountains of Mist and guard against incursion through the passes by Manetheren. It hasn't been used for military purposes since the Trolloc Wars; there's hardly need to worry about invasion from Two Rivers people who don't even remember the name Manetheren."

Min nodded. "Though, Arad Doman did get invaded by a shepherd from the Two Rivers."

Once that would have made him smile. She kept forgetting that he didn't do that anymore.

"A few centuries back," Rand said, eyes narrowed in thought, "the king of Arad Doman seized Natrin's Barrow back in the name of the throne. For some time before, it had been occupied by a minor noble family from Toman Head who had been trying to set up their own new kingdom. That happens on Almoth Plain occasionally. The Domani king liked the location, and used the fortress as a palace instead.

"He spent a great deal of time there, so much, in fact, that several of his merchant enemies gained too much power in Bandar Eban. The King fell, but his successors also used the fortress, and it became a popular retreat for the Crown when the King needed relaxation. The practice dwindled during the last hundred years or so, until it was granted to a distant cousin of the King about fifty years back. Their family has used it ever since. Among the general Domani populace, Natrin's Barrow has been largely forgotten."

"Except by Alsalam?" Min asked.

Rand shook his head. "No. I doubt he knew of it at all. I learned this history from the royal archivist, who had to search for hours to locate the name of the family using the place. There has been no contact with them for months, though they used to visit towns on occasion. The few farmsteaders in the area say that someone new seems to be living in the palace, though nobody knows where the former owner went. They seem surprised that they've never thought about how odd that is."

He eyed her. "This is exactly the sort of location Graendal would choose as her center of power. It's a jewel—a forgotten fortress of beauty and power, ancient and regal. Close enough to Bandar Eban for her to have a hand in ruling Arad Doman, but far enough away to be defensible and secluded. I made a mistake in my searches for her—I assumed she'd want a beautiful manor with gardens and grounds. I should have realized; it isn't just beauty that she collects, but prestige. A magnificent fortress for kings fits her just as much as an elegant manor house. Particularly since this one is more palace than fort now."

Footsteps in the entryway behind drew Min's attention, and a few seconds later a servant ushered in Nynaeve and the foppish Ramshalan, with his pointed beard and thin mustache. Today he had tiny bells at the end of the beard and wore a black velvet beauty mark on his cheek, also in the shape of a bell. He wore a loose silk costume of green and blue, the sleeves drooping, ruffled shirt poking out beneath. Min didn't care what fashion dictated, the man looked ridiculous. Like a disheveled peacock.

"My Lord called for me?" Ramshalan said, bowing extravagantly toward Rand.

Rand didn't turn away from the map. "I have a puzzle for you, Ramshalan," he said. "I want to know what you think."

"Please, don't hesitate, my Lord!"

"Then tell me this: How do I outthink an enemy I know is smarter than I am?"

"My Lord." Ramshalan bowed a second time, as if worried that Rand hadn't noticed the first one. "Surely you seek to trick me! There is nobody more intelligent than yourself."

"I wish that were true," Rand said softly. "I face some of the most crafty people who have ever lived. My current foe understands the minds of others in a way that I cannot hope to match. So how do I defeat her? She will vanish the moment I threaten her, running to one of a dozen other refuges she is sure to have set up. She won't fight me head-on, yet if I destroy her fortress in a surprise attack, I risk letting her slip away and never knowing if I've finished her."

"A problem indeed, my Lord," Ramshalan said. He looked confused.

Rand nodded, as if to himself. "I have to peer into her eyes, see into her soul, and know that it's *her* that I face and not some decoy. I have to do that without frightening her into running. How? *How* can I kill a foe who is more clever than myself, a foe who is impossible to surprise, yet who is also unwilling to confront me?"

Ramshalan looked overwhelmed by those demands. "I. . . . My Lord, if your foe is that clever, then perhaps your best course of action is to request the aid of someone *more* clever?"

Rand turned to him. "An excellent suggestion, Ramshalan. Perhaps I've already done just that."

The man swelled. *He thinks that's why Rand summoned him!* Min realized. She had to hide her smile with a turn of the head and a raised hand.

"If *you* had an enemy such as this, Ramshalan, what would you do?" Rand asked. "I grow impatient. Give me an answer."

"I'd make an alliance, my Lord," Ramshalan said without pausing for another second. "Anyone that powerful would make a better friend than foe, I say."

Idiot, Min thought. *If your enemy is that crafty and ruthless, an alliance will only end with an assassin's dagger in your back.*

"Another excellent suggestion," Rand said softly. "But I am still intrigued by the first comment you made. You said I need allies who are smarter than I am, and that is true. It is time for you to be off, then."

"My Lord?" Ramshalan said.

"You are to be my emissary," Rand said, waving his hand. A gateway suddenly split the air on the far side of the room, shearing through the fine rug at the floor. "Too many of the Domani bloodborn are hiding, scattered through the country. I would have them as my allies, but it would be a drain on my time to seek each one in person. Fortunately, I have you to go on my behalf."

Ramshalan looked excited about the prospect. Through the gateway, Min could see towering pines, and the air on the other side was cold and crisp. Min turned and glanced at Nynaeve—dressed in blue and white again. The Aes Sedai watched the exchange with calculating eyes, and Min could read her own emotions in Nynaeve's expression. What was Rand's game?

"Beyond that gateway," Rand said, "you will find a hill leading down to an ancient palace which is inhabited by a minor Domani merchant family. It is the first of many places I shall send you. Go in my name and seek those who rule the keep. See if they are willing to support me, or if they even know about me. Offer them rewards for allegiance; since you have proven yourself clever, I will let you determine the terms. I haven't the mind for those sorts of negotiations myself."

"Yes, my Lord!" the man said, swelling further, though he did eye the gateway with concern, distrustful—like most people—of the One Power, particularly when wielded by a man. If it were opportune, this man would switch loyalties as quickly as he had when Lady Chadmar had fallen. What was Rand thinking, sending a popinjay like this to meet with Graendal?

"Go," Rand said.

Ramshalan took a few hesitant steps toward the gateway. "Er, my Lord Dragon, could I perhaps have something in the way of an escort?"

"No need to frighten or alarm the people there," Rand said without turning from the map. Cold air continued to blow through the gateway. "Go quickly and return, Ramshalan. I will leave the gateway open until you are back. My patience is not limitless, and there are many I could turn to for this mission."

"I. . . ." The man seemed to calculate the risks. "Of course, Lord Dragon." He took a deep breath and walked through the portal, his steps uncomfortable, like those of a house cat venturing out into a puddle of water. Min found herself feeling sorry for the man.

Fallen needles crackled as Ramshalan moved off into the forest. A breeze hissed through the trees; it was an odd sound to hear while standing in the comfort of the mansion. Rand left the gateway open, still staring at his map.

"All right, Rand," Nynaeve demanded after a few minutes, her arms folded. "What game is this?"

"How would *you* beat her, Nynaeve?" Rand asked. "She won't be goaded into fighting me, like Rahvin or Sammael were. She won't be easily trapped either. Graendal understands people better than anyone. Twisted she may be, but she *is* crafty, and should not be underestimated. Torhs Margin made that mistake, I recall, and you know his fate."

Min frowned. "Who?" she asked, looking at Nynaeve. The Aes Sedai shrugged.

Rand glanced at them. "I believe in history he was known as Tohrs the Broken."

Again, Min shook her head. Nynaeve joined her. Neither was deeply versed in history, true, but Rand acted as if

they should know this name. Rand's face hardened, and he
blushed just faintly, turning away from them. "The question
remains," he said, voice soft but tense. "How would you
fight her, Nynaeve?"

"I don't care to play your games, Rand al'Thor," Nynaeve
replied with a huff. "You've obviously already decided what
you intend to do. Why ask me?"

"Because what I am about to do should frighten me," he
said. "It doesn't."

Min shivered. Rand nodded to the Maidens standing in
the doorway. Moving lightly, they crossed the room, leaped
through the gateway, and spread through the pine forest,
quickly vanishing from sight. All twenty together made less
noise than Ramshalan had.

Min waited. On the other side of the gateway, a distant
sun was hidden from sight, giving a late-afternoon light
to the shadowed forest floor. After a few moments, white-
haired Nerilea stepped into view and nodded to Rand. All
clear.

"Come," Rand said, and walked to the gateway. Min followed, though Nynaeve—breaking into a trot—beat her to
the gateway.

They stepped out onto a carpet of brown pine needles,
dirtied from a long slumber beneath the vanished winter
snows. Branches nudged one another in the breeze, and
the mountain air was more chilly than the breeze had indicated. Min wished for a cloak, but there wasn't time to go
fetch one. Rand strode directly through the forest, Nynaeve
trotting up to him and speaking in a low voice.

Nynaeve wouldn't get anything useful out of Rand, not
when he was in this kind of mood. They would just have
to see what he revealed. Min caught sight of some Aiel in
the woods, but only brief glimpses when they obviously
weren't taking care to hide. They certainly had taken well
to life in the wetlands. How did a people raised in the Waste
know so instinctively how to hide in a forest?

Up ahead, the trees broke. Min hastened to join Rand
and Nynaeve, who had stopped at the top of a gently slop-
ing ridge. Here, they could see over the forest, and the trees
continued down below like a sea of green and brown. The
pines parted at the shores of a small mountain lake, caught
in a triangular depression of the land.

Atop a ridge of its own, high above the water, was an impressive white stone structure. Rectangular and tall, it was built in the form of several towers stacked atop one another, each one slightly thinner than the one beneath. That gave the palace an elegant shape—fortified, yet palatial. "It's beautiful," she said breathlessly.

"It was built during a different time," Rand said. "A time when people still thought that the majesty of a structure lent it strength."

The palace was distant, but not so distant that Min couldn't make out the figures of men walking the battlements on guard, halberds at their shoulders, breastplates reflecting the late sunlight. A late party of hunters rode in through the gates, a fine buck deer lashed to the packhorse, and a group of workers chopped at a fallen tree nearby, perhaps for firewood. A pair of serving women in white carried poles, bucket at each end, up from the lake, and lights were winking on in windows the length of the structure. It was a living, working estate bundled up in a single massive building.

"Do you think Ramshalan found his way?" Nynaeve said, arms folded, obviously trying not to look impressed.

"Even a fool like him could not miss that," Rand said, eyes narrowing. He still carried the statuette in his pocket. Min wished he had left the thing behind. It made her uncomfortable, the way he fingered it. Caressed it.

"So you sent Ramshalan to die," Nynaeve said. "What will that accomplish?"

"She won't kill him," Rand said.

"How can you be sure of that?"

"It isn't her way," Rand said. "Not when she can use him against me."

"You don't expect her to believe that story you told him," Min said. "About sending him out to test the allegiance of the Domani lords?"

Rand slowly shook his head. "No. I hope for her to believe something of that tale, but I do not expect it. I meant what I said about her, Min—she's more crafty than I am. And I fear that she knows me far better than I know her. She will compel Ramshalan and pull from him that entire conversation we had. From there, she will find a way to use that conversation against me."

"How?" Min asked.

"I don't know. I wish I did. She'll think of something clever, then infect Ramshalan with a very subtle Compulsion that I won't be able to anticipate. I'll be left with the choice to keep him nearby and see what he does, or to send him away. But of course, she will think of that as well, and whatever I do will set in motion her other plans."

"You make it sound as if you can't win," Nynaeve said, frowning. She didn't seem to notice the chill at all. In fact, neither did Rand. Whatever that "trick" about ignoring cold and heat was, Min had never been able to figure it out. They claimed it had nothing to do with the power, but if that were so, why were Rand and the Aes Sedai the only ones who could manage it? The Aiel didn't seem to be bothered by the cold either, but they didn't count. They never seemed bothered by regular human concerns, though they could be very touchy about the most random and insignificant things.

"We can't win, you say?" Rand asked. "Is that what we're trying to do? Win?"

Nynaeve raised an eyebrow. "Do you not answer questions anymore?"

Rand turned, looking at Nynaeve. Standing on the other side of him, Min couldn't see what was in his face, but she could see Nynaeve grow pale. It was her own fault. Couldn't she sense how on edge Rand was? Perhaps Min's chill didn't just come from the cold. She moved up close to him, but he didn't put his arm around her as he might once have. When he finally turned away from Nynaeve, the Aes Sedai slumped slightly, as if she had been dangling, held up by his gaze.

Rand did not speak for some time, and so they waited quietly on the mountain ridge as the distant sun made its way toward the horizon. Shadows lengthened, fingers stretching away from the sun. Down below, by the fortress walls, a group of grooms began walking some horses to give them exercise. More lights had been lit in the fortress windows. How many people did Graendal have in there? Scores, if not hundreds.

A crashing sound in the brush suddenly drew Min's attention; it was accompanied by curses. She jumped as the noise cut off quite abruptly.

A small group of Aiel approached a few moments later,

leading a disheveled Ramshalan, his fine clothing stuck with needles and scratched from branches. He dusted himself off, then took a step toward Rand.

The Maidens held him back. He glanced at them, cocking his head. "My Lord Dragon?"

"Is he infected?" Rand asked of Nynaeve.

"By what?" she asked.

"Graendal's touch."

Nynaeve walked over to Ramshalan and looked at him for a moment. She hissed and said, "Yes. Rand, he's under a heavy Compulsion. There are a lot of weaves here. Not as bad as the chandler's apprentice, or maybe just more subtle."

"I say," Ramshalan said, "my Lord Dragon, what is going on? The lady of the castle down there was quite friendly—she is an ally, my Lord. You have nothing to fear from her! Very refined, I must say."

"Is that so?" Rand asked quietly. It was growing dark, sun setting behind the distant mountains. Besides the dim evening light, the only illumination came from the still-open gateway behind them. It shone with lamplight, an inviting portal back to warmth, away from this place of shadow and coldness.

Rand's voice sounded so hard. Worse than Min had ever heard it before.

"Rand," she said, touching his arm. "Let's go back."

"I have something I must do," he said, not looking at her.

"Think about it some more," Min said. "At least take some advice. We can ask Cadsuane, or—"

"Cadsuane held me in a box, Min," he said very softly. His face was clasped in shadow, but as he turned toward her, his eyes reflected the light from the open gateway. Orange and red. There was an edge of anger to his tone. *I shouldn't have mentioned Cadsuane,* she realized. The woman's name was one of the few things that could still get emotion out of him.

"A box, Min," Rand whispered. "Though Cadsuane's box had walls that were invisible, it was as binding as any that ever held me. Her tongue was far more painful a rod than any that was taken to my skin. I see that now."

Rand pulled away from Min's touch.

"What is the purpose of all this?" Nynaeve demanded. "You sent this man to suffer a Compulsion, *knowing* what

it would do to him? I won't watch another man squirm and
die because of this! Whatever she has compelled him to do,
I won't remove it! It will be your own fault if it brings your
death."

"My Lord?" Ramshalan asked. The growing terror in his
voice put Min on edge.

The sun set; Rand was now just a silhouette. The fortress
was only a black profile with lanterns lighting the holes in
its walls. Rand stepped up to the lip of the ridge, removing the access key from his pocket. It started to glow just
faintly, a red light coming from its very heart. Nynaeve inhaled sharply.

"Neither of you were there when *Callandor* failed me," he
said into the night. "It happened twice. Once I tried to use
it to raise the dead, but I got only a puppeted body. Once I
tried to use it to destroy the Seanchan, but I caused as much
death among my own armies as I caused among theirs.

"Cadsuane told me that the second failure came from a
flaw in *Callandor* itself. It cannot be controlled by a lone
man, you see. It only works if he's in a box. *Callandor* is
a carefully enticing leash, intended to make me surrender
willingly."

The access key's globe burst alight with a more brilliant
color, seeming crystalline. The light within was scarlet,
the core brilliant and bright. As if someone had dropped a
glowing rock into a pool of blood.

"I see a different answer to my problems," Rand said,
voice still almost a whisper. "Both times *Callandor* failed
me, I was being reckless with my emotion. I allowed temper to drive me. I can't kill in anger, Min. I have to keep that
anger inside; I must channel it as I channel the One Power.
Each death must be deliberate. Intentional."

Min couldn't speak. Couldn't phrase her fears, couldn't
find the words to make him stop. His eyes remained in the
darkness, somehow, despite the liquid light he held before him. That light hurled shadows away from his figure,
as if he was the point of a silent explosion. Min turned to
Nynaeve; the Aes Sedai watched with wide eyes, mouth
slightly open. She couldn't find words either.

Min turned back to Rand. When he'd been close to killing
her with his own hand, she hadn't feared him. But then,
she'd known that it wasn't Rand hurting her, but Semirhage.

But this Rand—hand aflame, eyes so intent yet so dispassionate—terrified her.

"I've done it before," he whispered. "I once said that I didn't kill women, but it was a lie. I murdered a woman long before I faced Semirhage. Her name was Liah. I killed her in Shadar Logoth. I struck her down, and I called it mercy."

He turned to the fortress palace below.

"Forgive me," he said, but it didn't seem directed at Min, "for calling this mercy as well."

Something impossibly bright formed in the air before him, and Min cried out, backing away. The air itself seemed to warp, as if pulling away from Rand in fear. Dust blew from the ground in a circle around him, and the trees groaned, lit by the brilliant white light, the pine needles rattling like a hundred thousand insects scrambling over one another. Min could no longer make out Rand, only a blazing, brilliant *force* of light. Pure power, gathered, making the hairs on her arms rise with the force of its nebulous energy. In that moment, she felt as if she could understand what the One Power was. It was there, before her, made incarnate in the man Rand al'Thor.

And then, with a sound like a sigh, he released it. A column of pure whiteness exploded from him and burned across the silent night sky, illuminating the trees below it in a wave. It moved as quick as a snap of the fingers, striking the wall of the distant fortress. The stones came alight, as if they were breathing in the force of the energy. The entire fortress glowed, transforming into living light, an amazing, spectacular palace of unadulterated energy. It was beautiful.

And then it was gone. Burned from the landscape—and the Pattern—as if it had never been there. The entire fortress, hundreds of feet of stone and everyone who had lived in it.

Something hit Min, something like a shocking wave in the air. It wasn't a physical blast, and it didn't make her stumble, but it twisted her insides about. The forest around them—still lit by the glowing access key in Rand's hands—seemed to warp and shake. It was as if the world itself were groaning in agony.

It snapped back, but Min could still feel that tension. In that instant, it seemed as if the very substance of world had been near to breaking.

"What have you done?" Nynaeve whispered.

Rand didn't reply. Min could see his face again, now that the enormous column of balefire had vanished, leaving behind only the glowing access key. He was in ecstasy, mouth agape, and he held the access key aloft before himself as if in victory. Or in reverence.

Then he gritted his teeth, eyes opening wide, lips parted as if he were under great pressure. The light flashed once, then immediately vanished. All became dark. Min blinked in the sudden darkness, trying to get her eyes to adjust. The powerful image of Rand seemed burned into her vision. Had he really done what she thought he had? Had he burned away an entire fortress with balefire?

All those people. Men returning from the hunt . . . women carrying water . . . soldiers on the walls . . . the grooms outside . . .

They were *gone*. Burned from the Pattern. Killed. Dead forever. The horror of it made Min stumble back, and she pressed her back against a tree to keep herself upright.

So many lives, ended in an instant. Dead. Destroyed. By Rand.

A light appeared from Nynaeve, and Min turned, seeing the Aes Sedai illuminated by the warm, soft glow of a globe above her hand. Her eyes seemed almost afire with a light of their own. "You are out of control, Rand al'Thor," she declared.

"I do what must be done," he said, speaking now from the shadows. He sounded exhausted. "Test him, Nynaeve."

"What?"

"The fool," Rand said. "Is her Compulsion still there? Is Graendal's touch gone?"

"I hate what you just did, Rand," Nynaeve snarled. "No. 'Hate' isn't strong enough. I *loathe* what you've done. What has happened to you?"

"Test him!" Rand whispered, voice dangerous. "Before condemning me, let us first determine if my sins have achieved anything beyond my own damnation."

Nynaeve breathed in deeply, then glanced at Ramshalan, who was still held in the grip of several Aiel Maidens. Nynaeve reached out and touched his forehead, concentrating. "It's gone," she said. "Erased."

"Then she is dead," Rand said from the darkness.

Light! Min thought, realizing what he'd done. *He didn't use Ramshalan as a courier, or as bait. He used the man as a way of proving to himself that Graendal was dead.* Balefire burned someone out of the Pattern completely, making it so that their most recent actions never occurred. Ramshalan would remember visiting Graendal, but her Compulsion no longer existed. In a way, she'd been killed *before* Ramshalan had visited her.

Min felt at her neck, where the bruises of Rand's hand on her neck hadn't yet faded.

"I don't understand," Ramshalan said, his voice nearly a squeak.

"How do you fight someone smarter than yourself?" Rand whispered. "The answer is simple. You make her think that you are sitting down across the table from her, ready to play her game. Then you punch her in the face as hard as you can. You have served me well, Ramshalan. I will forgive you for boasting to Lords Vivian and Callswell that you could manipulate me however you wished."

Ramshalan slumped in shock, and the Maidens let him fall to his knees. "My Lord!" he said. "I had too much wine that night, and—"

"Hush," Rand said. "As I said, you have served me well this day. I will not execute you. You will find a village two days' walk to the south."

With that, Rand turned; to Min's eyes, he was just a shadow rustling in the forest. He walked to the gateway and stepped through. Min hurried to follow him, and Nynaeve did likewise. The Maidens came last, leaving Ramshalan kneeling stupefied in the forest. When the last Maiden was through the gateway, the portal slid closed, cutting off the sounds of Ramshalan whimpering in the dark.

"What you have done is an abomination, Rand al'Thor," Nynaeve said as soon as the gateway was closed. "There looked to have been dozens, maybe hundreds, of people living in that palace!"

"Each one made into an idiot by Graendal's Compulsion," Rand replied. "She never lets anyone close to her without destroying their mind first. The boy she sent to work the jail barely knew a fraction of the torture most of her pets receive. She leaves them without ability to think or act—all they can do is kneel and adore her, perhaps run errands at her command. I did them a favor."

"A favor?" Nynaeve asked. "Rand, you used balefire! They were burned out of existence!"

"As I said," Rand replied softly. "A favor. Sometimes, I wish the same blessing for myself. Good night, Nynaeve. Sleep as well you can, for our time in Arad Doman is at an end."

Min watched him go, wishing to sprint after him, but holding herself back. Once he was gone from the room, Nynaeve slumped into one of the room's maroon chairs, sighing and leaning her head against her hand.

Min felt like doing the same. Until that moment, she hadn't realized just how drained she was. Being around Rand lately did that to her, even when he wasn't engaged in activities as terrible as the ones this night.

"I wish Moiraine were here," Nynaeve muttered softly, then froze, as if surprised to have heard herself say that.

"We have to do something, Nynaeve," Min said, looking at the Aes Sedai.

Nynaeve nodded absently. "Maybe."

"What do you mean by that?"

"Well, what if he's right?" Nynaeve asked. "Wool-headed fool though he is, what if he really *does* have to be like this to win? The old Rand could never have destroyed an entire fortress full of people to kill one of the Forsaken."

"Of course he couldn't have," Min said. "He still *cared* about killing then! Nynaeve, all those lives . . ."

"And how many people would still be alive now if he'd been this ruthless from the start?" Nynaeve asked, looking away. "If he'd been capable of sending his followers into danger as he did Ramshalan? If he'd been able to strike without worrying about whom he would have to kill? If he'd ordered his troops into Graendal's fortress, her followers would have resisted fanatically, and they would have ended up dead anyway. And she would have escaped.

"This might be what he has to be. The Last Battle is nearly upon us, Min. *The Last Battle!* Can we dare send a man to fight the Dark One who won't sacrifice for what needs to be done?"

Min shook her head. "Dare we send him as he is, with

that look in his eyes? Nynaeve, he's stopped caring. Nothing matters to him anymore but defeating the Dark One."

"Isn't that what we want him to do?"

"I. . . ." She stopped. "Winning won't be winning at all if Rand becomes something as bad as the Forsaken . . . We—"

"I understand," Nynaeve said suddenly. "Light burn me, but I do, and you're right. I just don't like the answers those conclusions are giving me."

"What conclusions?"

Nynaeve sighed. "That Cadsuane was right," she said. Nearly under her breath, she added, "Insufferable woman." She stood up. "Come on. We need to find her and discover what her plans are."

Min stood, joining Nynaeve. "You're certain she *has* plans? Rand was harsh with her. Maybe she's just staying with us to watch him flounder and fail without her."

"She has plans," Nynaeve said. "If there's one thing we can count on with that woman, it's that she's scheming. We just have to convince her to let us in on it."

"And if she won't?" Min asked.

"She will," Nynaeve said, looking at the place where Rand's gateway had split the rug. "Once we tell her about tonight, she will. I dislike the woman, and I suspect she returns the emotion, but neither of us can handle Rand alone." She pursed her lips. "I worry we won't be able to handle him together. Let's go."

Min followed. "Handle" Rand? That was another problem. Nynaeve and Cadsuane were both so concerned with *handling* that they failed to see that it might be best to *help* him instead. Nynaeve cared for Rand, but she saw him as a problem to be fixed, rather than a man in need.

And so Min accompanied the Aes Sedai out of the mansion. They walked into the dark courtyard—Nynaeve making a globe of light—and hurried around the back, past the stable and toward the gatekeeper's cottage. They passed Alivia on the way; the former *damane* looked disappointed. Likely, she'd been turned away by Cadsuane and the others again—Alivia spent a great deal of time trying to get the Aes Sedai to train her in new weaves.

They finally reached the gatekeeper's cottage—at least, the gatekeeper's cottage was what it *had* been until Cadsuane prevailed upon him to move out. It was a single-story, thatch-roofed structure of painted yellow wood. Light shone out between the shutters on the windows.

Nynaeve stepped up to the front and knocked on the sturdy oak door; it was answered shortly by Merise. "Yes, child?" the Green asked, as if intentionally trying to goad Nynaeve.

"I have to speak with Cadsuane," Nynaeve growled.

"Cadsuane *Sedai*, she has no business with you right now," Merise said, moving to close the cottage door. "Return tomorrow, and perhaps she will see you."

"Rand al'Thor just burned an entire palace full of people from existence with balefire," Nynaeve said, loud enough to be heard by those inside the cottage. "I was with him."

Merise froze.

"Let her in," Cadsuane's voice said from inside. Reluctantly, Merise pulled open the door. Inside, Min saw Cadsuane sitting on some cushions on the floor with Amys, Bair, Melaine and Sorilea. The front room—the main room—of the cottage was decorated with a simple brown rug on the floor, mostly obscured by the seated women. A gray stone fireplace burned with a calm flame at the back, the wood nearly consumed, the fire low. A stool sat in the corner, with a pot of tea on it.

Nynaeve barely gave the Wise Ones a glance. She pushed her way into the cottage, and Min followed more hesitantly.

"Tell us of this event, child," Sorilea said. "We felt the world warping from here, but did not know what had caused it. We assumed it to be the Dark One's work."

"I'll tell you," Nynaeve said, then took a deep breath, "but I want to be a part of your plans."

"We shall see," Cadsuane said. "Relate your experience."

Min took a seat on a wooden stool at the side of the room as Nynaeve gave her account of Natrin's Barrow. The Wise Ones listened, tight-lipped. Cadsuane just nodded occasionally. Merise, face full of horror, refilled cups of tea from the pot on the stool—by the smell it was Tremalking black—then set it to hang by the fire. Nynaeve finished, still standing.

Oh, Rand, Min thought. *This must be tearing you apart inside.* But she could feel him through the bond; his emotions seemed very cold.

"You were wise to come to us with this, child," Sorilea said to Nynaeve. "You may withdraw."

Nynaeve's eyes opened wide with anger. "But—"

"Sorilea," Cadsuane said calmly, cutting Nynaeve off. "This child could be of use to our plans. She is still close to the al'Thor boy; he trusted her enough to take her with him this evening."

Sorilea glanced toward the other Wise Ones. Aged Bair and sun-haired Melaine both nodded. Amys seemed thoughtful, but did not object.

"Perhaps," Sorilea said. "But can she be obedient?"

"Well?" Cadsuane asked of Nynaeve. They all seemed to be ignoring Min. "Can you?"

Nynaeve's eyes were still wide with anger. *Light,* Min thought. *Nynaeve? Obey Cadsuane and the others? She's going to explode at them!*

Nynaeve tugged on her braid with a white-knuckled grip. "Yes, Cadsuane Sedai," she said through clenched teeth. "I can."

The Wise Ones seemed surprised to hear her speak the words, but Cadsuane nodded again, as if she'd expected that response. Who could expect Nynaeve to be so . . . well, reasonable?

"Sit down, child," Cadsuane said with a wave of the hand. "Let's see if you *can* follow orders. You might be the only one of the current crop who is salvageable." That made Merise flush.

"No, Cadsuane," Amys said. "Not the only one. Egwene has much honor."

The other two Wise Ones nodded.

"What is the plan?" Nynaeve said.

"Your part in it is—" Cadsuane began.

"Wait," Nynaeve said. "My part? I want to hear the whole thing."

"You'll hear when we're ready to tell you," Cadsuane said curtly. "And don't make me regret my decision to speak in your behalf."

Nynaeve forced her mouth shut, eyes aflame. But she did not snap at them.

"Your part," Cadsuane continued, "is to find Perrin Aybara."

"What good will that do?" Nynaeve asked, then added, "Cadsuane Sedai."

"That is our business," Cadsuane said. "He has been traveling in the south recently, but we can't discover exactly where. The al'Thor boy might know where he is. Find out for us, and perhaps I'll explain the point."

Nynaeve nodded reluctantly, and the others turned to a discussion of how much strain from balefire the Pattern could take before unraveling completely. Nynaeve listened in silence, obviously trying to glean more about Cadsuane's plan, though there didn't seem to be many clues.

Min only half-listened. Whatever the plan, someone would need to watch out for Rand. His deed this day would be destroying him inside, no matter what he proclaimed. There were plenty of others worrying about what he would do at the Last Battle. It was her job to get him to that Last Battle alive and sane, with his soul in one piece.

Somehow.

CHAPTER
38

News in Tel'aran'rhiod

Egwene, see reason," Siuan said, faintly translucent because of the *ter'angreal* ring she had used to enter *Tel'aran'rhiod.* "What good can you do, rotting in that cell? Elaida will see that you're never let free, not after what you said you did at that dinner." Siuan shook her head. "Mother, sometimes you just have to face truth. You can only repair a net so many times before you need to toss the thing aside and weave a new one."

Egwene sat on a three-legged stool in the corner of the room, the front part of a cobbler's shop. She'd chosen the location at random, just in case, eschewing a location in the White Tower itself. The Forsaken knew that Egwene and the others walked the World of Dreams.

With Siuan, Egwene could be more relaxed, more her real self. The two of them both understood that Egwene was now the Amyrlin and Siuan her lesser, but at the same time, they shared a bond. A camaraderie due to the station they both had filled. That bond, strangely, had turned into something akin to friendship.

At the moment, Egwene was nearly ready to strangle her friend. "We've been over this," she said firmly. "I *cannot* flee. Each day I spend imprisoned—but do not break—is another blow to Elaida's rule. If I disappear before her trial, it will undermine everything we've worked for!"

"The trial will be a sham, Mother," Siuan said. "And if it isn't, the punishment will be light. From what you've told me, she didn't break any bones when she beat you—why, she didn't break the skin."

That was true. Egwene's bleeding had been from broken glass, not Elaida's stripes.

"Even a formal censure from the Hall will undermine her," Egwene said. "My resistance, my refusal to break my imprisonment, means something. The Sitters themselves come to visit me! If I were to flee, it would look as though I'd given in to Elaida."

"Didn't she declare you a Darkfriend?" Siuan asked pointedly.

Egwene hesitated. Yes, Elaida had done that. But she didn't have proof for it.

Tower law was intricate, and sorting out the proper punishments and interpretations could be complicated. The Three Oaths would have prevented Elaida from using the One Power as a weapon, and so Elaida must have *thought* that what she was doing wasn't a violation. Either she had gone farther than she'd planned, or she saw Egwene as a Darkfriend. She could argue for either position to defend herself; the latter would relieve her of the most guilt, but the former would be much easier to prove.

"She could succeed at having you convicted," Siuan said, apparently thinking along the same lines. "You would be slated for execution. What then?"

"She won't succeed. She hasn't any proof that I am a Darkfriend, and so the Hall will never allow it."

"And if you're wrong?"

Egwene hesitated. "Very well. If the Hall decides that I am to be executed, I will let you get me out. But not until then, Siuan. Not until then."

Siuan snorted. "You might not have an opportunity, Mother. If Elaida cows them, she will act quickly. The woman's punishments can be swift as a stormwind, take you unaware. I know *that* for certain."

"If that happens," Egwene said pointedly, "my death would be a victory. Elaida would be the one who gave up, not I."

Siuan shook her head, muttering, "Stubborn as a mooring post."

"We are finished with that discussion, Siuan," Egwene said sternly.

Siuan sighed, but said nothing further. She seemed to have too much nervous energy to sit, and ignored the stool on the other side of the room, instead going to stand by the shop window to Egwene's right.

The cobbler's salesroom showed signs of great traffic. A stout counter divided the room in half, the wall behind pocketed with dozens of shoe-sized nooks. At times, most of these were stuffed with sturdy work shoes of leather or canvas, laces hanging down the front or buckles gleaming in the phantom light of *Tel'aran'rhiod*. Yet each time Egwene glanced at the wall, the shoes had shifted, some vanishing, others appearing. They must not stay long in their cubbyholes in the real world, for they left only vague images behind in the world of dreams.

The front half of the shop was crowded with stools for customers to use. The shoes on the back wall were of different designs and patterns, along with test shoes for sizing. A person came into the shop, tried on the sizing shoes, then picked a style. The cobbler—or, likely, his assistants— would then craft a pair for later pickup. The wide glass windows at the front proclaimed the name of the cobbler in white painted letters to be Naorman Mashinta, and a smaller number "three" had been painted beside the name. This was the third generation of Mashintas to run the shop. Not uncommon at all among townsfolk. In fact, the part of Egwene that was still influenced by the Two Rivers found it odd that anyone would consider leaving their parent's trade for another, unless they were a third or fourth child.

"Now that we've dealt with the obvious," Egwene said, "what news is there?"

"Well," Siuan said, leaning on the window and staring out at the eerily empty Tar Valon street. "An old acquaintance of yours recently arrived in camp."

"Really?" Egwene asked absently. "Who?"

"Gawyn Trakand."

Egwene started. That was impossible! Gawyn had sided with Elaida's faction during the rebellion. He wouldn't have come over to the rebel side. Had he been captured? But that wasn't how Siuan had phrased it.

For a moment, Egwene was a trembling girl, caught in the power of his whispered promises. She managed to keep her form locked into that of the Amyrlin, however, and forced her thoughts back to the moment, driving herself to be casual as she responded. "Gawyn?" she asked. "How odd. I wouldn't have thought to find him there."

Siuan smiled. "That was nicely handled," she said. "Though you paused too long, and when you did ask for him, you were overly uninterested. That made you easy to read."

"Light blind you," Egwene said. "Another test? Is he really there?"

"I hold to the oaths, thank you," Siuan said, affronted. Egwene was one of the few who knew that, as a result of her stilling and Healing, Siuan had been released from the Three Oaths. But, like Egwene, she chose not to lie anyway.

"Either way," Egwene said, "I should think that the time for testing me has passed."

"Everyone you meet will always be testing you, Mother," Siuan said. "You must be prepared for surprises; at any moment someone could throw one at you just to see how you respond."

"Thank you," Egwene said coldly. "But I really don't need the reminder."

"Don't you?" Siuan said. "Sounds a little like something Elaida would say."

"That's unfair!"

"Prove it," Siuan said smugly.

Egwene forced herself to be calm. Siuan was right. Better to take the advice, particularly when it was good advice, than to complain. "You are right, of course," Egwene said, smoothing out her dress across her knees as she also smoothed the frustration from her face. "Tell me more of Gawyn's arrival."

"I don't know much more," Siuan confessed. "I really should have mentioned it yesterday, but our meeting was cut short." They were meeting more often now—each night of Egwene's imprisonment—but yesterday something had awakened Siuan before they had finished talking. A bubble of evil in the rebel camp, she had reported, involving tents coming alive and trying to strangle people. Three had died, one of them Aes Sedai.

"Anyway," Siuan continued, "Gawyn hasn't said much that I could hear. I think he's here because he heard that you were captured. He arrived with a spectacular flurry, but now he stays in Bryne's command post, visiting the Aes

Sedai regularly. He's mulling over something; keeps going
to speak to Romanda and Lelaine."

"That's troubling."

"Well, they *are* the obvious power in camp," Siuan said.
"Save when Sheriam and the others can wrench some authority away. Things haven't gone well without you; the
camp needs leadership. Actually, we crave it, as a starving
fisherman craves a catch. Aes Sedai are a people of order, I
suppose. It—"

She stopped herself. Likely, she had been about to bully
Egwene again to accept rescue. She glanced at Egwene,
then continued. "Well, it will be good for us when you return, Mother. The longer you stay away, the stronger the
factions become. You can almost see the lines down the
middle of the camp now. Romanda on one side, Lelaine on
the other, with a shrinking slice that doesn't want to take
sides."

"We *cannot* afford another division," Egwene said. "Not
among ourselves; we have to prove stronger than Elaida."

"At least our splits aren't along the lines of Ajah," Siuan
said defensively.

"Factions and breaks," Egwene said, getting up. "Infight-
ing and squabbling. We are better than this, Siuan. Tell the
Hall that I wish to meet with them. Perhaps in two days.
Tomorrow, you and I should meet again."

Siuan nodded hesitantly. "Very well."

Egwene eyed her. "You think it unwise?"

"No," Siuan said. "I worry about how hard you're pushing
yourself. The Amyrlin needs to learn to ration her strength;
some in your place have failed not because they lacked the
capacity for greatness, but because they stretched that capacity too thin, sprinting when they should have walked."

Egwene refrained from pointing out that Siuan herself had spent much of her tenure as Amyrlin sprinting at
a breakneck speed. But it could very well be argued that
Siuan *had* stretched herself too thin, and had fallen as a
result. Who better to speak on the dangers of such activities
than one who had been burned by them so deeply?

"The advice is appreciated, daughter," Egwene said. "But
really, there is little to worry about. My days are spent in
solitude, with the occasional beating to provide spice. These
meetings at night help me survive." She shivered, glancing

away from Siuan, out the window toward the dirty, vacant street.

"Is it difficult to endure?" Siuan asked softly.

"The cell is narrow enough for me to touch opposite walls at once," Egwene said. "And isn't very long, either. When I lie down, I have to bend my knees to fit. I can't stand, since the ceiling is so low it makes me stoop, and I can't sit without pain, for they no longer Heal me between beatings. The straw is old and itches. The door is thick and the cracks don't allow in much light. I wasn't aware that the Tower *had* cells such as this one." She glanced back at Siuan. "Once I am upheld fully as Amyrlin, this room and any like it will be removed, the doors ripped out and the cells themselves filled with bricks and mortar."

Siuan nodded. "We'll make certain of it."

Egwene turned away again, and noticed with shame that she'd let her gown shift to the *cadin'sor* of an Aiel Maiden, complete with spears and bow at her back. She forced the clothing back, taking a deep breath. "No person should be kept in such a manner," she said, "not even. . . ."

Siuan frowned as Egwene trailed off. "What was that?"

Egwene shook her head. "It just occurred to me. This is what it must have been like for Rand. No, worse. The stories say he was locked in a box smaller than my cell. At least I can spend part of the evenings chatting with you. He had nobody. He was without the belief that his beatings meant something." Light send that she didn't have to endure as long as he had. Her imprisonment had only been a few days so far.

Siuan fell silent.

"Regardless," Egwene said, "I have *Tel'aran'rhiod*. During the days, my body is captive, but my soul is free at night. And each day I endure is another proof that Elaida's will is *not* law. She cannot break me. Her support from the others is eroding. Trust me."

Siuan nodded. "Very well," she said, rising. "You *are* Amyrlin."

"Of course I am," Egwene said absently.

"No, Egwene," Siuan said. "I meant that from the heart."

Egwene turned, surprised. "But you've always believed in me!"

Siuan raised an eyebrow.

"At least," Egwene said, "from fairly near the beginning."

"I always believed you had potential," Siuan corrected. "Well, you've fulfilled it. Some of it at least. Enough of it. However this storm blows through, you've proven one thing. You *deserved* the place you hold. Light, girl, you may end up being the best Amyrlin this world has known this side of Artur Hawkwing's reign!" She hesitated. "And that's not an easy thing for me to admit, mind you."

Egwene took Siuan's arms, smiling. Why, Siuan almost looked teary-eyed with pride! "All I did was get myself locked in a cell."

"And you did it like an Amyrlin, Egwene," Siuan said. "But I should be getting back. Some of us can't spend our days relaxing the way you can. We need real sleep, otherwise we're likely to fall unconscious in our washwater." She grimaced, releasing herself from Egwene's hands.

"You could just tell him to—"

"Now, I'll have none of that," Siuan said, wagging a finger at Egwene. Had she forgotten that she'd just been complimenting Egwene's stature as an Amyrlin? "I gave my word, and I'll be fish guts before I'll break it."

Egwene blinked. "I wouldn't dream of making you," she said, covering a smile as she noticed that Siuan's shadowy form now had a bright red ribbon in its hair. "Off with you, then."

Siuan nodded sharply, then sat down and closed her eyes. She faded slowly from *Tel'aran'rhiod*.

Egwene hesitated, watching the area where Siuan had been. It was probably time to return to normal dreaming, letting her mind restore itself. But returning to her normal dreams would be a step toward waking, and when she woke she would find only that cramped dungeon and its stuffy darkness. She longed to stay in the World of Dreams just a little longer. She thought of visiting Elayne's dreams to ask for a meeting . . . but no, that would take too much time, assuming Elayne could make her dream *ter'angreal* work. She rarely could, these days.

She found herself stepping away from Tar Valon, the cobbler's shop vanishing around her.

She appeared in the rebel Aes Sedai camp. A foolish place to visit, perhaps. If there were Darkfriends or Forsaken in the World of Dreams, they could very well be studying this camp and looking for information, much as Egwene sometimes visited the Amyrlin's study in *Tel'aran'rhiod* to search for clues on Elaida's plans. But Egwene needed to come here. She didn't question why; she simply felt that it was true.

The streets of the camp were muddy, worn in ruts from passing wagons. Once just a field, the area had been appropriated by the Aes Sedai and turned into . . . something. Part a place of war, with Bryne's soldiers camped in a ring about them. Part town, though no town had ever boasted such a complement of Aes Sedai, novices and Accepted. Part monument to the weakness of the White Tower.

Egwene walked the camp's main thoroughfare, where weeds had been trampled to mud, then mud worn into a road. Walkways lined it, and tents covered the flat land beyond. There were no people, only the occasional fleeting glimpse of a sleeper who had stumbled into *Tel'aran'rhiod*. Here, a brief flash of a woman in a fine green gown. A dreaming Aes Sedai, perhaps, though it was just as likely to be a serving maid imagining herself to be a queen. There, a woman in white—a woman with stringy blond hair who was far too old to be a novice. That no longer mattered. The novice book should have long ago been opened to all. The White Tower was too weak to turn down any source of strength.

Both women were gone almost as quickly as they appeared. Few dreamers stayed long in *Tel'aran'rhiod*; to remain longer, one needed either a particular skill like Egwene's or a *ter'angreal* like the ring Siuan used. There was a third way. Getting caught up in a living nightmare. There were none of the latter about, thank the Light.

The camp seemed strange to be so deserted. Egwene had long since stopped being unnerved by the eerie lack of people in *Tel'aran'rhiod*. But this camp was different somehow. It looked as a war camp might after all of the soldiers had been slaughtered on the battlefield. Deserted, yet still a banner to proclaim the lives of those who had occupied it. Egwene felt as if she could see the division that Siuan had talked about, tents clumped together like bunches of sprouting flowers.

With individuals removed, she could see the patterns and the troubles they bespoke. Egwene might denounce

Elaida for the rifts among the Ajahs in the White Tower,
but Egwene's own Aes Sedai were beginning to fracture
as well. Well, three Aes Sedai could hardly gather without
two of them making an alliance. It was healthy to have the
women planning and preparing; the trouble was when they
began to regard others of their kind as enemies, rather than
just rivals.

Siuan was right, unfortunately. Egwene could not spend
much more time setting her hopes on reconciliation. What
if the White Tower *didn't* unseat Elaida? What if, despite
Egwene's progress, the rifts between the Ajahs never
healed? What then? Go to war?

There was another option, one that none of them had
brought up: that of giving up on reconciliation permanently.
Setting up a second White Tower. It would mean leaving
the Aes Sedai broken, perhaps forever. Egwene shuddered
at the prospect, and her skin itched, rebelling against the
thought.

But what if she had no other choice? She had to consider
the ramifications, and she found them daunting. How could
they encourage the Kin or the Wise Ones to tie themselves
to the Aes Sedai if the Aes Sedai themselves were not unified? The two White Towers would become opposed forces,
confusing the leaders of men as rival Amyrlins tried to use
nations for their own purposes. Allies and enemies alike
would lose their awe of the Aes Sedai, and kings very well
might start up their own centers for women talented in
channeling.

Egwene steeled herself, walking on the muddy road, the
tents along the way changing, their flaps open, then closed,
then open again in the strange ephemeral way of the World
of Dreams. Egwene felt the Amyrlin's stole appear around
her neck, too heavy, as if woven with lead weights.

She *would* bring the White Tower Aes Sedai to her side.
Elaida *would* fall. But if not . . . then Egwene would do
what was necessary in order to preserve the people, and the
world, in the face of Tarmon Gai'don.

She stepped away from the camp, the tents, ruts, and
empty streets vanishing. Again, she wasn't certain where
her mind would take her. Traveling in the World of Dreams
this way—letting *need* direct her—could be dangerous, but
it could also be very illuminating. In this case, she looked

not for an object, but for knowledge. What did she need to know, what did she need to see?

Her surroundings blurred, then snapped back straight. She stood in the middle of a small camp, fire smoldering in a firepit before her, a tiny tongue of smoke curling toward the sky. That was odd. Fire was usually too fleeting to reflect in *Tel'aran'rhiod*. There were no actual flames, despite the smoke and the orange glow warming the smooth riverstones that ringed the pit. She glanced upward, toward the too-dark, stormy sky. That silent storm was another irregularity for the World of Dreams, though it had become so common lately that she hardly noticed it anymore. Could anything be called regular for this place?

With shock, she noticed colorful wagons around her, green, red, orange and yellow. Had they been there a moment before? She was in a large clearing set inside a forest of phantom white aspen. The underbrush was thick, where spindly wild grass poked fingers out in jagged patches. An overgrown road meandered through the trees to her right; the colorful wagons sat in a ring around the fire. Bright paints colored the sides of the boxy vehicles, which had roofs and walls like tiny buildings. Oxen did not reflect in the World of Dreams, but plates, cups and spoons appeared, then vanished from places beside the firepit or on the seats of the wagons.

It was a camp of the Traveling People, the Tuatha'an. Why this place? Egwene walked idly around the firepit, looking at the wagons, the coats of paint kept fresh and free of cracks or stains. This caravan was much smaller than the one she and Perrin had visited so long ago, but it had much the same feel. She could almost hear the flutes and drums, could almost imagine those flickers from the firepit to be the shadows of dancing men and women. Did the Tuatha'an still dance, with that sky so full of gloom, the winds so full of ill news? What place was there for them in a world preparing for war? Trollocs cared nothing for the Way of the Leaf. Did this group of Tuatha'an seek to hide from the Last Battle?

Egwene settled herself on the side steps of a wagon, which was turned to face the nearby firepit. For a moment, she let her gown change to that of a simple, woolen Two Rivers dress of green, much like the one she'd worn during

her time visiting the Traveling People. She stared into those
nonexistent flames, remembering and pondering. What
had become of Aram, Raen and Ila? Likely they were safe
somewhere in a camp just like this one, waiting to see what
Tarmon Gai'don would do to the world. Egwene smiled,
thinking of those days when she'd flirted and danced with
Aram beneath Perrin's scowling disapproval. That had been
a simpler time; though the Tinkers always seemed able to
make a simpler time for themselves.

Yes, this group would still dance. They would dance right
up until the day when the Pattern burned away, whether or
not they found their song, whether or not Trollocs ravaged
the world or the Dragon Reborn destroyed it.

Had she let herself lose sight of those things which were
most precious? *Why* did she fight so hard to secure the
White Tower? For power? For pride? Or because she felt it
really was best for the world?

Was she going to suck herself dry as she fought this battle? She had chosen—or, would have chosen—the Green
and not the Blue. The difference wasn't just that she liked
the way the Greens stood up and fought; she thought that
the Blues were *too* focused. Life was more complicated
than a single cause. Life was about living. About dreaming,
laughing and dancing.

Gawyn was in the Aes Sedai camp. She said that she'd
chosen the Green for its aggressive determination—it was
the Battle Ajah. But a more secret, more honest, part of herself admitted that Gawyn was a motivation for her decision
as well. Among the Green Ajah, marrying one's Warder
was common. Egwene *would* have Gawyn for her Warder.
And her husband.

She loved him. She would bond him. Those desires of
her heart were less important than the fate of the world,
true, but they *were* still important.

Egwene rose from the steps as her dress transformed
back into the white and silver gown of the Amyrlin. She
took a step forward and let the world shift.

She stood before the White Tower. She turned her eyes
high, running them along the length of the delicate—yet
still powerful—white spire. Though the sky bubbled in
black turmoil, something cast a shadow from the Tower,
and it fell directly on Egwene. Was this a vision of some

sort? The Tower dwarfed her, and she felt its weight, as if she were holding it up herself. Pushing on those walls, keeping them from cracking and tumbling.

She stood for a long while there, sky boiling, the Tower's perfect spire throwing its shadow down on Egwene. She stared up at its peak, trying to decide if it was time to just let it fall.

No, she thought again. *No, not quite yet. A few more days.*

She closed her eyes, then opened them to blackness. Her body suddenly exploded with pain, her backside pounded raw from the strap, her arms and legs cramped from being forced to lie curled in the small room. It smelled of old straw and mold, and she knew that if her nose hadn't been used to it, she would have smelled the stench of her own unwashed body as well. She stifled a groan—there were women outside, guarding her and maintaining her shield. She wouldn't let them hear her offer complaint, not even in the form of a groan.

She sat up, wearing the same novice dress that she'd worn to Elaida's dinner party. The sleeves of the dress were stiff with dried blood, and this cracked as she moved, scraping against her skin. She was parched; they never gave her enough water. But she did not complain. No yells, no cries, no begging. She forced herself to sit up despite the pain, smiling to herself at how it felt. She crossed her legs, then leaned back and—one by one—stretched the muscles in her arms. Then she stood and stooped over, stretching her back and shoulders. Finally, she lay down on her back and stretched her legs up into the air, cringing as they complained. She needed to remain limber. Pain was nothing. Nothing at all compared with the danger the White Tower was in.

She sat back down, cross-legged, and took deep breaths, repeating to herself that she *wanted* to be locked in this room. She could escape if she wished, but she remained. By remaining she undermined Elaida. By remaining she proved that some would not bow and quietly accept the fall of the White Tower. This imprisonment meant something.

The words, repeated in her head, helped stave off the panic at considering yet another day within this cell. What would she have done without the nightly dreams to keep her sane? Again, she thought of poor Rand, locked away. She and he shared something now. A kinship beyond a common childhood in the Two Rivers. They had both suffered Elaida's punishments. And it hadn't broken either of them.

There was nothing to do but wait. Around noon, they would open the doors and drag her out to be beaten. It wouldn't be Silviana who did the punishing. Giving the beatings was seen as a reward, compensation to the Red sisters for having to spend all day sitting in the dungeons guarding her.

After the beating, Egwene would go back in the cell and be given a bowl of tasteless gruel. Day after day it was the same. But she would not break, particularly not while she could spend the nights in *Tel'aran'rhiod*. In fact, in many ways, those were her days—spent free and active—while these were her nights, in inactive darkness. She told herself that.

The morning passed slowly. Eventually, iron keys clanked as one turned in the ancient lock. The door opened, and a pair of slender Red sisters stood outside, barely silhouettes, the light so unfamiliar to Egwene that she couldn't make out their features. The Reds grabbed her roughly by the arms, though she never resisted. They pulled her out and threw her to the ground. She heard the strap as one slapped it against her hand in anticipation, and Egwene steeled herself for the blows. They would hear her laugh, just as they had every day before.

"Wait," a voice said.

The arms holding Egwene down grew stiff. Egwene frowned, cheek pressed against the cold tile floor. That voice . . . it had been Katerine's.

Slowly, the sisters holding Egwene relaxed their grips, pulling her to her feet. She blinked against the blazing light of the lamps to find Katerine standing in the hallway a short distance away, her arms folded. "She is to be released," the Red said, sounding strangely smug.

"*What?*" asked one of Egwene's captors. As her eyes adjusted, Egwene could see that it was lanky Barasine.

"The Amyrlin has realized that she is punishing the wrong person," Katerine said. "The failure lies not completely on the head of this . . . insect of a novice, but on the one who was to be manipulating her."

Egwene eyed Katerine. And then it clicked into place. "Silviana," she said.

"Indeed," Katerine said. "If the novices are out of control, then should not the blame fall on the one who was to train them?"

So Elaida *had* realized that she could not prove Egwene was a Darkfriend. Deflecting attention to Silviana was a clever move; if Elaida was punished for using the Power to beat Egwene, but Silviana was punished far more for letting Egwene get out of control, it would save face for the Amyrlin.

"I think the Amyrlin made a wise choice," Katerine said. "Egwene, you are to be . . . instructed from now on only by the Mistress of Novices."

"But Silviana is the one you said has failed," Egwene said, confused.

"Not Silviana," Katerine said; her smugness seemed to grow even further. "The new Mistress of Novices."

Egwene locked gazes with the woman. "Ah," she said. "And you believe that you will succeed where Silviana failed?"

"You will see." Katerine turned away and headed down the tiled hallway. "Take her to her quarters."

Egwene shook her head. Elaida was more competent than Egwene had assumed. She'd seen that the imprisonment wasn't working and had found a scapegoat to punish instead. But Silviana, removed from her position as Mistress of Novices? That would be a blow to the morale of the Tower itself, for many sisters considered Silviana an exemplary Mistress of Novices.

The Reds reluctantly began to walk Egwene toward the novices' quarters, now in their new location on the twenty-second level. They seemed annoyed to have missed out on the opportunity to beat her.

She ignored them. After spending so long locked up, it felt wonderful simply to be able to walk. It wasn't freedom, not with a pair of guards, but it certainly did feel like it! Light! She wasn't certain how many more days in that dank hole of a cell she'd have been able to stand!

But she'd won. The realization was just beginning to dawn on her. She'd *won*! She'd resisted the worst punishment Elaida could contrive, and had come out victorious! The Amyrlin would be punished by the Hall, and Egwene would go free.

Each familiar hallway seemed to shine with a congratulatory light, and each step she took seemed like the victory march of a thousand men across the battlefield. She
had won! The war was not over, but this battle went to
Egwene. They climbed some stairs, then entered the more
populated sections of the Tower. Soon, she saw a group of
novices passing; they whispered to one another as they saw
Egwene, then scattered away.

Within minutes, Egwene's little procession of three began to pass more and more people in the hallways. Sisters
of all Ajahs, looking busy—yet their steps slowed as they
watched Egwene pass. Accepted in their banded dresses
were far less covert; they stood at intersections, gawking as
Egwene was led past. In all of their eyes there was surprise.
Why was she free? They seemed tense. Had something
happened that Egwene wasn't aware of?

"Ah, Egwene," a voice said as they passed a hallway.
"Excellent, you are already free. I would speak with you."

Egwene turned with shock to see Saerin, the purposeful
Brown Sitter. The scar on the woman's cheek always made
her seem far more . . . daunting than most other Aes Sedai,
an air enhanced by the white locks of hair, indicating her
great age. Few members of the Brown could be described
as intimidating, but Saerin was certainly one of that select
group.

"We are taking her to her rooms," Barasine said.

"Well, I will speak to her as you do," Saerin said calmly.

"She is not to—"

"You deny me, Red? A Sitter?" Saerin asked.

Barasine blushed. "The Amyrlin will not be pleased to
hear of this."

"Then run along and tell her," Saerin said. "While I discuss some items of import with young al'Vere." She eyed
the Reds. "Give us some room, if you please."

The two Reds failed to stare her down, then backed away.
Egwene watched with curiosity. It appeared that the authority of the Amyrlin—indeed, that of her entire Ajah—was
somewhat dimmed. Saerin turned to Egwene and gestured,
and the two of them began to walk together through the
hallway, the Red sisters following behind.

"You take a risk being seen speaking to me like this,"
Egwene said.

Saerin sniffed. "Leaving one's quarters is taking a risk, these days. I'm growing too frustrated with events to bother with niceties anymore." She paused, then glanced at Egwene. "Besides. Being seen in your company can be rather worth that risk, these days. I wanted to determine something."

"What?" Egwene asked, curious.

"Well, I actually wanted to see if *they* could be pushed around. Most of the members of the Red are not taking your release well. They see it as a major failing on Elaida's part."

"She should have killed me," Egwene said with a nod. "Days ago."

"That would have been seen as a failure."

"As much a failure as being forced to remove Silviana?" Egwene asked. "Of suddenly deciding that your Mistress of Novices is to blame, a week after the fact?"

"Is that what they told you?" Saerin asked, smiling as they walked, her eyes forward. "That Elaida 'suddenly' came to this decision, all on her own?"

Egwene raised an eyebrow.

"Silviana demanded to be heard by the full Hall while it was sitting," Saerin explained. "She stood before the lot of us, before Elaida herself, and insisted that your treatment was unlawful. Which, likely, it was. Even if you aren't an Aes Sedai, you shouldn't have been placed in such terrible conditions." Saerin glanced at Egwene. "Silviana *demanded* your release. She seemed to respect you a great deal, I should say. She spoke with pride in her voice of how you'd received your punishments, as if you were a student who had learned her lesson well. She denounced Elaida, calling for her to be removed as Amyrlin. It was . . . quite extraordinary."

"By the Light . . ." Egwene breathed. "What did Elaida do to her?"

"Ordered her to take up the dress of a novice," Saerin said. "Just about caused an uproar in the Hall itself." Saerin paused. "Silviana refused, of course. Elaida has declared that she is to be stilled and executed. The Hall doesn't know *what* to do."

Egwene felt a stab of panic. "Light! She mustn't be punished! We must prevent this."

"Prevent it?" Saerin asked. "Child, the Red Ajah is crumbling! Its members are turning against one another, wolves attacking their own pack. If Elaida is allowed to go through with *killing* one of her own Ajah, whatever support she had from within the ranks will evaporate. Why, I wouldn't be surprised, when the dust settles, to see that the Ajah has undermined itself to the point that you could simply disband it and be done with them."

"I don't *want* to disband them," Egwene said. "Saerin, that's one of the problems with Elaida's way of thinking in the first place! The White Tower needs all of the Ajahs, even the Red, to face what is coming. We certainly can't afford to lose a woman like Silviana just to make a point. Rally what support you can. We have to move quickly to stop this travesty."

Saerin blinked. "Do you really think you're in control here, child?"

Egwene met her eyes. "Do *you* want to be?"

"Light, no!"

"Well, then stop standing in my way and get to work! Elaida must be removed, but we can't let the entire Tower collapse around us while it happens. Go to the Hall and see what you can do to stop this!"

Saerin actually nodded in respect before withdrawing down a side corridor. Egwene glanced back at her two Red attendants. "Did you hear much of that?"

They glanced at each other. Of course they'd been listening. "You'll want to go determine for yourselves what has happened," Egwene said. "Why haven't you?"

The two glanced at her with annoyance. "The shield," Barasine said. "We've been instructed to always have at least two to maintain it."

"Oh, for the. . . ." Egwene took a deep breath. "If I vow not to embrace the Power until I am properly back in the custody of another Red sister, will that be enough for you?"

The two regarded her with suspicion.

"I suspected as much," Egwene said. She turned to a group of novices who were standing in a side corridor, pretending to scrub the tiles on the side wall while they gawked at Egwene.

"You," Egwene said, pointing to one of them. "Marsial, isn't it?"

"Yes, Mother," the girl squeaked.

"Go and fetch us some forkroot tea. Katerine should have

some at the study of the Mistress of Novices. It's not far. Tell her that Barasine requested it for use on me; bring it to my quarters."

The novice scrambled off to do as asked.

"I'll dose myself with that, and then at least one of you can go," Egwene said. "Your Ajah is collapsing. They're going to need all of the clear minds they can get; maybe you can convince your sisters that it is unwise to let Elaida execute Silviana."

The two Reds glanced at each other uncertainly. Then the spindly one whose name Egwene didn't know cursed softly and hurried away with a flurry of rustling skirts. Barasine called after her, but the woman didn't return.

Barasine glanced at Egwene, muttered something under her breath, but remained in place. "We're waiting for that forkroot," she said, staring Egwene in the eyes. "Keep moving on to your quarters."

"Fine," Egwene said. "But each minute you delay could cost you deeply."

They climbed the stairs to the new novices' quarters, which were scrunched up alongside the remainder of the Brown section of the Tower. They stopped by Egwene's door to wait for the forkroot. As they stood there, novices began to crowd around. In the distant corridors, sisters and their Warders ran through hallways with a sense of urgency. Hopefully, the Hall would be able to do something to contain Elaida. If she really went so far as to execute sisters for simply disagreeing with her. . . .

The wide-eyed novice finally returned with a cup and a small packet of herbs. Barasine inspected the packet and apparently determined that it was satisfactory, for she dumped it into the cup and proffered it to Egwene expectantly. With a sigh, Egwene took it and downed the entire cup of warm water. It was enough of a dose that she wouldn't be able to channel a trickle, but hopefully wouldn't be strong enough to render her unconscious.

Barasine turned and hurried away, leaving Egwene alone in the hallway. Not just alone, but alone and able to do exactly as she wished. She didn't get many of these opportunities.

Well, she'd have to see what she could do with that. But first, she'd need to change out of this filthy, bloodstained

dress, and wash herself, too. She pushed open the door to
her quarters.

And found someone sitting inside.

"Hello, Egwene," Verin said, taking a sip from a steaming cup of tea. "My! I was beginning to wonder if I'd have
to break into that cell of yours in order to speak with you."

Egwene shook off her shock. Verin? When had the
woman returned to the White Tower? How long had it been
since Egwene had seen her? "There isn't time right now,
Verin," she said, quickly opening the small locker that contained her extra dress. "I have work to be about."

"Hmm, yes," Verin said, taking a calm sip of her tea. "I
suspect that you do. By the way, that dress you are wearing
is green."

Egwene frowned at the nonsense sentence, glancing
down at her dress. Of course it wasn't green. What was
Verin saying? Had the woman become—

She froze, glancing at Verin.

That had been a lie. *Verin could speak lies.*

"Yes, I thought that might get your attention," Verin said,
smiling. "You should sit down. We have much to discuss
and little time in which to do it."

CHAPTER
39

A Visit from Verin Sedai

"You never held the Oath Rod," Egwene accused her, still standing by the closet. Verin remained on the side of the bed, sipping her tea. The stout woman wore a simple brown dress with a matronly cut through the bosom and a thick leather belt at the waist. The skirts were divided, and judging from the dirty boots peeking out from under the hem, she had only just arrived back in the White Tower.

"Don't be silly." Verin brushed back a lock of hair that had escaped from her bun; the brown was marked with a pronounced streak of gray. "Child, I held the Oath Rod and swore upon it before your *grandmother* was born."

"Then you've had the Oaths removed," Egwene said. It was possible with the Oath Rod—after all, Yukiri, Saerin and the others had removed their oaths and replaced them.

"Well, yes," Verin said in a motherly way.

"I don't trust you," Egwene found herself blurting. "I don't think I ever have."

"Very wise," Verin said, sipping her tea. It was not a scent Egwene recognized. "I am, after all, of the Black Ajah."

Egwene felt a sudden chill, like an ice cold spike pounded directly through her back and down into her chest. Black Ajah. Verin was Black. Light!

Egwene immediately reached for the One Power. But of course the forkroot made that effort futile. And Egwene herself had been the one to suggest it be given to her! Light, had she taken leave of her senses? She'd been so confident and certain following her victory that she hadn't anticipated what might happen if she ran into a Black sister. But who could *anticipate* running into a Black sister? Finding one sitting calmly on your bed, drinking tea and looking at you with those eyes that always *had* seemed to know too much. What better way to hide than as an unassuming Brown, constantly dismissed by the other sisters because of your distracted, scholarly ways?

"My, but this *is* good tea," Verin said. "When you next see Laras, please thank her on my behalf for providing it. She promised that she had some that hadn't spoiled, but I didn't trust her. Can't trust much these days, can you?"

"What, is Laras a Darkfriend?" Egwene asked.

"Heavens, no," Verin said. "She's many things, but not a Darkfriend. You'd sooner find a Whitecloak marrying an Aes Sedai than find Laras swearing to the Great Lord. Extraordinary woman. And quite good at judging the flavor of teas."

"What are you going to do with me?" Egwene said, forcing herself to speak calmly. If Verin had wanted to kill her, the deed would have been done by now. Obviously Verin wanted to use Egwene, and that use would give Egwene opportunity. Opportunity for escape, opportunity to turn the situation around. Light, this was bad timing!

"Well," Verin said, "first I will ask you to sit. I would offer you some tea, but I sincerely doubt you want any of what I'm having."

Think, Egwene! she told herself. Calling for help would be futile; only novices were likely to hear, as her Red keepers had both run off. Of all the times to be alone! She'd never have thought that she'd wish for jailers nearby.

Anyway, if she yelled, Verin would undoubtedly bind and gag her with weaves of Air. And if any novices *did* hear, they'd run to see what was the problem—and that would only pull them into Verin's clutches as well. So Egwene pulled over the room's single wooden stool and sat upon it, backside protesting the uncushioned wood.

The small room was still and quiet, cold and sterile, as it had been unoccupied for four days. Egwene sought furiously for an avenue of escape.

"I compliment you on what you've done here, Egwene," Verin said. "I've followed some little of the foolishness going on between the Aes Sedai factions, though I decided not to get involved personally. It was more important to continue my research and keep an eye on young al'Thor. He's a fiery one, I must say. I worry about the lad. I'm not certain he understands how the Great Lord works. Not all evil is as . . . obvious as the Chosen. The Forsaken, as you'd call them."

"Obvious?" Egwene said. "The Forsaken?"

"Well, by comparison." Verin smiled and warmed her hands on her cup of tea. "The Chosen are like a bunch of squabbling children, each trying to scream the loudest and attract their father's attention. It's easy to determine what *they* want: Power over the other children, proof that they are the most important. I'm convinced that it isn't intelligence, craftiness, or skill that makes one Chosen—though of course, those things are important. No, I believe it is *selfishness* the Great Lord seeks in his greatest leaders."

Egwene frowned. Were they really having a quiet chat about the *Forsaken?* "Why would he choose that quality?"

"It makes them predictable. A tool you can depend upon to act as expected is far more valuable than one you cannot understand. Or perhaps because when they struggle against one another, it makes only the strong ones survive. I don't know, honestly. The Chosen are predictable, but the Great Lord is anything but. Even after decades of study, I can't be certain exactly what *he* wants or why he wants it. I only know that this battle isn't being fought the way that al'Thor assumes it will be."

"And what does this have to do with me?" Egwene asked.

"Not much," Verin said, *tsking* at herself. "I'm afraid I let myself get sidetracked. And with so little time, too. I really must pay attention." She *still* seemed like the pleasant, scholarly Brown sister. Egwene had always expected that Black sisters would be . . . different.

"Anyway," Verin continued. "We were talking about what you did here, in the Tower. I was afraid that I'd come and find you still dawdling with your friends outside. Imagine my amazement at finding that you'd not only infiltrated Elaida's regime, but had apparently turned half of the Hall itself against her. You've certainly riled some of my associates, I can tell you that. They are none too pleased." Verin shook her head, taking another sip of tea.

"Verin, I. . . ." Egwene paused. "What is—"

"No time, I'm afraid," Verin said, leaning forward. Suddenly, something about her seemed to change. Though she was still the aged—and at times motherly—woman, her expression grew more determined. She caught Egwene's eyes, and the intensity within that gaze shocked Egwene. *Was* this the same woman?

"Thank you for humoring a woman's rambles," Verin said, voice more soft. "It was so very nice to have a quiet chat over tea, at least once more. Now, there are some things you need to know. A number of years ago, I faced a decision. I found myself in a position where I could either take the oaths to the Dark One, or I could reveal that I had actually never wanted—or intended—to do so, whereupon I would have been executed.

"Perhaps another would have found a way around this situation. Many would have simply opted for death. I, however, saw this as an opportunity. You see, one rarely has such a chance as this, to study a beast from inside its heart, to see really what makes the blood flow. To discover where all of the little veins and vessels lead. Quite an extraordinary experience."

"Wait," Egwene said. "You joined the Black Ajah to *study* them?"

"I *joined* them to keep my skin intact," Verin said, smiling. "I'm rather fond of it, though Tomas *did* go on about these white hairs. Anyway, after joining them, the chance to study them was my making the best of the situation."

"Tomas. Does he know what you've done?"

"He was a Darkfriend himself, child," Verin said. "Wanting a way out. Well, there really isn't a way out, not once the Great Lord has his claws in you. But there *was* a way to fight, to make up for a little of what you've done. I offered that chance to Tomas, and I believe he was quite grateful to me for it."

Egwene hesitated, trying to take all of this in. Verin was a Darkfriend . . . but not one at the same time. "You said he 'was' quite grateful to you?"

Verin didn't answer immediately. She simply took another sip of her tea. "The oaths one makes to the Great Lord are quite specific," she finally continued. "And, when they are placed upon one who can channel, they are quite binding. Impossible to break. You can double-cross other Darkfriends, you can turn against the Chosen if you can justify it. Selfishness must be preserved. But you can never betray *him*. You can never betray the order itself to outsiders. But the oaths are specific. Very specific." She looked up, meeting Egwene's eyes. "'I swear not to betray the Great Lord, to keep my secrets until the hour of my death.' That was what I promised. Do you see?"

Egwene looked down at the steaming cup in Verin's hands. "Poison?"

"It takes a very special tea to make asping rot go down sweetly," Verin said, taking another sip. "As I said, please thank Laras for me."

Egwene closed her eyes. Nynaeve had mentioned asping rot to her; a drop could kill. It was a quick death, peaceful, and often came . . . within an hour of ingestion.

"A curious hole in the oaths," Verin said softly. "To allow one to effect a betrayal in the final hour of one's life. I cannot help wondering if the Great Lord knows of it. Why wouldn't he close that hole?"

"Perhaps he doesn't see it as threatening," Egwene said, opening her eyes. "After all, what kind of Darkfriend would *kill* themselves in order to advance the greater good? It doesn't seem the kind of thing his followers would consider."

"You may be right at that," Verin said, setting the cup of tea aside. "It would be wise to make certain that is disposed of with care, child."

"So that is it?" Egwene asked, chilled. "What of Tomas?"

"We made our farewells. He is spending his last hour with family."

Egwene shook her head. It seemed such a tragedy. "You come to me to confess, killing yourself in a final quest for redemption?"

Verin laughed. "Redemption? I should think that wouldn't be so easily earned. Light knows I've done enough to require a very *special* kind of redemption. But it was worth the cost. Worth it indeed. Or perhaps that is simply what I must tell myself." She reached to her side, pulling a leather scrip from beneath the folded blanket at the foot of Egwene's bed. Verin carefully undid the straps, then produced two items: two books, both bound in leather. One was larger, like a reference book, though it had no title on

its red binding. The other was a thin blue book. The covers
of both were a little worn from use.

Verin handed them to Egwene. Hesitantly she took them,
the larger volume heavy in her right hand, the blue book
light in her left hand. She ran a finger over the smooth
leather, frowning. She looked up at Verin.

"Every woman in the Brown," Verin said, "seeks to
produce something lasting. Research or study that will be
meaningful. Others often accuse us of ignoring the world
around us. They think we only look backward. Well, that is
inaccurate. If we are distracted, it is because we look forward, toward those who will come. And the information,
the knowledge we gather . . . we leave it for them. The other
Ajahs worry about making today better; we yearn to make
tomorrow better."

Egwene set the blue book aside, looking into the red
one first. The words were written in a small, efficient, but
cramped hand she recognized as Verin's. None of the sen-
tences made sense. They were gibberish.

"The small book is a key, Egwene," Verin explained. "It
contains the cipher I used to write this tome. That tome is
the . . . work. My work. The work of my life."

"What is it?" Egwene asked softly, suspecting she might
know the answer.

"Names, locations, explanations," Verin said. "Everything I learned about *them*. About the leaders among the
Darkfriends, about the Black Ajah. The prophecies they
believe, the goals and motivations of the separate factions.
Along with a list, at the back, of every Black Ajah sister I
could identify."

Egwene started. "Every one?"

"I doubt I caught them all," Verin said, smiling. "But
I think I got the large majority of them. I promise you,
Egwene. I can be *quite* thorough."

Egwene looked down at the books with awe. Incredible! Light, but this was a treasure greater than any king's
hoard. A treasure as great as the Horn of Valere itself. She
looked up, tears in her eyes, imagining a life spent among
the Black, always watching, recording, and working for the
good of all.

"Oh, don't go doing that," Verin said. Her face was beginning to look pale. "They have many agents among us, like

worms eating the fruit out from the core. Well, I thought it time that we had at least one of us among them. This is worth one woman's life. Few people have had a chance to create something as useful, and as wonderful, as that book you hold. We all seek to change the future, Egwene. I think I might just have a chance at doing so."

Verin took a deep breath, then raised a hand to her head. "My. That does work quickly. There is one more thing I must tell you. Open the red book, please."

Egwene did so, and found a thin leather strap with steel weights on the ends, the type used for marking one's place in a book, though it was longer than others she had seen.

"Wrap it around the book," Verin said, "place it marking any page, then twist the loose ends around the top."

Egwene did so, curious, tucking the strap into a random page and closing the book. She put the smaller book on top of the larger one, then took the long ends of the bookmark that dangled down and twisted them about one another. The weights, she noticed, fit together. She locked them into place.

And the books vanished.

Egwene stared. She could still feel them in her hands, but the books themselves were invisible.

"Only works on books, I'm afraid," Verin said, yawning. "Someone from the Age of Legends, it appears, was *very* worried about hiding his or her journal from others." She smiled slightly, but was growing very pale.

"Thank you, Verin," Egwene said, unclasping and unwrapping the bookmark. The volumes appeared again. "I wish there were some other way . . ."

"I will admit that the poison was a backup plan," Verin said. "I am not eager for death; there are still things I need to do. Fortunately, I have set several of them in motion to be . . . seen to, in case I do not return. Regardless, my first plan was to find the Oath Rod, then see if I could use it to remove the Great Lord's oaths. The Oath Rod appears to have gone missing, unfortunately."

Saerin, Egwene thought, *and the others. They must have taken it again.* "I'm sorry, Verin," she said.

"It might not have worked anyway," Verin said, settling back on the bed, arranging the pillow behind her streaked brown hair. "The process of making those oaths to the

Great Lord was . . . distinctive. I do wish I'd been able to discover one more tidbit for you. One of the Chosen is in the Tower, child. It's Mesaana, I'm certain of it. I had hoped to be able to bring you the name she was hiding under, but the two times I met with her, she was shrouded to the point that I couldn't tell. What I did see is recorded in the red book.

"Be careful where you tread. Be careful how you strike. I will leave it to you to decide if you want to try to get all of them at once, or if you want to take the most important ones separately in secret. Perhaps you will decide to watch and see if you can counter their plots. A good interrogation might yield light upon some of the questions I was not able to answer. So many decisions you must make, for one so young." She yawned, then grimaced as a pain stabbed her.

Egwene rose, walking to Verin's side. "Thank you, Verin. Thank you for choosing me to carry this burden."

Verin smiled faintly. "You did very well with the previous tidbits I gave you. That was quite the interesting situation. The Amyrlin commanded that I give you information to hunt the Black sisters who fled the Tower, so I had to comply, even though the leadership of the Black was frustrated by the order. I wasn't supposed to give you the dreaming *ter'angreal*, you know. But I've always had a feeling about you."

"I'm not certain I deserve such trust." Egwene looked down at the book. "Trust such as you've shown."

"Nonsense, child," Verin said, yawning again, eyes closing. "You will be Amyrlin. I'm confident of it. And an Amyrlin should be well armed with knowledge. That, among all things, is the most sacred duty of the Brown—to arm the world with knowledge. I'm still one of them. Please see that they know, although the word Black may brand my name forever, my soul is Brown. Tell them. . . ."

"I will, Verin," Egwene promised. "But your soul is not Brown. I can see it."

Her eyes fluttered open, meeting Egwene's, a frown creasing her forehead.

"Your soul is of a pure white, Verin," Egwene said softly. "Like the Light itself."

Verin smiled, and her eyes closed. The actual death was a few more minutes in coming, but unconsciousness came first and swiftly. Egwene sat, holding the woman's hand.

Elaida and the Hall could see to themselves; Egwene had prepared her seeds well. Showing up now and making demands would be to overextend her authority.

After Verin's pulse faded, Egwene took the cup of poisoned tea and set it aside, then raised the saucer up in front of Verin's nose. The shiny surface reflected no fog. It felt callous to double-check, but there were some poisons which could make one appear to be dead and breathe only very shallowly, and if Verin had wanted to trick Egwene and point a finger at the wrong sisters, this would have been a wonderful method. Callous indeed to double-check, and it made Egwene feel sick, but she was Amyrlin. She did that which was difficult and considered all possibilities.

Surely no truly Black sister would have been willing to die just to create such misdirection. Her heart trusted Verin, although her mind wanted to be certain. She glanced toward her simple desk, where she had set the books. At that moment, the door to her room opened without warning and a young Aes Sedai—new enough to the shawl that her face didn't show the ageless look yet—peeked in. Turese, one of the Red sisters. So someone had finally been assigned to watch over Egwene. Her period of freedom had come to an end. Well, there was no use crying over what could have been. The time had been well spent. She wished Verin had come to see her a week earlier, but what was done was done.

The Red sister frowned at seeing Verin, and Egwene quickly raised a finger to her lips and shot the young sister a harsh look.

Egwene hurried to the door. "She just got in, and wished to speak to me regarding a task she had set me upon long ago, back before the Tower split. They can be oddly single-minded at times, these Brown sisters." True words, every one of them.

Turese nodded ruefully at the comment about Browns.

"I do wish she'd chosen her own bed to lie down in," Egwene said. "I'm not sure what to do with her now." All true again. Egwene really *did* need to get her hands on that Oath Rod. Lying started to seem far too convenient at times like this.

"She must be tired from her travels," Turese said, voice soft but firm. "You let her do as she wishes; she is Aes Sedai, and you simply a novice. Do not disturb her."

With that, the Red closed the door, and Egwene smiled to herself in satisfaction. Then she glanced at Verin's corpse, and the smile faded. Eventually, she would have to reveal that Verin had died. How would she explain *that*? Well, she would think of something. If pressed, she might just tell the truth.

First, though, she needed to spend some time with that book. The chances of it being taken from her in the near future were great, even with the bookmark *ter'angreal*. She should probably store the cipher separate from the concealed book. Perhaps memorize and destroy the cipher. This would all be easier to plan for if she knew how events had gone in the Hall! Had Elaida been deposed? Was Silviana alive, or had she been executed?

There was little she could discover now, not while being guarded. She would simply have to wait. And read.

The code proved to be rather complex, requiring a good part of the smaller book to explain. That was both advantageous and frustrating. It would be very difficult to break the code without it, but the code would also be near impossible to memorize. She wouldn't be able to manage it before morning, by which time she would have to reveal Verin's true state.

She glanced over at the woman. Verin really did look as if she were sleeping peacefully. Egwene had pulled out the blanket and covered her up to the neck, then taken off her shoes and set them beside the bed to enhance the illusion. Feeling a little disrespectful, she decided to roll Verin onto her side. The Red sister had already peeked in a couple of times, and seeing Verin in another position would look less suspicious.

That finished, Egwene glanced at her candle to judge the passage of time. There were no windows in the room, not in a novice's quarters. She shoved aside the longing to embrace the Power and create a ball of light by which to read. She'd have to be satisfied with the single candle's flame.

She dug into her first task: deciphering the names of the Black sisters listed at the back of the tome. That was more important, even, than memorizing the cipher. She *had* to know whom she could trust.

The next few hours were among the most disturbing and discomforting in her life. Some of the names were unknown to her, many barely familiar. Others were women she had worked with, respected, and even trusted. She cursed when she found Katerine's name near the head of the list, then hissed in surprise when Alviarin's name came up. She'd heard of Elza Penfell and Galina Casban, though she didn't know some of the next few names.

She felt a sickening pit within her when she read Sheriam's name. Egwene had once suspected the woman, true, but that had been during her days as a novice and an Accepted. During those days—the days when she'd first begun hunting the Black Ajah—Liandrin's betrayal had still been fresh. Egwene had suspected everyone then.

During the exile in Salidar, Egwene had worked closely with Sheriam and had grown to like the woman. But she was Black. Egwene's own Keeper was Black. *Steel yourself, Egwene,* she thought, continuing to read down the list. She worked through the feelings of betrayal, the bitterness and the regret. She would not let emotions get in the way of her duty.

The Black sisters were spread across all Ajahs. Some were Sitters, others were the lowest and least powerful of Aes Sedai. And there were hundreds of them, a little over two hundred by Verin's own count. Twenty-one in the Blue, twenty-eight in the Brown, thirty in the Gray, thirty-eight in the Green, seventeen in the White, twenty-one in the Yellow, and a stunning forty-eight in the Red. There were names of Accepted and novices as well. The book noted that those had probably been Darkfriends before they joined the White Tower, as the Black Ajah did not recruit from any except Aes Sedai. It referred her to an earlier page for a longer explanation, but Egwene continued down the list of sisters. She needed to know the names of each woman. She *needed* to.

There were Black sisters among the rebel Aes Sedai and those of the White Tower, and even some among those unaligned who had been away from the Tower during the split. Other than Sheriam, the most disturbing discovery on the list were the sisters who were Sitters in either the Tower or among the rebels. Duhara Basaheen. Velina Behar. Sedore Dajenna. Delana Mosalaine, of course, and Talene Minly as well. Meidani had admitted to Egwene in confidence that Talene was the member of the Black Ajah that Saerin and the others had discovered, but she had fled the Tower.

Moria Karentanis. That last was a member of the Blue Ajah, a woman who had worn the shawl for over a hundred years, known for her wisdom and level-headedness. Egwene had conferred with her on numerous occasions, and had drawn on her experience, assuming that she—a Blue—would be one of the most reliable in her support. Moria had been one of those who had been eager to elect Egwene as Amyrlin, and had stood quickly in Egwene's favor at several crucial moments.

Each name was like a thorn through Egwene's skin. Dagdara Finchey, who had healed Egwene once when she'd stumbled and twisted her ankle. Zanica, who had taught Egwene lessons and had seemed so pleasant. Larissa Lyndel. Miyasi, for whom Egwene had cracked nuts. Nesita. Nacelle Kayama. Nalaene Forrell, who—like Elza—was bound to Rand. Birlen Pena. Melvara. Chai Rugan. . . .

The list went on. Neither Romanda or Lelaine were Black, which was somewhat irritating. Being able to throw one or both of those into chains would have been very convenient. Why Sheriam, but neither of those two?

Stop it, Egwene, she thought. *You aren't behaving rationally.* Wishing for certain sisters to be Black got her nowhere.

Cadsuane was not on the list. Neither were any of Egwene's dearest friends. She hadn't expected them to be, but it was still good to complete the list without seeing any of their names. The group hunting the Black Ajah in the White Tower really was true, as none of their names were on the list. The list also didn't contain the names of any of the spies sent from Salidar.

And Elaida's name wasn't on the list either. There was a notation at the end, explaining that Verin had looked very closely at Elaida, searching for proof that she was Black. But comments by Black sisters led her to believe strongly that Elaida was *not* herself Black. Just an unstable woman who was sometimes as frustrating to the Black as she was to the rest of the Tower.

It made sense, unfortunately. Knowing that Galina and Alviarin were Black had led Egwene to suspect that she wouldn't find Elaida's name on the list. The Blacks seemed more likely to choose someone they could manipulate to be Amyrlin, then install a Black Keeper to keep her in line.

They probably had used some kind of leverage against

Elaida through Galina—whom Verin noted had probably managed to make herself Head of the Red Ajah—or Alviarin. They had bullied or bribed Elaida to do as they wished without her knowing that she was serving the Black. And that helped explain Alviarin's strange fall. Had she gone too far, perhaps? Overstepped herself, earning Elaida's ire? It seemed plausible, though they wouldn't know for certain until Elaida spoke or Egwene could have Alviarin interrogated. Which she meant to do as soon as possible.

She closed the fat red book, thoughtful, her candle burned nearly down to the base. It was growing late in the day. Perhaps it was time to insist on being given some information about the state of the Tower.

Before she could decide how to go about that, a knock came at the door. Egwene looked up, hurriedly twisting the straps of the bookmark around and making both books vanish. A knock meant someone other than a Red was there.

"Come," she called.

The door opened to reveal Nicola, with her large dark eyes and slender build, standing outside beneath the watchful eye of Turese. The Red did not seem pleased that Egwene had a visitor, but the steaming bowl carried on Nicola's tray indicated why she'd been given leave to knock.

Nicola curtsied to Egwene, her white novice dress fluttering. Turese's scowl deepened. Nicola didn't notice, however. "For Verin Sedai," she said softly, nodding toward the bed. "By orders of the Mistress of Kitchens, after hearing how exhausted Verin Sedai was from her travels."

Egwene nodded, gesturing toward the table, hiding her excitement. Nicola approached quickly, setting the tray on the table, whispering under her breath, "I'm to ask if you trust her." She glanced at the bed again.

"Yes," Egwene answered, covering the sound by scooting her stool back. So her allies didn't know that Verin was dead. That was good; the secret was still safe, for the moment.

Nicola nodded, then spoke in a louder voice. "It would be good for her to eat it when it's warm, though I'll leave it to you if you wish not to wake her. I'm instructed to warn you not to touch it yourself."

"I won't do so unless it turns out that she has no need of it," Egwene replied, turning away. A few moments later, the door closed behind Nicola. Egwene waited a painful few minutes for Turese to open the door and check on her, passing the time by washing her face and hands, and putting on a clean dress. Finally, confident she wouldn't be interrupted, she grabbed the spoon and fished in the soup. Sure enough, she found a small glass vial with a rolled-up piece of paper in it.

Clever. Her allies had apparently heard of Verin's presence in Egwene's room and decided to use it as an excuse to get someone in. She unrolled the paper, which contained only one word. "Wait."

She sighed, but there was nothing to do. She didn't dare get out the book and continue reading, however. Soon, she heard voices outside, and what sounded like an argument. Another knock came at the door.

"Come," Egwene said, curious.

The door opened and Meidani stepped into the room. She pointedly closed the door on Turese. "Mother," she said, curtsying. The slender woman was wearing a tight gray dress which pulled a little too obviously across her ample chest. Had she been scheduled for a dinner with Elaida this evening? "I am sorry to keep you waiting."

Egwene waved dismissively. "How did you get past Turese?"

"It is known that Elaida . . . favors me with visits," she said. "And Tower law says that no prisoner can be forbidden visitors. She could not stop a sister from wishing to visit a simple novice, though she did try to make a point of arguing it."

Egwene nodded, and Meidani glanced at Verin, frowning. Then she paled. Verin's features had grown waxy and dull, and it was obvious that something was wrong. It was a good thing that Turese had never looked closely at the "sleeping" woman.

"Verin Sedai is dead," Egwene said, glancing at the door.

"Mother?" Meidani asked. "What happened? Were you attacked?"

"Verin Sedai was poisoned by a Darkfriend shortly before her conversation with me. She was aware of the poison, and came to pass on some important information to me during her last moments." It was incredible what a few true statements could conceal.

"Light!" Meidani said. "A murder *inside* the White Tower? We have to tell someone! Gather the guard and—"

"It will be dealt with," Egwene said firmly. "Keep your voice down and pull yourself together. I don't want the guard outside to hear what we are saying."

Meidani paled, then looked at Egwene, likely wondering how she could be so callous. Good. Let her see the collected, determined Amyrlin. As long as she didn't see a hint of the grief, confusion and anxiety inside.

"Yes, Mother." Meidani curtsied. "Of course. I apologize."

"Now, you bring news, I assume?"

"Yes, Mother," Meidani said, composing herself. "Saerin instructed me to come to you. She said you would need to know of the day's events."

"And I do," Egwene said, trying not to show her impatience. Light, but she'd already been able to figure out *that* part. Couldn't the woman get on with it? There were Black Ajah to deal with!

"Elaida is still Amyrlin," Meidani said, "but only by a hair. The Hall of the Tower met and censured her formally. They informed Elaida that the Amyrlin was *not* an absolute ruler, and that she couldn't continue to make decrees and demands without consulting them."

Egwene nodded. "Not an unexpected turn," she said. More than one Amyrlin had become only a figurehead because she'd overextended herself in a similar way. It was what Elaida had been heading for, and that would have been satisfactory, had these not been the end of days. "What of penance?"

"Three months," Meidani said. "One for what she did to you. Two for behavior unbecoming her station."

"Interesting," Egwene said, thoughtful.

"There were some who called for more, Mother. It seemed that for a moment she might be deposed right there."

"You were watching?" Egwene asked with surprise.

Meidani nodded. "Elaida asked for the proceedings to be Sealed to the Flame, but she gained no support in the move. I think that her own Ajah was behind that, Mother. All three of the Red's Sitters are out of the Tower. I still wonder where Duhara and the others went."

Duhara. A Black. What is she up to? And the other two?

Were the three together, and if so, could the other two be Black as well?

She'd have to address that later. "How did Elaida take all of this?"

"She didn't say much, Mother," Meidani said. "She sat and watched, mostly. She didn't look very pleased; I was surprised she didn't start ranting."

"The Reds," Egwene said. "If she is really losing support in her own Ajah, they'd have warned her ahead of time not to make more waves."

"That was Saerin's assessment as well," Meidani replied. "She also noted that your own insistence that the Red Ajah not be allowed to fall—spread by a group of novices who overheard you—was part of what kept Elaida from being deposed."

"Well, I wouldn't mind her deposed," Egwene said. "I just didn't want the entire Ajah disbanded. Still, this might be for the best. Elaida's fall has to come in a way that doesn't tear the Tower down with her." Though, if Egwene could do it again, she might retract those words said earlier. She didn't want anyone to think that Egwene had been *supporting* Elaida. "I assume that Silviana's sentence has been dismissed?"

"Not completely, Mother," Meidani said. "She is being held as the Hall decides what to do to her. She still defied the Amyrlin in a very public way, and there is talk of penance."

Egwene frowned. It smelled of a compromise; Elaida had probably met in closed conference with the head of the Red Ajah—whoever that was, now that Galina had vanished—hashing out the details. Silviana would still be punished, although not as strongly, but Elaida would submit to the will of the Hall. It indicated that Elaida was on shaky ground, but that she could still make demands. Her support wasn't as completely eroded within her own Ajah as Egwene had hoped.

Still, this was a fortunate turn of events. Silviana would live, and Egwene—it appeared—would be allowed to return to her life as a "novice." The Sitters were displeased enough with Elaida to reprimand her. Given just a little more time, Egwene was confident she could get the woman overturned and the Tower reunited. But dare she spend that time?

She glanced at the table, where the precious books lay hidden from eyes. If she staged a mass assault on the Black Ajah, would that precipitate a battle? Would she destabilize the Tower even further? And could she realistically hope to strike at all of them like that? She needed time to consider the information. For now, that meant staying in the Tower and working against Elaida. And, unfortunately, that meant letting most of the Black sisters run free.

But not all of them. "Meidani," Egwene said. "I want you to report to the others. They *must* take Alviarin into captivity and test her with the Oath Rod. Tell them to take any reasonable risk to achieve it."

"Alviarin, Mother?" Meidani asked. "Why her?"

"She's Black," Egwene said, stomach turning. "And near the head of their organization in the Tower. This was the information Verin died to bring me."

Meidani paled. "Are you certain, Mother?"

"I'm confident in Verin's trustworthiness," Egwene said. "But it would still be advisable to have others remove, then replace, Alviarin's oaths and ask her if she's Black. Every woman should be given that chance to prove herself, no matter the evidence. You have the Oath Rod, I assume?"

"Yes," Meidani said. "We needed it to prove Nicola's trustworthiness; the others wanted to bring some Accepted and novices in, as they can run messages where sisters cannot go."

It was wise, considering the divisions among the Ajahs. "Why her?"

"Because of how often she speaks to the others about you, Mother," Meidani said. "It's well known that she's one of your greatest advocates among the novices."

It was odd to hear that of a woman who had effectively betrayed her, but the girl couldn't really be blamed for that, all things considered.

"They didn't let her swear all three oaths, of course," Meidani said. "She's not Aes Sedai. But she did take the oath about lying and proved herself not a Darkfriend. They removed the oath after."

"And you, Meidani?" Egwene asked. "Have they removed the fourth oath from you?"

The woman smiled. "Yes, Mother. Thank you."

Egwene nodded. "Go, then. Pass on my message. Alviarin

must be taken." She glanced at Verin's body. "I'm afraid I'll have to ask you to take her with you as well. It will be better if she vanishes, as opposed to my having to explain her death in my room."

"But—"

"Use a gateway," Egwene said. "Skim if you don't know the area well enough."

Meidani nodded, then Embraced the Source.

"Weave something else, first," Egwene said thoughtfully. "It doesn't matter what; something that requires a lot of power. Perhaps one of the hundred weaves one takes in the test to become Aes Sedai."

Meidani frowned, but did as asked, weaving something very complicated and power-intensive. Soon after she began, Turese poked her head into the room suspiciously. The weave blocked her sight of Verin's face, fortunately, but Turese wasn't focused on the "sleeping" Brown. She focused on the weave, opening her mouth.

"She is showing me some of the weaves I will need to know if I take the test to become Aes Sedai," Egwene said curtly, cutting off Turese's words. "Is that forbidden?"

Turese glared at her, but pulled the door shut and withdrew.

"That was to prevent her from poking in and seeing the weaves for gateways," Egwene said. "Quickly now. Take the body. When Turese looks in again, I will tell her the truth—that you and Verin left through a gateway."

Meidani glanced at Verin's corpse. "But what should we do with the body?"

"Whatever seems appropriate," Egwene said, growing testy. "I'll leave that to you. I don't have the time to deal with it now. And take that cup with you; the tea is poisoned. Dispose of it carefully."

Egwene glanced at her flickering candle; it was burned nearly all the way down to the table itself. To the side, Meidani sighed softly, then created a gateway. Weaves of Air moved Verin's body in through the opening, and Egwene watched her go with a pang of regret. The woman had deserved better. Someday, it would be known what she had suffered and what she had accomplished. But not for a time yet.

Once Meidani was gone with the corpse and the tea, Egwene lit another candle, then lay down on her bed, trying not to think of the body that had occupied it previously. She relaxed herself, thinking of Siuan. The woman would be going to sleep soon. She needed to be warned about Sheriam and the others.

Egwene opened her eyes in *Tel'aran'rhiod*. She was in her room, or at least the dream version of it. The bed was made, the door closed. She changed her dress to that of a stately green gown fitting an Amyrlin, then moved herself to the Tower's Spring Garden. Siuan wasn't there yet, but it was probably still a little early for their meeting.

Here, at least, one could see none of the filth that piled up in the city or the corruption that worked at the roots of Ajah unity. The Tower gardeners moved like natural forces, planting, cultivating, and harvesting as Amyrlins rose and fell. The Spring Garden was smaller than most of the other Tower gardens; it was a triangular plot of land pressed between two walls. Perhaps in another city, this plot would have been used for storage or simply filled in with stone. But in the White Tower, both options would have been unsightly.

The solution was a small garden full of plants that thrived in the shade. Hydrangeas ran up the walls and surged around planters. Bleeding hearts sat in rows, with their tiny pink blossoms drooping from delicate three-pronged compound leaves. Flowering bristleboughs, with their thin, fingerlike leaves, and other small shade trees ran along the insides of the triangular walls, meeting in a single point.

Walking up and down the lines of trees as she waited, Egwene thought of Sheriam being Black. How many things had the woman had a hand in? She'd been Mistress of Novices for years during Siuan's tenure as Amyrlin. Had she used her position to bully, perhaps to turn, other sisters? Had she been behind the attack of the Gray Man so long ago?

Sheriam had been part of the group that Healed Mat. Surely she could have done nothing malicious while in a circle with so many other women—but anything involving the woman was suspect. That was so much! Sheriam had been one of those in charge of Salidar before Egwene's rise to power. What had Sheriam done, how much manipulation had she exerted then, how much had she betrayed to the Shadow?

Had she been aware ahead of time of Elaida's plans to depose Siuan? Galina and Alviarin were Black, and they had been two of the main instigators, so it seemed likely other Blacks had been warned. Were the exodus of half of the Tower, the gathering in Salidar, and the subsequent waiting and debating all part of the Dark One's plan? What of Egwene's own rise to power? How many of the Shadow's strings did she dance on without knowing it?

This is an exercise in futility, she told herself firmly. *Don't go down that path.* Even without Verin's books, Egwene had suspected that the breaking of the Tower was the Dark One's work. Of course he would be pleased that the Aes Sedai had split in two, rather than unifying behind one leader.

It was just more . . . personal now. Egwene felt dirtied, she felt duped. For a moment, she felt herself to be the country girl many thought her to be. If Elaida had been a pawn for the Blacks, then so had she. Light! How the Dark One must have laughed to see two rival Amyrlins, each with one of his loyal minions at her side, pitting them against one another.

I can't be certain exactly what he wants or why he wants it, Verin had said. *Even after years of study, I can't be certain. . . .* Who knew whether the Dark One laughed?

She shivered. Whatever his plan, she would fight him. Resist him. Spit in his eye, even if he won, just as the Aiel said.

"Well, that's a sight," Siuan's voice said.

Egwene spun, realizing with chagrin that she no longer wore the dress of the Amyrlin, but a full suit of armor like a soldier riding to battle. In her hand, she carried a pair of Aiel spears.

She banished armor and spears with a thought, resuming the dress. "Siuan," she said curtly. "You may want to summon yourself a chair. Something has happened."

Siuan frowned. "What?"

"First off, Sheriam and Moria are Black Ajah."

"What?" Siuan said, shocked. "What nonsense is this?" She froze. "Mother," she added belatedly.

"It is not nonsense," Egwene said. "The truth, I'm afraid. There are others, but I will have to give you their names later. We can't yet take them into custody. I need time to plan and think, an evening perhaps. We will strike soon. But until we do, I want Sheriam and Moria watched. Don't be alone around them."

Siuan shook her head in disbelief. "How certain are you about this, Egwene?"

"Certain enough," Egwene said. "Watch them, Siuan, and be thinking of what to do. I'll want to hear your suggestions. We'll need a way to take them quietly, then prove to the Hall that what we've done is justified."

"This could be dangerous." Siuan rubbed her chin. "I hope you know what you are doing, Mother." She emphasized the last word.

"If I err," Egwene said, "then it will be on my head. But I don't think that I do. As I said, much has changed."

Siuan bowed her head. "Are you still captive?"

"Not exactly. Elaida has—" Egwene hesitated, frowning to herself. Something was wrong.

"Egwene?" Siuan asked, anxious.

"I. . . ." Egwene began, then shuddered. Something was pulling on her mind, clouding it. Something was . . .

Pulling her back. *Tel'aran'rhiod* winked away and Egwene opened her eyes back in her room, an anxious Nicola shaking her arm. "Mother," she was saying. "Mother!"

The girl had a bloody gash on her cheek. Egwene sat up sharply, and at that moment the entire *Tower* shook as if from an explosion. Nicola grabbed her arm, yelping in fright.

"What is going on?" Egwene demanded.

"Shadowspawn!" Nicola cried. "In the air, serpents that throw flame and weaves of the One Power! They're destroying us! Oh, Mother. It's Tarmon Gai'don!"

Egwene felt a moment of primal, nearly uncontrollable panic. Tarmon Gai'don! The Last Battle!

She heard screams in the distance, followed by the shouts of soldiers or Warders. No . . . no, she needed to focus! Serpents in the air. Serpents that wielded the One Power . . . or with *riders* that wielded the One Power. Egwene threw off the blanket and leaped to her feet.

It wasn't Tarmon Gai'don, but it was nearly as bad. The Seanchan had finally attacked the White Tower, just as Egwene had Dreamed.

And she couldn't channel enough Power to light a candle, let alone fight back.

CHAPTER
40

The Tower Shakes

S iuan awoke with a start. Something was wrong. Something was very, *very* wrong. She scrambled off of her pallet. As she did, a dark figure moved suddenly on the other side of the tent, metal rasping against metal. Siuan froze, embracing the Source reflexively and summoning a globe of light.

Gareth Bryne stood alert, heron-marked steel drawn and ready. He wore only his smallclothes, and she had to keep herself from staring at his muscled body, which was in far better shape than that of most men half his age. "What is it?" he asked tensely.

"Light!" Siuan said. "You sleep with your sword?"

"Always."

"Egwene is in danger."

"What kind of danger?"

"I don't know," she admitted. "We were meeting and she vanished suddenly. I think . . . I think Elaida may have decided to execute her. Or at least pull her from her cell and . . . do something to her."

Bryne didn't ask for details. He simply sheathed his sword, then proceeded to put on a pair of trousers and a shirt. Siuan still wore her now-wrinkled blue skirt and blouse—it was her habit to change after her meetings with Egwene, once Bryne was sound asleep.

She felt an anxiety she couldn't quite define. Why was she so on edge? It wasn't uncommon for something to wake a person while they were dreaming.

But most people weren't Egwene. She was a master of the

World of Dreams. If something had awakened her unexpectedly, she would have dealt with it, then returned to calm Siuan's worries. But she hadn't, despite Siuan's waiting for what had seemed like an eternity.

Bryne stepped up to her, now wearing his stiff gray trousers and uniform coat. He'd buttoned up his high collar, marked with three stars on the left breast and golden epaulets on the shoulders.

A frenzied voice called from outside. "General Bryne! My Lord General!"

Bryne glanced at her, then turned toward the tent flaps. "Come!"

A youthful soldier with neat black hair pushed into the tent and gave a quick salute. He didn't apologize for coming so late—Bryne's men knew that their general trusted them to awake him if there was need. "My Lord," the man said. "Scout's report. Something is going on in the city."

"'Something,' Tijds?" Bryne asked.

"The scouts aren't certain, my Lord," the man said with a grimace. "With the cloud cover, the night is dark, and the spyglasses aren't much help. There have been bursts of light near the Tower, like an Illuminator's show. Dark shadows in the air."

"Shadowspawn?" Bryne asked, pushing out of the tent. With the globe of light, Siuan and the soldier followed. The moon would be barely a sliver, and with those perpetual clouds, it was difficult to see anything at all. The tents of the officers were slumbering banks of black on black around them, and the only really distinguishable lights were the watchfires of the guards at the palisade entrance.

"They could be Shadowspawn, my Lord," the soldier said, trotting after Bryne. "Stories tell of creatures of Shadow that fly in such a way. But the scouts aren't certain what they're seeing. The flashes of light are there for sure, though."

Bryne nodded, heading toward the watchfires. "Alert the night guard; I want them up and armored, just in case. Send runners to the city fortifications. And bring me more information!"

"Yes, my Lord." The soldier saluted and ran off.

Bryne glanced at Siuan, his face illuminated by the globe of light hovering above her hand. "Shadowspawn wouldn't

dare attack the White Tower," he said. "Not without a sub-
stantial ground assault waiting, and I sincerely doubt that
there are a hundred thousand Trollocs hiding in what little
cover these plains offer. So what in the blazes is going on?"

"Seanchan," Siuan said, a pit of ice forming in her stomach. "Fish guts, Gareth! It *has* to be. Egwene predicted it."

He nodded. "Yes. They ride Shadowspawn, some of the
rumors say."

"Flying beasts," Siuan said, "not Shadowspawn. Egwene
said that they're called *raken*."

He eyed her doubtfully, but said only, "What would make
the Seanchan so foolhardy as to attack without a ground
assault in tandem?"

Siuan shook her head. She'd always assumed that a Seanchan strike at the White Tower would mean a large-scale
invasion, and Egwene had guessed that the attack was still
months off. Light! It looked like Egwene could be wrong.

Bryne turned toward his watchfires, which were blazing
higher in the night, tossing light across the front of the palisade. Inside the ring of wood, officers were rousing, calling
to neighboring tents. Lamps and lanterns winked on.

"Well," Gareth said, "so long as they attack Tar Valon,
they are no problem of ours. We just need to—"

"I'm getting her out," Siuan said suddenly, surprising
herself.

Bryne spun toward Siuan, into the light of her globe. His
chin was shadowed by evening stubble. "What?"

"Egwene," Siuan said. "We *need* to go in for her. This
will provide a perfect distraction, Gareth! We can go in and
grab her before anyone is the wiser."

He eyed her.

"What?"

"You gave your word not to rescue her, Siuan." Light, but
it felt nice to hear him use her name!

Focus! she scolded herself. "That doesn't matter now.
She's in danger and needs help."

"She doesn't *want* help," Bryne said sternly. "We need to
make certain our own force is safe. The Amyrlin is confident that she can care for herself."

"I thought I could care for myself too," Siuan said. "And
look where it got me." She shook her head, glancing toward
the distant spire of Tar Valon. She could just faintly see a

burst of light along the spire, illuminating it briefly. "When Egwene speaks of the Seanchan, she always shivers. Very little upsets her—not the Forsaken, not the Dragon Reborn. Gareth, you don't know what the Seanchan *do* to women who can channel." She met his eyes. "We need to go for her."

"I will not be a party to this," he said stubbornly.

"Fine," Siuan spat. Fool man! "Go take care of your men. I think I know someone who *will* help me." She stalked away, heading toward a tent just inside the palisade.

Egwene steadied herself against the wall of the hallway as the entire Tower shook again. The very stones quivered. Flakes of mortar crumbled down from the ceiling, and a loose tile fell from the wall and shattered into a dozen shards on the floor. Nicola screamed, and clutched at Egwene.

"The Dark One!" Nicola wailed. "The Last Battle! It's come!"

"Nicola!" Egwene snapped, straightening up. "Control yourself. This isn't the Last Battle. It's the Seanchan."

"Seanchan?" Nicola said. "But I thought they were just a rumor!"

Fool girl, Egwene thought, hurrying down a side hallway. Nicola scuttled after her, carrying her lamp. Egwene's memory served her correctly, and the next hallway was at the edge of the Tower, giving her a window to the outside. She waved Nicola to the side, then risked a glance out into the darkness.

Sure enough, dark, winged forms flapped in the sky. Those were too big to be *raken*. *To'raken*, then. They swooped, weaves spinning around many of them, glowing and vibrant to Egwene's eyes. Blasts of fire sprang into existence, lighting pairs of women riding on the backs of the *to'raken*. *Damane* and *sul'dam*.

Portions of the Tower's wings below were alight with flames, and to her horror, Egwene saw several gaping holes directly in the sides of the Tower. *To'raken* clutched the side of the Tower, climbing up like bats clinging to a wall, unloading soldiers and *damane* into the building. As Egwene watched, a *to'raken* leapt free of the side of the Tower, the height allowing it to forgo its normal running start. The creature wasn't as graceful as one of the smaller *raken*, but its handler did a masterful job of directing it back into the air. The creature flew right by Egwene's window, the wind of its passing blowing back her hair. Egwene faintly heard screaming as the *to'raken* swept past. Terrified screaming.

It wasn't a full-scale attack—it was a raid! A raid to capture *marath'damane*! Egwene pulled to the side as a blast of fire shot by the window and hit the wall a short distance away. She could hear rock crumble, and the Tower shook violently. Dust and smoke exploded down a side passage off the hallway.

Soldiers would soon follow. Soldiers and *sul'dam*. With those leashes. Egwene shuddered, wrapping her arms around herself. The cool, seamless metal. The nausea, the degradation, the panic, despair, and—shamefully—guilt at not serving her mistress to the best of her abilities. She remembered the haunted look of an Aes Sedai as she was broken. Most of all, she remembered her own terror.

The terror of realizing that she would be like the others, eventually. Just another slave, happy to serve.

The Tower shook. Fire flashed in the distant hallways accompanied by shouts and wails of despair. She could smell smoke. Oh, Light! Could this really be? She wouldn't go back. She wouldn't let them leash her again. She had to run! She had to hide, flee, escape . . .

No!

She pushed herself upright.

No, she would *not* flee. She was Amyrlin.

Nicola huddled beside the wall, whimpering. "They're coming for us," the girl whispered. "Oh Light, they're coming!"

"Let them come!" Egwene roared, opening herself to the Source. Blessedly, enough time had passed to dull the forkroot slightly, and she was able to grab a faint trickle of the Power. It was tiny, perhaps the least amount of the Power she'd ever channeled. She wouldn't be able to weave a tongue of Air to shift a piece of paper. But it would be enough. It had to be. "We will fight!"

Nicola just sniffed, looking up at her. "You can barely channel, Mother!" she wailed. "I can see it. We *can't* fight them!"

"We can and will," Egwene said firmly. "Stand, Nicola! You're an initiate of the Tower, not a frightened milkmaid."

The girl looked up.

"I will protect you," Egwene said. "I promise."

The girl seemed to take heart, rising. Egwene glanced toward the distant hallway where the blast had hit. It was dark, the wall lamps unlit, but she thought she spotted shadows. They'd be coming, and they'd be leashing any women they found.

Egwene turned in the other direction. She could still faintly hear screams that way. They were the ones she'd heard just after she'd awakened. She didn't know where the guard at her door had gone, and didn't really care.

"Come," she said, striding forward, holding to her tiny bit of the Power like a drowning woman clinging to a rescue rope. Nicola followed, still sniffling, but she followed. Several moments later, Egwene discovered what she'd hoped to find. The hallway was filled with girls, some in their white dresses, others wearing their shifts. The novices clumped together, many of them screaming at each blast that shook the Tower. Likely, they wished that they were down below, where the novices' quarters had once been.

"The Amyrlin!" several exclaimed as Egwene entered the hallway. They were a sorry bunch, lit by candles in terrified hands. Their questions sprouted like rotwood mushrooms in the spring.

"What's happening?"

"Are we under attack?"

"Is it the Dark One?"

Egwene raised her hands, and the girls fell mercifully silent. "The Tower is under attack from the Seanchan," she said in a calm voice. "They have come to capture women who can channel; they have ways of forcing those women to serve them. It is *not* the Last Battle, but we are in grave danger. I don't intend to let them take a single one of you. You are mine."

The hallway grew still. Girls glanced at her, hopeful, nervous. There were a good fifty of them, perhaps more. They would have to do.

"Nicola, Jasmen, Yeteri, Inala," Egwene said, naming off some of the more powerful of the novices. "Come forward. The rest of you pay close attention. I'm going to teach you something."

"What, Mother?" one of the girls asked.

This had better work, Egwene thought. "I'm going to teach you how to link."

There were gasps. This wasn't a thing taught to novices, but Egwene would see that *sul'dam* did not find easy pickings in the novices' quarters!

Teaching the method took a worrisome length of time, each moment torn by more blasts and more screams. The novices were frightened, and that made it difficult for some of them to embrace the Source, let alone learn a new technique. What had taken Egwene only a few tries to master took the novices a heart-pounding five minutes to begin.

Nicola was a help—she had been taught to link back in Salidar—and could help demonstrating. As they practiced, Egwene had Nicola join a circle with her. The young novice opened herself up to the Source, but stayed just on the cusp of surrender and let Egwene pull power through her. It worked, bless the Light! Egwene felt a rush of exhilaration as the One Power—too long denied her in meaningful quantities—flooded into her. How sweet it was! The world was more vibrant around her, sounds more sweet, colors more beautiful.

She smiled at the thrill of it. She could feel Nicola, sense her fear, her emotions bubbling over. Egwene had been part of enough circles to know how to separate herself from Nicola, but Egwene remembered that first time, how she had felt swept up into something far larger than herself.

There was a special skill to opening oneself to a circle. It wasn't terribly difficult to learn, but they didn't have much time. Fortunately, some of the girls soon picked it up. Yeteri, a petite blonde still in her nightgown, was first. Inala, a coppery and lanky Domani, followed soon after. Egwene eagerly formed a circle with Nicola, and the two other novices. Power flooded into her.

Next, she set about getting the others to practice. She had some inkling, from discussions with the novices during her stay in the Tower, which among them were the most skilled with weaves and the most level-headed. Those weren't always the most powerful, but that wouldn't matter if they had a circle backing them up. Egwene hurriedly set them into groups, explaining how to accept the Source through a link. Hopefully, at least some of them would figure it out.

What mattered was that Egwene now had the Power. A

fair measure of it, almost as much as she was accustomed to without forkroot. She smiled in anticipation, then began a weave, the complexity of it awing several of the novices. "What you are seeing," Egwene warned, "is something that you are *not* to try, even those of you leading circles. It is far too difficult and dangerous."

A line of light split the air at the end of the hallway, rotating upon itself. She hoped that the gateway would open in the right location; she was going on Siuan's instructions, which had been somewhat vague, though she also had Elayne's original description of the place.

"Also," Egwene said to the novices in a stern voice, "you are *not* to repeat this weave for anyone without my express permission, not even other Aes Sedai." She doubted that would be an issue; the weave was complex and few novices would have the skill yet to repeat it.

"Mother?" a hawk-nosed girl named Tamala squeaked. "Are you escaping?" Her voice was edged with fear, and not a little hope, as if Egwene might take her, too.

"No," Egwene said firmly. "I'll return in just a moment. When I come back, I want at least five good circles formed!"

And with Nicola and her two other attendants in tow, Egwene stepped through the gateway into a dark room. She wove a globe of light, and the illumination revealed a storeroom with shelves lining the walls. She let out a relieved sigh. She'd gotten the location right.

Those shelves, along with two short rows of shelves out on the floor, were filled with items of curious design. Crystal globes, small exotic statues, here a glass pendant which reflected blue in the light, there a large set of metal gauntlets lined at the cuffs with firedrops. Egwene strode into the room, leaving the three novices to stare in wonder. They could likely sense what Egwene knew—these were objects of the One Power. *Ter'angreal, angreal, sa'angreal.* Relics of the Age of Legends.

Egwene scanned the shelves. Items of the Power were infamously dangerous to use if you didn't know exactly what they did. Any one of these items could kill her. If only. . . .

She smiled broadly, stepping up to a shelf and sliding a fluted white wand as long as her forearm off the top shelf. She'd found it! She held it reverently for a moment, then reached and pulled the One Power through it. An awesome, almost overpowering, torrent of power flooded through her.

Yeteri gasped audibly at sensing it. Few women had ever held such power. It surged into Egwene, like a deep breath drawn in. It made her long to roar. She looked at the three novices, smiling broadly. "*Now* we're ready," she announced.

Let the *sul'dam* try and shield her while she was wielding one of the most powerful *sa'angreal* that the Aes Sedai possessed. The White Tower would not fall while she was Amyrlin! Not without a fight to rival the Last Battle itself.

Siuan found Gawyn's tent illuminated, shadows playing on the walls as the man moved about inside. His tent was suspiciously close to the guard post; he was allowed to stay within the palisade, perhaps so that Bryne—and the watching guards—could keep an eye on him.

Bryne, being the stubborn devilfish he was, had *not* gone to his guard post as she'd instructed. He'd followed behind her, cursing and calling for his attendants to come find him, rather than meet him at the post. Even as she stopped at young Gawyn's tent, Bryne stepped up beside her, hand resting on the hilt of his sword. He eyed her with dissatisfaction. Well. She wouldn't let *him* be the judge of her honor! She would do what she pleased.

Although it was likely to make Egwene very, very annoyed with her. *She'll be thankful in the end,* Siuan thought. "Gawyn!" she barked.

The handsome youth burst out of his tent, hopping as he stomped on his left boot. He had his sheathed sword in hand, sword belt half on around his waist. "What?" he asked, scanning the camp. "I heard shouts. Are we being attacked?"

"No," Siuan said, glancing at Bryne. "But Tar Valon might be."

"Egwene!" Gawyn cried, hurriedly doing the last loops on his belt. Light, but the boy was single-minded.

"Boy," Siuan said, folding her arms. "I owe you a debt for getting me out of Tar Valon. Will you take my help getting you *in* to Tar Valon as repayment?"

"Gladly!" Gawyn said eagerly, sliding his sword in place. "Repayment and then some!"

She nodded. "Go get us some horses, then. It might just be the two of us."

"I'll risk it," Gawyn said. "Finally!"

"You won't be taking my horses for this fool's errand," Bryne said sternly.

"There are mounts in his stables owned by the Aes Sedai, Gawyn," Siuan said, ignoring Bryne. "Get one of them for me. A *mild* one, mind you. Very, very mild."

Gawyn nodded and ran away into the night. Siuan followed him at a more careful pace, plotting. This would all be so much easier if she could create a gateway, but she didn't have enough strength in the Power for that. She had before her stilling, but wishing for things to be different was about as useful as wishing the silverpike you'd caught was a fangfish instead. You sold what you had and were happy for any kind of catch at all.

"Siuan," Bryne said softly, walking beside her. Couldn't he just let her be! "Listen to me. This is insanity! How are you going to get in?"

Siuan glanced at him. "Shemerin got out."

"That was before there was a siege, Siuan." Bryne sounded exasperated. "The place is much tighter now."

Siuan shook her head. "Shemerin was being watched closely. She got out through a watergate; it's unwatched I'll bet, even now. I'd never heard of it, and I was Amyrlin. I have a map to its location."

Bryne hesitated. Then his face hardened. "It doesn't matter. The two of you still have no chance on your own."

"Then come with us," Siuan said.

"I will *not* be party to you breaking your oath again."

"Egwene said we could do something if it looked like she was in danger of execution," Siuan said. "She told me she'd let us rescue her then! Well, the way she vanished from the meeting with me tonight, I'm inclined to think she's in danger."

"It isn't Elaida who put her there, but the Seanchan!"

"We don't *know* for certain."

"Ignorance is not an excuse," Bryne said sternly, stepping closer to her. "You have made oathbreaking far too convenient, Siuan, and I don't want it to become a habit for you. Aes Sedai or not, former Amyrlin or not, people must have *rules* and *boundaries*. To say nothing of the fact that you're likely to get yourself killed attempting this!"

"And will you stop me?" She was still holding the source. "Do you think you could manage it?"

He ground his teeth. But he said nothing. Siuan turned and walked away from him, straight toward the fires at the palisade gate.

"Blasted woman," Bryne said from behind. "You'll be the death of me."

She turned, raising an eyebrow.

"I'll come," he said, hand gripping the hilt of his sheathed sword. He cut an imposing figure in the night, the straight lines of his coat matching the set cast of his face. "But there are two conditions."

"Name them," she said.

"The first is that you bond me as your Warder."

Siuan started. He wanted. . . . Light! Bryne wanted to be her Warder? She felt a surge of excitement.

But she hadn't considered taking a Warder, not since Alric's death. Losing him had been a terrible experience. Did she want to risk that again?

Did she dare pass the opportunity to have this man bonded to her, to feel his emotions, have him by her side? After all that she had dreamed and all that she had wished?

Feeling reverent, she stepped back up to Bryne, then laid a hand against his chest and wove the required weaves of Spirit and laid them over him. He breathed in sharply as new awareness blossomed inside of both of them, a new connection. She could feel his emotions, could sense his concern for her, which was shockingly powerful. It was ahead of his worry for Egwene and concern for his soldiers! *Oh, Gareth,* she thought, feeling herself smile at the sweetness of his love for her.

"I always wondered what that would feel like," Bryne said, raising his hand and making a fist a few times in the torchlight. He sounded amazed. "Would that I could give this to each man in my army!"

Siuan sniffed. "I highly doubt that their wives and families would approve of that."

"They would if it kept the soldiers alive," Bryne said. "I could run a thousand leagues and never want for breath.

I could stand against a hundred foes at once and laugh at them all."

She rolled her eyes. Men! She had given him a deeply personal and emotional connection to another person—the likes of which even husbands and wives would never know—and all he could think about was how much better he might have become at swordplay!

"Siuan!" a voice called. "Siuan Sanche!"

She turned. Gawyn, riding a black gelding, approached. Another horse trotted behind him—a shaggy brown mare.

"Bela!" Siuan exclaimed.

"Is she suitable?" Gawyn said, sounding slightly out of breath. "Bela was once Egwene's horse, I recall, and the stablemaster said she was the most placid he had."

"She'll do just fine," Siuan said, turning back to Bryne. "You said you had two requirements?"

"I'll tell you the second at a later time." Bryne still sounded a little breathless.

"That's rather ambiguous." Siuan folded her arms. "I don't like giving an open promise."

"Well, you'll have to do it anyway," Bryne said, meeting her eyes.

"Fine, but it had better not be indecent, Gareth Bryne."

He frowned.

"What?"

"It's odd," he said, smiling. "I can sense your emotions now. For instance I could tell. . . ." He cut off, and she could sense him growing just faintly embarrassed.

He can tell that I half want *him to demand something indecent of me!* Siuan realized, aghast. *Bloody ashes!* She felt herself blushing. This was going to be very inconvenient. "Oh, for the Blessed Light. . . . I agree to your terms, you lout. Get moving! We have to go."

He nodded. "Let me prepare my captains to take charge in case the fight spills out of the city. I'll bring a guard of my best hundred with us. That should be small enough to get in, assuming this gate really is passable."

"It will be," she said. "Go!"

He actually saluted her, his face straight, but she could sense his inward grin—and he likely knew it. Insufferable man! She turned to Gawyn, who sat his gelding, looking confused.

"What's happening?" Gawyn asked.

"We don't have to go in alone." Siuan took a deep breath, then steeled herself as she climbed up into Bela's saddle. Horses couldn't be trusted, not even Bela, though she was better than most. "That means our chances of surviving long enough to take Egwene just improved. Which is fortunate, since after what we're about to do, she'll undoubtedly want the privilege of killing us personally."

Adelorna Bastine ran through the hallways of the White Tower. For once, she rued the enhanced senses that holding the Power offered. Scents seemed more crisp to her, but all she could smell were burning wood and dying flesh. Colors were more vibrant, and all she could see were the ashen scars of broken stone where lashes or balls of flame had fallen. Sounds were more crisp, but all she heard were screams, curses, and the raucous calls of those horrible beasts in the air.

She scrambled down a darkened hallway, her breath coming in gasps, until she reached an intersection. She pulled to a stop, putting a hand to her breast. She had to find resistance. Light, they couldn't all have fallen, could they? A pocket of Greens had stood with her and fought. She had seen Josaine die as a weave of Earth had destroyed the wall beside her and had seen Marthera captured with some kind of metal leash around her neck. Adelorna didn't know *where* her Warders were. One was wounded. Another lived. The last . . . the last she didn't want to think about. Light send that she could at least reach the wounded Talric soon.

She pulled herself to her feet, wiping blood from her forehead where a chip of stone had grazed her. There were just so many of the invaders, with their strange helmets and women used as weapons. And they were so skilled with those deadly weaves! Adelorna felt ashamed. The Battle Ajah indeed! The Greens with her had stood only minutes before being defeated.

Breathing heavily, she continued down the hallway. She stayed away from the outer edge of the Tower, where the invaders were most likely to be found. Had she lost the ones who had been chasing her? Where was she? The twenty-second level? She'd lost count of the stairwells she'd fled through.

She froze; she sensed channeling coming from her right. That could mean invaders, or it could mean sisters. She hesitated, but gritted her teeth. She was the Captain-General of the Green Ajah! She couldn't just run and hide.

Torchlight sprang from the hallway in question, light accompanied by ominous shadows of men with strange armor. A squad of invaders burst around the corner, and they had a pair of women with them, the ones connected by a leash. Adelorna yelped despite herself, dashing away as fast as her feet could carry her. She felt a shield push at her, but she held to *saidar* too firmly, and it didn't get into place before she rounded a corner. She continued to flee, gasping, dazed.

She rounded another corner and nearly stumbled out of a rift in the side of the Tower. She teetered on the exposed ledge, looking out upon a sky filled with terrible monsters and lines of fire. She stumbled back with a cry, turning away from the hole. There was rubble to her right. She scrambled over the rocks. The hallway continued there! She had to—

A shield shoved between her and the Source, this time locking into place. She gasped, stumbling to the ground. She wouldn't be caught! She couldn't be caught! Not that!

She tried to continue forward, but a flow of Air tightened around her ankle and dragged her back across the broken-tiled floor. No! She was pulled directly up to the squad of soldiers, now accompanied by two sets of women connected by the leashes. In each pair there was a woman wearing a gray dress and another in red and blue, with the lightning-bolt pattern.

Another woman approached, wearing the red and blue. She held something silvery in her hands. Adelorna screamed in denial, pushing at the shield. The third woman calmly knelt and snapped a silver collar on Adelorna's neck.

This wasn't happening. It *couldn't* be happening.

"Ah, very nice," the third woman said in a slow drawl. "My name is Gregana, and you shall be Sivi. Sivi will be a good *damane*. I can see it. I have waited long for this moment, Sivi."

"No," Adelorna whispered.

"Yes." Gregana smiled deeply.

Then, shockingly, the collar unclipped from Adelorna's neck and fell to the floor. Gregana looked stunned for a moment before she was consumed in a blast of fire.

Adelorna's eyes opened wide, and she shied away from the sudden heat. A corpse in a blackened red and blue dress crumbled to the ground before her, smoking and reeking of burned flesh. It was then that Adelorna became aware of an extremely powerful source of channeling coming from behind.

The invaders screamed, the women in gray weaving shields. That proved to be the wrong choice, as both women's leashes unlocked, twisting lines of Air unclasping them with dexterous speed. Just a heartbeat after that, one of the women in red and blue disappeared in a flash of lightning while the other was set upon by tongues of flame, like striking serpents. She screamed as she died, and a soldier shouted. It must have been the command to fall back, for the soldiers fled, leaving two frightened women who had been unleashed by the tongues of Air.

Adelorna turned hesitantly. A woman in white stood atop the rubble a short distance away, a massive halo of power surrounding her, her arm outstretched toward the fleeing soldiers, her eyes intense. The woman stood like vengeance itself, the power of *saidar* like a storm around her. The very air seemed alight, and her brown hair blew from the wind of the open gap in the wall beside them. Egwene al'Vere.

"Quickly," Egwene said. A group of novices scrambled over the rubble and came to Adelorna's side, helping her to her feet. She stood, amazed. She was free! Several other novices hurried to grab the two unleashed women in gray—who, oddly, just kept kneeling in the hallway. They could channel; Adelorna could feel it. Why didn't they strike back? Instead, they seemed to be weeping.

"Put them with the others," Egwene said, striding over the rubble and glancing out the broken hallway gap. "I want—" Egwene froze, then raised her hands.

Suddenly, more weaves sprang up around Egwene. Light! Was that Vora's *sa'angreal* she carried in her hand, the white fluted wand? Where had Egwene gotten *that*? Blasts of lightning flew from Egwene's open hand, flashing through the opening in the wall, and something screeched and fell outside. Adelorna stepped up to Egwene, embracing

the Source, feeling a fool for having been captured. Egwene
struck again, and another of those flying monsters fell.

"What if they're carrying captives?" Adelorna asked,
watching one of the beasts fall amid Egwene's flames.

"Then those captives are better dead," Egwene said,
turning to her. "Trust me. I know this." She turned to the
others. "Back from the hole, everyone. Those blasts may
have drawn attention.

"Shanal and Clara, watch this hole from a safe distance.
Run to us if any *to'raken* land here. Do *not* attack them."

Two girls nodded, taking up positions by the rubble. The
other novices hurried away, chivvying the two strange in-
vader women along with them. Egwene marched down the
hallway behind them, like a general at the battle lines. And
perhaps she was. Adelorna hastened to join her. "Well," she
said. "You have done nicely to organize, Egwene, though
it's good that an Aes—"

Egwene froze. Those eyes were so calm, so in control. "I
am in command until this threat passes. You will call me
Mother. Give me penance later if you must, but for now my
authority must be unquestioned. Is that clear?"

"Yes, Mother," Adelorna found herself saying, shocked.

"Good. Where are your Warders?"

"One wounded," Adelorna said. "One safe, with the
other. One dead."

"Light, woman, and you're still standing?"

Adelorna straightened her back. "What other choice do
I have?"

Egwene nodded. Why did her look of respect make Adelorna swell with pride?

"Well, I'm glad to have you," Egwene said, resuming
her walk. "We've only rescued six other Aes Sedai, none
of them Green, and we're having trouble keeping the Seanchan bottled at the eastern stairwells. I'll have one of the
novices show you how to unlock the bracelets; but don't
take any risks. Generally, it's easier—and much safer—to
kill the *damane*. How familiar are you with the Tower's
angreal storerooms?"

"Very," Adelorna said.

"Excellent," Egwene said, absently weaving as complex a
weave as Adelorna had ever seen. A line of light broke the
air, then rotated around itself, creating a hole into black-

ness. "Lucain, run and tell the others to hold. I'll be bringing more *angreal* soon."

A brunette novice bobbed her head and rushed away. Adelorna was still staring at that hole. "Traveling," she said flatly. "You really *have* rediscovered it. I thought the reports wishful rumors."

Egwene looked at her. "I'd have never shown you this, save that I just had a report that Elaida has been spreading knowledge of this weave. Knowledge of Traveling has been compromised. That means the Seanchan are likely to have it by now, assuming they've taken any women Elaida taught."

"Mother's milk in a cup!"

"Indeed," Egwene said, eyes like ice. "We need to stop them and destroy any *to'raken* we see, with captives or not. If there's any chance of stopping them from returning to Ebou Dar with someone who can Travel, we must take it."

Adelorna nodded.

"Come," Egwene said. "I need to know what items in this storeroom are *angreal*." She stepped through the hole.

Adelorna stood, stunned, still thinking over what she'd been told. "You could have run," she said. "You could have fled at any time."

Egwene turned back to her, looking through the portal. "Fled?" she asked. "If I left, it wouldn't have been *fleeing* you, Adelorna, it would have been *abandoning* you. I am the Amyrlin Seat. My place is here. I'm certain you've heard that I Dreamed this very attack."

Adelorna felt a chill. She had indeed.

"Come," Egwene repeated. "We must be quick. This is just a raid; they'll want to grab as many channelers as possible and be off with them. I intend to see that they lose more *damane* than they gain Aes Sedai."

CHAPTER
41

A Fount of Power

W ell, tie a kerchief on my face and call me Aiel," said one of Bryne's soldiers, kneeling beside the general at the prow of their narrow boat. "It really *is* there."

Gawyn squatted at the prow of his own boat, the dark waters rippling and lapping at the sides of the vessel. They'd needed thirteen boats to carry them all, and had set into the river quietly and easily—at least, they had once Siuan Sanche had finished her inspection of the boats and decided they were riverworthy. Barely.

Each vessel carried a single, shielded lantern. Gawyn could barely make out the other boats sliding over the ebony water, the soldiers rowing them in near silence as they pulled up beside the stonework embankment on Tar Valon's southwestern side. The flashes of light in the sky were distracting, and Gawyn kept finding himself glancing up, to see serpentine beasts illuminated briefly by cold white lightning or blazing crimson fire.

The White Tower itself seemed to burn. It lit a daunting profile in the sky, all white and red, outlined by flames. Smoke boiled toward the midnight clouds above, fires blazed inside many Tower windows, and a glare at the base indicated that outlying buildings and trees were also alight.

The soldiers shipped oars as Gawyn's boat gracefully slid up beside that of Bryne, passing under the lip of ancient stonework where rock overhung the river. That blocked Gawyn's view of the furious battle—though he could still hear the rumblings and pops, and an occasional spray of broken stone falling to the cobbles, sounding like distant rain.

Gawyn raised his lantern, risking just a sliver of light from the shield. With that illumination, he could make out what Bryne's soldier had seen. Tar Valon's island was rimmed by Ogier-made bulwarks, part of the original city design; they kept the island from eroding. Like most Ogier work, the bulwarks were beautiful. Here, the stone delicately arched outward from the island five or six feet above the water, forming a lip that looked like the white tip of a crashing wave. In the soft light of Gawyn's lantern, the undersides of those stones were so realistic, so delicate, that it was difficult to tell where stone ended and river began.

One of those stone ripples hid a cleft, almost impossible to spot even from this close at hand. Bryne's soldiers were steering his boat into the narrow rift, which was enclosed on both sides and top by stone. Siuan's boat went next, and Gawyn waved for his rowers to go after her. The rift turned into a very narrow tunnel, and Gawyn unshielded his lantern further, as Bryne and Siuan had done ahead. The lichen-covered stones were ribboned on the sides by dark watermarks. In many years, this passage would have been completely under water.

"It was probably designed for workers," Bryne said from up ahead, his soft voice echoing in the damp tunnel. Even the movements of the oars in the water were amplified, as were distant drips and lappings of the river. "To go out and maintain the stonework."

"I don't care *why* they built it," Siuan said. "I'm just glad it's here. And mortified I didn't know about it earlier. One of the strengths of Tar Valon has always been that the bridges make it secure. You can keep track of who goes in and who goes out."

Bryne snorted softly, the sound echoing down the tunnel. "You can never control everything in a city this size, Siuan. Those bridges, in a way, they give you a false sense of control. Sure, for an invading army, this city is impenetrable—but a place like this, tighter than a tick, can still have a dozen holes big enough for fleas to slip through."

Siuan fell silent. Gawyn calmed himself, breathing steadily. At least he was *finally* doing something to help

Egwene. It had taken far longer than he'd wanted. Light send that he was coming soon enough!

The tunnel trembled from a distant explosion. Gawyn glanced over his shoulder at the other ten boats, packed with apprehensive soldiers. They were gliding directly into a war zone where both sides were stronger than they were, both sides had little reason to like them, and both sides were wielding the One Power. It took a special kind of man to stare those odds in the eyes.

"Here," Bryne said, silhouetted against the light. He raised a hand and halted the line of boats. The tunnel had opened up to the right, where a ledge of stone—a landing with a set of stairs—waited. The watery tunnel itself continued on.

Bryne stood, bending over, and stepped out onto the ledge, mooring his boat to a cleat. The soldiers in his boat followed, each carrying a small brown package. What were they? Gawyn hadn't noticed them loading the packages on the boats. When the final soldier in that boat stepped out, he pushed the vessel forward and handed its tow rope to a soldier in Siuan's boat. As the line continued forward, they tied each boat to the one ahead of it. The last man would secure his boat to the docking pillar, and it would hold them all in place.

Gawyn stepped onto the stone ledge when his turn came and he trotted up the steps, which opened into the floor of a small alley. This entrance had probably long since been forgotten by all save the few beggars who used it for shelter. Several of the soldiers were tying up a small group of such men at the back of the alleyway. Gawyn grimaced, but said nothing. More often than not, beggars would sell secrets to any who cared to listen, and news of a hundred soldiers sneaking into the city would be worth good coin from the Tower Guard.

Bryne stood with Siuan at the mouth of the alleyway, checking the street outside. Gawyn joined them, hand on his sword. The streets were empty. The people no doubt hid in their homes, likely praying that the raid would soon pass.

The soldiers gathered in the alley. Bryne quietly ordered a squad of ten to guard the boats. Then the rest opened the soft-looking brown packages that Gawyn had noticed earlier and removed folded white tabards. They pulled these over their heads, tying them at the waist. Each was marked with the flame of Tar Valon.

Gawyn whistled softly, though Siuan stood with arms akimbo, looking indignant. "Where did you get *those*?"

"I had the women in the outer camp make them," Bryne said. "It's always a good idea to have a few copies of your enemy's uniform."

"It's not proper," Siuan said, folding her arms. "Serving on the Tower Guard is a sacred duty. They—"

"They're your *enemy*, Siuan," Bryne said sternly. "For now, at least. You're not Amyrlin anymore."

She eyed him, but held her tongue. Bryne looked over the soldiers, then nodded in approval. "This won't fool anyone up close, but from a distance, it will serve. Out onto the streets and fall into ranks. Hustle toward the Tower, as if you're rushing to help with the battle. Siuan, a globe of light or two would help with the disguise—if those who see us also see an Aes Sedai at our head, they'll be more likely to assume what we want them to."

She sniffed, but did as requested, creating two globes of light, then setting them to float in the air beside her head. Bryne gave the command, and the entire group spilled out of the alley and formed ranks. Gawyn, Siuan and Bryne took up positions at the front—Gawyn and the general walking just ahead of Siuan, as if they were Warders—and they double-timed forward down the street.

All in all, the illusion was very good. On first glance, Gawyn himself would have bought the disguise. What would be more natural to see than a squadron of Tower Guard marching to the scene of the attack, guided by an Aes Sedai and her Warders? It was certainly better than trying to sneak a hundred men through the city in alleyways, unseen.

As they approached the Tower grounds they entered the nightmare. The billowing smoke reflected red firelight, enveloping the Tower in a menacing crimson haze. Holes and gashes broke the walls of the once-majestic building; fires blazed within several of them. *Raken* commanded the air, swooping and spinning about the Tower like gulls circling a dead whale in the waves. Screams and shouts permeated the air, and the thick, acrid smoke made Gawyn's throat itch.

Bryne's soldiers slowed as they approached. There seemed to be two points of combat in the raid. The base of the Tower, with its two flanking wings, showed flashes of light. The grounds were littered with the dead and the wounded. And up above, near the middle of the Tower, several gashes were spewing fireballs and lightning back out at the invaders. The rest of the Tower seemed silent and dead, though surely fighting was going on in the corridors.

The group pulled to a halt outside the Tower grounds' iron gates. Those gates were open and completely unguarded. That seemed ominous. "Now what?" Gawyn whispered.

"We find Egwene," Siuan answered. "We start at the base, then head down to the basement floors. She was locked down there somewhere earlier today, and it's probably the first place we should look."

A spray of stone chips fell from the ceiling and rained down on the table as the White Tower shook from yet another blast. Saerin cursed to herself, wiping the chips away, then unrolled a wide piece of parchment, weighting the sides with some broken chunks of tile.

Around her, the room was in virtual chaos. They were on the ground floor, in the forward gathering room, a large square chamber situated where the eastern wing met the Tower proper. Members of the Tower Guard pulled tables out of the way to make room for the groups passing through. Aes Sedai warily glanced out the windows, watching the skies. Warders stalked like caged animals. What were they to do about flying beasts? Their best place was here, guarding the center of operations. Such as it was. Saerin had only just arrived.

A sister in green swept up to her. Moradri was a long-limbed Mayener with dark skin, and she was trailed by two handsome Warders, both also Mayener. Rumors said that they were her brothers, come to the White Tower to defend their sister, though Moradri didn't speak of the matter.

Saerin demanded, "How many?"

"The ground floor has at least forty-seven sisters," Moradri said. "Spread across the Ajahs. That's the best count I could gather, as they're fighting in small groups. I told them

we were organizing a formal command center here. Most
seemed to think that was a good idea, though many were
too tired, too shocked or too dazed to respond with much
else besides a nod."

"Mark their locations on the map here," Saerin said. "Did
you find Elaida?"

Moradri shook her head.

"Blast," Saerin muttered as the Tower shook again. "What
of any Green Sitters?"

"I didn't find any," Moradri said, glancing over her shoulder, obviously eager to get back to the fighting.

"A pity," Saerin said. "They like to call themselves the
Battle Ajah, after all. Well, that leaves me to organize the
fighting."

Moradri shrugged. "I suppose." She glanced over her
shoulder again.

Saerin eyed the Green sister, then tapped the map. "Mark
the locations, Moradri. You can be back to the fighting soon
enough, but your knowledge is more important right now."

The Green sister sighed, but quickly began to make notations on the map. As she worked, Saerin was pleased to
note Captain Chubain entering. The man looked youthful
for his forty-some winters, without a speck of gray in his
black hair. Some men were inclined to disparage his abilities because of his too-pretty face; Saerin had heard of the
humiliation those men had received by his sword in return
for the insults.

"Ah, good," she said. "Finally something is going well.
Captain, over here if you will."

He limped over, favoring his left leg. His white tabard,
hanging over mail, was scorched; his face was smudged
with soot. "Saerin Sedai," he said, bowing.

"You are wounded."

"An inconsequential wound, Aes Sedai, in the glory of a
fight such as this."

"See yourself Healed anyway," she ordered. "It would be
ridiculous for our captain of the guard to risk death because
of an 'inconsequential' wound. If it makes you stumble for
a moment we could lose you."

The man stepped closer, speaking in a low voice. "Saerin
Sedai, the Tower Guard is all but useless in this fight. With

the Seanchan using those . . . monstrous women, we can barely reach them before being ripped to pieces or blasted to ashes."

"You need to change your tactics, then, Captain," Saerin said firmly. Light, what a mess! "Tell the men to switch to bows. Do *not* risk closing on the enemy's channelers. Shoot from a distance. A single arrow could turn the battle to our side; we have their soldiers grossly outnumbered."

"Yes, Aes Sedai."

"As a White might say, it's simple logic," she said. "Captain, our most important task is to form a center of operations. Aes Sedai and soldiers alike are scrambling about independently, acting like rats faced by wolves. We need to stand together."

What she didn't mention was how embarrassed she was. The Aes Sedai had spent centuries guiding kings and influencing wars, but now—with their sanctuary assaulted— they had proven woefully inadequate in defending it. *Egwene was right,* she thought. *Not just in predicting this attack, but in berating us for being divided.* Saerin didn't need reports from Moradri or scouts to know that the Ajahs were each fighting this battle independently.

"Captain," she said. "Moradri Sedai is marking pockets of fighters on the map. Ask her which Ajah is represented in each group; she has an excellent memory, and will be able to tell you specifics. Send runners in my authority to any group of Yellow or Brown sisters. Tell them to report here, to this chamber.

"Next, send runners to the other groups and tell them that we are going to send one Brown or Yellow sister to them for Healing purposes. There will also be a group of sisters here providing Healing. Anyone wounded is to report here immediately."

He saluted.

"Oh," she added. "And send someone to the outer grounds to spot the main breaches above. We need to know where the invasion is deepest."

"Aes Sedai, . . ." he said. "The outer grounds are dangerous. Those flying above fire on anyone they see moving."

"Then send men who are good at concealing themselves," she growled.

"Yes, Aes Sedai. We—"

"This is a disaster!" an angry voice shouted.

Saerin turned to find four Red sisters entering the room. Notasha was wearing a white dress bloodied up the left side, though if the blood was her own, she'd been Healed. Katerine's mass of long black hair was frazzled and tangled with chips of stone. The other two women wore ripped dresses, faces soiled with ash.

"How *dare* they strike here!" Katerine continued, crossing the room. Soldiers ducked out of her way, and several less-influential sisters who had gathered at Saerin's order suddenly found things to do at the corners of the room. Distant booms sounded, like the noises of an Illuminator's display.

"They dare because they have the means and the desire, obviously," Saerin replied, shoving down her annoyance and maintaining her calm. With difficulty. "So far, the strike has proven remarkably effective."

"Well, I'm assuming command here," Katerine growled. "We need to scour the Tower and eliminate each of them!"

"You will *not* take command," Saerin said firmly. Insufferable woman! Calm, remain calm. "Nor will we go on the offensive."

"And you will dare stop me?" Katerine snarled, the glow of *saidar* a burning light around her. "A *Brown*?"

Saerin raised an eyebrow. "Since when did the Mistress of Novices outrank a Sitter in the Hall, Katerine?"

"I—"

"Egwene al'Vere predicted this," Saerin said, grimacing. "We can assume, therefore, that the other things she told us about the Seanchan are true. The Seanchan seize women who can channel and use them as weapons. They have brought no ground force; it would be near impossible to march them this far through hostile territory anyway. That means this is a *raid*, intended to seize as many sisters as possible.

"The battle has already stretched long for a raid, perhaps because we've done such a poor job of resisting that they feel they can take their time. Either way, we need to form a unified front and hold our ground. Once the battle goes more roughly for them, they will withdraw. We are in no position whatsoever to 'scour the Tower' and force them out."

Katerine hesitated, considering that. Another boom sounded outside.

"Where *do* those keep coming from?" Saerin asked in annoyance. "Haven't they made enough holes?"

"That wasn't directed at the Tower, Saerin Sedai!" called one of the soldiers at the room's doorway, standing just outside in the garden.

He's right, Saerin realized. *The Tower didn't shake. It didn't the time before, either.* "What are they firing on? People down below?"

"No, Aes Sedai!" the guard said. "I think it was a blast thrown from within the Tower, launched from one of the upper floors out at the flying creatures."

"Well, at least *someone* else is fighting back," Saerin said. "Where was it launched from?"

"I didn't see," the soldier said, still watching the skies. "Light, there it goes again! And again!" Red and yellow reflected from the smoke above, bathing the garden in light barely visible through the door and windows. *Raken* screamed in pain.

"Saerin Sedai!" Captain Chubain said, turning from a group of wounded soldiers. Saerin hadn't seen them enter; she'd been too caught up with Katerine. "These men are down from the upper levels. It appears that there's a second rallying point for the defense, and it's doing very well. The Seanchan are breaking off their attack below to focus there."

"Where?" Saerin asked eagerly. "Specifically?"

"The twenty-second, Aes Sedai. Northeastern quarter."

"What?" Katerine asked. "The Brown Ajah sections?"

No. That was what had been there *before*. Now, with the swapping of the Tower's corridors, that area of the Tower was . . . "The *novices' quarters*?" Saerin said. That seemed even more ridiculous. "How in the world. . . ." She trailed off, eyes widening slightly. "*Egwene*."

Each faceless Seanchan that Egwene struck down seemed to be Renna in her mind's eye. Egwene stood at an open hole in the side of the White Tower, wind pulling at her white dress, tugging at her hair, howling as if in accompaniment to her rage.

Her anger was not out of control. It was cold and distilled. The Tower was burning. She had Foretold this, she had Dreamed it, but the reality was far worse than she had feared. If Elaida had prepared for the event, the damage would have been much less. But there was no point in longing for what had not been.

Instead, she directed her anger—the anger of justice, the wrath of the Amyrlin. She blasted *to'raken* after *to'raken* from the air. They were much less maneuverable than their smaller cousins. She must have felled a dozen by now, and her actions had drawn the attention of those outside. The attack below was breaking off, the entire raid focusing on Egwene. The novices fought Seanchan raiding parties on the stairs, forcing them back. *To'raken* winged about in the air, swooping around the Tower, trying to take Egwene with shields or blasts of fire. Smaller *raken* darted through the air, crossbowmen on their backs launching bolts at her.

But she was a fount of Power, drawn from deep within the fluted rod in her hands, channeled through a group of novices and Accepted hiding in the room behind, bound to her in a circle. Egwene was *part* of the fires that burned in the Tower, bloodying the sky with their flames, painting the air with their smoke. She almost seemed not a being of flesh, but one of pure Power, sending judgment to those who had dared bring war to the Tower itself. Blasts of lightning stormed from the sky, the clouds churning above. Fire sprouted from her hands.

Perhaps she should have feared breaking the Three Oaths. But she did not. This was a fight that needed to be fought, and she did not lust for death—though, perhaps, her rage against the *sul'dam* approached it. The soldiers and *damane* were unfortunate casualties.

The White Tower, the sacred dwelling of the Aes Sedai, was under attack. They were all in danger, a danger greater than death. Those silvery collars were far worse. Egwene defended herself and each woman in the Tower.

She would *make* the Seanchan withdraw.

Shield after shield came to sever her from the source, but they were like the hands of children trying to stem the roaring flow of a waterfall. With this much power, she could not be stopped save by a full circle, and the Seanchan didn't use circles; the *a'dam* prevented it.

The attackers prepared weaves to strike her down, but each time Egwene struck first, either deflecting the balls of fire with a blast of air or simply bringing down the *to'raken* who carried the women trying to kill her.

Some beasts had flown away into the night, bearing captives. Egwene had felled the ones she could, but there had been so many *to'raken* in this raid. Some would escape. Sisters would be captured.

She formed a ball of fire in each hand, blasting another beast from the sky as it swooped too close. Yes, some would escape. But they would pay dearly. That was another goal. She had to make certain they never attacked the Tower again.

This raid had to *cost* them.

"Bryne! Above you!"

Gareth dodged to the side, rolling with a grunt, breastplate digging into his sides and belly as he hit cobblestones. Something massive in the air passed just above him, and a thudding crash followed. He came up on one knee to see a burning *raken* tumbling across the ground where he had been standing, its rider—already dead from the fireblast that had killed his mount—tumbling free like a rag doll. The *raken* corpse, still smoldering, slumped to a rest beside the Tower wall. The rider lay where he had fallen, the helm bouncing away into the darkness. One of the corpse's boots was missing.

Bryne heaved himself to his feet and pulled his belt knife free—he'd dropped his sword in the roll. He spun, scanning for danger. There was plenty of it to be found. *Raken* swooped—big ones and small ones—though most were fixated on the Tower above. The inner green at the front of the Tower was studded with chunks of stone and bodies twisted into horrific positions. Bryne's men were fighting a squadron of Seanchan soldiers; the invaders in their insectile armor had piled out of the Tower moments ago. Were the Seanchan running away from something or just looking for a fight? There were a good thirty of them.

Had the soldiers come out to this courtyard to be lifted away? Well, either way, they had met an unexpected force in Bryne's soldiers. Light be blessed, there were no channelers in the group.

With over two-to-one odds, Bryne's men should have had an easy time of it. Unfortunately, there were some few of the bigger *raken* above dropping stones and fireballs on the courtyard's occupants. And these Seanchan fought well. Very well.

Bryne called for his men to stand fast, glancing about for his sword. Gawyn—the one who had warned him earlier—stood near it, dueling two Seanchan at once. Had the boy no sense? Gawyn's force had the upper hand. He should have a swordmate with him. He—

Gawyn dispatched both Seanchan with one fluid motion. Was that Lotus Closes Its Blossom? Bryne had never seen it used so effectively against two men at once. Gawyn wiped his weapon as part of the traditional finishing flourish, then sheathed it and kicked Bryne's fallen sword up into the air and snatched it. He fell into a guard position, holding the sword, wary. Bryne's line of men was holding, despite the attacks from above. Gawyn nodded to Bryne, waving him forward with the sword.

Metal on metal rang across the courtyard, shadows thrown across the scarred grass, lit by the fires above. Bryne took his sword back and Gawyn unsheathed his own blade, on edge. "Look up there," he said and pointed with his sword.

Bryne squinted. There was a great deal of activity near a hole in one of the upper floors. He pulled free his spyglass, focusing on the location, trusting in Gawyn to warn him if danger approached.

"By the Light . . ." Bryne whispered, focusing on the gap. A solitary figure wearing white stood in the Tower's rent. It was too distant to make out her face, even with the spyglass, but whoever she was, she was certainly doing some damage to the Seanchan. Her arms were upraised with fire glowing between her hands, the burning light throwing shadows across the outer Tower wall around her. Blasts of fire flew in a steady stream, flinging *raken* from the sky.

He raised his spyglass higher, scanning the length of the Tower, searching for other signs of resistance. There was activity on the flat, circular roof. It was so distant he could barely make it out. It looked like poles being raised, followed by *raken* swooping down and . . . What? Each time a *raken* swooped by, it left dragging something.

Captives, Bryne realized with a chill. *They're taking captive Aes Sedai to the roof, tying ropes to them, then the* raken *are snatching those ropes and towing the women into the air.* Light! He caught a glimpse of one of the captives being pulled away. It looked as if she had a sack tied over her head.

"We have to get into the Tower," Gawyn said. "This fight is just a distraction."

"Agreed," Bryne said, lowering the spyglass. He glanced to the side of the courtyard, where Siuan had said she'd wait while the men fought. Time to collect her and—

She was gone. Bryne felt a spike of shock, followed by one of terror. Where was she? If that woman had gotten herself killed. . . .

But no. He could sense her inside the Tower. She wasn't hurt. This bond was such a wondrous thing, but he was too unaccustomed to it. He should have noticed that she was gone! He scanned his line of soldiers. The Seanchan had fought well, but they were visibly routed now. Their line was breaking, scattering in all directions, and Bryne barked the order for his men not to follow.

"First and second squads, gather the wounded quickly," he called. "Carry them to the side of the courtyard. Those who can walk should head directly for the boats." He grimaced. "Those who can't walk will need to wait for Aes Sedai to Heal them." The soldiers nodded. The badly wounded would be abandoned into enemy hands, but they had been warned of that possibility before coming on this mission. Recovering the Amyrlin outweighed all other concerns.

Some men would die from their wounds while they waited. There was nothing he could do about that. Hopefully, most would be Healed by the White Tower Aes Sedai. That healing would be followed by imprisonment, but there was no other choice. The team of soldiers had to keep moving quickly, and there was no time for litters to carry the wounded.

"Third and fourth squads," he began, urgent. He stopped as a familiar form in a blue dress strode out of the Tower, towing a girl in white. Of course, Siuan herself looked only faintly older than the girl, now. At times, he had difficulty connecting her to the stern woman he had met years ago.

Feeling a surge of relief, he confronted Siuan as she approached. "Who is *that*?" he demanded. "Where did you go?"

She clicked her tongue, telling the novice to wait, then pulling Bryne away to speak to him in a low voice. "Your soldiers were busy, and I decided it would be a good time to gather some information. And, I might note, we're going to have to work on your attitude, Gareth Bryne. That's not the proper way for a Warder to speak to his Aes Sedai."

"I'll start worrying about that when *you* start acting like you have two bits of sense in your head, woman. What if you'd run into Seanchan?"

"Then I would have been in danger," she said, hands on hips. "It wouldn't have been the first time. I couldn't risk being seen by other Aes Sedai with you or your soldiers. Such simple disguises won't fool a sister."

"And if you'd been recognized?" he demanded. "Siuan, these people tried to *execute* you!"

She sniffed. "Moiraine herself wouldn't recognize me with this face. The women in the Tower will just see a young Aes Sedai who looks faintly familiar. Besides, I didn't run into any of them. Just this child." She glanced at the novice; the girl had a short bob of black hair and stared, terrified, at the battle in the sky above. "Hashala, come here," Siuan called.

The novice scurried over.

"Tell this man what you told me," Siuan commanded.

"Yes, Aes Sedai," the novice said with an anxious curtsy. Bryne's soldiers made an honor guard around Siuan, and Gawyn stepped up beside Bryne. The young man's eyes kept flicking toward the deadly sky.

"The Amyrlin, Egwene al'Vere," the novice said in a quivering voice. "She was released from the cells earlier today and allowed to return to the novices' quarters. I was down in the lower kitchens when the attack came, so I don't know what has happened to her. But she's probably up on the twenty-first or twenty-second level somewhere. That's where the novices' quarters are now." She grimaced. "The inside of the Tower is a mess, these days. Nothing is where it should be."

Siuan met Bryne's eyes. "Egwene's been given forkroot in heavy doses. She'll barely be able to channel."

"We've got to reach her!" Gawyn said.

"Obviously," Bryne said, rubbing his chin. "That's why we're here. I guess we go up instead of down, then."

"You're here to rescue her, aren't you?" The novice sounded eager.

Bryne eyed the girl. *Child, I wish you hadn't made that connection.* He hated the thought of leaving a mere novice tied up in the middle of this mess. But they couldn't have her running to give warning to the White Tower Aes Sedai.

"I want to go with you," the novice said fervently. "I'm loyal to the Amyrlin. The *real* Amyrlin. Most of us are."

Bryne raised an eyebrow, glancing at Siuan.

"Let her come," the Aes Sedai said. "It's the easier option anyway." She moved over to begin asking the girl a few more questions.

Bryne glanced to the side as one of his captains, a man named Vestas, approached. "My Lord," Vestas said urgently, his voice a deep whisper. "The wounded are sorted. We lost twelve men. Another fifteen are wounded but can walk and are heading for the boats. Six are wounded too badly to go with them." Vestas hesitated. "Three men won't last the hour, my Lord."

Bryne gritted his teeth. "We move on."

"I feel that pain, Bryne," Siuan said, turning around and eyeing him. "What is it?"

"We don't have time. The Amyrlin—"

"Can wait another moment. What is it?"

"Three men," he said. "I have to leave three of my men to die."

"Not if I Heal them," Siuan said. "Show me."

Bryne made no further objection, though he did glance at the sky. Several of the *raken* had landed elsewhere in the Tower grounds, vague black shapes, lit by the fires in flickering orange. The fleeing Seanchan were congregating at them.

Those were the ground assault troops, he thought. *They really are pulling out. The raid is ending.*

Which meant they were running out of time. As soon as the Seanchan left, the White Tower would start to reorganize. They needed to reach Egwene! Light send that she hadn't been captured.

Still, if Siuan wanted to Heal the soldiers, then it was her decision. He just hoped that these three lives did not end up costing the life of the Amyrlin.

Vestas had set the three soldiers by themselves at the side of the green, beneath the boughs of a large shade tree. Bryne brought a squad of soldiers, leaving Gawyn to organize the rest of the men, and followed Siuan over to the wounded. She knelt beside the first man. Her skill in Healing was not the best; she'd warned Bryne of this ahead of time. But perhaps she could make these three well enough that they would survive to be discovered and taken by the White Tower.

She worked quickly, and Bryne noticed that she'd done herself an injustice. She seemed to do a creditable job with the Healing. Still, it took time. He scanned the courtyard, feeling his anxiety rise. Though blasts were still being exchanged on the upper floors, the lower floors and grounds were silent. The only sounds nearby were those of the groaning wounded and the crackling of flames.

Light, he thought, surveying the rubble, running his eyes over the Tower's base. The east wing's roof and far wall had been leveled, and flames flickered inside the structure. The courtyard was a mess of rubble and gouges. Smoke hung in the air, pungent and thick. Would the Ogier be willing to return and rebuild this magnificent structure? Would it ever be the same again, or had a seemingly eternal monument fallen this evening? Was he proud or grieved to have witnessed it?

A shadow moved in the darkness beside the tree.

Bryne moved without thought. Three things in him mixed: years of training with the sword, a lifetime of practiced battlefield reflexes and a new bond-enhanced awareness. All came together in one motion. His sword was out in a heartbeat, and he performed Blacklance's Last Strike, slamming his sword straight into the neck of the dark figure.

All was still. Siuan, shocked, looked up from the man she was Healing. Bryne's sword extended directly over her shoulder and into the neck of a Seanchan soldier in pure black armor. The man silently dropped a wickedly barbed shortsword slathered with a viscous liquid. Twitching, he reached for Bryne's sword, as if to push it free. His fingers gripped Bryne's arm for a moment.

Then the man slid backward off of Bryne's blade and to the ground. He spasmed once, whispering something distinct despite the bubbling of his bleeding throat. "*Marath . . . damane . . .*"

"Light burn me!" Siuan breathed, raising a hand to her breast. "What was *that*?"

"He wasn't dressed like the others," Bryne said, shaking his head. "The armor is different. Assassin of some sort."

"Light," Siuan said. "I didn't even see him! He almost seemed part of the darkness itself!"

Assassins. They always seemed to look the same, regardless of the culture. Bryne sheathed his sword. That was the first time he'd ever used Blacklance's Last Strike in combat. It was a simple form, intended for only one thing: speed. Draw the sword and strike into the neck in one fluid motion. If you missed, you usually died.

"You saved my life," Siuan said, looking up at Bryne. Her face was mostly shadowed. "By the seas at midnight," she said, "the blasted girl was *right*."

"Who?" Bryne asked, warily scanning the darkness for more assassins. He waved curtly, and his men sheepishly opened their lanterns further. The assassin's attack had come so quickly that they had barely moved. If Bryne hadn't had the speed of a Warder bond. . . .

"Min," Siuan said, sounding tired. Those Healings seemed to have taken a lot out of her. "She said I had to stay near you." She paused. "If you hadn't come tonight, I would have died."

"Well," Bryne said, "I *am* your Warder. I suspect it won't be the only time I save you." Why had it grown so warm all of a sudden?

"Yes," Siuan said, standing up. "But this is different. Min said I'd die, and . . . No, wait. That's *not* what Min said exactly. She said that if I didn't stay close to you, we'd both die."

"What are you—" Bryne said, turning toward her.

"Hush!" Siuan said, taking his head in her hands. He felt a strange prickling sensation. Was she using the Power on him? What was going on? He recognized that shock, like ice in the veins! She was Healing him! But why? He wasn't wounded.

Siuan took her hands off his face, then teetered slightly

with a sudden look of exhaustion. He grabbed her, to help steady her, but she shook her head and righted herself. "Here," she said, grabbing his sword arm, twisting it so that the wrist was visible. There, pressed into his skin, was a tiny black pin. She yanked it free. Bryne felt a chill totally unrelated to the Healing.

"Poisoned?" he asked, glancing at the dead man. "When he reached for my arm, it wasn't a simple death spasm."

"Probably had a numbing agent on it," Siuan muttered angrily, letting him help her sit down. She tossed the pin aside and it suddenly burst into flames, the poison evaporating beneath the heat of her channeling.

Bryne ran a hand through his hair. His brow was damp. "Did you . . . Heal it?"

Siuan nodded. "It was surprisingly easy; there was only a little in your system. It would have killed you anyway. You'll have to thank Min next time you see her, Bryne. She just saved both of our lives."

"But I wouldn't have poisoned if I hadn't come!"

"Don't try to apply logic to a viewing or Foretelling like this," Siuan said, grimacing. "You're alive. I'm alive. I suggest we leave it at that. You feel good enough to keep going?"

"Does it matter?" Bryne said. "I'm not about to let you go on without me."

"Let's move, then," Siuan said, taking a deep breath and climbing to her feet. That rest hadn't been nearly long enough, but he didn't challenge her. "These three soldiers of yours will survive the night. I've done what I can for them."

Egwene sat, exhausted, on a pile of rubble, staring out of the hole in the White Tower, watching fires burning below. Figures moved about them, and one by one, the fires winked out. Whoever had been running the resistance was quick-minded enough to realize that the fires could prove as dangerous as the Seanchan. But a few sisters weaving Air or Water could make short work of the flames, preserving the Tower. What was left of it.

Egwene closed her eyes and lay back, resting against the fragments of a wall, feeling the fresh breeze blow across her. The Seanchan were gone, the last *to'raken* vanishing into the night. That moment, watching it flee, was the moment when Egwene realized how hard she'd taxed herself and the poor novices she'd been drawing through. She'd released them with orders to go directly to sleep. The other women she'd gathered were caring for wounded or working on the fires on the upper levels.

Egwene wanted to help. A part of her did, at least. A sliver. But Light, she was tired! She couldn't channel another trickle, not even using the *sa'angreal*. She'd pushed the limits of what she could manage. But she was so worn out now that she wouldn't be able to embrace the Source if she tried.

She'd fought. She'd been glorious and destructive, the Amyrlin of judgment and fury, Green Ajah to the core. And still, the Tower had burned. And still, more *to'raken* had escaped than had fallen. The count of wounded among those she'd gathered was somewhat encouraging. Only three novices and one Aes Sedai dead, while they'd gathered ten *damane* and killed dozens of soldiers. But what of the other floors? The White Tower would not come out ahead in this battle.

The White Tower was broken, physically now as well as spiritually. They'd need a strong leader to rebuild. The next few days would be pivotal. It made her more than exhausted to consider the work she'd need to do.

She had protected many. She had resisted and fought. But this day would still mark one of the greatest disasters in the history of the Aes Sedai.

Can't think of that, she told herself. *Have to focus on what to do to fix things. . . .*

She would get up soon. She would lead the novices and Aes Sedai on these upper floors as they cleaned up and assessed the damage. She would be strong and capable. The others would be tempted to fall into despair, and she needed to be positive. For them.

But she *could* take a few minutes. She just needed to rest for a little while. . . .

She barely noticed when someone picked her up. She tiredly opened her eyes, and—though numb of mind—was astonished to find that she was being carried by Gawyn Trakand. His forehead was smeared with crusty dried blood, but his face was determined. "I've got you, Egwene," he said, glancing down. "I'll protect you."

Oh, she thought, closing her eyes again. *Good. Such a pleasant dream.* She smiled.

Wait. No. That wasn't right. She wasn't supposed to be leaving the Tower. She tried to voice complaint, but she could barely mumble.

"Fish guts," she heard Siuan Sanche say. "What did they do to her?"

"Is she wounded?" another voice. Gareth Bryne.

No, Egwene thought numbly. *No, you have to let me go. I can't leave. Not now. . . .*

"They just left her there, Siuan," Gawyn said. His voice was so nice to hear. "Defenseless in the hallway! Anyone could have come upon her like that. What if the Seanchan had discovered her?"

I destroyed them, she thought with a smile, thoughts slipping away from her. *I was a burning warrior, a hero called by the Horn. They won't dare face me again.* She almost fell asleep, but being jostled by Gawyn's steps kept her awake. Barely.

"Ho!" She distantly heard Siuan's voice. "What's this? Light, Egwene! Where did you get *this*? This is the most powerful one in the Tower!"

"What is it, Siuan?" Bryne's voice asked.

"Our way out," Siuan said distantly. Egwene sensed something. Channeling. Powerful channeling. "You asked about sneaking back out with all the activity in the court-yard? Well, with this, I'm strong enough for Traveling. Let's go collect those soldiers with the boats and hop back to camp."

No! Egwene thought, clawing through her drowsiness, forcing her eyes open. *I'm winning, don't you see? If I offer leadership now, when the rubble is being cleared, they'll see me as Amyrlin for certain! I have to stay! I have to—*

Gawyn carried her through the gateway, leaving the hall-ways of the White Tower behind.

Saerin finally let herself sit. The gathering room that was her center of operations had also become a room for sepa-rating and Healing the wounded. Yellow and Brown sisters moved down the lines of soldiers, servants, and other sisters, focusing on the worst cases first. There were a frightful number of dead, including over twenty Aes Sedai so far. But the Seanchan had withdrawn, as Saerin had predicted. Thank the light for that.

Saerin herself sat at the far northwestern corner of the room, beneath a fine painting of Tear in spring, perched on a short stool and accepting reports as they came. The wounded groaned and the room smelled of blood and of healall, which was used on those whose wounds didn't demand immediate Healing. The room also smelled of smoke. That was ever-present tonight. More and more soldiers approached her, handing in reports of damage and casualties. Saerin didn't want to read further, but it was better than listening to those groans. Where under the Light was Elaida?

Nobody had seen anything of the Amyrlin during the battle, but much of the upper Tower had been cut off from the lower portions. Hopefully, the Amyrlin and the Hall could be gathered soon to present a strong leadership in the crisis.

Saerin accepted another report, then raised her eyebrows at what it said. Only three novices in Egwene's group of over sixty had died? And only one sister out of some forty she had gathered? *Ten* Seanchan channelers captured, over thirty *raken* blown from the air? Light! That made Saerin's own efforts seem downright amateur by comparison. And this was the woman Elaida kept trying to insist was simply a *novice*?

"Saerin Sedai?" a man's voice asked.

"Hmm?" she asked, distracted.

"You should hear what this Accepted has to say."

Saerin looked up, realizing that the voice belonged to Captain Chubain. He had his hand on the shoulder of a young Arafellin Accepted with blue eyes and a plump round face. What was her name? Mair, that was it. The poor child looked ragged. Her face sported a number of cuts and some scrapes that would likely bruise. Her Accepted dress was ripped on the sleeve and shoulder.

"Child?" Saerin asked, glancing at Chubain's worried face. What was wrong?

"Saerin Sedai," the girl whispered, curtsying, then wincing at the action. "I. . . ."

"Spit it out, child," Saerin demanded. "This isn't a night for dawdling."

Mair looked down. "It's the Amyrlin, Saerin Sedai. Elaida Sedai. I was attending her tonight, taking transcriptions for her. And. . . ."

"And what?" Saerin said, feeling a growing chill.

The girl started crying. "The entire wall burst in, Saerin Sedai. The rubble covered me; I think they thought I was dead. I couldn't do anything! I'm sorry!"

Light intercede! Saerin thought. *She can't be saying what I think she is. Can she?*

Elaida awoke to a very odd sensation. Why was her bed moving? Rippling, undulating. So rhythmic. And that wind! Had Carlya left the window open? If so, the maid would be beaten. She'd been warned. She'd been—

This was not her bed. Elaida opened her eyes and found herself looking down at a dark landscape hundreds of feet below. She was tied to the back of some strange beast. She couldn't move. Why couldn't she move? She reached for the Source, then felt a sudden, sharp pain, as though she had suddenly been beaten on every inch of her body with a thousand rods.

She reached up, dazed, feeling the collar at her throat. There was a dark figure riding in the saddle next to her; no lanterns lit the woman's face, but Elaida could *feel* her somehow. Elaida could just barely remember spending time dangling in the air, tied to a rope, as she fell in and out of consciousness. When had she been pulled up? What was happening?

A voice whispered from the night. "I shall forgive that little mistake. You have been *marath'damane* for very long, and bad habits are to be expected. But you will not reach for the Source again without permission. Do you understand?"

"Release me!" Elaida bellowed.

The pain returned tenfold, and Elaida retched at the intensity of it. Her bile and sick-up fell over the side of the beast and dropped far to the ground below.

"Now, now," the voice said, patient, like a woman speaking to a very young child. "You must learn. Your name is

Suffa. And Suffa will be a good *damane*. Yes she will. A very, very good *damane*."

Elaida screamed again, and this time, she didn't stop when the pain came. She just kept screaming out into the uncaring night.

CHAPTER
42

Before the Stone of Tear

W e don't know the names of the women who were
in Graendal's palace, Lews Therin said. *We
can't add them to the list.*

Rand tried to ignore the madman. That proved impossible. Lews Therin continued.

*How can we continue the list if we don't know the names!
In war, we sought out the Maidens who had fallen. We
found every one! The list is flawed! I can't continue!*

It's not your list! Rand growled. *It's mine, Lews Therin.
MINE!*

No! the madman sputtered. *Who are you? It's mine! I
made it. I can't continue now that they're dead. Oh, Light!
Balefire? Why did we use balefire! I promised that I would
never do that again. . . .*

Rand squeezed his eyes shut, holding tightly to
Tai'daishar's reins. The warhorse picked his way down the
street; the hooves hit packed earth, one after another.

What have we become? Lews Therin whispered. *We're
going to do it again, aren't we? Kill them all. Everyone
we've loved. Again, again, again. . . .*

"Again and again," Rand whispered. "It doesn't matter,
as long as the world survives. They cursed me before, swore
at Dragonmount and by my name, but they lived. We're
here, ready to fight. Again and again."

"Rand?" Min asked.

He opened his eyes. She rode her dun mare next to
Tai'daishar. He couldn't let her, or any of them, see him slipping. They mustn't know how close he was to collapsing.

So many names we don't know, Lews Therin whispered.
So many dead by our hand.

And it was just the beginning.

"I am well, Min," he said. "I was thinking."

"About the people?" Min asked. The wooden walks of
Bandar Eban were filled with people. Rand no longer saw
the colors of their clothing; he saw how worn that clothing
was. He saw the rips in the magnificent fabric, the threadbare patches, the dirt and the stains. Virtually everyone in
Bandar Eban was a refugee of one sort or another. They
watched him with haunted eyes.

Each time he'd conquered a kingdom before, he'd left it
better than when he'd arrived. Rand had removed Forsaken
tyrants, brought an end to warfare and sieges. He'd cast out
Shaido invaders, he'd delivered food, he'd created stability.
Each land he'd destroyed had, essentially, been saved at the
same time.

Arad Doman was different. He'd brought in food—but
that food had drawn even more refugees, straining his supplies. Not only had he failed to give them peace with the
Seanchan, he had appropriated their only troops and sent
them up to watch the Borderlands. The seas were still un-
safe. The tiny Seanchan empress hadn't trusted him. She
would continue her attacks, perhaps double them.

The Domani would be trampled beneath the hooves of
war, crushed between the invading Trollocs to the north
and the Seanchan to the south. And Rand was leaving them.

Somehow, the people realized that, and it was very hard
for Rand to look at them. Their hungry eyes accused him:
Why bring hope, then let it dry up, like a newly dug well
during a drought? Why force us to accept you as our ruler,
only to abandon us?

Flinn and Naeff had ridden before him; he could see their
black coats ahead as they sat their horses watching Rand's
procession approach the city square. The pins sparkled on
their high collars. The fountain in the square still flowed
among gleaming copper horses leaping from copper waves.
Which of those silent Domani continued to shine the fountain, when no king ruled and half the merchant council was
lost?

Rand's Aiel hadn't been able to track down enough of the
council to form a majority; he suspected that Graendal had

killed or captured enough of them to keep a new king from ever being chosen. If any of the merchant council members had been pretty enough, they'd have joined the ranks of her pets—which meant that Rand had killed them.

Ah, Lews Therin said. *Names I can add to the list. Yes. . . .*

Bashere rode up beside Rand, knuckling his mustaches, looking thoughtful. "Your will is done," he said.

"Lady Chadmar?" Rand asked.

"Returned to her mansion," Bashere said. "We've done the same with the other four members of the merchant council the Aiel were holding near the city."

"They understand what they are to do?"

"Yes," Bashere said, sighing. "But I don't think they'll do it. If you ask me, the moment we're gone they'll bolt from the city like thieves fleeing a prison once the guards leave."

Rand gave no reaction. He'd ordered the merchant council to choose new members, then pick a king. But Bashere was probably right. Already, Rand had reports from the other cities along the coast, where he'd told his Aiel to withdraw. The city leaders were vanishing, running before the presumed Seanchan assault.

Arad Doman, as a kingdom, was finished. Like a table laden with too much weight, it would soon collapse. *It is not my problem,* Rand thought, not looking at the people. *I did everything I could.*

That wasn't true. Though he'd wanted to help the Domani, his real reasons for coming had been to deal with the Seanchan, to find out what had happened to the king, and to track down Graendal. Not to mention to secure what he could of the Borderlands.

"What news from Ituralde?" Rand asked.

"Nothing good, I'm afraid," Bashere said grimly. "He's had skirmishes with Trollocs, but you knew that already. The Shadowspawn always withdraw quickly, but he warns that something is gathering. His scouts catch glimpses of forces large enough to overrun him. If the Trollocs are gathering there, then they're likely gathering elsewhere as well. Particularly the Gap."

Curse those Borderlanders! Rand thought. *I will have to do something about them. Soon.* Reaching the square, he reined in Tai'daishar and nodded to Flinn and Naeff.

At his signal, they each opened a large gateway in the city square. Rand had wanted to leave directly from Lady Chadmar's mansion grounds, but that would have been to vanish like a thief, there one day and gone the next. He would at least let the people see that he was leaving and know that they had been left to themselves.

They lined the boardwalks, much as they had when Rand had first entered the city. If possible, they were more quiet now than they had been. Women in their sleek gowns, men in colorful coats and ruffled sleeves beneath. There were many without the coppery skin of the Domani. Rand had lured so many to the city with promises of food.

Time to go. He approached one of the gateways, but a voice called out. "Lord Dragon!"

The voice was easy to hear, since the crowds were so silent. Rand turned in his saddle, seeking out the source of the voice. A willowy man in a red Domani coat—buttoned at the waist, open in a "V" up the front, with a ruffled shirt beneath. His golden earrings sparkled as he elbowed his way through the crowd. The Aiel intercepted him, but Rand recognized him as one of the dockmasters. Rand nodded for the Aiel to let the man—Iralin was his name—approach.

Iralin hurried up to Tai'daishar. He was uncharacteristically clean shaven for a Domani man, and his eyes were shadowed from lack of sleep.

"My Lord Dragon," the man said in a hushed voice, standing beside Rand's horse, "The food! It has spoiled."

"What food?" Rand asked.

"All of it," the man said, voice taut. "Every barrel, every sack, every bit in our stores and in the Sea Folk ships. My Lord! It's not just full of weevils. It's grown black and bitter, and it makes men sick to eat it!"

"*All* of it?" he repeated, shocked.

"Everything," Iralin said softly. "Hundreds upon hundreds of barrels. It happened suddenly, in the blink of an eye. One moment, it was good, the next moment. . . . My Lord, so many people have come to the city because they heard we had food! Now we have *nothing*. What will we do?"

Rand closed his eyes.

"My Lord?" Iralin asked.

Rand opened his eyes and kicked Tai'daishar into motion. He left the dockmaster behind, mouth open, and passed through the gateway. There was nothing more Rand could do. Nothing more he *would* do.

He put the coming starvation out of his mind. It was shocking how easy that was.

Bandar Eban vanished, those too-silent people vanished. The moment he passed through the gateway, cheers exploded from the waiting crowds. It was so shocking, such a contrast, that Rand pulled Tai'daishar up short, stunned.

Tear spread before him. This was one of the great cities, massive and sprawling, and the gateways opened directly into Feaster's Run, one of the main city squares. A short rank of Asha'man saluted with fists to chests. Rand had sent them on earlier in the morning to prepare the city for his arrival and clear the square for gateways.

The people continued their cheers. Thousands had gathered, and Banners of Light flapped atop dozens of poles held aloft by the crowd. The adulation hit Rand like a wave of reproach. He didn't deserve such praise. Not after what he had done in Arad Doman.

Must keep moving, he thought, kicking Tai'daishar into motion again. The horse's hooves fell on flagstones here, rather than rain-dampened dirt. Bandar Eban was a large city, but Tear was something else entirely. Streets snaked across the landscape, lined with buildings that most country folk would have called cramped, but that were ordinary to the Tairens. Many of the peaked slate or tile roofs had men or boys perched on their edges, hoping for a better view of the Lord Dragon. The building stones were a lighter hue here than they had been in Bandar Eban, and they were the preferred building material. Perhaps that was because of the fortress that loomed above the city. The Stone of Tear, it was called. A relic of a previous age, still impressive.

Rand trotted forward, Min and Bashere still riding nearby. Those crowds roared. So loud. Nearby, two flapping pendants got caught in the wind, and inexplicably entangled. The men holding them aloft, near the front of the crowd, lowered them and tried to pull them apart, but they were knotted tight, somehow twisted that way by the wind. Rand passed them with barely any notice. He'd stopped feeling surprise at what his *ta'veren* nature could do.

Rand was surprised, however, to see so many foreigners

in the crowd. That wasn't so unusual; Tear always saw a lot of outlanders—it welcomed those who would trade spices and silks from the east, porcelain from the seas, grains or tabac from the north, and stories from anywhere they could be gleaned. However, Rand had found that outlanders—no matter what the city—paid him less heed when he visited. This was true even when those outlanders were from another country he had conquered. When he was in Cairhien, the Cairhienin would fawn over him—but if he were in Illian, the Cairhienin would avoid him. Perhaps they didn't like being reminded that their lord and their enemy's lord were the same man.

Here, however, he had no trouble counting foreigners: Sea Folk with their dark skin and their loose, bright clothing; Murandians, in their long coats and waxed mustaches; bearded Illianers with upturned collars; pale-faced Cairhienin with stripes on their clothing. There were also men and women who wore simple Andoran wool. Fewer of the foreigners cheered than locals, but they were there, watchful.

Bashere scanned the crowd.

"The people seem surprised," Rand found himself saying.

"You've been away for a time." Bashere knuckled his mustaches in thought. "No doubt the rumors have flown swifter than arrows, and many an innkeeper has spun tales of your death or disappearance to encourage another round of drinks."

"Light! I seem to spend half of my life trampling down one rumor or another. When will it end?"

Bashere laughed. "When you can stop *rumor* itself, I'll get off my horse and ride a goat! Ha! And become one of the Sea Folk as well."

Rand fell silent. His followers continued to pile through the gateways. As the Saldaeans entered Tear, nearly to a man they held their lances up straighter, their horses prancing. The Aes Sedai wouldn't be caught preening, but they did look less wilted, their ageless faces regarding the crowd with a sagacious manner. And the Aiel—their prowling steps a little less wary, their expressions less guarded— seemed more comfortable with the cheering than they had with those quiet, accusing Domani eyes.

Bashere and Rand moved over to the side, Min following silently. She looked distracted. Nynaeve and Cadsuane had not been in the mansion when Rand had announced his departure. What could they be up to? He doubted they were together; those women barely tolerated being in the same room. Anyway, they would hear where he had gone, and they would find him. From this point on, Rand would be easy to locate. No more hiding in wooded manors. No more traveling alone. Not with Lan and his Malkieri riding to the Gap. There wasn't enough time left.

Bashere watched the open gateways, the Aiel passing through on silent feet. This method of voyaging was becoming familiar to them.

"Are you going to tell Ituralde?" Bashere finally asked. "About your withdrawal?"

"He will hear," Rand said. "His messengers were ordered to bring reports to Bandar Eban. They will soon discover I'm no longer there."

"And if he leaves the Borderlands to resume his war against the Seanchan?"

"Then he'll slow the Seanchan down," Rand said. "And keep them from nipping at my heels. That will be as good a use for him as any."

Bashere eyed him.

"What do you expect me to do, Bashere?" Rand asked quietly. That look was a challenge, if a subtle one, but Rand would not rise to it. His anger remained frozen.

Bashere sighed. "I don't know," he said. "This whole thing is a mess, and I don't see any way out of it, man. Going to war with the Seanchan at our backs, that's as bad a position as I can think of."

"I know," Rand said, looking over the city. "Tear will be theirs by the time this is through, probably Illian as well. Burn me, but we'll be lucky if they don't conquer all the way up to Andor while our backs are turned."

"But—"

"We have to assume that Ituralde will abandon his post once news of my failure reaches him. That means our next move *has* to be toward the Borderlander army. Whatever complaint your kinsmen have with me, it must be settled quickly. I have little patience for men who abandon their duties."

Have we done that? Lews Therin asked. *Who have we abandoned?*

Quiet! Rand growled. *Go back to your tears, madman, and leave me be!*

Bashere leaned back thoughtfully in his saddle. If he was thinking of Rand abandoning the Domani, he said nothing. Finally, he shook his head. "I don't know what Tenobia is about. Could be as simple as her anger at me for leaving to follow you; could be as difficult as a demand that you submit to the will of the Borderlander monarchs. I can't imagine what would draw her and the others away from the Blight at a time like this."

"We will soon find out," Rand said. "I want you to take a couple of the Asha'man and find out where Tenobia and the others are camped. Maybe we'll discover they've given up this fool's parade and turned back toward where they belong."

"All right, then," Bashere said. "Let me see my men settled and I'll be off."

Rand nodded sharply, then turned his mount and began to trot down the street. The people were lined up on either side, ushering him onward. The last time he had visited Tear, he had tried to come in disguise, for all the good it had done him. Anyone who knew the signs would have known he was in the city. Unusual events—banners tying themselves together, men falling from buildings and landing unharmed—were only the beginning. His *ta'veren* effect seemed to be growing more powerful, causing increasingly greater distortions. And more dangerous ones.

During his last visit, Tear had been besieged by rebels, but the city hadn't suffered. Tear had too much trade to be bothered by something as simple as a siege. Most people had lived as usual, barely acknowledging the rebels. Nobles could play their games, as long as they didn't disrupt more honest folks.

Besides, everyone had known that the Stone would hold, as it almost always had. It might have been rendered obsolete by Traveling, but for invaders who didn't have access to the One Power, the Stone was virtually impossible to take. In and of itself, it was more massive than many cities—a gargantuan sprawl of walls, towers and sheer fortifications without a single seam in its rock. It included forges, warehouses, thousands of defenders, and its own fortified dock.

None of that would be much use against an army of Seanchan with *damane* and *raken*.

Crowds lined the street up to the Stone Verge, the large open space that surrounded the Stone on three sides. *It's a killing field,* Lews Therin said.

Here, another crowd cheered Rand. The gates to the Stone were open, and a welcoming delegation awaited him. Darlin—once a High Lord, now King of Tear—sat astride a brilliant white stallion. Shorter than Rand by at least a head, the Tairen had a short black beard and close-cropped hair. His prominent nose kept him from being handsome, but Rand had found him very keen of mind and of honor. After all, Darlin had opposed Rand from the start, rather than joining those who had hastened to worship him. A man whose allegiance was hard to win was often one whose allegiance would also be secure when he was out of your sight.

Darlin bowed to Rand. Pale-faced Dobraine, dressed in a blue coat and white trousers, sat astride a roan gelding beside the King. His expression was unreadable, though Rand suspected he was still disappointed in being sent from Arad Doman so soon.

Lines of Defenders of the Stone stood before the wall, swords held before them, breastplates and ridged helmets shined near to glowing. Their puffy sleeves were striped with black and gold, and above them waved the banner of Tear, a half-red, half-gold field marked with three silver crescents. Rand could see that the square inside the wall was bursting with soldiers, many in the colors of the Defenders, but many wearing no uniform beyond a strap of red and gold tied around their arms. Those would be the new recruits, the men Rand had ordered Darlin to gather.

It was a display to produce awe. Or perhaps to stroke a man's pride. Rand stopped Tai'daishar before Darlin. Unfortunately, the rooster Weiramon accompanied the King, sitting his horse just behind Darlin. Weiramon was so lacking in wits that Rand would barely have trusted him to work a field unsupervised, let alone command a squad of troops. True, the short man was brave, but that was likely only because he was too slow of thought to consider most

dangers. As always, Weiramon looked even more the fool
for attempting to style himself as anything other than a buf-
foon; his beard was waxed, his hair was carefully arranged
to hide just how much he was balding and his clothing was
rich—a coat and breeches cut as if to be a field uniform, but
no man would wear such fine cloth into battle. No man but
Weiramon.

I like him, Lews Therin thought.

Rand started. *You don't like anyone!*

He's honest, Lews Therin replied, then laughed. *More
than I am, for certain! A man doesn't choose to be an idiot,
but he does choose to be loyal. We could do much worse
than have this man as a follower.*

Rand kept his tongue. Arguing with the madman was
pointless. Lews Therin made decisions without reason. At
least he wasn't humming about a pretty woman again. That
could be distracting.

Darlin and Dobraine bowed to Rand, Weiramon mim-
icking them. There were others behind the King, of course.
Lady Caraline was a given; the slender Cairhienin was as
beautiful as Rand remembered. A white opal hung on her
forehead, the golden chain woven into her dark hair. Rand
had to force himself to look away. She looked too much like
her cousin, Moiraine. Sure enough, Lews Therin started
naming off the names on the list, Moiraine at the forefront.

Rand steeled himself, listening to the dead man in the
back of his mind as he studied the rest of the group. All of
the remaining High Lords and Ladies of Tear were there—
atop their own mounts. Simpering Anaiyella sat her bay
horse beside Weiramon. And . . . was she wearing a handkerchief favor bearing his colors? Rand had thought her a
little more discriminating than that. Torean had a smile on
that lumpy face of his. A pity that he was still alive when
far better men among the High Lords had died. Simaan, Es-
tanda, Tedosian, Hearne—all four had opposed Rand, leading the siege against the Stone. Now they bowed to him.

Alanna was there, too. Rand didn't look at her. She was
sorrowful, he could tell through their bond. As well she
should be.

"My Lord Dragon," Darlin said, straightening in his saddle, "thank you for sending Dobraine with your wishes."
His voice conveyed his displeasure. He'd rushed to gather

an army at Rand's urgent command, and then Rand had forced him to do nothing for weeks. Well, the men would be glad for the extra weeks of training soon.

"The army is ready," Darlin continued, hesitant. "We are prepared to leave for Arad Doman."

Rand nodded. He'd originally intended to set Darlin in Arad Doman so he could pull Aiel and Asha'man out for placement elsewhere. He turned, glancing back at the crowds, absently realizing why there were so many foreigners among them. Most of the nationals had been recruited for the army, and now stood in ranks inside the Stone.

Perhaps the people in the square and on the streets hadn't been there to cheer Rand's arrival. Perhaps they thought they were cheering their departing armies off to victory.

"You have done well, King Darlin," Rand said. "It's about time someone in Tear learned to obey orders. I know your men are impatient, but they will have to wait a short time longer. Make rooms for me in the Stone and see to quartering Bashere's soldiers and the Aiel."

Darlin's confusion deepened. "Very well. Are we not needed in Arad Doman, then?"

"What Arad Doman needs, nobody can give," Rand said. "Your forces will be coming with me."

"Of course, my Lord. And . . . where will we be marching?"

"To Shayol Ghul."

CHAPTER

43

Sealed to the Flame

E gwene sat quietly in her tent, hands in her lap. She
controlled her shock, her burning anger and her incredulity.

Plump, pretty Chesa sat silently on a cushion in the corner, sewing embroidery on the hem of one of Egwene's
dresses, looking as content as a person could be, now that
her mistress had returned. The tent was secluded, set in
its own grove within the Aes Sedai camp. Egwene had allowed no attendants besides Chesa this morning. She had
even turned away Siuan, who had undoubtedly come to offer some kind of apology. Egwene needed time to think, to
prepare, to deal with her failure.

And it *was* a failure. Yes, it had been forced on her by
others, but those others were her followers and friends.
They would know her anger for their part in this fiasco. But
first she needed to look inward, to judge what she should
have done better.

She sat in her wooden chair, high-backed, with scroll-
work patterns across the armrests. Her tent was as she had
left it, desk orderly, blankets folded, pillows stacked in the
corner, obviously kept dusted by Chesa. Like a museum
used to instruct children of days past.

Egwene had been as forceful as possible with Siuan during their meetings in *Tel'aran'rhiod*, and yet they'd *still*
come against her wishes. Perhaps she had been too secretive. It was a danger—secrecy. It was what had pulled down
Siuan. The woman's time as head of the Blue Ajah's eyes-
and-ears had taught her to be parsimonious with information, doling it out like a stingy employer on payday. If the

others had known the importance of Siuan's work, perhaps they wouldn't have decided to work against her.

Egwene ran her fingers along the smooth, tightly woven pouch she wore tied to her belt. Inside was a long, thin item, retrieved secretly from the White Tower earlier in the morning.

Had she fallen into the same trap as Siuan? It was a danger. She had been trained by Siuan, after all. If Egwene had explained in more detail how well her work in the White Tower was going, would the others have stayed their hands?

It was a difficult line to walk. There *were* many secrets that an Amyrlin had to hold. To be transparent would be to lose her edge of authority. But with Siuan herself, Egwene should have been more forthcoming. The woman was too accustomed to taking action on her own. The way she had kept that dream *ter'angreal* against the Hall's knowledge and wishes was an indication of that. Yet Egwene had approved of that, unconsciously encouraging Siuan to defy authority.

Yes, Egwene had made mistakes. She could not lay all the blame on Siuan, Bryne and Gawyn. She had likely made other mistakes as well; she would need to look at her own actions in more detail later.

For now, she turned her attention to a greater problem. Disaster had struck. She'd been pulled from the White Tower on the brink of success. What was to be done? She did not get up and pace in thought. To pace was to show nervousness or frustration, and she had to learn to be reserved at all times, lest she unwittingly fall into bad habits. So she remained seated, arms on the hand rests, wearing a fine silken gown of green with yellow patterns on the bodice.

How odd it felt to be in that skirt. How *wrong*. Her white dresses, though forced upon her, had become something of a symbol of defiance. To change now meant an end to her strike. She was tired, emotionally and physically, from the night's battle. But she couldn't give in to that. This wouldn't be her first near-sleepless night before a very important day of decisions and problems.

She found herself tapping her armrest and forced herself to stop.

There was no way she could return to the White Tower

as a novice now. Her defiance had worked only because she had been a captive Amyrlin. If she went back willingly, she would be seen as subservient, or as arrogant. Besides, Elaida would certainly have her executed this time.

And so she was stuck, just as she had been when she'd first been taken by the White Tower's agents. She gritted her teeth. She'd once thought, mistakenly, that the Amyrlin wouldn't be so easily tossed about by random twists in the Pattern. She was supposed to be in control. Everyone else spent their days reacting, but the Amyrlin was a woman of action!

She was realizing more and more that being the Amyrlin *wasn't* different. Life was a tempest, whether you were a milkmaid or a queen. The queens were simply better at projecting control in the middle of that storm. If Egwene looked like a statue unaffected by the winds, it was actually because she saw how to bend with those winds. That gave the illusion of control.

No. It was not just an illusion. The Amyrlin *did* have more control, if only because she controlled herself and kept the tempest outside her. She swayed before the needs of the moment, but her actions were well-considered. She had to be as logical as a White, as thoughtful as a Brown, as passionate as a Blue, as decisive as a Green, as merciful as a Yellow, as diplomatic as a Gray. And yes, as vengeful as a Red, when necessary.

There was no returning to the White Tower as a novice, and she couldn't wait for negotiations. Not with the Seanchan bold enough to strike the White Tower, not with Rand completely unwatched, not with the world in chaos and the Shadow gathering its forces for the Last Battle. That left her with a difficult decision. She had a fresh army of fifty thousand troops, and the White Tower had suffered an incredible blow. The Aes Sedai would be exhausted, the Tower Guard broken and wounded.

In a few days' time, the Healings would be finished and the women rested. She didn't know if Elaida had survived the attack or not, but Egwene had to assume she was still in control. That gave Egwene a very narrow window for action.

She *knew* what the only right decision was. She didn't have time to wait for the sisters in the White Tower to make the right decision, she would have to *force* them to accept her.

She hoped that history would eventually forgive her.

She rose, threw open the flaps of her tent, and stopped dead. A man was sitting on the ground directly in front of her.

Gawyn scrambled to his feet, every bit as handsome as she remembered. He wasn't beautiful, like his half-brother. Gawyn was more solid, more *real*. Strikingly, that now made him *more* attractive to Egwene than Galad. Galad was like a being from beyond reality, a figure of legends and stories. He was like a glass statue to be placed on a table for admiration, but never touched.

Gawyn was different. Handsome, with that brilliant red-dish gold hair and those tender eyes. While Galad never worried about anything, Gawyn's concern made him genuine. As did his ability to make mistakes, unfortunately.

"Egwene," he said, righting his sword and dusting off his trouser legs. Light! Had he *slept* there in front of her tent? The sun was already halfway to its zenith. The man should have gone to take some rest!

Egwene squelched her concern and worry for him. It was not time to be a lovesick girl. It was time to be Amyrlin. "Gawyn," she said, raising a hand, stopping him as he stepped toward her. "I haven't *begun* to think about what to do with you. Other matters demand my attention. Has the Hall gathered, as I requested?"

"I think so," he said, turning to glance toward the center of camp. She could just barely make out the large gathering tent of the Hall through the scrub trees.

"Then I must appear before them," Egwene said, taking a deep breath. She began to walk forward.

"No," Gawyn said, stepping in front of her. "Egwene, we need to talk."

"Later."

"No, not *later*, burn it! I've waited months. I need to know how we stand. I need to know if you—"

"Stop!" she said.

He froze. She would *not* be taken in by those eyes, burn him! Not right now. "I said that I hadn't sorted through my feelings yet," she said coolly, "and I meant it."

He set his jaw. "I don't believe that Aes Sedai calmness,

Egwene," he said. "Not when your eyes are so much more truthful. I've sacrificed—"

"*You've* sacrificed?" Egwene interrupted, letting a little anger show. "What about what I sacrificed to rebuild the White Tower? Sacrifices that *you* undermined by acting against my express wishes? Did Siuan not tell you that I had forbidden a rescue?"

"She did," he said stiffly. "But we were worried about you!"

"Well, that *worry* was the sacrifice I demanded, Gawyn," she said, exasperated. "Don't you see what a distrust you have shown me? How can I trust *you* if you will disobey me in order to feel more comfortable?"

Gawyn didn't look ashamed; he just looked perturbed. That was actually a good sign—as Amyrlin, she needed a man who would speak his mind. In private. But in public she'd need someone who supported her. Couldn't he see that?

"You love me, Egwene," he said stubbornly. "I can see it."

"Egwene the woman loves you," she said. "But Egwene the Amyrlin is *furious* with you. Gawyn, if you'd be with me, you have to be with both the woman and the Amyrlin. I would expect you—a man who was trained to be First Prince of the Sword—to understand that distinction."

Gawyn looked away.

"You don't believe it, do you?" she asked.

"What?"

"That I'm Amyrlin," she said. "You don't accept my title."

"I'm trying to," he said as he looked back at her. "But bloody ashes, Egwene. When we parted you were just an Accepted, and that wasn't so long ago. Now they've named you Amyrlin? I don't know what to think."

"And you can't see how your uncertainty undermines anything we could have together?"

"I can change. But you have to help me."

"Which is why I wanted to talk *later*," she said. "Are you going to let me pass?"

He stepped aside with obvious reluctance. "We're not finished with this talk," he warned. "I've finally made up my mind about something, and I don't intend to stop chasing it until I have it."

"Fine," Egwene said, passing him. "I can't think about

that now. I have to go order people I care about to slaughter another group of people I care about."

"You'll do it, then?" Gawyn said from behind. "There's speculation in camp; I heard it though I barely left this place all morning. Some think you'll command Bryne to assault the city."

She hesitated.

"It would be a shame if it happened," he said. "I don't care a whit about Tar Valon, but I think I know what it would do to you to attack it."

She turned back to him. "I will do what must be done, Gawyn," she said, meeting his eyes. "For the good of the Aes Sedai and the White Tower. Even if it is painful. Even if it tears me apart inside. I will do it if it needs to be done. Always."

He nodded slowly. She headed for the pavilion at the center of camp.

"This was your fault, Jesse," Adelorna said. Her eyes were still red; she'd lost a Warder the night before. She was one of many. But she was also tough as a feral hound, and was obviously determined not to let her pain show.

Jesse Bilal warmed her hands on her cup of gooseberry tea, refusing to let herself be goaded. Adelorna's question had been inevitable. And perhaps Jesse deserved the reprimand. Of course, they *all* deserved it, in one way or another. Except perhaps for Tsutama, who hadn't been an Ajah head at the time. That was part of why the woman hadn't been invited to this particular meeting. That, and the fact that the Red Ajah wasn't in good favor with the others at the moment.

The small, cramped room was barely large enough for five chairs and the small potbellied stove at the wall, radiating a calm warmth. There wasn't room for a table, let alone a hearth. Just enough space for five women. The most powerful women in the world. And the five most foolish, it seemed.

They were a sorry sisterhood this morning, the morning following the greatest disaster in the history of the White Tower. Jesse glanced at the woman beside her. Ferane Neheran—First Reasoner of the White—was a small, stout woman who, oddly in a White, often seemed more temper than logic. Today was one of those times: she sat scowling, her arms folded. She'd refused a cup of tea.

Next to her was Suana Dragand, First Weaver of the Yellow Ajah. She was a beefy thing with a thrusting chin that matched her unyielding demeanor. Adelorna, the one to make the accusation against Jesse, was beside her. Who could blame the Captain-General for her spitefulness? She who had been birched by Elaida, and who had last night suffered near death at the hands of the Seanchan? The slim woman looked uncharacteristically disheveled. Her hair was pulled back in a serviceable bun, and her pale dress was wrinkled.

The last woman in the room was Serancha Colvine, Head Clerk of the Gray Ajah. She had light brown hair and a pinched face; she looked perpetually as if she'd tasted something very sour. The trait seemed more manifest today than usual.

"She has a point, Jesse," Ferane said, her logical tone a contrast with her obvious pique. "You *were* the one to suggest this course of action."

"'Suggest' is a strong word." Jesse took a sip of her drink. "I simply mentioned that in some of the . . . more private Tower records, there are accounts of times when the Ajah heads ruled instead of the Amyrlin." The Thirteenth Depository was known to the Ajah heads, though they could not visit it unless they were also Sitters. That didn't stop most of them from sending Sitters to gather information from it for them. "I may have been the messenger, but that is often the role of the Brown. You all were not so hesitant as to be *forced* into this course of action."

There were a few sideways glances at that, and the women found opportunity to study their tea. Yes, they were all implicated, and they understood it. Jesse would *not* take the blame for this disaster.

"There is little use in assigning blame." Suana attempted to be soothing, though her voice was laced with bitterness.

"I won't be deflected so easily," Adelorna growled. Some reacted to the loss of a Warder with sadness, others with anger. There was little doubt which was Adelorna's way. "A grave, grave error has been made. The White Tower burns, the Amyrlin has been captured by invaders, and the Dragon

Reborn *still* walks the earth unfettered. The entire world will soon know of our disgrace!"

"And what good will it do to blame one another?" Suana replied. "Are we so childish that we will spend this meeting squabbling about which one of us will hang, in a useless attempt to evade our responsibility?"

Jesse gave quiet thanks for the sturdy Yellow's words. Of course, Suana *had* been the first of the Ajah heads to agree to Jesse's plan. So she'd be next in line for the metaphorical hanging.

"She has a point." Serancha took a sip of her tea. "We must make peace among ourselves. The Tower needs leadership, and we're not going to get it from the Hall."

"That's partly our fault as well," Ferane admitted, looking sick.

It was. It had seemed like a brilliant plan. The division of the Tower, the departure of so many in rebellion and the raising of a new Amyrlin, had not been their fault. But it *had* presented several opportunities. The first had been the easiest to take hold of: send Sitters to the rebels to steer them and hasten a reconciliation. The most youthful of Sitters had been chosen, their replacements in the Tower intended to serve only a short time. The Ajah heads had been certain this ripple of a rebellion could be easily smoothed over.

They hadn't taken it seriously enough. That had been their first mistake. The second was more dire. There were indeed times in the past where the Ajah heads—not the Amyrlin Seat or the Hall of the Tower—had led the Aes Sedai. It had been done secretly, of course, but it had been very successful. Why, the reign of Cemaile Sorenthaine would have been a complete disaster if the Ajah heads hadn't stepped in.

This had seemed like a similar occasion. The days of the Last Battle's approach were a special time, requiring special attention. Attention from women of sound, rational minds and great experience. Women who could speak together in confidence and decide on the best course, avoiding the arguments that the Hall got into.

"Where did we go wrong, do you think?" Serancha asked quietly.

The women fell silent. None of them wanted to admit

outright that the plan had backfired. Adelorna settled back in her chair, arms folded, smoldering but no longer flinging out accusations.

"It was Elaida," Ferane said. "She wasn't ever . . . very logical."

"She was a bloody disaster is what she was," Adelorna muttered.

"It was more than that," Jesse admitted. "Directly choosing Sitters we could control to replace those sent to the rebels was a good decision, but perhaps too obvious. The women of our own Ajahs became suspicious; I know of several comments made by women of the Brown. We are not so oblivious as others would like to think us."

Serancha nodded. "It smelled of conspiracy," she said. "That made the women less trusting. And then there were the rebels. Far more difficult to control than presumed."

The women nodded. They, like Jesse, had assumed that with proper direction, the rebels would find their way back to the Tower and ask forgiveness. This division should have ended with no more damage than a few bruised egos.

But they hadn't counted on how resilient, or effective, the rebels would be. A full army, appearing on the shores around Tar Valon in the middle of a snowstorm? Led by one of the greatest military minds of the Age? With a new Amyrlin and a frustratingly effective siege? Who could have expected it? And some of the Sitters they had sent had begun siding with the rebels more than the White Tower!

We never should have let Elaida disband the Blue Ajah, Jesse thought. *The Blues might have been willing to come back, had it not happened. But it was such a dishonor that they dug in.* Light only knew how dangerous that was; the histories were filled with accounts of how dogged the Blues could be at getting their way, particularly when they were forced into a corner.

"I think it is time to admit that there is no hope to save our plans," Suana said. "Are we agreed?"

"Agreed," Adelorna said.

One by one, the sisters nodded their heads, and so did Jesse herself. Even in this room, it was difficult to admit fault. But it was time to cut their losses and begin rebuilding.

"This has its own problems," Serancha said, voice more

calm now. The other women looked more assured as well. They didn't trust one another, these five, but they were far closer to doing so than any other group with any authority in the Hall.

"Care must be taken," Ferane added. "The division must be mended."

"The rebellion was against Elaida," Adelorna said. "If she is no longer Amyrlin, then what is there to rebel against?"

"So we abandon her?" Jesse asked.

"She deserves it," Adelorna said. "She said time and time again that Seanchan were no threat. Well, now she is paying for her foolishness firsthand."

"Elaida is beyond rescue," Ferane added. "The Hall has already discussed this. The Amyrlin is buried somewhere in a mass of Seanchan captives, and we have neither the resources nor the information for a rescue."

Not to mention our total lack of desire, Jesse added to herself. Many of the Sitters who had brought those points before the Hall were ones who had been sent to penance by Elaida. Jesse wasn't one of those, but she *did* agree that Elaida had earned her reward, if only for the way she had driven the Ajahs to one another's throats.

"Then we need a replacement," Serancha said. "But who?"

"It has to be someone strong," Suana said. "But someone cautious, unlike Elaida. Someone whom the sisters can rally around."

"What about Saerin Asnobar?" Jesse asked. "She has shown uncanny wisdom of late, and she is well liked."

"Of course you'd choose a Brown," Adelorna said.

"And why not?" Jesse said, taken aback. "You all heard, I think, how well she did assuming command during the attack last night?"

"Seaine Herimon led her own pocket of resistance," Ferane said. "I should think this would be a time for a woman to lead who is of an unemotional temperament. Someone who can provide *rational* guidance."

"Nonsense," Suana said. "Whites are too emotionless; we don't want to alienate sisters, we want to bring them together. Heal them! Why, a Yellow—"

"You're all forgetting something," Serancha interjected. "What is needed now? A reconciliation. The Gray Ajah is

the one that has spent centuries practicing the art of nego-
tiation. Who better to deal with a divided Tower, and the
Dragon Reborn himself?"

Adelorna gripped the armrests of her chair and straightened her back. The others were growing tense as well. As
Adelorna opened her mouth to speak, Jesse cut her off.

"Enough!" she interjected. "Are we just going to squabble as the Hall has been doing all morning? Each Ajah offering its own members, and the others summarily rejecting
them?"

The room fell silent again. It was true; the Hall had been
in session for hours and had only just gone into a short re-
cess. No one Ajah was *close* to getting enough support for
one of its candidates. The Sitters would not stand for anyone not of their own Ajah; there was too much animosity
between them. Light, but this was a mess!

"Ideally, it should be one of us five," Ferane said. "That
makes sense."

The five looked at each other, and Jesse could read their
answers to *that* in their eyes. They were the Ajah heads,
the most powerful women in the world. Right now, they
were balanced in power, and while they trusted each other
more than most, there was no way any of them would allow
the elevation of another Ajah head to the Amyrlin Seat. It
would give the woman far too much power. After the failure of their plan, trust was wearing very thin.

"If we don't decide soon," Suana noted, "the Hall may
take the decision from us."

"Bah." Adelorna waved a hand. "They're so divided they
can't agree on what color the sky is. The Sitters have no
idea what they're doing."

"At least some of us didn't choose Sitters who were *years*
too young to be placed in the Hall," Ferane said.

"Oh?" Adelorna said. "And you got around that how, Ferane? By choosing *yourself* as a Sitter?"

Ferane's eyes widened with rage. It was *not* a good idea
to rile that woman's temper.

"We all made mistakes," Jesse said quickly. "Many sisters we chose were odd. We wanted women who would do
exactly as we said, but instead we got a group of squabbling
brats with inflated opinions of themselves, too immature
for more temperate minds to influence."

Adelorna and Ferane made a point of not looking at each other.

"This still leaves us with a problem," Suana said. "We need an Amyrlin. Healing must begin quickly, whatever the cost."

Serancha shook her head. "I honestly can't think of a single woman that a sufficient number of Sitters would support."

"I can," Adelorna said softly. "She was mentioned in the Hall several times today. You know of whom I speak. She is young, and her circumstances are unusual, but everything is unusual at the moment."

"I don't know," Suana said, frowning. "She was mentioned, yes, but by those whose motives I don't trust."

"Saerin seems quite taken with her," Jesse admitted.

"She's too young," Serancha said. "Weren't we just berating ourselves for choosing Sitters who lacked the necessary experience?"

"She is young, yes," Ferane noted, "but you have to admit, there's a certain . . . flair to her. I hardly think that anyone in the Tower stood up to Elaida as effectively as she. And while in such a position as she was, no less!"

"You've heard the reports of her actions during the attack," Adelorna said. "I can confirm that they are true. I was there with her for most of it."

Jesse started at this. She hadn't realized that Adelorna had been on the twenty-second level during the fighting. "Surely some of what was said is exaggeration."

Adelorna shook her head grimly. "No. It isn't. It sounds incredible . . . but it . . . well, it happened. All of it."

"The novices all but worship her," Ferane said. "If the Sitters will not stand for someone of another Ajah, what of a woman who never picked an Ajah? A woman who has some experience—however unjustified—in holding the very position we are discussing?"

Jesse found herself nodding. But how had the young rebel gained such respect from Ferane and Adelorna?

"I am uncertain," Suana said. "It seems like another rash decision."

"Didn't you yourself say that we had to heal the Tower, no matter what the cost?" Adelorna asked. "Can you honestly think of a better way to bring the rebels back to us?"

She turned to Serancha. "What is the best method of appeasing an offended party? Would it not be to give some ground to them, acknowledge what they have done right?"

"She has a point," Suana admitted. She grimaced, then downed the rest of her tea in one gulp. "Light, but she's right, Serancha. We have to do it."

The Gray looked at each of them in turn. "You aren't foolish enough to assume this woman will be led by the nose, are you? I won't stand for this if we're simply trying to create another puppet. That plan failed. It failed miserably."

"I doubt we'll find ourselves in that situation again," Ferane said, smiling faintly. "This one . . . is not the type to be bullied. Just look at how she dealt with Elaida's restrictions."

"Yes," Jesse found herself saying, to her own surprise. "Sisters, if we agree to this, it will end our dream of ruling from the shadows. For better or worse, we'll be setting up an Amyrlin of strength."

"I, for one," Adelorna said, "think that's a *splendid* idea. It's been too long."

One by one, the others agreed.

Siuan stood, unmoving, beneath the boughs of a small oak. The tree had been engulfed by the camp, and its shade had become a favored location for Accepted and novices taking lunches. There were none doing so at the moment; the sisters, showing remarkably good judgment this time, had set them tasks to keep them from congregating around the tent where the Hall was meeting.

And so Siuan stood alone, watching as Sheriam pulled the flaps to the large pavilion closed. She was able to attend now that Egwene was back. It was easy to sense when the ward against eavesdropping was woven, Sealing the meeting to the Flame and excluding prying ears.

A hand fell on Siuan's shoulder. She didn't jump; she'd sensed Bryne approaching. The general walked with stealth, although there was no need. He was going to make an excellent Warder.

He stepped up beside her, hand still comfortably on her shoulder, and she allowed herself the luxury of taking just a small step closer to him. His height and sturdiness felt good beside her. Like knowing that though the sky stormed and the sea raged, your hull was caulked and your sail crafted of the strongest cloth.

"What do you think she will tell them?" Bryne asked, his voice subdued.

"I honestly have no idea. She could call for my stilling, I suppose."

"I doubt that she will," Bryne asked. "She is not the vengeful type. Besides, she knows that you did what you felt you had to. For her own good."

Siuan grimaced. "Nobody likes being disobeyed, least of all the Amyrlin. I will pay for last night, Bryne. You're right that it probably won't be in a public way, but I worry that I've lost the girl's trust."

"And was it worth the cost?"

"Yes," Siuan said. "She didn't realize how close this band was to slipping away from her. And we couldn't know that she'd be safe within the Tower during the attack. If there's one thing my time in the White Tower taught me, it's that there is a time for gathering and planning, but one *also* has to act. You can't always wait for certainty."

She could feel Bryne's smile through the bond. Light, but it was good to have a Warder again. She hadn't realized how much she'd missed that comforting knot of emotions in the back of her mind. That stability. Men thought differently from women, and things she found complicated and baffling, Bryne saw as straightforward and simple. Make your decision and go. There was a helpful clarity to his way of reasoning. Not that he was simple—just less inclined to regret decisions he'd already made.

"And what of the other costs?" Bryne added.

She could feel his hesitation, his worry. She turned to him, smiling in amusement. "You're a fool, Gareth Bryne."

He frowned.

"Bonding you was never a cost," she said. "Whatever else happens because of this fiasco, *that* aspect of the night's events were pure profit on my part."

He chuckled. "Well, I'll have to make extra certain that my *second* demand is more unreasonable, then."

Fish guts, Siuan thought. She'd almost forgotten about that. Burning unlikely that Bryne would, though. "And when, precisely, are you going to make this unreasonable demand of me?"

He didn't respond immediately, instead looking down at her, rubbing his chin. "You know," he said, "I think I actually understand you now, Siuan Sanche. You *are* a woman of honor. It's just that nobody else's requirements of you can ever be more harsh or more demanding than your own requirements of yourself. You owe such a self-imposed debt to your own sense of duty that I doubt any mortal being could pay it back."

"You make me sound centered on myself," she said.

"At least I'm not comparing you to a boar again."

"So you *do* think I'm self-centered!" she said. Burn him! He could probably sense that she was actually bothered by his statement, rather than making argument for the sake of it. Burn him again!

"You're a driven woman, Siuan Sanche," he said. "Driven to save the world from itself. That's how you can shrug off an oath or an order so easily."

Siuan took a deep breath. "This conversation grew very tedious very quickly, Gareth Bryne. Are you going to tell me that other demand, or are you going to make me wait?"

He studied her stone face thoughtfully. "Well, frankly, I'm planning to demand that you marry me."

She blinked in surprise. Light! The bond said that he was honest.

"But only after you feel the world can care for itself. I won't agree to it before then, Siuan. You've given your life to something. I'll see that you survive through it; I hope that once you're done, you'll be willing to give your life to something else instead."

She reined in her shock. She wouldn't let a fool man make *her* speechless. "Well," she forced herself to say. "I see you have some sense after all. We shall see if I agree to this 'demand' of yours or not. I will think on it."

Bryne chuckled as she turned around to regard the pavilion, waiting for Egwene's reappearance. He could sense the truth from inside her, just as she could sense it from him. Light! Now she knew why Greens married their Warders so often. Feeling his affection for her while she felt the same for him made her giddy.

He was a fool of a man. And she no less a fool of a woman. She shook her head ruefully, but she did let herself lean back against him softly as they waited, and he replaced

his hand on her shoulder. Soft, not forceful. Willing to wait.
He *did* understand her.

Egwene stood before a group of smooth faces that were far
too good at hiding their anxiety. By custom, she had ordered Kwamesa to weave the ward against eavesdropping,
as the sharp-nosed Gray was the youngest among the Sitters in the large tent. It looked almost empty with so few
places taken. A dozen women, two from each Ajah—there
would have been three of each, but the Ajahs had all sent
one Sitter with the envoy to the Black Tower. The Grays had
already replaced Delana with Naorisa Cambral.

Twelve Sitters, along with Egwene and one other.
Egwene did not look at Sheriam, who sat in her place to the
side. Sheriam had seemed troubled as she entered. Did she
realize what Egwene knew? She couldn't. If she had, she'd
never have come to the meeting.

Still, knowing she was there—and knowing what she
was—made Egwene nervous. In the chaos of the Seanchan
attack, Siuan hadn't been able to watch Sheriam. Why *did*
the Keeper wear a bandage on her left hand? Egwene didn't
believe her excuse of an accident while riding, her little finger getting caught in her reins. Why had she refused Healing? Blast Siuan! Instead of watching Sheriam, she'd come
to kidnap Egwene!

The Hall grew still, the women waiting to see what
Egwene's response would be to her "freedom." Romanda,
gray-streaked hair up in a bun, sat primly in a yellow dress.
She oozed satisfaction, while Lelaine—on the opposite
side of the room—sulked while trying to act pleased at
Egwene's return. After what Egwene had been through in
the White Tower, this squabbling felt ridiculously petty.

Egwene took a deep breath, then embraced the Source.
It felt so good! No bitter forkroot to squeeze her power to a
trickle, no need to reach through other women to lend her
strength. No need for a *sa'angreal*. Sweet though the fluted
wand's power had been, being strong in and of herself was
even more satisfying.

Several of the women frowned at the action, and not a
few of them embraced the Source themselves, as if by re-
flex, looking about as if for danger.

"There will be no need for that," Egwene said to the women. "Not yet. Please release the Source."

They were hesitant, but—ostensibly—they accepted her as Amyrlin. One by one their power winked away. Egwene did not release it herself.

"I am very glad to see that you returned safely, Mother," Lelaine said. She skirted the Three Oaths by adding the word "safely."

"Thank you," Egwene said calmly.

"You said that there were important revelations to make," Varilin added. "Is this regarding the Seanchan attack?"

Egwene reached to the pouch on her skirt and pulled its contents free. A smooth white rod with the numeral three inscribed on it in the script of the Age of Legends, near the base. There were several gasps.

Egwene wove Spirit into the Rod, then spoke in a clear voice. "I vow that I will speak no word that is not true." She felt the oath fall over her like a physical thing, her skin growing tighter, prickling. It was easy to ignore; the pain was nothing compared with what she had been through. "I vow that I will make no weapon for one man to kill another. I vow that I will never use the One Power as a weapon except against Darkfriends and Shadowspawn, or in the last extreme of defending my life or that of my Warder or of another sister."

The Hall was silent. Egwene released her weave. Her skin felt so odd! As if someone had pinched the excess up at the base of her neck and along her spine, yanking it and binding it in place.

"Let it no longer be thought that I can avoid keeping the Three Oaths," Egwene announced. "Let it no longer be breathed that I am not fully Aes Sedai." None of them said anything about her not having taken the test to gain the shawl. She would see to that another day. "And now that you've seen me use the Oath Rod and know that I cannot lie, I will tell you something. During my time in the White Tower, a sister came to me and confided that she was Black Ajah."

The women's eyes bulged, and several gasped quietly.

"Yes," Egwene said. "I know we don't like to speak of them, but can any of us honestly claim that the Black Ajah does not exist? Can you hold to the oaths while saying that you've never considered the possibility—even the *likeli-hood*—of there being Darkfriends among us?"

Nobody dared to. The tent felt hot despite the early hour. Stuffy. None of them sweated, of course—they knew the age-old trick of avoiding that.

"Yes," Egwene said, "It is shameful, but it is a truth that we—as the leaders of our people—must admit. Not in public; but among ourselves there is no avoiding it. I have seen firsthand what distrust and quiet politicking can do to a people. I will *not* see the same disease infect us here. We are of different Ajahs, but we are single in purpose. We need to know that we can trust one another implicitly, because there is very little else in this world that can be trusted."

Egwene looked down at the Oath Rod, which she'd fetched early in the morning from Saerin. She rubbed her thumb on it. *I wish you'd been able to find this when you visited, Verin,* she thought. *Perhaps it wouldn't have saved you, but I would have liked to try. I could use your aid.*

Egwene looked up. "I am not a Darkfriend," she announced to the room. "And you know it cannot be a lie."

The Sitters looked perplexed. Well, they would soon see the point.

"It is time for us to prove ourselves," Egwene said. "Some clever women in the White Tower hit upon this idea, and I intend to expand it. We will each in turn use the Oath Rod to release ourselves from the Three Oaths, then reswear them in turn. Once we are all bound, we will be able to promise that we are not servants of—"

Sheriam embraced the Source. Egwene had been anticipating that. She slammed a shield between Sheriam and the Source, causing the woman to gasp. Berana cried out in shock, and several other women embraced the Source, looking this way and that.

Egwene turned and met Sheriam's eyes. The woman's face was nearly as red as her hair, and she was breathing in and out quickly. Like a captured rabbit, its leg in a snare, eyes wide with fright. She clutched her bandaged hand.

Oh, Sheriam, Egwene thought. *I had hoped that Verin was wrong about you.*

"Egwene?" Sheriam asked uncomfortably. "I was just—"

Egwene stepped forward. "Are you Black Ajah, Sheriam?"

"What? Of course not!"

"Do you consort with the Forsaken?"

"No!" Sheriam said, glancing to the sides.

"Do you serve the Dark One?"

"No!"

"Have you been released from your oaths?"

"No!"

"Do you have red hair?"

"Of course not, I never—" She froze.

And thank you for that trick as well, Verin, Egwene thought with a mental sigh.

The tent grew very, very still.

"I misspoke, of course," Sheriam said, sweating nervously. "I didn't know what question I was answering. I can't lie, of course. None of us can. . . ."

She trailed off as Egwene held out the Oath Rod. "Prove it, Sheriam. The woman who came to me in the Tower gave me your name as a leader among the Black Ajah."

Sheriam met Egwene's eyes. "Ah, then," the woman said softly, eyes mournful. "Who was it, now, who came to you?"

"Verin Mathwin."

"Well, well," Sheriam said, settling back on her chair. "Never expected it of *her*, I'll say. How did she get past the oaths to the Great Lord?"

"She drank poison," Egwene said, heart twisting.

"Very clever." The flame-haired woman nodded. "I could never bring myself to do such a thing. Never indeed. . . ."

Egwene wove bonds of Air and wrapped Sheriam in them, then tied off the weaves. She turned back to an incredulous group of women, white-faced. Some terrified. "The world marches to the Last Battle," Egwene said sternly. "Did you expect that our enemies would leave us alone?"

"Who else?" Lelaine whispered. "Who else was mentioned?"

"Many others," Egwene said. "Sitters among them."

Moria leaped to her feet and ran for the exit. She barely made it two steps. A dozen different sisters enclosed the former Blue with shields and bound her in weaves of Air. In seconds, she was hanging, gagged, tears leaking down the sides of her oval face.

Romanda clicked her tongue, walking around the woman.

"Both from the Blue," she noted. "This was a dramatic way to make the revelations, Egwene."

"You will address me as 'Mother,' Romanda," Egwene said, walking down from the dais. "And it is not so odd that there would be a higher percentage of them among the Blue here, since that entire Ajah fled the White Tower." She held up the Oath Rod. "The reason I had to make the revelation this way was simple. How would you have responded if I'd simply declared them to be Black without offering proof?"

Romanda nodded her head. "You are correct on both counts, Mother," she admitted.

"Then you wouldn't mind being the first to retake the oaths, I presume?"

Romanda hesitated only briefly, glancing at the two women bound in Air. Almost everyone in the room held to the Source, eyeing the others as if they might grow copper-snakes for hair at any moment.

Romanda took the Oath Rod, and did as instructed, releasing herself from the oaths. The process was obviously painful, but she held herself to a controlled, hissing intake of breath. The others watched carefully for a trick, but Romanda was straightforward in reswearing. She handed the rod back to Egwene. "I am not a Darkfriend," she said. "And I never have been."

Egwene accepted the Oath Rod back. "Thank you, Romanda," she said. "Lelaine, do you wish to be next?"

"Gladly," the woman said. She probably felt a need to vindicate the Blue. One by one, the other women forswore—gasping or hissing at the pain of it—then swore again and promised that they were not Darkfriends. Egwene let out a silent sigh of relief at each one. Verin had admitted that there would be sisters she didn't get, and that Egwene might discover other members of the Black among the Sitters.

When Kwamesa, the last, handed the Rod back to Egwene and declared herself not a Darkfriend, there was a visible release of tension in the room.

"Very good," Egwene said, returning to stand at the head of the room. "From now on, we continue as one. No more squabbling. No more fighting. We each have the best interests of the White Tower—and the world itself—at heart. The twelve of us, at least, are confident in one another.

"A cleansing is never easy. It is often painful. Today, we

have cleansed ourselves, but what we have to do next will be nearly as painful."

"You . . . know the names of many others?" Takima asked, for once looking not a bit distracted.

"Yes," Egwene said. "Over two hundred total, some from each Ajah. Some seventy among us here in this camp. I have the names." She had returned in the night to fetch Verin's books from her room. They were now safely hidden in her tent, invisible. "I propose that we arrest them, though it will be difficult, as we will have to seize all of them as simultaneously as possible." Their greatest advantage, beyond surprise, was going to be the inherently distrusting nature of the Black Ajah. Verin and other sources had indicated that few sisters in the Black knew more than a handful of other names. There was an entire write-up in the book about Black Ajah organization, and their system of groups known as "hearts" that had minimal interaction to keep them hidden. Hopefully, that very system would slow their realizing what was happening.

The Sitters looked daunted. "First," Egwene said, "we will claim that we need to spread important news to every Sister, but can't let it be overheard by the soldiers in camp. We'll call the sisters into this pavilion by Ajah—it's big enough to hold about two hundred people. I'll distribute to each of you the names of all the Black sisters. When each Ajah enters, I'll repeat to them what I told you and tell them they're all going to have to reswear on the Oath Rod. We'll be ready to seize Black sisters who try to escape. We'll tie them up and deposit them in the audience tent." That smaller tent was connected to the side of the Hall, and could be closed off so that entering sisters wouldn't see the captives.

"We'll have to do something about Warders," Lelaine said grimly. "Let them come in with their sisters, I suppose, and be prepared to seize them."

"Some of them will be Darkfriends," Egwene said. "But not all. And I don't know which ones." Verin had had some notes about this, but not many, unfortunately.

"Light, what a mess," Romanda muttered.

"It must be done," haughty Berana said with a shake of her head.

"And it must be done quickly," Egwene said. "So that the Black sisters don't have time to escape. I'll warn Lord

Bryne to create a perimeter of archers and sisters we trust to stop any trying to escape, just in case. But that will only work for those too weak to make gateways."

"We mustn't let it come to that," Lelaine said. "A war inside the camp itself . . ."

Egwene nodded.

"And what of the White Tower?" Lelaine said.

"Once we have cleansed ourselves," Egwene said, "then we can do what must be done to reunify the Aes Sedai."

"You mean—"

"Yes, Lelaine," Egwene said. "I mean to begin an assault on Tar Valon by this evening. Pass the word and tell Lord Bryne to prepare his men. The news will serve to distract the Black members among us, and will make them less likely to notice what we are doing."

Romanda glanced at Sheriam and Moria, hanging in the air at the side of the tent, both weeping openly, mouths bound with gags of Air. "It must be done. I put forth a motion before the Hall to take the action the Amyrlin has suggested."

The tent grew still. Then, slowly, each women rose to give consensus. It was unanimous.

"Light preserve us," Lelaine whispered. "And forgive us for what we are about to do."

My thoughts exactly, Egwene added.

CHAPTER
44

Scents Unknown

Tarwin's Gap is the place that makes the most sense!" Nynaeve argued.

She and Rand rode on an overgrown road in the open grassland of Maredo, accompanied by a crowd of Aiel. Nynaeve was the only Aes Sedai there; Narishma and Naeff rode near the back of the group, looking sullen. Rand had forced their Aes Sedai to stay behind. He seemed particularly determined to assert his independence from them, lately.

Nynaeve was astride a pure white mare named Moonlight, appropriated from Rand's stable in Tear. It still seemed odd that he would have his own stable at all, let alone one in each of the major cities of the world.

"Tarwin's Gap," Rand said, shaking his head. "No. The more I think about it, the more I realize that we don't want to fight there. Lan is doing me a favor. If I can coordinate an assault alongside his own, I can gain great advantage. But I don't want to distract my armies with the Gap. It would be a waste of resources."

A waste of resources? The Gap was where *Lan* was heading, like an arrow loosed from a Two Rivers longbow. Heading there to die! And Rand said helping was a waste? Wool-headed fool!

Gritting her teeth, she forced herself to calm down. If only he would *argue*, rather than speaking in that distant way he had recently adopted. He seemed so emotionless, but she had seen the beast get free and roar at her. It was coiled inside him, and if he didn't let his emotions out soon, they would devour him from the inside.

But how to make him see reason? She had prepared argument after argument—each of them distinctly reasoned and calmly explained—during their time in Tear. Rand had ignored all of them, spending the last two days meeting with his generals and planning strategy for the Last Battle.

Each day brought Lan one step closer to a fight he couldn't win. Each day made her more anxious; several times, she'd nearly abandoned Rand and ridden for the north. If Lan was going to fight an impossible battle, then she longed to be at his side. But she stayed. Light take Rand al'Thor, she stayed. What good would it do to help Lan, only to let the world fall into Shadow because of a stubborn sheepherder's stubborn . . . *stubbornness*!

She gave her braid a solid yank. The jeweled bracelets and rings on her hands glittered in the faint sunlight—the sky was cloudy, of course, just as it had been for weeks. Everyone tried to ignore how unnatural that was, but Nynaeve could still feel that storm building to the north.

Such a short time left until Lan reached the Gap! Light send that he was slowed down by the Malkieri who had come to support him in his ride. Light send that he was not alone. Thinking of him, riding into the Blight, facing the army of Shadowspawn who infested his homeland. . . .

"We *have* to attack there," Nynaeve said. "Ituralde says that the Blight is swarming with Trollocs. The Dark One is gathering his forces. You can bet that the bulk of them will be at the Gap, where it's easiest to get through and strike at Andor and Cairhien!"

"That is exactly why we will not attack at the Gap, Nynaeve," Rand said, voice cold and even. "We cannot let the enemy dictate our battlefield. The last thing we want to do is fight where *they* want us to, or where they expect us to." He turned eyes northward. "Yes, let them gather. They seek me, and I shall not deliver myself. Why fight at Tarwin's Gap? It makes the best sense to jump most of our armies right to Shayol Ghul."

"Rand," she said, trying to sound reasonable. Couldn't he see that she was reasonable? "There is no way that Lan has been able to gather a large enough force to hold back a mass assault by the Trollocs, particularly not with most of the Borderlander armies doing Light only knows what down here. He'll be overrun, and the Trollocs will invade!"

Mention of the Borderlanders made Rand's face tighten; they rode to meet with their messengers. "The Trollocs will invade," Rand repeated.

"Yes!"

"Good," Rand said. "It will keep them occupied as I do what needs to be done."

"And Lan?" Nynaeve asked.

"His attack will be well placed." Rand nodded. "He will draw my enemies' attention to Malkier and the Gap, and it will make them think that I am there. Shadowspawn can't move through gateways, so they can't move as quickly as I can. By the time they've engaged Lan, I'll be past them and attacking directly at the Dark One's heart.

"I don't plan to abandon the southern lands, not at all. When the Trollocs punch through the Gap, they will break up into fists to invade. That's when my forces will hit them, led by Bashere, Traveling by gateway to strike at each group of Trollocs from the sides or behind. That way, we can pick the best battlefields to suit our needs."

"Rand," Nynaeve said, her anger fading to horror. "Lan will die!"

"Then who am I to deny him that?" Rand said. "We all deserve the chance to find peace."

Nynaeve found her mouth hanging open. He actually believed that! Or he was convincing himself to believe it, at least.

"My duty is to kill the Dark One," Rand said, as if to himself. "I kill him, then I die. That is all."

"But—"

"That is enough, Nynaeve." Rand spoke softly in that dangerous voice of his. He would not be pressed further.

Nynaeve sat back, stewing, trying to decide how to press him on the topic. Light! He would leave the people of the Borderlands to suffer and die in the Trolloc invasions? The people there wouldn't care if the Dark One had been defeated—they would be cooking in stewpots. That would leave Lan and the Malkieri to fight alone, a tiny force to resist the might of every monster that the Blight could spit out.

The Seanchan would wage their war to the south and the west. The Trollocs would attack from the north and the east. The two would meet, eventually. Andor and the other kingdoms would be turned into a massive battleground, the people there—good people, like those in the Two Rivers—would have no chance against such warfare. They'd be crushed.

So what could she do to change it? She had to come up with a new strategy to influence Rand. Everything, in her heart, pointed at protecting Lan. She had to get him help!

The group rode through open grassland spotted occasionally with farms. They passed one on the right, a solitary farmstead not unlike many back in the Two Rivers. Yet, in the Two Rivers, she'd never seen a farmer watch travelers with such open hostility. The red-bearded man in dirtied trousers, with sleeves rolled nearly to his shoulders, leaned against a half-finished fence, his axe laid casually—but very visibly—on the logs beside him.

His field had seen better years; though the soil had been neatly plowed and harrowed, the furrows had spat forth only the smallest of sprouts. The field was spotted with empty patches where seeds had inexplicably refused to take root, and the plants that *were* growing had a yellowish cast to them.

A group of younger men were pulling a stump free from a neighboring field, yet to Nynaeve's practiced eye, they weren't actually trying to get any work done. They didn't have the harness hooked to their ox, and they hadn't loosened the stump in the earth by digging about it. Those lengths of wood lying in the grass were too stout and smoothly worked to be the shafts of tools. Quarterstaffs. It was almost an amusing display—considering the fact that Rand had two hundred Aiel with him—but it said something. These men expected trouble and were preparing for it. No doubt they could feel the storm themselves.

This area, close to trade routes and within reach of Tear, was relatively safe from bandits. It was also just far enough north to avoid being caught in squabbles between Illian and Tear. This should have been a place where farmers didn't need to turn good lumber into quarterstaffs, nor watch strangers with eyes that expected attack.

That wariness would serve them well when the Trollocs reached them—assuming the Seanchan hadn't conquered them and pressed them into their armies by that point. Nynaeve tugged her braid again.

Her mind turned back to Lan. She had to do something! But Rand wasn't seeing sense. That left only Cadsuane's mysterious plan. Fool woman, refusing to explain it. Nynaeve had made the first step, offering an alliance, and how had Cadsuane reacted? With presumptuous arrogance, of course. How dare she welcome Nynaeve into her little group of Aes Sedai like a child who had been wandering in the woods!

How would Nynaeve's task—discovering where Perrin was—help Lan? During the past week, Nynaeve had pressed Cadsuane for more information, but had failed. "Perform this task well, child," Cadsuane had said, "and perhaps we shall give you more responsibility in the future. You've proven yourself willful at times, and we can't have that."

Nynaeve sighed. Find out where Perrin was. How was she supposed to do that? The Two Rivers folk had been of little use. Many of their men were traveling with Perrin, but they hadn't been seen for some time. They were in the south somewhere, Altara or Ghealdan, likely. But that left a large area to search.

She should have known that the Two Rivers would not provide an easy answer. Cadsuane had obviously already tried reaching Perrin herself, and must have failed. That's why she'd given the task to Nynaeve. Had Rand sent Perrin on some secret mission?

"Rand?" she said.

He was muttering roughly to himself.

She shivered. "Rand," she said more sharply.

He stopped muttering, then glanced at her. She thought she could see the anger hidden there, deep within him, a flash of annoyance at her interruption. Then it was gone, replaced by the frighteningly cool control. "Yes?" he asked.

"Do you . . . know where Perrin is?"

"He has tasks set before him and performs them," Rand said, turning away. "Why do you wish to know?"

Best not to mention Cadsuane. "I'm still worried about him. And about Mat."

"Ah," Rand said. "You are particularly unaccustomed to lying, aren't you, Nynaeve?"

She felt her face flush in embarrassment. When had he learned to read people so well! "I *am* worried about him,

Rand al'Thor," she said. "He has a peaceful, unassuming nature—and always did let his friends push him around too much."

There. Let Rand think about *that*.

"Unassuming," Rand said musingly. "Yes, I suppose he is still that. But peaceful? Perrin is no longer too . . . peaceful."

So he had been in touch with Perrin recently. Light! How had Cadsuane known, and how had Nynaeve missed those communications? "Rand, if you have Perrin working on something for you, then why have you kept it secret? I deserve to—"

"I haven't been meeting with him, Nynaeve," Rand said. "Calm yourself. There are simply things that I know. We are connected, Perrin, myself and Mat."

"How? What do you—"

"That is all I will say on it, Nynaeve," Rand interrupted, slicing into her sentence with soft words.

Nynaeve settled back, gritting her teeth again. The other Aes Sedai spoke of being in control of their emotions, but obviously they didn't have to deal with Rand al'Thor. Nynaeve could be calm too, if she weren't expected to manage the most bullheaded fool of a man who had ever put on a pair of boots.

They rode in silence for a time, the overcast sky hanging above them like a distant field of graymoss peat. The meeting place with the Borderlanders was a nearby crossroads. They could have Traveled directly there, but the Maidens had prevailed upon Rand to arrive a short distance out and approach more carefully. Traveling was extremely convenient, but it also could be dangerous. If your enemies knew where you would appear, you could open a gateway and find yourself ambushed by a line of archers. Even sending scouts through the gateway first wasn't as safe as Traveling to a spot where nobody was expecting you.

The Aiel learned, and adapted, quickly. Surprising, really. The Waste was terribly unvaried; every part looked just about the same. Of course, she *had* overheard some Aiel guards saying something similar about the wetlands.

This particular crossroads hadn't been important in years. If Verin or one of the other Brown sisters had been there, they'd likely have been able to explain exactly why.

All Nynaeve knew was that the kingdom which had once held this land had fallen long ago, and the only remnant was the independent city of Far Madding. The Wheel of Time turned. The most grand of kingdoms fell, rusted and eventually changed into lazy fields, ruled only by farmers determined to grow a particularly good crop of barley. It had happened to Manetheren, and it had happened here. Great highways that had once transported legions now dwindled to obscure country roads in need of maintenance.

As they continued, Nynaeve let Moonlight fall back from Rand's position. That placed her riding near Narishma, with his dark, braided hair, bells tinkling on the ends. He wore black, like most Asha'man, and the Sword and Dragon twinkled on his collar. He'd changed in the months since being bonded as a Warder. She could no longer look at him and see a boy. This was a man, with the grace of a soldier, the careful eyes of a Warder. A man who had seen death and fought Forsaken.

"You're a Borderlander, Narishma," Nynaeve said. "Do you have any idea why the others left their posts?"

He shook his head, scanning the landscape. "I was a cobbler's son, Nynaeve Sedai. I know not the ways of lords and ladies." He hesitated. "Besides, I'm not a Borderlander anymore." The implication was clear. He would protect Rand, no matter what other allegiances tugged at him. A very Warder-like way of thought.

Nynaeve nodded slowly. "Do you have any idea what we're riding into?"

"They'll keep their word," Narishma said. "A Borderlander would sooner die than break his word. They promised to send a delegation to meet with the Lord Dragon. They'll do just that. I wish we'd been allowed to bring our Aes Sedai, though."

Reports held that the Borderlander army included thirteen Aes Sedai. A dangerous number: the number needed to still a woman or gentle a man. Thirteen women in a circle could shield the most powerful of channelers. Rand had insisted that the delegation that came to meet him include no more than four of those thirteen Aes Sedai; in return, he promised to bring no more than four channelers. Two Asha'man—Narishma and Naeff—Nynaeve and Rand himself.

Merise and the others had thrown the Aes Sedai equivalent of a fit—it involved a lot of downturned lips and questions like "Are you certain you want to do that?"—when Rand had forbidden them to come.

Nynaeve noted Narishma's tense posture. "You don't look as if you trust them."

"A Borderlander's place is guarding the Border," Narishma said. "I was a cobbler's son, and yet I was trained with the sword, spear, bow, axe and sling. Even before joining the Asha'man, I could best four out of five trained southern soldiers in a duel. We *live* to defend. And yet they left. Now, of all times. With thirteen Aes Sedai." He glanced at her with those dark eyes of his. "I want to trust them. I know them for good people. But good people can do the wrong thing. Particularly when men who can channel are involved."

Nynaeve fell silent. Narishma had a point, though what cause would the Borderlanders have to harm Rand? They'd fought the encroachment of the Blight and its Shadowspawn for centuries, and the struggle against the Dark One was imprinted on their very souls. They wouldn't turn against the Dragon Reborn.

The Borderlanders had a special honor about them. It could be frustrating, true, but it was who they were. Lan's reverence for his homeland—particularly when many other Malkieri had abandoned their identity—was part of what she loved about him. *Oh, Lan. I'll find someone to help you. I won't let you ride into the Shadow's jaws alone.*

As they neared a small green hill, several Aiel returned from scouting. Rand pulled the group to a halt, waiting for the *cadin'sor*-clad scouts to pad up to him, several wearing the red headbands marked with the ancient symbol of the Aes Sedai. The scouts weren't winded, despite the fact that they'd run all the way ahead to the meeting place and then back.

Rand leaned forward in his saddle. "Did they do as I asked? Did they bring no more than two hundred men, no more than four Aes Sedai?"

"Yes, Rand al'Thor," said one of the scouts. "Yes, they kept to your requirements admirably. They have great honor."

Nynaeve recognized the strange Aiel brand of humor in the tone of the man's response.

"What?" Rand asked.

"One man, Rand al'Thor," the Aiel scout said. "That is all that their 'delegation' consists of. He's a short little thing of a man, though he looks like he knows how to dance the spears. The crossroads is behind this hill."

Nynaeve looked ahead. Indeed, now that she knew to look, she could see another road running up from the south, presumably meeting with theirs just beyond the hill.

"What manner of trap is this?" Naeff asked, riding up beside Rand, his lean, warrior's face concerned. "An ambush?"

Rand held up a hand for silence. He kicked his gelding into motion, and the scouts kept up without a word of complaint. Nynaeve was nearly left behind; Moonlight was a far more placid animal than she would have chosen for herself. She'd have words with the stable master when she returned to Tear.

They rounded the hillside, finding a dusty square of ground, scarred by old firepits where caravans had stopped for the night. A roadway smaller than the one they'd been using twisted up to the north and down to the south. A solitary Shienaran man stood in the center, where roads met, watching the oncoming procession. His shoulder-length gray hair hung loose around a lean face which complemented his wiry build. His round face was lined with marks of age; his eyes were small, and he seemed to be squinting.

Hurin? she thought with surprise. Nynaeve hadn't seen the thief-taker since he'd accompanied her and a group of others back to the White Tower following the events at Falme.

Rand reined in his horse, allowing Nynaeve and the Asha'man to catch up. Aiel fanned out like leaves blown before a gust of wind, taking up watchful positions around the crossroads. She was fairly certain that both of the Asha'man had seized the Source, and likely Rand had as well.

Hurin shuffled uncomfortably. He looked much as Nynaeve remembered him. A tad more gray in the hair, but wearing the same simple brown clothing, with a swordbreaker and a shortsword at his waist. He had tied a horse to a fallen log nearby. The Aiel watched it suspiciously, as others might watch a pack of guard dogs.

"Why, Lord Rand!" Hurin called, voice uneven. "It *is*

you! Well, you've certainly come up in the world, I must say. Good to—"

He cut off as he was raised from the ground. He made an "urk" of surprise, being turned on unseen weaves of Air. Nynaeve suppressed a shiver. Would seeing men channel ever stop bothering her?

"Who chased after you and me, Hurin," Rand called, "the time when we were trapped in that distant shadow land? What nationality of men did I fell with the bow?"

"Men?" Hurin asked, voice almost a squawk. "Lord Rand, there were no men in that place! None that we met, beyond Lady Selene, that is. All I remember are those frog beasts, the same ones folk say those Seanchan ride!"

Rand spun Hurin around in the Air, regarding him with cold eyes. Then he urged his mount closer. Nynaeve and the Asha'man did as well.

"You don't believe that I'm me, Lord Rand?" Hurin asked as he hung in the air.

"I take very little as it is presented to me, these days," Rand said. "I assume the Borderlanders sent you because of our familiarity?"

Hurin nodded, sweating. Nynaeve felt a stab of pity for the man. He was absolutely devoted to Rand. They had spent a lot of time together, chasing down Fain and the Horn of Valere. On the return trip to Tar Valon, she'd seldom been able to stop Hurin from gossiping about this or that grand feat that Rand had accomplished. Being treated this way by the man he idolized was probably very unsettling for the lean thief-taker.

"Why only you?" Rand asked quietly.

"Well," Hurin said, sighing. "They did tell you—" He hesitated, seeming distracted by something. He sniffed audibly. "Now that . . . that's strange. Never smelled that before."

"What?" Rand asked.

"I don't know," Hurin said. "The air . . . it smells like a lot of death, a lot of violence, only not. It's darker. More terrible." He shuddered visibly. Hurin's ability to smell violence was one of those oddities that the Tower couldn't explain. Not something related to the Power, yet obviously not quite natural either.

Rand didn't seem to care what Hurin smelled. "Tell me why they sent only you, Hurin."

"I was saying, Lord Rand. See, this here, we're to discuss *terms*."

"Terms regarding your armies moving back where they belong," Rand said.

"No, Lord Rand," Hurin said uncomfortably. "Terms for setting up a *real* meeting with them. That part in their letter was kind of vague, I guess. They said you might be angry to find only me here."

"They were wrong," Rand said, voice softer. Nynaeve found herself straining to hear him, leaning forward.

"I no longer feel anger, Hurin," Rand said. "It serves me no useful function. Why would we need 'terms' to meet together? I presumed that my offer to bring only a small force would be acceptable."

"Well, Lord Rand," Hurin said, "you see, they really *want* to meet with you. I mean, we came all this way—marched through the bloody winter itself, my pardon, Aes Sedai. But it was the bloody *winter*! And a bad one, although it took a long time getting to us. Anyways, we did that coming for you, Lord Rand. So you see, they want to meet with you. Very badly."

"But?"

"But, well, last time you were in Far Madding there was—"

Rand held up a finger. Hurin quieted, and all grew still. Even the horses seemed to hold their breaths.

"The Borderlanders are in Far Madding?" Rand asked.

"Yes, Lord Rand."

"They want to meet with me there?"

"Yes, Lord Rand. You'll have to come inside the protection of the Guardian, you see, and—"

Rand waved a curt hand, cutting off Hurin. A gateway opened immediately. It didn't appear to lead to Far Madding, however; it just led back a short distance, to the road where Rand and the others had been riding a short time before.

Rand released Hurin, gesturing for the Aiel to let the man mount, then moved Tai'daishar through the gateway. What was going on? Everyone else followed. Once through, Rand created another gateway, this one opening into a small wooded hollow. Nynaeve thought she recognized it;

this was where they had stopped following their visit to Far Madding with Cadsuane.

Why the first gateway? Nynaeve thought, confused. And then it occurred to her. One didn't need to learn an area to Travel a short distance from it—and Traveling *to* a place taught someone that location well enough to create gateways from it.

So by Traveling a short hop first, Rand memorized the location well enough to create gateways wherever he wanted—while skipping the time needed to learn the area! It was extremely clever, and Nynaeve felt herself blushing that she hadn't seen the possibility before. How long had Rand known of this trick? Had memory of it come from that . . . voice in his head?

Rand rode Tai'daishar out into the hollow, the horse's hooves stirring fallen leaves as he worked his way through the underbrush. Nynaeve followed, trying to urge her docile mare to keep up with Rand. That stablemaster was going to hear from her for certain. His ears would burn when she was through with him!

Hurin trotted his horse out as well, and the Aiel loped along, subtly keeping him surrounded. They had their faces veiled, spears or bows in hand. Past the trees and underbrush, Rand stopped Tai'daishar, looking across the open meadow toward the ancient city of Far Madding.

It wasn't large, not by the measure of the Great Cities. Nor was it beautiful, not when compared with the Ogier-built wonders Nynaeve had seen. But it was big enough, and it was certainly home to fine architecture and ancient relics. Set upon an island in a lake, it was actually faintly reminiscent of Tar Valon. Three broad bridges crossed the calm waters, and were the only means of entering the city.

A very large army was encamped around the lake, perhaps covering more ground than Far Madding itself. Nynaeve counted dozens of different pennons marking dozens of different houses. There were lines upon lines of horses, and tents like rows of summer crops, carefully planted and organized, awaiting harvest. The Borderlander army.

"I've heard of this place," Naeff said, riding up, close-cropped, dark brown hair ruffling in the wind. He narrowed his eyes, rectangular face dissatisfied. "It's like a *stedding*, only not as safe."

Far Madding's massive *ter'angreal*—known as the Guardian—created invisible protective bubbles that blocked people from touching the One Power. That could be worked around through the use of a very specialized *ter'angreal*, one of which Nynaeve happened to be wearing. But it would help only slightly.

The army looked close enough to be within the bubble that prevented men from channeling, which extended about a mile out around the city.

"They will know we've come," Rand said softly, eyes narrowed. "They'll have been waiting for it. They expect me to ride into their box."

"Box?" Nynaeve asked hesitantly.

"The city is a box," Rand said. "The whole city and the area round it. They want me where they can control me, but they don't understand. Nobody controls me. Not anymore. I've had enough of boxes and prisons, of chains and ropes. Never again will I put myself into the power of another."

Still staring at the city, he reached to its place on his saddle and removed the statuette of a man holding aloft a globe. Nynaeve felt a sharp chill. Did he have to bring *that* with him everywhere he went?

"Perhaps they need to be taught," Rand said. "Given encouragement to do their duty and obey me."

"Rand. . . ." Nynaeve tried to think. She couldn't let this happen again!

The access key began to glow faintly. "They want to capture me," he said softly. "Hold me. Beat me. They did it once in Far Madding already. They—"

"Rand!" Nynaeve said sharply.

He stopped, looking at her, seeing her as if for the first time.

"These are not slaves with their minds already burned away by Graendal. That is an entire city full of innocent people!"

"I wouldn't harm the people of the city," Rand said, voice emotionless. "That army deserves the demonstration, not the city. A rain of fire upon them, perhaps. Or lightning to strike and bite."

"They have done nothing other than ask you to meet with

them!" Nynaeve said, edging her horse closer to him. That *ter'angreal* sat like a viper in his hand. Once, it had cleansed the Source. If only it had melted away as the female one had!

She wasn't certain what would happen if he aimed a weave into the protective bubble of Far Madding, but she suspected it would still work. The Guardian didn't stop weaves from being made; Nynaeve had been able to craft weaves just fine, when she'd drawn upon her Well.

Either way, she knew that she had to stop Rand from turning his anger—or whatever it was he felt—upon his allies. "Rand," she said softly. "If you do this, there will be no turning back."

"There's already no turning back for me, Nynaeve," he said, his eyes intense. Those eyes shifted, sometimes seeming gray, sometimes blue. Today, they looked iron gray. He continued, voice flat. "My feet started on this path the moment Tam found me crying on that mountain."

"You don't have to kill anyone today. Please."

He turned to look back at the city. Slowly, mercifully, the access key stopped glowing. "Hurin!" he barked.

He must be close to fraying, Nynaeve thought. *His anger is slipping out in his voice.*

The thief-taker rode up to the front of the group. The Aiel kept their distance, however. "Yes, Lord Rand?"

"Return to your masters inside of their box," Rand said, voice under control again. "You are to give them a message for me."

"What message, Lord Rand?"

Rand hesitated, then slipped the access key back in its place. "Tell them that it will not be long before the Dragon Reborn rides to battle at Shayol Ghul. If they wish to return to their posts with honor, I will provide them with transport back to the Blight. Otherwise, they can remain here, hiding. Let them explain to their children and grandchildren why *they* were hundreds of leagues away from their posts when the Dark One was slain and the prophecies fulfilled."

Hurin looked shaken. "Yes, Lord Rand."

With that, Rand turned his horse about and rode back toward the clearing. Nynaeve followed, too slowly. Beautiful though Moonlight was, she'd have traded the beautiful mare in an instant for a biddable, dependable Two Rivers horse like Bela.

Hurin stayed behind. He still looked shaken. His reunion with "Lord Rand" had obviously been far from what he expected. Nynaeve gritted her teeth as the trees obscured her view of him. Inside the clearing, Rand had opened another gateway, a direct gateway to Tear.

They rode out into the Traveling ground prepared outside the Stone of Tear's stableyards. The air was hot and muggy in Tear, despite the overcast sky, and thick with the sounds of men training and gulls shrieking. Rand rode out to where stablehands waited, then dismounted, his face unreadable.

As Nynaeve climbed off of Moonlight and handed the reins to a ruddy-faced stable worker, Rand walked past her. "Look for a statue," he said.

"What?" she asked with surprise.

He glanced back at her, stopping. "You asked where Perrin was. He's camped with an army beneath the shade of an enormous fallen statue shaped like a sword stabbing the earth. I'm certain scholars here can tell you where it is; it's very distinctive."

"How . . . how do you know that?"

Rand just shrugged. "I just do."

"Why tell me?" she asked, walking alongside him across the yard of packed earth. She hadn't expected him to give up the information—he had gotten into the habit of holding onto whatever he knew, even if that knowledge was meaningless.

"Because," he said, striding toward the keep, voice growing almost too soft to hear, "I . . . have a debt to you for caring when I cannot. If you seek Perrin out, tell him that I will soon need him."

With that, he left her.

Nynaeve stood in the horse yard, watching him go. There was a wet scent to the air, the smell of new rain, and she could feel that she'd missed a sprinkle. Not enough to clear the air or muddy the ground, but enough to leave wetted sections of stone in shaded corners. To her right, men galloped and exercised horses beneath the dun sky, riding across sandy earth between pickets. The Stone was the only fortress she knew of with exercise areas for cavalry—but, then, the Stone was far from ordinary.

The rumble of hoofbeats was like the sound of a distant storm, and she found herself glancing northward. The storm there felt *closer* than it had before. She'd assumed it was gathering in the Blight, but now she wasn't so certain.

She took a deep breath, then hastened to the keep. She passed Defenders in their immaculate uniforms, the upper arm portions ribbed and puffy, breastplates smooth and curved. She passed stableboys, each probably dreaming of one day wearing that same uniform, but for now only leading horses back to the stables for hay and currying. She passed dozens of servants in linens, doubtless far more comfortable than Nynaeve's maroon wool.

The keep itself was a towering rock of a structure, sheer walls broken only by windows. Except that she could still spot the place where Mat had destroyed a section of stone with his Illuminator's fireworks when coming to rescue Nynaeve and the others from their imprisonment. Fool boy. Where was he? She hadn't seen him in . . . in quite a long time. Since Ebou Dar had fallen to the Seanchan. In a way, she felt as though she'd abandoned him, though she'd never admit that. Why, she'd embarrassed herself enough in front of the Daughter of the Nine Moons when she'd defended that scoundrel! She still didn't know what had come over her.

Mat could care for himself. He was probably carousing in some inn while the rest of them worked to save the world—drinking himself silly and playing at dice. Rand was another matter. He'd been so much easier to deal with when he'd continued to act like other men—stubborn and immature, but predictable. This new Rand with the cold emotions and the cold voice was truly unnerving.

The narrow corridors of the Stone were still unfamiliar to Nynaeve, and she often got lost. Her disorientation wasn't helped by the fact that hallways and walls sometimes changed places. She'd tried to discount such tales as superstitious nonsense, but the day before, she'd woken to discover that her room had indeed suddenly and mysteriously *moved*. Her door had opened to a smooth wall of the same seamless rock as the Stone itself. She'd been forced to escape through a gateway, and had been shocked to learn that her window looked out from a location two stories higher than it had the previous night!

752   THE GATHERING STORM

Cadsuane said it was the Dark One's touch on the world, causing the Pattern to unravel. Cadsuane said a lot of things, and few of them were things that Nynaeve wished to hear.

Nynaeve got lost twice as she wove her way through the corridors, but she eventually arrived at Cadsuane's room. At least Rand hadn't forbidden his stewards to grant her rooms. Nynaeve knocked—she'd learned that she'd better—then entered.

The Aes Sedai from Cadsuane's group—Merise and Corele—sat in the room, knitting and sipping tea, trying to look like they were *not* waiting on the infernal woman's whims. Cadsuane herself was speaking quietly with Min, whom she had all but appropriated in recent days. Min herself didn't seem to mind, perhaps because it wasn't easy to spend time with Rand these days. Nynaeve felt a stab of sympathy for the girl. Nynaeve only had to deal with Rand as a friend; all of this would be much harsher on the one who shared his heart.

All eyes turned toward Nynaeve as she closed the door. "I think I've found him," she announced.

"Who is that, child?" Cadsuane said, leafing through one of Min's books.

"Perrin," Nynaeve said. "You were right; Rand did know where he was."

"Excellent!" Cadsuane said. "You did well; it appears that you *can* be of use."

Nynaeve wasn't certain which annoyed her more—the backhanded compliment, or the fact that her heart swelled with pride at hearing it. She was no girl, without her braid, to be stroked by this woman's words!

"Well?" Cadsuane looked up from the book. The others remained silent, though Min did shoot Nynaeve a congratulatory smile. "Where is he?"

Nynaeve's opened her mouth to reply before she caught herself. What was it about this woman that made her want to obey? It wasn't the One Power or anything to do with it. Cadsuane simply projected the air of a stern, but fair, grandmother. The type you never spoke back to, but who would give you some baked sweets in reward for sweeping the floor when told.

"First, I want to know why Perrin is important." Nynaeve

stalked into the room and took the only remaining seat, a painted wooden stool. When she sat, she found herself sitting a few inches below eye level. Like a student before Cadsuane. She almost stood up, but realized that would draw more attention.

"Phaw!" Cadsuane said. "You'd hold this knowledge back, even if it means the lives of those you hold dear?"

"I want to know what I've gotten myself into," Nynaeve said stubbornly. "I want to know that this information isn't going to end up hurting Rand further."

Cadsuane snorted. "You presume to think that I'd *hurt* the fool boy?"

"I'm not going to presume otherwise," Nynaeve snapped. "Not until you *tell* me what you are doing."

Cadsuane closed the book—*Echoes of His Dynasty*—and looked perturbed. "Will you at least tell me how the meeting with the Borderlanders went?" she asked. "Or is that information held for ransom as well?"

Did she think she'd distract Nynaeve that easily? "It went poorly, as one might expect," she said. "They've hunkered down outside Far Madding and refuse to meet with Rand unless he comes within range of the Guardian, cutting himself off from the Source."

"Did he take it well?" Corele asked from her cushioned bench at the side of the room. She smiled faintly; she seemed to be the only one who thought the changes in Rand were amusing, rather than terrifying. But, then, she *was* one of the women who had bonded an Asha'man at practically the first opportunity.

"Did he take it well?" Nynaeve repeated flatly. "That depends. Does pulling out that blasted *ter'angreal* and threatening to rain down fire on the army strike you as 'Taking it well'?"

Min paled. Cadsuane raised an eyebrow.

"I stopped him," Nynaeve said. "But just barely. I don't know. It . . . it might be getting too late to do anything to change him."

"That boy *will* laugh again," Cadsuane said quietly, but intensely. "I didn't live this long to fail now."

"What does it matter?" Corele said.

Nynaeve turned in shock.

"Well?" Corele set down her mending. "What *does* it matter? We're obviously going to succeed."

"Light!" Nynaeve said. "What gave you *that* idea?"

"We've just spent all afternoon drilling this girl about her visions." Corele nodded to Min. "They always come true, and she's seen things that obviously can't happen until *after* the Last Battle. So we know that Rand is going to defeat the Dark One. The Pattern has already decided it. We can stop worrying."

"No," Min said. "You're wrong."

Corele frowned. "Child, are you saying that you lied about the things you've seen?"

"No," Min said. "But if Rand loses, there *is* no Pattern."

"The girl is correct." Cadsuane sounded surprised. "What this child sees are weavings in the Pattern from a time still distant—but if the Dark One wins, he will *destroy* the Pattern entirely. This is the only way the visions could fail to occur. The same holds for other prophecies and Foretellings. Our victory is by no means sure."

That stilled the room. They weren't playing at village politics or national dominance. At stake was creation itself.

Light. Can I withhold this information if there's any chance of it helping Lan? It wrenched her heart to think of him, and she had few options. In fact, Lan's only hope seemed to rest in the armies Rand could marshal and the gateways his people could form.

Rand had to change. For Lan. For them all. And she had no idea what to do other than, unfortunately, to trust Cadsuane. Nynaeve swallowed her pride and spoke. "Do you know the location of a statue of an enormous sword, fallen to the earth as if stabbing it?"

Corele and Merise glanced at each other in confusion.

"The hand of the *amahn'rukane*." Cadsuane turned from Min with a raised eyebrow. "The full statue was never finished, from what scholars can tell. It rests near the Jehannah Road."

"Perrin is camping in its shadow."

Cadsuane pursed her lips. "I assumed he would go eastward, toward lands al'Thor has captured." She took a deep breath. "All right. We are going for him *right now*." She hesitated, then glanced at Nynaeve. "In answer to your question earlier, child, Perrin actually isn't important to our plans."

"He isn't?" Nynaeve asked. "But—"

Cadsuane raised a finger. "There are people with him who are *vital*. One in particular."

CHAPTER

45

The Tower Stands

E gwene walked slowly through the rebel camp, wearing a crimson gown, its skirts divided for riding. The color raised not a few eyebrows. Considering what the Red Ajah had done, these Aes Sedai weren't likely to wear the hue. Even the camp's serving women had noticed, selling their red and maroon dresses or cutting them up for rags.

Egwene had asked for the crimson specifically. In the Tower, sisters had formed the habit of wearing only their own Ajah's color, and the practice had helped fuel the division. While it was good to be proud of your Ajah affiliation, it was dangerous to begin assuming that you couldn't trust anyone wearing other colors.

Egwene was all Ajahs. Today, the red symbolized many things to her. The impending reunification with the Red Ajah. A reminder of the division that needed to be righted. A sign of the blood that would be spilled, the blood of good men who fought to defend the White Tower.

The blood of the dead Aes Sedai, beheaded not an hour ago by Egwene's order.

Siuan had found her Great Serpent ring; it felt very good to have it on her finger again.

The sky was an iron gray, and the scent of dirt rose into the air, accompanying the bustling motion around the camp. Women hurriedly washed clothing, as if they were late in getting their patrons ready for a festival. Novices ran—literally ran—from lesson to lesson. Aes Sedai stood about with arms folded, eyes ready to burn any who didn't keep up the tempo.

They sense the tension of the day, Egwene thought. *And*

can't help but be made anxious by it. The night before, with
its attack by the Seanchan. Followed by the return of the
Amyrlin, who had spent the morning cleansing the Aes Sedai. And now afternoon, and the beating drums of war.

She doubted that Bryne's own camp was in such a state.
He'd have his men ready for attack; he probably could have
assaulted the White Tower at a moment's notice on any
given day of the siege. His soldiers would decide this war.
Egwene would *not* have her Aes Sedai riding into battle,
wriggling around their oaths not to use the Power to kill.
They would wait here, to be called only for Healing.

Or called if the White Tower sisters joined the fight in
earnest. Light send that Elaida saw wisdom in forbidding
that. If the Aes Sedai turned the Power against one another,
it would be a dark day indeed.

Can this day grow any darker? Egwene wondered. Many
of the Aes Sedai she passed in the camp gave her looks
of respect, awe, and a little horror. After a long absence,
the Amyrlin had returned. And she had brought destruction
and judgment in her wake.

Over fifty Black Sisters had been stilled, then executed.
Egwene felt sick, thinking of their deaths. Sheriam had
seemed almost relieved when her turn came, though she'd
soon begun to struggle, sobbing and desperate. She'd confessed to several disturbing crimes, as if hoping that her
willingness to speak would gain her amnesty.

They'd placed her head on the block and taken it off,
just like the others. That scene would always be vivid in
Egwene's mind—her former Keeper, lying with her head
pressed against the stump, blue dress and fiery red hair suddenly bathed in warm golden light as a thinner section of
clouds moved in front of the sun. Then the silvery axe, falling to claim her head. Perhaps the Pattern would be kinder
to her next time she was allowed a thread in its great tapestry. But perhaps not. Death was not an escape from the
Dark One. Sheriam's horror at the end indicated that she
might have been thinking that very thing as the axe took
her head.

Now Egwene understood fully how the Aiel could laugh
at a simple beating. Would that she could go through a few
days beneath the rod rather than have to order the execution
of women she had liked and worked with!

Some of the Sitters had argued for interrogation instead of execution, but Egwene had been insistent. Fifty women were far too many to shield and guard, and now that they knew stilling could be Healed, that wasn't an option. No, history proved how slippery and dangerous members of the Black could be, and Egwene was tired of worrying about what *could* happen. She had learned with Moghedien that there was a price to be paid for greed, if just greed for information. She and the others had been too eager—too proud of the "discoveries" they'd made—to see the world rid of one of the Forsaken.

Well, she would not allow a similar mistake here. The law was known, the Hall had made its judgment, and it had not been done in secret. Verin had died to stop these women, and Egwene would see that her sacrifice meant something.

You did well, Verin. So very well. Every Aes Sedai in the camp had been made to swear the Three Oaths over again, and only three members of the Black had been discovered beyond the ones Verin had located. Her research had been thorough.

The Blacks' Warders were under guard. They would have to be sorted through at a later date, when attention could be given to separating those who were really Darkfriends from those who were just enraged by the loss of their Aes Sedai. Most of them would seek death, even the innocent ones. Perhaps the innocent could be convinced to remain alive long enough to throw themselves into the Last Battle.

Nearly twenty of the Black sisters on Verin's list had still escaped, despite all of Egwene's precautions. She wasn't certain how they had known. Bryne's guards had caught some weaker ones trying to flee, and soldiers had fallen to delay them. But many had still escaped.

No use crying over that. Fifty Black were dead; that was a victory. A frightening one. But a victory nonetheless.

And so she walked through the camp, in riding boots and a dress of red, brown hair free to stream in the wind and tied with crimson ribbons to mark the streams of blood she had shed not an hour before. She did not blame the sisters around her for their sly glances, their masked concern, their fear. And their respect. If there had been any doubt that Egwene was Amyrlin, it had been dispelled. They accepted her, they feared her. And she would never quite fit in with them again. She was separate, and always would be.

A determined figure in blue made her way through the tents and approached Egwene. The dignified woman curtsied appropriately, though since they were walking so quickly, Egwene didn't stop to let her kiss the Great Serpent ring. "Mother," Lelaine said, "Bryne sends word that all is at ready for the assault. He says that the western bridges would be the ideal point of attack, though he suggests that gateways be employed to send a flanking force of his men behind the White Tower lines. He asks if this would be possible."

It wasn't using the Power as a weapon, but it was close. A fine distinction. But being Aes Sedai was *about* fine distinctions. "Tell him I will make the gateway myself," she said.

"Excellent, Mother," Lelaine said, bowing her head, the perfect, loyal attendant. It was remarkable, how quickly the woman's bearing toward Egwene had changed. She must have realized that her only choice was to attach herself to Egwene completely and give up on her attempts to secure power. This way, she didn't look like a hypocrite and would perhaps gain position through Egwene. Assuming Egwene was able to stabilize herself as a powerful Amyrlin.

It was a good assumption.

Lelaine must have been frustrated by Romanda's change of temperament. The Yellow waited beside the road ahead, as if on cue. She wore a dress after the color of her Ajah, hair back in a stately bun. She curtsied as Egwene reached her and barely spared a glance for Lelaine before falling into position on Egwene's right, away from Lelaine. "Mother," Romanda said, "I have made the inquiries you requested. There has been no contact with those sent to the Black Tower. Not a whisper."

"Does this strike you as odd?" Egwene asked.

"Yes, Mother. With Traveling they should have been there and back by now. They should have at least sent word. This silence is disturbing."

Disturbing indeed. Even worse, that delegation contained Nisao, Myrelle, Faolain *and* Theodrin. Each of the women had sworn fealty to Egwene. An unsettling coincidence. The departure of Faolain and Theodrin was particularly suspicious. Supposedly, they had gone because they had no Warders, but the sisters in the camp didn't consider those two full Aes Sedai—though nobody would dare say such to Egwene directly.

Why had those four, out of the hundreds of Aes Sedai in the camp, been placed in the delegation? Was it mere coincidence? It stretched plausibility. But what did it mean, then? Had someone intentionally sent away those loyal to Egwene? If so, why not send Siuan? Was this perhaps Sheriam's work? The woman had confessed to several things before her execution, but this hadn't been one of them.

Either way, something was happening with those Asha'man. The Black Tower would need to be dealt with.

"Mother," Lelaine said, drawing her attention back. The Blue didn't glance at her rival. "I have other news."

Romanda sniffed quietly.

"Speak," Egwene said.

"Sheriam wasn't lying," Lelaine said. "The *ter'angreal* used for dreams are gone. All of them."

"How is this possible?" Egwene demanded, letting a hint of her anger slip out.

"Sheriam was Keeper, Mother," Lelaine said quickly. "We kept the *ter'angreal* together, as is custom in the White Tower, under guard. But . . . well, what reason would those guards have had to turn Sheriam away?"

"And what do you suppose she was planning to tell us?" Egwene asked. "This theft could not have been kept hidden for long."

"I don't know, Mother," Lelaine said, shaking her head. "The guards said that Sheriam seemed . . . flustered . . . when she took the *ter'angreal*. This was just last night."

Egwene clenched her teeth, thinking of Sheriam's final spilled confessions. The theft of the *ter'angreal* had been far from the most shocking tidbit she'd mentioned. Elayne would be livid; she had made all of the copies that were stolen. While none of her copies worked as well as the original, they worked well enough. She would not be happy that they were in the hands of a Forsaken.

"Mother," Lelaine said, more softly. "What of Sheriam's . . . other claim?"

"That one of the Forsaken is in the White Tower, impersonating an Aes Sedai?" Egwene said. Sheriam claimed she'd given the *ter'angreal* to this . . . person.

Lelaine and Romanda walked silently, both staring forward, as if speculation were too daunting.

"Yes, I suspect that she is right," Egwene said. "They infiltrated not only our camp, but the aristocracies of Andor, Illian and Tear. Why not the White Tower as well?" She didn't add that Verin's book confirmed the presence of one of the Forsaken. It seemed best to keep the extent of Verin's notes secret.

"I wouldn't worry about it too much," Egwene said. "With the assault on the Tower, and our return, it seems likely that the Forsaken—whoever she is—will find it prudent to slip away and find an easier target for her scheming."

Lelaine and Romanda didn't seem comforted by that comment. The three of them reached the edge of the Aes Sedai camp, where mounts awaited them, as well as a large group of soldiers and one Sitter from each of the Ajahs, other than the Blue and Red. There wasn't a Blue because Lelaine was the only one remaining in camp; the reason there wasn't a Red was obvious. This was part of why Egwene had chosen to wear red, a subtle hint that all Ajahs should be represented in the action they were about to take. It was for the good of all.

As Egwene mounted, she noticed that Gawyn was following her, again, at a respectful distance. Where had he come from? They hadn't spoken since the early morning. As she mounted, so did he, and as she turned to ride out of camp with Lelaine, Romanda, the Sitters and the soldiers, Gawyn followed at a safe distance. Egwene wasn't certain what to do with him yet.

The army camp was mostly deserted. Tents sat empty, ground trampled by feet and hoofs, hardly any soldiers remaining behind. Egwene embraced the Source soon after leaving their camp, and she held to it, ready with weaves should someone attack her during the ride. She still didn't trust that Elaida wouldn't use a gateway to interfere with the assault. True, the false Amyrlin probably had her hands full with the aftermath of the Seanchan attack. But expectations like that one—assuming that she was safe—were what had gotten Egwene captured in the first place. She was

Amyrlin. She couldn't risk herself. It was frustrating, but she knew that an end had come to her days of solitary action, striking out as she saw fit. She could have been killed, rather than captured, all those weeks ago. The Salidar rebellion would have floundered, and Elaida would have continued as Amyrlin.

So it was that her force rode up to the battle lines outside the village of Darein. The White Tower still smoldered, a wide field of smoke trailing up in a ring from the center of the island, shrouding the white spire. Even from a distance, the scars of the Seanchan attack were evident on the building. Blackened holes, like spots of corruption on an otherwise healthy apple. The Tower almost seemed to groan as she looked at it. It had stood for so long, had seen so much. Now it had been wounded so deeply that it still bled a day later.

And yet it stood. Light bless them, it *stood*. It rose high, wounded but sound, pointing toward a sun hidden by clouds above. It stood defiant of those who would break it, within and without.

Bryne and Siuan waited for Egwene at the back of the army. A disparate couple they were. The battle-hardened general, with temples of gray and a face like an unyielding piece of armor. Strong, made of lines. And beside him Siuan, the diminutive woman in pale blue, her face lovely, looking young enough to be Bryne's granddaughter, for all the fact that they were near the same age.

Siuan made a horseback curtsy as Egwene approached, and Bryne saluted. His eyes were still troubled. He seemed ashamed of his part in the rescue, though Egwene bore him no grievance. He was a man of honor. If he had been bullied into coming along to protect foolhardy Siuan and Gawyn, then Bryne was to be commended for keeping them alive.

As Egwene joined them, she noted that Siuan and Bryne were riding close together. Had Siuan finally admitted her attraction to the man? And . . . there was a certain familiar grace to Bryne now. It was slight enough that she could have just been seeing things, but coupled with the relationship between the two. . . .

"You've taken another Warder, at last?" Egwene asked Siuan.

The woman narrowed her eyes. "Aye," she said.

Bryne did seem surprised, and a tad ashamed.

"Do your best to keep her out of trouble, General," Egwene said, staring Siuan in the eyes. "She has been in quite a bit of it lately. I have half a mind to give her to you to use as a foot soldier. I believe that the military organization might be good for her, and remind her that sometimes, *obedience* overrides initiative."

Siuan wilted, glancing away.

"I haven't decided what to do with you yet, Siuan," Egwene said in a softer voice. "But my anger has been kindled. And my trust has been lost. You will need to soothe the first and stoke the second if you wish to enter my confidence again."

She turned from Siuan to the general, who looked sick. Probably from being forced to feel Siuan's shame.

"You are to be commended for your bravery, letting her bond you, General," Egwene said, turning to Bryne. "I realize that keeping *her* from trouble is a nearly impossible charge, but I have confidence in you."

The general relaxed. "I shall do my best, Mother," he said. Then he turned his horse, glancing along the rows of soldiers. "There is something you should see. If you will?"

She nodded, turning her horse and riding beside him down the roadway. The village was cobbled here, the population evacuated, the main thoroughfare lined with thousands of Bryne's soldiers. Siuan accompanied Egwene, and Gawyn followed. Lelaine and Romanda stayed with the other Sitters at a wave of Egwene's hand. Their newfound obedience was proving useful, particularly since they had apparently decided that they would now be trying to outdo one another for Egwene's approval. Likely, they were both vying to be her new Keeper, now that Sheriam was gone.

The general led Egwene to the front lines, and Egwene prepared a weave of Air just in case an arrow was shot in her direction. Siuan eyed her, but said nothing at the precaution. It shouldn't have been needed—Tower Guards would never fire on an Aes Sedai, not even in a conflict like this one. However, the same couldn't be said of Warders, and accidents *did* happen. It would be very convenient for Elaida if a stray arrow took her rival in the throat.

They made their way through the village, finally coming

to a stop near the Darein Bridge, a majestic white construction that spanned the river to Tar Valon. Here was the thing Bryne wanted her to see: Gathered just west of the high point of the bridge, bunkered down behind a blockade of stones and large logs, was a force of Tower Guard. They looked to be about three hundred strong. Across the river, more soldiers stood atop the walls. They brought the total to no more than a thousand.

Bryne's assault force here was ten thousand strong.

"Now, I know it was never numbers that were keeping us from attacking," Bryne said. "But the Tower Guard should be able to field more men than that, particularly with conscriptions out of the city proper. I doubt they've been spending these months carving pegs by the fire and reminiscing about old times. If Chubain has half a mind, he's been training a new set of recruits."

"So where is everyone?" Egwene asked.

"Light only knows, Mother," Bryne said, shaking his head. "We'll lose some men getting past that force, but not many. It will be a rout."

"Could the Seanchan have really hurt them *that* much?"

"I don't know, Mother," Bryne said. "It was bad last night. A lot of fire, a lot of men dead. But I'd have pegged the cost at hundreds, not thousands. Perhaps the Tower Guard is clearing out rubble and stopping the fires, but I still think they'd have gathered a larger force when they saw me forming up here. I've taken a spyglass to those lads over there, and I've noted more than one set of bleary red eyes."

Egwene sat thoughtfully, glad for the breeze blowing in along the river from downstream. "You haven't questioned the wisdom of this assault, General."

"It's not my habit to question where I'm pointed, Mother."

"And your thoughts on the matter, if asked?"

"If asked?" Byrne said. "Well, attacking makes tactical sense. We've lost Traveling as an edge, and if our enemy can resupply at will and send envoys in and out whenever they want, then what's the purpose of a siege? It's time to either attack or pack up and leave."

Egwene nodded. And yet, she found herself hesitating. That ominous smoke in the sky, the maimed Tower, the frightened soldiers without reinforcements. It all seemed to whisper a warning.

"How long can we wait before you absolutely *must* begin this assault, General?" she asked.

He frowned, but didn't question her. He glanced at the sky. "It's getting late. An hour, perhaps? After that, it will be too dark. With numbers this favorable, I'd rather not add the randomness of a night battle to the mix."

"We wait, then, for an hour," Egwene said, settling back on her mount. The others seemed confused, but they said nothing. The Amyrlin Seat had spoken.

What was she waiting for? What were her instincts telling her? Egwene thought on it as the minutes extended, eventually realizing what had made her pause. Once this step had been taken, there was no turning back. The White Tower had suffered the previous night; it was the first time an enemy force had used the One Power against it. Egwene's assault would be another first: the first time one group of Aes Sedai had led troops in battle against another group. There had been fights between factions in the Tower before; clashes between one Ajah and another, some turning to bloodshed, like what had happened after Siuan's ousting. The Secret Histories mentioned such events.

But never had the dissension extended beyond the doors of the Tower itself. Never had Aes Sedai led troops across those bridges. To do so now would attach the event forever to Egwene's tenure as Amyrlin. Whatever else she achieved, it would likely be overshadowed by this day.

She had hoped to liberate and unite. Instead, she would turn to war and subjugation. If it had to be so, then she would give the command. But she wanted to wait until the last possible moment. If that meant a grim hour beneath the overcast sky, horses snorting as they sensed their riders' tension, then so be it.

Bryne's hour came and passed. Egwene hesitated for a few minutes longer—as long as she dared. No relief came to the poor soldiers standing on the bridge. They just stared out from behind their little barricade, resolute.

Reluctantly, Egwene turned to give the command.

"Here now." Bryne leaned forward in his saddle. "What is this?"

Egwene turned back to the bridge. Distantly, just barely visible, a procession was coming over the top. Had she waited too long? Had the White Tower sent reinforcements?

Had she cost the lives of her men by her stubborn reluctance?

But no. That group wasn't soldiers, but women in skirts. Aes Sedai!

Egwene held up her hand, staying any attacks by her soldiers. The procession rode directly up to the Tower Guard fortification. A moment later, a woman in a gray dress stepped out in front of the blockade, accompanied by a single Warder. Egwene squinted, trying to make out the woman's features, and Bryne hastily handed her his spyglass. Egwene accepted it thankfully, but had already recognized the woman. Andaya Forae, one of the new Sitters to the Hall chosen after the split. Gray Ajah. That implied a willingness to negotiate.

The glow of power surrounded the woman, and Siuan hissed, causing several nearby soldiers to raise their bows. Again Egwene held up a hand. "Bryne," she said sternly, "I will *not* have the first shot fired until I give permission."

"Stand down, men!" Bryne bellowed. "I'll have your hides if you so much as nock an arrow!" The men snapped their bows back down from the ready.

The distant woman used a weave Egwene couldn't make out, and then spoke in a voice that was obviously amplified. "We would speak with Egwene al'Vere," Andaya said. "Is she in attendance?"

Egwene made her own weave to amplify her voice. "I am here, Andaya. Tell the others with you to come out so that I can see them."

Surprisingly, they obeyed the command. Nine more women filed out, and Egwene studied each one. "Ten Sitters," she said, handing Bryne back his spyglass and releasing her weave so that she could speak without her words being projected. "Two from each Ajah except the Blue and the Red."

"That's promising." Bryne rubbed his chin.

"Well, they could be here to demand my surrender," Egwene noted. "All right," she said, amplifying her voice with the Power again. "What do you wish of me?"

"We have come," Andaya said. She hesitated. "We have come to inform you that the Hall of the White Tower has chosen to raise you to the Amyrlin Seat."

Siuan gasped in shock, and Bryne cursed quietly to himself. Several of the soldiers muttered about it being a trap. But Egwene just closed her eyes. Dared she hope? She'd assumed that her unwanted rescue had come too soon. But if she'd laid enough groundwork before being taken by Siuan and Gawyn. . . .

"What of Elaida?" Egwene demanded, opening her eyes, her voice booming across the expanse. "Have you deposed yet another Amyrlin?"

The other side was silent for a moment. "They're conferring." Bryne had raised his spyglass.

Andaya spoke a moment later. "Elaida do Avriny a Roihan, Watcher of the Seals, the Flame of Tar Valon, the Amyrlin Seat . . . was taken in the raid last night. Her whereabouts are unknown. She is presumed dead or otherwise unable to fulfill her duties."

"By the Light!" Bryne lowered the glass.

"No more than she deserved," Siuan muttered.

"No woman deserves that," Egwene said to Siuan and Bryne. Absently she raised fingers to her neck. "Better she had died."

Bryne said, "This could be a trap."

"I don't see how," Siuan said. "Andaya is bound by the oaths. She wasn't on your list of Black, was she, Egwene?"

Egwene shook her head.

"I'm still hesitant, Mother," Bryne said.

Egwene restored her weave. "You will let my army enter? You will accept the other Aes Sedai back in fellowship and will reinstate the Blue Ajah?"

"We anticipated these demands," Andaya said. "They will be met."

There was silence, the only sound that of the waters lapping against their banks below.

"Then I accept," Egwene said.

"Mother," Siuan said cautiously. "This might be rash. Perhaps you should speak with—"

"It is not rash," Egwene released her weave and felt a surge of hope. "It is what we've wanted." She eyed Siuan. "Besides. Who are you to lecture me on being rash?" Siuan looked down. "General, prepare your men to cross, and bring the Sitters at the back forward. Send runners back to the Aes Sedai camp with the news, and make certain your men at the other bridges know to stand down."

"Yes, Mother." Bryne wheeled his horse about and gave the necessary orders.

Taking a deep breath, Egwene kicked her horse into motion onto the bridge. Siuan muttered a fisher's curse and followed. Egwene could hear Gawyn's horse following as well, then a squad of soldiers obeying a curt command from Bryne.

Egwene rode across the waters, hair blowing out behind her, laced with red ribbons. She felt an odd sense of moment—a weight of realization—as she considered what they had all just avoided. It was soon replaced with growing satisfaction and joy.

Her white mare bucked her head slightly, brushing a silky mane across Egwene's hands. On the bridge, the Sitters turned to make their way into the city. The Tower rose just ahead. Wounded. Bleeding.

But it still stood. Light, it *stood*!

CHAPTER

46

To Be Forged Again

After crossing the bridge to Tar Valon as a victor, the day nearly became a blur for Egwene. She hastened to the White Tower, Siuan and Gawyn barely managing to keep up with her. At the Tower, Egwene was met by a group of servants; the Sitters themselves were waiting in the Hall for Egwene.

The servants led her to an unadorned, wood-paneled chamber set with a pair of leather-padded chairs. Egwene had never been here before; it appeared to be a kind of waiting room near the Hall. It smelled of leather, and a small brazier burned coals in the corner.

Soon, a short, toadlike Brown sister named Lairain entered and instructed Egwene on the proper way to go about the ceremony. The little curly-haired woman seemed completely indifferent to the importance of the moment, and Egwene had never met her before. Likely, she was one of the Browns who spent her life roaming the back library stacks, and only surfaced once a century or so to recite instructions to prospective Amyrlins. Egwene listened carefully; she'd gone through the ceremony once, but it was very complex.

She could still remember her nervousness on that day, months ago, when she'd been raised in Salidar. Back then, she'd still been confused as to what was happening. Her? Amyrlin?

That hesitation was gone. She did not really worry about getting the ceremony wrong. It was only a ceremony, and the important decision had already been made. As Egwene listened to Lairain, she heard Siuan arguing outside the doors with one of the sisters, claiming that Egwene had already been raised, and that this ceremony wasn't needed. Egwene quieted Lairain with a raised hand and called out to Siuan.

Siuan peeked in the door.

"I was raised by the rebels, Siuan," Egwene said sternly. "These women deserve the chance to stand for me as well. Otherwise, I will never have a claim to their loyalty. The ceremony must be performed again."

Siuan scowled, but nodded. "Very well."

Lairain opened her mouth to continue instructions, but Egwene silenced her with another motion, earning a huff. "What news have you, Siuan?"

"Well," Siuan said, cracking the door a little wider, "Bryne moved most of his troops across the bridges, and has relieved the Tower Guard from their positions at the fortifications, sending them in—along with a number of his own squads—to help put out flareups around the city. The Seanchan set some homes on fire to cover their retreat as they fled."

That explained the lack of troops at the barricade—that, along with the knowledge that the Hall was busy debating whether or not to raise Egwene. They likely didn't realize how close they'd come to war.

"What do you want to do with the sisters from your camp?" Siuan asked. "They're starting to wonder."

"Tell them to gather in front of the Sunset Gate," Egwene said. "Have them stand in ranks by Ajah, with Sitters in a line at the front. Once I am finished with the ceremony, I will greet them and formally accept their apology for their rebellion and welcome them back into the Tower."

"Accept their *apology*?" Siuan asked incredulously.

"They rebelled against the Tower, Siuan," Egwene said, looking at her. "Whatever the need of what they did, there is reason for apology."

"But you were with them!"

"I no longer represent just them, Siuan," Egwene said firmly. "I represent the Tower. The entire Tower. And the Tower needs to know that the rebels regret the division. They needn't lie and say that they wished they had stayed, but I think it *is* appropriate for them to express sorrow over the hardships the division caused. I will acquit them, and we can get on with healing."

"Yes, Mother," Siuan said in resignation. Egwene caught

sight of Tesan standing behind, the woman nodding her Taraboner-braided head at Egwene's words.

Egwene let Lairain continue her instructions, then repeated back to her the lines she would have to say and the actions she'd have to take. When the Brown was satisfied, Egwene rose, pulled open the door and found that Siuan had left to relay her orders. Tesan stood in the hallway outside, arms folded, regarding Gawyn. He leaned against the wall a short distance away, his hand resting on the pommel of his sheathed sword.

"Your Warder?" Tesan asked of Egwene.

She regarded Gawyn, and was forced to confront a whole mess of emotions. Anger, affection, passion and regret. What a strange mix. "No," she said. She stared Gawyn in the eyes. "What I am going to do next you cannot be part of, Gawyn. Wait here."

He opened his mouth to object, thought better of it, then stood up stiffly and bowed. That gesture felt even more insolent than an argument would have.

Egwene sniffed softly—yet loud enough for him to hear—then allowed Tesan to lead her to the Hall of the Tower. The Hall: both a place and a group of people. For they were one, just as the Amyrlin Seat was a person, yet was also the chair in which she sat.

She stopped before the doors to the Hall, the dark wood inlaid with the silver Flame of Tar Valon, and felt her heart flutter rebelliously. Siuan suddenly appeared, with a pair of slippers, gesturing at Egwene's riding boots. Of course; the Hall floor was delicately painted. She changed into the slippers; Siuan took her boots away. There was no need to be nervous! *I've been here before,* she thought suddenly. *Not just in Salidar. In my testing. I've faced this door, confronted the women beyond. In my testing . . .*

A gong suddenly sounded; it seemed loud enough to shake the entire Tower, ringing to warn that an Amyrlin was about to be raised. The gong rang again, then again, and those ornate doors swung open. Yes, this was a different experience entirely from the one she'd had back in that humble wooden building where she'd been raised by the Salidar Aes Sedai. In many ways, her performance in Salidar had been but a rehearsal.

The doors finished opening, and Egwene stifled a gasp.

The grand, domed room beyond now had a blasted hole—a gaping emptiness—directly across from the entrance. It looked out at Dragonmount. The chamber wasn't as damaged as some had been in the Seanchan attack; the rubble was minimal, and the destruction had barely reached past that outer wall. The raised platform still ran around the outside of the room, and the chairs it held were undamaged. Eighteen of them, in clusters of three, each painted and cushioned to declare the Ajah of its inhabitant.

The Amyrlin Seat stood by the far wall, directly in front of the broken wall, its back to the sprawling landscape beyond and distant Dragonmount. If the Seanchan blast had gone a few feet farther inward, the Seat would have been destroyed. Thank the Light, it was unmarred.

Egwene could faintly smell paint in the air. Had they hurriedly had the Seat repainted to bear all seven colors again? If so, they'd worked quickly. They hadn't had time to replace the seats of the Blue Sitters, however.

Egwene noted Saerin, Doesine and Yukiri sitting with their respective Ajahs. Seaine was there as well, regarding Egwene with those calculating blue eyes. How much power had these four women wielded in these events? Square-faced Suana, of the Yellow, was smiling openly in satisfaction as she regarded Egwene, and while most of the faces bore the serene, unemotional faces of Aes Sedai, Egwene sensed approval in their postures. Or, at least, a lack of hostility. More than just the Black Ajah hunters had been behind this decision.

Saerin stood up from her chair in the Brown section. "Who comes before the Hall of the Tower?" she asked in a ringing voice.

Egwene hesitated, still looking over the Sitters, their seats arranged around the outer platform, equally spaced. Too many of those chairs were empty. There were only two Green Sitters; Talene had fled weeks ago. The Gray were missing Evanellein, who had vanished earlier in the day. Velina and Sedore were gone as well. That didn't bode well; those two were on Verin's list of Black Ajah. Had they been warned? Did Evanellein's disappearance mean Verin had missed her?

There were no Red sisters either. With a start, Egwene remembered that Duhara had left the Tower some weeks before—nobody knew why, but some said it had been on a mission for Elaida. Perhaps she was about Black Ajah business. The other two red Sitters, Javindhra and Pevara, had vanished mysteriously.

That left eleven Sitters. Not enough to raise an Amyrlin by the old laws of the Tower—but those had been revised with Elaida's disbanding of the Blue. Fewer Sitters meant fewer women needed to raise an Amyrlin, and now only eleven were required. It would have to do. At least each and every Sitter currently in the Tower knew of this event; it wasn't in secret, like Elaida's raising. And Egwene could be reasonably certain no Black Sitters would stand for her.

Saerin cleared her throat, glancing at Egwene uncertainly, and called again, "Who comes before the Hall of the Tower?"

Tesan leaned in from the side, as if to hiss the proper response to Egwene. Egwene, however, cut her off by holding up a hand.

There was something Egwene had been considering, something audacious. Yet it was appropriate. She knew that it was. She could *feel* that it was. "The Red Ajah is in disgrace?" she asked quietly of Tesan.

The White nodded, braided hair brushing the sides of her face. "The Reds, you needn't worry about them," she said in her light Taraboner accent. "Following Elaida's disappearance, they retreated back to their quarters. The Sitters here, they worried that the Red would choose new Sitters quickly and send them to this proceeding. I believe some . . . curt missives from the Hall of the Tower were enough to cow them."

"And Silviana Brehon? Still imprisoned?"

"She is, as far as I know, Mother," Tesan said, slipping for a moment and using the title, though Egwene hadn't been formally raised by the Hall yet. "Don't worry, Leane—she has been freed. We had her escorted out to stand with the other rebels, awaiting your forgiveness."

Egwene nodded thoughtfully. "Have Silviana brought here, to the Hall of the Tower, immediately."

Tesan's brow wrinkled. "Mother, I don't think this is the time—"

"Just do it," Egwene hissed, then turned to face the Hall. "One who comes obediently, in the Light," she pronounced in a firm voice.

Saerin relaxed. "Who comes before the Hall of the Tower?"

"One who comes humbly, in the Light," Egwene responded. She stared at each of the Sitters. A firm hand. She would have to be firm. They needed leadership.

"Who comes before the Hall of the Tower?" Saerin finished.

"One who comes at the summons of the Hall," Egwene said, "obedient and humble in the Light, asking only to accept the will of the Hall."

The ceremony proceeded, each of the Sitters stripping to the waist to prove she was a woman. Egwene did the same, and barely gave a blush at the thought of Gawyn, who had clearly thought she should bring him along to the event.

"Who stands for this woman?" Saerin asked after the Sitters had re-dressed. Egwene had to remain stripped to the waist for now, and the cool breeze through the broken wall was chill on her skin. "And pledges for her, heart for heart, soul for soul, life for life?"

Yukiri, Seaine and Suana stood quickly. "I so pledge," each of them announced.

The first time Egwene had experienced this ceremony, she had been in shock. At each step, she'd been terrified she'd make an error. Worse, she'd been terrified that it would all turn out to be a ruse or a mistake.

That fear was gone. As the ritual questions were asked—as Egwene stepped forward three steps and knelt on the smooth floor, repainted by Elaida's order with only six colors spiraling out of the mark of the Flame of Tar Valon—Egwene saw through the pomp and looked at the core of what was happening. These women were terrified. As had been the women in Salidar. The Amyrlin Seat was a force of stability, and they reached for it.

Why had she been chosen? Both times, it seemed the same answer. Because she was the only one they could all agree upon. There were smiling faces in this group. But they were the smiles of women who had succeeded in keeping rivals off of the Seat. Either that, or they were the smiles of women who were relieved that *someone* was stepping up to take leadership. And, perhaps, there were some who smiled because they weren't the ones who had to take the Seat. Its recent history had been fraught with danger, dissension, and two dramatic tragedies.

Originally, in Salidar, Egwene had thought the women

were being idiots. She was more experienced now, and hopefully wiser as well. She could see that they hadn't been fools. They'd been Aes Sedai—covering their fear by being overly cautious, yet brazen at the same time. Choosing someone they wouldn't mind seeing fall. Taking a risk, but not putting themselves in direct danger.

These women were doing the same. They covered their fear with smooth faces and acts of control. When the time came for the Sitters to stand in her support, Egwene was not surprised that all eleven rose to their feet. Not a single dissent. There would be no foot washing during this ceremony.

No, she was not surprised. They knew that there was no other option, not with an army on their doorstep, not with Elaida as good as dead. The Aes Sedai thing to do was act as if there had never been any argument. The consensus must be reached.

Saerin looked surprised that nobody had chosen to remain seated, if only to prove that she would not be bullied. In fact, more than one of the Sitters seemed surprised, and Egwene suspected that they were regretting their decision to stand up so quickly. One could gain some measure of power by being the only person who remained seated, forcing Egwene to wash her feet and ask for permission to serve. Of course, that also could have singled the woman out, and earned her the dislike of the new Amyrlin.

The women slowly took their seats. Egwene needed no guidance, and none was offered. She rose and strode across the hall, her slippered feet silent on the painted stone of the Flame. A gust of wind blew through the room, ruffling shawls, blowing across Egwene's bare skin. It said something for the strength of the Hall that they had chosen to meet here, despite the dizzying view out of the far wall.

Saerin met Egwene at the Seat. The olive-skinned Altaran began to button Egwene's bodice with careful fingers, then reverently lifted the Amyrlin's stole from the Seat. It was the one with all seven colors, recovered from wherever Elaida had discarded it. Saerin regarded Egwene for a moment, hefting the stole, as if judging it.

"Are you certain you want to bear this weight, child?" Saerin asked in a very soft voice. This was not part of the ceremony.

"I bear it already, Saerin." Egwene's reply was almost a whisper. "Elaida cast it aside when she tried to slice it and divide it as she wished. I took it up and have carried it since. I would bear it to my death. And will."

Saerin nodded. "I think that might be why you deserve it," she said. "I doubt anything in the histories will compare to the days ahead. I suspect that, in the future, scholars will look back on our days and judge them to be more difficult—more trying of mind, body and soul—than the Time of Madness or the Breaking itself."

"Then it's a good thing the world has us, isn't it?" Egwene asked.

Saerin hesitated, then nodded. "I suppose it is at that." She raised the stole and set it upon Egwene's shoulders. "You are raised to the Amyrlin Seat!" she declared, the voices of the other Sitters joining in, "In the glory of the Light, that the White Tower may endure forever. Egwene al'Vere, the Watcher of the Seals, the Flame of Tar Valon, the *Amyrlin Seat*!"

Egwene turned to regard the group of women, then sat down in the chair. She felt as if she had returned home after a very long journey. The world bowed beneath the stress of the Dark One's touch, but it felt a little more right—a little more secure—the moment she took her place.

The women arranged themselves before her in order of age, with Saerin at the very end. One at a time they curtsied deeply before her, asked her permission to serve, then kissed her Great Serpent ring and stepped aside. As they did so, Egwene noticed that Tesan had finally returned. She peeked in to be certain everyone was dressed, then returned a moment later leading a group of four guards with the Flame of Tar Valon burning white on their chests. Egwene suppressed a sigh. They'd brought Silviana in chains, it appeared.

After kissing her ring, the Sitters returned to their chairs. There was some little more to the ceremony, but the important part was through with. Egwene was Amyrlin, really and truly, at long last. She had waited so long for this moment.

Now it was time for some surprises.

"Release the prisoner's chains," Egwene said.

Reluctantly, the soldiers outside the room did as demanded, the metal clinking. The Sitters turned with confused expressions.

"Silviana Brehon!" Egwene declared, standing up. "You may approach the Amyrlin Seat."

The soldiers stepped aside and allowed Silviana to enter. Her red dress had once been fine, but she had not been well treated by Elaida's confinement. Her black hair—normally kept in a bun—was instead coarsely braided. Her dress was rumpled, the knees dirty. And yet her square face was serene.

Surprisingly, she knelt before Egwene after walking across the room. Egwene lowered her hand and let the woman kiss her ring.

The Sitters watched, confused that Egwene had broken the ceremony. "Mother," Yukiri finally asked. "Is this the best time to be dispensing judgment?"

Egwene withdrew her hand from the kneeling Silviana and looked directly at Yukiri, then turned her gaze across the waiting Sitters. "You all bear a great deal of shame," she said.

Stiff-faced Aes Sedai raised eyebrows and opened eyes wider. They seemed angry. They had no right! Their anger was nothing beside hers.

"This," Egwene said, gesturing toward the broken wall. "You bear responsibility for this." She pointed at Silviana, still kneeling. "You bear responsibility for *this*. You bear responsibility for the way our sisters regard one another in the halls, and you bear responsibility for letting the Tower remain so long in division. Many of you bear responsibility for that division in the first place!

"You are a *disgrace*. The White Tower—the pride of the Light, the power for stability and truth since the Age of Legends—has nearly been shattered because of you."

Eyes bugged out, and a few women choked in shock. "Elaida—" one began.

"Elaida was a madwoman, and you all know it!" Egwene said sternly, standing tall, staring them down. "You knew it these last few months as she worked unwittingly to destroy us. Light, many of you probably knew it when you *raised* her in the first place!

"There have been foolish Amyrlins before, but none have come as close to tearing down the entire Tower! *You* are a check upon the Amyrlin. *You* are to keep her from doing things like this! *You* allowed her to disband an entire Ajah? What were you *thinking*? How is it that you allowed the Tower

to fall so far? And when the *Dragon Reborn* himself walks
the land, no less!

"You should have removed Elaida the moment you heard
of her disastrous attempt to confine Rand al'Thor. You should
have removed her when you saw how her bickering and petti-
ness was turning Ajahs against one another. And you should
certainly have removed her when she refused to do what was
needed to bring the Tower together again, whole as one!"

Egwene looked down the lines of sisters, staring at each
one in turn, meeting each set of eyes until they looked away.
None dared hold her gaze for long. Finally, she saw shame
begin to peek through their masks. As well it should!

"None of you would stand up to her," Egwene spat. "You
dare call yourself the Hall of the Tower? You who were
cowed? You who were too frightened to do what was needed?
You who were too caught up in your own squabbles and politicking to *see* what was needed?"

Egwene looked down at Silviana. "Only one woman in
this room was willing to stand up for what she knew to be
right. Only one woman dared defy Elaida, and she accepted
the price of doing so. And you think I brought this woman
here to exact *vengeance* on her? Are you really so blinded
that you think I'd punish the only person in the entire Tower
who did anything of decency these last few months?"

They were all looking down, now. Even Saerin wouldn't
meet her eyes.

Silviana looked up at her.

"You did your duty, Silviana," Egwene said. "And you did
it well. Rise."

The woman stood. She looked haggard, eyes puffy from
lack of sleep, and Egwene suspected she was having trouble
standing. Had anyone seen to bringing her food or water during the chaos of the last few days?

"Silviana," Egwene said, "a new Amyrlin has been raised.
And, it shames me to say, it was done with subterfuge similar
to Elaida's raising. Of the seven Ajahs, only five were represented. The Blue I know would support me, were they here.
But the Red were not even given a chance to voice their dissent or approval."

"There are good reasons for that, Mother," Silviana said.

"That may be true," Egwene said, "but it all but ensures
that my reign will be marked with tension between myself

and the Red. They will perceive ill will where there is none, and I will lose the strength of hundreds of women. Women that will be sorely needed."

"I . . . don't see any way around that, Mother," Silviana said, honestly.

"I do," Egwene said. "Silviana Brehon, I would have you as my Keeper of the Chronicles. Let it not be said that I spurned the Red."

Silviana blinked in surprise. There were a few gasps from the Sitters, though Egwene did not mark whose they were.

She stared Silviana in the eyes. Just a short time ago, this woman had had Egwene over the side of the desk, paddling her at Elaida's command. But Silviana now knelt; she had done so without needing an order. She accepted the Hall's authority to raise Egwene. Did she accept Egwene herself?

Egwene's offer would place her on a difficult and dangerous road. The Reds might see it as a betrayal. What would Silviana's response be? Egwene blessed the trick that kept her from sweating, otherwise she knew that drops would have been trickling down the sides of her face.

"I would be honored, Mother," Silviana said, kneeling again. "Truly honored."

Egwene let out a breath. Her task of reuniting the fractured Ajahs would be difficult—but if the Reds saw her as an enemy, it would be nearly impossible. With Silviana on her side, she would have an envoy to the Reds who would not be rejected. Hopefully.

"This will be a difficult time for the Red Ajah, daughter," Egwene said. "Their nature has always been to capture men who can channel, but reports claim that *saidin* is cleansed."

"There will still be rogue channelers, Mother," Silviana said. "And men are not to be trusted."

Someday, we will have to move beyond that last sentiment, Egwene thought. *But for now, it is true enough to let stand.* "I didn't say that your purpose would vanish, only that it would change. I see great things for the Red Ajah in the future—an expanding of vision, a renewal of duty. I am pleased to have you at my side to help guide them."

Egwene looked up at the Sitters, who were watching in stunned silence. "I'd order you all to do penance," Egwene said, "save for the fact that I know some of you, at least, were working behind the scenes to stop the crumbling of the

White Tower. You didn't do enough, but you did something. Beyond that, I think that the penance we often demand of ourselves is ridiculous. What is physical pain to Aes Sedai?"

Egwene took a deep breath. "And I am not guiltless either. I share some of your shame, for it was during my tenure that these disasters occurred. I sided with the rebels, allowed myself to be raised by them because it was the only choice. But that choice still gives me culpability.

"Bear your shame, Sitters, but bear it with determination. Do not let it break you. The time for healing has begun, and there is no longer any use in pointing fingers. You failed. But you are all that we have. *We* are all that the world has."

The women began to look up.

"Come," Egwene said, striding through the room, Silviana smoothly falling into step beside her. "Let us greet the rebels."

They passed through the hallways of the Tower, which still smelled of smoke and were strewn with rubble in places. Egwene tried not to look at the bloodstains. The Sitters followed behind, clustering in Ajah groups, despite Egwene's recent chastisement. There would still be a lot of work to heal them.

"Mother," Silviana said quietly as they walked, "I can only assume that you had a Keeper already, among the rebels. Do you intend to maintain two of us?" Her tense voice revealed what she thought of such an unconventional arrangement.

"No," Egwene said. "My previous Keeper was executed for being of the Black Ajah."

Silviana paled. "I see."

"We can't dance around these things, Silviana," Egwene said. "I received a very important visitor just before my . . . rescue. She was of the Black, and betrayed to me the names of other Black sisters. I have confirmed each of those who were among the rebel Aes Sedai through use of the Oath Rod."

"The Oath Rod?" Silviana exclaimed.

"Yes," Egwene said as they entered a stairwell. "I was given it last night by an ally in the Tower. Though, it occurs to me that we'll have to move the room with the *ter'angreal*. And keep the location secret and constantly warded. It won't be long before every sister with sufficient power knows the weave for Traveling, and I wouldn't put it past many of

them—including those I trust—to 'borrow' *angreal* now and
again."

"Yes, Mother," Silviana said. Then, in a quieter voice. "I'm
going to have to get used to a lot of things changing, I suspect."

"I'm afraid so," Egwene said. "Not the least of which will
be the need to choose a proper Mistress of Novices, one who
can deal with hundreds of new initiates—many of whom are
not of the standard age. I've already begun the process of
accepting for training any woman, no matter how old, who
shows some measure of ability with channeling. I suspect
that before long, the White Tower will be bursting at the
seams with novices."

"I shall consider suggestions for a replacement quickly
then, Mother," Silviana said.

Egwene nodded in approval. Romanda and Lelaine would
undoubtedly be livid when they discovered what Egwene
had done in choosing Silviana, but the more she considered
it, the more satisfied Egwene was. Not just because Silviana
was Red, but because she was so capable. Saerin would have
been a fair choice, but many would have seen her as being
Egwene's guide, and perhaps the real power behind the Seat.
Picking a Blue would have been too divisive for the current
state of the Tower. And besides, with an Amyrlin who was
one of the rebels—nobody would soon forget that, no matter
what Egwene said or did—it would go a long way toward
healing relations to have a Keeper who had been a loyalist.

Before long, they reached the Tower's Great Square, on
the east side of the building. The square was filled—as per
her orders—by women in ranks by Ajah. Egwene had chosen this position because of the tall steps leading up to the
Tower, topped by a spacious landing. She stood there, back to
the majestically carved doors. It was a perfect location from
which to address a crowd.

It was also situated between the wings, which had taken
the worst damage during the attack the previous night. The
east wing still smoldered; the dome had collapsed; one of the
walls had fallen in. However, from this vantage, the Tower
itself was relatively free of scars, and neither of the gaping
holes was directly visible.

Egwene could see faces lining the lower windows. Aes Sedai and novices alike watched her. It seemed that in addition

to the rebels, Egwene had an opportunity to address the majority of the remaining occupants of the Tower. She made a weave to enhance her voice. Not to booming levels, but enough to let her be heard both from behind and below.

"Sisters," she said, "daughters. I have been raised properly to the Amyrlin Seat. Both sides of this conflict have chosen me. Both followed the prescribed methods, and both now accept me as their Amyrlin. It is time to join together again.

"I will not pretend that our division did not take place. We of the White Tower are sometimes too eager to forget those facts we don't want to acknowledge. This one cannot be hidden, not from us who lived it. We were divided. We nearly came to war with one another. We have disgraced ourselves.

"You rebels before me have done something terrible. You have shattered the Tower and raised up a rival Amyrlin. For the first time, troops have been marshaled by Aes Sedai against Aes Sedai. I led those troops. I know of this shame.

"Necessary or not, it *is* a shame. And so it is that I require your admission of guilt. You must take responsibility for your crimes, even those performed in the name of the greater good."

She looked down at the Aes Sedai below. If her action of forcing them into ranks—then making them wait upon her will—hadn't made them aware of her attitude, then perhaps her words would.

"You did not come here in glory," Egwene said to them. "You did not come here victorious. For there *is* no victory, and could have been no victory, when sister fought sister and Warder died to Warder." She noted Siuan standing near the front of the ranks and met her eyes across the distance. Leane was there, too, looking disheveled from her long imprisonment, but standing erect.

"Mistakes have been made on both sides," Egwene said. "And we will all have to work hard to repair what we have done. It is said by blacksmiths that a sword can never be whole again once it has been shattered. It must be completely reforged, the metal melted down to slag, then reworked and re-formed.

"These next few months will be our re-forming. We have been broken, then torn down nearly to roots. The Last Battle approaches, and before it arrives, I mean to see that we are once again a sword forged with strength, whole and unbroken! I will make demands of you. They will be harsh. They will stretch you to the limits of what you think you can bear. I will take these burned holes and fill them! Accommodations will have to be made, for between us there are far too many Sitters for the Hall, not to mention five too many Ajah heads. Some of you will have to step down and bow yourselves in humility before those you dislike.

"These days will test you! I will force you to work with those you saw as enemies just hours ago. You will march alongside those who spurned you, or hurt you, or hated you.

"But we are stronger than our weaknesses. The White Tower stands, and we shall stand with it! We *will* become one again. We will be an assembly that tales will tell of! When I am finished with you, it will not be written that the White Tower was weak. Our divisions will be forgotten in the face of our victories. We will be remembered not as the White Tower who turned against itself, but as the White Tower who stood strong in the face of the Shadow. These days will be *legendary*!"

Cheers burst out, mostly from novices and soldiers, as the Aes Sedai were too reserved for that sort of behavior. Generally. Some younger ones did call out, caught up in the moment. Thankfully, those cheers came from both sides. Egwene let them roar for a moment, then raised her arms, quieting them.

"Let it go forth across the land!" she shouted. "Let it be spoken of, let it be relied upon, and let it be remembered. The White Tower is whole and complete. And no one— man, woman or creation of the Shadow—will see us divided again!"

The cheers were nearly deafening this time, and surprisingly, more Aes Sedai joined in. Egwene lowered her hands.

She hoped they would still cheer her in the months to come. There was a great deal of work to be done.

CHAPTER

47

The One He Lost

Rand did not return to his rooms immediately. The failed meeting with the Borderlanders had left him feeling unhinged. Not because of their tricky attempt to pull him into Far Madding—that was frustrating, but it was not unexpected. People always tried to control and manipulate him. The Borderlanders were no different.

No, it was something else that had unsettled him, something he couldn't quite define. And so he stalked through the Stone of Tear, two Aiel Maidens trailing behind him, his presence startling servants and unnerving Defenders.

The corridors twisted and turned. The walls—where unadorned by tapestry—were the color of wet sand, but they were far stronger than any rock Rand knew, alien and strange; each smooth span a reminder that this place was not natural.

Rand felt the same way. He had the form of a human. Indeed, he had the mannerisms and history of one. But he was a thing that no human—not even he himself—could understand. A figure of legend, a creation of the One Power, as unnatural as a *ter'angreal* or a fragment of *cuendillar*. They dressed him up like a king, just as they dressed these corridors with tasseled gold and red rugs. Just as they hung the walls with those tapestries, each one depicting a famous Tairen general. Those decorations were intended for beauty, but they were also intended to obscure. The patches of naked wall highlighted how alien the place was. Rugs and tapestries made it all feel more . . . human. Just as giving Rand a crown and a fine coat allowed them to accept him. Kings were supposed to be a little different. Never mind his much more alien nature, hidden beneath the crown. Never mind his heart of a man long dead, his shoulders created to bear the weight of prophecy, his soul crushed by the needs, wants and hopes of a million people.

Two hands. One to destroy, the other to save. Which had he lost?

It was easy to go astray in the Stone. Long before the Pattern had begun to unravel, these twisting corridors of brown rock had been misleading. They were designed to befuddle attackers. Intersections came unexpectedly; there were few landmarks, and the inner corridors of the keep didn't have windows. The Aiel said they had been impressed with how difficult it had been to seize the Stone. It hadn't been the Defenders who had impressed them, but the sheer scope and layout of the monstrous building.

Fortunately, Rand had no particular goal. He simply wanted to walk.

He had *accepted* what he needed to be. Why was he so bothered by it, then? A voice deep down—one not in his head, but in his heart—had begun to disagree with what he did. It was not loud or violent like Lews Therin's; it just whispered, like a forgotten itch. Something is wrong. Something is wrong. . . .

No! he thought. *I must be strong. I have finally become what I must be!*

He stopped in the corridor, teeth gritted. In his deep coat pocket, he carried the access key. He fingered it, its contours cold and smooth. He didn't dare leave it to the care of a servant, no matter how trusted.

Hurin, he realized. *That's what is bothering me. Seeing Hurin.*

He resumed walking, straightening his back. He had to be strong—or at least appear strong—at all times.

Hurin was a relic from an earlier life. Days when Mat had still mocked Rand's coats, days when Rand had hoped that he'd marry Egwene and somehow return to the Two Rivers. He had traveled with Hurin and Loial, determined to stop Fain and get back Mat's dagger, to prove that he was a friend. That had been a much simpler time, although Rand hadn't known it. He'd have wondered if anything could grow more complicated than thinking his friends hated him.

The colors shifted in his vision. Perrin walking through a dark camp, that stone sword looming in the air above him.

The vision changed to Mat, who was still in that city. It was Caemlyn? Why could he be near Elayne, when Rand had to remain so far away? He could barely feel her emotions through the bond. He missed her so. Once they had stolen kisses from one another in the halls of this very fortress.

No, he thought. *I am strong.* Longing was an emotion he mustn't feel. Nostalgia got him nowhere. He tried to banish both, ducking into a stairwell and moving down the steps, working his body, trying to make his breath come in gasps.

Do we run from the past, then? Lews Therin asked softly. *Yes. That is well. Better to run than to face it.*

Rand's time with Hurin had ended at Falme. Those days were indistinct in his mind. The changes that had come upon him then—realizing that he had to kill, that he could never return to the life he had loved—were things he could not dwell on. He'd headed out toward Tear, almost delirious, separated from his friends, seeing Ishamael in his dreams.

That last one was happening again.

Rand burst out onto one of the lower floors of the keep, breathing deeply. His Maidens followed him, not winded. He strode down the hallway and into a massive chamber with rows of pillars, stout and broad, wider than a man could wrap his arms around. The Heart of the Stone. Several Defenders came to attention and saluted as Rand passed them.

He walked to the center of the Heart. Once, *Callandor* had hung here, glistening with light. The crystal sword was now in Cadsuane's possession. Hopefully, she hadn't bungled that and lost *it* as she had the male *a'dam.* Rand didn't really care. *Callandor* was inferior; to use it, a man had to subject himself to the will of a woman. Besides, it was powerful, but not nearly as powerful as the Choedan Kal. The access key was a much better tool. Rand stroked it quietly, regarding the place where *Callandor* had once hung.

This had always bothered him. *Callandor* was the weapon spoken of in the prophecies. The Karaethon Cycle said that the Stone would not fall until *Callandor* was wielded by the Dragon Reborn. To some scholars, that passage had implied that the sword would *never* be wielded. But the prophecies did not work that way—they were made to be fulfilled.

Rand had studied the Karaethon Prophecy. Unfortunately, teasing out its meaning was like trying to untie a hundred yards of tangled rope. With one hand.

Taking the Sword That Cannot Be Touched was one of the first major prophecies that he had fulfilled. But was his taking of *Callandor* a meaningless sign, or was it a step? Everyone knew the prophecy, but few asked the question that should have been inevitable. Why? *Why* did Rand have to take up the sword? Was it to be used in the Last Battle?

The sword was inferior as a *sa'angreal*, and he doubted that it was intended to be used simply as a sword. Why did the prophecies not speak of the Choedan Kal? He had used *those* to cleanse the taint. The access key gave Rand power well beyond what *Callandor* could provide, and that power came with no strings. The statuette was freedom, but *Callandor* was just another box. Yet talk of the Choedan Kal and their keys was absent from the prophecies.

Rand found that frustrating, for the prophecies were—in a way—the grandest and most stifling box of them all. He was trapped inside of them. Eventually, they would suffocate him.

I told them . . . Lews Therin whispered.

Told them what? Rand demanded.

That the plan would not work, Lews Therin said, voice very soft. *That brute force would not contain him. They called my plan brash, but these weapons they created, they were too dangerous. Too frightening. No man should hold such Power . . .*

Rand struggled with the thoughts, the voice, the memories. He couldn't recall much at all of Lews Therin's plan to Seal the Dark One's prison. The Choedan Kal—had they been built for that purpose?

Was that the answer? Had Lews Therin made the wrong choice? Why, then, was there no mention of them in the prophecies?

Rand turned to leave the empty chamber. "Guard this place no more," he said to the Defenders. "There is nothing here of worth. I'm not sure if there ever was."

The men looked shocked, mortified, like children just chastised by a beloved father. But there was a war coming, and he wouldn't leave soldiers behind to defend an empty room.

Rand gritted his teeth and strode into a hallway. *Callandor.* Where had Cadsuane hidden it? He knew she'd taken rooms in the Stone, again pushing the limits of his exile. He would have to do something about that. Cast her from the Stone, perhaps. He hurried up the stone steps, then left the stairwell on a random floor, continuing to *move*. Sitting now would drive him mad.

He worked so hard to keep from being tied with strings, but at the end of the day, the prophecies would see that he did what he was supposed to. They were more manipulative, more devious, than any Aes Sedai.

His anger welled up inside him, raging against its constraints. The quiet voice deep within shivered at the tempest. Rand leaned his left arm against the wall, bowing his head, teeth gritted.

"I will be strong," he whispered. And yet, the anger would not go away. And why should it? The Borderlanders defied him. The Seanchan defied him. The Aes Sedai pretended to obey him, yet dined with Cadsuane behind his back and danced at her command.

Cadsuane defied him most of all. Staying right near him, flouting his words of command and twisting his intentions. He pulled out the access key, fingering it. The Last Battle loomed, and he spent what little time he had riding to meetings with people who insulted him. The Dark One was unraveling the Pattern more each day, and those sworn to protect the borders were hiding in Far Madding.

He glanced around, breathing deeply. Something about this particular hallway seemed familiar. He wasn't certain why; it looked like all of the others. Rugs of gold and red. An intersection of hallways ahead.

Maybe he shouldn't have let the Borderlanders survive their defiance. Perhaps he should go back and see that they learned to fear him. But no. He didn't need them. He could leave them for the Seanchan. That Borderlander army would serve to slow his enemies here in the south. Perhaps that would keep the Seanchan from his flanks while he dealt with the Dark One.

But . . . was there, perhaps, a way to stop the Seanchan for good? He looked down at the access key. Once he had tried to use *Callandor* to fight the foreign invaders. He hadn't yet understood why the sword was so difficult to control: only after his disastrous assault had Cadsuane explained what she knew about it. Rand needed to be in a circle with two women before he could safely wield the sword that was not a sword.

That had been his first major failure as a commander.

But he had a better tool now. The most powerful tool ever created; surely no human could hold more of the One Power than he had when cleansing *saidin*. Burning Graendal and Natrin's Barrow away had required only a fraction of what Rand could summon.

If he turned *that* against the Seanchan, then he could go to the Last Battle with confidence, no longer worried about what was creeping along behind him. He had given them their chance. Several chances. He had warned Cadsuane, told her that he'd bind the Daughter of the Nine Moons to him. One way . . . or another.

It would not take long.

There, Lews Therin said. *We stood there.*

Rand frowned. What was the madman babbling about? He glanced around. The wide hallway's floor was tiled in red and black patterns. A few tapestries fluttered on the walls. With shock, Rand realized that several of them depicted *him*, taking the Stone, holding *Callandor*, killing Trollocs.

Fighting the Seanchan wasn't our first failure, Lews Therin whispered. *No, our first failure happened here. In this hallway.*

Exhausted, following the battle with the Trollocs and Myrddraal. His side throbbing. The Stone still ringing with the cries of the wounded. Feeling he could do anything. *Anything.*

Standing above the corpse of a young girl. Just a child. *Callandor* glowing in his fingers. The body suddenly jerked.

Moiraine had stopped him. Bringing life to the dead was beyond him, she'd said.

How I wish she was still here, Rand thought. He had often been frustrated with her, but she—more than anyone else—had seemed to grasp just what it was he was expected to do. She'd made him more willing to do it, even when he'd been angry with her.

He turned away. Moiraine had been right. He could not bring life to those who were dead. But he was *very* good at bringing death to those who lived. "Gather your spear-sisters," Rand called over his shoulder to his Aiel guards. "We are going to battle."

"Now?" one of them asked. "It is nightfall!"

Have I been walking that long? Rand thought with surprise.

"Yes," he said. "The darkness won't matter; I shall create light enough." He fingered the access key, feeling a thrill and a horror at the same time. He had driven the Seanchan back into the ocean once. He would do so again. Alone.

Yes, he would drive them back—at least, the ones he left alive.

"Go!" he shouted at the Maidens. They left him, loping down the hallway. What had happened to his control? The ice had grown thin lately.

He walked back to the stairway and climbed a few flights up toward his rooms. The Seanchan would know his fury. They dared to provoke the Dragon Reborn? He offered them peace, and they *laughed* at him?

He threw open the door to his rooms, silencing the eager Defenders on guard outside with a sharply upraised hand. He was not in the mood for their prattle.

He stormed inside, and was annoyed to find that the guards had allowed someone inside. An unfamiliar figure stood with his back to Rand, looking out the open balcony doors. "What—" Rand began.

The man turned. It was *not* a stranger. Not a stranger at all. It was Tam. His father.

Rand stumbled back. Was this an apparition? Some twisted trick of the Dark One? But no, it was Tam. There was no mistaking the man's kindly eyes. Though he was a head shorter than Rand, Tam had always seemed more solid than the world around him. His broad chest and steady legs could not be moved, not because he was strong—Rand had met many men of greater strength during his travels. Strength was fleeting. Tam was *real*. Certain and stable. Just looking at him brought comfort.

But comfort clashed with who Rand had become. His worlds met—the person he had been, the person he had become—like a jet of water on a white-hot stone. One shattering, the other turning to steam.

Tam stood, hesitant, in the balcony doorway, lit by two flickering lamps on stands in the room. Rand understood Tam's hesitation. They were not blood father and son. Rand's blood father had been Janduin, clan chief of the Taardad Aiel. Tam was just the man who had found Rand on the slopes of Dragonmount.

Just the man who had raised him. Just the man who had

taught him everything he knew. Just the man Rand loved and revered, and always would, no matter what their blood connection.

"Rand." Tam's voice was awkward.

"Please," Rand said through his shock. "Please sit."

Tam nodded. He closed the balcony doors, then walked forward and took one of the chairs. Rand sat, too. They stared across the room at one another. The stone walls were bare; Rand preferred them unornamented with tapestries or paintings. The rug was yellow and red, and so large it reached to all four walls.

The room felt too perfect. A vase of freshly cut dara lilies and calima blossoms sat there, right where it should. Chairs in the center, arranged too correctly. The room didn't look *lived* in. Like so many places he stayed, it wasn't home. He hadn't truly had a home since he'd left the Two Rivers.

Tam sat in one chair, Rand in another. Rand realized he still had the access key in his hand, so he set it on the sun-patterned rug before him. Tam glanced at Rand's stump, but said nothing. He clenched his hands together, probably wishing he had something to work on. Tam was always more comfortable talking about uncomfortable things when he had something to do with his hands, whether it be checking the straps on a harness or shearing a sheep.

Light, Rand thought, feeling a sudden urge to enfold Tam in a hug. Familiarity and memories flooded back into his mind. Tam delivering brandy to the Winespring Inn for Bel Tine. The pleasure Tam took in his pipe. His patience and his kindness. His unexpected heron-mark sword. *I know him so well. And yet I've rarely thought of him recently.*

"How . . ." Rand said. "Tam, how did you get here? How did you find me?"

Tam chuckled quietly. "You've been sending nonstop messengers to all the great cities these last few days, telling them to marshal their armies for war. I think a man would have to be blind, deaf *and* drunk not to know where to find you."

"But my messengers haven't gone to the Two Rivers!"

"I wasn't in the Two Rivers," Tam said. "Some of us have been fighting alongside Perrin."

Of course, Rand thought. Nynaeve must have contacted Perrin—the colors swirled—she was so worried about him and Mat. It would have been easy for Tam to come back with her.

Was Rand really having this conversation? He had given up on returning to the Two Rivers, on ever seeing his father again. It felt so good, despite the awkwardness. Tam's face held more lines than it had before, and the few determined streaks of black in his hair had finally given in and gone silver, but he was the same.

So many people had changed around Rand—Mat, Perrin, Egwene, Nynaeve—it was a wonder to meet someone from his old life who was the same. Tam, the man who had taught Rand to seek the void. Tam was a rock that seemed to him stronger than the Stone itself.

Rand's mood darkened slightly. "Wait. Perrin has been using Two Rivers folk?"

Tam nodded. "He needed us. That boy's put on a balancing act to impress any menagerie performer. What with the Seanchan and the Prophet's men, not to mention the Whitecloaks and the queen—"

"The queen?" Rand said.

"Aye," Tam said. "Though she says she's not queen anymore. Elayne's mother."

"She *lives*, then?" Rand asked.

"She does, little thanks to the Whitecloaks," Tam said with distaste.

"Has she seen Elayne?" Rand asked. "You mentioned Whitecloaks—how did he run into Whitecloaks?" Tam began to answer, but Rand held up his hand. "No. Wait. I can get a report from Perrin when I wish it. I will not have our time together spent with you acting the messenger."

Tam smiled faintly.

"What?" Rand asked.

"Ah, son," he said, shaking his head, broad hardworking hands clasped before him, "they've really done it. They've gone and made a king out of you. What happened to the gangly boy, so wide-eyed at Bel Tine? Where's the uncertain lad I raised all those years?"

"He's dead," Rand said immediately.

Tam nodded slowly. "I can see that. You . . . must know then. . . . About. . . ."

"That you're not my father?" Rand guessed.

Tam nodded, looking down.

"I've known since the day I left Emond's Field," Rand replied. "You spoke of it in your fever dreams. I refused to believe it for a time, but I was eventually persuaded."

"Yes," Tam said. "I can see how. I. . . ." He gripped his hands together tightly. "I never meant to lie to you, son. Or, well, I guess I shouldn't call you that, should I?"

You can call me son, Rand thought. *You are my father. No matter what some may say.* But he couldn't force the words out.

The Dragon Reborn couldn't have a father. A father would be a weakness to be exploited, even more than a woman like Min. Lovers were expected. But the Dragon Reborn had to be a figure of myth, a creature nearly as large as the Pattern itself. He had difficulty getting people to obey as it was. What would it do if it were known that he kept his father nearby? If it were known that the Dragon Reborn relied upon the strength of a shepherd?

The quiet voice in his heart was screaming.

"You did well, Tam," Rand found himself saying. "By keeping the truth from me, you likely saved my life. If people had known that I was a foundling, and discovered near Dragonmount no less—well, word would have spread. I might very well have been assassinated as a child."

"Oh," Tam said. "Well, then, I'm glad I did it."

Rand picked up the access key—it too brought him comfort—then stood. Tam hastily joined him, acting more and more like just another retainer or servant.

"You have done a great service, Tam al'Thor," Rand said. "By protecting and raising me, you have ushered in a new Age. The world owes you a debt. I will see that you are cared for the rest of your life."

"I appreciate that, my Lord," Tam said. "But it isn't necessary. I have what I need."

Was he hiding a grin? Perhaps it *had* been a pompous speech. The room felt stifling, and Rand turned, crossing the fine rug and throwing open the balcony doors again. The sun had indeed set, and darkness had fallen on the city. A crisp ocean breeze blew across him as he stepped out to the balcony railing, into the night.

Tam stepped up beside him.

"I'm afraid I lost your sword," Rand found himself saying. It felt foolish.

"That's all right," Tam said. "I don't know that I ever deserved the thing anyway."

"Were you really a blademaster?"

Tam nodded. "I suppose. I killed a man who was one, did it in front of witnesses, but I've never forgiven myself for it. Though it needed doing."

"The ones that need to be done often seem the ones that we least like to have to do."

"That's the truth if I've ever heard it," Tam said, sighing softly, leaning on the balcony railing. Lit windows were beginning to shine in the darkness below. "It's so strange. My boy, the Dragon Reborn. All of those stories I heard when traveling the world, I'm part of them."

"Think how it feels for me," Rand said.

Tam chuckled. "Yes. Yes, I suppose you understand exactly what I mean, don't you? Funny, isn't it?"

"Funny?" Rand shook his head. "No. Not, that. My life isn't my own. I'm a puppet for the Pattern and the prophecies, made to dance for the world before having my strings cut."

Tam frowned. "That's not true, son. Er, my Lord."

"I can't see it any other way."

Tam crossed his arms on the smooth stone railing. "I guess I can understand. I remember some of those emotions myself, during the days when I was a soldier. You know that I fought against Tear? You'd think I would have painful memories, coming here. But one enemy often comes to seem like another. I don't bear any grudges."

Rand rested the access key on the railing, but held it tightly. He did not lean down; he remained straight-backed.

"A soldier doesn't have a lot of choices for his own destiny either," Tam said, tapping softly on the railing with an idle finger. "More important men make all the decisions. Men, well, I guess men like you."

"But my choices are made for me by the Pattern itself," Rand said. "I have *less* freedom than the soldiers. You could have run, deserted. Or at least gotten out by legal means."

"And you can't run?" Tam asked.

"I don't think the Pattern would let me," Rand said. "What I do is too important. It would just force me back in line. It has done so a dozen times already."

"And would you really *want* to run?" Tam asked.

Rand didn't reply.

"I could have left those wars. But, at the same time, I couldn't have. Not without betraying who I was. I think it's the same for you. Does it matter if you *can* run, when you know that you're not going to?"

"I'm going to die at the end of this," Rand said. "And I have no choice."

Tam stood up straight, frowning. In an instant, Rand felt that he was twelve years old again. "I won't have talk like that," Tam said. "Even if you're the Dragon Reborn, I won't listen to it. You *always* have a choice. Maybe you can't pick where you are forced to go, but you still have a choice."

"But how?"

Tam laid a hand on Rand's shoulder. "The choice isn't always about *what* you do, son, but *why* you do it. When I was a soldier, there were some men who fought simply for the money. There were others who fought for loyalty—loyalty to their comrades, or to the crown, or to whatever. The soldier who dies for money and the soldier who dies for loyalty are both dead, but there's a *difference* between them. One death meant something. The other didn't.

"I don't know if it's true that you'll need to die for this all to play out. But we both know you aren't going to run from it. Changed though you are, I can see that some things are the same. So I won't stand any whining on the subject."

"I wasn't whining—" Rand began.

"I know," Tam said. "Kings don't whine, they deliberate." He seemed to be quoting someone, though Rand had no idea who. Oddly, Tam gave a brief chuckle. "It doesn't matter," Tam continued. "Rand, I think you can survive this. I can't imagine that the Pattern won't give you some peace, considering the service you're doing for us all. But you're a soldier going to war, and the first thing a soldier learns is that you might die. You may not be able to choose the duties you're given. But you *can* choose why you fulfill them. Why do you go to battle, Rand?"

"Because I must."

"That's not good enough," Tam said. "To the crows with that woman! I wish she'd come to me sooner. If I'd known—"

"What woman?"

"Cadsuane Sedai," Tam said. "She brought me here, said that I needed to talk to you. I'd stayed away, previously, because I thought the last thing you needed was your father stomping across your field!"

Tam continued, but Rand stopped listening.

Cadsuane. Tam had come because of *Cadsuane.* It wasn't because Tam had noticed Nynaeve and taken the opportunity. Not because he'd just wanted to check on his son. But because he'd been *manipulated* into coming.

Would the woman never leave Rand alone!

His emotions seeing Tam were so strong that they had worn away the ice. Too much affection was like too much hatred. Either one made him *feel*, which was something he could not risk.

But he had. And suddenly, *feeling* nearly overcame him. He shuddered, turning away from Tam. Had their conversation all been another one of Cadsuane's games? What was Tam's part in it?

"Rand?" Tam asked. "I'm sorry. I shouldn't have brought up the Aes Sedai. She said you might be angry if I mentioned her."

"What else did she say?" Rand demanded, spinning back toward Tam. The stout man took a hesitant step backward. Night air blew around them, lights from the city dots below.

"Well," Tam said, "she told me that I should talk about your youth, remind you of better times. She thought—"

"She manipulates me!" Rand said softly, meeting Tam's eyes. "And she manipulates you. Everyone ties their strings to me!"

The rage boiled inside. He tried to shove it back, but it was *so* difficult. Where was the ice, the quiet? Desperately, Rand sought the void. He tried pouring all of his emotions into the flame of a candle, as Tam had taught so long ago.

Saidin was waiting there. Without thought, Rand seized it, and in doing so was overwhelmed with those emotions he thought he'd abandoned. The void shattered, but somehow *saidin* remained, struggling against him. He screamed as the nausea hit him, and he threw his anger against it in defiance.

"Rand," Tam said, frowning. "You should know better than—"

"*BE SILENT!*" Rand bellowed, throwing Tam to the floor with a flow of Air. Rand wrestled with his rage on one side and *saidin* on the other. They threatened to crush him between them.

This was why he needed to be strong. Couldn't they see? How could a man laugh when confronted by forces like these?

"I am the Dragon Reborn!" Rand roared at *saidin*, at Tam, at Cadsuane, at the Creator himself. "I will not be your pawn!" He pointed at Tam with the access key. His father lay on the stone floor of the balcony. "You come from Cadsuane, pretending to show me affection. But you unwind another of her strings to tie about my throat! Can I not be free of you all?"

He had lost control. But he didn't care. They wanted him to feel. He would *feel*, then! They wanted him to laugh? He would laugh as they burned!

Screaming at them all, he wove threads of Air and Fire. Lews Therin howled in his head, *saidin* tried to destroy both of them, and the quiet voice inside Rand's heart vanished.

A prick of light grew in front of Rand, sprouting from the center of the access key. The weaves for balefire spun before him, and the access key grew brighter as he drew in more power.

By that light, Rand saw his father's face, looking up at him. Terrified.

What am I doing?

Rand began to shake, the balefire unraveling before he had time to loose it. He stumbled backward in horror.

What am I DOING? Rand thought again.

No more than I've done before, Lews Therin whispered.

Tam continued to stare at him, face shadowed by the night.

Oh, Light, Rand thought with terror, shock and rage. *I am doing it again. I am a monster.*

Still holding tenuously to *saidin*, Rand wove a gateway to Ebou Dar, then ducked through, fleeing from the horror in Tam's eyes.

CHAPTER
48

Reading the Commentary

Min sat in Cadsuane's small room, waiting—with the others—to hear the result of Rand's meeting with his father. A low fire burned in the fireplace and lamps at each corner of the room lent light to the women, who worked at various busying activities—embroidery, darning, and knitting—to keep their minds off of the wait.

Min was past regretting her decision to make an alliance with Cadsuane. Regret had come early, during the first few days when Cadsuane had kept Min close, asking after every viewing she had had about Rand. The woman was meticulous as a Brown, writing down each vision and answer. It was like being in the White Tower, again!

Min wasn't certain why Nynaeve's submission to Cadsuane had given the woman license to interrogate Min, but that was how Cadsuane seemed to interpret it. Mix that with Min's discomfort around Rand lately and her own desire to figure out just what Cadsuane and the Wise Ones were planning, and she seemed to spend practically all of her time in the woman's presence.

Yes, regret had come and gone. Min had moved on to resignation, tinged with a hint of frustration. Cadsuane knew quite a bit about the material Min was studying in her books, but the woman doled out her knowledge like cloudberry jam, a little reward for good behavior, always hinting that there was more to come. That kept Min from fleeing.

She *had* to find the answers. Rand needed them.

With that thought in mind, Min leaned back on her cushioned bench and reopened her current book, a work by Sajius that was simply titled *Commentary on the Dragon*. One line in it teased at her, a sentence mostly ignored by those who had written commentary. *He shall hold a blade of light in his hands, and the three shall be one.*

The commentators felt it was too vague compared with other passages, like Rand taking the Stone or Rand's blood being spilled on the rocks of Shayol Ghul.

She tried not to think about that last one. The important thing was that many of the prophecies—with a little consideration and thought—generally made sense. Even the lines about Rand being marked by the Dragons and the Herons made sense, looking at it now.

But what of this line? A blade of light almost certainly meant *Callandor*. But what of the "three shall be one"? Some few scholars claimed that "the three" were three great cities—Tear, Illian and Caemlyn. Or, if one happened to be a scholar from Cairhien, then they were said to be Tear, Illian and Cairhien. The problem was that Rand had united far more than three cities. He'd conquered Bandar Eban as well, not to mention the fact that he would need to bring the Borderlanders to his banner.

But he was ruler—or near to it—in three kingdoms. He'd given up Andor, but Cairhien, Illian and Tear were directly beneath his control, even if he personally wore only one crown. Maybe this passage did mean what the scholars said, and Min was chasing nothing.

Were her studies as useless as the protection she'd thought to offer Rand? *Min,* she told herself, *self-pity will get you nowhere.* All she could do was study, think and hope.

"This is wrong," she found herself saying out loud.

She heard Beldeine's softly derisive snort from across the room. Min looked up, frowning.

The women who had sworn to Rand—Erian, Nesune, Sarene and Beldeine—had found themselves less welcome in his presence as he had grown less trusting of Aes Sedai. The only one he regularly allowed to see him was Nynaeve. It wasn't odd, then, that the others had found their way to Cadsuane's "camp."

And what of Min's own relationship with Rand? She was still welcome in his presence; that hadn't changed. But there was something wrong, something *off*. He put up walls when she was near—not to keep her out, but to keep the real him in. As if he was afraid of what the real him would do, or could do, to those he loved. . . .

He's in pain again, she thought, feeling him through the bond. *Such anger.* What was going on? She felt a spike of fear, but shoved it down. She had to trust in Cadsuane's plan. It was a good one.

Corele and Merise—almost constant attendants of Cadsuane these days—continued their embroidery in matching chairs by the hearth. Cadsuane had suggested the work to them to keep their hands busy while they waited. It seemed the ancient Aes Sedai rarely did anything without intending to teach someone a lesson.

Of the Aes Sedai sworn to Rand, only Beldeine was there at the moment. Cadsuane sat near Min, perusing her own book. Nynaeve walked back and forth, up and down, occasionally tugging on her braid. Nobody spoke of the tension in the room.

What *were* Rand and Tam discussing? Would Rand's father be able to turn him?

The chamber was cramped. With three chairs on the rug beside the hearth, a bench along the wall, and Nynaeve crossing back and forth before the door like a spotted hound, there was barely room to move. The smooth stone walls made the place feel like a box, and there was only one window, open to the night air, behind Cadsuane. Light shone from the coals in the hearth and the lamps. The Warders were speaking in low tones in the adjoining room.

Yes, it was cramped, but considering her banishment, Cadsuane was lucky to have rooms in the Stone at all.

Min sighed and turned back to *Commentary on the Dragon.* That same phrase popped out at her again. *He shall hold a blade of light in his hands, and the three shall be one.* What did it mean?

"Cadsuane," Min said, holding up the book. "I think the interpretation of this phrase is wrong."

Again, Beldeine let out a small—almost imperceptible— sniff of disdain.

"You have something to say, Beldeine?" Cadsuane asked, not looking up from her own book, a history called *The Proper Taming of Power.*

"Not in so many words, Cadsuane Sedai," Beldeine replied lightly. The Green had a face that some might have called pretty, bearing traces of her Saldaean heritage. Young enough to not yet have the ageless face, she often seemed to try too hard to prove herself.

"You obviously thought *something* when Min spoke, Beldeine," Cadsuane replied, turning a page. "Out with it."

Beldeine flushed slightly—one noticed these things, if one spent a lot of time with Aes Sedai. They *did* have emotional reactions, they were just subtle. Unless, of course, the Aes Sedai in question was Nynaeve. Although she'd grown better at controlling her emotions, she . . . well, she was still Nynaeve.

Beldeine said, "I simply think that the child is amusing in the way she pokes through those tomes, as if she were a scholar."

Min would have taken that as a challenge from most people, but from Beldeine, the words were matter-of-fact.

Cadsuane turned another page. "I see. Min, what was it you were saying to me?"

"Nothing important, Cadsuane Sedai."

"I didn't ask if it was important, girl," Cadsuane said briskly. "I asked you to repeat yourself. Out with it."

Min sighed. Nobody could humiliate one more soundly than an Aes Sedai, for they did it without malice. Moiraine had explained it to Min once in simple terms: Most Aes Sedai felt it was important to establish control when there was no great conflict, so that if a crisis *did* happen, people would know where to look.

It was very frustrating.

"I said," Min repeated, "that a passage is wrong. I'm reading commentary on the Karaethon Cycle. Sajius claims that this line about the three becoming one speaks of the unification of three kingdoms beneath the Dragon's banner. But I think he's wrong."

"And why," Cadsuane said, "is it that you think you know more than a respected scholar of the prophecies?"

"Because," Min said, bristling, "the theory doesn't make sense. Rand only really holds one crown. There *might* have been a good argument here if he hadn't given away Tear to Darlin. But the theory doesn't hold any longer. I think the passage refers to some way he has to use *Callandor*."

"I see," Cadsuane said, turning yet another page in her own book. "That is a very unconventional interpretation."

Beldeine smiled thinly, turning back to her embroidery. "Of course," Cadsuane added, "you are quite right."

Min looked up.

"It was that very passage that led me to investigate *Callandor*," Cadsuane continued. "Through a great deal of searching I discovered that the sword could only be used properly in a circle of three, led by a woman. That is likely the ultimate meaning of the passage."

"But that would imply that Rand had to use *Callandor* in a circle sometime," Min said, looking at the passage again. He'd never done so, as far as she knew.

"It would," Cadsuane said.

Min felt a sudden thrill. A hint, perhaps. Something that Rand didn't know, that might help him! Except . . . Cadsuane had already known it. So Min hadn't discovered anything of real import after all.

"I should think," Cadsuane said, "that an acknowledgment is due. Bad manners are not to be tolerated, after all."

Beldeine looked up from her needlework, face dark. Then, unexpectedly, she stood and left the room. Her Warder, the youthful Asha'man Karldin, followed quickly from the side chamber, crossing the room with the Aes Sedai and following Beldeine out into the hallway outside. Cadsuane gave a sniff, then turned back to her book.

The door closed, and Nynaeve eyed Min before returning to her pacing. Min could read a lot in that glance. Nynaeve was annoyed that nobody else seemed nervous. She was frustrated that they hadn't found some way to listen in on Rand and Tam's conversation. And she was obviously terrified for Lan. Min understood. She felt similarly about Rand.

And . . . what was that vision that was suddenly hovering above Nynaeve's head? She was kneeling over someone's corpse in a posture of grief. The viewing was gone a moment later.

Min shook her head. That hadn't been a viewing she could interpret, so she let it pass. She couldn't waste her time trying to unravel all of those. For instance, the black knife that spun around Beldeine's head recently could mean anything.

She focused on the book. So . . . Rand was to use *Callandor* as part of a circle, then? The three becoming one? But for what reason and with whom? If he was to fight the

Dark One, then it didn't make sense for him to be in a circle with someone else in control, did it?

"Cadsuane," she said. "This is still wrong. There's more here. Something we haven't discovered."

"About *Callandor*?" the woman asked.

Min nodded.

"I suspect so as well," Cadsuane replied. How odd to hear her being frank! "But I haven't been able to determine *what*. If only that fool boy would revoke my exile, we could get on with more important—"

The door to Cadsuane's room slammed open, causing Merise to jump in shock. Nynaeve hopped back from the door—it had nearly hit her.

Standing in the doorway was a very angry Tam al'Thor. He glared at Cadsuane. "What have you done to him?" he demanded.

Cadsuane lowered her book. "I have done *nothing* to the boy, other than to encourage him toward civility. Something, it seems, other members of the family could learn as well."

"Watch your tongue, Aes Sedai," Tam snarled. "Have you seen him? The entire *room* seemed to grow darker when he entered. And that face—I've seen more emotion in the eyes of a corpse! What has happened to my son?"

"I take it," Cadsuane said, "that the reunion did not go as hoped?"

Tam took a deep breath, and the anger seemed to suddenly flow out of him. He was still firm, his eyes displeased, but the rage was gone. Min had seen Rand take control of himself that quickly, before things had started to go wrong in Bandar Eban.

"He tried to kill me," Tam said in a level voice. "My own son. Once he was as gentle and faithful a lad as a father could hope for. Tonight, he channeled the One Power and turned it against me."

Min raised her hand to her mouth, feeling a panicked terror. The words brought back memories of Rand looming over her, trying to kill her.

But that hadn't been him! It had been Semirhage. Hadn't it? *Oh, Rand,* she thought, understanding the pain she'd felt through the bond. *What have you done?*

"Interesting," Cadsuane said, her voice cold. "And did you speak the words I prepared for you?"

"I began to," Tam said, "but I realized that it wasn't working. He wouldn't open up to me, and well he shouldn't. A man using an Aes Sedai script with his own son! I don't know what you did to him, woman, but I recognize hatred when I see it. You have a lot to explain to—"

Tam cut off as he was suddenly lifted into the air by unseen hands. "You recall, perhaps, what I said about civility, boy?" Cadsuane asked.

"Cadsuane!" Nynaeve said. "You don't need to—"

"It's all right, Wisdom," Tam said. He looked at Cadsuane. Min had seen her treat others like this, including Rand. He had always grown frustrated, and others she did it to were prone to bellowing.

Tam stared her in the eyes. "I've known men who, when challenged, always turn to their fists for answers. I've never liked Aes Sedai; I was happy to be rid of them when I returned to my farm. A bully is a bully, whether she uses the strength of her arm or other means."

Cadsuane snorted, but the words had irked her, for she set Tam down.

"Now," Nynaeve said, as if she'd been the one to defuse the exchange, "perhaps we can get back to what is important. Tam al'Thor, I'd have expected you of all people to handle this better. Didn't we warn you that Rand had grown unstable?"

"Unstable?" Tam asked. "Nynaeve, that boy is right near *insane*. What has happened to him? I understand what battle can do to a man, but. . . ."

"This is irrelevant," Cadsuane said. "You realize, child, that might have been our last opportunity to save your son?"

"If you'd explained to me how he regarded you," Tam said, "it might have gone differently. Burn me! This is what I get for listening to Aes Sedai."

"This is what you get for being wool-headed and ignoring what you are told!" Nynaeve interjected.

"This is what we all get," Min said, "for assuming we can *make* him do what we want."

The room fell still.

And suddenly Min realized that through their bond, she could feel Rand. Distant, to the west. "He's gone," she whispered.

"Yes," Tam said, sighing. "He opened one of those gateways right on the balcony. Left me alive, though I could have sworn—looking in his eyes—that he meant to kill me. I've seen that look in the eyes of men before, and one of the two of us always ended up bleeding on the floor."

"What happened, then?" Nynaeve asked.

"He ... seemed to be distracted by something, suddenly," Tam said. "He took that little statue and dashed through the gateway."

Cadsuane raised an eyebrow. "And did you see, by chance, where that gateway took him?"

West, Min thought. *Far to the west.*

"I'm not certain," Tam admitted. "It was dark, though I thought. . . ."

"What?" Nynaeve prodded.

"Ebou Dar," Min said, surprising them all. "He's gone to destroy the Seanchan. Just as he told the Maidens he would."

"I don't know about that last part," Tam said. "But it *did* look like Ebou Dar."

"Light preserve us," Corele whispered.

CHAPTER
49

Just Another Man

Rand walked, stump shoved in the pocket of his coat, head down, carrying the access key securely wrapped in white linen and looped to his belt at his side. Nobody paid attention to him. He was just another man walking the streets of Ebou Dar. Nothing special, despite the fact that he was taller than most. He had reddish gold hair, maybe suggesting some Aiel blood. But a lot of strange people had fled to the city recently to seek Seanchan protection. What was one more?

As long as a person wasn't able to channel, he or she could find stability here. Safety.

That bothered him. They were his enemies. They were conquerors. He felt their lands shouldn't be peaceful. They should be terrible, full of suffering because of the tyrannical rule. But it wasn't like that at all.

Not unless you could channel. What the Seanchan did with this group of people was horrifying. Not all was well beneath this happy surface. And yet, it was shocking to realize how well they treated others.

Tinkers camped outside the city in large groups. Their wagons had not moved for weeks, and it seemed they were forming villages. As Rand had moved among them, he'd heard some of them speak of settling down. Others had objected to this, of course. They were the Tinkers, the Traveling People. How would they find the Song if they did not search for it? It was as much a part of them as the Way of the Leaf.

Last night, Rand had listened to them at one of the camp-fires. They'd welcomed him in, fed him, never asking who he was. He'd kept the dragon on his hand hidden and the access key carefully tucked in his coat pocket, looking at that fire burning down to coals.

He hadn't ever been to Ebou Dar itself; he'd only visited the hills to the north, where he'd fought the Seanchan while wielding *Callandor*. That had been a place of failure. Now he had returned to Altara. But for what?

In the morning, when the gates to the city had opened, he made his way inside with the others who had arrived at night. The Tinkers had taken them all in; apparently, they were receiving a ration of food from the Seanchan to house after-hour travelers. That was only one of their many occupations. They mended pots, sewed uniforms and did other odd jobs. For this, they received the protection of rulers for the first time in their long history.

He'd spent long enough with the Aiel to pick up some of their disdain for the Tinkers. Yet that disdain warred with his knowledge that the Tuatha'an—in many ways— followed more true, traditional Aiel ways. Rand could *remember* what it was like to live as they had. In the visions of Rhuidean, he had followed the Way of the Leaf. He'd also seen the Age of Legends. He'd lived those lives, the lives of others, for a few brief moments.

He walked along the packed streets of the muggy city, still in something of a daze. Last night, he had traded his fine black coat to a Tinker for a common brown cloak, ragged on the bottom and stitched in places. Not a Tinker cloak, just one that a Tinker had sewn up for a man who had never returned to claim it. It made him stand out less, even if it did require him to carry the access key looped to his belt, rather than his deep pocket. The Tinker also gave him a walking staff, which Rand used as he walked, slouching slightly. Height might make him memorable. He wanted to be invisible to these people.

He had nearly killed his father. He hadn't been forced to by Semirhage, or by Lews Therin's influence. No excuses. No argument. He, Rand al'Thor, had tried to kill his own father. He'd drawn in the Power, made the weaves and nearly released them.

Rand's rage was gone, replaced by loathing. He'd wanted to make himself hard. He'd *needed* to be hard. But this was where hardness had brought him. Lews Therin had been able to claim madness for his atrocities. Rand had nothing, no place to hide, no refuge from himself.

Ebou Dar. It was a busy, bulging city, split in half by its large river. Rand walked the west side, through squares edged with beautiful statues and streets lined with row upon row of white houses, many several stories high. He often passed men fighting with fists or knives, and nobody making any effort to break them apart. Even the women wore knives at their necks in jeweled scabbards, hanging above low-cut dresses worn over colorful petticoats.

He ignored them all. Instead, he thought on the Tinkers. Tinkers were safe here, but Rand's own father wasn't safe in his empire. Rand's friends feared him; he had seen it in Nynaeve's eyes.

The people here weren't afraid. Seanchan officers moved through the crowds, wearing those insectlike helms. The people made way for them, but out of respect. When Rand heard commoners speaking, they were glad for the stability. They actually praised the Seanchan for conquering them!

Rand crossed a short, canal-spanning bridge. Small boats idled down the waterway, boatmen calling greetings to one another. There didn't seem to be any sense of order to the city layout; where he expected houses, he found shops, and instead of similar shops clustering together—as was common in most cities—here they were scattered, haphazard. On the other side of the bridge, he passed a tall, white mansion, then a tavern right next to it.

A man in a colorful silk vest jostled Rand on the street, then offered a lengthy, overly polite apology. Rand hurried on, lest the man want to start a duel.

This did not seem like an oppressed people. There was no undercurrent of resentment. The Seanchan had a much better hold on Ebou Dar than Rand had on Bandar Eban, and the people here were happy—even prosperous! Of course, Altara—as a kingdom—had never been very strong. Rand knew from his tutors that the Crown's authority hadn't extended much beyond the borders of the city. It was much the same for the other places the Seanchan had conquered. Tarabon, Amadicia, Almoth Plain. Some were more stable than Altara, others less, but all would welcome security.

Rand stopped and leaned against another white building,

this one a farrier's shop. He raised his stump to his head, trying to clear his mind.

He didn't want to confront what he had nearly done back in the Stone. He didn't want to confront what he *had* done: weaving Air and shoving Tam to the ground, threatening him; raving.

Rand couldn't focus on that. He had not come to Ebou Dar to gawk like a farmboy. He had come to destroy his enemies! They defied him; they needed to be eliminated. For the good of all nations.

But if he drew that much power through the access key, what damage would he cause? How many lives would he end? And would he not simply light a beacon for the Forsaken, as he had in cleansing *saidin*?

Let them come. He straightened up. He could defeat them.

It was time to attack. Time to burn the Seanchan off the land. He set aside his staff and took the key off its strap at his belt, but could not force himself to unwrap it from its linen shroud. He stared at it in his hand for a time, then continued to walk, idly leaving the staff behind. It felt so odd to be just another foreigner. The Dragon Reborn walked among this people, and they did not know him. To them, Rand al'Thor was far off. The Last Battle was secondary to whether or not they could get their chickens to market, or whether their son would recover from his cough, or whether they would be able to afford that new silk vest they had been wanting.

They would not know Rand until he destroyed them.

It will be a mercy, Lews Therin whispered. *Death is always a mercy.* The madman didn't sound as crazy as he once had. In fact, his voice had started to sound an awful lot like Rand's own voice.

Rand stopped atop another bridge, looking over at the city's massive white-walled palace, home to the Seanchan court. It rose four stories high, with rings of gold at the base of its four domes and more gold at the tips of its many spires. The Daughter of the Nine Moons would be found in there. He could give those walls a purity they had never known, a perfection. That would make the building complete, in a way, in the moment before it faded into nothingness.

He unwrapped the access key, just another foreigner,

standing on the muddy bridge. After destroying the palace, he would have to be quick. He'd send off bursts of bale-fire to destroy the ships in the harbor, then use something more mundane to rain fire on the city itself, throw it into a panic. The chaos would delay his enemies' reaction. After that, he would Travel to the garrisons at the city gates and destroy them. He vaguely remembered scout reports of supply camps to the north, well stocked with both soldiers and foodstuffs. He would destroy them next.

From there, he'd need to move on to Amador, then to Tanchico and others. He'd Travel quickly, never remaining in one place long enough to be caught by the Forsaken. A flickering light of death, like a burning ember, flaring to life here, then there. Many would die, but most would be Seanchan. Invaders.

He stared down at the access key. Then he seized *saidin*.

The sickness washed across him more powerfully than it ever had before. The force of it knocked him to the ground like a physical blow. He cried out, barely noticing when he hit the stones. He groaned, gripping the access key, curling around it. His insides seemed to burn, and he turned his head, rolling onto his shoulder and vomiting onto the bridge.

But he held on to *saidin*. He needed the power. The succulent, beautiful power. Even the stench of his own vomit seemed more real to him, more sweet, for the power within him.

He opened his eyes. People were gathered around him, concerned. A Seanchan patrol was approaching. Now was the time. He had to strike.

But he could not. The people looked so concerned. So worried. They cared.

Screaming in frustration, Rand made a gateway, causing the people to jump back in shock. He stumbled to his feet and threw himself through, scrabbling on all fours, as the Seanchan soldiers drew swords and yelled unfamiliar words.

Rand landed on a large stone disc of black and white, the air around him a void of darkness. The portal closed behind, locking Ebou Dar away, and the disc began to move. It floated through the void, lit by some strange ambient light. Rand curled up on the disc, cradling the access key, breathing deeply.

Why can't I be strong enough? He didn't know if the thought was his or if it was Lews Therin's. The two were the same. *Why can't I do what I must?*

The disc traveled for a short time, the only sound in the void that of his breathing. The disc looked like one of the seals to the Dark One's prison, split with a sinuous line dividing the black from the white. Rand lay directly atop it. They called the black half the Dragon's Fang. To the people, it symbolized evil. Destruction.

But Rand was *necessary* destruction. Why had the Pattern pushed him so hard if he didn't need to destroy? Originally, he had tried to avoid killing—but there had been little chance of that working. Then he'd made himself avoid killing women. That had proven impossible.

He was destruction. He just had to accept that. *Someone* had to be hard enough to do what was necessary, didn't they?

A gateway opened, and he stumbled to his feet, clutching the access key. He stepped from the Skimming platform and out onto an empty meadow. The place where he'd fought the Seanchan once with *Callandor*. And failed.

He stared at this place for a long time, breathing in and out, then spun another gateway. This one opened onto a field of snow, and icy wind blasted at him. He stepped through, feet crunching into the snow, and let the gateway close.

Here, the world spread before him.

Why have we come here? Rand thought.

Because, Rand replied. *Because we made this. This is where we died.*

He stood on the very point of Dragonmount, the lone peak that had erupted where Lews Therin had killed himself three thousand years before. To one side, he could see down hundreds of feet to where the side of the mountain opened into a blasted-out chasm. The opening was enormous, larger than it looked from profile. A wide oval of red, blazing, churning rock. It was as if a chunk of the mountain were simply missing, torn away, leaving the peak to rise into the air but the entire side of the mountain gone.

Rand stared down into that seething chasm. It was like the maw of a beast. Heat burned from below and flakes of ash twisted into the sky.

The dun sky was clouded above him. The ground seemed

equally distant, barely visible, like a quilt marked with patterns. Here a patch of green that was a forest. There a stitch that was a river. To the east, he saw a small speck in the river, like a floating leaf caught in the tiny current. Tar Valon.

Rand sat down, the snow crunching beneath his weight. He set the access key into the bank before him and wove Air and Fire to keep himself warm.

Then he rested his elbows on his knees and his head on his hand, staring at the diminutive statue of the man with the globe.

To think.

CHAPTER
50

Veins of Gold

Wind blew around Rand as he sat at the top of the world. His weaving of Air and Fire had melted away the snow around him, exposing a jagged gray-black tip of rock about three paces wide. The peak was like a broken fingernail jutting into the sky, and Rand sat atop it. As far as he could tell, it was the very tip of Dragonmount. Perhaps the highest point in the world.

He sat upon his small outcropping, the access key sitting on the rock in front of him. The air was thin here, and he'd had trouble breathing until he'd found a way to weave Air so that it compressed slightly around him. Like the weave that warmed him, he wasn't certain how he'd done it. He vaguely remembered Asmodean trying to teach him a similar weave, and Rand hadn't been able to get it right. Now it came naturally. Lews Therin's influence, or his own growing familiarity with the One Power?

Dragonmount's broken, open mouth lay several hundred feet beneath him, to the left. The scents of ash and sulphur were pungent, even at this distance. The maw was black with ash and red from molten rock and blazing fires.

He still held to the Source. He didn't dare let go. This last time he'd seized it had been the worst he could remember, and he feared that the sickness would overpower him if he tried again.

He had been here for hours. And yet he did not feel tired. He stared at the *ter'angreal*. Thinking.

What was he? What was the Dragon Reborn? A symbol? A sacrifice? A sword, meant to destroy? A sheltering hand, meant to protect?

A puppet, playing a part over and over again?

He was angry. Angry at the world, angry at the Pattern, angry at the Creator for leaving humans to fight against the Dark One with no direction. What right did any of them have to demand Rand's life of him?

Well, Rand had offered that life to them. It had taken him a great while to accept his death, but he *had* made his peace. Wasn't that enough? Did he have to be in pain until the end?

He had thought that if he made himself hard enough, it would take away the pain. If he couldn't feel, then he couldn't hurt.

The wounds in his side pulsed in agony. For a time, he'd been able to forget them. But the deaths he had caused rubbed his soul raw. That list starting with Moiraine. Everything had begun to go wrong at her death. Before that, he'd still had hope.

Before that, he'd never been put in a box.

He understood what would be required of him, and he'd changed in the ways he thought he needed. Those changes were to keep him from being overwhelmed. Die to protect people he didn't know? Chosen to save mankind? Chosen to force the kingdoms of the world to unite behind him, destroying those who refused to listen? Chosen to cause the deaths of thousands who fought in his name, to hold those souls upon his shoulders, a weight that must be borne? What man could do these things and remain sane? The only way he had seen had been to cut off his emotions, to make himself *cuendillar*.

But he had failed. He hadn't been able to stamp his feelings out. The voice inside had been so small, but it had pricked at him, like a needle making the smallest of holes in his heart. Even the smallest of holes would let the blood leak free.

Those holes would bleed him dry.

The quiet voice was gone now. It had vanished when he'd thrown Tam to the floor and nearly killed him. Without that voice, did Rand dare continue? If it was the last remnant of the old Rand—the Rand who had believed that he knew what was right and what was wrong—then what did its silence mean?

Rand picked up the access key and stood up, boots scraping stone. It was midday, though the sun still lay hidden behind the clouds. Below, he could see hills and forests, lakes and villages.

"And what if I don't *want* the Pattern to continue?" he bellowed. He stepped forward, right to the edge of the rock, clutching the access key to his chest.

"We live the same lives!" he yelled at them. "Over and over and over. We make the same mistakes. Kingdoms do the same *stupid* things. Rulers fail their people time and time again. Men continue to hurt and hate and die and kill!"

Winds buffeted him, whipping at his brown cloak and his fine Tairen trousers. But his words carried, echoing across the broken rocks of Dragonmount. It was cold and crisp, the air new. His weave kept him warm enough to survive, but it did not stop the chill. He hadn't wanted it to.

"What if I think it's all meaningless?" he demanded with the loud voice of a king. "What if I don't *want* it to keep turning? We live our lives by the blood of others! And those others become forgotten. What *good* is it if everything we know will fade? Great deeds or great tragedies, neither means anything! They will become legends, then those legends will be forgotten, then it will all start over again!"

The access key began to glow in his hands. The clouds above seemed to grow darker.

Rand's anger beat in rhythm with his heart, demanding to be set free.

"What if *he* is right?" Rand bellowed. "What if it's better for this all to end? What if the Light was a lie all along, and *this* is all just a punishment? We live again and again, growing feeble, dying, trapped forever. We are to be tortured for all time!"

Power flooded into Rand like surging waves filling a new ocean. He came to life, glorying in *saidin*, not caring that the display must be brilliantly visible to men everywhere who could channel. He felt himself alight with the Power, like a sun to the world below.

"NONE OF THIS MATTERS!"

He closed his eyes, drawing in more and more power, feeling as he had only twice before. Once when he had cleansed *saidin*. Once when he had created this mountain.

Then he drew in more.

He knew that much power would destroy him. He had stopped caring. Fury that had been building in him for two years finally boiled free, unleashed at long last. He spread his arms out wide, access key in his hand. Lews Therin had been right to kill himself and create Dragonmount. Only he hadn't gone far enough.

Rand could remember that day. The smoke, the rumbling, the sharp pains of a Healing bringing him back to lucidity as he lay in a broken palace. But those pains had paled compared with the agony of realization. Agony from seeing the beautiful walls scarred and broken. From seeing the piles of familiar corpses, tossed to the floor like discarded rags.

From seeing Ilyena a short distance away, her golden hair spread out on the ground around her.

He could *feel* the palace around him shaking from the earth's own sobs. Or was that Dragonmount, throbbing from the immense power he had drawn into himself?

He could smell the air thick with blood and soot and death and *pain*. Or was that just the scent of a dying world, spread before him?

The winds began to whip at him, spinning, enormous clouds above twisting upon themselves, like ancient leviathans passing in the profound black deep.

Lews Therin had made a mistake. He had died, but had left the world alive, wounded, limping forward. He'd let the Wheel of Time keep turning, rotating, *rotting* and bringing him back around again. He could not escape it. Not without ending everything.

"Why?" Rand whispered to the twisting winds around him. The Power coming to him through the access key was greater than he'd held when cleansing *saidin*. Perhaps greater than any man had ever held. Great enough to unravel the Pattern itself and bring final peace.

"Why do we have to do this again?" he whispered. "I have already failed. She is dead by my hand. Why must you make me live it *again*?"

Lightning cracked above, thunder buffeting him. Rand closed his eyes, perched above a drop that plummeted thousands of feet downward, in the middle of a tempest of icy wind. Through his eyelids, he could sense the blazing light of the access key. The Power he held inside dwarfed that light. He was the sun. He was fire. He was life and death.

Why? Why must they do this over and over? The world could give him no answers.

Rand raised his arms high, a conduit of power and energy. An incarnation of death and destruction. He would end it. End it all and let men rest, finally, from their suffering.

Stop them from having to live over and over again. *Why? Why had the Creator done this to them? Why?*

Why do we live again? Lews Therin asked, suddenly. His voice was crisp and distinct.

Yes, Rand said, pleading. *Tell me. Why?*

Maybe . . . Lews Therin said, shockingly lucid, not a hint of madness to him. He spoke softly, reverently. *Why? Could it be . . . Maybe it's so that we can have a second chance.*

Rand froze. The winds blew against him, but he could not be moved by them. The Power hesitated inside him, like the headsman's axe, held quivering above the criminal's neck. *You may not have a choice about which duties are given you,* Tam's voice, just a memory, said in his mind. *But you can choose* why *you fulfill them.*

Why, Rand? Why do you go to battle? What is *the point? Why?*

All was still. Even with the tempest, the winds, the crashes of thunder. All was still.

Why? Rand thought with wonder. *Because each time we live, we get to love again.*

That was the answer. It all swept over him, lives lived, mistakes made, love changing everything. He saw the entire world in his mind's eye, lit by the glow in his hand. He remembered lives, hundreds of them, thousands of them, stretching to infinity. He remembered love, and peace, and joy, and hope.

Within that moment, suddenly something amazing occurred to him. *If I live again, then she might as well!*

That's why he fought. That's why he lived again, and that was the answer to Tam's question. *I fight because last time, I failed. I fight because I want to fix what I did wrong.*

I want to do it right this time.

The Power within him reached a crescendo, and he turned it upon itself, drove it through the access key. The *ter'angreal* was connected to a much greater force, a massive *sa'angreal* to the south, built to stop the Dark One. Too powerful, some had said. Too powerful ever to use. Too frightening.

Rand used its own power upon it, crushing the distant globe, shattering it as if in the grip of a giant's hands.

The Choedan Kal exploded.

The Power winked out.

The tempest ended.

And Rand opened his eyes for the first time in a very long while. He knew—somehow—that he would never again hear Lews Therin's voice in his head. For they were not two men, and never had been.

He regarded the world beneath him. The clouds above had finally broken, if only just above him. The gloom dispersed, allowing him to see the sun hanging just above.

Rand looked up at it. Then he smiled. Finally, he let out a deep-throated laugh, true and pure.

It had been far too long.

EPILOGUE

Bathed in Light

Egwene worked by the light of two bronze lamps. They were shaped like women holding their hands into the air, a burst of flame appearing in each set of palms. The calm yellow light reflected on the curves of their hands, arms and faces. Were they symbols of the White Tower and the Flame of Tar Valon? Or were they instead depictions of an Aes Sedai, weaving Fire? Perhaps they were simply relics of a previous Amyrlin's taste.

They sat on either side of her desk. A proper desk, finally, with a proper chair to sit upon. She was inside the Amyrlin's study, purged of any and all references to Elaida. That left it bare, the walls empty, the wood paneling unadorned by picture or tapestry, the end tables empty of works of art. Even the bookshelves had been emptied, lest something of Elaida's offend Egwene.

The moment Egwene had seen what the others had done, she had ordered all of Elaida's effects gathered and placed under secure lock, guarded by women Egwene trusted. Hidden among those effects would be clues to Elaida's plans. They might simply be hidden notes slipped between the pages of books, left for further review. Or they might be as obscure as connections between the types of books she'd been reading or the items she'd had in the desk drawers. But they didn't have Elaida herself to question, and there was no telling what schemes of hers would return to bite the White Tower at a later date. Egwene intended to look over those objects, then interview each and every Aes Sedai who had been in the Tower and determine what clues they hid.

For now, she had her hands full. She shook her head, turning over the pages of Silviana's report. The woman was proving to be an effective Keeper indeed, far more skilled than Sheriam had ever been. The loyalist women respected Silviana, and the Red Ajah seemed to have accepted—at least in part—Egwene's offer of peace in choosing one of their own as her Keeper.

Of course, Egwene also had two stiff letters of disapproval—one from Romanda and one from Lelaine—on the bottom of her stack. The two women had withdrawn their effusive support almost as quickly as they'd given it. Right now, they were arguing over what to do with the *damane* Egwene had captured during the White Tower raid, and neither one liked Egwene's plan to train them as Aes Sedai. Romanda and Lelaine would trouble her for years yet, it appeared.

She set the report aside. It was late afternoon, and light peeked through the slits of the louvered shutters to her balcony. She didn't open them, preferring the quiet dimness. The solitude felt nice.

For now, she didn't mind the room's sparse decorations. True, it reminded her just a little too much of the study of the Mistress of Novices, but no number of wall hangings would banish her memory of those days, not when Silviana herself was Egwene's Keeper. That was fine. Why would Egwene want to banish those days? They contained some of her most satisfying victories.

Though she certainly didn't mind being able to sit without cringing.

She smiled faintly, scanning the next of Silviana's reports. Then she frowned. *Most* of the Black Ajah in the Tower had escaped. This report, written in Silviana's careful, flowing script, told that they had managed to seize some of the Blacks in the hours following Egwene's raising, but only the weakest of the lot. The majority of them—some sixty Black sisters—had escaped. Including one Sitter, as Egwene had noticed before, whose name had not been on Verin's list. Evanellein's disappearance indicated strongly that she was Black.

Egwene picked up another report, frowning to herself. It was a list of all the women in the White Tower, an extensive list several pages long, broken down by Ajah. Many names had a notation beside them. Black, escaped. Black, captured. Taken by the Seanchan.

That last group was galling. Saerin—acting with foresight—had taken a census following the attack to determine exactly who had been captured. Nearly forty initiates—over two dozen of them full Aes Sedai—snatched in the night and carried off. It was like a story told to children at bedtime, warning of Fades or Halfmen who stole wicked children. Those women would be beaten, confined and turned into nothing more than tools.

Egwene had to steel herself from reaching up to feel her neck, where the collar had held her. She wasn't focusing on that right now, burn it all!

Each of the Black Ajah members on Verin's list had been seen healthy and alive following the Seanchan attack. But most had escaped before Egwene arrived at the Tower to take her seat. Velina was gone. So were Chai and Birlen. And Alviarin; the Black hunters hadn't managed to get to her in time.

What had tipped them off? Unfortunately, it had probably something to do with Egwene seizing the Black Ajah in the rebel camp. She had worried about overplaying her hand. But what else should she have done? Her only hope had been to seize every Black in the camp and hope that word didn't spread to the White Tower.

But it had. She'd captured the ones who remained, and had them executed. Then she'd resworn every sister in the Tower on the Oath Rod. They hadn't liked it, of course. But the knowledge that all of the women in the rebel camp had done it had swayed them. If it hadn't, the news that Egwene had ordered the execution of her own Keeper probably did. It had certainly been a relief when Silviana had offered to swear first, in front of the entire Hall, to prove herself. Egwene had followed by reswearing herself, then told the Hall truthfully that she had watched each and every woman in the camp prove that she wasn't a Darkfriend. They'd captured three more Black sisters who hadn't been on Verin's list. Only three. What accuracy! Verin had proven herself once again.

Egwene set aside the report. Knowledge of those who had escaped still chewed at her. She had known the names of sixty Darkfriends, and they had escaped her grasp. That

number reached to eighty if she included those who had escaped from the rebel camp.

I will find you, Alviarin, Egwene thought, tapping the
sheet with her finger. *I will find you all. You were a rot
within the Tower itself. The worst kind of rot. I will not let
you spread it.*

She set the sheet aside and picked up another. This one
bore only a few names. A list of all the women in the Tower
who had *not* been on Verin's list and who had either been
taken by the Seanchan, or had disappeared following the
attack.

Verin had believed that one of the Forsaken, Mesaana,
was hiding in the Tower. Sheriam's confession corroborated
this. Egwene's task of reswearing every Aes Sedai on the
Rod had revealed no Darkfriends of great power. Hopefully, the reswearing itself would ease the tension between
the Ajahs. They could stop worrying if there were Blacks
in their midst. Of course, it could very well weaken the Aes
Sedai by giving proof that the Black Ajah *had* indeed existed in the first place.

Either way, Egwene had a problem. She looked over
the sheet before her. Each woman in the White Tower had
proven that she was not a Darkfriend. Each woman on Verin's list was accounted for. She'd been executed, she'd been
captured, she'd fled the White Tower the day of Egwene's
ascension, she'd been taken by the Seanchan or she was out
of the Tower at the moment—and had been for some time.
The sisters had instructions to watch for those.

Perhaps they'd been lucky, and the Forsaken was one
of those women who had been taken by the Seanchan.
But Egwene didn't believe in that kind of luck. One of the
Forsaken would not be captured so easily. She'd probably
known about the attack in the first place.

That left the three names on the list in front of Egwene.
Nalasia Merhan, a Brown; Teramina, a Green; and Jamilila
Norsish, a Red. All were very weak in the Power. And the
women on this list had all been in the Tower for years. It
seemed implausible that Mesaana had been impersonating
one of them and doing it so well that her subterfuge hadn't
been noticed.

Egwene had a feeling. A premonition, perhaps. At the
very least, a fear. These three names were the only ones

who could have been the Forsaken. But none of them fit, not at all. That gave her a chill. Was Mesaana still hiding in the Tower?

If so, she somehow knew how to defeat the Oath Rod.

A soft knock came at her door. It cracked a moment later. "Mother?" Silviana asked.

Egwene looked up, raising her eyebrows.

"I thought you might want to see this," Silviana said, entering, her hair back in its tidy black bun, the red Keeper's stole around her shoulders.

"What is it?"

"You should come and see."

Curious, Egwene rose. There was no tension to Silviana's voice, so it couldn't be anything too dire. The two of them left the study behind, walking around the outside of the building to the Hall of the Tower. When they reached it, Egwene raised an eyebrow. Silviana gestured for her to enter.

The Hall wasn't in session, and the chairs sat empty. A scattering of mason's tools lay on white sheets in the corner, and a group of workers in thick brown overalls and white shirts—sleeves rolled up—were collected in front of the gap in the wall that the Seanchan had left. Egwene had ordered a rose window fitted into the opening instead of having it sealed up completely, a remembrance for the time the White Tower had been attacked. A warning to prevent its happening again. Before the window could be installed, however, stonemasons were busy shoring up the sides and creating the fitting.

Egwene and Silviana glided into the room, walking down the short ramp to the floor, which had again been properly painted with the colors of all seven Ajahs. The stonemasons saw them, then backed away respectfully, one man pulling off his cap and clutching it to his chest. Reaching the edge of the room, just before the opening, Egwene finally saw what Silviana had brought her to see.

After all this time, the clouds had finally broken. They had pulled back in a ring around Dragonmount. The sun shone down, radiant, lighting the distant, snowcapped crag. The broken maw and uppermost peak of the blasted mountainside were bathed in light. It was the first time Egwene could remember seeing direct sunlight in weeks. Perhaps longer.

824 THE GATHERING STORM

"Some novices noticed it first, Mother," Silviana said, stepping up beside her. "And news spread quickly. Who would have thought that a little ring of sunlight would cause such a stir? It's such a simple thing, really. Nothing we haven't seen before. But. . . ."

There was something beautiful about it. The light streaming down in a column, strong and pure. Distant, yet striking. It was like something forgotten, but somehow still familiar, shining forth from a distant memory to bring warmth again.

"What does it mean?" Silviana asked.

"I don't know," Egwene said. "But I welcome the sight of it." She hesitated. "That opening in the clouds is too even to be natural. Mark this day on the calendars, Silviana. Something has happened. Perhaps, eventually, we shall know the truth of it."

"Yes, Mother," Silviana said, looking out through the gap again.

Egwene stood with her, rather than returning to her study immediately. It felt relaxing to stare out at that distant light, so welcoming and noble. "Storms will soon come," it seemed to say. "But for now, I am here."

I am here.

At the end of time,
when the many become one,
the last storm shall gather its angry winds
to destroy a land already dying.
And at its center,
the blind man shall stand
upon his own grave.
There he shall see again,
and weep for what has been wrought.

—from *The Prophecies of the Dragon,*
Essanik Cycle. Malhavish's
Official Translation, Imperial Record
House of Seandar,
Fourth Circle of Elevation.

The End

of the Twelfth Book of

The Wheel of Time

GLOSSARY

A Note on Dates in This Glossary. The Toman Calendar (devised by Toma dur Ahmid) was adopted approximately two centuries after the death of the last male Aes Sedai, recording years After the Breaking of the World (AB). So many records were destroyed in the Trolloc Wars that at their end there was argument about the exact year under the old system. A new calendar, proposed by Tiam of Gazar, celebrated freedom from the Trolloc threat and recorded each year as a Free Year (FY). The Gazaran Calendar gained wide acceptance within twenty years after the Wars' end. Artur Hawkwing attempted to establish a new calendar based on the founding of his empire (FF, From the Founding), but only historians now refer to it. After the death and destruction of the War of the Hundred Years, a third calendar was devised by Uren din Jubai Soaring Gull, a scholar of the Sea Folk, and promulgated by the Panarch Farede of Tarabon. The Farede Calendar, dating from the arbitrarily decided end of the War of the Hundred Years and recording years of the New Era (NE), is currently in use.

Aelfinn: A race of beings, largely human in appearance but with snakelike characteristics, who will give true answers to three questions. Whatever the question, their answers are always correct, if frequently given in forms that are not clear, but questions concerning the Shadow can be extremely dangerous. Their true location is unknown, but they can be visited by passing through a *ter'angreal*, once a possession of Mayene but in recent years held in the Stone of Tear. There are reports that they can also be

reached by entering the Tower of Ghenjei. They speak
the Old Tongue, mention treaties and agreements and ask
if those entering carry iron, instruments of music or de-
vices that can make fire. *See also* Eelfinn.

Arad Doman: A nation on the Aryth Ocean, currently
racked by civil war and by wars against those who have
declared for the Dragon Reborn. Its capital is Bandar
Eban, where many of its people have come for refuge.
Food is scarce. In Arad Doman, those who are descended from the nobility at the time of the founding of
the nation, as opposed to those raised later, are known
as the bloodborn. The ruler (king or queen) is elected
by a council of the heads of merchant guilds (the Council of Merchants), who are almost always women. He or
she must be from the noble class, not the merchant, and
is elected for life. Legally the king or queen has absolute authority, except that he or she can be deposed by
a three-quarter vote of the Council. The current ruler is
King Alsalam Saeed Almadar, Lord of Almadar, High
Seat of House Almadar. His present whereabouts are
much shrouded in mystery.

Area, units of: (1) Land: 1 ribbon = 20 paces × 10 paces
(200 square paces); 1 cord = 20 paces × 50 paces (1000
square paces); 1 hide = 100 paces × 100 paces (10,000
square paces); 1 rope = 100 paces × 1000 paces (100,000
square paces); 1 march = 1000 paces × 1000 paces (¼
square mile). (2) Cloth: 1 pace = 1 pace plus 1 hand × 1
pace plus 1 hand.

Asha'man: (1) In the Old Tongue, "Guardian" or "Guard-
ians," but always a guardian of justice and truth. (2) The
name given, both collectively and as a rank, to the men
who have come to the Black Tower, near Caemlyn in Andor, in order to learn to channel. Their training largely
concentrates on the ways in which the One Power can be
used as a weapon, and in another departure from the us-
ages of the White Tower, once they learn to seize *saidin*,
the male half of the Power, they are required to perform
all chores and labors with the Power. When newly en-
rolled, a man is termed a Soldier; he wears a plain black
coat with a high collar, in the Andoran fashion. Being
raised to Dedicated brings the right to wear a silver pin,
called the Sword, on the collar of his coat. Promotion

to Asha'man brings the right to wear a Dragon pin, in gold and red enamel, on the collar opposite the Sword. Although many women, including wives, flee when they learn that their men actually can channel, a fair number of men at the Black Tower are married, and they use a version of the Warder bond to create a link with their wives. This same bond, altered to compel obedience, has recently been used to bond captured Aes Sedai as well. Some Asha'man have been bonded by Aes Sedai, although the traditional Warder bond is used. The Asha'man are led by Mazrim Taim, who has styled himself the M'Hael, Old Tongue for "leader."

Band of the Red Hand: *see Shen an Calhar.*

Blood, the: Term used by the Seanchan to designate the nobility. There are four degrees of nobility, two of the High Blood and two of the low, or lesser, Blood. The High Blood let their fingernails grow to a length of one inch and shave the sides of their heads, leaving a crest down the center, narrower for men than for women. The length of this crest varies according to fashion. The low Blood also grow their fingernails long, but they shave the sides and back of the head, leaving what appears to be a bowl of hair, with a wide tail at the back allowed to grow longer, often to the shoulder for men or to the waist for women. Those of the highest level of the High Blood are called High Lady or High Lord and lacquer the first two fingernails on each hand. Those of the next level of the High Blood are called simply Lord or Lady and lacquer only the nails of the forefingers. Those of the low Blood also are called simply Lady or Lord, but those of the higher rank lacquer the nails of the last two fingers on each hand, while those on the lowest level lacquer only the nails of the little fingers. The Empress and immediate members of the Imperial family shave their heads entirely and lacquer all of their fingernails One can be raised to the Blood as well as born to it, and this is frequently a reward for outstanding accomplishment or service to the Empire.

Brown Ajah Council: The Brown Ajah is headed by a council instead of an individual Aes Sedai. The current head of the council is Jesse Bilal in the White Tower; the other members in the White Tower and all of those in the rebel camp are unknown.

calendar: There are 10 days to the week, 28 days to the month and 13 months to the year. Several feast days are not part of any month; these include Sunday (the longest day of the year), the Feast of Thanksgiving (once every four years at the spring equinox) and the Feast of All Souls Salvation, also called All Souls Day (once every ten years at the autumn equinox). While the months have names (Taisham, Jumara, Saban, Aine, Adar, Saven, Amadaine, Tammaz, Maigdhal, Choren, Shaldine, Nesan and Danu), these are seldom used except in official documents and by officials. For most people, using the seasons is good enough.

Captain-General: The title given to the head of the Green Ajah. This position is currently held by Adelorna Bastine in the White Tower, and Myrelle Berengari among the rebel faction.

Children of the Light: Society of strict ascetic beliefs, owing allegiance to no nation and dedicated to the defeat of the Dark One and the destruction of all Darkfriends. Founded during the War of the Hundred Years by Lothair Mantelar to proselytize against an increase in Darkfriends, they evolved during the war into a completely military society. They are extremely rigid in their beliefs, and certain that only they know the truth and the right. They consider Aes Sedai and any who support them to be Darkfriends. Known disparagingly as Whitecloaks, a name they themselves despise, they were formerly headquartered in Amador, Amadicia, but were forced out when the Seanchan conquered the city. Galad Damodred became Lord Captain Commander after he killed Eamon Valda in a duel for assaulting his stepmother, Morgase. Valda's death produced a schism in the organization, with Galad leading one faction, and Rhadam Asunawa, High Inquisitor of the Hand of the Light, leading the other. Their sign is a golden sunburst on a field of white. *See also* Questioners.

***Commentary on the Dragon*:** A book by Sajius of which little is known.

Comprehensive Discussion of Pre-Breaking Relics, A: A book of which little is known (other than its title).

Corenne: In the Old Tongue, "the Return." The name given by the Seanchan both to the fleet of thousands of ships and to the hundreds of thousands of soldiers, craftsmen and others carried by those ships, who came behind the Forerunners to reclaim the lands stolen from Artur Hawkwing's descendants. The *Corenne* is led by Captain-General Lunal Galgan. *See also Hailene, Rhyagelle.*

cuendillar: A supposedly indestructible substance created during the Age of Legends. Any known force used in an attempt to break it, including the One Power, is absorbed, making *cuendillar* stronger. Although the making of *cuendillar* was thought lost forever, new objects made from it have surfaced. It is also known as heartstone.

currency: After many centuries of trade, the standard terms for coins are the same in every land: crowns (the largest coin in size), marks and pennies. Crowns and marks can be minted of gold or silver, while pennies can be silver or copper, the last often called simply a copper. In different lands, however, these coins are of different sizes and weights. Even in one nation, coins of different sizes and weights have been minted by different rulers. Because of trade, the coins of many nations can be found almost anywhere, and for that reason, bankers, moneylenders and merchants all use scales to determine the value of any given coin. Even large numbers of coins are weighed.

The heaviest coins come from Andor and Tar Valon, and in those two places the relative values are: 10 copper pennies = 1 silver penny; 100 silver pennies = 1 silver mark; 10 silver marks = 1 silver crown; 10 silver crowns = 1 gold mark; 10 gold marks = 1 gold crown. By contrast, in Altara, where the larger coins contain less gold or silver, the relative values are: 10 copper pennies = 1 silver penny; 21 silver pennies = 1 silver mark; 20 silver marks = 1 silver crown; 20 silver crowns = 1 gold mark; 20 gold marks = 1 gold crown.

The only paper currency is "letters-of-rights," which are issued by bankers, guaranteeing to present a certain amount of gold or silver when the letter-of-rights is presented. Because of the long distances between cities, the length of time needed to travel from one to another and the difficulties of transactions at long distance, a letter-of-rights may be accepted at full value in a city near to the bank which issued it, but it may only be accepted at a lower value in a city farther away. Generally, someone intending to be traveling for a long time will carry one or more letters-of-rights to exchange for coin when needed. Letters-of-rights are usually accepted only by bankers or merchants, and would never be used in shops.

da'covale: (1) In the Old Tongue, "one who is owned," or "person who is property." (2) Among the Seanchan, the term often used, along with "property," for slaves. Slavery has a long and unusual history among the Seanchan, with slaves having the ability to rise to positions of great power and open authority, including authority over those who are free. It is also possible for those in positions of great power to be reduced to *da'covale*. *See also so'jhin*.

Deathwatch Guards, the: The elite military formation of the Seanchan Empire, including both humans and Ogier. The human members of the Deathwatch Guard are all *da'covale*, born as property and chosen while young to serve the Empress, whose personal property they are. Fanatically loyal and fiercely proud, they often display the ravens tattooed on their shoulders, the mark of a *da'covale* of the Empress. The Ogier members are known as Gardeners, and they are not *da'covale*. The Gardeners are as fiercely loyal as the human Deathwatch Guards, though, and are even more feared. Human or Ogier, the Deathwatch Guards not only are ready to die for the Empress and the Imperial family, but believe that their lives are the property of the Empress, to be disposed of as she wishes. Their helmets and armor are lacquered in dark green (so dark that it is often mistakenly called black) and blood-red, their shields are lacquered black and their swords, spears, axes and halberds carry black tassels. *See also da'covale*.

Delving: (1) Using the One Power to diagnose physical condition and illness. (2) Finding deposits of metal ores with the One Power. That this has long been a lost ability among Aes Sedai may account for the name becoming attached to another ability.

Depository: A division of the Tower Library. There are twelve publicly known Depositories, each having books and records pertaining to a particular subject, or to related subjects. A Thirteenth Depository, known only to some Aes Sedai, contains secret documents, records and histories which may be accessed only by the Amyrlin Seat, the Keeper of the Chronicles, and the Sitters in the Hall of the Tower. And, of course, by that handful of librarians who maintain the depository.

der'morat-: (1) In the Old Tongue, "master handler." (2) Among the Seanchan, the prefix applied to indicate a senior and highly skilled handler of one of the exotics, one who trains others, as in *der'morat'raken. Der'morat* can have a fairly high social status, the highest of all held by *der'sul'dam,* the trainers of *sul'dam,* who rank with fairly high military officers. *See also morat-.*

Echoes of His Dynasty: A book of which little is known.

Eelfinn: A race of beings, largely human in appearance but with foxlike characteristics, who will grant three wishes, although they ask for a price in return. If the person asking does not negotiate a price, the Eelfinn choose it. The most common price in such circumstances is death, but they still fulfill their part of the bargain, although the manner in which they fulfill it is seldom the manner the one asking expects. Their true location is unknown, but it was possible to visit them by means of a *ter'angreal* that was located in Rhuidean. That *ter'angreal* was taken by Moiraine Damodred to Cairhien, where it was destroyed. It is also reported that they may be reached by entering the Tower of Ghenjei. They ask the same questions as the Aelfinn regarding fire, iron and musical instruments. *See also* Aelfinn.

Falling Shale: A history of which little is known.

Fel, Herid: The author of *Reason and Unreason* and other books. Fel was a student (and teacher) of history and philosophy at the Academy of Cairhien. He was discovered in his study torn limb from limb.

First Reasoner: The title given to the head of the White Ajah. This position is currently held by Ferane Neheran, an Aes Sedai in the White Tower. Ferane Sedai is one of only two Ajah heads to sit in the Hall of the Tower at present.

First Selector: The title given to the head of the Blue Ajah. The First Selector is currently unknown, although it is suspected that Lelaine Akashi fills this position.

First Weaver: The title given to the head of the Yellow Ajah. This position is currently held by Suana Dragand in the White Tower. Suana Sedai is one of only two Ajah heads to sit in the Hall of the Tower at present. Among the rebel Aes Sedai, Romanda Cassin holds this position.

Forcing; forced: When someone with the ability to channel handles as much of the One Power as they can over long periods of time and channels continually, they learn faster and gain strength more rapidly. This is called forcing, or being forced, by Aes Sedai, who abjure the practice with novices and Accepted because of the danger of death or being burned out.

Forerunners, the: See Hailene.

Forsaken, the: The name given to thirteen powerful Aes Sedai, men and women both, who went over to the Shadow during the Age of Legends and were trapped in the sealing of the Bore into the Dark One's prison. While it has long been believed that they alone abandoned the Light during the War of the Shadow, in fact others did as well; these thirteen were only the highest-ranking among them. The Forsaken (who call themselves the Chosen) are somewhat reduced in number since their awakening in the present day. Some of those killed have been reincarnated in new bodies.

Hailene: In the Old Tongue, "Forerunners," or "Those Who Come Before." The term applied by the Seanchan to the massive expeditionary force sent across the Aryth Ocean to scout out the lands where Artur Hawkwing once ruled. Originally under the command of the High Lady Suroth, it has now been subsumed into the *Corenne. See Corenne, Rhyagelle.*

Hand: In Seanchan, Hand refers to a primary assistant or one of a hierarchy of Imperial functionaries. A Hand of the Empress is of the First Rank, and Lesser Hands will be found at lower ranks. Some Hands operate in secret, such as those who guide the Seekers and Listeners; others are known and display their rank by wearing the appropriate number of golden hands embroidered on their clothing.

Hanlon, Daved: A Darkfriend, also known as Doilin Mellar, who was captured with Lady Shiaine, Chesmal Emry, Eldrith Jhondar, Temaile Kinderode, Falion Bhoda and Marillin Gemalphin. They are currently being held prisoner in the Royal Palace of Andor.

Head Clerk: The title given to the head of the Gray Ajah. This position is currently held by Serancha Colvine in the White Tower.

Head of the Great Council of Thirteen: The title given to the head of the Black Ajah. This position is currently held by Alviarin Freidhen.

heart: The basic unit of organization in the Black Ajah. In effect, a cell. A heart consists of three sisters who know each other, with each member of the heart knowing one additional sister of the Black who is unknown to the other two of her heart.

Highest: The title given to the head of the Red Ajah. This position is currently held by Tsutama Rath.

Illuminators, Guild of: A society that held the secret of making fireworks. It guarded this secret very closely, even to the extent of doing murder to protect it. The Guild gained its name from the grand displays, called Illuminations, that it provided for rulers and sometimes for greater lords. Lesser fireworks were sold for use by others, but with dire warnings of the disaster that could result from attempting to learn what was inside them. The Guild once had chapter houses in Cairhien and Tanchico, but both are now destroyed. In addition, the members of the Guild in Tanchico resisted the invasion by the Seanchan and were made *da'covale*, and the Guild as such no longer exists. However, individual Illuminators still exist outside of Seanchan rule and work to make sure that the Guild will be remembered. *See also da'covale*.

Ishara: The first Queen of Andor (circa FY 994–1020). At the death of Artur Hawkwing, Ishara convinced her

husband, one of Hawkwing's foremost generals, to raise
the siege of Tar Valon and accompany her to Caemlyn
with as many soldiers as he could break away from the
army. Where others tried to seize the whole of Hawkwing's empire and failed, Ishara took a firm hold on a
small part and succeeded. Today, nearly every noble
House in Andor contains some of Ishara's blood, and the
right to claim the Lion Throne depends both on direct
descent from her and on the number of lines of connection to her that can be established.

Kaensada: An area of Seanchan that is populated by less-
than-civilized hill tribes. These tribes fight a great deal
among themselves, as do individual families within the
tribes. Each tribe has its own customs and taboos, the
latter of which often make no sense to anyone outside
that tribe. Most of the tribesmen avoid the more civilized
residents of Seanchan.

Lance-Captain: In most lands, noblewomen do not personally lead their armsmen into battle under normal circumstances. Instead, they hire a professional soldier, almost
always a commoner, who is responsible both for training and leading their armsmen. Depending on the land,
this man can be called a Lance-Captain, Sword-Captain,
Master of the Horse or Master of the Lances. Rumors of
closer relationships than Lady and servant often spring
up, perhaps inevitably. Sometimes they are true.

Legion of the Dragon, the: A large military formation, all
infantry, giving allegiance to the Dragon Reborn, trained
by Davram Bashere along lines worked out by himself
and Mat Cauthon, lines which depart sharply from the
usual employment of foot. While many men simply walk
in to volunteer, large numbers of the Legion are scooped
up by recruiting parties from the Black Tower, who first
gather all of the men in an area who are willing to follow
the Dragon Reborn, and only after taking them through
gateways near Caemlyn winnow out those who can be
taught to channel. The remainder, by far the greater number, are sent to Bashere's training camps.

Length, units of: 10 inches = 1 foot; 3 feet = 1 pace; 2
paces = 1 span; 1000 spans = 1 mile; 4 miles = 1 league.

Listeners: A Seanchan spy organization. Almost anyone in the household of a Seanchan noble, merchant or banker may be a Listener, including *da'covale* occasionally, though seldom *so'jhin*. They take no active role, merely watching, listening and reporting. Their reports are sent to Lesser Hands who control both them and the Seekers and decide what should be passed on to the Seekers for further action. *See also* Seekers, Hand.

marath'damane: In the Old Tongue, "those who must be leashed," and also "one who must be leashed." The term applied by the Seanchan to any woman capable of channeling who has not been collared as a *damane*.

march: *see* Area, units of.

Marks and Remarks: A history of which little is known.

Master of the Horse: *See* Lance-Captain.

Master of the Lances: *See* Lance-Captain.

Meditations on the Kindling Flame: A history dealing with the rise of various Amyrlins.

Mellar, Doilin: *See* Hanlon, Daved.

Mera'din: In the Old Tongue, "the Brotherless." The name adopted, as a society, by those Aiel who abandoned clan and sept and went to the Shaido because they could not accept Rand al'Thor, a wetlander, as the *Car'a'carn*, or because they refused to accept his revelations concerning the history and origins of the Aiel. Deserting clan and sept for any reason is anathema among the Aiel; therefore their own warrior societies among the Shaido were unwilling to take them in, and they formed this society, the Brotherless.

Moiraine Damodred: A Cairhienin Aes Sedai of the Blue Ajah. Long presumed dead. Thom Merrilin has, however, revealed the receipt of a letter purporting to be from her. It is reproduced here:

My dearest Thom,
There are many words I would like to write to you, words from my heart, but I have put this off because I knew that I must, and now there is little time. There are many things I cannot tell you lest I bring disaster, but what I can, I will. Heed carefully what I say. In a short while I will go down to the docks, and there

I will confront Lanfear. How can I know that? That secret belongs to others. Suffice it that I know, and let that foreknowledge stand as proof for the rest of what I say.

When you receive this, you will be told that I am dead. All will believe that. I am not dead, and it may be that I shall live to my appointed years. It also may be that you and Mat Cauthon and another, a man I do not know, will try to rescue me. May, I say because it may be that you will not or cannot, or because Mat may refuse. He does not hold me in the affection you seem to, and he has his reasons which he no doubt thinks are good. If you try, it must be only you and Mat and one other. More will mean death for all. Fewer will mean death for all.

Even if you come only with Mat and one other, death also may come. I have seen you try and die, one or two or all three. I have seen myself die in the attempt. I have seen all of us live and die as captives.

Should you decide to make the attempt anyway, young Mat knows the way to find me, yet you must not show him this letter until he asks about it. That is of the utmost importance. He must know nothing that is in this letter until he asks. Events must play out in certain ways, whatever the costs.

If you see Lan again, tell him that all of this is for the best. His destiny follows a different path from mine. I wish him all happiness with Nynaeve.

A final point. Remember what you know about the game of Snakes and Foxes. Remember, and heed.

It is time, and I must do what must be done.

May the Light illumine you and give you joy, my dearest Thom, whether or not we ever see one another again.

                                                        Moiraine

Monuments Past: A history of which little is known.

morat-: In the Old Tongue, "handler." Among the Seanchan, it is used for those who handle exotics, such as *morat'raken*, a *raken* handler or rider, also informally called a flier. *See also der'morat-.*

Pelateos: Author of *Pelateos' Ponderings*.

Proper Taming of Power, The: A history of which little is known.

Prophet, the: More formally, the Prophet of the Lord Dragon. Once known as Masema Dagar, a Shienaran soldier, he underwent a revelation and decided that he had been called to spread the word of the Dragon's Rebirth. He believed that nothing—nothing!—was more important than acknowledging the Dragon Reborn as the Light made flesh and being ready when the Dragon Reborn called, and he and his followers would use any means to force others to sing the glories of the Dragon Reborn. Those who refused were marked for death, and those who were slow might find their homes and shops burned and themselves flogged. Forsaking any name but "the Prophet," he brought chaos to much of Ghealdan and Amadicia, large parts of which he controlled, although with him gone, the Seanchan are reestablishing order in Amadicia and the Crown High Council in Ghealdan. He joined with Perrin Aybara, who was sent to bring him to Rand, and, for reasons unknown, stayed with him even though this delayed his going to the Dragon Reborn. He was followed by men and women of the lowest sort; if they were not so when they were pulled in by his charisma, they became so under his influence. He died under mysterious circumstances.

Queen's Guard, the: The elite military formation in Andor. In peacetime the Guard is responsible for upholding the Queen's law and keeping the peace across Andor. The uniform of the Queen's Guard includes a red undercoat, gleaming mail and plate armor, a brilliant red cloak and a conical helmet with a barred visor. High-ranking officers wear knots of rank on their shoulder and golden lion-head spurs. A recent addition to the Queen's Guard is the Daughter-Heir's personal bodyguard, which is composed entirely of women since the arrest of its former captain, Doilin Mellar. These Guardswomen wear much more elaborate uniforms than their male counterparts, including broad-brimmed hats with white plumes, red-lacquered breastplates and helmets trimmed in white and lace-edged sashes bearing the White Lion of Andor.

Questioners, the: An order within the Children of the Light. They refer to themselves as the Hand of the Light—they intensely dislike being called Questioners—and their avowed purposes are to discover the truth in disputations and uncover Darkfriends. In the search for truth and the Light, their normal method of inquiry is torture; their normal manner is that they know the truth already and must only make their victim confess to it. At times they act as if they are entirely separate from the Children and the Council of the Anointed, which commands the Children. The head of the Questioners is the High Inquisitor, at present Rhadam Asunawa, who sits on the Council of the Anointed. After Galad Damodred killed Lord Captain Commander Valda and assumed Valda's position, there was a schism in the organization, with Galad leading one faction, and Asunawa leading the other. Their sign is a blood-red shepherd's crook.

Redarms: Soldiers of the Band of the Red Hand, who have been chosen for temporary police duty to make sure that other soldiers of the Band cause no trouble or damage in a town or village where the Band has stopped. So named because, while on duty, they wear very broad red armbands that reach from cuff to elbow. Usually chosen from among the most experienced and reliable men. Since any damages must be paid for by the men serving as Redarms, they work hard to make sure all is quiet and peaceful. A number of former Redarms were chosen to accompany Mat Cauthon to Ebou Dar. *See also Shen an Calhar.*

Return, the: *See Corenne.*

Rhyagelle, the: Old Tongue for "Those Who Come Home." Another name for the Seanchan who have returned to the lands once held by Artur Hawkwing. *See also Corenne, Hailene.*

Sajius: Author of *Commentary on the Dragon.*

Seandar: The Imperial capital of Seanchan, located in the northeast of the Seanchan continent. It is also the largest city in the Empire. After the death of Empress Radhanan, it descended into chaos.

Seekers: More formally, Seekers for Truth, they are a po-
lice/spy organization of the Seanchan Imperial Throne.
Although most Seekers are *da'covale* and the property
of the Imperial family, they have wide-ranging powers.
Even one of the Blood can be arrested for failure to answer any question put by a Seeker, or for failure to coop-
erate fully with a Seeker, this last defined by the Seekers
themselves, subject only to review by the Empress. Their
reports are sent to Lesser Hands, who control both them
and the Listeners. Most Seekers feel that the Hands do
not pass on as much information as they should. Unlike
the Listeners', the Seekers' role is active. Those Seekers
who are *da'covale* are marked on either shoulder with a
raven and a tower. Unlike the Deathwatch Guards, Seekers are seldom eager to show their ravens, in part because
it necessitates revealing who and what they are. *See also*
Hand, Listeners.

sei'mosiev: In the Old Tongue, "lowered eyes," or "downcast eyes." Among the Seanchan, to say that one has
"become *sei'mosiev*" means that one has "lost face." *See
also sei'taer.*

sei'taer: In the Old Tongue, "straight eyes," or "level eyes."
Among the Seanchan, it refers to honor or face, to the
ability to meet someone's eyes. It is possible to "be" or
"have" *sei'taer,* meaning that one has honor and face,
and also to "gain" or "lose" *sei'taer. See also sei'mosiev.*

Shara: A mysterious land to the east of the Aiel Waste
which is the source of silk and ivory, among other trade
goods. The land is protected both by inhospitable natural features and by man-made walls. Little is known
about Shara, as the people of that land work to keep
their culture secret. The Sharans deny that the Trolloc
Wars touched them, despite Aiel statements to the con-
trary. They deny knowledge of Artur Hawkwing's attempted invasion, despite the accounts of eyewitnesses
from the Sea Folk. The little information that has leaked
out reveals that the Sharans are ruled by a single absolute monarch, a Sh'boan if a woman and a Sh'botay
if a man. That monarch rules for exactly seven years,
then dies. The rule then passes to the mate of that ruler,
who rules for seven years and then dies. This pattern
has repeated itself since the time of the Breaking of

the World. The Sharans believe that the deaths are the "Will of the Pattern."

There are channelers in Shara, known as the Ayyad, who are tattooed on their faces at birth. The women of the Ayyad enforce the Ayyad laws stringently. A sexual relationship between Ayyad and non-Ayyad is punishable by death for the non-Ayyad, and the Ayyad is also executed if force on his or her part can be proven. If a child is born of the union, it is left exposed to the elements, and dies. Male Ayyad are used as breeding stock only. They are not educated in any fashion, not even how to read or write, and when they reach their twenty-first year or begin to channel, whichever comes first, they are killed and the body cremated. Supposedly, the Ayyad channel the One Power only at the command of the Sh'boan or Sh'botay, who is always surrounded by Ayyad women.

Even the name of the land is in doubt. The natives have been known to call it many different names, including Shamara, Co'dansin, Tomaka, Kigali and Shibouya.

Shen an Calhar: In the Old Tongue, "the Band of the Red Hand." (1) A legendary group of heroes who had many exploits, finally dying in the defense of Manetheren when that land was destroyed during the Trolloc Wars. (2) A military formation put together almost by accident by Mat Cauthon and organized along the lines of military forces during what is considered the height of the military arts, the days of Artur Hawkwing and the centuries immediately preceding.

Sisnera, Darlin: A High Lord in Tear, he was formerly in rebellion against the Dragon Reborn. After serving for a short period as Steward of the Dragon Reborn in Tear, he was chosen to be the first king of Tear.

Snakes and Foxes: A game that is much loved by children until they mature enough to realize that it can never be won without breaking the rules. It is played with a board that has a web of lines with arrows indicating direction. There are ten discs inked with triangles to represent the foxes, and ten discs inked with wavy lines to represent the snakes. The game is begun by saying, "Courage to strengthen, fire to blind, music to dazzle, iron to bind," while describing a triangle with a wavy line through it with one's hand. Dice are rolled to determine moves for the players and the snakes and foxes. If a snake or fox lands on a player's piece, he is out of the game, and as long as the rules are followed, this always happens.

so'jhin: The closest translation from the Old Tongue would be "a height among lowness," though some translate it as meaning "both sky and valley" among several other possibilities. *So'jhin* is the term applied by the Seanchan to hereditary upper servants. They are *da'covale*, property, yet occupy positions of considerable authority and often power. Even the Blood step carefully around *so'jhin* of the Imperial family, and speak to *so'jhin* of the Empress herself as to equals. *See also* Blood, the; *da'covale*.

Standardbearer: A Seanchan rank equivalent to Bannerman.

Succession: In general, when one House succeeds another on the throne. In Andor, the term is widely used for the struggle for the throne that arose upon Mordrellen's death. Tigraine's disappearance had left Mantear without a Daughter-Heir, and two years passed before Morgase, of House Trakand, took the throne. Outside of Andor, this conflict was known as the Third War of Andoran Succession.

Sword-Captain: *See* Lance-Captain.

Tarabon: A nation on the Aryth Ocean. Once a great trading nation, a source of rugs, dyes and the Guild of Illuminators' fireworks among other things, Tarabon has fallen on hard times. Racked by anarchy and civil war compounded by simultaneous wars against Arad Doman and the Dragonsworn, it was ripe for the picking when the Seanchan arrived. It is now firmly under Seanchan control, the chapter house of the Guild of Illuminators has been destroyed and the Illuminators themselves have been made *da'covale*. Most Taraboners appear grateful that the Seanchan have restored order, and since the Seanchan allow them to continue living their lives with minimal interference, they have no desire to bring on more warfare by trying to chase the Seanchan out. There are, however, some lords and soldiers who remain outside the Seanchan sphere of influence and are fighting to reclaim their land.

Thoughts Among the Ruins: An ancient work of history.

***Wake of the Breaking, The*:** A book of which little is known.

weight, units of: 10 ounces = 1 pound; 10 pounds = 1 stone; 10 stone = 1 hundredweight; 10 hundredweight = 1 ton.

Winged Guards, the: The personal bodyguards of the First of Mayene, and the elite military formation of Mayene. Members of the Winged Guards wear red-painted breastplates and helmets shaped like rimmed pots that come down to the nape of the necks in the back, and carry red-streamered lances. Officers have wings worked on the sides of their helmets, and rank is denoted by slender plumes.

PROLOGUE

A preview of
Towers of Midnight

The Thirteenth Book of
The Wheel of Time

Distinctions

Mandarb's hooves beat a familiar rhythm on broken ground as Lan Mandragoran rode toward his death. The dry air made his throat rough, and the earth was sprinkled white with crystals of salt that precipitated from below. Distant red rock formations loomed to the north, where sickness stained them. Blight marks, a creeping dark lichen.

He continued riding east, parallel to the Blight. This was still Saldaea, where his wife had deposited him, only narrowly keeping her promise to take him to the Borderlands. It had stretched before him for a long time, this road. He'd turned away from it twenty years ago, agreeing to follow Moiraine, but he'd always known he would return. This was what it meant to bear the name of his fathers, the sword on his hip, and the *hadori* on his head.

This rocky section of northern Saldaea was known as the Proska Flats. It was a grim place to ride; not a plant grew on it. The wind blew from the north, carrying with it a foul stench. Like that of a deep, sweltering mire bloated with corpses. The sky overhead stormed dark, brooding.

That woman, Lan thought, shaking his head. How quickly

Nynaeve had learned to talk, and think, like an Aes Sedai.
Riding to his death didn't pain him, but knowing she feared
for him . . . that did hurt. Very badly.

He hadn't seen another person in days. The Saldaeans had
fortifications to the south, but the land here was scarred with
broken ravines that made it difficult for Trollocs to assault;
they preferred attacking near Maradon.

That was no reason to relax, however. One should never
relax, this close to the Blight. He noted a hilltop; that would
be a good place for a scout's post. He made certain to watch
it for any sign of movement. He rode around a depression
in the ground, just in case it held waiting ambushers. He
kept his hand on his bow. Once he traveled a little farther
eastward, he'd cut down into Saldaea and cross Kandor on
its good roadways. Then—

Some gravel rolled down a hillside nearby.

Lan carefully slid an arrow from the quiver tied to Mandarb's saddle. Where had the sound come from? *To the right,*
he decided. Southward. The hillside there; someone was approaching from behind it.

Lan did not stop Mandarb. If the hoofbeats changed, it
would give warning. He quietly raised the bow, feeling the
sweat of his fingers inside his fawn-hide gloves. He nocked the
arrow and pulled carefully, raising it to his cheek, breathing in
its scent. Goose feathers, resin.

A figure walked around the southern hillside. The man
froze, an old, shaggy-maned packhorse walking around beside him and continuing on ahead. It stopped only when the
rope at its neck grew taut.

The man wore a laced tan shirt and dusty breeches. He
had a sword at his waist, and his arms were thick and
strong, but he didn't look threatening. In fact, he seemed
faintly familiar.

"Lord Mandragoran!" the man said, hastening forward,
pulling his horse after. "I've found you at last. I assumed
you'd be traveling the Kremer Road!"

Lan lowered his bow and stopped Mandarb. "Do I know
you?"

"I brought supplies, my Lord!" The man had black hair
and tanned skin. Borderlander stock, probably. He continued
forward, overeager, yanking on the overloaded packhorse's
rope with a thick-fingered hand. "I figured that you wouldn't

have enough food. Tents—four of them, just in case—some water too. Feed for the horses. And—"

"Who *are* you?" Lan barked. "And how do you know who I am?"

The man drew up sharply. "I'm Bulen, my Lord. From Kandor?"

From Kandor . . . Lan remembered a gangly young messenger boy. With surprise, he saw the resemblance. "*Bulen?* That was twenty years ago, man!"

"I know, Lord Mandragoran. But when word spread in the palace that the Golden Crane was raised, I knew what I had to do. I've learned the sword well, my Lord. I've come to ride with you and—"

"The word of my travel has spread to *Aesdaishar?*"

"Yes, my Lord. El'Nynaeve, she came to us, you see. Told us what you'd done. Others are gathering, but I left first. Knew you'd need supplies."

Burn that woman, Lan thought. And she'd made him *swear* that he would accept those who wished to ride with him! Well, if she could play games with the truth, then so could he. Lan had said he'd take anyone who wished to *ride* with him. This man was not mounted. Therefore, Lan could refuse him. A petty distinction, but twenty years with Aes Sedai had taught him a few things about how to watch one's words.

"Go back to Aesdaishar," Lan said. "Tell them that my wife was wrong, and I have *not* raised the Golden Crane."

"But—"

"I don't need you, son. Away with you." Lan's heels nudged Mandarb into a walk, and he passed the man standing on the road. For a few moments, Lan thought that his order would be obeyed, though the evasion of his oath pricked at his conscience.

"My father was Malkieri," Bulen said from behind.

Lan continued on.

"He died when I was five," Bulen called. "He married a Kandori woman. They both fell to bandits. I don't remember much of them. Only something my father told me: that someday, we would fight for the Golden Crane. All I have of him is this."

Lan couldn't help but look back as Mandarb continued to walk away. Bulen held up a thin strap of leather, the *hadori,* worn on the head of a Malkieri sworn to fight the Shadow.

"I would wear the *hadori* of my father," Bulen called, voice growing louder. "But I have nobody to ask if I may. That is the tradition, is it not? Someone has to give me the right to don it. Well, I would fight the Shadow all my days." He looked down at the *hadori*, then back up again and yelled, "I would stand against the darkness, al'Lan Mandragoran! Will you tell me I cannot?"

"Go to the Dragon Reborn," Lan called to him. "Or to your queen's army. Either of them will take you."

"And you? You will ride all the way to the Seven Towers without supplies?"

"I'll forage."

"Pardon me, my Lord, but have you *seen* the land these days? The Blight creeps farther and farther south. Nothing grows, even in once-fertile lands. Game is scarce."

Lan hesitated. He reined Mandarb in.

"All those years ago," Bulen called, walking forward, his packhorse walking behind him. "I hardly knew who you were, though I know you lost someone dear to you among us. I've spent years cursing myself for not serving you better. I swore that I would stand with you someday." He walked up beside Lan. "I ask you because I have no father. May I wear the *hadori* and fight at your side, al'Lan Mandragoran? My King?"

Lan breathed out slowly, stilling his emotions. *Nynaeve, when next I see you* . . . But he would not see her again. He tried not to dwell upon that.

He *had* made an oath. Aes Sedai wiggled around their promises, but did that give him the same right? No. A man was his honor. He could not deny Bulen.

"We ride anonymously," Lan said. "We do *not* raise the Golden Crane. You tell nobody who I am."

"Yes, my Lord," Bulen said.

"Then wear that *hadori* with pride," Lan said. "Too few keep to the old ways. And yes, you may join me."

Lan nudged Mandarb into motion, Bulen following on foot. And the one became two.

Perrin slammed his hammer against the red-hot length of iron. Sparks sprayed into the air like incandescent insects. Sweat beaded on his face.

Some people found the clang of metal against metal grating. Not Perrin. That sound was soothing. He raised the hammer and slammed it down.

Sparks. Flying chips of light that bounced off his leather vest and his apron. With each strike, the walls of the room—sturdy leatherleaf wood—*fuzzed,* responding to the beats of metal on metal. He was dreaming, though he wasn't in the wolf dream. He knew this, though he didn't know *how* he knew.

The windows were dark; the only light was that of the deep red fire burning on his right. Two bars of iron simmered in the coals, waiting their turn at the forge. Perrin slammed the hammer down again.

This was peace. This was *home.*

He was making something important. So very important. It was a piece of something larger. The first step to creating something was to figure out its parts. Master Luhhan had taught Perrin that on his first day at the forge. You couldn't make a spade without understanding how the handle fit to the blade. You couldn't make a hinge without knowing how the two leaves moved with the pin. You couldn't even make a nail without knowing its parts: head, shaft, point.

Understand the pieces, Perrin.

A wolf lay in the corner of the room. It was large and grizzled, fur the color of a pale gray river stone, and scarred from a lifetime of battles and hunts. The wolf laid its head on its paws, watching Perrin. That was natural. Of *course* there was a wolf in the corner. Why wouldn't there be? It was Hopper.

Perrin worked, enjoying the deep, burning heat of the forge, the feel of the sweat trailing down his arms, the scent of the fire. He shaped the length of iron, one blow for every second beat of his heart. The metal never grew cool, but instead retained its malleable red-yellow.

What am I making? Perrin picked up the length of glowing iron with his tongs. The air warped around it.

Pound, pound, pound, Hopper sent, communicating in images and scents. *Like a pup jumping at butterflies.*

Hopper didn't see the point of reshaping metal, and found it amusing that men did such things. To a wolf, a thing was what it was. Why go through so much effort to change it into something else?

Perrin set the length of iron aside. It cooled immediately, fading from yellow, to orange, to crimson, to a dull black. Perrin had pounded it into a misshapen nugget, perhaps the size of two fists. Master Luhhan would be ashamed to see such shoddy work. Perrin needed to discover what he was making soon, before his master returned.

No. That was wrong. The dream shook, and the walls grew misty.

I'm not an apprentice. Perrin raised a thick-gloved hand to his head. *I'm not in the Two Rivers any longer. I'm a man, a married man.*

Perrin grabbed the lump of unshaped iron with his tongs, thrusting it down on the anvil. It flared to life with heat. *Everything is still wrong.* Perrin smashed his hammer down. *It should all be better now! But it isn't. It seems worse somehow.*

He continued pounding. He hated those rumors that the men in camp whispered about him. Perrin had been sick and Berelain had cared for him. That was the end of it. But still those whispers continued.

He slammed his hammer down over and over. Sparks flew in the air like splashes of water, far too many to come from one length of iron. He gave one final strike, then breathed in and out.

The lump hadn't changed. Perrin growled and grabbed the tongs, setting the lump aside and taking a fresh bar from the coals. He *had* to finish this piece. It was so important. But what was he making?

He started pounding. *I need to spend time with Faile, to figure things out, remove the awkwardness between us. But there's no time!* Those Light-blinded fools around him couldn't take care of themselves. Nobody in the Two Rivers ever needed a lord before.

He worked for a time, then held up the second chunk of iron. It cooled, turning into a misshapen, flattened length about as long as his forearm. Another shoddy piece. He set it aside.

If you are unhappy, Hopper sent, *take your she and leave. If you do not wish to lead the pack, another will.* The wolf's sending came as images of running across open fields, stalks of grain brushing along his snout. An open sky, a cool breeze, a thrill and lust for adventure. The scents of new rain, of wild pastures.

Perrin reached his tongs into the coals for the final bar of iron. It burned a distant, dangerous yellow. "I can't leave." He held the bar up toward the wolf. "It would mean giving in to being a wolf. It would mean losing myself. I won't do that."

He held the near-molten steel between them, and Hopper watched it, yellow pinpricks of light reflecting in the wolf's eyes. This dream was so odd. In the past, Perrin's ordinary dreams and the wolf dream had been separate. What did this blending mean?

Perrin was afraid. He'd come to a precarious truce with the wolf inside of him. Growing too close to the wolves was dangerous, but that hadn't prevented his turning to them when seeking Faile. Anything for Faile. In doing so, Perrin had nearly gone mad, and had even tried to kill Hopper.

Perrin wasn't nearly as in control as he'd assumed. The wolf within him could still reign.

Hopper yawned, letting his tongue loll. He smelled of sweet amusement.

"This is not funny." Perrin set the final bar aside without working on it. It cooled, taking on the shape of a thin rectangle, not unlike the beginnings of a hinge.

Problems are not amusing, Young Bull, Hopper agreed. *But you are climbing back and forth over the same wall. Come. Let us run.*

Wolves lived in the moment; though they remembered the past and seemed to have an odd sense for the future, they didn't worry about either. Not as men did. Wolves ran free, chasing the winds. To join them would be to ignore pain, sorrow and frustration. To be free . . .

That freedom would cost Perrin too much. He'd lose Faile, would lose his very *self.* He didn't want to be a wolf. He wanted to be a man. "Is there a way to reverse what has happened to me?"

Reverse? Hopper cocked his head. To go backward was not a way of wolves.

"Can I . . ." Perrin struggled to explain. "Can I run so far that the wolves cannot hear me?"

Hopper seemed confused. No. "Confused" did not convey the pained sendings that came from Hopper. Nothingness, the scent of rotting meat, wolves howling in agony. Being cut off was not a thing Hopper could conceive.

Perrin's mind grew fuzzy. Why had he stopped forging?

He had to finish. Master Luhhan would be disappointed! Those lumps were terrible. He should hide them. Create something else, show he *was* capable. He *could* forge. Couldn't he?

A hissing came from beside him. Perrin turned, surprised to see that one of the quenching barrels beside the hearth was boiling. *Of course,* he thought. *The first pieces I finished. I dropped them in there.*

Suddenly anxious, Perrin grabbed his tongs and reached into the turbulent water, steam engulfing his face. He found something at the bottom and brought it out with his tongs: a chunk of white-hot metal.

The glow faded. The chunk was actually a small steel figurine in the shape of a tall, thin man with a sword tied to his back. Each line on the figure was detailed, the ruffles of the shirt, the leather bands on the hilt of the tiny sword. But the face was distorted, the mouth open in a twisted scream.

Aram, Perrin thought. *His name was Aram.*

Perrin couldn't show *this* to Master Luhhan! Why had he created such a thing?

The figurine's mouth opened farther, screaming soundlessly. Perrin cried out, dropping it from the tongs and jumping back. The figurine fell to the wood floor and shattered.

Why do you think so much about that one? Hopper yawned a wide-jawed wolf yawn, tongue curling. *It is common that a young pup challenges the pack leader. He was foolish, and you defeated him.*

"No," Perrin whispered. "It is not common for humans. Not for friends."

The wall of the forge suddenly melted away, becoming smoke. It felt natural for that to happen. Outside, Perrin saw an open, daylit street. A city with broken-windowed shops.

"Malden," Perrin said.

A smoky, translucent image of himself stood outside. The image wore no coat; his bare arms bulged with muscles. He kept his beard short, but it made him look older, more intense. Did Perrin really look *that* imposing? A squat fortress of a man with golden eyes that seemed to glow, carrying a gleaming half-moon axe as large as a man's head.

There was something wrong about that axe. Perrin stepped out of the smithy, passing through the shadowy version of himself. When he did, he became that image, axe heavy in his hand, work clothes vanishing and battle gear replacing it.

He took off running. Yes, this *was* Malden. There were Aiel in the streets. He'd lived this battle, though he was much calmer this time. Before, he'd been lost in the thrill of fighting and of seeking Faile. He stopped in the street. "This is wrong. I carried my hammer into Malden. I threw the axe away."

A horn or a hoof, Young Bull, does it matter which one you use to hunt? Hopper was sitting in the sunlit street beside him.

"Yes. It matters. It does to me."

And yet you use them the same way.

A pair of Shaido Aiel appeared around a corner. They were watching something to the left, something Perrin couldn't see. He ran to attack them.

He sheared through the chin of one, then swung the spike on the axe into the chest of the other. It was a brutal, terrible attack, and all three of them ended on the ground. It took several stabs from the spike to kill the second Shaido.

Perrin stood up. He did remember killing those two Aiel, though he had done it with hammer and knife. He didn't regret their deaths. Sometimes a man needed to fight, and that was that. Death was terrible, but that didn't stop it from being necessary. In fact, it had been wonderful to clash with the Aiel. He'd felt like a wolf on the hunt.

When Perrin fought, he came close to becoming someone else. And that was dangerous.

He looked accusingly at Hopper, who lounged on a street corner. "Why are you making me dream this?"

Making you? Hopper asked. *This is not my dream, Young Bull. Do you see my jaws on your neck, forcing you to think it?*

Perrin's axe streamed with blood. He knew what was coming next. He turned. From behind, Aram approached, murder in his eyes. Half of the former Tinker's face was coated in blood, and it dripped from his chin, staining his red-striped coat.

Aram swung his sword for Perrin's neck, the steel hissing in the air. Perrin stepped back. He refused to fight the boy again.

The shadowy version of himself split off, leaving the real Perrin in his blacksmith's clothing. The shadow exchanged blows with Aram. *The Prophet explained it to me . . . You're really Shadowspawn. . . . I have to rescue the Lady Faile from you. . . .*

The shadowy Perrin changed, suddenly, into a wolf. It leaped, fur nearly as dark as that of a Shadowbrother, and ripped out Aram's throat.

"No! It didn't happen like that!"

It is a dream, Hopper sent.

"But I didn't kill him," Perrin protested. "Some Aiel shot him with arrows right before. . . ."

Right before Aram would have killed Perrin.

The horn, the hoof, or the tooth, Hopper sent, turning and ambling toward a building. Its wall vanished, revealing Master Luhhan's smithy inside. *Does it matter? The dead are dead. Two-legs do not come here, not usually, once they die. I do not know where it is that they go.*

Perrin looked down at Aram's body. "I should have taken that fool sword from him the moment he picked it up. I should have sent him back to his family."

Does not a cub deserve his fangs? Hopper asked, genuinely confused. *Why would you pull them?*

"It is a thing of men," Perrin said.

Things of two-legs, of men. Always, it is a thing of men to you. What of things of wolves?

"I am not a wolf."

Hopper entered the forge, and Perrin reluctantly followed. The barrel was still boiling. The wall returned, and Perrin was once again wearing his leather vest and apron, holding his tongs.

He stepped over and pulled out another figurine. This one was in the shape of Tod al'Caar. As it cooled, Perrin found that the face wasn't distorted like Aram's, though the lower half of the figurine was unformed, still a block of metal. The figurine continued to glow, faintly reddish, after Perrin set it down on the floor. He thrust his tongs back into the water and pulled free a figure of Jori Congar, then one of Azi al'Thone.

Perrin went to the bubbling barrel time and time again, pulling out figurine after figurine. After the way of dreams, fetching them all took both a brief second and what seemed like hours. When he finished, hundreds of figurines stood on the floor facing him. Watching. Each steel figure was lit with a tiny fire inside, as if waiting to feel the forger's hammer.

But figurines like this wouldn't be forged; they'd be cast. "What does it mean?" Perrin sat down on a stool.

Mean? Hopper opened his mouth in a wolf laugh. *It means there are many little men on the floor, none of which you can eat. Your kind is too fond of rocks and what is inside of them.*

The figurines seemed accusing. Around them lay the broken shards of Aram. Those pieces seemed to be growing larger. The shattered hands began working, clawing on the ground. The shards all became little hands, climbing toward Perrin, reaching for him.

Perrin gasped, leaping to his feet. He heard laughter in the distance, ringing closer, shaking the building. Hopper jumped, slamming into him. And then . . .

Perrin started awake. He was back in his tent, in the field where they'd been camped for a few days now. They'd run across a bubble of evil the week before that had caused angry red, oily serpents to wiggle from the ground all through camp. Several hundred were sick from their bites; Aes Sedai Healing had been enough to keep most of them alive, but not restore them completely.

Faile slept beside Perrin, peaceful. Outside, one of his men tapped a post to count off the hour. Three taps. Still hours until dawn.

Perrin's heart pounded softly, and he raised a hand to his bare chest. He half-expected an army of tiny metal hands to crawl out from beneath his bedroll.

Eventually, he forced his eyes closed and tried to relax. This time, sleep was very elusive.

About the Authors

Robert Jordan was born in 1948 in Charleston, South Carolina. He taught himself to read when he was four with the incidental aid of a twelve-years-older brother, and was tackling Mark Twain and Jules Verne by five. He was a graduate of the Citadel, the Military College of South Carolina, with a degree in physics. He served two tours in Vietnam with the U.S. Army; among his decorations are the Distinguished Flying Cross with bronze oak leaf cluster, the Bronze Star with "V" and bronze oak leaf cluster, and two Vietnamese Gallantry Crosses with Palm. A history buff, he also wrote dance and theater criticism. He enjoyed the outdoor sports of hunting, fishing, and sailing, and the indoor sports of poker, chess, pool, and pipe collecting. He began writing in 1977 and continued until his death on September 16, 2007.

Brandon Sanderson was born in 1975 in Lincoln, Nebraska. After a semester as a biochem major, Brandon came to his senses and recognized writing as his true vocation. He switched to English, graduating from Brigham Young University, then returning for a master's in creative writing. During this time Brandon wrote thirteen novels, finally publishing his sixth, *Elantris,* in 2005. He has since released books for both adults and young readers, including the Mistborn trilogy, *Warbreaker,* and the Alcatraz series. He lives with his wife and children in Utah, where he often plays Magic: The Gathering, regularly eats mac-and-cheese, and occasionally teaches writing at BYU. Find more at www.brandonsanderson.com.